Liepaja

Baltic Sea

• Siauliai

Klaipeda

LITHUANIA

Vilnius

Kaunas

Kaliningrad

Smorgon

Chernyakhovsk

St. Petersburg

Suwalki

Lida

0   20   40   60   80   Statute miles

0   50   100   150   Kilometers

RUSSIA

• Moscow

COMMONWEALTH

OF

INDEPENDENT

STATES

Osmansky Highlands

• Minsk

LORUSSIA

NIA

VIA

• Kiev

UKRAINE

0   100   200   Statute miles

0   100   200   300   400   Kilometers

NIGHT
OF THE
HAWK

NIGHT
OF THE
HAWK

Dale Brown

DONALD I. FINE, INC./G. P. PUTNAM'S SONS
New York

BRO

G. P. Putnam's Sons
Publishers Since 1838
200 Madison Avenue
New York, NY 10016

Endpaper maps by Lisa Amoroso.

Library of Congress Cataloging-in-Publication Data
Brown, Dale, date
Night of the hawk / Dale Brown.
p.   cm.
ISBN 0-399-13739-4 (acid-free paper)
I. Title.
PS3552.R68543N54   1992
813'.54—dc20   92-14138 CIP

Printed in the United States of America

1 2 3 4 5 6 7 8 9 10

This book is printed on acid-free paper.

∞

One of the most stirring sights I have ever witnessed was in Vilnius, Lithuania, in May of 1991, only four months after the Soviet Army occupied the capital and massacred thirteen civilians in the street. I saw hundreds of Lithuanians waving their (then illegal) national flag, erecting posters and memorials, chanting slogans and singing songs of freedom and defiance—right in front of the Red Army tanks surrounding the national television studio. I didn't know how long it would be before Lithuania and the Baltic states would regain their freedom, but I knew they deserved it. They wanted freedom, and they were willing to fight for it.

Night of the Hawk is dedicated to the peace-loving people of the world, and especially our friends in the now-independent republics of the former Soviet Union. May the entire world's transition to democracy and freedom be a peaceful one.

This book is also dedicated to the memory of my aunt, Mary Kaminski, and my uncle, Richard Brown. They have left behind some very fond memories and the most wonderful relatives a guy like me could have.

Acknowledgments

W hen you talk about infantry weapons, you can learn only so much from a book—you eventually have to get out to the range, get a gun in your hand, and return some lead to the earth. I was lucky enough to find the best in the business to help me. Thanks to Jefferson "Zuma Jay" Wagner, surfer chief and president of Movie Arms Management, Inc., and his partners, Ben Sherrill and Jared Chandler ("Razor" in the movie *Flight of the Intruder*), for taking me out to the range and showing me how to use some of the weapons described in *Night of the Hawk*. It was an awesome experience I'll never forget. Special thanks also to Bill Hazen, also of Movie Arms Management, who gave me specific suggestions and details on U.S. Special Forces tactics employed in many of the scenarios I built for this novel.

Special operations is very much a multiservice tasking, and I've received assistance from just about all of them.

Although not officially a part of U.S. Special Operations Command, the U.S. Marine Corps is usually the spearhead in most military operations overseas and has a wealth of experience and talent in the world of special operations—I hope I've done justice to the time and attention they've given me. I'd like to thank Major Mark Hughes and Chief Warrant Officer Charles Rowe, USMC Public Affairs in New York, for a great wealth of information on Marine Corps special operations. Special thanks also to First Lieutenant Mike Snyder, who provided me with tons of information on Marine Corps weapons and equipment.

Very special thanks go to First Lieutenant Todd Yeatts, deputy public affairs officer, Marine Corps Recruiting Depot, Parris Island, S.C. When I needed information on the USMC Confidence Course, Todd went out with a videotape camera and ran it for me, each and every obstacle, without a single hitch. That's an American Marine!

Thanks to Lieutenant Colonel Terry Meehan, U.S. Army, of the Office of the Assistant Secretary of Defense, Public Affairs, for the information he provided on the U.S. Special Operations Command; to Lieutenant Colonel Les Grau and Lieutenant Colonel Tim Thomas, U.S. Army, Office of Foreign Military Studies, Fort Leavenworth, Kansas, for data on Soviet troop deployments in the Baltic states, the Commonwealth republics, and the former USSR; Kent Lee; Dr. Jacob Kipp, Russian military historian at Fort Leavenworth; and Peter Ernest, public affairs officer, Central Intelligence Agency.

Special thanks to Army Staff Sergeant Vincent Lobello, California Air National Guard, Mather AFB, California, for an incredible tour of the Army's AH-1 Cobra gunship and an explanation of tactics involved with night-vision equipment.

Thanks to Captain Kimberley Urie, U.S. Air Force, and Shirley Sikes, public affairs officers at Air Force Special Operations Command, Hurlburt Field, Florida, for information on Air Force special operations aircraft, weapons, and tactics; and Major Norm Hils, MH-53J helicopter pilot, Captain Randy Garratt, AC-130 gunship pilot, and Captain David Tardiff, MC-130 electronic-warfare officer, for their help with their respective special-operations weapon systems and the helpful criticism they provided on my manuscript.

Thanks to Jeff Richelson, author of *Sword and Shield;* Amy Knight, at the Library of Congress; and David Colton, White & Case Attorneys at Law, New York City, for information on Soviet paramilitary forces; William E. Burrows, author of "Deep Black" and "Exploring Space," for information on Defense Department satellites; also David McClave and Ronald Grimm, at the Library of Congress; Ian Cuthbertson, Institute for East-West Studies; David Shakley, Magnavox Defense Group, Inc.; Caroline Russell, Boeing Aircraft Inc. Product Support Division; and Mr. Evan H. Whildin, Sr., of Colt's Manufacturing Co., Inc.

An excellent source of information on U.S. Marine Corps special operations on which I relied is the book *Strike Force* by Agostino von Hassell, published by Howell Press. A good source of general information on Marine Corps history and training is *The Marine Book* by Chuck Lawliss, published by Thames & Hudson.

Part of the research for this book was a trip I took to the Soviet Union and the three Baltic states in April and May of 1991. Thanks to Jurga Sakalauskaite, a guide with GT International, the first private travel agency in Lithuania, for the information she provided on Lithuania, Vilnius, and the Baltic states. Thanks also to Intourist, the Soviet government travel agency, and its representatives for being so honest and open about their country and the status and future of the breakaway republics.

The best source of historical, cultural, and geographical information on the Baltic states that I used was *A Guide to the Baltic States,* edited by Ingrida Kalnins, published by Inroads, Inc.

A continuing source of information, morale, inspiration, and encouragement were Lieutenant General Robert Beckel, commander of Fifteenth Air Force, Strategic Air Command (soon to be part of USAF Air Mobility Command); Major General James Meier, Fifteenth Air Force deputy commander; and Lieutenant Colonel Fredric Lynch, Fifteenth Air Force Chief of Public Affairs, March Air Force Base, Riverside, California. They have helped me immeasurably by sharing their time and enthusiasm for their profession with me over the past several months.

It has been a wild and woolly time trying to keep up with the changes going on in the old Soviet Union, and I couldn't have done it without help. As ever, I wish to thank my wife, Jean, for helping me cook up these stories; my editor and friend, George Coleman, at Putnam; and especially my executive assistant and friend, Dennis T. Hall, for chasing down information sources, handling the phones, checking my sources and contacts, and helping me straighten out the kinks in a rapidly changing real-world political scene. I can't wait to see what happens next. . . .

Dale Brown
Folsom, CA
March 1992

Actual News Excerpts

WASHINGTON POST, 8 December 1991—The leaders of Russia, the Ukraine and Byelorussia formally announced the dissolution of the Soviet Union today and said they had agreed to establish a "Commonwealth of Independent States" in its place.

The decision to liquidate the 69-year-old Communist-forged union and halt activity of all Soviet government organs came during a closed-door meeting at a Byelorussian hunting lodge near the Polish border in the absence of Soviet President Mikhail Gorbachev.

There was no immediate comment from Gorbachev, whose constitutional position as president and commander in chief of the 4-million-member Soviet armed forces has now been challenged throughout the Slavic heartland of the former Soviet superpower.

In Washington, Secretary of States James A. Baker III said in a television interview that "the Soviet Union as we've known it no longer exists," but he warned that there is still a risk of civil war amid the ruins of the Soviet empire.

NEW YORK TIMES, 24 December 1991—. . . The nuclear weapons issue [in the new Commonwealth of Independent States], while the subject of reassuringly worded promises in the Kremlin, remains to be worked out in its critical details by the new commonwealth.

The republic leaders are to gather . . . in Minsk, the commonwealth headquarters, to try to resolve their differences over how to craft a common defense council that does not smack of the old union. They also will be facing resistance by [many Soviet republics] to a plan under which Russia ultimately becomes the guarantor of disarmament and repository of the entire Soviet nuclear armory.

WASHINGTON POST, 20 February 1992—A classified study prepared as the basis for the Pentagon's budgetary planning through the end of the century casts Russia as the gravest potential threat to U.S. vital interests and presumes the United States would spearhead a NATO counterattack if Russia launched an invasion of Lithuania.

U.S. intervention in Lithuania, which would reverse decades of American restraint in the former Soviet Union's Baltic sphere of influence, is one of seven hypothetical roads to war that the Pentagon studied to help the military services size and justify their forces through 1999. In the study, the Pentagon neither advocates nor predicts any specific conflict.

The Lithuanian scenario contemplates a major war by land, sea and air in which 24 NATO divisions, 70 fighter squadrons and six aircraft carrier battle groups would keep the Russian navy "bottled up in the eastern Baltic," bomb supply lines in Russia and use armored formations to expel Russian forces from Lithuania. The authors state that Russia is unlikely to respond with nuclear weapons, but they provide no basis for that assessment.

An unclassified draft preface to the seven scenarios describes them as "illustrative" of the demands that might be placed on the U.S. military in coming years, adding, "They are neither predictive nor exhaustive."

The Lithuanian scenario judges the likelihood of war with Russia as "low," but goes on to say that economic and political tensions "could compel political leaders to make decisions that appear irrational" and asserts that a Russian invasion of Lithuania "is plausible in light of recent events in the former Soviet Union."

More striking to analysts inside and outside the government has been the Pentagon document's description of Lithuania as a "U.S. vital interest." The language of vital interests traditionally describes something that the U.S. government would use military force to protect. Though applying the term to Lithuania, the document, titled "1994–1999 Defense Planning Guidance Scenario Set for Final Coordination," does not propose to represent current U.S. policy.

National security officials outside the Pentagon sharply disputed the scenario's premise, noting that the United States never recognized the Soviet Union's World War II conquest of the Baltic states but steered clear of interference there for fear of nuclear war.

ANNUAL REPORT TO THE PRESIDENT AND THE CONGRESS, Secretary of Defense Dick Cheney, February 1992—Special operations forces are essential contributors to strategic deterrence and defense. The ongoing proliferations of weapons of mass destruction and the means to deliver them threaten to erode strategic stability . . . SOF special reconnaissance and direct action capabilities can help to locate and destroy storage facilities, control nodes, and other strategic assets . . . SOF are one of the few instruments available to precisely apply measured force to deal with an adversary's nuclear weapons capabilities.

ASSOCIATED PRESS, 12 March 1992—Russia's vice-president confirmed Wednesday that nuclear weapons are stored in both Armenia and Azerbaijan, the former Soviet republics embroiled in a vicious conflict over the Nagorno-Karabakh enclave.

. . . It was not known what kind of nuclear weapons were in the republics, although they are assumed to be tactical—or "battlefield"—weapons.

BEE NEWS SERVICES, 13 March 1992—Ominous new concerns were raised Thursday about the safety of the former Soviet Union's nuclear arsenal when Ukraine said it has stopped returning nuclear weapons to Russia for dismantling.

. . . Perfilyev [advisor to the Russian vice-president] accused Kravchuk [Ukrainian president] of using nuclear weapons to prove Ukraine's independence, and said that Russia would react harshly.

Note

This story is not intended to chronicle or explain actual U.S. government, U.S. Marine Corps, U.S. Special Operations Command, or military contractors' tactics, doctrines, procedures, equipment, or capabilities. The scenarios, units, equipment, and tactics described in *Night of the Hawk* are purely products of my imagination. I have made every effort to be accurate, but this is a work of fiction and none of the persons, units, equipment, scenarios, or tactics I describe are intended to accurately depict the real thing. I hope I've done our special operations forces some justice (at least so they won't be out gunning for *me*!), but my intention was not to tell their story for them. I hope to be qualified to do so someday.

I don't especially care for sequels, but I do like bringing back many of the characters from previous stories—they are like old friends. The plot and settings for this story stand alone, but in general occur after *Flight of the Old Dog* and *Hammerheads,* but before the events described in *Day of the Cheetah* and *Sky Masters.*

I still refer to the B-1B bomber as "Excalibur," although its official Air Force nickname is "Lancer."

Freedom suppressed and again regained bites with keener fangs than freedom never endangered.
—CICERO

Prologue

This was not the way the flight of the Old Dog was supposed to be ending, First Lieutenant David Luger, United States Air Force, thought grimly.

Not at all.

And yet here they were, in the very northeastern tip of the Soviet Union, forced to land at this snowy, bitterly cold enemy backwater base to steal fuel because their B-52 (I) Megafortress was running on fumes. Holding a gun to the head of the base chief's custodian, they had commandeered one of his fuel trucks and put whatever they could into the plane. The custodian had escaped and obviously put in a frantic call to the regional militia. Luger shook his head. During the course of this mission—one of the most highly classified in the annals of American military warfare—they'd successfully penetrated restricted Soviet airspace, fought off waves upon waves of surface-to-air missiles, swarms of deadly MiG fighters, and, with a Striker glide-bomb, knocked out the most sophisticated weapon the USSR had ever developed.

The mission should have been a success, but now they were going to be captured by the fucking Red Army. Luger was sure of it. Even in a backwater, the Red Army was going to protect the Motherland—at all costs.

The tall, lean, twenty-six-year-old Texas-born crew navigator was alone in the bitterly cold belowdecks section of the crew compartment aboard the Megafortress, an experimental B-52 "test-bed" aircraft that had been pressed into service on this unusual and dangerous mission. He felt an uncontrollable shiver of fear, frustration, and sheer anger take hold of his body. Maybe it was finally going to be over.

They certainly weren't in any condition to fight—maybe they should just surrender. The stolen fuel they had pumped into their tanks was

19

contaminated fuel oil, not jet fuel. One of their eight engines had been destroyed, and another was leaking oil so badly that it was all but useless. The Old Dog's fuselage was full of holes, and their stabilators—the odd-looking V-tail assembly that served both as rudder and horizontal stabilizer—had been shot out. The plane's wheels were frozen in knee-deep snow, and it was doubtful that the plane could even taxi on six engines, let alone attempt a takeoff on the short, snow-covered Soviet runway. The pilot, Lieutenant General Bradley Elliott, had been dragged upstairs by some of the other crew, unconscious and nearly frozen to death.

Now they were surrounded by Russian militia.

Luger had been strapping himself into his ejection seat in the downstairs compartment, but had stopped when he realized how ridiculous the idea of trying to launch the Megafortress seemed right now—not much use in strapping in if there was no way the plane would ever get off the ground—so he laid the straps aside.

There was a gaping hole in the downstairs crew compartment big enough that he could see footprints in the snow outside. Just a few hours earlier his right leg had been in back of that jagged hole. For the first time since arriving at the Russian base, Luger surveyed the damage on his leg—and felt his stomach turn at the sight. Even heavily wrapped in bandages from the first-aid kit, he could feel his kneecap gone, see the limb twisted and his right foot pointing at an unnatural angle. The leg had frozen into an unrecognizable stick, thanks to both the windblast inflight and then spending several hours in freezing temperatures outside. He was probably going to lose the leg or, at best, be crippled for life. Most of the navigation equipment was damaged or in reset, and the weapons were probably shut down. Were they kidding themselves, or what?

Luger's partner, Captain Patrick McLanahan, had finished helping Lieutenant General Elliott and the two women crew members up the ladder and was going to strap into the seat beside Luger when copilot Lieutenant Colonel John Ormack called McLanahan upstairs. Ormack had kept one engine running while they had refueled the Megafortress, and incredibly had started engine number five just a few minutes ago. The contaminated fuel was causing tremendous explosions in each engine during ignition, but amazingly the engines kept running. Now more engines were starting. Luger thought McLanahan was probably acting as copilot with Elliott incapacitated. He put on his headphones to block out the bangs and screams of the engines. He could hear Ormack and McLanahan on the interphone.

"If we start a firefight here . . ." Ormack said.

"We may not have any choice," McLanahan replied.

Maybe we are *going to fight it out,* Luger thought. But with what? Half the crew was injured, the plane was shot to hell, they were surrounded by Soviet militiamen . . .

"He wants us to shut down," Luger heard Ormack say over interphone. "Patrick, we're running out of time . . ."

There were several loud bangs on both wings this time and the Old Dog began to buck and rumble as if its insides had been seized by a coughing fit. Down in the lower deck of the Megafortress, alone and shot up and half frozen, Luger felt useless to the crew who needed him the most. But they were continuing the engine start, and Luger realized Ormack and McLanahan weren't giving up. They were going to get the Megafortress in the air or die trying. He smiled. Good old McLanahan. A real give-a-shit crew dog who was giving the finger to the Russians in their own backyard. If you're gonna fight, this was the way to do it. The way they'd been taught. Never give up.

Lights popped on in the belowdecks compartment as the generators were brought on-line. No, the nav equipment was okay—the GPS (Global Positioning System) satellite navigation system was working, the TDC (terrain-data computer) and COLA (computer-generated lowest altitude) terrain-avoidance computer was operable, even the AIM-120 Scorpion air-to-air missiles were on-line. Out of force of habit, if not by optimistic thinking, Luger moved the data cartridge lever on the TDC from LOCK to READ and got a TERRAIN DATA LOAD OK message on his computer terminal. But seconds later, when the generators popped off-line and put the entire system back into reset, he gave up trying to get the computers running.

The engines were now screaming louder than ever, up to taxi power and almost to full military power. The Megafortress wasn't moving. But Ormack and McLanahan were running through checklists, starting more engines, putting internal power back on-line . . .

Suddenly the unmistakable rattle of a heavy-caliber machine gun split the air.

They're shooting at us . . . the motherfuckers! Luger cursed to himself.

McLanahan, upstairs, went on with the engine start. Over interphone, he called, "Everyone on interphone? Report by compartment."

The engines were cut to IDLE. McLanahan said, "Crew, we've got a Russian armored vehicle about a hundred yards off our left wing. They've got a machine gun. They've ordered us to cut our engines—"

Alone downstairs, Luger seethed. *Cut our engines? As they say in Texas, when pigs fly . . .*

Luger rose out of his ejection seat and pulled himself aft, dragging his shattered right leg like a sack of heavy wet sand alongside him. He glanced up through the between-decks ladder well and saw electronic-warfare officer Wendy Tork kneeling beside General Elliott on the upper deck. She was removing her flight jacket and laying it over Elliott to try to warm him up. Wendy saw Luger and her eyes raised an unspoken question. Luger stared expressionlessly at her, then removed his flight jacket, passed it upstairs to Wendy, and gave her a thumbs-up—and her eyes widened in disbelief.

"Thanks, Dave," Wendy Tork said, words that could not be heard over the screaming of the six operable turbofan engines. Luger smiled anyway, then dropped out of sight below the rim of the between-decks ladder well. She got a glimpse of his horribly injured leg and wondered where he was going. To repair a damaged relay? Close the aft bulkhead door? Double-check the lock on the entry hatch?

Then she realized that he was not just offering his jacket to help Elliott keep from freezing to death . . . he was going to leave the plane.

And she did nothing to stop him.

Luger dropped to his left side on the deck, reached down, slid the hatch-lock lever over, and pulled the latch lever back. The belly hatch flopped open. He swung his good left leg through the hatch and braced himself in the hatch for a moment, sitting on the rear sill looking forward at the navigator's crew stations, catching his breath.

So the Soviets want us to cut our engines? No way. If Ormack and McLanahan can bite the bullet, then I'm sure as hell going to do my part. Sitting alone, strapped in my seat, freezing to death with a bad leg and a bad eye, isn't doing jack-shit to help. But there may be a way . . .

Luger saw a trail of thick dark blood staining the entry ladder and lower deck and realized there would be rivers of blood pouring out of this black beast if he didn't do something—and do it now.

Crew dogs rarely talked of things like fear, but he knew the rest of the crew had to be as scared as he was. But fear was no reason to bail out; fear accelerated one's courage. It certainly did his. Feeling the blasts of frigid air rushing through the open hatch below him, hearing the scream of the engines, Luger reached down and felt the .38-caliber survival revolver strapped against his torso. He withdrew it and counted the cartridges—five, with the hammer down on the empty chamber. It was a small gun, but it helped melt the last of his fear away. He slipped off the entry hatch rear sill, dropped down to the hard-packed snow below, and closed the hatch behind him.

Upstairs, the HATCH NOT CLOSED AND LATCHED light on the forward instrument panel snapped on then, and before either Ormack and McLanahan could react it popped out.

"What was *that?*" asked Ormack.

"I don't . . . Dave, did you open the hatch?" No reply. "Luger. Report."

There was no answer.

Luger had never been outside a B-52 with the hatch closed and the engines running. It was a weird, almost overpowering feeling.

For an instant he visualized the faces of everyone he had just left behind. But one look at the menacing-looking armored half-track parked between two hangars off to the left of the nose of the bomber and he knew what he had to do.

The roar of the engines was deafening, acutely painful. Staying under the left wing, careful not to get either in front or behind the running engines, oblivious to the ear-shattering noise, he moved away from the Megafortress and toward the half-track, the gun in his fist.

Luger was only a few feet from the Megafortress's shattered left wing-tip when he inadvertently tried to put weight on his right leg. It immediately gave way, and he sprawled to the snow into a patch of black oil that had spilled out of the damaged number-two engine. The shock of the slimy snow on his face sent a surge of energy—or panic—through his body, and he half-stumbled, half-crawled to the fuel truck, which was still parked just off the left wingtip.

He heard several rapid-fire *pop-pop-pop-pop* shots coming from the Megafortress, turned, and saw Colonel Ormack firing a big pistol—General Elliott's big .45, he realized—out the left cockpit window. Luger couldn't see what he was shooting at, but he assumed it was the half-track. The heavy-caliber gun would slice the cockpit into ribbons in a few seconds . . .

Luger reached the fuel truck, crawled around to the driver's side, and was about to get in when he saw the half-track's gunner take aim at the Megafortress.

Luger threw himself forward onto the hood of the fuel truck, took aim, and fired his .38 at the gunner. The gun's puny reports nevertheless sent slaps of shock waves against his face and eyes, but he held the gun as steady as his frozen fingers could manage. He wasn't sure if he took proper aim or even opened his eyes, but to his amazement Luger saw the Russian gunner clutch his chest and fall down into the half-track.

"Luger! Get back here!" It was Ormack shouting at him over the roar of the engines.

In pain, Luger dropped the pistol and made his way around to the front of the fuel truck, starting back for the Old Dog. He had taken only three steps when another soldier appeared from behind the half-track, lifted a rifle with a long, curved cartridge magazine, and fired. Suddenly his left leg was thrust violently to his right and out from underneath him. He collapsed onto his left side, screaming at the pain from his left thigh—a bullet hole the size of a damn Ping-Pong ball had carved out a gory tunnel in the side of his thigh. He screamed again as the sounds of gunfire erupted all around him, and he kept on screaming—for Patrick, for his mother, for help from God—as he clawed to the relative safety and protection of the fuel truck.

Ormack could only fire his pistol again, forcing the Russian at the back of the half-track to retreat, but he didn't notice another soldier sliding into the machine-gun mount on the half-track.

The soldier took aim on the Old Dog and let the machine gun rip.

The 20-millimeter shells plowed through the Old Dog's left side . . .

Somehow Luger pulled himself up inside the cab of the fuel truck and lay down on the frozen bench seat, peeking out the side windows at the horrifying display outside.

The left cockpit windows were gone, and little black puffs of fibersteel were bursting all over the nose and left side of the crew compartment. A huge cloud of smoke erupted from the number-four engine, the one closest to the pilot's side windows, and the bomber was shaking and bucking enough to make the big wings flap.

They're killing the Old Dog, Luger thought. Ormack couldn't have survived that gunfire—my God, the whole cockpit was gone. *"You sons of bitches,"* Luger screamed at the Russian half-track's gunner. *"You're killing them!"*

Luger's shattered right leg touched the fuel truck's accelerator and the engine revved—McLanahan or defensive-systems officer Angelina Pereira must have left it running when they'd used it to get the stolen fuel. Luger found the parking brake, eased it off, then reached down with his hand to lift his bloody left leg onto the clutch. He put the transmission into first gear, eased his left leg off the clutch, and stomped with all his might on the accelerator, leaving his near-frozen right leg on it, and steered the fuel truck toward the armored personnel carrier.

The fuel truck lurched ahead, bouncing and clattering on ages-old springs. He was about ten meters from the half-track before the gunner noticed him coming, swiveled the gun turret around toward him, and opened fire. Nearly passing out from the pain and the shock, screaming like an animal caught in a trap, Luger dived out the open driver's side door . . .

. . . just as a fusillade of bullets shattered the windshield and ripped the interior of the truck apart.

Luger was lying facedown in two feet of snow, unconscious, when the fuel truck plowed into the half-track. Bullets from the half-track's gun tore open the fuel tank, igniting the fuel-oil fumes inside, which turned both the truck and the half-track into balloons of fire. The concussion of the double explosion tossed Luger's body another fifty feet away like a rag doll, but mercifully the young navigator was not awake to experience that final blast.

9 FEBRUARY 1989, 0531 MOSCOW

The bullets from the half-track had continued to walk down the left side of the Megafortress, eventually reaching the leading edge of the left wing and causing a terrific explosion as the red-hot shells found the fuel oil in the mains. Luger hadn't stopped the half-track—it had missed, or the fuel truck exploded before reaching it, he didn't know what had happened—but the Megafortress was dying. The left wing was afire and the left-center wing tank exploded and sheared the entire wing off. Wendy and Angelina scrambled out of the hatch just as the Old Dog flopped onto its right wing, crushing it instantly and causing a huge explosion as the rest of the fuel tanks ruptured. The resulting fireball was at least a mile in diameter, swallowing up the two civilian women and engulfing the huge bomber in sheets of flame.

"Patrick!" Luger shouted. "Patrick! Eject! Get out! Patrick! Patrick . . . !"

Luger's muscles convulsed. They quivered uncontrollably, but for some reason none of them wanted to function—he could move each one only a centimeter or two before they retreated into fits of spasms. Gasping for air, Luger fought for control, trying to ignore the waves of fear rising in his chest.

Something was wrong . . .

Slowly, the spasms ceased, and Luger was able to breathe evenly again. He felt as if he had run a marathon—his entire body felt weak. His fingertips felt puffy and soft, and the slightest exertion, like lifting the index finger of his right hand, caused the spasms to return. He decided to lie quietly and get his bearings—at least his eyes still functioned.

He was in a dimly lit room. He saw light fixtures overhead, and out of the corners of his eyes he saw hospital beds. So he was in a hospital ward. Luger could make out dingy white curtains surrounding some beds, a few intravenous bottle stands—thankfully, none near his bed. By straining, he could see railings on his bed and, thank God, even his feet under the white linen. Whatever had happened, they had saved his shot-up legs.

And then he realized there were sounds of pain coupled with the sights. A *lot* of men in pain. He could make out a door at the far right side of the ward, and by the sound and numbers of men moaning, he expected a nurse or doctor or even an orderly to enter the room—but none did. Luger waited several minutes, but the men's cries went unanswered. He could see shadows move past the doors, but no one entered.

What kind of hospital was this? If this was a Russian military hospital, Luger could understand getting poor treatment as a prisoner—but these other men weren't foreigners. Some of them cried out in the Russian language. Didn't they bother taking care of their own?

Luger extended a shaking hand to the railing on his bed. It rattled easily. He continued to rattle it and was rewarded a moment later with the rail collapsing alongside the bed. The sudden noise caused the moans to intensify, as if the men knew a nurse was nearby and wanted to be sure they were heard. Luger waited for what he thought was a few more minutes to see if anyone would come, and was surprised to find he had dozed off—for how long, he did not know.

But the brief rest was helpful. He found he now had the strength and control to move his legs to the edge of the bed. As first his right leg, and then his left emerged from under the sheets, he was overjoyed to see little evidence of his injuries—a lot of deep scars, large hairless spots where skin grafts were taken from farther up his thigh, thick bandages all around his legs, but little pain or discomfort. Skinny as hell, but all in one piece. He commanded his toes to wiggle, and after having to wait a measurable moment, was rewarded with a faint movement. He was weak and obviously emaciated, but he was in one piece, and the collective pieces seemed to be operable. Thank God for that.

With renewed vigor Luger swung his legs off the right edge of the bed and onto the floor. The linoleum was gritty and cold, but at least he could feel it. The movement forced his torso to turn to the right, and he let his body roll right until he was facedown on the bed with his knees almost touching the floor. Luger dragged his feet closer to the bed, took a deep breath, braced himself, and began putting weight on his feet. His legs immediately began to shake, but with a lot of effort he managed to push himself upright.

Success!

Luger found a plastic hospital I.D. bracelet around his wrist, but there was not enough light to read it. He was dressed in a long armless hospital gown, much like a poncho, made of rough white cloth with the back slit open but with no ties to close it. No matter—he was going right back to bed anyway, right after he explored a little and got someone's attention at the nurses' station outside. The thought of escape crossed his mind, but the room was really cold and he didn't think he had a chance—even if he did manage to get out of the hospital, he was probably still in eastern Siberia. Where was he going to go? Alaska? Yeah, right. Not even if he had two men's strength.

For an instant his mind drifted back to the Old Dog. Had the rest of the crew made it out of Siberia? Or had the Old Dog given out before they could take off? And if so, where was McLanahan? Ormack? Wendy and the rest? Were they here as well? Or had the Soviet Union already "dealt" with them? He blocked out the thought. If the latter had happened, he could only imagine . . . Glimpses of those final moments, hazy as they now were, drifted through.

No, Luger decided, they *must* have made it out.

He was the only one who had not.

Depressed by the thought, Luger took in more of the room. There wasn't a condition chart at the foot of his bed, which was unfortunate. It could have told him a lot about himself. Still, that didn't mean he couldn't find out about himself on his own. He heard voices coming from outside the room. He didn't want to get caught wandering around the ward, but he had to get to know this room and then slip back into bed—then, at least, he could figure out a way to escape while his body rested. After all, he was going to need his strength to resist the interrogations he knew were waiting for him. Luger counted the other beds, noted the other doorways, found lockers and washbasins, a bathroom, and a drug cabinet. Perfect. Steal a little something every opportunity you get, hide it under the mattress—you never knew what could be used as a weapon, or an escape tool, or a signaling device.

Painfully, unsteadily, he made his way over to the cabinet and tried the first large stainless-steel knob. Locked. He tried another, and this one opened. *All right, let's see what we got . . .*

"*Ay!*" a voice shouted from the bed to his right. "*Stoy! Stoytyee yeevo!*"

The voice startled Luger and he stumbled backwards, bounced off the adjacent bed, and fell forwards. His jaw slammed on the cold linoleum hard enough to draw blood and send a shower of stars obliterating his vision.

The man kept on screeching, "*Ay! Vrahchyah! Ay! Pahzahveetyee bistrah kahvonyeebood nah pomahshch!*"

His head pounding, Luger said, "Oh, shut up, will ya?" His voice was raspy and hoarse, barely audible. The alarmed Russian looked at Luger in shock, muttered something, then continued his shouting even louder, more in fear than in warning. Luger wiped blood off his chin from a fairly deep gash—and was suddenly blinded as the ward lights snapped fully on. The lights made him dizzy . . . weak . . .

Luger was lifted off the floor by two strong sets of hands and dragged back to his bed. He couldn't see who carried him, but he could hear their voices, and they seemed surprised, not angry. He was effortlessly hoisted back onto his bed, and they held his arms and legs securely on it, obviously not realizing Luger didn't have the strength to resist even if he wanted to. A few minutes later he felt the inevitable prick of a needle in his arm. That was unnecessary, too—his exertion had left him totally drained.

Seconds later he was once again unconscious.

* * *

"Welcome back to the land of the living, Lieutenant Luger."

David Luger opened his eyes. His vision was blurred, and he couldn't move his hands to clear them. After a command was given in Russian, someone wiped his eyes with a cold washcloth, and he was able to focus.

He saw two doctors, two nurses, and a man in civilian clothes—no military uniforms around. One nurse was taking a pulse and blood pressure reading, while the other was copying the readings in a medical chart. When they were finished, the medical personnel were dismissed and the door was closed behind them.

"Can you hear me, Lieutenant Luger?" the man in civilian clothes asked. Luger noticed his ankle-length coat was rich-looking black leather, and the collar of the white shirt underneath it was clean and starched, with a gold clasp under the Windsor knot of his necktie. Luger's eyes returned to meet the man's eyes, which were bright blue, with lines around the corners. But the face was chiseled, the jaw firm, the neck was gaunt—a runner's neck, the colonels back at Ford Air Force Base called it. Not a desk jockey . . .

"How are you feeling, Lieutenant?" The words were clipped and precise, with only a trace of accent. "Can you hear me all right, Lieutenant?"

Luger decided not to answer. He was *not* going to answer. Period. Lessons taught in the Air Force Survival School interrogation-resistance training facility—the "POW camp"—Fairchild Air Force Base, Washington, were mostly long forgotten, but one lesson wasn't—keep your mouth shut. Getting trapped by clever interrogators was something no crew dog ever learned to forget.

"Please answer me, Lieutenant," the civilian said. "The doctors have said you are fit and able to respond, but only you can tell us if your needs are being met. Are you well enough to talk to me?"

No reply.

The guy seemed perturbed but not angry. "Very well. I see by your expressions that you can understand me, but choose not to reply. So I will do the talking: You are in a hospital in Siberia, the location of which I am not permitted to reveal to you. You have been here for many months. We have cared for you as we would care for a Soviet fighting man, except no one has been notified of your presence here.

"By order of the Chief of Staff of the Military Forces of the Union of Soviet Socialist Republics, I am here to tell you that you are a prisoner of the people of the USSR. You are not a prisoner of war under the Geneva Conventions, but are a prisoner of crimes against the state and the people. Do you understand?"

Again Luger did not reply, but he heard the litany of charges against him: "You face fourteen counts of criminal murder, one count of attempted murder, willful destruction of government property, willful destruction of private property, violating the sovereignty of the state, and seeking to make war against the people of the Soviet Union, among other somewhat lesser crimes. Since the nature of your crimes does not lend itself to a public trial, and since you were deathly ill and in hospital for so long, a military tribunal was convened without your presence, evidence was presented, judgment was passed, and a sentence was delivered—a sentence of death."

Luger had been only half-listening, staring at a corner of the room to take his mind off the man's words, but "sentence of death" made him glare at the man's face.

A death sentence?

Luger's mouth became dry, and his heart pumped heavily. His blood pressure was rising, he could feel it, but for the first time since he'd regained consciousness, he was genuinely, truly scared. He tried to think—quickly—even in the glare of the lights and the foreign surroundings. Outwardly he fought to remain composed. He'd survived the explosion of the fuel truck which, hopefully, had allowed his fellow crew members an exit out to their final destination of Nome, Alaska, only now to be told he was going to die anyway.

Well, he had been prepared to die when he'd left the Old Dog . . . so what did it matter if he died now?

The civilian continued expressionlessly: "Since a criminal found guilty of murder and sentenced to death in the Soviet Union gives up all rights, you have no rights of appeal, not to the Soviet government or to any other government, nor are we required to notify anyone else of the sentence—and in fact we have not done so. Because of the severity of your crimes and the sensitive nature of the acts which you committed, you may not have the opportunity to have your sentence stayed, pardoned, or commuted. Carrying out your punishment cannot be delayed for any reason, even for psychological evaluation or to wait for your injuries to completely heal. A final review of your case will be accomplished by our civilian counterparts—only a formality, please understand—then witnesses will be summoned and a place of execution will be chosen. Within seven days, it will be done." The man paused for a few heartbeats, then added, "Death will be by a seven-member firing squad, the traditional means of execution for one convicted of capital crimes against the military."

Luger tried to hide the fear that was finally overcoming him, a fear far different from the adrenaline-rushed courage he'd shown during those final moments of the Old Dog mission. Then, he'd gambled not knowing what the outcome of his actions would be, if any. Now he knew. The outcome was predetermined. He was going to face death anyway.

Or was he? He avoided the man's eyes, all the while trying to think. If they were going to execute him, why hadn't they done so before now? Why go through all the trouble of trying to heal him, keep him in this hospital, only to kill him?

No, the Soviets had something else in mind. They were going to torture him, a fate often worse than death, depending on the techniques. They would do it for weeks, perhaps months. They wouldn't sit still for the basic Geneva Convention crap like name, rank, serial number. Hell, they already *knew* his name and rank. He was a prize, he realized, and they were going to use him. They'd try to pull everything they could out of him—information about the Strategic Air Command, about "Dreamland"—the top-secret Nevada military installation run by General Brad Elliot where ideas became reality, theories became machines and weapons—or even what he knew about SIOP, the Single Integrated Operations Plan the U.S. had developed for fighting World War III.

He was, Luger realized, more than a prize. He was their guinea pig, their lab rat . . .

The Russian civilian saw Luger's reflective eyes and struggled to repress a smile. He knew what the American was thinking. There he was, helpless in a hospital bed . . . Weighing his options, considering his chances, evaluating his life. Dependent on them. Yes, he decided, Luger would eventually talk. He might have been one tough bastard at Anadyr Base, but everyone has their breaking point. Even the Americans. Sometimes especially the Americans. And Luger *would* break.

And after that? The brainwashing would begin. The civilian was looking forward to *that*. It was, after all, one of his specialties, with a stellar record of success.

"If you talk to me, explain your circumstances, and agree to cooperate in our investigation," the man droned on, "the tribunal may be inclined to show you some leniency, perhaps commute your sentence to one of imprisonment. They may decide to notify your government that you are alive so a prisoner exchange can be arranged. I cannot guarantee any of this—it all depends on your willingness to cooperate.

"But I will tell you that this is no time for silence, bravado, or misplaced heroics, Lieutenant. You are alone and far from home. Even your crew has given you up for dead."

Luger's eyes narrowed at that—he knew *that* was a lie. These bastards weren't as smart as they thought.

"A court of law in a land foreign to you has sentenced you to death. You are alone, Lieutenant Luger. Remain silent and you remain alone. Speak to me, Lieutenant. If you do not, you will lose your identity—and eventually your life. Is life worth so little to you?"

Still no reply.

Stone-faced, the man continued. "I am not asking you to reveal military or state secrets, Lieutenant David Luger. We already know quite a bit about you. Frankly, I doubt if you have anything of real value to tell us. It would be a pity for you to undergo any . . . hardships for nothing."

Again no reply. Luger licked his lips and tried to move his arms—they were securely fastened to the sides of the bed. This man had just given away his real intentions, Luger reminded himself—they *were* going to torture him. All this talk of execution was bullshit . . .

"We can start with your date of birth, Lieutenant. How old are you?" Silence. "Come, come, Lieutenant. Surely your age is of no military value to the Soviet Union. Your code of honor says you may reveal your date of birth, as does the International Red Cross. What is your date of birth, Lieutenant?" No reply.

The man's mood suddenly turned dark. He moved a few inches closer to Luger's face. He reached into his pocket and withdrew a small round metal container and held it up so Luger could clearly see it.

"Do you know what this is, Lieutenant?" the man asked in a low, rumbling, menacing tone. "It is mentholated jelly. You place some of it under your nose, like so." The man unscrewed the cap, dipped on index finger into it, and roughly smeared a small blob of it on Luger's upper lip. Even through the jelly, the man's finger felt ice-cold. The jelly smelled like stale, pungent grass—undoubtedly a drug mixed with it, perhaps a mild hallucinogen such as LSD. The scent was strong enough to make Luger's eyes water—or *was* it from the jelly? "This is given to those who must work in this place because it filters out the stench of death. Prisoners come here to die, Lieutenant. Few prisoners leave this place alive . . . or as whole human beings. You can spend the last seven days of your life here, just another one of the breathing corpses, or you can stop this childish John Wayne game and speak to me."

The man—Luger still didn't know his name, or had forgotten it—stepped back but kept his eyes affixed on Luger's. "Maintain this stubborn silence and we have no use for you," he said, "in which case we will either be forced to attempt to make you talk or, if that proves to be too tedious, we will simply eliminate you. In any case, you will die within seven days. Speak to us as a soldier and as a man, and we will treat you like one and spare your life."

Luger closed his eyes, trying to block out the gamut of emotions running through him. Luger knew the guy was playing with his mind, trying to get him to take that first step . . . *One word, Dave, and you won't be able to back away. One word leads to another, then a few more, then eventually idle chat, then substantive chat. Remember your POW training. Remember your country, your crew members, remember the Old Dog . . .*

"I order you to answer me, Lieutenant!" the man shouted. Luger jumped at the sudden sound, and he sought to refocus his eyes on his captor. "I show you respect because you are a soldier and a professional—do me the same courtesy. Tell me your date of birth, a simple request, and I'll see to it that your sentence is delayed for a month. Refuse me, and I will throw you to the wolves that wait outside. They do not see you as an officer and as an aviator—they see you as a tough piece of meat that must be *tenderized*. Speak, for your own damned good, you fool. If I walk out that door unhappy, your days will be numbered . . ."

Luger's pulse was racing, his breathing labored. He tried to block out what this sonofabitch was saying, but his mind . . . was cloudy. His neurons weren't firing at their usual speed. They must have drugged him. Had, in fact, probably kept him pumped with drugs during his recovery. He swallowed hard, trying to focus, trying to think of his options, if any. But his thinking was muddled, fatigued . . .

His captor's patience ran out. "To hell with you, Luger," the man said in a low, murderous tone. "Why should I show you any respect? You invaded my country. You attacked my people, you destroyed my land, you violated my rights," he hissed, his visage turning darker and darker. "Yet here you lie, in a clean, warm hospital bed, receiving care from a physician that could otherwise be caring for a Soviet citizen. You deserve none of this, do you hear me? *None* of this!"

The man found a set of hospital shears on a nearby table—Dave did not realize the incongruity of those shears being so handy—and began slicing away at the bandages covering Luger's right leg. "You don't deserve these bandages . . . this dressing . . ." He exposed Luger's right leg. "My God, look at this! They have given you an artificial kneecap! A Soviet citizen must wait years for surgery such as this, if he is lucky enough to have access to a hospital at all! What have you done to deserve such treatment? Nothing! *Nothing!*"

Luger's weakened right leg jumped when he felt the cold steel of the shears against the side of his knee and the razor-sharp edge digging into a suture. "By God, I will not stand for this! I don't care if I'm punished for this, but a dead man does not need a kneecap!"

Luger cried aloud as he felt the first stitch rip free. He tried to shake his foot free to kick the man away, but his captor held the leg like a carpenter holding a piece of lumber.

"Give us back what you stole from us, you American pig!"

His leg began convulsing, flopping against the restraints.

The man ripped open a second suture, and Luger screamed—not from the pain, but from the fear that this guy was going to open up his entire leg . . .

This time, though, his scream was answered by a shout from the doorway as the doctors and nurses rushed into the room. The shears were pulled from sight, and the man was escorted from the room. Luger heard him shouting, "Seven days, you filthy pig! Seven days and you're dead! Seven days!"

The doctors and nurses were frantically examining Luger's right leg. To Luger's surprise, the doctor said in English, "Do not worry, Comrade. He did no serious harm. There is danger of infection, but we have the bleeding under control." Luger was urged to lean back and ignore the pain as antiseptic and sutures were brought to the bedside.

"Is . . . is he crazy?" Luger gasped. "Will he kill me?"

The doctor appeared not to be surprised to hear Luger speak. The doctor looked behind himself as if to check to see that the door was securely closed, then said quietly, "He is in charge here . . . I cannot say more."

"That sonofabitch," Luger muttered. "Sonofabitch." He was shaking. The touch of those blades, the sound of his flesh ripping, the eerie feel of his warm blood running over his skin . . .

"Relax, Comrade, relax," the doctor said soothingly. "My mission is to heal, not to harm." Luger failed to notice that the physician's English was just as precise as the interrogator's. He held up a syringe of clear fluid. "This will help you to relax . . ."

"No!" Luger rasped. "No drugs! I don't need drugs . . . !"

The syringe disappeared from view. "Very well, Comrade," the doctor said. "If you insist. But you really must rest. Can you relax?"

Luger's chest was heaving, his eyes wide with anger and fear, but he managed a nod. "Yeah . . . but no drugs, though. And wipe this stuff from under my nose. I think he tried to drug me."

"As you wish," the doctor replied, wiping away the jelly, all the while making mental notes about his patient. If Luger was concerned about drugs in the jelly, that indicated a couple of things: he was lucid and he was already paranoid, concocting grim scenarios about his "fate." Good, that was just the way the doctor wanted it. He saw Luger's eyes thanking him as the last of the jelly was wiped away. Thanking him was the first step, trusting him was the next. It was a building process, albeit sometimes a slow one, depending upon the subject. An American flyer like this, well, they were sometimes tougher. Like captured spooks. But eventually most turned. Especially if they bonded with their control, which was the doctor's job. And if they didn't, well . . .

"I will try to be present if Major Teresov—" The doctor stopped, closing his mouth as if he had just made a grievous error.

"Teresov? Major Teresov?" Luger asked. The American's face was smiling now. "That's his name? Teresov? Is he KGB?"

"I should say no more . . ."

"Is he KGB?" Luger demanded.

"You did not hear his name from me," the doctor said. "You did *not* hear it from me."

"Don't worry. I won't tell anyone."

The doctor looked relieved. He extended a hand, and Luger grasped it. "I am Petyr Kaminski."

"You're a Pole?"

"Yes," the doctor replied. "From Legnica, near the German border. I was brought here to Siberia five years ago . . . how do you say it, 'shanghaied'? Yes—shanghaied."

"David Luger, United States Air—" Luger stopped, realizing he was talking too much—but the doctor was a glorified prisoner too, he thought. He had to find out if he was as real as he seemed. Besides, they already seemed to know he was in the Air Force. "—Force," Luger finished. "I guess we're both pretty far from home."

"I must go," the doctor said, and leaned conspiratorially toward Luger. "This room is not . . . bugged, now, but since you are now awake it will be, so we must be careful in our conversations. I will bring something that will mask our voices." The doctor gave Luger a sly wink. "I have done this before." He then held up the syringe and squirted its contents onto the wall behind the bed. "Act sleepy or they might be suspicious. I will try to help you. Be careful of Teresov. Trust no one. I will return. Be brave." And the doctor rapidly departed.

Luger sank back in bed after the doctor left, feeling more drained than ever, but with a glimmer of hope that he clung to with all his might. Here, in the middle of Siberia, there was a co-conspirator, a confidant.

Or was there? How could you ever know? How could you be sure it wasn't just another mind game? Luger, cold and aching from head to toe, had never felt so alone—or unsure—in all of his twenty-six years.

Maybe there was still a chance to survive . . .

"Dr. Petyr Kaminski" walked into his office a few minutes later. Inside were two plainclothesmen, and Teresov was sitting at his desk with headphones against one ear. Teresov stood at attention as Kaminski—otherwise known as KGB General Viktor Gabovich—entered. Teresov asked in Russian, "How did it go, sir?"

"Better than I ever hoped," General Gabovich replied, taking the desk from Teresov. "The young fool couldn't wait to talk to me—he practically kissed my hand when I told him I'd watch out for him. One, maybe two days, and he will be committed. It is true—Americans trust doctors without question. You could have sawed off his entire leg, but he will eventually tell me his whole life story simply because I appear to be a doctor."

"Did he tell you anything else, sir?"

"If I started to interrogate him, he would have gotten suspicious of me," Gabovich said. "No, but he will talk when he's ready. He's young, afraid, and facing death otherwise. What choice will he have?"

"So we proceed as planned?"

"Yes," Gabovich replied. "Pump sleeping gas into his room in five minutes—low dose only. Then wake him up in two hours. He'll think one day has already gone by. You'll interrogate him some more, then I'll come back and see what he has to say. The closer we get to his 'execution' day, the more he'll talk. In five days, no more than six, he'll be ready to move."

"Move?" Teresov echoed incredulously. "Sir, you're still planning on taking him to the Fisikous Institute?"

"Of course," Gabovich replied. "Luger is an aeronautical engineer, an honor graduate of the Air Force Academy, a highly trained aircrew member, a trained Strategic Air Command navigator, and his last assignment was the High Technology Aerospace Weapons Center. If we turn Luger without destroying his intellect, he can supply enough information to put Fisikous in the lead in new aircraft technology. It will be the intelligence coup of the century—we can turn Fisikous into a bigger aircraft-design bureau than Sukhoi or Mikoyan-Gurevich."

"But Lithuania is becoming a battle zone," Teresov said. "The pro-independence movement there is gathering too much momentum—and attracting too much attention. Fisikous could be easily jeopardized."

"We will never lose Fisikous," Gabovich said. "The Party will never allow it. I think we will never lose the Baltic states, but even if we do, Fisikous will *always* belong to the Soviet Union, like the Baltic Sea Fleet headquarters in Riga and the Tupolev-92 bomber base in Tallinn. We built those places—they belong to us forever."

"Are you willing to bet everything on that, sir?" Teresov asked. "The Fisikous design bureau is being moved to Kaliningrad in a few years— perhaps Luger should be transferred there or kept here in Moscow . . ."

"We are in no danger," Gabovich repeated. "This independence movement will eventually die out."

General Gabovich was being blind, Teresov thought, trusting another organization or unit for his own security. "But, sir . . ."

"Luger can be moved quickly enough if the situation warrants—until then he belongs in Vilnius," Gabovich insisted. "I will see to it. The government insists that Vilnius and the Fisikous Institute are secure—all KGB apparatuses have been moved there—so I can trust it."

"Yes, sir," Teresov said. Gabovich had made up his mind—there seemed no dissuading him. "Now, as to Luger . . ."

"He ceases to exist as Luger now, except to 'Kaminski,' " Viktor

Gabovich said. "From now on he will be known by his file designation, 41 dash Zulu. We will begin the disorientation cycle immediately. Wake him up in two hours for his first session, then drug him to sleep, then wake him up two hours later. He will think another day has gone by. After twelve hours, he will be begging us not to execute him—if he lasts that long," he sneered.

NIGHT
OF THE
HAWK

V-22 Osprey Joint Service Aircraft

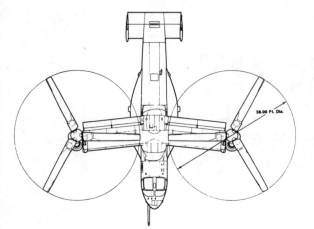

Aircraft Characteristics

Spread	
Length	57' 4"
Width	84' 7"
Height	22' 7"

Folded	
Length	62' 7"
Width	18' 5"
Height	18' 1"

Take-Off Weights	
VTOL/STOL	55,000 lb
Self Deploy STOL	60,500 lb
Fuel Capacity	2015 gal

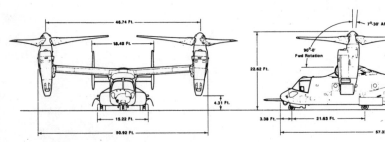

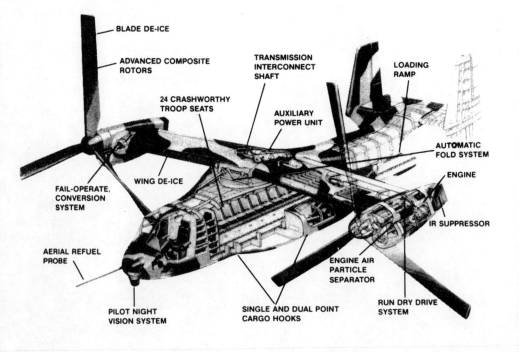

BLADE DE-ICE

ADVANCED COMPOSITE ROTORS

TRANSMISSION INTERCONNECT SHAFT

LOADING RAMP

24 CRASHWORTHY TROOP SEATS

AUXILIARY POWER UNIT

AUTOMATIC FOLD SYSTEM

ENGINE

WING DE-ICE

FAIL-OPERATE, CONVERSION SYSTEM

IR SUPPRESSOR

AERIAL REFUEL PROBE

ENGINE AIR PARTICLE SEPARATOR

PILOT NIGHT VISION SYSTEM

SINGLE AND DUAL POINT CARGO HOOKS

RUN DRY DRIVE SYSTEM

ONE

ABOARD THE USS *VALLEY MISTRESS*
OFF THE COAST OF THE LATVIAN REPUBLIC
29 NOVEMBER, YEARS LATER, 1233 LATVIAN TIME (0633 ET)

"S tand by for team launch," Air Force Colonel Paul White radioed on the intercom. "All decks, get ready to rock and roll." Captain Joseph Marchetti, the senior ship's officer standing beside White, looked at his colleague in amusement and consternation. Rock and roll? Things were going to get critical here very, very fast . . .

Paul White was fifty-one years old, but, as he himself would readily admit, capriciously, only seventeen or eighteen. And he could not have been more out of place than on this ship—or having more fun than if he had an A-pass at Disneyland. It was at times like this that White longed for the flying skill and combat nerve needed to get knee-deep in the action. Although he had designed trainers and simulators for the Strategic Air Command and other organizations over the years, he had never earned a flying rating nor seen combat—but anyone who had flown in his modified super-realistic simulators back at Ford Air Force Base would have sworn they'd just been in combat when they finished a grueling session.

His current assignment with the Intelligence Support Agency—a support agency of the Director of Central Intelligence—was also not considered a combat assignment, but if something went wrong on this mission, or if they were discovered, they could be just as dead as if they were in the middle of World War III.

The twenty-nine-year veteran Air Force officer was on the bridge of what had to be the most unusual vessel in the world, as befitting one of the most dedicated yet unusual men in the world. The USS *Valley Mistress* was a maritime salvage and deep-sea construction vessel registered under the U.S. flag. Officially, the *Mistress* was part of the U.S. Navy's Ready Reserve Fleet, leased from a private company from Larose, Louisiana, but for the past few months she was detached from her reserve duties and was on a "privately contracted" voyage to northern Europe, performing a variety of jobs in Finland, Sweden, Germany, Poland, and even the Commonwealth of Independent States, or CIS—what used to be known as the Soviet Union. Three hundred and twenty feet long, sixty feet in width, with a draft of twelve feet and a manifested crew of only twenty, the *Mistress* had put in a considerable number of miles on voyages all over the world.

Originally an oilfield support tug, the *Mistress* had been converted to an undersea construction, salvage, and rescue vessel with the addition of a large steel pressure enclosure on the middeck specifically designed to support a Navy deep-submergence rescue vehicle, or DSRV, which was its primary Naval Reserve Fleet assignment. The *Mistress* also sported a thirty-five-ton crane abaft the main superstructure, ostensibly to load and unload the DSRV, and it had a large helicopter landing pad on the fantail, so big that the sides of the pad hung out over the ship's gunwales and several feet behind the transom. Her hull had been ice-strengthened to be able to operate in the Arctic and Antarctic, and a pressurized recovery hatch had been added in the hull to allow a DSRV or pressure-suited divers to be raised and lowered directly inside the enclosure. Her three big fourteen-thousand-brake-horsepower diesels propelled the three-thousand, five-hundred-ton vessel at a snappy twenty knots; computer-controlled stabilizers ensured a relatively smooth ride in all but the most treacherous waters; and side-thrusters and a sophisticated navigation and electronics suite allowed her to be positioned anywhere near a rescue site with great precision, or to locate submerged objects in up to two thousand feet of water.

Paul White was not her skipper—on the unclassified manifest he was listed as purser, in charge of everything from buying water while in port to filling out customs forms—but he loved this ship as if he was her master. It was a strange and overwhelming feeling of pride for a man from Wyoming who had never been near the sea or owned a boat, whose whole career had been in the United States Air Force, designing and building mechanical and electronic devices for aircrews. His particular talent was engineering . . . things. He was into gadgets, big and small.

And the *Valley Mistress* was Paul White's biggest and best gadget of all.

The vessel, and Colonel White as her operational commander, were known by the code name MADCAP MAGICIAN. The vessel's real purpose: conduct unconventional warfare, direct action, reconnaissance, counterterrorist, foreign internal defense, and special rescue operations to support the National Command Authority and unified military commands worldwide. It was one of four oceangoing vessels modified by

White and secretly operated by the Intelligence Support Agency, the CIA's "troubleshooters." When the CIA needed more firepower than they normally used, but did not want to directly involve the military, it called on the Intelligence Support Agency. When ISA needed a tough job done quickly and effectively, it called on MADCAP MAGICIAN.

Although perfectly capable of acting as a salvage vessel—she had already earned several million for her nonexistent Louisiana salvage company, an unexpected bonus for the U.S. government treasury—she was not doing so now. The *Valley Mistress* had transferred her DSRV onto another cargo ship, this one the Italian-flag vessel *Bernardo LoPresti,* which had been contracted by the Intelligence Support Agency to act as the *Valley Mistress*'s support ship, and had secretly taken aboard a very different kind of cargo: six mission-specific cargo containers, or MISCOs, and a CV-22 PAVE HAMMER tilt-rotor special-operations aircraft, now nestled in the DSRV chamber and ready to go.

Her present, covert mission: a Lithuanian-born officer in a mostly Byelorussian unit of the CIS Army in Lithuania who had been delivering military and state secrets to the CIA for several months. He had been discovered and was now in danger of being captured. As part of his double-agent deal, the U.S. agreed to extract him by whatever means when the time came.

This was it.

"Gimme the downlink from PATRIOT, Carl," White said to his operations officer, Air Force Major Carl Knowlton. "Tell the Intel section to stand by."

The skipper of the *Mistress* watched and listened as White gave his orders—although Marchetti was commander of the vessel and in overall command of the entire mission, it was White who ran this show.

"You got it, boss," Knowlton replied casually, then relayed the order down to the Intel section. The Air Force crew had long ago dispensed with traditional military courtesies while deployed—in fact, no one on board could easily be recognized as military men. They wore civilian work clothes, not uniforms, and some sported long hair and scraggly beards. Their military I.D. cards were in a hidden safe in the Engineering section and would not be reissued to the crew until they arrived back at their home port in Kittery, Maine.

Moments later a phone rang on the bridge. White picked it up himself: "Bridge, White here. Go ahead, PATRIOT."

The snaps and crackles of the secure radio link were audible on the radio channel: "This is PATRIOT controller S-3. Radar plot description follows. Plot describes mission essential data." PATRIOT was a NATO E-3B AWACS radar aircraft, orbiting over the Baltic Sea between Poland and Sweden. The plane's powerful radar could track hundreds of aircraft and vessels for many miles in all directions and then feed that digitized data directly to White's crew on the *Valley Mistress.* Even though the Warsaw Pact had disbanded, East Germany had fallen, and the Soviet Union had broken up into many fragments, a NATO radar surveillance plane was still on patrol twenty-four hours a day over Eastern Europe, tracking aircraft and vessels over the horizon and correlating the information with civilian and military sources. The Cold War may have been over, but President Ronald Reagan's famous words, "Trust, but verify," were the new watchwords in West-East relations in the 1990s.

The current political situation in the old USSR was confusing, complicated, and extremely dangerous. The new Commonwealth of Independent States (CIS) had replaced the USSR in 1992, but the new entity was more of a collection of bickering ministers than any sort of true union. The Red Army had disbanded, split along ethnic or religious lines, but the splits were inequitable and destructive: the Russian Army found itself with most of the skilled technicians and almost all of the officers but no one willing to do the "menial" tasks, while the armies of Belarus (Byelorussia), Ukraine, and Kazakhstan—the three most powerful members of the CIS besides Russia—were left with few well-trained, knowledgeable leaders but a lot of soldiers with little technical training or formal education. To say it was a mess was an understatement.

But all four republics still had one thing in common: nuclear weapons.

Despite the Commonwealth's initial pledge to destroy its intercontinental weapons, move all tactical weapons to the Russian interior or into storage, and place the remaining ones in joint command, no republic was willing to give up the nuclear weapons inside its borders unless the other republics gave them up first. As a result, no one gave them up. All four republics—Belarus, Ukraine, Kazakhstan, and Russia—had intercontinental-range nuclear weapons and the skilled soldiers to use them.

Officially, the role of the United States government in regard to the fledgling Commonwealth was simple: encourage democratic reforms and a free market, but otherwise hands off. The Commonwealth had pledged to adhere to treaties already in force between the U.S. and the old USSR, and that satisfied the White House for the time being. Talks on new trade agreements between the Commonwealth, the individual states, and the U.S. and other countries were laid, in preparation for full diplomatic recognition and lifting of all trade barriers. World markets were eagerly awaiting the millions of new consumers being unleashed by the republics; everyone seemed willing to overlook the devalued, nearly worthless ruble (the adopted currency of the CIS) and bet that the future was going to be much brighter.

The White House feeling in private was much different: monitor the nuclear weapons and military movements in all Commonwealth-member republics and develop strategies and doctrines for dealing with a possible breakup of the Commonwealth and a loss of central control for each republic's nuclear arsenal. For the Central Intelligence Agency, that meant stepping up covert operations in the various republics, especially the strategically and politically important Baltic states.

That's where Paul White and MADCAP MAGICIAN came in.

The radar operator aboard PATRIOT read off his position, altitude, surveillance track, date-time group of the surveillance run, and his equipment status—all in encoded format, even on the secure anti-eavesdrop channel—then continued: "Nearest vessel of interest is off your port beam, range three point one nautical miles, possible ELINT vessel. Numerous smaller vessels all quadrants appear to be at anchor, adrift, or moored to navigation aids, none considered a mission risk. Largest vessel in projected flight path confirmed identity as ferry *Baltic Star.* Additional vessel, the *LoPresti,* west-northwest of your position, is scheduled to rendezvous with you in approximately twelve hours. He is just leaving port at this time."

White muttered a curt "Copy."

The ELINT (electronic intelligence) vessel, a Soviet-CIS Gagarin-class research ship about the same size as the *Valley Mistress,* was a serious threat to this mission. Primarily used for spacecraft tracking and recovery, it was crammed full of communications and radar gear. Based in St. Petersburg, it had been on its way to the Atlantic when it had slowed and begun shadowing the American vessel in the Baltic, using its radar to constantly monitor the skies and seas around the *Mistress.* White thought that the CIS spy ship would go away after they had made their schedule port call in Tallinn, Estonia, but it had not. Then, after their inspection by Estonian customs officials in Tallinn—many of whom, White was sure, were former KGB agents—he thought the spy ship would definitely leave. Again, it had not, although it was no longer scanning them with radar. The *Mistress* had moved back into the Baltic, headed toward its next port of call in Norway, and the Gagarin-class research ship was right on his tail.

It was wrong, but probably prudent, to always believe that your cover was blown. The Gagarin-class vessel was not now using its radar, but it had lots of other sophisticated sensors—infrared, laser, low-light TV, super-sensitive optical, and plain old trained "weather-eye" crewmen— with which to watch over the *Mistress.* Or it could be just hanging out, tracking its own satellites, conducting training missions, anything. White's mission was too important to scrub, so some chances had to be taken. . . .

The report from PATRIOT continued: "Possible military rotary-wing aircraft will be within ten miles of target vicinity at feet-dry. Subject aircraft has been observed orbiting the vicinity since sunset. Analysis indicates the target may have been compromised. Recommend postponement additional twenty-four hours. Radar downlink to follow. PATRIOT standing by. Out."

Well, things did not look good. A spy ship nearby, and now a military chopper in the target area. "Looks like we've been blown," Knowlton said. "We don't have a choice but to bug out."

"Shit," White muttered. "You're probably right." But Knowlton knew White had no intention of leaving. White turned to Marchetti and said, "Let's start putting a little distance between us and that Gagarin, Joe. Try to get us over his radar horizon."

"It'll look suspicious . . ."

"We *already* look suspicious," White said. "I'm going down to Intel. Keep an eye on things up here," he ordered Knowlton, then hurried off the bridge.

The confusing status of White's HUMINT (human intelligence) target underscored the dangerous situation that now existed in the region. Even though the Baltic states had been independent for quite a long time, all still had foreign troops on their soil. Worse, those troops had a continuing identity crisis of their own. They had gone from being Soviet Red Army troops to Union of Sovereign Socialist Republic troops to Union Treaty troops to Commonwealth of Independent States troops, all in the space of a few months. Now most of those troops didn't even belong to the Commonwealth. The Soviet troops of Byelorussian heritage in the Baltic states pledged allegiance to Belarus, while the Russian troops pledged loyalty to the Russian Federation, and Lithuanian troops supported Lithuania.

Aggravating this identity problem was the status of the many former Soviet military installations and other important government facilities in the Baltic states. Lithuania had twenty such installations, ranging from radar sites to research laboratories to fighter and bomber bases. The land belonged to Lithuania—that was clear. The structures, equipment, and products within these facilities belonged to the Commonwealth of Independent States, subject to transfer negotiations between Minsk, the capital of the CIS, and Vilnius, the capital of Lithuania. But occupying some of these bases were Soviet scientists and engineers, some of whom never agreed to or wanted a new commonwealth to upset their system of rank and privileges assured them under the old Soviet system. Some facilities were under the control of former KGB officers who still wielded considerable power. Other facilities were guarded by heavily armed troops who were loyal to who was the richest, the most powerful, or the most influential at the moment—the KGB, the CIS, Belarus, or themselves.

The main objective of CIA operations in the Baltics was to study the complicated, potentially disastrous mixture being brewed here in Lithuania. The best way to do that was to cultivate HUMINT resources. In a poor, unorganized land such as this, the CIA found lots of willing informants. But it wasn't long before the CIA needed help in order to successfully run all their informants, so they had called on MADCAP MAGICIAN.

Since the *Valley Mistress* was a real, privately-owned salvage vessel, subject to searches by all seagoing navies when not operating on behalf of the U.S. Navy, she could not have normal intelligence sections in her—no Commonwealth or non-aligned nation would allow such a vessel in its territorial waters. But White devised a system to solve that problem. The *Mistress*'s specially designed cargo containers (MISCOs) could be shipped like any other container or easily transferred by the *Mistress*'s big crane between vessels while under way. The containers were completely self-enclosed, with all necessary subsystems installed, and were fully functional once ship's power was applied. The *Valley Mistress*'s six MISCOs were strapped down to the middeck area abaft the crane. Three belonged to the CV-22 aircraft's maintenance and support crew, one was a heavy-weapons armory for the CV-22 and the assault crew, and two made up the mission command center, or Intel, which contained all of the classified radar, communications, and intelligence-gathering equipment necessary to run the mission and communicate with U.S. Special Operations Command headquarters in Florida. All six MISCOs could be slid overboard in case of an unexpected boarding or attack, and self-destruct charges and incendiaries would ensure complete destruction of most of the incriminating evidence.

The CV-22 PAVE HAMMER aircraft itself was the newest addition to the Air Force Special Operations Command arsenal. This unusual tilt-rotor aircraft had the ability to take off and land vertically like a helicopter, but then fly like a conventional turboprop airplane. It had twice the range, speed, and payload capability of a helicopter, but had all the advantages of vertical flight. It carried a crew of three—pilot, copilot, and engineer/loadmaster—plus a combat crew of eight soldiers, and was armed with one 20-millimeter Hughes Chain Gun on one outrigger pod and one twelve-round Stinger missile pod on another; both pods were steerable by either the pilot or copilot with helmet-pointing fire-control systems. The CV-22 PAVE HAMMER folded itself into a compact 58-foot by 18-foot by 18-foot unit that fit perfectly into the DSRV chamber on the *Valley Mistress*.

The V-22 family of tilt-rotor aircraft had made a name for itself in the fledgling U.S. Border Security Force, or "Hammerheads," which was to receive sixty of the hybrid aircraft for border patrol and drug-interdiction duty. Hidden within that appropriation bill had been six other birds, modified by the Air Force, General Bradley Elliott's High Technology Aerospace Weapons Center (HAWC) in Nevada, and transferred to the Special Operations Command. This was to be one of its first actual missions . . .

. . . If it was to go at all.

In the cramped, cold interior of the second container that formed the new Intel offices aboard ship, Paul White watched as five days' worth of radar plots were replayed on a digital situation board. The map of the target area—a spot ten miles north of a small port and resort town called Liepaja, on the Baltic coast of Latvia, a few miles north of the Lithuanian border—showed numerous aircraft transiting the area. "Which one are we looking at?" White asked.

"PATRIOT says it's this one," an intelligence officer explained. He pointed at a persistent radar dot just north of the town, farther away from the other aircraft that seemed to circle near the town. "Liepaja has a large civil airfield here, called Liepaja East, used by the CIS Baltic Sea Fleet to resupply the naval patrol base. Lots of helicopter activity. There's another base, a CIS air-defense fighter base, thirty nautical miles east-southeast of Liepaja at Vainode. Mostly older MiG-19s and MiG-21s—daylight fighters—but once in a while they'll deploy a couple of MiG-29s there. They've also deployed Sukhoi-25 'Frogfoot' attack planes and 'Hind-D' attack choppers, too. I'd assume they have 'em there now."

White nodded impatiently—he was well familiar with the deployment of the Commonwealth troops in the Baltic states. Technically those jets and choppers might have belonged to the CIS, but the pilots and commanders who controlled them were Byelorussian. In recent months Belarus had stepped up military activities in Lithuania, ostensibly to protect Byelorussian citizens moving out of Lithuania and to guard products and shipments being transferred across Lithuania from Kalinin, the small sliver of land on the Baltic Sea coast between Lithuania and Poland.

But Lithuania was no threat to Belarus. The real reason for the increased military activity, White feared, was a move by Belarus to at some point occupy Lithuania.

Like Iraq before its invasion of Kuwait, Belarus seemed on the brink of breaking out of its isolation and claiming some valuable, unprotected neighboring territory. All the elements were there, and the parallels between Iraq and Belarus were frightening: Belarus was industrially advanced but cash- and resources-poor; Belarus had a large, well-equipped, and well-trained military, whose officers had seen a great decline in their prestige and perquisites after it joined the CIS; Belarus had no outlet to the sea and had to bargain with others for access to ports and commercial overseas-shipping facilities; and it was very dependent on the CIS, Poland, and Lithuania for raw materials for its factories. It would be difficult to stop Belarus if it decided to stretch its legs a bit.

So far his theory had no basis in fact, but White could see the signs. Something was brewing out there. . . .

"The pickup point is here," the intelligence officer continued, pointing to a forested area several miles north of Liepaja, "and here's the helicopter they're looking at. It's been in the target area for two days and seems to be hanging on for another day. The area is flat and marshy, and land navigation is pretty bad. Farther south is a resort area, very popular in the summer, but this is too early in the season. Railroad tracks and a highway farther east, very well traveled and patrolled."

"What a damned stupid place for an exfiltration," White muttered. "Less than ten miles from a military base. Hell, let's just pick him up in a limo *at* the base!" But White knew they had no choice. According to the CIA, their subject, a lieutenant stationed at a research facility in Vilnius, Lithuania, had gone home to Siauliai, a town between the coast and the Lithuanian capital of Vilnius. The young Lithuanian Army officer had been a longtime informant for the CIA, code-named RAGANU (Lithuanian for "witch"), but he was not a professional spy. He had inadvertently delivered a batch of fake data on a CIS Air Force deployment to Lithuania, an error that pointed directly at him as the infiltrator. Fortunately RAGANU was home on leave when the Americans discovered his cover blown, and he was told by his American handlers not to return to his unit but to execute one of his pre-planned exfiltration plans, the best of which was to send RAGANU to the coast to await pickup.

RAGANU was obviously clever enough to keep out of sight for one or two days, but as soon as his disappearance was noticed, the hunt for him would be on. From his hometown of Siauliai, they would track him down easily. After four days AWOL, the net would be very, very tight around him. He was probably a dead man, White thought, at least by daylight if not right now. The pickup plan was for RAGANU to meet at a predetermined spot and monitor it. Eventually someone would be inserted to retrieve him at that location.

That "someone" was MADCAP MAGICIAN.

White looked at his watch and cursed again—time was running out. It would take the Marines almost two hours to paddle into the drop area and travel overland to the target area—then they had to find RAGANU, travel to the pickup point, and find the CV-22, all before daylight. To make matters worse, the *Valley Mistress*'s cover was going to run out soon. She was scheduled for a port call in Kalmar in southern Sweden just seventy miles away, and it would attract a *lot* of attention if she was late. The Italian-flagged cargo vessel *Bernardo LoPresti* was going to rendezvous with the *Valley Mistress* in twelve hours to off-load the mission containers before the *Mistress* pulled into port—the mission had to be over by then. A decision had to be made.

White left the Intel section and made his way to the aft chamber, where the CV-22 aircraft was stowed. In the subdued night-vision red lights of the chamber, the CV-22 looked as if it were damaged. Its main wing was swiveled parallel to the fuselage instead of perpendicular, and the fifteen-foot-long rotors were folded flat against the engine nacelles. It looked as if it would never be able to untangle itself. But White knew that the CV-22 could go from completely stowed to ready for engine start in five minutes, all with the push of three buttons.

When White entered the chamber, the CV-22's eight-man Marine Corps Maritime Special Purpose Force (MSPF) crew snapped to their feet in anticipation. Even after working with these guys for so many months, White was still in awe of them. They were members of "Cobra Venom," Tenth Force Reconnaissance Company, 26th Marine Expeditionary Unit (Special Operations Capable), deployed in the Mediterranean with the U.S. Navy's Sixth Fleet aboard LHD-1 *Wasp* and detached for service in Oslo. The MSPF were the elite of the elite and consisted of only fifty Marines in the United States specially trained for deep reconnaissance and covert penetration missions. The men in the MSPF could walk across cables stretched between two buildings, climb a ten-story building without a rope, swim ten miles in bone-chilling water—and kill with absolute precision, stealth, and speed. Most were unmarried, but the meaner ones were—meaner because they had more to fight for than just themselves.

The eight men here had received extra training in working not with Marine air-combat elements, but with U.S. Air Force special-operations forces, which they considered inferior but tolerable to their own. MADCAP MAGICIAN, on the other hand, seemed insane and dangerous enough for them, so they took him in stride.

None of them said a word as White strode to the CV-22's cockpit. Inside were two Air Force pilots, Major Hank Fell and Major Martin J. Watanabe. The black-suited soldiers circled in behind White as he stepped inside the tilt-rotor aircraft and squatted between the two pilots' seats. The crew engineer and loadmaster, Master Sergeant Mike Brown, left his place at the compartment doors and hurried to join them. The assault team leader, Marine Corps Gunnery Sergeant Jose Lobato, squatted behind the left-hand copilot's seat to listen in as well.

"Visit from the boss just before a mission," Fell quipped as White was about to speak. "Looks serious. Decision time, eh?"

"You got it. Listen up. The same fucking spy ship is still out there, but I think we can radar-shadow you enough to get away clean—we're at ten miles now, and we'll probably be right on the edge of his radar horizon by launch time. The problem is in the target area. There's a chopper circling the pickup point, the same one we've seen the past two days."

"Still just one chopper?" Fell asked. White nodded. "No other activity from Liepaja?"

"Plenty of activity, but nothing associated with the lone chopper or with us—at least I don't think so," White replied uneasily. "Radar pictures from two hundred miles away are not enough to accurately estimate enemy movements, but I think they're still looking for RAGANU. They may be close, but I don't think they got him. In any case, eyes are in the target area, and maybe eyes on us right now. It's looking very risky. We have to off-load the MISCO trailers tomorrow morning before we enter Swedish waters or we'll be in deep shit if we're caught with them on board.

"My question is, do we go or cancel? The book says cancel." He paused, gave a sly smile that went unappreciated by the black-suited warriors, then continued: "My gut says we go for it! But since it's your asses on the firing line, I wanted to hear from you."

"I need to see the radar plots," Fell said. A technician came up a few moments later and delivered several large sheets of paper, each with different four-color screen dumps of the digitized radar picture from the AWACS radar plane. Fell examined them briefly, then handed them over to Watanabe, who began correlating the radar targets with his mission chart. "Any idea what aircraft they have at Liepaja other than the patrol and supply choppers?" Fell asked. "Any fixed-wing stuff? Any of the attack planes or helicopters from that squadron in Kaliningrad move north into Latvia?"

"Still the same info," White replied. "Light-patrol, medium–search and rescue, medium-troop, and heavy-cargo helicopters only." He referred to the screen dump. "Maybe a twin-engine liaison plane shuttling between Riga, Liepaja, and Vilnius, but no armed fixed-wings from Liepaja East. No apparent increase in numbers which might signify a reinforcement of the garrison already there. Except for that one chopper, it's business as usual out there. Vainode is a large Soviet fighter base thirty miles east, but we haven't seen much activity from there except in daylight hours."

Fell gave a sarcastic snort. "Yeah, right. Business as usual—meaning ten thousand troops, a spy ship, several gunboats, and thirty choppers within ten miles of the target zone." Fell looked over at Watanabe. "Got all those targets plotted, Marty?"

"Plotted and laid in the mission computer," Watanabe replied, handing the printouts to Gunny Lobato for him and his men to peruse. The CV-22's advanced AN/AMC-641 computer would warn the crew of any known enemy positions and would use the multimode radar to update that information during the flight; during withdrawal it would plot a best-guess evasion route out of the area and offer suggestions for safe escape-and-evasion routes in case they were shot down. Watanabe looked at his watch. "We need to start pulling out on deck if we want to recover before first light."

"I take it you vote 'go,'" Fell said dryly. Watanabe nodded and began strapping himself in. Fell turned to Lobato. "Gunny?"

"Walk in the park," the dark Marine said quietly. "We go."

"We go, then," Fell said. "Turn us loose, Colonel."

"One last sweep of the area and you're on your way," White said, stepping out of the CV-22 PAVE HAMMER. "Good hunting, gents. See you in a few." White stood and watched as the Marine assault team loaded aboard the CV-22, the aft pressure-chamber access doors were opened, and the aircraft was winched out of the chamber onto the helicopter pad. White headed back to the bridge as the CV-22's on-board auxiliary power system was started.

By the time White made his way back onto the bridge, the CV-22 had begun its transformation from a wadded-up puzzle into a flying machine. The rear-engine nacelle swiveled until it was horizontal, allowing it to clear its stowed position between the twin tail rudders; then the entire wing began to swivel from its stowed position parallel to the fuselage into its normal perpendicular position. As the wing moved into position, the aft-engine nacelle swiveled vertically into position and, like the petals of a rose, the rotors began to unstow themselves on each wingtip nacelle. By the time the wing was in flight position, the rotors were extended to their full thirty-eight-foot diameter and the engines were being started.

"Pre-launch sweep," White called out to Operations Officer Knowlton.

"In progress, Paul," Knowlton replied. "Radar reports negative. That Gagarin radar ship is over our horizon at one-five miles—Ladybug needs to stay below one hundred feet and no less than fifteen miles to stay outside of his normal radar horizon." Knowlton said "normal" because the Gagarin-class ship was reported to have shipborne over-the-horizon radars that they very well could employ. "Data being transmitted to Ladybug—he'll have it on his tactical computer and should have a course to keep him well out of range. His initial heading should be one-six-zero, no farther east than that. Pre-launch report from PATRIOT coming in now."

The pre-launch radar scan was worse than before; the helicopter was still in the target area, and there were more boats than before along the coastline. "Looks like fishing vessels to me," White said to Knowlton.

His operations officer gave him a questioning expression—how could White know they were only fishing boats?

"It's about the right time for them to head out," White added, as if he had heard Knowlton's unspoken question. Then again, they might *not* have been fishing boats—they could have been Soviet patrol boats. But no great numbers of patrol boats had ever been deployed like this before, so either they were indeed just fishermen . . . or the Soviets somehow knew they were coming.

"Pre-launch from PATRIOT shows clear," Knowlton reported as a teletype machine on the bridge clattered away. He went to the small repeater scope, which had a smaller version of the Intel section's digital situation screen. "Can't tell about those boats—they're not traveling in much of a straight line, as if they're on a course to a particular spot. But only a few I can see are coming from the military docks—the rest look like they're coming from the commercial docks. No aircraft up, except for our friend—but it looks like he might be heading back to base."

"Must be refueling," White said. "How long does it take to refuel a helicopter?"

"Not long," Knowlton replied. "He'll be up again by the time Ladybug is feet-dry." He paused, looking at White with growing concern. "But we can't delay the launch or we'll run out of daylight."

"I know, I know," White exclaimed. "We're committed. If Fell or PATRIOT sees a problem developing, we'll wave Ladybug off, and RAGANU will have to go deep into hiding—or make a run for Poland. Jesus, what we need right now is a good thunderstorm to hide in."

But they did not even have the good luck of bad weather to help them on this one.

White had reported that they needed to be no higher than one hundred feet to go under the radar from the Gagarin-class radar ship. One hundred feet would have seemed like a mile to Fell and Watanabe right now, because they were flying their CV-22 in full airplane mode only thirty feet above the Baltic Sea. The plane's engine nacelles swiveled down to full horizontal, so the helicopter rotors were now airplane propellers. Aided by the high-resolution infrared scene projected onto their helmet-mounted sights by the AAR-50 thermal-imaging navigation set, and by their AN/APQ-174 multimode terrain-following radar, the tiny warplane streaked inbound, changing course every ten to twenty seconds, skirting as far as possible around the growing number of vessels they picked up on radar. In OVERWATER mode, a tiny beam of radar energy measured the distance between the CV-22's belly and the water, and a warning light would illuminate if the distance dipped below twenty feet.

The pilot was responsible for keeping the aircraft a safe distance above the water—no autopilot in existence had the precision to hold such a low altitude. Flight and sensor information was electronically projected onto

Fell's helmet visor, so he didn't have to look down into the cockpit for vital information—a fraction of a second's distraction could kill them all. As long as there were no sheer obstructions such as ships or towers in the flight path—the radar altimeter did not look *forward,* only *downward*—they were safe.

That is, if flying less than a wingspan's distance above the water at four miles per minute could be considered safe.

The plane was to drop the MSPF team about ten to twelve miles from the coast, but obviously the closer to shore they could get before running into hostile detection systems, the better. In their case it was not hostile Soviet radars—it was the huge number of boats that kept popping up on radar. But there was an "obstacle" to contend with—the port town of Liepaja, now only fifteen miles away. The piers and warehouses along the coast were so bright now that they threatened to destroy their night vision—and if they could see the town, someone could well see them. They managed to get closer than ten miles to shore before encountering boats they could not safely circumnavigate, but the closer they got to shore, the harder it was to avoid them.

"All right, I think we've gotten as close as we can get," Fell told Watanabe. "I can't go far enough around these sonsofbitches. If they get an eyeball on us, the game is up. Alert the team and get the cargo doors open."

Watanabe made the interphone calls. The glow from Liepaja was so bright now that it created glare on the CV-22 **PAVE HAMMER**'s windscreen.

"Christ, it feels like the whole world can see us up here," Fell muttered on interphone. "Double-check switches, Martin. If we make one squeak on the radio or forward-looking radar, they'll pick it up all the way to fucking St. Petersburg."

Watanabe carefully checked to see that all the radio switches were on STANDBY or RECEIVE, the APQ-174 was not in TFR mode, all other radios that could transmit a signal were in STANDBY, such as the instrument-landing system, and that all exterior lights were off.

The AAR-50 infrared scanner showed the area around them was clear for at least eight miles, the optimal range limit for the FLIR. "Clear on cargo doors." As Watanabe hit the switch to open the rear cargo ramp, Fell rotated a small switch on his control stick, which rotated the engine nacelles on the wingtips of the PAVE HAMMER and transformed the bird from a conventional turboprop plane to a helicopter, and the CV-22 began slowing from two hundred and fifty to only thirty miles per hour.

In the back of the cargo section of the aircraft, the ramplike cargo door lowered and a blast of frigid air washed over the MSPF team waiting in the back. The team was ready: they had a large twenty-foot rubber boat, called Combat Rubber Raiding Craft (CRRC), or "Rubber Raider," complete with a 75-horsepower gasoline engine and extra fuel tanks, waiting in the open cargo hatch. The team was dressed in "Mustang suits"—black nylon water suits that protected the wearer from the cold, provided flotation, sealed out water, and allowed much more mobility than divers' wet suits. Their weapons, radios, and other gear were sealed in black waterproof bags slung around their shoulders.

When the signal was given, the MSPF team members picked up the boat by its rope handles and ran out the cargo ramp into space, dropping into the ice-cold water below. The weight of the Marines on the handlines kept the CRRC from flipping over, and they began pulling themselves into the boat, stabilizing it against the hurricane-like turbulence from the CV-22's rotor downwash. Seconds later the CRRC's outboard engine was started, team members loaded and checked their MP-5 submachine guns and .45-caliber automatics and, with Lobato providing directions from a compass and from his intense advance study of the area, they raced off for shore.

Aboard the CV-22, Sergeant Brown reported that the Marines were safely away, and Fell wheeled his plane westward once again and sped away from shore, staying below fifty feet but carefully avoiding all boats that popped up on his FLIR sensor. At that same time, Watanabe relayed a single message on the command channel: *"Teviske,"* which meant "Motherland" in Lithuanian, the signal to Paul White and the rest of the assault team that the Marines were headed ashore.

Marines, especially Recon or special-operations teams, never fought alone. No matter how big or how small the team was, Marine Corps infantry units were always supported by a command, air, and logistics element. That simple "go" message would send the rest of the players into action:

As PAVE HAMMER returned to the *Valley Mistress* for fuel and to rearm with a two-man assist team, a Marine Corps KC-130 aerial-re-fueling tanker began its takeoff roll from Sandefjord Air Base, south of Oslo, a NATO training base where the U.S. Marines had established a Northern Europe operations center. Flying along with the KC-130 was a CH-53E Super Stallion helicopter—a huge transport helicopter—with a reinforced rifle platoon called a "Sparrowhawk" on board ready to assist Gunny Lobato's team if necessary. Watanabe's message also alerted other detached members of the 26th Marine Expeditionary Force in Denmark and Germany that the operation was in progress and that intelligence and planning teams were standing by, waiting for word on the team's progress and preparing alternate plans of action.

The U.S. Air Force also had a support network ready to go, with even more firepower than the Marines. Launching from Rhein-Main Air Base in Germany and under command of the Air Force Special Operations Command, was an MC-130P special-operations tanker aircraft—designed to refuel other aircraft at low altitude and over hostile territory or near a target area—accompanied by two F-16C Fighting Falcon fighters. Carrying mine dispensers, rocket pods, and antiradar missiles as well as air-to-air missiles, the heavily armed F-16s could assist the Marines on the ground to break away from hostile ground units, or they could clear the skies if the Soviets decided to scramble fighters against the rotary-wing aircraft. Additionally, the MC-130H COMBAT TALON aircraft from England, code-named WILEY COYOTE, and its fighter escorts from Norway, would begin their rendezvous orbit near the southern tip of the island of Gotland, ninety-six miles west of Liepaja, ready to pick up RAGANU and take him to safety. The *Valley Mistress* itself would dispatch several small, innocent-looking power boats—armed to the teeth by COBRA VENOM Marines—into the Baltic to act as a safety recovery team in case the CV-22 was damaged during its egress.

Lobato and his crew were dropped only eight miles offshore, but it took them nearly an hour to reach the sandy shore north of Liepaja—they would stop the heavily muffled outboard engine every few minutes, and Lobato and his men would carefully scan the horizon, using PVS-5 night-vision goggles, checking for any sign of pursuit.

The assault team relied on their training and experience to filter out the noise of waves and water—and suppress their own fear and discomfort—and be ready to take action against any possible threat. Despite carefully donning their insulated "Mustang suits," leaks were common, and the wet patches against their fire-resistant flight suits soon felt raw and numb from the wind-enhanced cold. Thick wool face masks and caps did little to protect against the wind-driven spray—they would hunker down as far as possible under the CRRC's gunwales, exposing as little of their bodies as possible to the elements while constantly scanning all around them for signs of danger. The radio operator, using a small 5.5-pound Motorola MX-300 tactical radio, had to struggle to listen to the radio as well as scan his area of responsibility. Every sweep of a nearby lighthouse's high-intensity white beam made the Marines tense up as they neared the shore, and Lobato was careful to keep that lighthouse as far away as possible.

Finally they heard the crashing of waves on the beach, and the assault team was ready to land. Every eye was trained on the beach, searching for anything that might be a threat—patrols were common, but civilians out for a late-night stroll were encountered even more frequently, and posed just as great a risk. Lobato made the decision to move the beaching spot an extra mile south because of an object that resembled a truck or large car parked near the coast highway, but otherwise their beachhead was clear.

With a soft hiss of sand, the CRRC slid onto Soviet soil. Immediately the Marines were out of the boat, ignoring the shock of cold water in their boots as they dragged the rubber raft out of the surf, across the fifty-yard-wide beach, and up onto a sandy ridge a few dozen yards from the coast highway. The CRRC was quickly buried in the sand and covered with brush, the area was policed and tracks erased, and the assault team spread out to search for threats along the highway.

Their task was only beginning—they had five miles to trek before reaching the extraction point.

USS *VALLEY MISTRESS*
29 NOVEMBER, 0100 (28 NOVEMBER, 1900 ET)

"All air assets are up," Knowlton relayed to Paul White in the number-two MISCO trailer, where the tactical communications gear was set up to monitor the mission. "All reporting in the green."

White smiled: ten sophisticated aircraft, about thirty highly trained men, plus a three-hundred-million-dollar high-tech spy vessel, directly involved in an operation to extract a non-American individual from a republic in the Commonwealth of Independent States (CIS). In two hours they would all converge on the eastern Baltic and the game would be played to its conclusion. If you included the men and women of the 26th Marine Expeditionary Unit, standing by in Norway and in the Mediterranean Sea, and the 93rd Air Force Special Operations Wing in England, there were nearly six thousand Americans involved in trying to get *one* man out of Lithuania.

Countering them, of course, was the awesome might of the CIS-Byelorussian Army, Air Force, and Navy in the occupied Baltic states. Even after wholesale troop withdrawals in recent years, there were still over fifty thousand foreign troops in the three Baltic republics themselves, plus over a half-million more Belarus troops within a few hours' flying time.

The odds clearly were not in the Marines' favor.

Only three things gave the Americans any chance for success—the speed, bravery, and stealth of the eight men who at that very moment were setting foot on Lithuanian soil to put their hands on a Lithuanian peasant officer.

"Urgent message from PATRIOT," Knowlton said, grabbing White's attention. "That chopper is heading back to the target area. It'll be on top of the assault team in ten minutes, maybe less."

"Shit," Paul White swore. They all knew the helicopter was going to be a factor. "Have PATRIOT relay the contact to the assault team. I'll get on the horn to Colonel Kline."

White hustled to the communications console and put his hand on the phone that was tied directly to the Amphibious Task Force commander, Marine Corps Colonel Albert Kline, commander of the 26th MEU's (SOC) Ground Combat Element, on the amphibious-assault carrier *Wasp*—then stopped. What would he recommend? He had sent this team on its way knowing the helicopter, which had been dogging them for days, was in the area and would probably be a factor. Should White now recommend additional assets be brought in? One of the F-15's escorting COMBAT TALONs could make short work of a helicopter, but it would blow the whole mission if the Gagarin radar ship saw it barreling in toward the coast.

No, they had to use the CV-22. "I need a status report from Ladybug," White snapped. "Give me the location of WILEY COYOTE as well."

The locations of both aircraft and an estimate of the CV-22's aircraft's fuel status were laid out for White on a chart in the MISCO trailer. The MC-130 COMBAT TALON special-operations support aircraft was in its standby orbit seventy-five miles north, near the southern tip of the Swedish island of Gotland, well within view of the Gagarin-class spy ship but presently being left pretty much alone. The CV-22 was headed back to the *Valley Mistress* for refueling and rearming, sweeping well to the south and west to stay away from the Soviet radar ship.

White made the only decision he could: "Tell the MC-130 and the CV-22 that they need to perform an emergency rendezvous. I need Ladybug back in the target area without delay." White himself found a plotter and a pair of dividers and, using a base refueling speed of 180 knots, computed a rough rendezvous point about forty-three miles west of Liepaja: "Clear COMBAT TALON for 'music,' and keep the escorts in the rendezvous area. Send it."

"Pojorna, nas razyidinili, butti lubezni, paftariti," the Marine assault-crew radio operator suddenly heard in Russian on the radio. It came over the receive-only command channel—a broadcast from PATRIOT, the E-3B AWACS radar plane. Translated, "Squad, reply not received, repeat message." It was meant for Lobato and his crew, a warning message saying that the helicopter that had been working the target area was on its way and heading toward them. For maximum reliability, emergency radio messages from the AWACS to the assault crew were not scrambled or encoded with complex algorithms, which meant that intercepting and decoding a message was easier for the enemy—hence the code words in Russian.

The Marine carrying the radio moved quietly to Lobato's side and passed the word to him, and Lobato nodded. They knew all about the helicopter, and Lobato had been expecting it—the wise play would be to assume the helicopter would arrive just as the Marines approached the target area. Lobato increased the assault team's speed, still using extreme caution but picking up the pace slightly.

But he wasn't expecting what happened next. The unit had traveled within one mile of the estimated pickup point when they heard the faint *whupwhupwhupwhup* of a helicopter in the distance.

The CIS helicopter that had been scouring the area for days looking for RAGANU was closing in on the Marines' position.

"Message from PATRIOT," the radio operator reported to Lobato. "The chopper is inbound, slowing to patrol speed."

Lobato seethed: "Shit . . . we're running out of time." Lobato signaled the rest of the squad and they fanned out and headed for the pickup spot. The Marines hastily split up and dashed into the treelines on both sides of a small dirt road, carefully staying just within sight of each other, MP5 submachine guns at the ready.

They moved as if linked: they would stop for a long sixty seconds, scanning the woods and the road, listening for sounds of men, vehicles, aircraft; then, together move another twenty or thirty yards and repeat the process. They used their night-vision goggles to carefully sweep the area.

After another ten minutes of movement, Gunny Lobato was beginning to get nervous—the target was nowhere to be seen. He signaled the radio operator to join up with him as the squad moved cautiously ahead. Lobato searched the forest, but with no luck. The target was still south of them; he *had* to be.

He had to be very—

Someone was kneeling at the base of a tree, just thirty feet ahead of Lobato. He appeared out of nowhere. He was slowly getting to his feet, but he was still hidden to Marine Corps Corporal John Butler, who was moving in his direction to Lobato's right. Butler had just crouched down as he heard the faint rustle of leaves—he knew that something was out there, but he couldn't see or identify it yet.

Lobato had raised his MP5 and had clicked on the small infrared sniperscope searchlight, which would provide bright illumination for anyone wearing PV-5 goggles, when suddenly the stranger whispered loudly, "Hey, Marine, I here. Here."

Butler swung around, saw the stranger, and was about to fire when the man said quickly, "Top of the morning, Marine, top of the morning," in a thick, Transylvanian-sounding accent.

"Hands up!" Lobato hissed, praying silently that Butler wouldn't pull the trigger. He didn't. The man's hands shot up in the air. His right hand was empty; his left held a thin briefcase. "Drop the briefcase!" Lobato shouted.

"No!" the man shouted back.

In a flash Butler leaped toward the man, driving the butt of his rifle into the stranger's solar plexus and dropping him to the ground. With an animal-like *wooof!* of air forced out of his lungs, the man collapsed, and Butler jumped on top of him, scrambling for the man's hands.

Two other assault-team members rushed to Lobato's side. They pried the man's fingers off the briefcase, and one Marine took it away to examine it away from the others in case it was booby-trapped. Lobato knelt to the man and searched him, loosening all his clothing, running his gloved hands next to his skin to check for wires or weapons. It took several seconds, but finally the man began to regain his breath, grunting, "Top of the morning, top of the morning," in a hoarse whisper.

The sound of the helicopter was getting closer—this guy's identity had to be verified before they dared take off with him. "Midnight jaybird," Lobato challenged. It was one of the code-word challenges devised with a nonverbal response, used in just these situations where the subject was unable to speak or wearing a gas mask. Butler took his knees off the man's wrists, and he promptly interlaced his fingers together, thumbs bent. It was the right response. Wordlessly, Lobato ordered Butler to gag RAGANU and bind his hands in front of his body; then he reached down to his web belt and activated a tiny radio transmitter.

No sooner had he done that than a brilliant searchlight flared to life. The intense white beam focused squarely on the small group of American soldiers at the edge of the trees. The CIS attack helicopter had suddenly popped out from over the trees and had emerged practically right on top of them.

"Pilot, engineer, pickup signal." The PAVE HAMMER CV-22's crew chief, Master Sergeant Brown, dared not say anything more on interphone because he knew they were only milliseconds away from going into battle—or dying in a fiery crash. They had to save *themselves* before going back to save the assault team.

The PAVE HAMMER CV-22 was skimming over the dark waves of the Baltic Sea, less than six hundred feet above the surface—it would have been lower, except the north winds had picked up considerably and the turbulence threatened to throw them into the sea at any moment. Forty feet in front of the CV-22, at the same altitude, was the MC-130H COMBAT TALON aircraft. The huge dark cargo plane had unreeled one of its "hose-and-drogue" aerial-refueling systems—a three-foot lighted basket at the end of a fuel line—from a pod on the right wingtip, and Fell had plugged his refueling probe into the tiny lighted basket. The CV-22 was taking on fuel at two hundred gallons per minute. The lighted ring around the edge of the basket was the only light on these two aircraft—at night, about three wingspans above the sea, traveling at four miles a minute. The two airplanes sped through the night with only a thin hose between them and disaster.

Hank Fell's hands were grasping the controls with a hard death's grip as he fought to maintain control. He knew the MC-130H was in front of him, somewhere, but he would see it only at less than twenty-feet range—just before a collision—so the probe kept on disconnecting from the drogue and he had to struggle to reconnect. Fell had swiveled the engine nacelles on the CV-22 to 30 degrees, an intermediate position between airplane and helicopter modes, to give him as much altitude control as possible while maintaining maximum forward airspeed—the COMBAT TALON aircraft was designed to refuel helicopters at low speeds, but in this turbulence and at this low altitude, a sudden wind shear could send the one-hundred-and-forty-thousand-pound special-operations plane into the sea without warning.

As if to underscore his fear, the MC-130H suddenly dipped precariously down by the tail as if wallowing in heavy seas. Fell could feel the buffeting of the plane's four huge turboprops as the prop wash rolled over the CV-22, and he could hear power being applied. The hose dipped suddenly, then shot up and swayed from side to side as the COMBAT TALON pilot fought for control. The drogue popped off the CV-22's probe, whipped violently in the swirling winds, and the padded canvas-covered basket hit the tilt-rotor aircraft's windscreen with a loud *thump!* The MC-130H pilot pulled power back to try to get back into position.

Fell turned the nacelle angle-control upwards, moving the CV-22 more into HELICOPTER mode so he could safely decelerate. "Dammit! Signal breakaway!" Fell shouted. Watanabe flicked the exterior lights four times in rapid succession, and the drogue disappeared as the MC-130H pilot applied power again and climbed an extra one hundred feet. "How much fuel now, Marty?"

"We took on five thousand pounds," Watanabe replied. "We have ten thousand total."

"Is it enough?"

"Barely," Watanabe replied. "Just barely. In, out, land back on the *Mistress* with one thousand pounds. Oslo is out unless we can get the MC-130 back after exfiltration—and that's unlikely since *he* must be low on fuel."

"Signal 'terminate refueling,' then," Fell said. "We're going in with what we got." Watanabe gave the MC-130H crew six flashes of the lights—flash-flash, pause, flash-flash, pause, flash-flash—and the ghostly outline of the COMBAT TALON disappeared.

They were headed east, back toward the target point east of the town of Liepaja—in fact, after air refueling they were only six miles from the coast. Things had changed very quickly. PATRIOT was no longer using Russian code words to warn the CV-22 crew of airborne threats—instead, he was on the secure HAVE QUICK scrambled channel, issuing threat information directly to Ladybug. Brown had set the CV-22's entire INEWS (Integrated Electronic-Warfare System) jamming suite to full automatic, which would jam all surface-to-air and air-to-air radars, radio communications, and laser illuminators detected by the threat receiver. INEWS also automatically modulated the heat emissions from the CV-22 itself, effectively "jamming" its own infrared signature to provide limited protection against heat-seeking missiles.

The threat scope had come alive a few minutes later as the CV-22 crossed the coastline—the search radar at Liepaja got a solid skin paint on them when they climbed to their highest altitude, three hundred feet, when Fell yanked the aircraft up to avoid a transmission tower that the AN/APQ-174 terrain-following radar suddenly detected directly ahead. Soon afterward plenty of VHF radio transmissions and fast-sector radar scans were detected.

The bad guys had spotted them.

The Marines had sprinted off into the forest as soon as the helicopter appeared. Lobato dragged RAGANU along after him as though the young CIS Army officer had been a sack of dirty laundry. Quickly, the Marines had turned the tables on the chopper pilot—eight sets of MP5 submachine guns were trained on the helicopter's cockpit and engine compartment, ready to send it crashing to earth in a blazing fireball. The chopper, a Kamov-27 "Helix-B" amphibious-warfare helicopter, was fitted with a rocket pack on one side and a 12.5-millimeter gun pod on the other. Seconds after it popped on its searchlight on the group, it suddenly sped off into the night, extinguishing the searchlight and all other external lights.

"Move out!" Lobato shouted. "Scatter!" There was something else he remembered about the Helix—it had a bomb bay. With one hand firmly under RAGANU's left arm, and his other hand holding his MP5, Lobato scrambled off into the forest.

Just then the chopper could be heard coming back. Lobato quickened his pace, his pulse thrumming in his ears. When he heard the chopper almost directly overhead, he wheeled left, ran hard until the throb of the chopper's rotors seemed to replace the heartbeat in his chest, then dived behind a tree opposite the sound. He dragged RAGANU behind the tree with him, closed his eyes tightly, and yelled "Cover!" just before a series of loud explosions tore into the forest. The Helix had dropped two

explosive mine canisters and the four hundred tiny bomblets began ripping the foliage into green shreds.

RAGANU was screaming like a wounded lamb, and Lobato had to
put a hand over his mouth. "Shut the fuck up!" yelled Lobato.
RAGANU seemed to understand—Lobato wanted RAGANU alive, but
he would not put himself or his squad in any more danger because of the
Lithuanian soldier; the Marines had RAGANU's briefcase, the contents
of which were probably as important as the man himself. As he listened
for a follow-on attack, Lobato followed RAGANU's hand up his arm
and felt blood.

Lobato unrolled a thick field-dressing pad from a pouch on his web
belt, pressed it onto where he thought the center of the wound was, put
the Lithuanian soldier's free hand on the wound, and tightened the man's
fingers around it. "Press hard," Lobato ordered. "Hard!"

Once Lobato was convinced that RAGANU was finally helping himself, he raised up to a knee and tried to scan the area with his night-vision
goggles. The device was useless, broken in a desperate race to get away
from the mines. Unaided vision was an exercise in futility. Still, Marines
had fought for decades without them. . . .

The area underneath the chopper's flight path was probably strewn
with delayed-arming antipersonnel mines, so Lobato reminded himself to
avoid it. He shouted, "Assemble foxtrot two, foxtrot two! Assemble!"
then ducked and listened. After a few minutes he heard the familiar
rustling of feet behind him and he knew his men were on the move.

Time to get the hell out of Dodge.

"Ladybug, target ten o'clock, three miles, altitude seven hundred feet,
climbing, airspeed one-zero-five knots," the radar controller aboard
PATRIOT reported. "Target turning left . . . target turning left to intercept . . ."

The chopper appeared out of nowhere, but fortunately its appearance
was telegraphed by a series of small flashes on the ground ahead—and
then Fell wondered if the Marines might be down there under those
flashes. But there was no time to think about them.

Fell saw that the chopper was doing more than turning to intercept—a
second later he could see tiny winks of light and a few bright-yellow lines
arc in the night sky. "Target shooting!" he cried out. He hauled back on
his control stick, zooming up and over the tracers. The helicopter tried to
climb and keep its muzzle pointing at Ladybug, but it didn't have the
airspeed that the CV-22 did. Seconds later, after climbing less than two
hundred feet, it suddenly lowered its nose again and banked hard to the
right.

Fell was expecting that right turn—the pilot sits on the right side of most helicopters, even Eastern Bloc helicopters, so that's the direction chopper pilots prefer to turn—so Fell was banking hard left and descending as soon as he saw the hostile helicopter couldn't pursue. "Stinger coming on-line," Fell shouted as he flicked the weapon-arming switch on his control stick. After one more turn to the right to line up on the helicopter, Fell heard the growl of one Stinger missile's seeker head locking on to the helicopter's hot exhaust. "One away!" he warned Watanabe as he pressed the trigger. The CIS chopper banked once more, hard to the right, but the tiny Stinger missile tracked it easily. There was a small puff of white flame, a tiny flicker of fire, then darkness.

"Ladybug, splash one," PATRIOT reported. "Area clear of airborne targets. Steer heading one-five-four for pickup, range six miles." Fell did not acknowledge—flying the suggested heading was acknowledgment enough, and there would be plenty of time to thank the crew of the E-3B after the assault team and RAGANU were safely on board the *Valley Mistress.* He re-engaged the TFR system and resumed his nap-of-the-earth flight back to the pickup point.

The small dirt road they had worked around all night had a peculiar hairpin turn in it that showed up remarkably well on satellite photos they studied while planning this extraction, and now Lobato knew why—there was a small religious monument, a *janseta,* in the curve. This was the "foxtrot two" assembly area, the closest one away from the area where the Helix attack chopper could have strewn mines. Lobato took up a position south of the *janseta* and sat and waited. After five minutes he used hand gestures to tell RAGANU to stay put, and he carefully inched his way toward the monument.

Stealth and patience were more important now than in almost any other time in the mission, but after the helicopter attack Lobato's men were really anxious to get out of the country. No sooner had Lobato reached the monument than the seven other members of the team came in—the last, Corporal Butler, practically sprinting. Lobato took them back into the forest and set up a security watch. Except for a few serious-looking scrapes and one possible broken wrist from a fall, the rest of the team members appeared well.

The arrival of the CV-22 a few minutes later was like watching an angel descend from heaven. Four Marines guarded the front and rear of the landing zone and two others carried RAGANU up the cargo ramp. Ladybug was on the ground less than thirty seconds before lifting off again and tree-hopping away back to the Baltic. RAGANU was given water, a life vest, and careful medical attention by the team's corpsman.

He had received a deep, six-inch-long gash in his right bicep, and a three-inch piece of metal was embedded in the wound—one last chilling reminder of what would probably be his last moments in the CIS.

The CV-22 took the long way back to the *Valley Mistress* this time— giving the Gagarin-class research vessel a wide berth and avoiding all large vessels and shore radar sites, it took twice as long to get back to the salvage ship as it did to reach shore. As soon as Ladybug touched down on the helipad, crew members were on deck doing an engines-running refueling, checking for damage, and removing the weapons pods from the aircraft. All possible evidence of the incident had to be erased.

Paul White was on board as soon as it was safe to approach the aircraft. He saw four Marines surrounding a smiling young man. White went over to the newcomer, extending a hand. "Lieutenant Fryderyk Litwy?"

The young man nodded enthusiastically, shaking White's hand with both mittened hands. It was the first time Lobato had realized that this guy might have a *real* name.

White had been studying Lithuanian phrases for a week just for this moment. *"Labas vakaras.* Glad to see you. Welcome to America." To the Marines surrounding RAGANU, White said, "Excellent job. Bring him inside and get him something to eat."

As the Marines escorted Lieutenant Litwy out of the CV-22 and into the pressure chamber, White met up with Lobato, who pressed the brief-case into White's hands. "Mission accomplished. We checked it over and swept it for bugs and transmitters. Clean. Pretty good-quality set of photos in there. Definitely a worthwhile trip, I'd say."

"Fantastic," White said gleefully. "I'll make copies and uplink them to HG, then send the package with a destruct mechanism with you to Norway. Good job, Gunny. Pass a well-done to your troops."

The fuel lines were being retracted and the assault team was returning back to the plane as White crossed through the pressure chamber to the first MISCO trailer and turned the briefcase over to the technicians waiting inside the darkened room. The CV-22 was not going to stay on the *Valley Mistress*—the ship needed to be transformed back into a salvage vessel as quickly as possible. The CV-22 would take the Marines, the photos, and Lieutenant Litwy to U.S. Embassy officials in Oslo as quickly as possible so formal political asylum proceedings could begin. Litwy would be yet another American intelligence success story.

Before they could leave, however, the photos that they had risked so much to retrieve from occupied Lithuania had to be successfully copied, and the originals taken back to the United States. It was not enough to simply take a picture of a picture—too many successful exfiltration oper-ations were ruined by careless handling of retrieved photos. White was determined not to let this happen to him, and he had designed MISCO number two to safely, quickly, and redundantly process photos without damaging them or triggering some secret destruct process.

One by one, Litwy's photos were examined with a variety of methods, principal among which were plain sight and feel. Many photos were treated with chemicals to kill the person handling them, or to self-destruct if handled too much or if exposed to flash photography. But these appeared to be standard 8-by-10 and 5-by-7 matte-finish photos—judging by their brittle, curled appearance. They were processed hastily in an amateur-photography darkroom with old enlarging paper and old, cold chemicals, then allowed to air-dry. White photographed each one with high-resolution video and still cameras without using any extra light or flash units, followed thereafter by Xerox copies and digitized computer scans. The digitized pictures were transmitted via satellite to U.S. Special Operations Command headquarters in Florida and to the National Security Agency intelligence-data collection center in Virginia. White waited impatiently as the data was transmitted to the satellite, relayed to other satellites ringing the globe, then dumped to the NSA's ground station in Ft. Belvoir, Virginia.

Major Carl Knowlton arrived at the MISCO 2 trailer a few moments later, just as the last of the photos were being successfully uplinked to the satellites. "PATRIOT reports rotary-wing choppers from Liepaja about forty miles out, heading this way," Knowlton reported. "ETA, twenty minutes. They're surface-scanning. No air radars reported."

"We're finished here," White said, packing the original photos in waterproof bags, then turning them over to a technician for packing in a special transfer case. "Ladybug will be halfway to Oslo in twenty minutes. What is the Gagarin doing?"

"It's headed our way as well," Knowlton replied. "ETA to radar horizon crossing, forty-five minutes."

"If the Russkies launch fighters from Vainode, Riga, or Kaliningrad, we'll be in for a rough time," White said soberly. The photos were ready to go; White inspected the self-destruct package himself, locked the photos up, and armed the package. If the lock was tampered with, or if someone attempted to cut the case open, an incendiary charge would burn the photos inside and probably kill anyone standing within a few feet. "We better get permission from the Swedish government for an overflight. Are the weapons pods off the bird?"

"You bet. Checked on that myself. The fire-control boxes were pulled also."

"Good." The U.S. government would have to certify to the Swedish government that any aircraft requesting overflight were unarmed—if the CV-22 crashed in Sweden with weapons aboard, even a few 20-millimeter cannon shells, it would create a disastrous international incident, akin to the embarrassment of Soviet submarines running aground in Swedish waters, and U.S. aircraft and ships would be barred from Sweden for years. White began to flip through the copies of the photos as he continued: "First sign of anyone trying to board us, we deep-six the gun pods and the Intel MISCO trailers."

"Everything's ready to jettison," Knowlton said. "The pods are in the pressure chamber. If those choppers try to deliver a boarding party, we can dump the weapon pods and most of the classified stuff out the recovery hatch. We can also—"

"Shit! Look at this!" White exclaimed, staring at a photo. It was a blurry but very readable picture of what had to be the most unusual-looking aircraft either of them had ever seen. "What the hell is it?"

"It looks like a . . . like a fighter, I think," Knowlton said. "Like a stealth fighter, only with a curved fuselage and wings. It reminds me of the alien spacecraft from the movie *War of the Worlds,* except with a pointed nose. You think the Russians have a fighter like this in development—in *Vilnius,* of all places? They're building a bomber in the middle of a revolution?"

"Well, Fisikous *is* a major aerospace research-design complex," White explained. "They probably got a dozen models like this . . ." White found a magnifying glass and peered intently at the photo. "I don't think this is a model. It's too big! See the sentry standing over here? The lower root edge of that wing has to be twenty feet high. It's gotta be bigger than the B-2 bomber. And they've got pneumatic and electrical cables running to it. Maybe it's a prototype. The Pentagon is gonna love this."

"Think it's a fake? A decoy?"

"Could be," White admitted. "If young Lieutenant Litwy was blown, they might have set up some fake aircraft at Fisikous."

"*Or* Litwy could be a fake," Knowlton observed. "The real Litwy could have been tortured for the passwords and responses, a mole put in his place. This whole thing could be a big ruse."

White gave Knowlton a lopsided grin and a shrug of his thin shoulders. "That's above our pay grade, Carl," he said, flipping to another photo. "It's up to Defense Intelligence and the CIA to find out if Litwy's for real. We don't kiss 'em or shoot 'em—we just snatch 'em. Let the guys in the bad brown suits worry about—"

Paul White froze. He was staring at a photo he'd just flipped to, his eyes riveted to it, not believing what he was seeing.

Knowlton saw his superior officer's wide-eyed look. "Paul? What is it? Litwy bring back a gory one? Let me see—"

White glanced up, confusion and disbelief spreading across his face. He lowered the photo, handing it over to Knowlton. It was a picture of a

group of three soldiers—all elite Black Beret troops who occupied many
of the more important ex-Soviet facilities in the Baltic states, including
the Fisikous Research Institute—surrounding a younger man. One
couldn't tell whether the Black Berets were protecting an important civilian or if he was a prisoner.

But it was the man, dressed in plain brown slacks and a sweater, who
had grabbed White's attention.

Knowlton prodded. "Hey, Paul, who is he? A long-lost brother or
something? You know this guy?"

White nodded, taking the photo back. "A guy I knew at Ford—"

"Ford Air Force Base? You're kidding, right? Maybe he just looks like
him."

But White had thought of that and instantly discarded it. He remembered hearing the reports of Lieutenant Dave Luger's death, three years
ago in a plane crash in Alaska, test-flying a supersecret bomber. He'd
never fully believed the report—the facts didn't wash and everything was
too neatly wrapped.

He'd heard the rumors circulating through the Air Force about a
preemptive strike against a ground-based laser site in Siberia, and about
the aircraft that accomplished the mission: a modified B-52, reportedly
from the High Technology Aerospace Weapons Center. How or why a
research center had a strike aircraft in its inventory was still unclear. But
there was never any inquiry or details about the mission and the threat
from the Soviet laser—if there ever had been one—had suddenly disappeared . . .

. . . As did two navigators from Paul White's old B-52 wing at Ford Air
Force Base, Patrick McLanahan and David Luger.

They had gone TDY several weeks before the alleged incident. Neither
had returned to Ford. Later, Paul White found out about Luger's death,
and learned that his crew partner, Patrick McLanahan, had suddenly
received a new duty assignment. White did not know where McLanahan
had gone, or why—but he was one of the most gifted bombardiers in the
nation, so White never thought McLanahan had gotten himself in trouble
or kicked out of the Air Force. White had liked both men—they were
sharp, very sharp—though Luger could be a bit of a hothead. Still, he'd
done well at Ford, as had McLanahan.

And now Luger had, it seemed, turned up alive at a secret Commonwealth research center in Lithuania. White rubbed his chin. What was
going on? Was Luger a defector? A mole? He turned to Knowlton: "It's
the guy from Ford, I'm sure of it. An American military officer in fucking
Lithuania, of all places. This guy was declared *dead* in 1989."

Knowlton looked skeptical. "Paul, how can an American Air Force
officer killed years ago suddenly turn up in Vilnius, Lithuania?"

"Stranger things have happened. Look at some of the Vietnam vets we'd written off for dead who've suddenly turned up in the past few years."

"But Vietnam was a *war,* Paul. You're bound to have misreported casualties. This guy—"

"David Luger. That's his name."

"Okay, this guy, Luger . . . wasn't in a war. Was he?"

White ignored the question. "I'm going to upchannel this one immediately. This can't wait. The mission Luger was on, well—if he's there and alive, people need to know it. The . . . uh, mission was too important."

Knowlton shook his head. "You can't make a call like that from the *Mistress,* Paul. You know that. An unnecessary secure communication this close to Russia, to Belarus, hell, that'll compromise us and the satellite channel both."

"Look, I *know* this guy. I ran him through my course at Ford."

"You gonna risk the entire MADCAP MAGICIAN program to help him? If the Russians get wind that we're anything but a marine salvage-and-rescue ship, everything goes down the drain. Years of *your* work, Paul."

He could tell White was mulling it over. Knowlton hadn't seen him this agitated in ages, which meant he was pretty damn sure of his I.D. of this guy. White had long joked he'd always forget a name, but never a face. Now he'd remembered both. "Look, Paul . . . send an urgent message in the photo packet to alert the intelligence section, then wait until we get to Oslo—the embassy has the facilities you need, and everything will be waiting for us. We can delay the CV-22 a few minutes until you draft a message."

White was ready to go connect the channel himself, but realized the best thing to do was wait. If he alerted Intel, God knows where it would end up. Some asshole looking for one less problem to deal with would just sweep it under the rug. And Paul White was damned if *that* was going to happen.

OVER WESTERN LITHUANIA
LATER THAT MORNING

"There it is," the Lithuanian Self-Defense Force helicopter pilot radioed to his passenger. "My God, look at what the bastards have done to that farm." He nodded toward the crash site. Several helicopters, dozens of vehicles—including some BTR armored combat vehicles—and hundreds of soldiers had surrounded a small dark splotch on the muddy ground.

The troops had used combat-engineering vehicles to carve a wide path from the main road to the crash site, shearing straight through several hundred meters of wire, wood, and stone fencing, bulldozing down a corral and six acres of corn and cutting down about four acres of pine forest to get to the crash site. The three kilometers from the main road to the crash site looked like the path of a tornado.

"The Byelorussian infantry is efficient, that's for sure," General Dominikas Palcikas, commander of the Lithuanian military, said as he studied the area carefully from the front copilot's seat. "The trucks have been dispersed throughout the area," he told the pilot. "See? They're blocking all the roads and open areas nearby with armored vehicles. They don't want us to land."

The chopper pilot nodded in understanding. Although Lithuania had separated from the Soviet Union in 1990, it wasn't until the USSR fell and the Commonwealth of Independent States was created that a transition treaty between the CIS and Lithuania allowed a CIS military presence within the Baltics—ostensibly to keep the peace. But it was a concern of every Lithuanian that these forces—especially the Byelorussians—would overstep their "obligations" and someday make a play for Lithuania.

"What do you want me to do, sir?" the pilot asked.

"Try the bastards again on the radio. Get them to clear that parking area there."

The pilot radioed, trying to get a reply.

Palcikas waited for a response from the Byelorussians, his expression getting angrier and darker with every passing second. General Dominikas Palcikas was a fifty-three-year-old combat veteran, born in Lithuania but trained and educated in the former Soviet Army. His father had been a Russian general, commander of a Lithuanian division nicknamed the Iron Wolf Brigade after the Lithuanian Grand Duke's fierce armies of medieval times. Palcikas' father's brigade became heroes in World War II, making Palcikas' own rise within the military easy. He rose quickly through the ranks to Colonel, served in the Far East Military District, then in Afghanistan as commander of a tank battalion. Later he was reassigned to the Western Military District after the withdrawal of troops from Afghanistan. But his career suffered because of the military defeat in Afghanistan, and he was reassigned to the Byelorussian SSR in the Interior Ministry's Troops of the Interior, in charge of a border patrol regiment. The sudden halt in his career affected his outlook on the Soviet Union: what the Soviet Union was turning Lithuania into was not much better than the poverty he saw in Afghanistan. He became a student of Lithuanian history, and his disenchantment with the Soviet occupation of Lithuania grew and peaked in 1989 and 1990 with the bloody massacres in Riga and Vilnius at the hands of special units of the Soviet Interior Troops called the Black Berets. He resigned his commission in the Soviet Army in 1990 and emigrated to Lithuania. Upon the independence of Lithuania in mid-1991, he accepted a commission in the Forces of Self-Defense, in the rank of General and Commander in Chief. He named his initial cadre of officers and enlisted volunteers the Iron Wolf Brigade, invoking not only the spirit of the Grand Dukes of Lithuania, but the memory of the World War II unit, led by his father, that saved Lithuania.

"No reply, sir," the pilot reported. "Only a warning to stay away."

Palcikas was boiling: "This is *my* country and *my* airspace, and no one will tell me what I will do. Hover near that group of vehicles, the one with the flag. Tell the other helicopters to stay by."

"But sir, that appears to be the investigation team chief's vehicle."

"I said hover near it. About twenty meters upwind and ten meters overhead." Palcikas unstrapped from the copilot's seat and made his way aft. On his way to the cargo section of the small Soviet-made twin-engine Mil-8 assault helicopter, he passed his aide-de-camp and headquarters executive officer, Major Alexei Kolginov, a young, Russian-born infantry officer who had served with Palcikas for many years. "Follow me, Alexei."

"Are we going to—?" And then Kolginov stopped and looked at Palcikas in surprise—his superior had just put a pair of heavy, rough leather gloves on his hands and had unstowed a four-centimeter-thick rope from its overhead storage bin. He checked that it was secure on its anchor hook on the ceiling of the helicopter's cabin. "Sir, what are you—?"

"Just follow me." Palcikas checked his sidearm, a Soviet-made Makarov TT-33 automatic, then slid open the portside entry door and peered outside. Kolginov knew what Palcikas had in mind, and scrambled to put on his gloves and secure his AKSU submachine gun.

The three-star commander of all Byelorussian forces in the western part of his country, General Lieutenant Anton Osipovich Voshchanka, cursed aloud as the Lithuanian assault helicopter moved nearly overhead. It quickly drowned out all voices around him. He grabbed his service cap before it twisted away in the wind, raised his voice, and turned to his commander of detached forces in Lithuania and Kaliningrad, Colonel Oleg Pavlovich Gurlo, and yelled, "Get that asshole's tail number and find out who the pilot is! I want him brought before me in thirty minutes!"

The Colonel had been in command of all Byelorussian armor and infantry units in Lithuania for many months. The loss of the attack helicopter the night before, and the subsequent appearance of his commanding general at the crash site, was turning into a real nightmare for him. This irritation was going to ice it for him—he would be lucky to hold on to his position for another hour.

The Colonel looked aloft and squinted against the swirling dust. "It is a damned Lithuanian helicopter," he said. "I will deal with—"

Suddenly a man leaped out the portside cargo door of the hovering helicopter. At first it looked like a suicide attempt, because the man virtually leaped headfirst. But the shock wore off quickly, and the Colonel recognized the maneuver—a man doing an Australian rappel, the fastest assault rappel known. In only two seconds the man reached the ground, pulling himself upright three meters before his face smashed into the earth. He was followed shortly thereafter by another man, accomplishing a more conventional feetfirst rappel from the same rope a few moments later.

Soldiers accompanying the two Byelorussian officers unslung their weapons and held them at the ready, but the first rappeller ignored them all as he strode right up to General Voshchanka. "What in hell do you mean by ordering me away from this area?" the Lithuanian officer yelled after waving the helicopter that he and the second man had dropped in safely. The chopper veered away. "I demand to know what in hell is going on here."

Voshchanka's colonel recognized the man as none other than Palcikas himself, commander of Lithuania's puny self-defense force.

"Who are you?" General Voshchanka demanded. "What is the meaning of this? Colonel Gurlo, arrest this man."

The Colonel knew he was not authorized to touch Palcikas—it would be an act of war for a foreign officer to touch a general on his own soil—but he motioned for two security officers to move closer. They immediately surrounded Palcikas but did not touch him. In Russian, the Colonel said, "General Voshchanka, may I present General Dominikas Palcikas, commander of the Self-Defense Forces of the Lithuanian Republic. General Palcikas, I present General Lieutenant Voshchanka, commander, Western Corps Armies, Republic of Belarus, and commander of security forces of the Baltic states for the Commonwealth of Independent States."

Neither man saluted the other.

Palcikas' face remained dark as he removed his thick rappelling gloves. But Voshchanka said, "Palcikas! We finally meet. I've heard a lot about you. That was quite a stunt for an old war horse."

"I'd be happy to teach it to you, General," Palcikas said in very good, well-disciplined Russian, "but it is not a maneuver for the faint of heart . . . or those with big bellies and soft hands."

Voshchanka, a rather short, stocky man who had never even been inside an assault helicopter, let alone jumped from one, calmly smiled away the offhanded remark.

Palcikas, eyes dead-on Voshchanka, said, "General, you will explain to me why your troops have destroyed this farm, and why your unit has been ordering my aviation and ground units away from this area."

"There was an attack last night, General Palcikas," Voshchanka explained. "A Lithuanian deserter from a Commonwealth unit stationed in Vilnius was being pursued by a patrol helicopter when suddenly the helicopter pilot reported that he was under attack by an unknown aircraft. Seconds later he was shot down by a heat-seeking missile of Western design. The Lithuanian *traitor* has vanished. We are investigating."

Palcikas' eyes flared at "Lithuanian traitor," which pleased Voshchanka. Palcikas said, "I sympathize with the loss of your flyers and your aircraft, General Voshchanka, but look at what your men are doing to this farmer's land—you are causing thousands of liths' worth of damage. The forests you've decimated can't be replaced for decades. And you're in violation of the treaty of security and cooperation by bringing your troops here. You will assemble them and move out immediately."

"We were . . . concerned about destruction of evidence, General," Voshchanka said lamely, not acknowledging Palcikas' orders. "Having untrained, undisciplined farm boys roving around where they are not supposed to will hinder our investigation."

"My men or these farmers could not possibly destroy more evidence than your men have done so far," Palcikas said.

Voshchanka knew that was true. He had obtained all the evidence he needed after the first few minutes on the crash scene. "I'll issue orders to my men to be more careful, and I will personally see to it that these farmers are reimbursed for the damage."

"Very well, General," Palcikas acknowledged. He stepped toward a plywood table covered with white canvas, where several pieces of a missile were being reassembled. The lower section of a one-and-a-half-meter-long missile, blackened and twisted, rested on the cloth, with several guidance fins still intact. "I see you've already collected quite a bit of evidence," he said. "A Stinger missile?"

"Very observant, General," said Voshchanka.

"Distinctive shape of the tail fins, distinctive blast pattern of the war-head section—I saw many like it in Afghanistan after they shot down our attack helicopters." He took a closer look, then added, "These tail fins are somewhat larger, however, and there appears to be an attachment point for an extra set of fins in the forward section, in addition to the normal set of retractable nose fins. An AIM-92C air-launched Stinger missile, perhaps?"

"Excellent," Voshchanka said. "And the origin of the missile?"

"Difficult to say, General Voshchanka. Many countries now fly the AIM-92C," Palcikas said. "We can narrow it down to six or seven European countries outside NATO. And they are readily available on the black market, I should think. They are license-built in Belgium, and their plant security is reputed to be poor."

"I see that we can do away with our investigation team, General Palcikas," Voshchanka said facetiously. "You've done all the detective work for us."

"Good," Palcikas said evenly. "Now you can get off this farmer's property and remove all these vehicles to Byelorussia."

"The proper name of our country is *Belarus*," Voshchanka said. "The distinction is important to us."

"As you wish," Palcikas said distractedly. For decades the western Soviet republic had been called Byelorussia, loosely translated as "White Russia," which, although most scholars attributed the name to mean that this part of the Slavic territory was never conquered by the dark-skinned Mongols, some said gave the people of this region a decidedly negative connotation, as in weak or enslaved people. When it became an independent nation, the republic proclaimed itself as the Republic of Belarus, which translated more closely to "Great Russia," or "Mother Russia," the native land of the original Rus conquerors of early Europe. The distinction was meaningless to Palcikas except for the fact that he knew how it would aggravate the hawkish right-wing advocates in the Byelorussian military.

"The presence of all these vehicles and soldiers violates the security and cooperation agreement between Lithuania and the Commonwealth of Independent States," Palcikas continued, and then recited the treaty provisions.

Voshchanka remained impassive, with the same amused smile on his lips, but the Colonel with him hissed: "Who in hell do you think you're talking to, Palcikas? General Voshchanka does not answer to you or to any Lithuanian!"

Voshchanka held up a hand. "What the Colonel is saying in a rather inelegant way, General Palcikas, is that I take my orders from the commander in chief of military forces of the Commonwealth of Independent States. Because of the nature of this mission—an attack against a Commonwealth helicopter by an unknown, hostile aircraft—I personally took charge of this mission when the order was delivered from Minsk, and I did not inquire into the treaty or legal ramifications of those orders."

"General Voshchanka, I did not ask you for an excuse," Palcikas interrupted. "You may submit your explanation in writing to the Lithuanian government directly, through me, or through the Commonwealth. I am only concerned with these Belarus troops violating the treaty. I hereby order you again to comply with the joint cooperation treaty and return to Belarus or to your bases. Will you comply with my orders or ignore them?"

Voshchanka pointed to the black smear of metal and burnt debris. "Three men died in that crash, General Palcikas. Three highly trained, professional aviators. Are you not concerned about the men who died here?"

"As concerned as you appear to be about complying with any treaties with Lithuania," Palcikas said.

"You insolent bastard!" Colonel Gurlo retorted. "The General has told you that he has orders to investigate this incident, and he will accomplish that mission with or without your cooperation or any trash about treaties. Now step out of the way and we will complete our assigned duty."

Now Palcikas chuckled. "Does this pitiful excuse for a colonel speak for you, General Voshchanka?"

The Byelorussian colonel said something in unintelligible Russian, and he drew his sidearm. "You Lithuanian bastard. I will put a bullet in your head for that."

Just then three helicopters popped from over a nearby treeline, encircled the group of Byelorussian vehicles, and hovered about two hundred meters away from the group. Voshchanka and his colonel could see that the first helicopter was Palcikas' Mil-8 transport helicopter, with door gunners standing in each side door and out the back of the rear cargo ramp, aiming huge Degtyarev 12.7-millimeter machine guns at the vehicles and soldiers below. The other two helicopters were small, almost toylike American-made McDonnell-Douglas Model 500 Defender attack models, but each one carried a rocket and gun pods on fuselage-mounted pylons. They may have looked like toys, but there was nothing childlike about the threat. At the same time, Palcikas' aide had raised his AKSU assault rifle, ready to open fire.

"Tell your aide to lower his rifle or there will be bloodshed," the Byelorussian colonel said. He had aimed his sidearm at Palcikas' aide when he had raised his own. The two men eyed each other, neither daring to move; then Kolginov turned the muzzle of his weapon away. The Colonel smiled, as though he had just won a major victory, then holstered his sidearm.

"This is how you want to conduct business with the Commonwealth, General Palcikas?" Voshchanka asked, taking only a momentary glance at the attack choppers before turning back to the Lithuanian general. "Aim a gun pod at a fellow officer—in peacetime? Threaten us with violence while in the midst of negotiations? You should re-evaluate your actions, I think."

"I am no threat to you or your Byelorussian soldiers, General Vosh-chanka," Palcikas said. "I am sure six antiaircraft guns are targeted against each one of my helicopters. They, or I, would not survive a firefight. But neither would you, and I assure you, I would be satisfied with that outcome."

"You Lithuanian *pig*," Voshchanka's colonel spat.

"I have asked you twice to depart this area. I shall ask a third time. After that I will consider this detachment an invasion force and deal with it with all the power in my command—right here, right now. You will pack up your troops and your vehicles and return to your CIS base in Siauliai or to Kaliningrad immediately. Will you comply?"

Voshchanka's confident smile had vanished with the appearance of those attack helicopters. True, he had more than enough counterbattery units to destroy this pathetic force, especially hovering as they were in plain view, but one rocket from one helicopter could kill all of them instantly. No, this was not the time nor place for a showdown.

"Colonel Gurlo, order your units to assemble and return to base immediately," Voshchanka said, keeping his gaze affixed on Palcikas. "Tell the gunners to lower their antiaircraft guns right now."

The Colonel looked mad enough to spit bullets, but he relayed the order.

Palcikas remained as he was, staring at Voshchanka as the big BMP-1 and BMV-3 armored personnel carriers scattered around the farm fired up their big diesels and started to move toward the main road, their 30-millimeter machine guns lowered and pointing far away from the helicopters. As the armored vehicles moved, the two Defender helicopters moved along with them, leaving Palcikas' Mil-8 nearby ready to pick up the Lithuanian general.

"I'd say that was a very risky move, General Palcikas," General Vosh-chanka said. "Sacrificing ten men and three helicopters, plus yourself and your aide—that would be more than your poor country could afford, I think. You might be better off letting your politicians do the fighting for you and to direct your forces from a desk instead of leaping out of helicopters and threatening superior officers." He moved a bit closer to Palcikas. "It could get very dangerous out here, you know, surrounded by superior forces . . ."

"On Lithuanian soil you are nothing but a trespasser, General," Palcikas replied. "I respect you and your soldiers, but I won't let that alter my responsibility to defend my homeland." This time Palcikas paused, then glanced at the retreating armored vehicles. "This is a large number of vehicles for a simple aviation incident, General."

"Perhaps I expected trouble from you Lithuanians."

"Or perhaps you have some other mission in mind, General," Palcikas said. "What else do you have planned for Lithuania, General? Or shall I guess?"

"You seem to enjoy the sound of your own prattle very much, General, so please continue," Voshchanka said magnanimously.

"I have watched most of the Commonwealth's Fifth Army in western Byelorussia being replaced by Byelorussian troops over the past several months," Palcikas said. "Now the Commonwealth's 103rd Guards Division appears to be replaced by Byelorussia's Tenth Lancers in Vilnius, Kaunas, and Kaliningrad . . ."

"Your intelligence is commendable but spotty," Voshchanka said smugly.

Palcikas ignored the remark. "Your forces are widely dispersed, but there is a solid line of Byelorussian troops forming from the Baltic to Minsk. There are almost no Commonwealth forces at all west of the thirtieth meridian."

"We are Commonwealth forces, Palcikas," the Byelorussian colonel said irritably. "What the hell do you think we're doing in your rat's nest of a country?"

Palcikas knew the Colonel was blowing smoke at him. While Voshchanka *was* commander of the Commonwealth of Independent States' military forces in the Baltics, set up as a part of the mutual-defense treaty of the Baltics, he was also commander of *all* Byelorussian forces. When Byelorussia became independent, Voshchanka simply assumed control of the troops and equipment that had been his to command when he was head of Soviet forces in Byelorussia. Besides being a convenient way to hold on to the rank and privileges Voshchanka enjoyed under Soviet rule, it was also a nice way to expand his power—and Palcikas would bet his next paycheck that Voshchanka would do it with *Byelorussian* troops.

"Never mind replying to his fiction, Colonel," General Voshchanka said. "He is trying to impress us with his supposed knowledge of Commonwealth troop deployment and strengths, when in fact he couldn't be further off the mark. He has asked us to withdraw, so we will." He turned back toward Palcikas and, raising his voice to be heard over the roar of the helicopters nearby, added, "Bringing your helicopter gunships over my troops is like pulling a gun on me, General. Next time you had better be prepared to use it. I will not warn you again." He turned and headed for his vehicle, leaving Palcikas and Kolginov alone in the middle of the muddy, disheveled corral.

"General, you took a very big chance there," Kolginov said in Lithuanian. He shouldered his rifle and held tightly to the sling, hoping that he could keep his hands from shaking. "True, they had at least six twenty- and thirty-millimeter guns on the Defenders, but they also had a few twelve-point-sevens trained on us. I thought we were dead."

"We *were* dead," Palcikas stressed. "I saw the murder in Voshchanka's eyes. He would have ordered his men to open fire, had he himself not been in the area. Colonel Gurlo was ready to mow us all down, too."

Palcikas motioned for the Mil-8 to land in a clearing a few hundred meters away. "Unfortunately, we haven't seen the last of him. He'll be back, with more troops, sooner than we think. He's a hungry pig."

Kolginov watched his superior officer searching the skies and the fields around him as if he were already commanding the battle he knew was coming.

Finally Palcikas said, "Let's go check the farmer and his family; they're probably scared out of their minds right now."

They found the farmer, who was mad enough to chew on horseshoes, a few moments later. Palcikas and Kolginov had no choice but to endure the old man's blistering tirade against all military men in general and Byelorussian soldiers in particular. "Why, they can't even drive a tank properly!" the old man shouted. "In the Great Patriotic War, I drove all kinds of vehicles, from sidecar motorcycles to tanks. I was half their age and I could maneuver a tank around a fencepost or outhouse like nobody's business!"

"If the General could just get your name, sir . . ." Kolginov tried, but the man ranted on for a few minutes more until a young woman entered the room.

"His name is Mikhaus Egoro Kulikauskas," the woman said. She touched the old man's shoulder to silence him. "He is my father. He doesn't hear very well, and he has seen more strangers this morning than he has all month."

"And you are Anna Kulikauskas, the famous young revolutionary," General Palcikas said. "I recognize you from your photos in the Sajudis newspapers. I now see where you get your temper from."

The woman, no older than her late thirties, nodded and smiled as she carefully returned Palcikas' gaze. Anna Kulikauskas was one of the new breed of young, fiery politicians in the "new" Lithuania, a left-wing (many, including Palcikas, would call her "radical") advocate of making Lithuania part of a "New European Order." Palcikas recalled that her idea of a New European Order did not include such things as armies, navies, military facilities of any kind, nuclear-power plants, taxes, heavy industrial plants that could pollute the environment, and foreign companies that wanted to invest in Lithuanian businesses that owned farms and forests. Anna Kulikauskas was active in the formation of the Sajudis independent political party and first gained international prominence as the leading voice of protest that finally resulted in the closing of the Ignalina Nuclear Power Plant in northwestern Lithuania—photos of her facing down hundreds of armed Red Army and Black Beret soldiers were published worldwide. She was strong-willed, intelligent, quick-tempered, bold, and aggressive.

She wore a homespun "peasant's skirt" that was now all the rage in Europe—especially in the Baltic states—and being copied by famous designers and dressmakers all over the world. Like most Slavic women, she had light-brown curly hair which was worn long and unbound, big blue eyes, full lips, and a nose just a bit out of proportion with the rest of her face. But there must have been a Viking in the barn one night, because Anna was also curvaceous and full-figured, with a thin waist bisecting healthy hips and a deep, sexy bosom that made Palcikas stare.

Kolginov coughed politely, stifling an amused smile.

Palcikas quickly asked, "Was anyone hurt here?"

"Human, no," Anna replied. "Animal, yes. Some of the soldiers claimed two of our horses jumped over a fence and ran away, but I think they took them. Some other animals were killed or chased away—a few thousand liths' worth."

"Make a list of the damage and the missing livestock, sign it, and deliver it to my headquarters at Trakai," Palcikas said. "The government will reimburse you immediately. My men will also help rebuild your barns and fences."

"I don't need your help to rebuild my farm!" the old man retorted. "I just need to be left alone! I used every ruble of my pension savings to buy this farm, and I won't have it torn apart by you soldiers again!"

"Those were Commonwealth soldiers, Mr. Kulikauskas," Palcikas' aide, Kolginov, said. "Not Lithuanians."

"And who are you?" the old man demanded, his eyes widening at Kolginov's slight Russian accent. "A Russian? First we have Commonwealth soldiers, then Byelorussians, and now Russians . . . ?"

Kolginov gave him a wry smile, but Palcikas interceded for him: "Major Kolginov is a naturalized Lithuanian and a member of the Iron Wolf Brigade, Mr. Kulikauskas," he said.

"The Iron Wolf Brigade!" the old man cried out. "How dare you! How dare you debase the name of the Grand Duke's army!" The old eyes sought out Palcikas' uniform and rested with shock on a red patch with a mounted knight on a rearing charger in white in the center. "You wear the Grand Duke's Vytis like a patch to mend tattered clothing? Do you have a Vytis sewn in your crotch as well? Why, that is . . . that is *unholy* . . . *!*"

"Mr. Kulikauskas, I do not defile the name of the Grand Duke—I honor it," Palcikas said. "The men in my unit who wear the Vytis have sworn an oath, with one hand on the Bible and one hand on the Sword of State, to protect this nation."

"What do you know about honor, or fidelity, or—"

"We follow the very same ritual of training and service, and swear the very same oath, as King Gediminas prescribed in centuries past," Palcikas said. "The training period is two years, as it was then. Major Kolginov accomplished the additional rigors of naturalization before performing the training, and he has earned the right to receive the Sword and make the oath. You are a veteran: if you wish to view this ritual at Trakai, you may do so as my guest. The next full moon, be at Trakai at eleven P.M. The ritual begins at midnight." Kolginov produced a memo sheet with instructions for the castle guard. Palcikas signed it, handed it over to the old man, and turned to depart.

Anna Kulikauskas met up with the two officers outside. "That was a good thing you did for my father," she said. "He is somewhat of a student of history."

"As am I," Palcikas said. "Please be sure he submits a full report on the damage, and advise me when my men can come over to rebuild your damaged farm."

"Thank you," she said. "Although I must admit this is a side of the military I have not seen. Are you sure you're not doing all this because of who I am?"

"I didn't know who owned this farm before I knocked on your door," Palcikas replied. "I give all our people equal attention, and what I do is what I do—I'm not quick enough to put on an act for everyone I see who I think might be an opinion leader. But I hope at least I've changed your attitude about the military—and about myself—a bit."

He knew she was controversial, a firebrand, even potentially dangerous to the continued existence of the Iron Wolf Brigade. Besides being a strong advocate for a completely demilitarized Lithuania and complete neutrality, with no more than regional police units to offer protection, she also advocated no military ties to any other nation or organization. But somehow that didn't really matter now.

"I'm not convinced that all military commanders are as caring and as sensitive as you appear," she admitted. "But yes, I'm willing to look a little harder for the good in everyone, even a man with a uniform and a gun." She paused, her eyes scanning the road that the Byelorussian soldiers used to depart the farm. "Will those Commonwealth troops be back?"

"I don't think so," Palcikas replied. "If they do return, notify my office at once. We must begin assembling a case against them for the government to take to the United Nations. It's obvious there are numerous violations of the transitional treaty. As for the helicopter crash, I will send an investigation team of my own to get your statement and one from your father, and anyone else that was here."

"We saw nothing," Anna said. She looked at her father, who stared at his daughter with questioning eyes, then turned toward Palcikas with defiance. To Palcikas, there was an unspoken message between father and daughter, heard and felt all too much in Palcikas' career: Don't get involved. Stay out of it. If they did see something last night, and the odds were good that they did, they were not going to volunteer the information.

"I would appreciate your cooperation, Mr. Kulikauskas, Miss Kulikauskas. If you have anything that I might find useful, anything at all, please notify me at once. Good day." He and Kolginov departed.

Outside, Kolginov had just finished signaling for the Mil-8 to return. "Well? They give you anything on the crash?"

"No, but they know something—they probably saw the whole thing," Palcikas said irritably. "A helicopter gun battle, unidentified planes flying low, reports of bomb blasts—they saw something. Hopefully, after their corral is rebuilt, they'll be a bit more helpful."

"At least the follow-up interviews will be a pleasure," Kolginov said with a smile. He looked at Palcikas and saw the trace of a thin smile on his lips. "I see you thought so too. It's funny—when she's on the podiums or on the evening news, she looks like a crackpot. In person, she's quite attractive and—"

"I think you need a dunk in the Salantai River," Palcikas said. "You're overheating."

"And you weren't, General?" Kolginov said with a laugh.

"You're crazy, Alexei."

"You're right, of course, sir. What would a woman like that see in an old war horse like you?"

"Thank God your ritual days are approaching," Palcikas said. "There's nothing like some good old-fashioned debasement and sacrifice to instill discipline in a man."

The Mil-8 swung overhead, translating to the touchdown area, but Palcikas flashed a sign to the pilot. Instead of landing, the crew chief on board threw the rappelling rope out the portside cargo hatch, and the pilot brought the aircraft to a hover about ten meters above ground. "Up you go, Major," Palcikas said.

"What? You want me to climb up, under a hovering helicopter?"

"You are the expert on love, I am the expert in soldiering," Palcikas said with a laugh as the sound of the rotors overhead nearly drowned out his voice. "We'll see who has the greater power. Follow me!" At that, Palcikas gave a loud cry, jumped onto the rope, and began climbing. In less than thirty seconds he was on-board the helicopter and waving for Kolginov to follow.

But as he leaned out the cargo door watching his young aide pull himself up the rope, he caught a glimpse of Anna Kulikauskas watching them from inside the house. Her hand was upraised, and he thought he saw her wave at him. It was hard to tell if she did, but the thought of her doing so made something stir within him.

FISIKOUS INSTITUTE OF TECHNOLOGY, VILNIUS, LITHUANIA
6 DECEMBER, **0839** VILNIUS **(0239** ET)

The scale aircraft model, ten meters in length and almost the same in width, dominated the conference room on the second floor of the main research center of the sprawling Fisikous Institute. The model, hanging from hydraulic arms a few meters above the conference table, looked nothing like a conventional plane. Its wings were undulating curves tapering to narrow points; its body was blended into the wings, giving it a huge manta-ray appearance. Its cockpit windows were narrow slits on the upper side near the pointed nose. Two sharply angled vertical stabilizers jutted out of the tail section, atop narrow engine exhausts.

The Fisikous Institute of Technology was one of perhaps a dozen government aircraft-design bureaus in the former Soviet Union. Like the High Technology Aerospace Weapons Center (HAWC) the U.S. government had in Nevada, Fisikous was an ultrasecret, highly classified development center that the official Soviet government never officially or publicly acknowledged. Normally, products developed in the compound housing the Fisikous labs in Lithuania went to one of the other major design bureaus—Sukhoi, Mikoyan-Gureyvich, or Tupolev, among others—in Moscow for incorporation in their designs. This radical aircraft was one of Fisikous' first designed from the wheels up by the Lithuanian lab itself, and it was one of the most important—it was the Soviet Union's first stealth bomber, designed to avoid detection by advanced radar systems.

One of the scientists gathered in the room activated a switch on a console at his seat, which rotated the model along its longitudinal axis so that the two vertical stabilizers could be clearly seen by all. "The tailplane on the Fisikous-170 stealth bomber is an all-moving, hydraulically operated fly-by-light control surface, made of all composite materials," Dr. Pyotr Fursenko, the senior project scientist, said, continuing his informal talk about the newest changes in his design. "It provides stability in all three axes of flight—yaw, roll, and pitch. In addition, the tailplanes can be retracted downwards toward the fuselage, like so." He hit another switch and the vertical stabilizers lowered until they were almost flush with the aft end of the weird-looking model. "This can be done during several phases of flight, but mostly during high-speed portions of a mission at either high or low altitude, when normal pitch-and-roll control can be accomplished by the mission-adaptive wing structure. The stabilizers are quite strong in their fully extended position, and their composite construction increases radar cross-section by only one one-thousandth of a percent—far less than the radar return from the pilot's helmet through the cockpit windscreen.''

The scientists in the room nodded their approval, but in the low murmur of approving voices there was one voice that caused the other delegates to the conference to stop and turn toward the speaker with a great deal of surprise. "Excuse me," Fursenko said irritably to the one attendee. "Would you repeat what you just said?"

"I said bullshit, *tovarisch,*" David Luger said in rather stilted pidgin Russian. The other delegates peeled away from the tall, thin man as if he were glowing with radioactivity. Luger went on: "That vertical surface will increase the aircraft's radar cross-section by a factor of at least four hundred, whether extended or retracted."

"We have run dozens of tests on the design, Dr. Ozerov," Fursenko replied. "The data show that radar cross-section is reduced significantly, as close to zero as possible, with the vertical control surfaces retracted."

"You're talking about a computer model that merely computes an RCS factor based on the square footage of the control surface in the slipstream," Luger said. Most of his words, especially the technical terms, came out in English, and his pronunciation of most of the Russian words was barely understandable—the other scientists shook their heads in exasperation, trying to understand him as he continued: "Your computer model doesn't take into account the lobal-propagation properties of RF energy coming off the wings and fuselage and the wave pattern associated with reflections from the control surfaces, especially when the main wing trailing edge deflects in greater increments during high-speed turns."

Fursenko rolled his eyes in exasperation. "I did not understand you, Doctor Ozerov. Would you kindly—"

Luger sneered. "Don't you know anything about stealth characteristics?"

Fursenko let out a resigned sigh and, searching the attendees, let his eyes rest on a man sitting as unobtrusively as possible in the back of the room. The man noticed Fursenko searching for him, and he smiled with great amusement at the scientist. The man in the back of the room made a gesture at Fursenko as if to say, "Answer the man, Doctor."

But before Fursenko could, Luger proceeded: "Stealth isn't just a factor of the structural or material composition of an aircraft. You can't just build anything you want out of composites and call it stealthy. You'll always have radar reflections because of structural members beneath the skin. But even if the entire thing were built out of plastic, it doesn't mean you'll have a stealthy aircraft. What you got there doesn't even come *close*. I haven't run a computer model of the aircraft with those stabilators, but just judging by the light reflecting off those things, you don't have a stealthy bomber there.

"The key is to *channel* whatever radar energy is reflected into lobes, with specific direction and amplitude, and you have to be careful not to let the lobes cross with other lobes from other parts of the aircraft. If you can aim the lobes away from the emitter, bingo! You have a stealthy design. The lobes are real, and they're powerful, just like regular RF energy—if you cross them or blend them, you'll destroy whatever stealth characteristics you had. Is that clear now?"

"Thank you for your input, Doctor Ozerov," Fursenko finally said to Luger. "You have certainly explained your arguments . . . er, succinctly and positively . . ."

"So run your computer models again, but this time you have to plot the lobes from the vertical stabilizers in every possible position, then combine it with the lobe structure from the main mission-adaptive wings in every possible position and see if you have any cases where the lobes enhance or blend with each other."

"Thank you, Doctor Ozerov."

"It may take a while, but it'll be worth it," Luger said, his voice more excited, his words more clipped. "You can compute the lobal propagation for the plane by hand, but it'll take weeks. But if you freed up the computer a little, I'd run the model for you and have an answer in a few days. If you ask me, you should just take the damn vertical stabs off. Increase the range of motion of the MAW actuators, and you'll have full roll-and-pitch control at all speeds—"

"I said, *thank you,* Doctor."

Luger scratched his head, his other hand patting nervously against his right leg. He glanced quickly at his colleagues, but something had suddenly gone out of his eyes. He was feeling confused, disoriented. "And another thing. I . . ." He looked around, frustration and anxiety giving way to anger. "Dammit, I was going to say something else, but I've lost . . . my train of thought. I . . . ." He scratched his head again, pacing back and forth. "I . . . don't know what's wrong . . . what I'm doing."

Fursenko's eyes darted to the back of the room, but the man who had been watching Luger was already moving toward him from behind.

Luger felt a hand on his shoulder. "Hey, Doc. Hey . . ." Luger's face fell into despair, then brightened somewhat. "Hey, Doc where have *you* been?"

"I think it is time to go, Ivan," Viktor Gabovich—known to David Luger as Dr. Petyr Kaminski—said gently. "That was a very good presentation."

"So why are these guys looking at me like this?" Luger asked. "Why are they staring at me?" He glared at one of the delegates and raged in English, "You got a problem? I'm right about those vertical stabilizers, man. You gotta take those suckers off—"

"Speak Russian, Ivan," Gabovich urged him quietly. "Some of these gentlemen don't understand English too well."

"Well, I suppose that's *my* fucking fault too, huh?" Luger shouted. A tiny drop of spittle rested on a corner of his mouth. "Just like it's my fault I can't get to sleep at night, right? And my fault the first prototype crashed . . . and now you're saying it's my fault that these morons can't understand me? Well, *fuck you,* Kaminski."

By this time Gabovich had led Luger out of the conference room and into an anterior hallway. "Hey, I wasn't finished with my points, friend, I gotta go back there—"

A fist plunged hard and deep into Luger's solar plexus, knocking the wind out of his lungs. Luger tried to take a breath, failed, wheezed, and sank to his knees, gasping for breath. Gabovich's deputy, Vadim Teresov, rubbed his knuckles for a moment, then pulled Luger's head up by his hair. "Quit whining, Luger!"

"Nyet," Gabovich said. "You idiot—his name is *Ozerov."* The two Russians helped Luger to his feet. Luger's face was turning red from the pain and exertion, but Gabovich could see he was taking deeper breaths. "You must learn not to get so excited, Ivan Sergeiovich," Gabovich told him. "You will just get yourself and those around you upset for no reason."

"Why the fuck did you do that?" Luger croaked. "Why did you do that . . . ?"

"Colonel Teresov was only trying to get your attention," Gabovich said. "Your excitement raises a lot of concern among your colleagues here."

"No one listens to me," Luger muttered. "I don't know any of these people . . . I don't know . . . I don't know who I am . . . sometimes . . ."

It was happening again, Gabovich thought.

Luger was losing his carefully regimented programming. After years of hard work, the effects they had so wondrously achieved were being nullified. This was the third incident in just two weeks. Gabovich wondered if Luger wasn't getting addicted to the pain to which he was being subjected, because it always took more and more of a booster to get him through a day's work.

"You must not get so excited," Gabovich said patiently. He snapped his fingers for some nearby guards, both known personally to him— Luger was too valuable to be entrusted to an uncleared person. "Come,

Ivan. Go back to the dormitory with these men. You've had a very long day." To the guards, Gabovich hissed, "Take him to the Zulu facility immediately. No one is to speak with him—*no one.*"

Luger seemed steady enough on his feet, so the two ex-Soviet guards began escorting him to the back exit and a waiting car outside which would take him to the security building, also in the compound. Luger looked downtrodden, as if the pain in his stomach was nothing compared to the hopelessness he felt as he thought of all the months of work that still lay ahead.

As they proceeded down the corridor, they noticed a Lithuanian Self-Defense Force officer, with a sergeant at his side, standing nearby watching them. "You. Come here," Gabovich ordered. The two soldiers walked over to him. "You are?"

"Major Alexei Kolginov, deputy commander, Iron Wolf Brigade headquarters," the officer replied. "This is Command Sergeant Major Surkov, Brigade NCOIC. I was—"

"Kolginov? Surkov? You are Russians?" General Gabovich asked with an expression of surprise and amusement.

Kolginov nodded.

"You are officers in a Lithuanian Boy Scout army . . . ?"

"We are part of the Lithuanian Self-Defense Force," Kolginov asserted.

"Ah yes, the Iron Wolf Brigade," Gabovich said derisively. "Such a tough name for such a playschool army."

Kolginov let the insult roll off his back. "We are on a facilities inspection, checking for treaty compliance as part of the deactivation of this facility, when I noticed you taking this man out of the security conference room. He appears to be ill or disoriented. Is there a problem here? Is he all right?"

Gabovich made an expression of undisguised exasperation. The security problems here at the Fisikous Institute were becoming a joke.

When the facility, and Lithuania, belonged to the old USSR, security at the Fisikous Research Institute was handled by the MVD, the Soviet Troops of the Interior. From the MVD troops stationed in Lithuania, a special detachment of highly trained troops was formed specifically to handle security here in Fisikous and in other critical Soviet offices in Vilnius. That unit was called OMON, or *Otriad Militisiia Osobennoga Naznachenaia,* meaning "Special Purpose Military Detachment." Because they wore black berets to distinguish them from other MVD troops, they were called the Black Berets by many in Lithuania and in the West. They soon gained a terrible reputation as ruthless enforcers, and were charged with murdering many Lithuanian citizens, along with citizens of the other Baltic republics, before those countries declared their independence from the Soviet Union.

When Lithuania became independent in 1991, the Black Berets were supposedly disbanded. But they weren't. They still existed, in smaller numbers, in the most important Soviet facilities in the Baltic states. At the Fisikous Institute in Vilnius, they were called "private security employees" and placed under the command of Viktor Gabovich, who was no longer part of the KGB (since technically the KGB did not exist as of 1992) but was an officer of the Commonwealth of Independent States' Inter-Republican Council for Security, or MSB, charged with maintaining security for Commonwealth facilities in Lithuania during the transition period.

But because of the treaty for the transition of control of former Soviet facilities between Lithuania and the Commonwealth, Commonwealth troops and Lithuanian officials had equal access to Fisikous to monitor compliance. Military personnel wearing all sort of uniforms paraded around the place all the time, making it nearly impossible for the scientists to get anything done. This went up Viktor Gabovich's ass sideways. The Institute was his domain, his base of operations, and even though he wasn't a scientist, he sure as hell had authority over what they did. Turning Fisikous into *the* premier weapons-and-aircraft-design facility in the Commonwealth was not only his goal, it was his obsession.

It was the reason he had brought the American from that hellhole in Siberia, and the reason he'd expended so much time and energy turning him from a prisoner into a collaborator.

It was also the reason he put up with these petty interruptions by the Lithuanians, on whose soil the Institute unfortunately sat. Every day he was tempted to simply lock the doors and gates, tell these Boy Scouts to fuck off, and seal off access. But Viktor Gabovich knew that his Black Berets did not have the numbers needed to keep the Lithuanians at bay, let alone the might of the Byelorussian-equipped Commonwealth forces.

But just because Gabovich had to let these popinjays in did not mean he had to stand for their petty interrogations. To Kolginov he replied, "You asked if he's all right? That is none of your business."

Kolginov's eyes narrowed, and Surkov instinctively took a defensive step backwards, immediately drawing his walkie-talkie to summon help. "Your identification cards, please," Kolginov demanded.

Gabovich produced his identification card and replied hotly, "What the problem is, Major, is that you are skulking around here and observing private research activities that do not concern you."

Kolginov examined the card and recognized the man's name immediately—although they had not met before, Kolginov knew Gabovich was the head of security for Fisikous, hired by the scientists themselves to provide "special" security procedures and services for parts of the facility not yet open to inspection by Lithuania. Kolginov also knew that Gabovich and his aide, a man named Teresov, were former KGB officers and most likely still had their entire KGB apparatus intact. Kolginov had never seen the third man. He motioned to Luger and asked, "And that man . . . ?"

"Doctor Ivan Sergeiovich Ozerov. He is under my supervision. He is not required to show you his identification," Gabovich said testily. "Now, what is your reason for being in this wing of the facility, Major Iron Wolf?"

"I am on an inspection tour of—"

"There are no guard posts down this corridor, Major," Gabovich pointed out. "I suggest you keep your nose out of business that does not concern you."

"If you have a problem with my actions, Comrade Gabovich," Kolginov said loudly, "you—"

But he never had a chance to finish. Gabovich, flushed with anger as his patience finally snapped, pulled out a huge Makarov pistol and aimed it at Kolginov, silencing him immediately. Teresov pulled a gun on Surkov before the NCO could reach into his holster.

"I am ordering you to close your mouth, move away from this area immediately, and keep your mouth closed about this incident, or I will shut you up *permanently,*" Gabovich said. "This is a private operation, underwritten by the Commonwealth of Independent States. Ozerov is a CIS scientist under my care, and you are in violation of internal-security regulations. If you have damaged this operation with your actions, I will see to it that General Voshchanka goes to your government and has you stripped of your rank. If you don't believe we have the power to do that, just try it. Now *go.*"

Kolginov glanced at Surkov and shook his head. He knew that Surkov could probably disable Teresov in the wink of an eye, and he might even reach Gabovich, but eventually one or both of the CIS officers would gun them down. There was no use fighting it out here and now—better to wait. Kolginov and Surkov stepped backwards away from the two MSB agents, and Teresov made sure that they were retreating away from the conference level before rejoining Gabovich.

"Damn those Lithuanian busybodies," Teresov cursed. "Do you think they heard what we were saying?"

"I do not know," Gabovich snapped. "See to it that access by Lithuanian security forces is restricted or denied."

"How do I do that?" Teresov asked. "The Commonwealth offers equal access to the Lithuanian Self-Defense Forces as it does to us. They let everyone in this place—Latvians, Byelorussian troops, Polish investors, everyone. We don't have the strength or influence to get the CIS to keep the Lithuanians out."

Gabovich was about to reprehend Teresov for asking such a question—it was *his* job to find ways to do things—but he fell silent. This was beginning to become a problem in all operations in Fisikous as the prospect of turning over the facility to the Lithuanians got closer and closer to reality. As part of the treaty between the Commonwealth of Independent States and Lithuania, the CIS was to turn over possession of all former Soviet land, bases, and facilities to Lithuania by the year 1995. The CIS could take all products and equipment made or brought into the country prior to the first of June 1991 out of those facilities and return them to the Commonwealth, subject to continuous scrutiny and verification by the CIS and Lithuania.

According to the treaty, the research and products made in the Fisikous Research Center, including the stealth bomber, belonged to the CIS. The problem was, the CIS did not know anything about it. The Fisikous-170 bomber was developed in near-total secrecy by a group of Soviet scientists, and its existence was kept off the books by the KGB and the Soviet Air Force for years. Viktor Gabovich, as senior KGB officer in Lithuania, became the driving force behind the project, tightening security at the facility, building a defense force around the facility of near-regiment strength, and recruiting the best and brightest scientists and engineers to work there—including his prisoner, David Luger.

When the Fisikous-170 program was canceled by the Soviet government in mid-1991, just after the August coup attempt, work continued on a part-time basis, with funds supplied by the Gabovich's "special projects" account. As a "black" program, the Fi-170 enjoyed almost unlimited funding and support until 1992, when the newly formed Commonwealth of Independent States disbanded the KGB and the CIS-Lithuania treaty went into effect. Gabovich still enjoyed considerable power in Lithuania and throughout the region, mainly because of the strength of the "private" army and his former KGB intelligence network, which was still intact, but the gradually weakening Commonwealth and the rapidly strengthening Lithuanian influences in the area weakened that power.

When he lost Fisikous, he would lose all he cherished—power, wealth, and influence. He, along with most of the Soviet scientists in the Fisikous Research Center, had nothing to return to back in the Commonwealth. They would lose everything they had if Fisikous closed down.

Dr. Fursenko met up with Gabovich a few moments later, after the Lithuanians had departed. "Is Doctor Ozerov going to be all right?" he asked, worried.

"I think so, Doctor." He paused for a moment, then added, "I should apologize for my colleague's behavior—"

"Nonsense, General," Fursenko interrupted. "Doctor Ozerov may be a little . . . eccentric, but he is a welcome addition to the engineering team. You know he's right, of course—our computer models *do* computer radar cross-section as a function of area and structural composition and not by lobal propagation. But, General . . . will Ivan . . . uh, Doctor Ozerov, be able to finish the modifications to the stealth computer-model applications as you said he would? He seemed very discombobulated this morning."

"Doctor Ozerov is under a great deal of *stress* right now, Doctor," Gabovich replied, "but he *will* be back in the lab to finish that program tomorrow."

Fursenko looked so relieved that Gabovich expected him to kiss his hand, and he all but skipped back to the conference room.

"And, Doctor . . ." Gabovich said.

Fursenko turned back to Gabovich, his big grin still on his face. "Please remember, Doctor, that Doctor Ozerov's presence here at Fisikous is still very classified. His name is not to be mentioned or published outside these walls. I will know about it if there is a leak."

Fursenko nodded his understanding and departed.

Gabovich let out a sigh of relief. The program was humming along nicely thanks to Luger. Never in his wildest dreams did Gabovich expect the American to be able to contribute to it on the level that he had. The knowledge Luger had gained at the High Technology Aerospace Weapons Center in Nevada was proving priceless. And he, Viktor Gabovich, was the reason why—he had turned a man others would have regarded simply as a prisoner to be shot into a *collaborator*. Dr. Ivan Sergeiovich Ozerov, né David Luger, was a natural-born worker, as intelligent or more so than the scientists at Fisikous, but as easily controlled as a dog that could be tied up, kicked, and trained.

The one infuriating fly in the ointment was the programming. Gabovich tried to put it out of his mind, but there wasn't any denying that Luger was having . . . problems. The behavior modification and assumption of Dr. Ozerov's identity weren't holding as well or as long as Gabovich had hoped.

The "booster" had better take care of that . . .

Or he would.

They called it the Zulu area, but the fancy name referred only to a dark, smelly, damp section of the second subfloor of the Fisikous Aircraft-Design Center Security Facility. The security facility—whose ex-KGB personnel were separate from the Commonwealth security forces for the main Fisikous installation—had four upper floors and two lower floors. Luger's apartment was on the top floor, along with surveillance and support rooms, and this was closed off to all personnel. Classified-document storage facilities were on the third floor; a complete arsenal for the four-hundred-man OMON Black Beret security force was on the second floor; offices and training rooms for Gabovich, his staff, and the security teams were on the ground floor; and more offices and storage areas were on the first subfloor. The Zulu area was a series of concrete-block cells and security systems amidst the mechanical equipment, boilers, and incinerators of the second subfloor.

The original idea behind Luger's interrogation and brainwashing in the Zulu area when he had been brought to Fisikous was implementation of the traditional *Shtrafnoi Izolyator,* or punishment-isolation cell system, which usually guaranteed that a prisoner would break within ten to fourteen days. The usual technique was isolation and sleep deprivation, sometimes for days, followed by alternating "good" and "bad" interrogators. He was given about 800 to 1700 calories of food and no more than a half-liter of water per day, most times laced with neuroleptic drugs such as haloperidol or triftazin, and stimulants such as methylphenidate. Physical torture was rarely used, especially with military or government-trained personnel, since most prisoners with resistance training could shut off the pain and could even use their pain against their torturers.

But David Luger was different.

Extracting information was not enough—Gabovich had wanted Luger to be able to use his education and experience to contribute hands-on to the growing Fisikous-170 stealth-bomber project. A beaten, battered, psychologically devastated Luger would not produce a workable collaborator. Since Fisikous had some of the finest electrical-engineering minds in the world working there, Gabovich had them design a machine to his specifications to try to "turn" David Luger without creating any psychological damage. His finely tuned intellect had to be left intact, even as his consciousness and short-term memory were being trashed and replaced with an alternate identity, that of Dr. Ivan Sergeiovich Ozerov.

Inside one of the cells, David Luger was strapped to a waveless waterbed, heated precisely to his skin temperature to help deaden his sense of feel and sever any sensory input. He was naked, covered with a thin cotton sheet to keep moisture from the cold, sweating walls from dripping on his skin and awakening him. An intravenous drip with a computerized metering device had been started in his left arm, which alternated a sedative, haloperidol, and phencyclidine hydrochloride—PCP, the powerful hallucinogen "angel dust"—in tune with an electroencephalograph. A tube had been inserted into Luger's mouth both to deaden his taste buds, to keep his teeth apart (the sound of teeth grinding or clicking was carefully controlled), and to keep him from swallowing his tongue in case of an induced epileptic episode. His eyes were covered by a tight blindfold. On his head was strapped a pair of headphones, through which instructions, messages, propaganda, noise, news, information, and other aural stimulation were introduced—or, if desired, no sound at all was allowed.

In his third year of captivity in the Fisikous Institute, First Lieutenant David Luger, United States Air Force, had become one of the greatest KGB mind-alteration experiments in history.

By controlling Luger's sensory inputs and altering his normal brain functions, Gabovich and his KGB associates were able to mold Luger's consciousness in whatever way they felt necessary. They tried to completely empty his short-term memory and introduce their own personality, Dr. Ozerov, in its place.

Viktor Gabovich entered the cell a few minutes later, still aggravated from the episode upstairs. "What in hell happened up there?" he demanded of the senior doctor in charge of the Zulu area. "He completely went to pieces!"

The doctor put a finger to his lips and motioned outside. Once the door was closed and locked, the doctor replied, "His tape program and narcotic regimen have not been started yet, Comrade General. Silence is important . . ."

"Going haywire in front of those eggheads could have jeopardized this entire project! He is *not* holding together!"

"Comrade General, this sensory-deprivation process is *not* an exact science," the doctor said. "The subject's mind is strong and resilient. Drugs and hypnotherapy with the audio system can unlock only so many levels of the human subconscious—the other deeply seated levels are bound to surface sooner or later. They can counteract weeks, even months of work."

"Ozerov has been hard at work on the Fisikous-170 project for over a year without so much as an English burp—now, three times in two weeks he's begun to unravel!" Gabovich said. "We are at a *critical* point in the development. He's got to stay together until we finish that aircraft."

"I cannot guarantee success, Comrade General," the doctor said. "We will continue with the treatments."

"*Accelerate* the treatments," Gabovich said. "Double the doses."

"Not if you want a cohesive, functioning engineer. Let me take care of it, Comrade General. Ozerov will be back at work by tomorrow morning, fresh and ready to go."

Gabovich narrowed his burning eyes: "He'd better be." He then stormed out of the cell.

VILNIUS INTERNATIONAL AIRPORT, LITHUANIA
6 DECEMBER, 1437 VILNIUS (0837 ET)

In the months since the collapse of the Soviet Union, the formation of the Commonwealth of Independent States, and the treaty defining the withdrawal of all foreign powers from Lithuanian soil, Viktor Gabovich of the KGB and General Lieutenant Anton Voshchanka of the Byelorussian Army had never met, although their paths had crossed often in southeastern Lithuania. Even though Gabovich, as a member of the Commonwealth of Independent States' Council of Inter-Republican Security, and Voshchanka, as an officer of the Commonwealth's central military command, ostensibly were part of the same organization, their minds still worked as separate entities: Gabovich was still KGB, and Voshchanka was still a Belarus general. The KGB had no business in Belarus's affairs, and Belarus had no business mucking around in KGB operations.

It was because of this that their first meeting, called by Gabovich's aide, Teresov, as a suggestion to his superior officer, started out very quiet and strained. He had picked a neutral location—the VIP lounge of the Vilnius International Airport. It turned out to be the perfect place. Since the airport adjoined the Fisikous Research Institute, Gabovich's KGB officers and Black Beret soldiers patrolled the eastern side of the facility; and because the airport was one of the locations that Commonwealth forces were allowed to stage out of according to treaty, it was heavily fortified with Belarus soldiers, tanks, armored vehicles, and aircraft.

Both men felt safe and secure.

Except for initial greetings, the two had not yet said anything to each other. Teresov re-introduced himself to the Byelorussian general, then said in Russian, "Sir, we have asked you here today to discuss the status of security measures here in Lithuania. As you know, the treaty between the Commonwealth of Independent States and the Lithuanian Republic calls for the complete withdrawal of all foreigners and the removal of all foreign equipment excluding real property. Most of these treaty provisions take effect by the first of next year.

"As an officer in the Commonwealth Inter-Republican Council for Security and director of security for the Fisikous Research Institute, General Gabovich has expressed his concern that . . . the right interests are not being met by these arrangements."

"What do you mean by 'the right interests,' Major?" Voshchanka asked, in heavily accented, sloppy Russian. "Are your interests not those of the Commonwealth?"

The old Byelorussian war horse had come right to the point, Gabovich thought. Good—maybe this would be a short meeting. Gabovich said, "Let's save both of us some time here, General. We both know that the treaty will hurt both Belarus and my principals."

"Your principals? Who are your principals, General Gabovich?" Voshchanka asked. "Do you not serve the Commonwealth?"

"I owe no loyalty to the CIS, General," Gabovich said irritably. Why was Voshchanka challenging him? All indications from Gabovich's sources in Minsk said that he was as dissatisfied with CIS policies and its future as Gabovich. Was Voshchanka saying all this to bait him, or was he truly that wedded to this damned Commonwealth? What if he had seriously misjudged Voshchanka? Well, it was too late now . . .

Gabovich continued. "When Fisikous closes, I will be out of work. I have a small pension, in worthless Russian currency. The same goes for the scientists, engineers, and administrators that work at the Institute. They will all be out of work. When the plant closes, their life's work will undoubtedly be sold or destroyed or . . . handed over to the *West.*"

Voshchanka nodded. No matter how much one espoused the benefits of openness with the West, Voshchanka and those like him, including Gabovich, were vehemently distrustful of the reforms and especially of the West. He had spent his entire career serving the Soviet Union only to see the collapse of his life's work, the USSR, and his own Belarus, dominated by countries like Russia and the Ukraine, even Lithuania and Latvia.

"Many things have changed," Voshchanka said. "In many ways this Commonwealth is worse than the old Soviet Union. It seems the government has no control. Why have a government if it will not assume control?" He looked at Gabovich warily. He had to remember that this man was . . . KGB. Even if he was no longer working for a Soviet government, the old KGB ways were undoubtedly still in him. "So, the scientists in Fisikous are your principals?"

"They offer a solution to the problems we face," Gabovich said. "An opportunity for us to break out of the stagnant cesspool we find ourselves being dragged into."

"Indeed? And what sort of things are your . . . 'principals' working on in Fisikous?" Voshchanka asked.

"The future," Gabovich said. "The state of the art in Soviet aerospace weapons. Antimissile and aircraft systems unlike anything in the Commonwealth's inventory. Cruise missiles that rival anything in the West, let alone the Commonwealth." He paused to make sure that the old fart Voshchanka was following him.

"But the best thing of all," Gabovich continued, "is that we have an operating breeder reactor—a facsimile of an efficient German model, not a Soviet one—capable of producing small amounts of weapons-grade plutonium. Once we return to full production, we can produce three hundred thermonuclear warheads per year, all with a yield of over one hundred kilotons."

The old general's eyes widened in surprise, and his mouth dropped open. "Three . . . *hundred* . . . nuclear warheads?"

Gabovich knew that the Byelorussian general would be impressed. "They are only very small nuclear warheads, weighing perhaps . . . oh, sixteen or seventeen kilos." He knew that was about the size of a 100-

millimeter artillery shell—small, easy to transport, easy to store, and adaptable to almost every kind of delivery system—which, Gabovich calculated, should make Voshchanka's mouth water even more. "Electronically adjustable yield and detonation triggers, a quite soldier-proof design. As I said, it is state-of-the-art. But when Fisikous is closed, *all* those weapons and *all* that technology will be either destroyed or sold— by the Commonwealth. They keep the money or the weapons. I doubt if Belarus will see *one kopek.*"

Voshchanka sat staring at General Gabovich, a slow, sly smile spreading across his face. The implications hung in the air like a thick, heavy fog. A twinkle sparkled in Voshchanka's eyes, his mind casting about the possibilities, all exciting, all dangerous . . . "What is it you want to do, Comrade Gabovich? My government does not have the money to buy the Fisikous Institute, and I seriously doubt if we will be permitted to buy any of these weapons ourselves. We probably couldn't even afford one of your scientists."

Gabovich nodded sympathetically, but shrugged. He was going to let out a bit more line before reeling this one in. "Yes, funds are scarce everywhere, General Voshchanka. The price of reform, no? Belarus is spending billions of rubles on building its own military—why, you must be knee-deep in requisitions for boots and socks alone . . . forget any modern weapons of war."

Voshchanka's eyes flared at Gabovich, his cheeks a flash of red. "How dare—"

Gabovich held up a hand. "No offense intended, General. After all, *I* don't have all the answers. Only . . . more questions. For example, I've often wondered what the arrangement will be between Belarus, the Commonwealth, and Lithuania when all Belarus forces depart Lithuania. When the treaty concludes, all of your forces go home—but where does that leave Kalinin? Will Belarus be separated from Kalinin forever? Will your troops be granted access to its industrial centers and ports? Or will you have to pay tolls and duties to . . . Lithuania just to get wheat and oil from the ports that *you* built and protected? Will a television set or farm tractor cost double the normal price because of transit and excise fees imposed by Vilnius?"

Gabovich had hit another nerve.

Kalinin.

Located between Poland, Lithuania, and Byelorussia, the tiny industrial territory of Kalinin, with its large year-round Baltic Sea port city of Kaliningrad, its extensive air and rail transportation network facilities, and its very high standard of living, was the best-kept secret of the old Soviet Union. Temperate climate, lush forests, and arable, well-drained farmland, beautiful beyond compare, Kalinin oblast was an ideal place for both a military assignment and a permanent residence, despite its industrial pollution and the hectic life-style of its affluent citizens. Kalinin was officially part of the Russian Federation, but the rail lines and superhighways from Kaliningrad through Vilnius to Minsk were the life's blood of the people of Belarus. As long as the rail lines and highways were open, Belarus did not have to depend on Moscow for anything. Belarus, without any other outlet to the sea, was landlocked without Kaliningrad . . .

. . . and Lithuania could close the railroad and the highways. According to the treaty between it and the Commonwealth, independent Lithuania was expected to maintain the highways and rails inside its own country, a multibillion-lith challenge. Lithuania, in an act seen by many in Belarus as economic retaliation against the Commonwealth (Voshchanka had at once called it "war" against Belarus), immediately set tolls and tariffs on imported goods brought in by rail or by truck. Since the railroads and highways were still the best way to get large amounts of food and supplies from Kaliningrad to Minsk, the price of using those facilities had now nearly doubled.

Financially strapped Belarus was beginning to feel the pinch.

"We are in negotiations with Lithuania on their schedule of tariffs and restrictions on transportation," Voshchanka said irritably. "Those negotiations . . . umm, will be resolved soon . . ."

"Resolved, yes." Gabovich chuckled. "But in Belarus's favor? I think not, unless you want to help the Lithuanians build new highways and railroads. No, *Belarus* will suffer."

"Never," Voshchanka growled. "My troops still maintain a presence along the railroads and in Kaliningrad. We have unrestricted access."

Gabovich noted Voshchanka's proprietary use of "my troops." Voshchanka had tipped his hand. He disliked and distrusted the Commonwealth as much as Gabovich. "What will happen when Russia takes control away from your forces of the port facilities at Kaliningrad?" Gabovich asked. "Belarus will be at the mercy of other countries for its very existence. You will have to deal with Ukraine, with Russia, with Poland, with Lithuania . . . Belarus will become the whore of Europe."

"Never!" Voshchanka declared angrily, rising to his feet, his face beet red. "We will take orders from *no* country, do you hear me? We will determine our own destiny."

"What about the Commonwealth? Do you serve the Commonwealth, General? Don't you believe the Commonwealth will protect Belarus, as the Soviet Union did? Where does *your* loyalty lie? Who is *your* principal, General—the Commonwealth of Independent States or Belarus?"

"Belarus!" Voshchanka raged, spittle flying. "The fucking Commonwealth is a *joke!* It is an attempt by Russia to impose its will on all of Europe and the Transcaucasus once again!"

"I agree, General," Gabovich said, nodding sympathetically. "But why is the headquarters of the Commonwealth located in Minsk? Why not Moscow? Kiev? Tblisi? Riga? Because Belarus is the key to solidarity. It is the most powerful, wealthy, industrialized city in the Commonwealth besides Moscow. Minsk leads the way. Subdue Minsk, and Belarus is forfeit. Subdue Belarus, and the rest are automatically held prisoner. And with Commonwealth troops swarming into Minsk, they can handcuff you rather effectively, can't they?"

"The Commonwealth does not control Minsk. *I* control Minsk!"

"There is little doubt of that," Gabovich soothed, "although I do know Commonwealth forces are garrisoned near your capital. No matter—you can subdue them easily if you have to. But that may not be true for the Baltic states. You have considerable forces in Lithuania, but *Russia* controls Latvia, *not* Belarus. If you had to fight Russia, you would fight from weakness, not strength. A landlocked country, surrounded by CIS forces . . ."

"We will never be subdued by anyone," Voshchanka said confidently. "This is all a fantasy. There is no conflict . . ."

"If the Commonwealth falls apart or is taken by Russia, Belarus withers and dies away," Gabovich said. *"You,* however, have the opportunity to seize the upper hand *before* it collapses. You have the position—and I and my principals can help."

"Help with what, General Gabovich?" Voshchanka asked suspiciously.

Gabovich leaned closer to the Byelorussian general, and in a low, conspiratorial voice, said, "Take Lithuania and Kalinin. *Now.*"

"What?" Voshchanka breathed. The old war horse seemed genuinely surprised at the suggestion. "Invade Lithuania . . . take Kalinin . . . ?"

Gabovich nodded. "Come now, don't act so surprised. You know it's the only solution. Belarus must have access to the Baltic and to those rail lines and highways. Not to mention a buffer zone between it and Russia. The only solution is to . . . take Lithuania."

Voshchanka said nothing, the wheels of thought turning.

Gabovich went on. "What's your biggest concern? How to counter the strength of the Commonwealth armies? You have hundreds of nuclear-capable launchers, from aircraft to artillery pieces to rockets. You also have several dozen warheads that you have not returned to Russia." Voshchanka narrowed his gaze at Gabovich and was about to speak, but Gabovich raised a hand. "I know you do, Comrade. So don't even bother protesting. But what you do not have is the means to unlock and pre-arm these weapons. Well, my principals in Fisikous *do* have the knowledge— they probably designed and built many of the tactical nuclear warheads still stored in your country. They also have the means of making your army one of the most powerful and technologically advanced in the world."

Voshchanka stared at Gabovich, not sure if he was a savior or the devil himself. Slowly, the Byelorussian general sank back into his seat, trying to sort out everything. "Your idea is absurd, General Gabovich," he said finally. "What makes you think I will not report your treason to the Commonwealth?"

"Because I'm the last hope you have of Belarus determining its own destiny," Gabovich said. "You report me and I'll deny this conversation ever took place—and I believe I have the political strength to neutralize your allegations. You would then have made yourself a powerful enemy in me."

Voshchanka looked at the ex-KGB officer as if sizing up this man who was so free with his threats. He was wondering if Gabovich really had the power to challenge a general of the CIS Army. "What if your connections did not save you?" Voshchanka asked. "The Commonwealth would order me to take *you* and occupy Fisikous myself. I would have its technology in any case."

"My principals would prefer to deal with you, General," Gabovich replied, "but they are certainly able to do so without you. If you tried to take Fisikous, my security forces would simply hold you off long enough to destroy all records and all devices. Believe me, we have the strength to hold off an entire army, even without thermonuclear weapons."

"A few scientists in a small research center, with no government support? How long do you think you'd last?"

"My OMON forces are handpicked and specially trained, General," Gabovich said. "We were trained to hold this entire country against well-organized militants."

"You obviously failed at that task." Voshchanka smirked.

"Perhaps. But now we control Fisikous. Now we control the weapons and defensive systems developed at Fisikous. We can stand against any army, at least long enough to destroy all the weapons inside and make our escape. After your army loses thousands of men trying to take Fisikous, you would find nothing but a booby-trapped, burned-out hulk. And if we face certain disaster from a sneak attack or airborne raid, one nuclear-tipped cruise missile aimed at your headquarters in Minsk should avenge our deaths. Where will *you* be when the fighting starts, General?"

Voshchanka clenched his fists, barely controlling his anger. "How dare you threaten my country. Do you expect me to trust you after making a threat like *that . . . ?*"

"General Voshchanka, I want to work *with* you, for the benefit of my principals and the benefit of Belarus," Gabovich said calmly. "Think about it. We can build a new Soviet state, ruled under Communist ideals, with the central government, led by Belarus, firmly in charge. And if Belarus wishes to remain in the Commonwealth, you can deal with Moscow on *equal* terms. I'm offering you a way to take advantage of the weakness of Lithuania and the weaknesses in the Commonwealth. Decline it, and we will both lose. Accept it, and we both have a chance to win."

Gabovich shrugged his shoulders. He knew an incohesive, disorganized, turbulent Commonwealth would leave Fisikous alone. He gave Voshchanka a mischievous smile. "If we fail, *tovarisch,* at least we gave it a good try. You will be praised as a patriot who wanted nothing but greatness for his country. The Commonwealth might bury you in an unmarked grave, but the people would remember you always."

Voshchanka couldn't believe Gabovich's balls—and that last remark! Gabovich's allegory was from a famous Byelorussian legend about a general from Minsk in the Great Patriotic War who commanded one of the armies that helped drive the Nazis from Russia; when the Byelorussian general reported back to Stalin that Moscow and Leningrad had been saved, he was reportedly shot and buried in a shallow grave because his fame might make him a political nemesis. "You know your Byelorussian history, *tovarisch,*" Voshchanka said finally. Then he stood up, nodded to his aide, and headed for the door. "I will be in contact with you, General Gabovich. *Doh svedanya.*"

LENINGRADSKY VOKZAL (LENINGRAD RAIL TERMINAL), MOSCOW
23 DECEMBER, 1035 MOSCOW (0235 ET)

Even in winter, the Leningrad Rail Station in central Moscow was normally one of the most beautiful public buildings in Europe. With soaring concourses, wide entryways, intricately carved relief sculptures on every wall, and ornate clocks everywhere, it was one of the main tourist attractions of Moscow. Even after the city of Leningrad changed its name back to its imperial, historic name of St. Petersburg in 1991, the Leningrad Station kept its name—there was no debate.

Today, it resembled a makeshift relief center for victims of some widespread natural disaster. Hundreds of men, women, and children were huddled against radiators and steam vents hoping for a trickle of warm air that would never come. Farmers from the countryside were selling the last bits of rotting food from their barns and cellars for exorbitant prices, just for a chance to buy a good coat or boots that did not exist anywhere in the city. Roving gangs of thieves were common, so the city police, Russian Federation army soldiers, and Commonwealth Army soldiers patrolled the station. Yet the soldiers, who had to give every ruble and every ration coupon they earned to their families, stole almost as much from the hapless, cowering merchants, and from each other, as the gang members.

Moscow, even in the best of times and weather, was never a particularly uplifting place to be. Now, in early spring, with heavy snowfall and freezing temperatures still lingering and after years of shortages leading to outright famine, it was a perfectly miserable place to be assigned.

Political Affairs Officer Sharon Greenfield, of the U.S. Embassy in Moscow, had been in the city now for three years, longer than anyone else in the American delegation. Greenfield was in her late thirties, tall, dark hair gradually turning gray, but with bright blue eyes that she used to advantage to rivet any man who would dare take her for granted.

Greenfield had seen every form of the human condition here. When the first McDonald's was opened, there was dancing in the streets. When the first foreign businesses opened that would accept the new convertible ruble, there were more celebrations. When full reforms failed to be enacted and the foreign stores closed, people were depressed. When the food ran out, there were riots. When the new Lithuanian Republic sold its former master its first one thousand metric tons of wheat, there was resentment and anger everywhere. Now, she was seeing simple, abject poverty—people dying in the streets, looting and lawlessness combined with severe martial law. The new Commonwealth of Independent States was powerless to help. The new law in Moscow was the army, whether local or state, and the "Russian Mafia" cartels that bought their protection.

Most of the ticket windows at Leningrad Station were boarded up and the doors locked, but Sharon went directly to one door and entered. A Moscow City Police officer immediately stood in front of her, arms outstretched, and reached for her left breast. She slapped it away. The officer's face flushed with anger and he took a menacing step forward until a firm voice behind him said, "As you were, Corporal." The cop backed away but gave Greenfield another satisfied glance.

Today he's groping me, Sharon thought. *Tonight he'll be booted out of his unit for insubordination, and tomorrow he'll be either in the gangs, dead after drinking himself into oblivion and passing out on the cold streets, or pounding on the outside gate of the U.S. Embassy, looking for asylum or work or trying to sell worthless information.* She had seen it a hundred times.

Her defender—if you could call him that—was Boris Georgivich Dvornikov, formerly the Moscow bureau chief of the KGB and now a high-level official with the Moscow City Police. He was tall, with wavy gray hair, an infectious smile, and big, meaty hands. Dvornikov was sometimes a Communist Party member, most times not; sometimes heterosexual, sometimes not; sometimes credited with a bit of integrity; most times not. They met on an irregular basis, depending on what either of them—or both—needed from the other. Today he had called her.

"My apologies, Sharon Greenfield, for that corporal's crude and inelegant action. Times are difficult, but I'll handle his insolence later."

Of that, Sharon Greenfield had no doubt. Boris Dvornikov was known to be ruthless, even sadistic—traits that had served him well in the KGB and certainly would continue to do so in the new Commonwealth. "Thank you, Boris Georgivich," replied Greenfield, using the respectful custom of the Russian's first name with his father's.

"My pleasure," Dvornikov said, then motioned to the door behind her. "Pitiful sight, is it not, Miss Greenfield? Three hundred eighty-seven new souls out there today alone. The total is well over three thousand homeless and living in the Leningrad Rail Station."

"And how many are removed every night?" Greenfield asked. She knew that, with a wide-open press in Russia now, the squalor in Leningrad Station was a political eyesore for the Russian government, so the police had been charged with helping "clean it up." For Dvornikov, that meant carting away hundreds of lost souls, probably for a long train ride to the farthest reaches of the Russian Federation, and certain death.

"We must deal with the situation as best we can."

"The pity is that much of their suffering could be avoided."

"Ah. The noble offer by the United States and the so-called industrialized nations," Dvornikov sneered. "And all Russia must do is give up our right of self-determination, our national identity, condemn our economic system, and leave ourselves defenseless."

Greenfield said, "Free elections, free emigration, institute a market economy, and do away with your offensive nuclear weapons. Russia spends billions of dollars—dollars, Boris Georgivich, not rubles—every year in maintaining a three-million-man army, a stockpile of ten thousand nuclear warheads, and a fleet of intercontinental bombers."

" 'It is hard for an empty bag to stand upright,' " Dvornikov quoted with his usual raconteur's flair. "Benjamin Franklin. Sometimes a nation needs something as awful as a military to help it stand upright. You have homeless in your country as well, Miss Greenfield, yet you too have bombers and nuclear warheads."

He paused, then smiled. "Why, you've even built and deployed a new aircraft that can take off and land like a helicopter but cruises like an airplane. Your Congress and your Secretary of Defense say you're going to cancel it, but here you've gone and built dozens of them, for the Air Force, for the Coast Guard, for the Marine Corps. I wonder who else?"

Greenfield's eyes widened in surprise, which pleased him.

He went on. "I see it being used by your new Border Security Force—but there are other applications for that wonderful machine. Civil transportation, law enforcement, offshore oil derrick supply—the possibilities are *endless."* He paused, making sure he had Sharon's full attention, then added with a smile, "Why, I'll bet you can launch one or two of those things off the deck of, say, an old cargo ship right in the Baltic Sea. You could even fly it into Liepaja, land it, retrieve a Commonwealth spy, a band of U.S. Marines . . ."

Sharon Greenfield hoped some color was still left in her face. Things were bad in the capital, and the Soviet Union was history, but the old KGB spy network was still intact. And Dvornikov was the master.

"I don't have any idea what you're talking about, Boris Georgivich," Sharon Greenfield said. "It would make a very good book, though. Perhaps an American publisher will offer you a deal, and you can become a novelist. You know, like John Le Carré."

"Now, that is a fine idea, Sharon Greenfield." He paused, his smile disappearing, and in clipped, stern Russian ordered the soldier to leave. Sharon took a moment and searched the adjacent rooms and found them all empty. Dvornikov did not question or impede her search—he would have done the same thing if the situation was reversed.

"Let me help you write chapter two of your novel, Boris," Greenfield said finally. "You invented this Soviet man that was kidnapped by Marines . . ."

"A Commonwealth officer of Lithuanian birth. A lieutenant," Dvornikov corrected her. "And not kidnapped. He went willingly. Obviously he was feeding information to the Americans for months and was about to be caught."

"You can work out the details in your book later, Boris," Greenfield said, still disturbed by how much Dvornikov knew about the RAGANU operation. "Let's go to chapter two. Say the Commonwealth officer told his benefactors some interesting tales—like about an American military officer being held captive in a certain Commonwealth research institute for several years. The Americans might want this officer back."

Dvornikov's eyes widened in complete surprise.

Sharon had been around Soviet and Commonwealth agents, bureaucrats, and other government officials long enough to know when they were really surprised and only faking it—the CIA teaches a class in body language—and Dvornikov was *really* surprised. "What do you think, Mr. Dvornikov?"

"I think," he said slowly, "that you are a better novelist than I am."

Sharon could only guess what Boris was thinking. She had information he did not have. That meant that the CIS or Russian government—Dvornikov had high-level contacts in both places and probably in many other government houses as well—probably didn't know it, either. But that also meant that REDTAIL HAWK, the new code name of the Air Force officer inside the Fisikous Institute, most likely wasn't under the control of the Commonwealth or Russian government. Whoever had REDTAIL HAWK had him in secret. Bleed the man dry, discard him, and no one, not even the central government, would know about it. She was gambling with REDTAIL HAWK's life. She knew that. Dvornikov had all he needed to know to find out about the American officer in Fisikous himself, and then he could just walk away. But Dvornikov had called this meeting, not she. Dvornikov wanted something.

Maybe he was willing to trade for it. His government contacts would pay big money for this information, especially if it meant destroying a political foe or helping set up a new political friend. The power struggles in the new regimes created from the shattered Soviet Union were endless.

"What else might you put in my novel?" he finally asked.

"Here's where the story could start getting interesting," Greenfield said. "This could be the first novel where the good guys and the bad guys actually help one another."

"Now this certainly *is* fiction."

"Fine. Then make up your own story, Boris," Greenfield said irritably. "Listen, I'm very busy. Can we—?"

"Not just yet. I asked you here not to discuss novels, but the situation in the Baltic." He motioned to an insulated pot and two cups, and poured very rich, dark coffee into two china cups. "You see? I've even prepared a small libation for us." He withdrew a silver flask from his coat pocket and offered some to Greenfield, who declined. It was an interesting gesture, since Sharon knew that Dvornikov disliked alcohol except as a policy-making tool directed against others. This had to be part of the act. Of course he knew that she would refuse a drink, so Dvornikov could have just plain water in that hip flask. Or maybe things here in Moscow *were* driving him to drink . . .

"As you know, Sharon, my country imports much food, dairy products, eggs, and other such necessities from our former Baltic republics as well as from other former Soviet states. We would like to keep this arrangement in operation, as distasteful as it is to many former Soviet bureaucrats who dislike paying huge sums of hard currency to a former republic. But there appears to be a move afoot to perhaps *reunite* one or more of the Baltic republics with its parent republic."

"Reunite? You mean one of the Commonwealth states might invade the Baltic states?"

"There appears to be strong historical precedent for a . . . reunion to take place between certain Commonwealth and Baltic states," Dvornikov said warily. "All of the Baltic states once belonged to Russia, even before the advent of the Soviet Union; and other states, such as Byelorussia and the Ukraine, were closely allied to the Baltics. But history lesson aside, what might be the American response?"

"You know damned well what the response would be, Dvornikov," Greenfield replied, dropping all politeness despite herself. "The United States has always stood in defense of any country whose government is freely elected by the people and that operates under a set legal standard."

"But, dear, you have also propped up dictatorships and oppressive governments: Marcos, Noriega, Pinochet, the Shah; shall I go on?"

"Let's stick to the Baltics, Dvornikov," Greenfield said testily. "They're as independent as the United States or Ireland or the United Kingdom. If one or more of them asked the United States for support, the President would be inclined to give it."

"Military support? Your president would go to war against the Commonwealth to protect the Baltics?"

"Yes," Greenfield replied firmly. "The President may have slashed the U.S. military budget by one-third and closed a hundred military bases in three months, but he knows his role as leader of the free world. *Yes,* he would commit troops to Europe to back the Baltics."

"Even if it meant a nuclear confrontation?"

"Nuclear confrontation?" Greenfield's eyes registered her surprise. "Russia would risk a nuclear war to occupy the Baltics?"

"That was a very amateurish diversion, Sharon," Dvornikov said with a smile—obviously he enjoyed verbal jousting as much as Greenfield hated it. "I never said Russia wanted to invade the Baltics."

Greenfield was seething. "Look, can I be blunt? Let's cut the shit. If you really called me here to play political mind-games, then it's time I left. An attack on the Baltics could re-ignite the Cold War and erase all the gains that have been made over the years."

"Sharon . . ." Dvornikov sighed, lost in thought. "What the West sees as gains are seen by many in the former Soviet Union as losses. Some say that all perestroika has resulted in is confusion and uncertainty."

"Your current political and economic mess is a result of decades of mismanagement in the communist government, *not* of democracy and peace," Greenfield said. "Attacking the Baltics—which are now as free and independent as any other country in the world, despite your so-called historical precedent—is a serious act of aggression. The United States will respond as such."

"Sharon, there are immense pressures on the Commonwealth and the Russian government to do something about the current state of affairs. Citizens are starving on a massive scale. There is unrest everywhere. Deep factions are developing in the central government. The peace of the entire world may be threatened if a military junta is successful or even attempted in Russia. If the Commonwealth breaks apart and Russia becomes a military dictatorship, the whole world will be affected."

"So what do you want the United States to do about it?" Greenfield asked. "You've spurned all attempts to reform your government and your society. Your government leaders can't stand the thought of some successful private-venture sausage-stuffer wielding more political power and becoming wealthier than they."

"I tell you, Sharon Greenfield, some government leaders will be forced to act just to hold on to their lives—not just their political life, their *earthly* life," Dvornikov said seriously.

"What will the Commonwealth do if one of the member republics invades the Baltic states?" Greenfield asked.

"What can they do? What power do they have?"

"What power? The Commonwealth has a three-million-man army, two-thirds of which are in the western half."

"And many of the member republics have *nuclear* weapons," Dvornikov said. "They were supposed to be deactivated or sent back to Russia, and most of the intercontinental weapons were deactivated, but most of the tactical and battlefield weapons were not. At worst, a nuclear confrontation between Commonwealth states is very likely if one state acts independently of the others. But more likely, the Commonwealth might endorse an invasion of the Baltics in order to prop up its own government. Either way, a nuclear conflict is possible—*very* possible—if the West gets itself involved. This is not like Iraq and the Persian Gulf War, Sharon Greenfield—the nuclear weapons, and the resolve to use them, truly exist here." Dvornikov stepped closer to Sharon and said, "The United States must *not* act if there is an invasion of the Baltic states."

Well, there you go, Sharon thought. *He's put it on the table.* "Is this how it sounded in the conversation between Hitler and Stalin in 1939? 'In exchange for peace and solidarity, you can take Estonia, Latvia, and Lithuania; I will take Czechoslovakia and Hungary . . .' "

"Ah, Sharon, that delightful sense of humor I love so well. You haven't lost it in all our years together."

"Get off it, Boris," Greenfield snapped. "I've been here too long already. The information you've given me is very valuable, but we've been monitoring the situation in the Baltics carefully. Your information is nothing but a big 'so what?' What I want is the American at Fisikous. Information on him would be extremely valuable, and direct assistance might buy you an entry visa and green card, courtesy of the CIA. You can go on the lecture circuit and make more than the President of the United States. Let me get a person close enough to the American, check him out, and help me set up an extraction, and you can name your price."

"How intriguing," Dvornikov said, "but the lecture circuit sounds dull. Besides, why would I leave my beautiful Russia? The place is falling apart at the seams, and I may be able to put together enough pieces for myself."

She turned to the door. "Fine. Just get me the information I want, Boris, and you'll get whatever you want. You know how to contact me. But make it quick."

After she'd departed, Boris Dvornikov thought about what she had said. Greenfield was so smug in her assumptions, so confident in her position. Well, he *would* help her with this matter concerning the American at Fisikous. The only question Boris had was, how much and in what manner would he extract payment from the Americans—and from her. He felt a stirring in his loins. Yes, what price will you be, Sharon Greenfield? He had wanted that bitch for a very long time. He had tried, but each time she had rejected him. Not merely declined, but made him feel worthless and undesirable.

That was okay. Her time would come. Boris massaged his crotch, fantasizing about all the things he would to do her. The pain she would suffer. Yes, that would be quite wonderful . . . seeing her in pain . . . and ecstasy.

To no surprise, Boris realized he had grown quite hard just thinking about her.

TWO

Lieutenant General Bradley Elliott, commander of the U.S. Air Force's top-secret flight-test facility known as HAWC (nicknamed Dreamland because of the highly classified high-tech equipment they developed and tested there), looked at the colonel standing before him, trying to make an assessment. Elliott poured some coffee from a pot, his memory kicking into overdrive.

Paul White, the Air Force colonel in Elliott's office, was someone Elliott knew, or knew *of,* rather. He was regarded as one of the most intelligent and creative engineers in the Air Force. Elliott himself had once recruited him for an assignment at HAWC, and if memory served him correctly, White had also been involved in training Patrick McLanahan and Dave Luger at Ford Air Force Base. But that was a while ago, and since then some other organization had snapped White up—which organization, Elliott did not know. His staff had tried to find out, but White's whereabouts were harder to track, which meant classified work, as was Elliott's. Still, Elliott's chief of security, Captain Hal Briggs, had tried to pull whatever he could on White—only to run into a brick wall at the White House.

The big blank in White's current life made Elliott uneasy, especially since the White House was involved, but White was on Elliott's turf now—in a meeting White had requested.

"Sir," White said, scanning the room with his eyes, "is there somewhere we can speak in private?"

"This *is* private, Colonel. If there is something I need to hear, spill it."

White glanced directly at a signed and remarqued Dru Blair lithograph of an F-117A stealth fighter hanging over Elliott's desk—the only one of eight such framed posters in the office that had a hidden microphone and security camera behind it. It was pure luck that he'd guessed it, but Elliott followed the gaze of his eyes and tried to ignore it.

105

A lot of people were intimidated by HAWC's intense security measures. The facility, located in the south-central part of Nevada, a hundred miles north of Las Vegas, was one of the most restricted in the world. Its overflight airspace was off-limits for *all* aircraft, from the surface to *infinity*. There were warnings of "Deadly Force Authorized" everywhere, which meant that security guards could shoot first, ask questions later. Armed patrols roamed the streets and hallways. Every building had its own special security setup, customized for the individuals and projects within. A request for a visit to HAWC set off a chain of security scrutiny of the kind Colonel White had been subjected to.

If he hadn't passed, he sure as hell wouldn't have been in Elliott's office, which was all the more aggravating for Elliott.

"Can't you at least turn off . . . the recording and video equipment?" White asked.

"I cannot and *will* not," snapped Elliott. "Well, Colonel, what is it? I'm extremely busy."

"Sir, the information I want to pass on to you is not only very unofficial, it's strictly between you and me. What you do with it is up to you, but I've risked my very career coming here, not to mention the possibility of arrest."

Elliott stared coldly at White. "Colonel, you may be enjoying this, but I'm about to put an end to it right now."

"Then kick me out. I've only come halfway around the world to try and see you. I've tried other channels, other ways to find a solution to this."

Elliott saw something in White's eyes—desperation, and determination. Whatever had brought him here had been bothering him for some time. He wanted to resolve it and didn't seem to care about the consequences one way or another. "There's always a way to get something done without ruining your life to do it. I think I know you, Colonel. We're a lot alike. You're an innovator, a dreamer. If things aren't working right, you fix them. Certainly you can fix—"

"No, General Elliott, I can't. You can. I went through the channels I was supposed to use. By the book. Nothing's happened. Believe me, *I* would've known."

Elliott had been around long enough—including two tours of Vietnam, where he was the youngest squadron commander in the Air Force, several command positions in Strategic Air Command tactical units, commander of the Eighth Air Force, and his current position as director of HAWC— to know a true soldier. An honorable soldier. White had pretty much convinced him he was on the level. He could see it in White's eyes, his body language. *"Known* what?" Elliott demanded.

"That something had been done about . . . David Luger."

Elliott froze, trying to recover from his surprise and the reaction he'd just given White. He averted his eyes to his desktop, then back to White: "Luger, you say? . . . David Luger? The name doesn't ring a bell."

"Your face says something else, General."

"You've got one more chance to get off this track before the locomotive wipes you out—and I *promise* you, it will. The subject of Lieutenant Luger is highly classified."

"I have a clearance . . ."

"Colonel, *I* would need clearance to begin any inquiries into David Luger, and I'd probably be denied," Elliott said. "You don't know *what* you're fooling with here, Colonel. You could have a security clearance to wipe God's ass for all I care, but you have no need to know—"

"I think I do," White said. He unzipped his Air Force blue lightweight jacket, then pulled a manila envelope from the inside lining.

"You sneaked a photograph inside the lining of your jacket?" Elliott asked incredulously.

"You'll see why in a second." White opened it and handed a photograph to Elliott. "He's alive, General. We got that photo several months ago from an informant in Lithuania. That's him. I know it is."

There was no mistaking it. Elliott assumed it would be one of the typically fuzzy photos taken from long distance, or deliberately fuzzied to protect the informant's identity or methods used to obtain the photograph—but it wasn't. It *was* Dave Luger. He was going through a security checkpoint, emerging from a metal detector. The photo was taken from slightly above head level—with the photographer or informant standing halfway up a staircase in front of the security area perhaps—but it was clear and sharp, perhaps computer-enhanced.

Luger looked thin and pale, but it was definitely him—the eyes, the shape of the head, the long legs, the slight slouch, the big Texas-sized hands with long fingers. Luger was carrying a briefcase. He was wearing a simple brown overcoat, no gloves, no hat, even though the men accompanying him wore thick fur hats and leather gloves against the obvious cold outside.

"Want to kick me out now, General?" White asked, a hint of a smile on his face.

"Shut up, White," Elliott grumbled. "Another word and I'll personally close that mouth of yours." Elliott sat down, running his hand through his hair, studying the picture more closely, trying to see if there was anything . . . anything at all . . . that indicated a setup. God knows he'd seen a lot of them in the press over the years, especially the faked POW pictures coming out of Vietnam. Elliott sighed. This one looked real, which actually made things harder: It meant Luger hadn't died . . . and that raised a lot of questions. Where was he? What had happened? Had he been captured and turned by the Soviets? Or, worse, had he . . . Elliott dismissed the thought immediately. Yes, someone would probably *wonder* if it was possible Luger had always been working for . . . someone else . . . but Elliott knew that was absurd. He'd spent too much time with Luger. Elliott knew Luger as well as he knew McLanahan and the rest of the crew.

No, David Luger was no traitor. At least, he *hadn't* been. He was, if anything, a prisoner. Or a brainwashed collaborator. It happened to the best of them. Elliott had seen it himself, with his own men, back in 'Nam. But if they could get him back . . .

White couldn't stand the silence any longer. "We've got to talk about this, General Elliott."

"Hold it. Just shut up for a second." He paused for another moment, then pressed his interoffice intercom button and said, "Sergeant Taylor, I've got the ceremony taken care of. See to it I'm not interrupted except by a priority-one call."

"Yes, sir," came the reply.

"We call our office recording devices 'sandwich' instead of 'ceremony,' " White said with a smile. "We find we can use it in more conversations."

"This is not funny, White," Elliott said. "I've never shut that tape recorder off in over six years of working behind this desk—I'm not even sure how to do it. Let's dispense with the cute comments now. Who do you work for, White?"

"The Intelligence Support Agency," White replied immediately.

Elliott knew they were the troubleshooters of the Director of Central Intelligence, the special team that assisted and augmented the regular field-intelligence forces of the United States. They were the ones who were called when the spooks got in trouble or when something needed doing outside normal DCI channels. "What program?"

White hesitated. It was a normal reaction to his highly classified position. But to Elliott it was a sign of insincerity, that this really *was* a trap. "You better not clam up on me now, White!"

"MADCAP MAGICIAN," White replied.

"Never heard of it."

"And I'm sure you've got a few things inside these hangars I've never heard of, General," White said. "We're a combined-forces military unit, mostly Air Force and Marine Corps special ops, based on the cargo ship USS *Valley Mistress.* We use some of the CV-22 PAVE HAMMER aircraft that were developed here. Human intelligence is our specialty."

"You were handling this informant in Lithuania?"

"CIA was handling him, but they lost him when he rabbited. The KGB was closing in on him."

"There *is* no KGB anymore."

"Wrong, sir. There's plenty of KGB, especially in the Baltic states. They call them the MSB, the Inter-Republican Council for Security, but they're all KGB, Internal Troops. OMON, Black Berets—the names have changed, but the faces have not. They were too powerful to destroy; now they're rogue elephants, guns for hire. They don't work for Moscow anymore—they work for whoever offers them the most money. We've been tracking this KGB cell in Vilnius, particularly around the Fisikous Research Institute, where the KGB provides 'specialized' security services—bribes, threats, and executions—in order to convince local Lithuanian officials not to close down Fisikous. We run up against them all the time."

"So you were sent in to get the informant?"

"He was a Lithuanian officer in a Byelorussian outfit representing the Commonwealth and based in Vilnius," White explained. "The informant was an intelligence officer in a unit in Vilnius. One of his unit's tasks, along with harassing Lithuanian citizens and helping the Byelorussians get rich while 'guarding' the country, was to guard the Fisikous Institute of Technology."

"The Institute *itself*? He was *in* it? That means Luger's in Fisikous?"

"Apparently so," White replied. "He's been working in the aircraft-design bureau for a while, perhaps years, under the name Doctor Ozerov. Ivan Sergeiovich Ozerov."

"I know the names of every scientist and every engineer working in every aircraft-design bureau in the Commonwealth," Elliott said, turning in his seat to look at White, "and I've *never* heard of Ozerov."

"Our informant indicates that he's not a part of the normal staff," White explained, "but he's there all right, under constant guard by the KGB contingent at Fisikous. He is very well respected, considered a bit of an oddball—very freewheeling. But he commands respect and admiration throughout the facility."

"So maybe it's someone that just looks like Luger."

"Maybe." White was silent for a moment. Then: "But your reaction was the same as mine when I saw that picture, and the others the informant brought out. It's David Luger all right. He looks like he's been mistreated, perhaps drugged or brainwashed, but it's him. His primary project is some large, weird aircraft that looks like something out of *Star Trek.*"

"Tuman?" Elliott gasped. "My God . . . Luger is working on *Tuman?"*

"What is it? Some new bomber?"

"It could be the world's most sophisticated warplane," Elliott said. "It's a combination and enhancement of the B-1 and B-2 bombers. Stealth technology, supercruise capability at high gross weights—that means a four-hundred-thousand-pound stealth bomber traveling over the speed of sound without afterburner—self-protection technology, slow-flight and close-air-support technology, terrain-following, air-to-air capability, even fractional orbital bombardment capability—it's the only advanced warplane in the world still being developed, after our B-2 stealth bomber program was canceled. You saw it?"

"The informant got pictures of it."

"Jesus. *Tuman* really exists," Elliott exclaimed. "It's been rumored to be on the drawing board for five years." Elliott began thinking out loud: "Who would've thought it would be at Fisikous? With Lithuania a free nation, Fisikous was the last place you'd expect a bunch of old Soviet sympathizers to keep a multibillion-dollar aircraft project—"

"Let's try to keep on the subject, sir," White said. "Namely, what do we do about Dave Luger?"

Elliott scooped up the photo and jammed it back into its envelope. "This had better be for real, Colonel, or you won't be facing a courts-martial or a firing squad—I'll deal with you myself, with my bare fucking *hands.* Dave Luger meant the world to me. I'd give everything, *everything,* to help him. But the mission is classified. Reopening the files could damage the careers of many individuals, from here all the way to the White House. I hope you realize the huge can of worms you've opened up here, Colonel."

"Believe me, it hurts me as much as it does you, General. I need your help, not your retribution. Dave Luger is alive. If we leave him up to the 'proper channels' to deal with, he'll be there forever. We have to get him out. You've got to—"

Suddenly the door behind him burst open. Three men, dressed in dark-blue jumpsuits, helmets with clear plastic face masks, and bulletproof vests dashed in, automatic weapons trained on Paul White's forehead. "Hands up! Now!" Captain Hal Briggs, General Elliott's chief of security at the High Technology Aerospace Weapons Center, shouted.

White raised his hands. When he looked at Brad Elliott again, the three-star general had a big .45 caliber automatic pistol in his hand, aimed at White as well. "Hey, General," White said, an amused smile on his face, "these guys are *good.*"

"You're under arrest, Colonel, for revealing classified information and attempting to exchange classified information. I want him Mirandized, hooded any time he is outside a building, searched—body cavity and X-ray—booked, and held in maximum security until a full identity check has been accomplished. No phone calls, no contact with any individuals whatsoever until *I* authorize it. Move out." White did not say another word as a black hood was placed over his head and he was dragged off.

"Good job, Hal," Elliott said, sitting back down.

"Don't thank me. Thank Sergeant Taylor. He recognized the duress code word 'ceremony' and called me the second you mentioned it. What was he trying to sell you?"

"An unbelievable story, Hal," Elliott said. "An incredible story. Half of me prays it's not true and half of me prays it is. We have some phone calls to make."

"You gonna let me bust this guy, sir?" Briggs said enthusiastically. "It's been a slow week and I could use the—"

"If his story doesn't pan out, I'll authorize a full national-security investigation and you can dismantle the guy piece by piece—with his defense counsel present, of course. But first I want to find out if what I've heard has any truth to it. I've got to ask General Curtis. He should get involved."

"Curtis? *The* General Curtis? The Chairman of the Joint Chiefs of Staff Curtis?"

"If what White said is true—and a lot of it seems to be irrefutable— then Curtis needs to know immediately. If this is all some big con game, then he can squash it quick and neat."

ABOARD AIR FORCE ONE, SOMEWHERE OVER KANSAS
17 MARCH, 0130 CT (0030 ET)

The President of the United States, on an evening flight back to Washington, D.C., after a trip to the West Coast, had just retired for the evening into the front section of Air Force One, which was outfitted as a full luxury suite for him and the First Lady. As usual, he left his staff with another two or three hours' work to do before the plane landed. Fortunately, Air Force One was well suited for work, with impeccable service, eighty-five phones on board, plus the assistance of no less than three operators, not to mention fax machines, word processors, and a rack of computers.

That evening flight found the White House Chief of Staff Robert "Case" Timmons, Chairman of the Joint Chiefs of Staff Wilbur Curtis, and National Security Advisor George Russell, together in the staff lounge, the plush "living room" in the center of the modified Boeing 747 reserved for the President's staff. Several soft leather chairs were arranged along the fuselage wall around a large, low coffee table, where magazines and English-language newspapers from all over the world were scattered. Aides for each Cabinet officer were nearby, taking copious notes and instructions as their superiors tossed orders to them.

In the adjacent staff/secretarial area, secretaries with Compaq laptop computers were hard at work, while several staff members shuttled between the presidential staff area and the other sections of the plane, delivering messages and retrieving memos. A steward had just brought coffee and dessert rolls from one of Air Force One's two kitchens and had departed. The presidential staff lounge could hold twelve, but with three senior Cabinet members on-board they took the room all to themselves for the entire trip.

"The President mentioned in his speech tonight sending a verification team to inspect military bases in the Commonwealth republics to check the destruction of nuclear weapons," Russell said to Curtis. "How soon can we get a team together?"

"I can have one ready to brief by tomorrow afternoon," Curtis replied. He then looked at his watch and smiled sheepishly: "I mean, later on *this* afternoon. I'll need State to draw up diplomatic passports, travel visas for the individual republics, arrange security, get access privileges . . ."

"The Commonwealth promised they'd cooperate," George Russell said. "I'll get a briefing from you at . . . what? Three?"

Curtis nodded.

"I'll brief the Old Man at three-thirty. How does that sound, Case?" asked Russell.

"Three-thirty's no good," the Chief of Staff said, checking the President's itinerary on a small electronic notebook. "I can squeeze you in at three-fifteen or it'll have to wait till five. The President's meeting with the Congressional leadership on the inspection at four. It'll have to be three-fifteen."

"Squeeze me in, then," Russell said. "I'll need your briefing as soon as you can get it, Wilbur."

General Curtis nodded. "I'll need a rep from the DCI's office in the meeting with the inspection team," Curtis suggested. "Any idea who that will be?"

Russell gave some names of persons in the office of the Director of Central Intelligence who were experts on the disposition of nuclear weapons in what used to be known as the Soviet Union, which was now just an amalgamation of rival states and confederations. Curtis had his aide make the calls for him from Air Force One's communications center.

"Speaking of the DCI," Curtis said, "there was something I wanted to ask you about, George."

"Shoot."

"There was a project run not too long ago that I heard about that I wanted to get an update on."

The National Security Advisor took a sip of coffee, put a napkin on his lap, and reached for a roll. "Can you be a bit more specific?"

"Sure." Curtis affixed Russell with a cold stare: "REDTAIL HAWK."

Russell was reaching for a sweet roll but stopped midway. His eyes returned Curtis's glare with one just as cold, then shifted over to Chief of Staff Timmons, who saw the sudden exchange and needed no prompting—he murmured some contrived excuse and left the room along with the aides.

After the door to Air Force One's living room was shut, George Russell said, "All right, Wilbur, who the *hell* told you about that?"

"Never mind. I found out. We *always* find out. Now, what's the story, George?"

"I'll find out who leaked that to you, Wilbur. And then I'll roast their balls on a spit."

Curtis shook his head. These guys were all alike. Everyone in the White House was on an ego trip, trying to be the top banana, all the while keeping the Pentagon, and most especially the Joint Chiefs of Staff, out of the loop. Typical. Wilbur Curtis, fourth-generation graduate of the Citadel, four-star General of the Air Force, swore if any of his own seven children ever went into politics he'd wring their neck.

Curtis looked straight at Russell. "Roast whomever you want, but do you or do you not have information on one of my troops being held in Vilnius, Lithuania, by the KGB?"

Russell ignored the question. Instead he peered out of one of the 747's oval windows: darkness, but far below, the tiny, twinkling lights of an American city. Finally, he turned back to General Curtis, still shaken by the lack of internal security that was often apparent in the White House.

"This is a DCI matter, Wilbur, not your concern."

Curtis tore off the end of a cigar, hunting for a match. "That's bullshit and you know it. Do you know who this prisoner is? He was part of a very special, select operation, a man who risked everything to prevent World War Three!"

"I know *who* REDTAIL HAWK is, Wilbur, but how the hell do you know who he is? What does he have to do with the Joint Chiefs?"

"Didn't you ever read the Old Dog file?" asked Curtis, chomping on his cigar. "Anyone ever tell you about that mission?"

Russell rolled his eyes, sipping now cold coffee. "I've never heard of this Old Dog or whatever you're talking about, Wilbur. What I *do* know is we've got a former Air Force officer, a B-52 crew member at that, who probably knows more about the Single Integrated Operations Plan and nuclear warfighting than *I* do. Now he's over there, in a KGB-run facility, posing as a Soviet scientist, helping a group of hard-liners build a stealth bomber. *I* didn't send him there, *you* didn't send him there, so he's not working for *us.* Which means he's working for *them,* spilling his guts."

Curtis jabbed out his cigar in a nearby ashtray, frustrated by the cut-and-dry attitude of politicians like Russell. There was never enough time—or interest—by the people sitting in the ever-changing seat of power in Washington to learn about the projects and details of the past. The Old Dog mission was only a few years old and already it was long forgotten by the very ones who should remember it. The flight of the Old Dog was a mission that had driven everyone involved in the episode into virtual isolation at HAWC. Not to mention the isolation David Luger had suffered behind the walls of Fisikous. Even if Luger was helping at the Institute, Curtis knew him as well as his own sons. Curtis was sure Luger's cooperation wasn't of his own volition.

"Look," Curtis said, "I'm going to pull the Old Dog file for you, and you'll have it when we arrive in Washington. Your eyes only." He scribbled a note to his aide, then said, "Now tell me, what's the status of REDTAIL HAWK?"

Curtis saw the slight hesitation, the aversion of the National Security Advisor's eyes, and a sinking feeling came over him.

"I don't know what his status is . . . at this point," Russell said.

Curtis exploded, eyes ablaze: "You didn't order a *sanction,* did you?"

Russell said nothing.

"Goddammit, you're going to have him *executed?* Whatever happened to *extraction?* Especially for one of our *own?"*

Russell loosened his tie, wishing he could simply leave the room. But Curtis would follow him all over the damn plane. "Wilbur, the last briefing I had on this guy said he was an Air Force officer who'd died in a plane crash in Alaska on a training mission. When we did some checking, DIA found out there was no plane crash and no mission. Now the guy turns up in a Soviet aircraft-design facility and doesn't show any obvious signs of duress. What were we supposed to think? How did I know it was some classified operation?"

"Let me guess," Curtis interrupted. "You just happen to have a guy very close to REDTAIL HAWK, close enough to, say, poison him."

Russell cleared his throat. "One of our Moscow section officers has an ex-KGB contact that still throws around a lot of weight," he explained. "This contact helped us . . . uh . . . place an agent very close to REDTAIL HAWK. It's verified. Wilbur—your 'friend' is a major player in this aircraft-design center. He's advanced the state of the art in Soviet aircraft design by at least five years."

"I don't believe it."

"It's true."

"No doubt on his identity?"

"Our agent got fingerprints, photos, shoe size, eye color, the works. No doubt at all."

"Well, it doesn't matter," Curtis said, still shaking his head in disgust. "You'll find Luger's a hero, a genuine hero, when you read the Old Dog file. He's obviously been brainwashed and forced to work for the Soviets. We've got to pull him out of there."

Russell's eyes lit up in surprise. "Pull him out? How the hell am I supposed to get this guy out of one of the most top-secret and secure places in the Soviet—I mean, in Europe?" Russell asked. "If he was in a gulag or a prison, maybe. But he's in the European version of Dreamland or China Lake. It would take a damned battalion to get him out!"

"Leave that to me, George," Curtis said confidently. "You give me the details and I'll show you how we can get him out. But tell your mole to watch Luger and keep us updated constantly on his position. For God's sake, don't *kill* him."

"Fine," Russell said. He picked up a roll, looked at it with distaste, then put it back on the tray. "That part of the game's not in my blood anyway."

"What about this bomber being built in Fisikous? Is this *Tuman* the stealth bomber the Soviets were supposedly working on before the empire crumbled?"

"I guess," Russell replied absently. "The staff convinced me we should keep an eye on it, although I think it's a lot of worrying over nothing. These Soviets holed up in Fisikous don't have the money to produce carrots, let alone an intercontinental bomber. They've lost all their privileges under the new system. When the facility's turned over to the Lithuanians, they'll be out of work."

"What if they get the money from somewhere else?"

"Who? Russia? They don't have the money either. Poland? Bulgaria? The IRA . . . ?"

"How about Iran? Iraq? Syria? Libya . . . ?"

"I'm telling you, nothing's going to happen. The plant will be closed, the production stopped, and the Lithuanians will put the stealth bomber on display or sell it to us for hard currency. The thing isn't going anywhere," Russell reiterated. "We've been monitoring things in Fisikous and all the other design bureaus, and they're ghost towns. We can shut Fisikous down immediately if there's any hint that the technology will be exported outside the CIS."

"Then Luger'll be killed," Curtis pointed out. "They wouldn't want it made public that they've been keeping an American military officer locked up in that place all these years."

"Or maybe Luger will go with the scientists. Voluntarily."

"We'll pull him out immediately then," Curtis said. "We can't take a chance."

Russell thought it would be easier to kill the guy than to risk lives trying to rescue him, but he didn't say it. In his present mood, Curtis would go ballistic. "All right, Wilbur. If you're gonna extract him, then work up a plan. But this guy is going to have a *lot* of explaining to do!"

"You didn't seem too interested in hearing him tell his story a little while ago, George," Curtis said.

"I can't stomach traitors," Russell said. "A career military guy, turning tricks for the other side—I can't stand it. I'd plug the guy myself if I could. But if you still want him, if he means something to you, then we'll sit on him until you cook up a plan. All right?"

"He means something to a lot of very important, highly placed people, believe me," Curtis said. "Some of those people owe him their lives. I think you'll find, when you read the Old Dog file, that the world probably owes him for helping bring down the Soviet Union itself."

OVER CENTRAL BELARUS, COMMONWEALTH OF INDEPENDENT STATES
17 MARCH, 0330 BELARUS (16 MARCH, 2030 ET)

Central Belarus is very flat.

One hundred kilometers south of Minsk and four hundred kilometers east of Warsaw, its thick forests, vast empty plains, and marshlands extending for hundreds of thousands of acres are not a great challenge for low-level flying. But an hour into the flight, they were still nearly a thousand meters above ground, and Dave Luger was ready to tear his hair out. The boredom was making him think about how stiff and uncomfortable the instructor pilot's seat—a metal bolt-in seat between the two cockpit officers'—really was. He was itching to see some action.

"Pilot, this is I-One," Luger said over the aircraft interphone. "How about taking it down now?"

There was a pause; Luger was about to repeat his question, but just then the weapons-systems officer in the copilot seat, nicknamed "Strike," replied, "We have high terrain at twenty kilometers, pilot. Recommend zero-point-eight K meters altitude."

Like the B-2 Black Knight bomber, this aircraft used a pilot-trained navigator in the right seat to manage the navigation, weapons, and defensive systems; an engineering officer, located in a forward-facing ejection seat behind the weapons officer, monitored essential aircraft, flight, and engine systems.

"Copy. Zero point eight. Descending." The aircraft descended the scant two hundred meters, and the autopilot came back on. Luger fell silent, biting his lip to keep from yawning into his oxygen mask.

Normally Luger wouldn't have been so bored flying at night on a simulated low-level bombing mission, especially since he was in the flight engineer's station of the incredible Fisikous-170 *Tuman* stealth bomber. But he *was* bored because the Soviet-trained pilots and engineers flew the thing like a couple of old women, which he really didn't understand. Somewhere, deep within the far reaches of his mind, something tugged at him, telling him a flight like this could be so much more exciting . . .

Still, even the by-the-book pilots and engineers didn't diminish Luger's growing love for the Fi-170. With two hundred and eight thousand kilos of composites and muscles, nearly half of that fuel, Luger usually felt like he was king of the sky in the bomber. Externally, nothing compared to the deadly war machine. It was shaped like a giant manta ray, with thin, curved wings that rolled upwards away from the center, then gently downwards toward the rounded wingtips. The four engines were buried within the oblong body, with grilles screening both the inlets and exhausts to prevent radar energy from reflecting off the compressor blades and to cut down on heat emissions. A split aileron system replaced rudders, with the ailerons deflecting up or down depending on the desired degree of roll or pitch—*Tuman* had no vertical surfaces whatsoever that might reflect radar energy. *Tuman* had three long, spindly landing gear—it was not designed for rough-field operations—and two twenty-five-meter-diameter drag chutes for stopping itself after landing.

Although *Tuman* had been first designed in the early 1980s, its weapon fit was not finalized until just a few years ago, with the arrival to the design- and flight-test program of Dr. Ivan Sergeiovich Ozerov—it was David Luger who almost singlehandedly decided and designed the weapons fit. *Tuman* was designed for very long-range strike missions against the United States and China, and also designed to be self-sufficient, with a minimum of support from other aircraft. Long-range bombers were inherently vulnerable to fighter and surface-to-air missile attack, so Luger designed *Tuman* to protect itself and still pack a significant offensive wallop.

No one, not even David Luger himself, realized that Dr. Ozerov developed that concept from an American bomber called the EB-52 Megafortress. Just as Viktor Gabovich of the KGB hoped, Luger had dredged up vital technical memories of his years in the United States Air Force and had applied his knowledge to a Soviet design—and the aircraft he remembered the most was the Old Dog. With the help of Viktor Gabovich's extensive brainwashing and personality-reprogramming procedures, Luger had unconsciously duplicated the Old Dog's weapons fit on the *Tuman* Fi-170, and in doing so made it a much more formidable aircraft.

Although it was a stealth aircraft, *Tuman* had three hardpoints on each wing for external stores, the philosophy being that all external stores would be jettisoned, and its stealth characteristics restored, long before it got within hostile radar range. On its two outboard wing hardpoints, *Tuman* carried two 1,500-dekaliter fuel tanks, which had already been jettisoned (on this mission, both tanks were empty and fitted with parachutes so they could be recovered and reused). On each center hardpoint, *Tuman* carried four long-range AS-17 rocket-powered antiradar cruise missiles, developed at Fisikous and designed to destroy coastal early-warning and fighter-intercept radars before the bomber got within the enemy radar's effective range. The AS-17, which had a range of nearly two hundred kilometers, used inertial guidance to get close to the radar; it would then activate a seeker that would home in on the radar emissions and destroy the radar. On each inboard hardpoint, *Tuman* carried four AA-9 radar-guided air-to-air missiles for long-range bomber self-defense.

Tuman had two bomb bays along its centerline, each four meters wide and seven meters long, capable of carrying nine thousand kilograms of ordnance each. It would eventually be adapted to carry every air-launched weapon in the Soviet inventory—or whoever's inventory *Tuman* would eventually be in, although that was not a concern of the scientists at Fisikous. For this test-bombing mission, however, it carried four huge 500-kilo gravity bombs in the aft bomb bay and two AS-11 laser-guided missiles in the forward bomb bay.

Internally, *Tuman* was something of a throwback; it served to highlight the Soviets' deficiencies in advanced electronics. *Tuman* did have an electronic flight-control system and fly-by-wire technology, but it was a relatively low-tech analog system instead of a high-speed digital suite. The navigation system was a simple Doppler flight computer, operated by "Strike" sitting in the copilot's seat, with intermittent position and velocity updates provided by the Commonwealth of Independent States' GLOSNASS satellite navigation system or by ground-mapping radar. The low-level navigation system was a standard ground-mapping radar, set into a cavernous nose bay that destroyed the plane's nose-on stealth characteristics, with a terrain-avoidance system spliced on top of it, similar to the G-model B-52—it simply painted a profile view of the terrain ahead. It provided no inputs whatsoever to the flight-control system, nor would it keep a pilot from flying into the hills.

Although stealth aircraft usually did not require a terrain-following system, Luger was sure this system was not developed for *Tuman* simply because the pilots would not trust it, and that definitely seemed to be the case now. "Listen, Comrades," Luger said in pidgin Russian over interphone, "flying around at eight hundred meters with the autopilot on is crazy for any strike aircraft unless you're in the vicinity of significant antiaircraft artillery units that can get a lucky shot off at you. Take it down and let 'er unwind, all right?"

"Our mission is to test the weapons-delivery systems," the pilot replied testily, "not test our enemy-avoidance techniques. Besides, what do we have to fear from antiaircraft defenses? No radar can see us; and the Americans do not have significant air-defense weapons anyway."

"You don't train for the best-case situation, you train for the worst."

"Are you suggesting we break the weapon-delivery parameters, Doctor Ozerov?"

"You can re-establish the weapon-release parameters immediately before delivery," Luger replied. "All other times you should be avoiding the enemy. Don't give him an opportunity to see you."

"The enemy cannot see us," the crew engineer said. "Machulishche Airport, south of Minsk, is only ninety kilometers away, and the detection-energy threshold is almost too low to be measured. That is the most powerful radar in the western Commonwealth. We do not need to descend and expose ourselves to ground hazards."

No use arguing with these guys, Luger thought. He checked his chart and the navigation displays on the right side of the cockpit and saw they still had almost one hundred kilometers to go until they reached the first missile-launch point. At only six hundred kilometers per hour, it would take another ten minutes to reach the IP. The assigned flight corridor, surveyed to avoid major towns and industrial areas, was twenty kilometers wide, which left them a lot of room to maneuver. "Push the airspeed up to seven hundred kph," Luger said, "and let's try some steep turns."

"That is not in the test-flight itinerary."

"No, but this is the twentieth test flight, the tenth low-level flight, and the fourth with weapons aboard," Luger snapped, not mentioning that it was also *his* sixth flight and by far the most boring, "and we've done nothing but fly straight and level. Let's crank this baby up."

To the three Russian crew members, Ozerov had a peculiar and annoying habit of lapsing into English when excited. Words like "crank" and "unwind," although they knew each word's meaning, did not make sense a lot of times. They often wondered about Ozerov's use of jargon, but they had the good sense not to ask—Ozerov was very close to the chief of security, General Gabovich. They also had the good sense not to deviate from the set program. Still . . .

. . . Perhaps Ozerov might get himself kicked off the program if he broke the rules. That would certainly make everyone's life more bearable.

"You are qualified to fly in the right seat, Doctor," the pilot said, smiling behind his oxygen mask. "If you would like to take command of this aircraft, you are most welcome." The pilot said that for the benefit of the continually running cockpit voice recorder, which was carefully reviewed after each flight. If control of the aircraft was not positively transferred, blame for a mishap could be misplaced. Surely, the pilot thought, not even the unorthodox Ozerov would want to disrupt this test flight, only minutes from the first bomb run.

"Climb up to min safe altitude and climb out of there, Strike," Luger said. The pilot had no choice—he directed the copilot to switch seats with Ozerov. In less than a minute Ozerov was strapped in.

"All right, let's not wait until the bomb run to run the weapon checklist," he said. Without prompting from the pilot, Ozerov accomplished every step of the "Before Weapons Release" checklist, from memory, not missing a step—although no one but the ground crew examining the recordings would know after post-mission analysis, because the pilot, engineer, and instructor could hardly keep up. Ozerov had the pilot activate his switches when prompted. Minutes later the checklist was done. Ozerov used nonsensical little rhymes and ditties, mostly in English, to run the checklists: "Bomb-cursor-man, as fast as you can; aim-cursor-auto, don't get into trouble . . . Turn-time-track-tweak-tune-trackbreakers-triple . . . checklist complete."

"Okay, we're ready to go. I just need to hit the BOMB button, recheck switches, and we're done. From now on we jink and jive until we reach the weapon-release point."

The turnpoint at the bomb run initial point came, but Ozerov did not turn. "Turnpoint five kilometers ago, Strike . . ."

"Too early," Ozerov said. "The autopilot only turns at fifteen degrees bank. The turn radius is too large—we wake too many bad guys up that way. Tight turns IP inbound." He grabbed the throttles in the middle of the center console and pushed them all the way up to military thrust. "And we go balls-to-the-wall, too—none of this ten-klicks-per-minute shit." Ozerov waited until nearly ten kilometers past the turnpoint, then threw the huge bomber into a 40-degree bank turn to the right. As the plane went into its steep turn, its supercritical wings lost lift, and the aircraft edged downwards. But that was exactly what Ozerov had in mind. As he rolled out on the new heading, he leveled off only one hundred meters above ground.

"High terrain, one o'clock, twelve kilometers," Ozerov reported. "Now, terrain calls *mean* something." Both Soviet pilots were frantically scanning outside the cockpit windscreen, trying to spot terrain, buildings, transmission towers, tall antennae—why, Ozerov couldn't figure, since it was pitch-black outside . . .

Well, not *totally* dark. Just then they caught a glimpse of a few trucks in a convoy rolling down a highway—the M7, the main east-west highway running between Baranovichi, the town of Slutsk, and the city of Bobruysk. Their track crossed the M7 at a steep angle. Unconsciously, Ozerov altered course so he was flying right down the highway, heading west, and dipped the bomber to only eighty meters above the ground. The headlights of the trucks heading east were getting brighter and brighter—it seemed they were close enough to see their occupants . . .

"You are at eighty meters altitude, Ozerov," the pilot warned nervously, placing his objection on the cockpit voice recorder. "And you are heading right for those trucks."

"No, I'm at least a hundred meters north of the highway," Ozerov said. *Well, maybe not that far, but what's a few dozen meters between friends?*

on the SRAM computer. Three seconds after bomb release, at their altitude and airspeed, should put them right over the target—if McLanahan had hit the target.

To Luger's immense surprise, the green ACCEPT *light illuminated on the SRAM panel.*

"It took the fix," Luger said, his voice incredulous.

"We nailed 'em, guys," McLanahan shouted.

"Sure, sure," Luger said. McLanahan was carrying the act a little too far.

"Tone!" The high-pitched radio tone came on.

Luger flipped the AUTOMATIC LAUNCH *switch down.*

"Missile counting down . . . doors are already open . . . missile away. Missile two counting down . . . missile two away. All missiles away. Doors coming closed . . ."

"Missile away, missile away," Martin called to the bomb-scoring site.

"Very good, boys," McLanahan said, finally opening his eyes.

What was all *this?* Luger wondered. He was in a cockpit, surrounded by men in strange helmets and flight suits. *Where am I? What am I doing here?*

Luger started to undo his shoulder harness and seat belt, frantically trying to get out of the copilot's seat. "I gotta get out of here," he muttered in English, wondering if he was in a bad dream. "Who *are* you guys?"

"Ozerov! Sit down!" the pilot screamed in Russian. Luger heard the words, but they sounded so loud and so foreign he winced. He ripped off his oxygen mask and helmet. As he rose, his body leaned against the control stick, and the Fisikous-170 dipped earthward—one fifty, one hundred, fifty, twenty . . .

"Pull up!" the engineer shouted. "My God, *pull up!"*

"Get off the stick!" the pilot shouted. "We're going to crash!"

The copilot dragged Luger down against the center console and leaned across him, grabbing for the control wheel. He and the pilot finally got the nose up as *Tuman* passed ten meters—barely thirty feet above ground. They heard a loud explosion and a tremendous rumble through the aircraft. The pilot had to lower the nose to prevent a stall as the bomber careened through two thousand meters with barely enough airspeed to keep flying.

"Hydraulic leak on the left flaperon," the engineer cried out. "Going to stand by on the number-two hydraulic system. Looks like we took some blast damage from those bombs."

Luger had half-crawled, half-fallen over the center console and was now in the narrow walkway behind the pilot's station, lying on the floor beside the engineer.

The noise was deafening.

Luger put his hands to his ears and pressed, trying to drown out not just the sounds from outside, but the pain and confusion *inside*. What in the hell was going on?

He wanted to scream.

COMMONWEALTH DEFENSE FORCE MILITARY HEADQUARTERS
KALININGRAD, RUSSIA
17 MARCH, 0845 KALININGRAD (0045 ET)

General Anton Osipovich Voshchanka replaced the telephone handset on its cradle, staring straight ahead at the wall in disbelief. His chief of ground forces, Colonel Oleg Pavlovich Gurlo, knocked and entered the office a few moments later. "Excuse me, sir, but I require—sir, is something wrong?"

"Orders . . . orders from Minsk," Voshchanka said. "I have been relieved of command."

"What . . . ?"

"It's true," Voshchanka said in despair. "That Lithuanian ass Palcikas complained to his president, who brought the matter of our . . . um, investigation of the helicopter crash to the Commonwealth Council of Ministers. The Council of Ministers ordered that I be relieved of command of Commonwealth forces in the Baltic states."

"They cannot do that!" Colonel Gurlo gasped.

"There's more," Voshchanka said. "The Defense Ministry of Belarus is opening an investigation into whether we were authorized to release weapons and overfly Lithuanian airspace in chasing down that Lithuanian traitor. They are upset at the loss of the helicopter and the crew."

"As are we!" Gurlo retorted. "They should be investigating where that other attack aircraft came from, not persecuting you for the loss!"

"It doesn't matter," Voshchanka said wearily. "I'm to return to Minsk to sit before a review board." He looked at Gurlo with pained, almost destitute eyes. "Oleg, I could lose my rank! I could lose everything! A dismissal before a review board could ruin me. No one goes before a review board without suffering."

Colonel Gurlo was thunderstruck—he was watching his commanding officer, his mentor, almost reduced to tears by the Lithuanians. "What can we do, sir? Who else but you is qualified to take command of your deployed forces? Everything will unravel."

"That was the third part of the message," Voshchanka said. "As part of the conference held between Lithuania and the Commonwealth, the

Commonwealth Council of Ministers is ordering all Commonwealth forces out of Lithuania and back to Belarus. A civilian liaison group will be established in Lithuania to oversee treaty verification and transitional procedures. Our forces in Kalinin are to be removed as well—until 'other' Commonwealth forces can replace them. You know what this means?"

"These 'other' Commonwealth forces—the *Russians?*"

"Exactly," Voshchanka said. "A detachment from Latvia and one from St. Petersburg will arrive within two to three weeks to set up patrols in the port city and along the highways. Belarus forces will not take part except during annual exercises."

"It's happening." Gurlo sighed. "Just like General Gabovich said— everything is falling apart, sir. We're going to lose all that we—"

"Shut up," Voshchanka said, rising from his chair to pace the room. "Just be quiet. I have to *think.*" The room was silent for a few moments when the telephone interrupted. "I don't want to talk to anyone," Voshchanka said as Gurlo picked up the receiver.

Colonel Gurlo listened for a few moments, then said to the caller, "Hold on." Voshchanka turned to admonish Gurlo for disobeying his orders, but Gurlo said quickly, "It's General Gabovich, calling from Vilnius on the secure line. He says he knows about your orders and he is repeating his offer to help."

"Gabovich? How in the—?" But Voshchanka fell silent. Yes, Gabovich certainly did have his spy network intact—he knew about the orders at the same time as Voshchanka himself, perhaps even earlier. He picked up the phone: "This is General Voshchanka."

"Dobraye Outrah, General Voshchanka. I am truly sorry to hear of the Commonwealth minister's decision. It must have been quite a shock."

"How in hell did you find out about that?" But it was no use asking, Voshchanka thought, so he skipped waiting for an answer. "What do you want?"

"The moment is at hand, General," Gabovich said. "History waits for no man."

"What are you talking about?" Voshchanka grumbled.

"The future, dear General. Your future. We are talking about whether you will meekly accept condemnation and ridicule from Moscow and from Minsk, or if you will stand up and take the lead in forming a new union and protecting the old way of government. Now is the time to decide."

"I don't know what you're talking about."

"In ten days, General, there will be a major antinuclear demonstration at Denerokin," Gabovich said. "These demonstrations have become more violent and more dangerous every time. The security of the entire Fisikous Research Center is at risk. The protection of Fisikous and the security of Commonwealth personnel and property within is your responsibility."

"No longer."

"You must convince the Commonwealth Council of Ministers of the danger," Gabovich said. "You think air support and troops will be needed to keep the peace. You are concerned about installations all over Lithuania being attacked by rioters. The rioters, led by Anna Kulikauskas and supported by Palcikas, of the Lithuanian Self-Defense Force, and foreign terrorists hired by imperialist plotters from Iceland, Poland, England, and the United States, are increasingly well armed and will stop at nothing."

"No one will believe that," Voshchanka said. "The protesters are peace freaks. They are nothing more than flower children."

"You believe they will forcibly storm and attack Fisikous with bombs and poison gas. You have arrested several suspects in connection with the downing of your helicopter. They say that the anti-Commonwealth terrorists have sophisticated weapons such as Stinger missiles and chemical grenades."

An attack on Fisikous during an antinuclear demonstration? That would be the perfect opportunity, Voshchanka thought. "Will other installations be affected? Can this be a widespread terrorist movement?"

"Our influence outside Fisikous is minimal," Gabovich said, "but I think other military and Commonwealth facilities can be affected."

"The Commonwealth's response will be swift," Voshchanka said. "What of the . . . special weapons we discussed? Can those be made available to me immediately?"

"They are ready," Gabovich said. "My principals want to see what sort of commitment you have to this endeavor, but they are ready to give you all the firepower you need to hold off the Commonwealth and the imperialists."

Voshchanka's head was swimming. Could this be the time? Could he trust Gabovich to come through? He tried one more test. "I will need one more thing," Voshchanka said. "The commanders of the Russian regiments in Kalinin oblast are not under my authority—they are not happy with the new Commonwealth, but they owe me no loyalty. They can be subdued easier with money than by force. I will need money to get those commanders to lay down their arms."

"That was not in the bargain."

"History waits, my dear General," Voshchanka said. "I will need at least one million American dollars for—"

"That is ridiculous," Gabovich retorted. "You are looking to set yourself up as some rich Brazilian arms dealer."

"One million dollars," Voshchanka said, "or the deal is off and you can take your chances with the Commonwealth."

There was a lengthy pause on the other end; then a frustrated Gabovich said, "I will have one million Swedish kroner delivered to you after the Denerokin demonstration. Another million kroner will be delivered to you when the country is secured. My principals will extend another two million kroner in credits for weapons over a two-year period after that point. That is my final offer."

"Done," Voshchanka said. "I will see you in Fisikous in ten days—or I will see you in hell." He hung up the phone.

Gabovich was crafty—Voshchanka had considered precisely that option: grabbing all the cash he could lay his hands on and fleeing to a hacienda in Brazil—but he was also for real. Four million kroner over two years was excellent wages, even after he used half of it to pay off the Russian warlords in Kalinin and the Commonwealth's military bureaucrats in Belarus. All he had to do was organize his forces and convince the government—by force if necessary, although it should not be needed—to keep him in power until after the upcoming demonstrations at Fisikous's nuclear power facility.

Well, if this was entrapment by the Commonwealth, it no longer mattered—Voshchanka's career was at an end no matter which way things went. He turned to Gurlo and asked, "How long would it take to get the senior regimental commanders in here or on a conference-call line?"

Gurlo was stunned, but he replied, "Ten minutes, I think."

"Get them together. I want every available field commander and senior staff officer and NCO in here or on the conference call. The question of our involvement in Lithuania and in the Commonwealth must be called—*right now.*"

OFFICE OF THE PRESIDENT'S NATIONAL SECURITY ADVISOR
WEST WING OF THE WHITE HOUSE, WASHINGTON, D.C.
26 MARCH, 0730 ET (1430 MINSK)

George Russell, the President's National Security Advisor, thumbed through the small stack of brown cardboard file folders marked USAF UNIT PERSONNEL RECORD, INDIV., the standard military-personnel file jacket. The jackets had been pulled from the Department of the Air Force's copy of military personnel records kept in its seemingly endless storage vaults at Randolph AFB. It was odd to be holding such an antiquated thing in this day and age. With computers invading every other aspect of life, especially in the high-tech, remote-controlled, kill-from-a-distance military, the Air Force still relied on these old sheaves of paper in their very low-tech prong clips to function. Russell himself was only in his late forties—typical of the younger, liberal new administration—and had been weaned on the incredible potential of the computer. Why the military had not converted over was another one of the aggravating mysteries he had to deal with.

The first place Russell had looked on each jacket was the sign-out space where the folders had been requested lately, and the list on each of the four jackets was impressive indeed—half the Pentagon had already seen these jackets, as had some of Russell's subordinates, including the Central Intelligence Agency, the Defense Intelligence Agency, and other intelligence and service support agencies. Each of the persons represented by these folders had passed some of the most rigorous scrutiny the government could undertake. Well, the career military people had screened them—now it was time for the politicians to do it.

Russell flipped through the folders, stopping briefly at the 8-by-10 black-and-white photo in each. There were four Air Force officers. The highest-ranking one was Air Force Lieutenant General Bradley Elliott, known throughout the National Command Authority as a brilliant but sometimes rambunctious and certainly unorthodox troubleshooter.

Elliott's file was impressive. Trained as an aircraft mechanic but rose quickly through the ranks to command positions and was offered a commission through Operation BOOTSTRAP in 1960. Elliott attended pilot training at Williams AFB, Arizona, and continued through B-52 training. He did two tours of Vietnam, where he was awarded two Distinguished Flying Crosses, three Air Medals, and two Purple Hearts. He then returned to the States and attended Air War College, had several command positions at SAC, went to the National War College, and now headed up the very classified High Technology Aerospace Weapons Center.

"What is General Elliott up to these days?" Russell asked the general officer in the office with him. "Still practicing for the big one?"

"Still commanding HAWC," Joint Chiefs Chairman Wilbur Curtis replied. "The White House seems to prefer Brad Elliott to—how should I say this—"

"—to stay out of sight and out of mind," Russell said. "And no wonder. Elliott's a loose cannon. We're not trying to start World War Three, just trying to get into one facility and get out. Quietly. We can do without him, Wilbur."

"That might be the inclination, but Elliott's facility in Nevada is a lot like Fisikous in Lithuania," Curtis reminded the National Security Advisor. "If you were going to plan on breaking into such a facility, better to bring along someone who has built one. He's also got an array of aircraft and weapons we might use. After all, Elliott was the one who validated the designs of the weapon systems now used in the MADCAP MAGICIAN program, among others."

Russell shook his head. "If the President sees Elliott's name on the tasking order, he'll have a coronary."

"We can sell the President on Elliott and his people," Curtis said. "You want someone who knows the target, who has the weapons, and who is completely covert and completely deniable—Brad Elliott and his troops are the ones for the job. Look what they did on Old Dog."

Russell was unimpressed, but he decided to delay his final decision for the moment.

Russell didn't recognize the other three faces in the folders. One was a brigadier general with command pilot's wings, named Ormack, the second one a Lieutenant Colonel McLanahan with command navigator's wings, and the last a captain Hal Briggs, wearing senior Army Airborne wings, an Air Force security police badge with command star, and, of all things, a U.S. Army Ranger tab. Only one out of a hundred men in the armed forces was selected for the Army Ranger school, Russell knew, and only six out of every ten of *those* men completed the course and wore the coveted Ranger tab—it was doubly surprising to see an Air Force man wearing it, let alone an officer. The star atop the Airborne wings meant that he had retained his parachutist's rating for at least six consecutive years. "What about this Briggs?" Russell asked. "An Air Force guy wearing Army insignia?"

"Volunteered for Ranger school after completing the Air Force combat-air-controller's course," Curtis continued. "Briggs could have played tight end on any pro-football team in the country—probably still could—but he's chief of security and Brad Elliott's aide-de-camp at HAWC. Nothing in the regs specifically prohibiting him from wearing Army insignia. On him, they fit. Believe me. He was picked not only because he knows the target, but he's a very highly trained and skilled commando type himself."

"He can wear Mickey Mouse ears for all I care," Russell said irritably, "as long as he does his job." The military was truly another world to Russell, one that he would never understand—a huge, hulking machine that didn't come with an instruction manual or documentation. Having to interface between the civilian and military worlds was turning out to be a very unenviable part of his job. But there was one thing he was learning about the American military machine that had been built in the past fifteen years—no matter what the politicians decided should be done, the military could devise a way to do it.

"Tell me about these other guys," Russell said distractedly as he thumbed through the other jackets. "What about McLanahan?"

"Probably the key to the whole operation," Curtis said, lighting a cigar. "Tough, intelligent, dedicated, and still the best bombardier in the country. He was Luger's partner on the Old Dog mission—he brought the plane back after the other two pilots were hurt. Early forties, pretty good shape—with a little training at Camp Lejeune or Quantico, he'll be able to keep up with the Special Ops guys, as will Briggs."

"Any engineering or scientific training?"

"Very little, all informal," Curtis replied, "but he's one of the best pure-systems operators in the Air Force, and he's got a good eye for weapons systems." Curtis motioned to the last jacket sitting on the National Security Advisor's desk. "General John Ormack is the man you want to go in and extract the data on the Soviet Fi-170 stealth bomber. He was the Old Dog crew copilot, but he was also the Megafortress's chief designer. Late forties. Racquetball freak—Air Force champ two years in a row now. He's both a Ph.D. in aeronautical engineering and a command pilot—with help, he should be able to go along with the assault team without hindering them. Out of all the Old Dog crew members, these are the best suited for this mission."

The Old Dog crew. Russell's mind wandered to the day he opened that classified file, several hours after getting off Air Force One with Curtis, and read the details of the B-52 mission that undoubtedly spelled the beginning of the end of the Cold War and the USSR. Russell was just a grade-school kid during the Cuban Missile Crisis, so he knew virtually nothing about "finger on the red button" tensions, but from what he read, the world had stepped right up to the brink that day. A lone B-52, nicknamed the Old Dog, had flown thousands of miles and had run an incredible gauntlet of Soviet air defenses to destroy a Soviet ground-based laser site in Siberia that had been shooting down American satellites and aircraft.

The mission was a success, and the ripples of shock, surprise, and fear that shot back and forth between Washington and Moscow could be felt all over the world, even though Old Dog was classified at the highest possible level. Although the episode was often presented as a breakdown in diplomacy, an abuse of power by the President of the United States, and a circumvention of the normal military chain of command, Old Dog set the stage for a successful U.S. military strategy and doctrine—hit hard, hit swiftly, hit stealthily, hit with the best you've got—for years to come.

Now Curtis wanted to bring back members of the same crew for the extraction of Luger.

"General, everyone you've picked on this mission was part of the other one," Russell said, an exasperated sigh in his voice. "This really isn't the time for a class reunion."

"And this isn't the time for making jokes, George."

"I don't make jokes," Russell said with an even voice. "I do, however, think that you're injecting a little personal bias in this. After all, you were heavily involved in the mission that eventually led to Luger being caught. You sure this isn't a bit of guilt drifting into the planning?"

"You asked for recommendations with specific objectives and problems," Curtis replied. "You wanted engineers to study the Soviet stealth bomber and be able to pick up the right documents, you wanted someone close to Luger, and you wanted them all in a hurry. Well, I got them for you. Whatever other motivations there may be, real or imagined, I have fulfilled your selection criteria. Now you can reject the candidates and I can have the J-staff come up with a new list of names, or I can instruct Special Operations Command to come up with their own team members. Now tell me what you want, George."

Russell considered all that was said; then, with a resigned nod, said, "All right. Let's go meet 'em."

Russell, Curtis, and their aides left the office, down past the President's second-floor office, and to the elevator which took them to the second underground floor. After checking in with the Secret Service agent's desk, they walked down a long corridor to the White House Situation Room, a large conference room with a sophisticated adjoining communications center.

The room was crowded with attendees, who all stood as Russell and Curtis entered the room and took their seats.

Among those assembled that Russell knew were the Commandant of the Marine Corps, General Vance K. Kundert, a medium-height, powerful-looking man in his mid-fifties, with the de rigueur "high and tight" haircut; Army General Mark V. Teller, the tall, silver-haired, athletic commander of the U.S. Special Operations Command, with a similar short haircut like Kundert's; and Kenneth Mitchell, the Director of Central Intelligence, with one of his Defense Intelligence Agency deputy chiefs.

Russell recognized Elliott, McLanahan, Ormack, and Briggs from the personnel records he had just reviewed. The others assembled were officers and aides who would conduct the more detailed briefing afterward. Russell didn't know them and probably never would, but he did know they did the lion's share of the work.

"Let's get started," Russell said brusquely as he took his seat. "General Curtis, please start."

"The following information is classified top secret, not releasable to foreign nationals, sensitive sources involved," Curtis began immediately. "Recently, a secret noncombatant personnel-extraction mission was conducted by a joint Air Force and Marine Corps special ops unit in the Republic of Lithuania. This unit brought back information from the Fisikous Institute of Technology in Vilnius on a Soviet aircraft that, after analysis, we believe is their latest strategic bomber, an intercontinental stealth bomber.

"The Pentagon would like to propose a covert infiltration of this Fisikous Institute to gather more data on the bomber."

Russell watched their reactions.

Kundert was unemotional—his men had already had a starring role in gathering the data; they would certainly be the prime movers in the next stage. McLanahan and Briggs, both just in from Elliott's High Technology Aerospace Weapons Center in Nevada, leaned a bit closer, their eyes alert, their faces sporting mischievous grins, hoping they would be a part of whatever operation developed. Ormack, the deputy commander of HAWC, also had anticipation written all over him. Russell remembered the file on Ormack. Like Elliott, another wild card.

And then the National Security Advisor looked at Lieutenant General Bradley Elliott only to find Elliott staring right at him. Elliott's look was one that could kill. Eyes burning with accusation.

Russell unconsciously swallowed, then sighed, realizing Elliott knew about Luger being at Fisikous. *Shit.* Of all the people he *didn't* need on his back . . . Would Curtis have told Elliott? He dismissed the thought. Curtis wouldn't have lasted a day as Chairman of the Joint Chiefs if he had. No, Elliott found out another way, but how?

"Excuse me, sir," Captain Hal Briggs said, raising his hand. "Why us? Why not just send in the CIA or use HUMINT resources?"

Curtis's eyes darted to Russell, who gave a slight nod to proceed. Chomping on his cigar, he said, "We've got a lot of resources planned for use, but you don't need to know about them. Nevertheless, there *is* another reason we're sending this particular team in." Curtis took a deep drag on the cigar and placed it in a nearby ashtray. "For some time now there's been a Western engineer at Fisikous, possibly working with the Fisikous design team. The, uh, engineer is ex–U.S. military. Ex–Air Force, in fact . . ."

Elliott couldn't stand it any longer.

He was on his feet, staring directly at Russell, who'd been staring at him. "You sonsofbitches! You've known for four months that he's been there and you didn't do diddly about it. Now we're finally getting around to an extraction mission? This is *criminal!*"

Confusion swept over the room. Everyone began talking at once, their voices echoing off the walls of the Situation Room, hitting Elliott with a barrage of questions. Ormack had risen, trying to calm Elliott down. "Brad, go easy, now. What's going on . . . ?"

Curtis was banging his ashtray on the table, trying to restore order.

"Tell them, Mr. National Security Advisor," Elliott snapped. "Tell 'em who's over there."

"Take your seat, General, or I'll see to it that you're out *permanently!*"

Russell ordered. "I don't know how you found out, but if you blabbed this it could kill your friend and ruin this whole operation. Now sit *down!"*

Elliott all but spat in disgust as he complied, but he did return to his chair.

Now all eyes were on Russell, who was furious with Elliott for setting him up like this. *I'll be lucky to get out of here alive,* he thought wearily.

"Who's General Elliott talking about?" Lieutenant Colonel McLanahan asked Russell with concern. "Who's been at Fisikous for five months?"

Russell noticed that this blond-haired, blue-eyed bomber jock got right to the point—and didn't even add a "sir" when addressing a Cabinet member. Half the time, general officers wouldn't speak up at all at these meetings, but that certainly wasn't this colonel's problem. Elliott's influence, no doubt.

Curtis cleared his throat, having decided to pull Russell's ass out of the sling. He looked straight at McLanahan, but addressed the entire room: "Well, he's been there longer than five months, but it's . . . David Luger."

"What?" McLanahan asked incredulously. *"Luger?"*

Everyone in the room leaned forward. Voices started coming at Curtis and Russell all at once.

"Are you sure?"

"Thought he'd died . . ."

"Must be a mistake . . ."

"Some kinda joke . . ."

"Bad intelligence . . ."

Russell, who had just about had enough, said, "Shut up, gentlemen, or I'll clear this room."

Curtis took a long drag off his cigar. "We believe Luger has undergone extensive psychological and personality alteration at the hands of the KGB, or ex-KGB. Luger goes by the name of Doctor Ivan Sergeiovich Ozerov, a Russian scientist. The contact we've got in place says Luger has been undergoing this KGB indoctrination training at Fisikous for some time."

"What kind of indoctrination training?" asked McLanahan. "The KGB disbanded—"

Curtis looked at him as if he should have known better. "Right. Anyway, he's in poor physical condition, which is consistent with the use of depressive drugs and physical torture. To make matters worse, he's been reported to have mood swings and discombobulation, which means they've been working overtime on his, uh, modification."

"So what's the deal?" McLanahan interrupted. "A prisoner exchange? How are you getting him out?"

"That hasn't been decided yet," Curtis replied uneasily. "If we acknowledge to the Soviets that we know about Luger, it's possible Luger and the stealth bomber will disappear."

"Well, you can't just leave him in there," McLanahan said emphatically. "The guy saved our lives. This country makes trades all the time—for the biggest sleazebuckets in the world—certainly you're going to get an American airman, a hero at that."

"Interesting you should bring that up, Colonel," CIA director Mitchell interjected. "Deputy Director Markwright here has been doing an extensive investigation into the Old Dog incident."

"What kind of investigation?" General John Ormack interjected.

Markwright turned to Ormack. "The DIA had closed the investigation on Old Dog and declared Luger legally dead, according to your testimony as commander of the aircraft and the last person to see Luger alive. His reappearance has reopened that investigation and introduced a number of allegations."

"Such as?"

"Such as why, after operating for months in total secrecy, did the High Technology Aerospace Weapons Center in Nevada suddenly come under attack only days after Lieutenant Luger was assigned to it?"

"What are you talking about?" Ormack demanded. "We'd been threatening to send a strike mission for days, and there was four hundred percent more activity at Dreamland after the Soviets knocked out our satellites than before. All other military bases had virtually ceased flying activity and put their birds on alert, ready to go if the balloon went up—all bases except HAWC. If the Soviets wanted to hit a base with a terrorist attack, Dreamland was the logical place."

"No, the logical place would have been Ellsworth, the home base for the B-1s scheduled to perform the strike against the Kavaznya laser site," Markwright argued. "The B-52 test-bed aircraft was never considered for the mission—yet it came under direct attack by Soviet-trained terrorists."

"Well, why wouldn't the informant have told the Soviets to attack Ellsworth?"

"Because Luger . . . I mean, the informant, didn't know that the B-1s would come out of Ellsworth," Markwright said. "He *did* know that your team was developing weapons, hardware, and tactics for B-1 and other strike aircraft, and he *did* know that there were B-1 bombers at Dreamland that were being loaded with the data being used on the test-bed B-52—he could have assumed that the aircraft to be used on the actual strike were the B-1s already at Dreamland, not at some other operational unit. The B-1s from Dreamland departed from there, went to Ellsworth to pick up their strike crews, then staged from there—but Luger thought they were going to strike from Dreamland—so he could have ordered the attack on Dreamland."

"That's crazy!" Ormack raged, furious at the implications. "You've been reading too many Tom Clancy novels."

McLanahan was nodding in agreement, trying to contain his anger. "We didn't know anything about an actual strike. We were told we were doing tests."

"Oh, come on, Colonel," Markwright said. "It would have been easy enough to deduce that your activities were related to real-world events— the entire Kavaznya incident and the state of East-West tensions were in the news for months. HAWC's mission is to produce mission-ready aircraft."

"But *we* didn't know that."

"You may not have been *told* that, but a lot of people in the military know what goes on at Dreamland. Don't be so naive."

"And don't you tell me what I think or what I know," McLanahan shot back angrily. "Our job was to fly the modified B-52, do what we were told, and keep our mouths shut. That's what we did."

"I'm making hypotheses based on your own testimony, Colonel," Markwright said, "not putting words in your mouth." He turned to Ormack. "General, think about your testimony on Luger's performance on the flight: the overly pessimistic fuel reports, the missed radar terrain calls, his attempts to continually force you to fly higher altitudes so you'd be detected."

"That's crazy!" Ormack repeated. "He did no such thing."

"He was doing his job," McLanahan said, running an exasperated hand through his blond hair. "Navigators are trained to err on the side of safety and prudence. Besides, Luger didn't make the decisions, he just reported information."

"Information that was consistently wrong, and always erring on the side of danger or turning the sortie back," Markwright said. "Colonel McLanahan, you even testified that Luger seemed hesitant to release the weapon on the Kavaznya facility, and that he suggested that the plane be crashed into the facility."

"We were under attack by a goddammed advanced *laser,*" McLanahan said. "Our equipment was faulted or destroyed. We didn't know if the weapon we had would work."

"Is crashing your aircraft into a target an approved method for ensuring mission success, Colonel?" Markwright asked skeptically.

"No, but—"

"Then why would Luger suggest such a thing? Why would he risk your lives on an idea that had no merit?"

"Our assignment was to destroy the laser site. Period. Crashing the bomber into the site would've done that."

"And then, once you survived the attack," Markwright pressed, ignoring McLanahan's arguments, "Luger suggests that you land at a *Soviet* airfield."

"It was a *crew* decision," Elliott said. "Luger guided us by radar and provided the data."

"And when you land at Anadyr, Luger leaves the aircraft and escapes into the hands of the Soviets."

McLanahan felt his face growing warmer. He was beginning to get pissed. Really pissed. Keeping his temper under control was something this eldest son of Irish immigrants usually didn't have to work at. McLanahan's strength had always been his understated ability to keep things under control. But this asshole wasn't a part of Old Dog and didn't know what the fuck he was talking about.

"He distracted the Soviet militiamen long enough for us to get away," McLanahan said angrily. "He sacrificed his life to save us."

"He didn't sacrifice anything," Markwright said dismissively. "He's still alive, living under an assumed name—and working to design Soviet stealth bombers."

"Bullshit!" McLanahan hissed. "You don't know what happened— you weren't *there!* You people never are. You shuffle papers and stay out of the line of fire, only to do postmortems with reports twisted to fit the circumstances. You said it yourself: Luger's been drugged or brain-washed into cooperating."

"The informant saw no evidence that Luger was being brainwashed, tortured, or drugged," Markwright said calmly. "General Curtis's *independent* analysis, based on the reports from the informant, suggest the possible use of drugs, but it could also be due to fatigue or stress due to overwork. In fact, the informant said that Ozerov enjoyed a certain notoriety, a wide circle of friends and colleagues, and many perquisites commensurate with a high Soviet official."

"Who the hell are you going to believe?" McLanahan said. "Us, or this informant?"

Ormack pointed his finger at Markwright. "We're telling you that David Luger sacrificed himself to save us. If he survived, it's up to us to get him out."

Markwright saw that he was clearly outnumbered and outshouted, so he stopped, took an exasperated breath, and looked at Central Intelligence Director Mitchell, who said, "My recommendation to Mr. Russell and the Joint Chiefs of Staff is that we attempt a covert extraction mission to get Luger and to recover as many photographs or documents of the bomber as possible."

"What do you mean, 'get him'?" McLanahan asked. "You mean rescue him?"

Markwright did not answer. Mitchell hesitated.

McLanahan exploded: "What the hell do you plan on doing? You've got to bring him back. At least then you'll be able to answer the questions you have about his loyalties."

"We understand, Colonel," Russell said. "Yes, we're going to bring Luger back. Director Mitchell will put assets in place to monitor Luger's whereabouts and even make contact if possible. We'll open discreet channels into the Soviet government to see if an exchange can be made, but that may be too risky. When the time's right, we'll assemble a personnel-extraction team and go in and exfiltrate him. If they can take him, they will. If they can't take him safely—"

"We'll plan it so we can get the information *and* Luger," Elliott said firmly.

"You're not in charge here, General Elliott," Russell reminded him. Russell remembered all too well the stories of Elliott taking his high-tech toys out of the desert and flying them all over the globe. The last thing he wanted was a man like Elliott operating outside strict civilian control. Jesus . . . what a nightmare that would be. "General Lockhart of European Command will be in overall command, with General Teller as air-operations commander and General Kundert as ground-and-naval-operations commander. I want no free-lancing or wild-ass theatrics on this one, General Elliott. We do this by the book, we get our people out, and we get the hell out of Lithuania. Period."

It was going to be a strange combination, Elliott thought as he nodded in assent to the National Security Advisor. General Lockhart, one of the "old guard" Army commanders and a good friend of Elliott's, was the right man to be in charge of this mission. He was strong, no-nonsense, a classic three-dimensional strategist. Teller and Kundert working together were the wild cards. For some strange reason, Marine Corps special-operations-capable assets were never placed under the jurisdiction of the newly formed U.S. Special Operations Command. Although General Teller, as commander of all Army, Navy, and Air Force special operations forces, had worldwide authority for this kind of mission, Kundert's Marines were usually the first to react and usually the best to send. Choosing between the two was as much a political struggle as an operational decision. The White House was uncomfortable enough with the military without having two competing forces vying for his attention.

Trouble was, the Joint Chiefs of Staff these days had become a political organism, not a true union of military commanders—even Curtis, who was as much an old crew-dog as he was in the early years of the Air Force, had become more of a mouthpiece of the White House's wishes than a true strategist and representative of the armed services. Curtis, who was on his second wife and seventh child, was savvy enough to have survived, unscathed, a change in administrations. He was now so respected on the

Hill and at the Pentagon that the White House couldn't deep-six him even if they wanted to. The Joint Chiefs still had considerable power and influence, but they were all basically Presidential cheerleaders. Joining the Marines and Special Operations Command on this mission clearly smacked of politics, of the President straddling the fence to keep the services happy.

Peace had turned the Joint Chiefs of Staff into uniformed politicians, and that was what Luger was being forced to bet his life on. Well, Elliott told himself, not if he could help it.

"I realize I'm not in charge," Elliott finally said to Russell. "But I've got aircraft and weapons you might consider for this extraction. They're designed for maximum stealth for the penetration, and they can be launched from—"

"Thank you, General Elliott," General Teller interrupted, "but we can handle it from now on. All we need from you is your staff officers here. They'll go into training with the MEU and Delta Force team members so they can keep up with the infiltration team. Colonel McLanahan's and Captain Briggs' job is to help escort the target out of the facility and assist General Ormack; General Ormack, you'll examine the laboratory where the target is working and procure any important documents you may find in connection with the Fi-170 project. It'll be quick, hard, silent, and surprising."

Elliott fell silent. It sounded like a good basic plan: go in, find Luger, toss a few desks and safes, and get out. Several special ops teams from all branches of the service practiced this type of mission almost every day. But Elliott thought it seemed too easy—way too easy . . .

"You three will fly to Camp Lejeune and report to the commanding general of the Marine Corps Special Operations Training Group," Kundert said. "We'll give you a physical, a fitness test, then send you off to join the 26th MEU in Norway when you have completed the fitness test and demonstrated that you can keep up with my Marines. The MEU will complete your evaluation and report back to me on whether or not you are qualified to go on this mission."

Kundert looked the three men over. His eyes showed muted appreciation for Briggs, then a bit of amusement as he looked at Ormack and McLanahan. "I hope you've been keeping yourselves in shape, ladies," he said, "because by this time tomorrow morning you'll experience a Marine Corps confidence course that'll chew you up and spit you out if you're not ready. If you can't cut the course by the end of the week, or can't handle an assault rifle, you're out. Colonel Kline will not risk the safety of his men for any out-of-shape Air Force officers. My aide'll issue you your orders." He turned to George Russell and General Teller. He was finished with these outsiders.

"You can go," Russell said. "General Elliott, nice to finally meet you.

We'll keep you briefed on the progress of the mission." Elliott shook hands cordially enough with all, then departed with the rest of his officers.

Outside the Situation Room, the four HAWC officers headed for the elevator that would take them upstairs to the West Wing's ground level. A couple of Secret Service agents fell in step beside them as escorts.

McLanahan looked numb but elated by the revelations that he'd just heard in the meeting. "After all this time . . . Luger's still alive. We'd all written him off. And now . . . now, it's just amazing."

Elliott shook his head as they stepped into the elevator and rode up. Although the Secret Service had clearances of their own, the subject was still too highly classified even for them to hear. Besides, reporters and White House staffers were flitting in and out all around the offices of the West Wing.

When they were inside the Pentagon car ordered for them and heading out the White House gates, they began to talk.

General Ormack turned to Elliott. "Who would've thought—Luger in Lithuania? Unbelievable. Now tell us about that little outburst you had with the NSA. Did you really know in advance that it was Luger?"

"Yeah, but I can't tell you how," Elliott said. "Someone knew he was there and got upset when several months had gone by and nothing had been done to pull him out. Even after going through the right channels. This person told me, then I told Curtis. The General took it from there."

"Well, thank God he did." Briggs grinned. "Man, I can't wait to see Luger. Think of the party we'll throw for that sonofabitch!"

Elliott darted him a stern glance.

"Sorry, sir . . . uh, naturally he'll have to be debriefed. Then probably hospitalized until they clean him up and detox him. But after that . . ."

"Just think of it," McLanahan said excitedly. "We get Luger back, *plus* the latest info on the Soviets' stealth bomber. All in one trip. It's like Christmas!"

Murmurs of agreement went around, with the exception of Brad Elliott, who remained silent.

"Problem, sir?" Ormack asked.

Elliott made a "no-big-deal" gesture and stared out the window. It was almost springtime in Washington, normally one of the more beautiful seasons to be in the nation's capital. But today the skies were heavily overcast, and a light, steady drizzle covered the lighted streets, the cars. A day that should have been spectacular was depressing and gray. Elliott wondered if it wasn't a portent of things to come. He turned to Ormack. "I guess I'm just not comfortable with handing over my troops without HAWC or myself in on the mission. Especially with Dave involved. It seems *we* ought to be the ones who get him. We have the hardware, the skills . . ."

"Not for an opposed personnel-extraction, we don't," Briggs said.

"We could train for it, but it would take us too long to get ready. The Marines and Delta Force train for contingencies like this all the time."

"And we already developed the CV-22 for them," Ormack added. "That's a significant contribution."

"You don't have to soothe my ego, John," Elliott said, a hint of impatience in his voice. "HAWC is a support group, not a combat outfit. I'm used to taking a backseat in important operations."

"So why the silent routine?"

"No reason," Elliott said. "I know you guys'll kick ass with these Marines."

"I'm not so sure about that," McLanahan said. "Run twenty kilometers with a pack? I run twenty kilometers a week, at the most, and the heaviest thing I carry is a Walkman."

"I told you months ago, Patrick," Briggs teased, "that you gotta lay off the leaded Coke and run with me at lunchtime instead of taking your girl out to the O-Club all the time. Looks like I'm going to have to carry you now."

"Carry *me?* In your dreams!"

Elliott half-listened to them, his mind returning to the operation. He knew the Marines' and Army's plan to rescue Luger was going to be well coordinated and executed with precision and speed—the most critical decisions of every special ops mission were made in the planning sessions—but he was still uncomfortable with the operation. Why? He didn't know. But he wasn't going to leave the success or failure to get Luger out to Special Operations alone. No, he was going to do a lot of mission planning of his own, bringing to bear every last resource under his command.

If their rescue mission somehow failed, he'd be ready with one of his own.

TRAKAI CASTLE, OUTSIDE VILNIUS, LITHUANIAN REPUBLIC
27 MARCH, 1930 VILNIUS (**1330** ET)

Ever since the Lithuanian Self-Defense Force (LSDF) was reactivated, their headquarters had been Trakai Castle, eighteen miles outside Vilnius. Located on an island on sparkling Lake Galve, Trakai was the first capital city of Lithuania, established in the early 13th century. The castle itself had been the official residence of the Grand Duke's family from the end of the 14th century until the monarchy was dissolved by the Bolsheviks in 1918. Still a museum and monument to the medieval Lithuanian state, Trakai also served as the ceremonial hall and conference center of the LSDF headquarters staff.

Anna Kulikauskas, with her father, parked their Volvo sedan in the parking lot and then walked across the well-lit wooden bridge across Lake Galve to the castle. Two armed guards—armed not with medieval swords, but with AK-47 rifles with bayonets affixed—checked their identification and the letter of authorization, and another guard led them across the drawbridge into the ancient castle.

The castle had been beautifully restored, and served as a tourist attraction as well as a historical monument and a military headquarters. Inside the outer castle wall was a large courtyard surrounded by shops where artisans practiced silversmithing, woodworking, ironworking, and other crafts in the medieval fashion, and small stores and restaurants that catered to castle tourists. Those shops were all closed. The guard led the two civilians down a long wooden boardwalk and across another drawbridge, across a wide moat and through a two-meter-thick wall to the main ten-story castle residence.

The courtyard of the castle residence was much smaller than the main courtyard. Oil lanterns illuminated the entire area, and guards in medieval costumes stood at attention in the doorways. Wooden stairs led up to each floor, and stone stairs to the left led down to the storage areas, jails, and armory. "I wonder if this castle could stand against modern-day invaders?" Anna asked.

"This castle fared none too well in its own day," her father replied in a whisper, as if raising his voice in that cathedral-like setting would be sacrilegious. "The castle was used only in times of peace. King Gediminas built the Tower in Vilnius as his main residence because Trakai was harder to defend in times of war."

"I'll bet the king didn't have one of those," Anna said, pointing toward the sky. Highlighted against a beautiful backdrop of stars on that chilly night was a revolving radar array. "They certainly have done some remodeling."

"Modern problems call for modern solutions," a voice said behind them. General Dominikas Palcikas walked over and greeted his guests. He was dressed in what appeared to be a red cassock, a simple cotton robe belted at the waist by a black sash. It was hard to see when he wore baggy fatigues, but now Anna could see how well-defined the man was—he had a broad, deep chest, a thick neck, and powerful arms. "Actually, we take the radar down at daybreak—it spoils the look of the castle for the tourists—and we use it only at night, for training, or in case of national emergency."

"Expecting trouble tonight, General?" Anna asked.

"Since the incident with the Byelorussian helicopter, we've been on guard twenty-four hours a day," Palcikas said. "I always expect trouble. But tonight we won't talk of trouble. This is a night for celebration. Come this way and we'll view the candidates."

Palcikas led them up two flights of thick wooden stairs. As they climbed, Anna said, "You look like a priest tonight, General."

"As a matter of fact I'm an ordained deacon in the Roman Catholic church," Palcikas explained. "I have been for ten years, since returning from Afghanistan. I can perform all rites and administer the sacraments."

"And must you remain celibate as well?"

Palcikas laughed. "No, I'm not a priest. My actual duties in the Church are limited to what you'll see tonight." He turned toward her as they reached the third floor of the castle, smiled mischievously, and said to her in a low voice, "But thank you for asking, Miss Kulikauskas."

They emerged onto a long balcony overlooking the castle residence's chapel, and saw what was for Anna and her father an astonishing sight. In the glare of lanterns and torches, twelve men were dressed in rough black robes, lying facedown before the altar, their arms outstretched beside them, their legs together, forming the shape of a cross with their bodies. Four guards dressed in full, polished-chrome knight's armor and carrying long-handled axes surrounded them.

"What in God's name is this?" Anna whispered.

Palcikas smiled and turned to Anna's father. "Perhaps you can explain it to your daughter, Mr. Kulikauskas?"

The old man beamed with pride at the request and said, "My dear, you are watching the initiation of those twelve men into knighthood."

"Knighthood? As in medieval times?"

"Not just medieval times, Anna," Palcikas said. "I have continued the tradition of the training and the ritual of acceptance. Any man or woman can join my units, and any person can become an officer; but only certain qualified candidates can carry or wear the Vytis, the war banner of the Grand Dukes of Lithuania. These men have completed two years of training to be able to do so."

"Those men have been like that for a full day and a full night," the old man said. Palcikas nodded—the old man did indeed know his history. "They are deep in prayer, reciting the codes of knighthood, allowed only one cup of water an hour, and asking for the strength to carry out the responsibilities of a knight." He pointed to a soldier who had just entered the chapel. "Watch this, Anna. This might amuse you."

The newcomer, an officer in one of Palcikas's units, dressed in full-dress uniform, genuflected at the foot of the altar, made the sign of the cross, then reported in to one of the guards surrounding the twelve candidates. The guard saluted. The officer returned it and then walked over to a small prayer bench. He knelt, prayed for a few moments, then picked up a long, black leather whip from the bench.

Anna gasped. "What—"

The officer walked to the front of the altar, genuflected once again, turned toward the twelve candidates lying before him, and said in a loud voice, "May the blessings of God and Jesus Christ be upon you. Glory to God and peace be upon our land."

In unison, the twelve candidates chanted aloud, "Glory to God and peace be upon our land."

The officer cried out, "Who present claims to be worthy of receiving the Cross and the Sword?"

"We do, the humble squires before you," came the response. At that, all twelve candidates reached back and pulled down the tops of their robes, exposing their bare backs, then resumed their original position. Anna's mouth dropped open; her father's eyes gleamed in wonder.

The officer walked to the first candidate and said, "Squire, what is your wish?"

The candidate replied in a loud voice, "Sire, I wish the discipline so that I might prove myself worthy to receive the power."

At that, the officer raised the whip and brought it down, hard, on the candidate's back. The crack of the whip against bare flesh echoed loudly throughout the chapel. The officer moved to the next candidate, repeated the same words, and the whip cracked again. After every crack, all the candidates chanted loudly, "Lord, grant me the power."

"How dare"—Anna gasped—"that's a real whip! He *beat* that man!"

"It's the ordeal, Anna," the old man said, a surprised and pleased smile on his face. "The candidates will receive one hundred lashes from the other knights in the twenty-four hours they are lying before the altar."

"How barbaric! How humiliating . . . degrading . . ."

"It's the old way, Anna," Mikhaus Kulikauskas said proudly. "A candidate who truly doesn't want to make the sacrifice will not stand for it. It's a test of loyalty, of commitment. King Gediminas was performing this very same ritual in Lithuania—probably in this very same chapel— over seven hundred years ago."

"But why? Beating them like animals?"

"Because soldiers back then were tough, far tougher than men today," the old man replied. "An eighteen-year-old squire in the fourteenth century could run for many kilometers in a full suit of iron armor—very little lightweight steel around back then. He could wield an eight-kilogram pig-iron sword in one hand all day without tiring. They were all but oblivious to cold, snow, or even pain. These men didn't break easily. Physical torture was ineffective—but full, complete obeisance, as a dog is to his master, was effective."

Dominikas Palcikas could see Anna wince every time the crack of the whip split the air, and he could see her eyes first round with terror, then narrow as if she were feeling the sting of the whip herself, so he took her arm and led her off the balcony. She allowed herself to be led through a modern-looking conference room and into an office a short distance away. He led her to a dark-black leather chair in front of his desk, then went to a nearby bar in a corner of the room and poured two small snifters of brandy. She took it but did not drink from it.

"That . . . that was one of the stupidest, most asinine, cruelest things I have ever seen in my life," she huffed. "Grown men being beaten like animals."

"We make it up to them afterward," Palcikas said idly. "During the Mass, the other knights bathe the candidates and dress them in clean white robes. Before they make the Oath, they are dressed in suits of armor."

"You really tap their shoulders with a sword and all that stuff?" Anna asked condescendingly.

"The Grand Dukes never tapped shoulders—I believe that's a British custom," Palcikas replied seriously. "I anoint their foreheads with oil. Then they place one hand on the Bible and another on the Lithuanian Sword of State, which is kept here at Trakai, and recite the Oath of Acceptance from memory. After Mass, the other knights treat them to a big feast in the Great Hall. As master of ceremonies, I pour them their first goblet of wine at supper."

"The whole thing seems perverse . . . ridiculous, if nothing else," Anna said. "I mean, this *is* the twentieth century!"

"I've got over a hundred men—including eighteen women, by the way—in training right now, and I've got over *five hundred* on the waiting list," Palcikas said. "They don't get paid extra, they don't get a title, and they don't get any special privileges. They wear a funny red patch on their uniform, and their coffin gets draped by a red Vytis when they're buried. We do it because it's a way to prove their loyalty and dedication to the country they live in and the cause they believe in."

"Prove to whom? You? Or the government?"

"Themselves—only themselves," Palcikas replied. "I don't require it, and I don't use appointment for or against anyone. But it seems we have so few things in this country that we can really believe in, and this gives citizens an opportunity to express their beliefs and desires. A belief is just a wish unless you can relate to it emotionally. The ritual gives these men a way to experience the significance of what they do on a historical, and emotional, level. Some can trace their ancestors who took the ritual; others want to be the first in their line, or to continue the tradition, since so many men's families were exterminated by the Russians and the Nazis during the Great Patriotic War. Whatever the reason, it helps them relate to their job—protecting their homeland."

"Some would call it a pagan ritual," Anna pointed out. "They'll point to Adolf Hitler's Nazi Youth, the SS's branding rituals, or the Ku Klux Klan's cross-burnings."

"Or a wedding ceremony? Or a swearing-in of a new member of Parliament? I think we all have our pagan rituals." He paused, watching the brandy swirling in his glass, then added, "Like protesters carrying fake coffins and wearing orange bedsheets like irradiated bodies in protest marches."

"So you've heard about our march at the Fisikous Research Institute coming up next week."

"Ah, yes . . . the Denerokin nuclear-power plant. You could have given me a bit more warning, Miss Kulikauskas," Palcikas said. "It takes time to set up a proper security team and to notify all the proper officials."

"We don't need permission or security to march in our own country," Anna said defiantly. "We can march anytime and anywhere we choose."

"But not inside the Denerokin gates," Palcikas noted. "The facility is still guarded by Commonwealth troops. Legally, they still own the facility, the nuclear-power plant, everything, until 1995. They don't have to let you inside."

"Then we'll stay outside the gate," Anna said boldly, "but we're going to stage the rally. Why do they still have that reactor operating? It doesn't produce power for Lithuania. Are they still conducting experiments in there?"

"What they do in the Fisikous Research Institute is Commonwealth business until 1995," Palcikas said. "The Denerokin reactor inside Fisikous is to be shut down by the end of this year. That's in the treaty."

"It was a bad treaty shoved down our government's throat by the United Nations, without one U.N. official ever setting foot in Lithuania," Kulikauskas declared irritably. "They gave permission for the Commonwealth to poison Lithuania and kill another couple thousand citizens."

"I agree with you, Anna," Palcikas said. "I wanted Denerokin shut down at the same time you got the Ignalina plant near Siauliai shut down. But it didn't happen. Now I must obey the law and do as I'm told."

"That makes you a good little soldier, then," Kulikauskas said. "Keep your mouth shut and do as you're ordered—while thousands of Lithuanians die from contaminated water, contaminated air, contaminated beef."

"As a Lithuanian soldier, I can't do more than the law allows," Palcikas insisted. "As a lawmaker yourself, you know that." She gave him an exasperated glare—Anna was a representative in the hundred-person Lithuanian Parliament. She knew he was right.

"But as a soldier I can tell you this, Anna: the situation is very, very dangerous right now. The Byelorussian and Commonwealth armies are all over the countryside, and I can't contain all of them. They harass our citizens every day; there are daily treaty violations; and their numbers are *increasing,* not decreasing. Fisikous itself seems to have more Byelorussian troops inside than ever, along with those ex-OMON troops still stationed there.

"Anna, I'm trying to build a case to present to the government for the United Nations that shows all the treaty violations and calls for stricter compliance or even direct U.N. supervision, but my case isn't strong enough yet. Until then it's better not to fan the flames by marching on Fisikous. That's their last major facility in Lithuania, and it's still an active installation. If they see it threatened, they may react violently."

"We have a right to peaceful protest in this country," Kulikauskas insisted.

"I don't dispute that, but I also don't see a reason to twist the tiger's tail. What I'm asking is this: keep your protesters all on the northeast side of the facility, near the Denerokin gate—don't try to mass along the south gates, because security there is not as strong and the troops might get anxious and do something stupid."

"They had better *not* do something stupid!"

"Stupid—and deadly—things happen all the time, Anna—I'm just trying to avoid some of them. Keep the bulk of your protesters across the street in the railroad-yard parking lot—you can set up your speaker's platform and podium there—and have no more than one hundred persons near the Denerokin gate. I will station my troops between the gate and the protesters. My troops will be no closer than fifty meters to the gate. You can block traffic on the Denerokin road, erect signs, hang anyone you want in effigy—just don't go near the gate or the fence. If we can agree to all these provisions, I can take them to the director of plant security in Fisikous and give him a heads-up as to what will happen. As long as everyone stays involved, I think everything will be okay. Agreed?"

Anna paused for a long moment. The thought of restrictions on any peaceful protester's movement was irritating, but safety was important and Palcikas obviously knew what he was doing.

"All right, General," she said, holding out her hand. "I'll present it to the rally committee, but I think you can count on their support." He rose from his chair and took her hand in his. "It's nice to be working with you."

"And with you," Anna replied.

Dominikas rolled up a sleeve of his cassock and looked at his watch. "Mass starts in twenty minutes. I'll escort you and your father to your seats, and then I've got to get ready." He motioned to a standing suit of armor in a corner of the office—it was the largest suit of armor Anna had ever seen, obviously "tailored" to fit Palcikas. "It takes a long time to put on all that damned armor, you know."

HIGH TECHNOLOGY AEROSPACE WEAPONS CENTER, NEVADA
27 MARCH, 2145 PT (28 MARCH, 0645 VILNIUS)

"Time to come to Jesus, Colonel."

Colonel Paul White rose from his bed to find an armed Air Force security policeman, a security police officer, and Lieutenant General Brad Elliott standing in the doorway of White's room. Since being arrested several days earlier, White had been staying in the small transient officers' quarters at Dreamland—not quite under house arrest, but his movements were carefully monitored and regulated nonetheless. Not that it mattered much—there wasn't anyplace to go within a hundred miles of that small desert base.

"I was surprised that it took you this long to come get me," White said. "I've been staying dressed until late, and dress very early, for days now. Just to be sure you're not inconvenienced when you come to take me on a tour of your facility."

"Tour . . . my . . . facility?" Elliott muttered in disbelief. Elliott motioned for the guards to wait outside, then closed the door behind him. White stayed where he was, sitting on the edge of his bed. Elliott stepped toward White and lowered his voice: "You think you're funny, Colonel?" Elliott said. "Do you see anyone laughing? Let me assure you, this is not a joke: You are here only because the Department of Justice and the Pentagon asked me to keep an eye on you until they can present formal charges of treason and divulging classified information."

"So I'm out?"

"Your discharge papers will be on the DCI's desk by seven A.M., and signed by the Secretary of the Air Force shortly thereafter. You'll be a civilian by seven-fifteen. By eight o'clock you'll be in front of a judge who will put you in prison without bail on conspiracy charges that will rival the Walker spy ring. Your trial will be sometime in the future. I'm here to place you under arrest, advise you of your Constitutional rights and your rights under the Uniform Code of Military Justice, and transfer you to the detention center to await transfer to Department of Justice agents."

"Well, I was afraid of all that," White said simply. He clapped his hands on his lap, took a deep breath, then looked back at Elliott and asked, "So, General, how did you lose your leg?"

Elliott looked at the ceiling in abject amazement. "Colonel, you don't seem very upset at the fact that you could be spending the rest of your life in prison."

"When are they going in to get Luger?"

"None of your goddamned business."

"Then it's on," White said with a Cheshire grin when he saw the scarcely hidden exasperation in Elliott's face. "Great. I was afraid the CIA might have put a contract out on David or something crazy like that." When he saw Elliott's face grimace, he added, "Jesus—they *did* put a contract out on him! That means we got to him in time! Thank God . . ."

"I said, that's enough. Now shut up, White," Elliott said angrily. Elliott read White his Miranda rights and his UCMJ rights from a card; then he stepped over to White, leaning closer to him, and asked, "Tell me about MADCAP MAGICIAN."

"I *knew* it!" White enthused. *"We* are going after Luger!"

"What . . . ?"

"Let me guess," White said energetically. "You met with the Director of Central Intelligence, maybe even with the National Security Advisor or even the President himself. They were going to bump off Luger but you talked them out of it. Now they say they're going to rescue Luger and maybe try to grab *Tuman,* the Soviet stealth bomber, along the way. Except you don't believe them. You think if the going gets tough they'll turn tail and leave Luger to his fate—i.e., kill him. They'll protect themselves and maintain the cover story above all else. I agree—that's what I'd do."

Despite his irritation, Elliott was starting to warm to this guy's bizarre, disjointed way of thinking. He said, "White, can't you stop talking just for a minute?"

"MADCAP MAGICIAN, General, is just what you need," White said excitedly. "What I've got, General, is a ship that looks like a cargo vessel but carries two CV-22 tilt-rotor aircraft, fully equipped for low-level assault and rescue, and I can carry another big helicopter like a CH-53 Jolly Green or H-60 Blackhawk up on deck. I can cruise anywhere in the Baltic—I'm fully documented, fully manifested, and rarely boarded because of my Civil Naval Reserve Fleet designation. I've got Marines and ISA agents that are as tough as anyone the Soviets or the CIA have.

"What I don't have is air support. I can get my choppers over Lithuania, but I need tankers to refuel the helicopters and air- and ground-defense support if the bad guys show up. You must have—"

"That's enough. Keep your mouth closed from now until I see you again or you'll regret it." The warning in Elliott's voice was clear; White did not doubt it for a moment. He wiped the grin off his face immediately. Elliott opened the door and admitted the security guards. "Lieutenant, Colonel White is formally under arrest. Take him to the van," he ordered. "I'll meet up with you later." With a grim face, the security officer pulled White to his feet and turned him around. White automatically put his hands behind his back, and the other guard wrapped plastic handcuffs on his wrists and led him to the door and into a waiting van.

The van drove through the early-morning darkness for what seemed like hours but was only about ten minutes. The terrain outside the darkened windows of the security police van was desolate, interrupted only occasionally by a traffic sign or stretch of strong, reinforced fencing. It reminded White of his two-hour-long drive from Nellis Air Force Base near Las Vegas to Dreamland—miles and miles of nothingness.

They finally stopped at a guard shack, and the guard went inside and had his identification checked—a rigorous check for an officer assigned to the base, White thought. A guard came by and shined a flashlight in White's face, studied him for a moment, noted that he was handcuffed, checked the face against a photo on a clipboard, then went away. After the I.D. check and an inspection of the van by bomb dogs and mirrors, the van continued on for several long minutes through pitch-black territory. Clouds obscured the sky, so White had no sense of direction.

After a long ride on both paved and unpaved roads, the van stopped several meters away from a large, featureless building. The van door was opened and White was led outside to a steel-sheathed door. The security officer punched a combination into a CypherLock next to the door, and the other guard pulled it open when he heard the door buzz.

"We go through one at a time," the officer told White. "Walk straight ahead to the second door. Do not stop. I'll be watching you." He went in. A few minutes later the door buzzed again, and the guard opened it and let White pass inside.

The room inside was dark green and the floor felt spongy, as if it were made of rubber instead of concrete. An illuminated sign and an electroluminescent line on the floor told him where to walk. As he moved through the room, the temperature suddenly jumped, and he felt flushed and uncomfortable for several brief moments. Was he getting nervous? What was going on? He always knew that HAWC would have some pretty tight security, but a rubber room inside the security facility?

The door on the other end opened just as White got there. The security officer was waiting. He led him into an adjacent office, where his identification was checked once again.

"Tell me about the pins in your foot, sir," a security guard asked.

"The pins in my . . . ?" White hesitated. Both security officers looked at him, waiting for a response. White noticed their impatience and quickly replied, "I stepped on an unexploded mine. Village of Bun Loc, Vietnam. Tet offensive. July, nineteen sixty-eight. The pins were put in at a hospital in Saigon."

The guards were reading from a computer screen at the same time that White related his story—obviously a hookup to the personnel records at Defense or the National Security Agency. "How many pins?" he asked.

"Four."

"What is your mother's maiden name?"

The sudden shift in topics momentarily confused White, but he was accustomed to such questions—rapid changes in topic was a standard interrogation technique. A mole or impostor relying on rote memorization could not recall facts fast enough to look believable during such quick changes. "I don't know my natural mother's maiden name; I was adopted. My adoptive mother's maiden name was Lewis." Suddenly White broke into a slight grin. "Hey . . . was that an X-ray chamber? I've heard of those things! You check for implants, microdots, miniature transmitters, that kind of stuff, right?"

"Very good, colonel," Lieutenant General Brad Elliott said, appearing from the outer hallway. "I think you passed. The Intelligence Support Agency verifies that you're for real. Take the cuffs off." The security officer cut off the handcuffs. Elliott led White down a darkened hallway in which small displays resembling memorials were highlighted by a single small spotlight.

"Pretty snazzy security you got here, General," White said. "Even better than ISA. We only have—" White passed a large aircraft-control wheel that looked like it was from a B-52. He wanted to stop and read the inscription on a plaque underneath it, but Elliott kept on walking ahead, so White stepped quickly to catch up. "As I was saying, we use a broadcast interferometer to detect implants and transmitters. I suppose you—"

White passed a glassed-in display case in the hallway, and this time he stopped. A single spotlight overhead illuminated a standard Air Force-issue heavyweight Nomex flying jacket, displayed upright in the case. The olive-drab jacket was nearly completely covered with dark splotches, and the normally light-green quilted lining was stained nearly black. "Uh, General, what's—?" White's eyes were drawn to the glossy-black vinyl name tag on the jacket . . .

. . . the name tag, with silver navigator's and jump wings on it, said simply: LUGER.

"Yes, that's his," Elliott said. He had come back to stand beside White. "The blood is mine. He passed it up to the officer that was treating my wounds, just before he left the plane. David knew he wasn't going to need it." Elliott motioned across the hallway. "I made this hallway a sort of shrine to the crew, and to the mission we flew." He pointed at the control wheel. "That's the control wheel from the Old Dog, the B-52 we flew to take out Kavaznya. We gave it to Patrick after the mission, but of course he couldn't keep it or take it anywhere."

"Patrick? *McLanahan?* He's here? He's all right?"

"He's all right, but he's not here," Elliott said. "He's with the Marines that have gone to try to rescue David from Lithuania. Thanks to you, we got that chance."

White smiled. What a great time he'd had with McLanahan and Luger at Ford Air Force Base, putting them both through the loops of his B-52 Ejection and Egress Trainer. What a time those two had had. White had almost felt sorry for them, especially when they'd had to do a *manual* bailout. But they'd come out of the session with flying colors, even with all the tricks White had tossed at them, and McLanahan and Luger ended up being a great team.

"You know, I always figured McLanahan and Luger were together, and that they were mixed up in something like this," White said. "I'd heard the rumors about the Kavaznya laser, that it wasn't really a nuclear accident, that in reality the United States bombed the thing. I only half-believed it anyway, and the government wasn't giving out details, so everyone just dropped it."

"The National Security Advisor didn't know about any of this until a few days ago."

"Amazing. Well, that certainly restores my faith in our appointed government officials." White looked at Elliott, then glanced down the hallway to the door they had not yet taken. "Can you tell me about the Old Dog? Can you tell me about the mission . . . ?"

"Are you serious about helping me?" Elliott asked. "I need to know, right now, without any bullshit and without any nonsense."

"First I need to know if I'm right," White said. "Could the person in the photo really be Luger? If the mission you flew was against the Kavaznya site, how could David have gotten to Lithuania?"

"That part I don't know," Elliott said. "But yes, we did fly the bombing mission against Kavaznya. Patrick; David; my deputy, John Ormack; and some civilian engineers that were under contract by HAWC—Angelina Pereira and Wendy Tork."

"Pereira? Tork? Christ, those are the biggest names in electrical engineering in the country," White said. "Campos was another one. Pereira's associate, I believe. He disappeared right around the same time."

"Campos was with us. He was killed before the mission began."

"My God . . ." White sighed. "Everyone thought there was this black hole that just sucked in the world's best scientists one night. Who would've guessed they were all in on the Kavaznya 'accident'?"

"The mission was a success," Elliott explained, turning and looking at the displays on the wall one by one. "Somehow . . . we made it out of there alive. We started the operation with damaged wings on our bomber. We faked a crash off the coast of Seattle to hide our whereabouts. We had to threaten an Air Force colonel with death to get an aerial refueling. The Soviet defenses were a nightmare come true—wave after wave of fighters, SAM sites popping up in front of us, terrain all around us. Then we were attacked by the laser itself. I still tremble at night, thinking about the energy they unleashed on us."

"What happened to David Luger?"

"We had no choice," Elliott explained. "We landed at a Soviet fighter base in Siberia."

"You *what . . . ?*"

Elliott motioned to another display. "Here's David's bastardized flight plan and fuel calculations—we launched with no flight plans, no proper charts, not even oxygen masks and helmets. The computers weren't working, blasted all to hell. But David was . . . is . . . the consummate navigator. Always be able to reconstruct the mission. Never trust the gadgets. Plan for the worst and hope for the best. He was hurt, real bad, but he dead-reckoned his way across eastern Russia and guided us into a Soviet fighter base. We found enough fuel to make it home. But we almost got caught."

Elliott told the rest of the story—about the fuel truck, about holding off the militia, and their eventual escape without Luger. When he was finished, he became very quiet.

White couldn't think of anything to say. It was the most incredible saga he had ever heard.

At last Elliott said, "Somehow he survived. They brainwashed him, took him to Lithuania, and made him work on the Soviet stealth-bomber project. Now we're going to get him out of there."

"You said Patrick and the Marines were going after him?"

"They're sending in a small Marine assault force," Elliott explained. "A Force Recon Team. Thirty-two soldiers."

"Standard-sized Marine special ops team," White said. "They're good, General. Very good. They can enter, search, and exit a three-story office building in less than seven minutes. They'd have no problem searching, demolishing, and capturing a single man on this installation, I can guarantee that."

"But against Commonwealth infantry? Against the Byelorussian Army? Against the KGB? Besides, I'm worried about the political side of this as well. Invading this facility will be politically unpopular, and I don't think the President is willing to risk any Marines to get Luger out. They think he's been turned. They're ready to have him assassinated, for God's sake. No, the White House will pull the Marines out if there's any chance of discovery. If that happens I want to be ready with our own assault team."

"Well, I've got sixty of the best Marines in the world assigned to MADCAP MAGICIAN," White said, "plus another twenty ex-Marines in the ISA task force group that I can recall for extended duty afloat. But I can't send my guys all the way to Vilnius without tanker support, and I won't do it without air and ground support. That's another reason I came to you."

"Follow me," Elliott said. He walked down the hallway, punched a code into yet another CypherLock security lock, and pushed the door open. White stepped inside a huge hangar, meticulously clean, with strong overhead floodlights bathing the entire space in an unearthly glow . . .

. . . and parked within that hangar was the most unusual aircraft White had ever seen. "What in God's name is it?" White breathed.

"Meet the Old Dog," Elliott said. "It's what started this whole friggin' mess—and it's what's going to end it."

The aircraft was enormous, but it was unlike any B-52 White had ever seen. It was completely black, low and menacing. White saw it from the tail end first. The rear empennage was a streamlined, graceful swept-back V-tail assembly—but it was immense, with each diagonal stabilizer a full twenty feet wide and easily fifty feet long. The muzzle of a large, unusual gun protruded out the back of the tail—not a Gatling gun, but some huge steerable cannon. The wings looked like standard B-52 wings, but there was something unusual about them.

"The wings . . . they don't sag," White said after finally realizing what was different. "They look the same size as a BUFF's wings, but they don't curve."

"The Old Dog has composite wings and radar-absorbent fibersteel skin," Elliott explained. "The wings are far stronger than the original wings, but twenty percent lighter. That gives the Old Dog much greater performance."

White noticed what was hanging under the wings, and he stepped over to the plane to examine it more closely. "Missiles? You put air-to-air missiles on a B-52 . . . ?"

"This is not really a B-52 anymore," Elliott said. "We call it a strategic flying battleship. It can escort other aircraft like a fighter, attack targets like a bomber, detect and destroy enemy defenses like a Wild Weasel, launch cruise missiles, conduct reconnaissances, even launch satellites into orbit. We're modifying four B-52s a year, converting them into battleships. I've got six of them here at HAWC."

"Six of them? You're kidding."

"That's not the best part," Elliott said proudly. They walked over to the open bomb bay, where Elliott had to have his I.D. checked once again by a security guard. They ducked under the open bomb-bay doors and peered inside. On a rotary drumlike launcher in the aft part of the bomb bay were several oblong objects resembling surfboards, with pointed tips and small fins on the back.

"The newest generation of 'smart' conventional cruise missiles," Elliott said. "They're called MARS missiles—Multi-target Anti-Armor Reattack System. MARS was developed after the Persian Gulf War as a force multiplier against large waves of armored vehicles. It uses a combination of high-speed computers, a stealth cruise missile, and sensor-fused weapons to autonomously detect, identify, and attack tanks and other large vehicles, or the navigator can reprogram the missile to attack several different areas.

"The cruise missile carries twenty-four cylinders in belly ejectors. The missile is programmed to cruise around in a target 'basket' about twenty by twenty miles, for as long as twenty minutes. Radars and infrared seekers in the cruise missile help it home in on columns of tanks or other large vehicles. When the missile flies over the vehicle, it drops the sensor-fuzed weapon cylinders, which float down by parachute. Each cylinder contains six copper disks in front of an explosive charge and mates with an infrared sensor. The infrared sensors lock on to nearby vehicles as the cylinder descends, then the cylinder automatically explodes about fifty feet above the vehicle's target. The copper disks turn into white-hot molten metal bullets that can penetrate six inches of steel or ceramic armor.

"The cruise missile is designed to loiter over a target area until all its antitank rounds are expended—it'll even reattack any vehicles that were hit but not seriously damaged—but it's smart enough to figure out if the vehicles it detects are 'live' targets or targets on fire or severely damaged. The Old Dog can carry up to twelve MARS missiles internally and twelve on the wing pylons. With only six MARS missiles, one Old Dog can attack armored vehicles over a fifteen-hundred-square-mile area—and the Old Dog can be miles away, attacking other targets."

"Absolutely incredible," White said, his eyes wide in wonder. "I knew there were unbelievable things going on at HAWC, but I never expected something like this!"

"I'm assembling my crews and doing the mission planning—secretly, of course," Elliott said sotto voce. "I think it's about time for HAWC and MADCAP MAGICIAN to join forces, don't you? I pray we won't be used, but I'm also not going to stand by and watch David Luger be killed in the name of political expediency."

"I'm with you, General," White said. "You know, I was so afraid you wouldn't believe me that I almost gave up hope." He paused, his smile dimming, and asked, "But if I'm being taken into custody by the Department of Justice, how are we going to do this?"

"As you pointed out yourself, Colonel," Elliott said with an amused smile, "this is HAWC. When I want to conduct an investigation into a possible security breach, I do it—everyone else, including the Department of Justice, either stands aside or cooperates fully. I've already had your ship impounded in Norway under full security, the aircraft and MISCO trailers returned, and your entire operations and support crew assembled.

They are being flown back here right this minute, every last one of them. We'll plan this mission, then we'll execute it if the Marines fail."

FISIKOUS INSTITUTE OF TECHNOLOGY, VILNIUS, LITHUANIA
28 MARCH, 0820 VILNIUS (0220 ET)

Ever since his brainwashing had been completed and his name was changed from his coded file designation, 41 dash Zulu, to Dr. Ivan Sergeiovich Ozerov, David Luger's life as a "permanent staff member in residence"—as much a laboratory animal as the rats, monkeys, and dogs at Fisikous—was pretty much the same every day. He was awakened at five-thirty A.M. and reported to the exercise room for calisthenics, fifteen minutes on a treadmill under a sunlamp—Luger rarely saw daylight except through the one window in his room—a fast checkup by a nurse or MSB medic, a shower, shave (using a nonelectric windup razor that was inspected for tampering every day), and breakfast. His performance in his exercises was carefully monitored and recorded, as was his caloric intake, energy level, even the amount of liquid and solid waste produced. His movements were monitored constantly by closed-circuit TV or by guards.

There was only one place where Luger was neither under direct guard nor monitored by cameras, and that was the dining facility in the Fisikous Research Center; since the dining hall was used all day, mostly by security guards, and since Luger usually ate alone or with his former KGB handlers, no security was thought necessary.

It was here that Mizschasis "Mike" Jonzcich decided to make his move.

Jonzcich was a member of the United States' Central Intelligence Agency, Intelligence Support Agency, assigned to what he thought had to be the most whacked-out but unusual intelligence-support unit in the free world: MADCAP MAGICIAN, led by Air Force Colonel Paul White. First-generation Lithuanian-American by heritage but true-blue American in politics and spirit, twenty-eight-year-old Jonzcich was recruited from Boston College to work for the CIA soon after graduation. Because Jonzcich and the rest of his family still spoke Lithuanian, the "old language," he went right to work for the Baltic desk, compiling data from covert and volunteer sources on almost all aspects of life in occupied Lithuania.

Sometime after that, Jonzcich was approached first by the Director of Central Intelligence General Services Recruiting Branch, then by the Deputy Director for Operations of the CIA himself, asking him to join the ISA and go undercover in his family's native land to spy on the Soviets occupying that country. Naturally Jonzcich agreed. He was sent to Lithuania and kept "inactive" by the ISA, working a variety of jobs and establishing his credentials, until four months ago when he was called and told to report to the Fisikous Research Institute for his first assignment.

That assignment was REDTAIL HAWK.

Dr. Ivan Sergeiovich Ozerov—the "Hawk"—was no stranger around the plant. Although the Hawk's face often looked grim and expressionless, he always seemed polite. He wasn't standoffish or full of attitude toward the Lithuanian workers, like most of the Russian-born scientists. He was usually left alone, mostly because the ex-KGB officer in charge of security at Fisikous, General Viktor Gabovich, was usually accompanying him. Everyone at the facility gave Gabovich a wide berth.

Jonzcich and the Hawk had never spoken—until today, when the Hawk was carrying his tray to his table and was "accidentally" bumped by Jonzcich as the worker emerged from a doorway right in the Hawk's path. The Hawk tripped sideways, hit a chair, and went down, his tray of food scattering in all directions.

Jonzcich was there in a flash to help him to his feet. A few soldiers nearby saw what had happened, and a few got to their feet to assist, but they saw that Ozerov was all right and that someone was there with a bucket and mop, so they returned to their breakfast.

"Are you all right, Doctor?" Jonzcich asked him in Russian.

"Goddamn it," Ozerov said in slightly accented English—thankfully, it was not too loud, or it might have attracted even more attention. Then, without hesitation, he slipped into Russian and said, "I guess I had better watch where I am walking."

"It's my fault. I just washed the floor—it might have been slippery," Jonzcich said, surprised that Ozerov could speak English so well. Jonzcich decided to test him. In English, he asked, "Are you hurt?"

"No," Ozerov replied in English. There was absolutely no change in his expression—it was as if he were thinking just as plainly in English as he was in Russian, without being able to register any surprise that he was using both languages. Ozerov continued in English: "The coffee will help."

Jonzcich began to clean up the spilled mess. No one came near them, but he knew that the Hawk was more closely guarded than that. He had very little time. Now was his chance. "Listen to me carefully," Jonzcich said in English. "You are Lieutenant David Luger, United States Air Force. Do you understand? *David Luger, United States Air Force.*"

Ozerov nearly dropped his breakfast tray again—Jonzcich almost gasped. The shock, the surprise, the recognition came immediately—and there was much more. A tiny spark ignited in the Hawk's brain.

"What did you say? Who *are* you?" Luger demanded in English.

"Don't speak to me," Jonzcich replied sotto voce. "Your handler will be back any minute. Listen to me carefully. Your life depends on your concentrating on my words. Remember them. This will save your life.

"You have been drugged. The man you know as Kaminski has been giving you poison. This will help you. Do not cry out or we are both dead."

At that, Jonzcich reached under the waist of his pants into a secret pocket and withdrew a tiny device that looked like a tiny piece of plastic, about the size of a .22-caliber bullet. He twisted off the round top of the device, exposing a needle about a half an inch long.

Luger's eyes widened when he saw the needle, but before he could react, Jonzcich stuck the needle into Luger's left forearm, jabbed it in all the way, and squeezed the bottom part of the miniature syringe.

In a flash Jonzcich put it back into his secret pocket, just as he had been rehearsing for the past several days. The tiny bit of coagulant in the antidote kept all but a tiny spot of blood from appearing, and Luger's shirtsleeve hid that.

"That was an antidote. It will take time to work. Remember what I am about to tell you, because it will save your life.

"You are Lieutenant David Luger, *not* Ivan Sergeiovich Ozerov. Lieutenant David Luger. You are an American military officer born in Amarillo, Texas, *not* a scientist from the Soviet Union. The American government knows you're here, and they're coming to get you. When you hear the name Ivan Sergeiovich Ozerov, you will think, 'God bless America.' *Remember that.* When you hear your false name, Ivan Sergeiovich Ozerov, you will think, *'God bless America.' "*

The Hawk put a hand up to his left temple as if in a great deal of pain—or confusion. His eyes were curious and puzzled. "But how can you . . . ?"

"Don't talk to me," Jonzcich whispered. "Tell me to clean this mess up, and go get more food. And prepare yourself. God bless America."

Was the Hawk going to do it? Jonzcich knew this was the turning point, the most critical step in his mission. Luger had been a prisoner here for years. He was so brainwashed, so compliant, that he might tell his handler, Gabovich, all about this. Jonzcich might not have an hour left to live if Luger got scared and blabbed about him to the KGB.

But Jonzcich had seen the spark, the recognition in Luger's eyes . . . Well, he had done what he had to do. Jonzcich's assignment in Fisikous was over.

Luger got to his feet and said in clear, strong Russian, "Please clean this mess up for me," then walked back to the serving line.

Mission accomplished.

FISIKOUS AIRCRAFT-DESIGN BUREAU SECURITY FACILITY
28 MARCH, 0935 VILNIUS **(0335** ET**)**

General Viktor Gabovich entered David Luger's room in the security building of the Institute. The upper floor of the building had been remodeled, transformed into a typical Soviet-style public-housing apartment floor, complete with cheap paneling, a "floor mother," or common housekeeper and caretaker for all residents of each floor, and a social area. As far as Luger knew, he lived in a standard Soviet apartment with other residents who were scientists like himself. In reality there were no other residents. The other apartments contained listening posts, control centers for monitoring Luger and controlling his activities, plus medical facilities for his brainwashing procedures.

Gabovich found Luger sitting in a chair beside the room's lone window, which was now closed by heavy metal shutters that allowed only small lines of light to penetrate. "Good morning, Ivan Sergeiovich," Gabovich said pleasantly. "How do you feel today, my friend?"

"The shutters are closed," Ozerov said. "They won't open."

Although Luger had a pull cord that opened and closed the shutters, those shutters were really controlled by a security officer in the command center; they were going to remain closed for the rest of the day until the demonstration at Denerokin was over. Luger would find a carefully measured amount of static and snow on his television set as well, to prevent him from getting news broadcasts about the demonstration, and his radio was "out for repairs" for two days. Almost everything in the room, from the amount of oxygen, to the sounds present, to the content of drugs in the bathroom tap water, could be controlled by Gabovich and his men. "The windows were being washed, I think, Comrade," Gabovich said. "They were barred from the outside until they are completed."

"I wanted to watch the demonstration."

Gabovich fought to control his surprise. "What demonstration are you talking about, Ivan?"

"I heard several hundred protesters are going to be outside today."

"Not that I know of, Comrade," Gabovich said sincerely, masking his aggravation at having to begin *another* investigation into security leaks in the "dormitory." His staff performed no-notice inspections every few weeks, but security always seemed to relax in spite of their precautions. "A new squad of trainees are going to be given their first orientation tour of the facility—perhaps that's what you are referring to," explained Gabovich.

Luger paused for a moment, confused. He wanted to believe Gabovich, since he liked and trusted him, but . . . his mind was cloudy.

Gabovich seized upon Luger's hesitation: "I brought you the first printouts of the new RCS computational models. Excellent work, Ivan. We found a few bugs, mostly formatting corrections. But I think—"

"My name is *not* Ivan," Luger interrupted. "Why . . . why do you keep calling me Ivan?" He began massaging his forehead, where a spot of pain was growing in his temple. "I'm not . . . I'm not Ivan Ozerov."

"Ivan, are you not feeling well? What are you talking about? Of course that's your name. Ivan Sergeiovich Ozerov. Born in Leningrad, educated in Moscow—"

Luger was shaking his head. "That's bullshit and you know it." The pain in Luger's temple increased. He squinted away the pain but it kept on coming. "I'm not David . . . no, Ivan. I'm not . . ."

Gabovich said, "You're getting confused, Ivan. I think you're working too hard. You really don't seem yourself when you're like this."

"I don't *feel* like myself," Luger said, exasperated by the pain, his confusion. "Why do I keep thinking I'm David?"

Gabovich thought quickly. "Ah, well . . . you are Ivan Ozerov, but a long time ago you were working as an operative for us in another country. It was a horrible assignment. Perhaps you're just remembering back to those awful days."

Now Luger was really confused.

But somewhere in the back of his head he heard a small voice say: *Mind-fucking. That's what they're doing to you, Dave, my man.*

Luger opened his eyes and Gabovich could see that the pain had subsided. Good. All those years of hypnotherapy, all those long nights of conditioning and drugs and beatings, were paying off. One of the things Gabovich and his men had learned during Luger's modification was that they could not prevent his subconscious from dredging up memories of the past. The doctors had not yet discovered a way to erase the subconscious. What they were able to do was form physiological associations with certain thoughts, so whenever those undesirable thoughts came back, they would cause severe, debilitating pain. When Luger was reminded that thinking proper thoughts ended the pain, the conscious mind was usually able to suppress the subconscious, unbidden thoughts and eliminate the pain—and Luger appeared to be doing that now.

It was not a perfect science by any means, as Gabovich had witnessed over the past few weeks. He remembered the couple of incidents in the design bureau as well as the reports he'd had on the test flight over Belarus.

Dreaming was the real test, the real torture. The pain would be at its height whenever Luger dreamed, and he would awaken several times a night screaming in agony. Luger had not had a proper night of REM sleep in almost four years, until he learned to control it. While some persons have severe REM-sleep nightmares only once or twice in their entire lives, Luger had had them every night for almost three years. It was a wonder, and certainly a tribute to Luger's excellent, strong, highly intelligent mind, that he hadn't at some point killed himself throughout those horrifying months.

But Luger was getting stronger, physically as well as mentally, and the hypnotherapy would soon have less and less effect. His eyes were narrow and tortured from the pain as the undesirable thoughts returned, but he was fighting it—and winning. "Ozerov . . . Ozerov is a Russian name," he said. "I'm not Russian." Suddenly, in English, he said, "I am not a *Russian . . .*"

"You are a Russian air-crew member and an aeronautical engineer who was offered a chance to work here at the Fisikous Institute," Gabovich said. "You were in a terrible accident test-flying a new bomber, but you have recovered fully. Don't you remember, Ivan? I am Petyr Kaminski, your doctor and your friend."

"You're a Russian . . ."

"I am a Polish immigrant who has come to the Fisikous Institute for the same reasons as you," Gabovich said. "We are here to help the Soviet Union become a better, more secure place." It was important not to lose patience with the subject—any show of anger or aggression might trigger a defensive mechanism and they would have to start over with his conditioning. Patience was important, but Gabovich's was wearing thin. "Please, Ivan Sergeiovich, snap out of it."

God bless America . . .

"My . . . name . . ." The stress was beginning to tear Luger in half. Gabovich was worried—Luger was fighting the pain better and better every time. But the fight was short-lived this time.

A few moments later Luger finally looked at Gabovich with clear, round eyes. Gabovich smiled and said, "Feeling better? Good. Would you care to look at the printouts, over coffee or cocoa perhaps?"

"No."

"I heard you had an accident in the dining hall this morning."

Ozerov looked up at Gabovich, then looked away again—and it was then that Gabovich realized that something *had* happened. There *was* a breach of security.

"It was nothing. I tripped over a chair."

"Are you hurt?"

"No."

"Did Mr. Biletris bother you?"

Luger looked up at Gabovich. "Who?"

"Biletris. The orderly who helped you clean up."

Luger looked a little panicked. *So,* Gabovich decided, *he was the one.*

Security will have to pick up the young Lithuanian bastard before he gets away.

"No. No," Luger insisted. "He was very helpful."

I'll bet he was. Gabovich cursed silently, careful not to show his annoyance. Besides, Luger could clam up in an instant if he thought his new contact was blown, and Luger still had a lot of work to do. "As you wish." Gabovich opened the bag he carried, presenting Luger with a small container of snacks. "At least nibble on a doughnut or an apple while I let you know what your new assignment will be."

Luger was compliant, but he did sneak a curious glance at Gabovich every now and then, which the ex-KGB officer returned with a reassuring smile. Within a few more minutes, Luger was beginning to work at his usual efficient, intelligent pace. He even began to eat the sedative-laced apples that had been laid out for him—Gabovich was careful to choose an apple with no stem on it, to distinguish them from the tainted ones.

Well, at least that little episode was over. Still, Gabovich worried. Unfortunately, Luger seemed to be at the beginning of the end of his usefulness as a designer and engineer. His periods of lucidity were becoming more frequent, and it was increasingly harder to adjust his thinking back to the Russian alias. And now there was a foreign contact in the facility, someone who had to be taken care of.

"Excuse me, Ivan. I need to use your bedroom phone. I hope it is working today. Someday they will fix this thing for good, eh, Ivan?"

God bless America . . .

Usually the phone was out of order—shut down by the guards secretly monitoring Luger—but Gabovich suspected it would work when he picked it up. He ordered Teresov to conduct a full search for Biletris, starting in Vilnius and encompassing all major transportation networks.

In the living room, Luger was about to take another bite of the apple when he noticed it had a peculiar smell. Something also didn't taste quite right. He was going to ignore it, but the smell wouldn't go away, so he went to the kitchen to toss it out. But just as he opened the door to the cupboard space under the sink where the garbage can was, his stomach churned. Before he realized what was happening or before he could stop it, he vomited into the trash can. His stomach knotted, expelling its entire contents, and the sudden spasms didn't stop until several long moments of dry heaves.

Because he was stooped down under the kitchen sink, the security cameras in Luger's apartment never saw him get sick.

Luger couldn't understand what was happening—he didn't have a fever, he didn't feel bad, and the apple had tasted okay at first. He sniffed it again.

"Are you all right, Ivan Sergeiovich?" Gabovich asked pleasantly, back in the living room.

"Ivan *who?*"

God bless America . . . David Luger . . .

And then, in an instant, other thoughts flooded in . . .

"If we start a firefight here . . ." Ormack said.

"We may not have any choice," McLanahan replied.

Maybe we are *going to fight it out, Luger thought.*

The memories came unbidden. He shut his eyes, trying to block them out. *What is going on?* he asked as a sting of pain shot through him. *Am I losing my mind? Going crazy?*

Fight it out with what? Half the crew was injured, the plane was shot to hell, they were surrounded by Soviet militiamen . . .

"He wants us to shut down," Luger heard Ormack say over the interphone. *"Patrick, we're running out of time . . ."*

"Ivan . . . ?"

You are First Lieutenant David Luger, United States Air Force . . . not Ozerov.

What did Dr. Kaminski call the orderly? Biletris? Luger tried to block the pain, to remember exactly what the orderly had said. *You are not Ozerov.* And something about being drugged . . .

Luger looked at the apple he'd just tossed away, now covered with his vomit. Things were coming together, beginning to make sense. The needle stick. The antidote. All for the *apple,* which Kaminski must have poisoned. Or *someone* must have poisoned. When the poison met up with the antidote in his body, he threw up.

Luger got to his feet and turned toward Gabovich. "Just throwing out that apple, Doctor Kaminski," he said in Russian. "Didn't agree with my stomach. Let's get back to work, shall we?"

Gabovich watched Luger closely. Except for a little weakness and a slightly distracted expression, he looked completely normal. Still . . . something in Gabovich's gut told him this one was going to take even closer monitoring than before.

If Gabovich had had the time, it might have been worth it to try an entirely new reprogramming sequence on Luger. Spend another few years breaking down every last remnant of the Luger persona and implanting a new one. Granted, nobody had ever survived two reprogramming sequences, but Luger had the strength to do it. At the very least it would be an interesting experiment. The problem was, there was no time. Luger would have to die soon, before the Fisikous-170 project was rolled out—only a few weeks away—because nobody knew Luger was here. The Commonwealth would not appreciate the Fisikous Research Institute using brainwashed Western engineers to design its military aircraft. By midspring the great Dr. Ivan Sergeiovich Ozerov would disappear just as mysteriously as he appeared.

THE MARINE CORPS SPECIAL OPERATIONS TRAINING GROUP FACILITY
CAMP LEJEUNE, NORTH CAROLINA
28 MARCH, 0835 ET (1435 VILNIUS)

"I am not impressed with you, sir," Marine Gunnery Sergeant Chris Wohl shouted through a megaphone. "You have lowered my opinion of the United States Air Force considerably, sir. If you are the best of the best, sir, my country is in serious jeopardy, sir."

Gunny Wohl was standing atop a tall log wall, watching as three men continued through "Confidence Course," the simplest level of obstacle courses at the Marine Special Operations Training Group (SOTG) school at Camp Lejeune. SOTG is the training course for all special-operations-capable Marines. Every six months a Marine Expeditionary Unit is selected for special operations training, which lasts six full months. Only two MEUs per year receive this training, and the competition to qualify is intense. The courses at SOTG concentrate on eighteen "unconventional-warfare" missions that the unit might be given, such as amphibious raids, reinforcement operations, security operations, counterintelligence, and MOUT, or Military Operations in Urban Terrain. At the end of training, the MEU receives the Special Operations Capable (SOC) designation and deploys either in the Pacific theater or in the Mediterranean Sea region.

The Confidence Course was not designed to be physically demanding, since the Marine officers who arrived at this school were already in top condition and would find this course pathetically easy, but it was designed to challenge a Marine both psychologically and physically. It did that by emphasizing one thing: moving at height, sometimes dozens of feet above ground, with nothing more than a four-foot-deep pool of water underneath. That pool of water didn't look like much of a safety net when you were twenty feet above it.

McLanahan, Briggs, and Ormack had just negotiated the "amphibious-landing" section of the course, designed to loosely simulate a World War II–style beach assault. Carrying an M-16A2 rifle with sixteen blank cartridges loaded in its magazine, the three Air Force officers had already climbed down a cargo net, waded across a fifty-yard mud-bottomed pool, run across fifty yards of sand with obstacles and up a sand hill, while keeping the rifle clean. All that was just to get to the main portion of the course, called the Jungle Gym.

Gunny Wohl was not impressed at all. He was bound by tradition and discipline to call these three officers "sir," but these men were sure not up to Marine Corps standards and he was going to let them know it. The way he looked at it, their softness challenged him and everyone in the Corps, and that was completely *unacceptable.*

This was the fourth time that Ormack, McLanahan, and Briggs had been on the course in the past week, but they were no better at it from their first encounter—the ropes seemed more slippery, the walls a bit higher, the mud a bit deeper. The fifth time was the qualifying test, and it was only the second time that the students would be armed and had to protect each other during their run against instructors who were gunning for them.

The Jungle Gym had seven obstacles that tested a student's upper-body strength and exposed any fear of heights or other fears. Vertigo or disorientation were not a problem with the two trained aviators, but upper-body strength was. Briggs could breeze through the course with ease, but even McLanahan, who was a semiserious weight lifter, found himself relying more and more on Briggs for help.

The course started with the "Dirty Name," a seventeen-foot-high wall of three logs spaced four to six feet apart. Next was the "Run, Jump, and Swing," where the student ran up a ramp, jumped onto a suspended rope, and swung across a mud-filled ditch. The "Inclining Wall" was the third obstacle, a sixteen-foot wall with a thick rope to climb, except the wall was tilted toward the climber, which put much more emphasis on arm strength than leg strength.

John Ormack was having the worst time of it. He got what he thought was a lot of exercise: racquetball three days a week, and the monthly Air Force fitness test, which was a two-mile run in jogging shoes, ten pull-ups, thirty sit-ups, and thirty push-ups. Ormack was slender, well-toned, and looked damned good in a uniform. But he had poor upper-body strength, limited long-range endurance, and his thin body carried no energy reserves. By the time he finished the Inclining Wall, Gunny Wohl noticed that he could barely hold on to the rope on the way down, and he dropped a good eight feet. He was not hurt, but Wohl thought he was seeing the beginning of the end of General John Ormack in this school.

McLanahan's muscular strength was far better, but he had no aerobic endurance and just couldn't seem to be able to catch his breath.

Hal Briggs, on the other hand, could have finished the course twice by the time they reached the fourth obstacle, the "Confidence Climb," a thirty-foot-tall ladder made of railroad ties. McLanahan had always thought that Briggs's impossibly thin body had no strength, but the man was like a finely tuned Italian race car—slim and racy, but loaded with power. "C'mon, you guys," Briggs huffed. "I can see the finish line. We're almost there."

"Fuck you," McLanahan gasped. "We're coming . . ."

"Don't talk," Briggs panted. Along with being out of shape, one other by-product of becoming a staff weenie, Briggs noticed, was that McLanahan didn't take coaching very well. Even when the Marine Corps drill instructor's mocking tone, which Briggs found comical, was making McLanahan angry—and making him take his mind off his job. "Save your breath. Concentrate on what you're doing, Patrick. You too, John. Breathe through your nose. Breathe deep. Flush the crud out of your lungs and muscles. Your strength will come back."

"I . . . don't . . . think so," Ormack gasped.

"You guys are in good shape," Briggs lied. "This course is easy. It's just Gunny Wohl getting you down."

"Fuck him too . . ."

"I said don't talk," Briggs ordered. "You got one thing to think about, and that's Dave. Think about *him*. He's not going to make it out alive unless you help him."

McLanahan and Ormack pumped their legs a little harder . . .

After a lot of sweat and strain, they reached the obstacle that was one of the worst ones on the course, appropriately named "The Tough One." After climbing a fifteen-foot rope, the three officers stepped across a platform of logs spaced about three feet apart, climbed up a pyramid-shaped structure of beams that rose another twenty feet in the air, and climbed down a rope all the way to the ground. Ormack made it up to the platform, but after stepping over the logs, found he barely had enough strength to guide himself up the pyramid. Briggs was right beside him, negotiating the pyramid like a chimpanzee, ready to help. But after a few long pauses, Ormack managed to get atop the pyramid by himself.

The toughest part was getting off the pyramid and onto the rope for the climb back down. "I can't do it, Hal," Ormack said. "Man, my arms would give out in a second . . ."

"C'mon, General, you've done this one before. Remember, the trick is using your feet. Wrap the rope around your leg, brace it against your foot, then press against it with your other foot." Ormack did as he was told, but the strength wasn't in his feet either. He slid down the rope at too high a speed and collapsed to the ground, weary but unhurt. McLanahan was also breathing heavily as he joined them a few moments later.

They struggled through the next obstacle, the "Reverse Ladder," which was a twelve-foot-high ladder of eight metal bars inclined toward the candidate and one that had to be climbed totally by arm power.

Finally, they made their way to the last obstacle.

It was a variation of the age-old "Slide for Life" obstacle that has been a part of Marine Corps boot camps for over a hundred years. The student had to climb a twenty-foot-high cargo net to a platform, straddle a thick rope leading from the top of the platform to the ground, and then begin to descend the rope headfirst, pulling himself down the rope. A four-foot pool of water was his only safety net. One-third the way down the rope, the student had to flip over until he was hanging down under the rope, and he continued down headfirst until he was to the two-thirds point. But in this variation, the student had to stop and perform a reversal—cross the arms and re-grip the rope, let go with the legs, hang down from the rope as the body swivels around, then swing the legs back up onto the rope and shimmy headfirst back up to the platform.

During the course, John Ormack had never finished this obstacle. "I'll go first," Briggs said. "John, watch me. You can do this."

"Let's go, girls!" Wohl said. "I'm not going to wait all damned day!"

"Patrick, you gotta keep guard," Briggs said. "Be ready in case we need you. Watch me, John. Rest up." Briggs swung onto the first rope and shimmied out to the first crossover point. He took his time, holding on to the rope a few moments longer on each crossover until Wohl would start yelling, then worked his way through the obstacle. McLanahan did the same, allowing Ormack the most time possible to rest up.

"Okay, John," McLanahan said as he pulled himself off the rope. "You can do it, man. Do it for Luger."

Ormack's adrenaline was pumping. He performed the first changeover easily, worked his way down the rope, and paused at the last changeover. He looked confident, bouncing a bit on the rope to get a good grip. He took a firm grip and let go of the rope with his legs. He did not fall this time. He swung his legs up, grasping the rope with his legs. They hooked over the rope securely, and he began working his way back up to the platform.

"Way to go, John!" McLanahan shouted. "You did it!"

Ormack gave out a victory cry himself—he had never been able to hang on long enough to get his legs back up.

They did not notice Gunnery Sergeant Wohl standing beside the safety pool—he wasn't yelling, he wasn't screaming, he wasn't doing anything. Calmly, he pulled a baseball-sized object from a pocket in his BDU pants, pulled a pin, and threw the object into the pool. Seconds later the safety pool erupted into a massive geyser of water as the small training grenade exploded. Ormack yelled, flipped off the rope, and thankfully did not land headfirst as he plummeted into the muddy water.

Wohl stepped into the safety pool and helped Ormack out, and they were both out of the water by the time Briggs and McLanahan made it down the cargo net and landed beside them. Wohl was ready for a chewing-out, even a push or shove—but what he wasn't ready for was a right cross by the usually quiet Colonel McLanahan.

The haymaker staggered Wohl, but he kept his feet, holding his chin to feel for any broken bones or loose teeth. "That's it, Wohl," McLanahan shouted. "You've crossed the line now, you motherfucking sonofabitch."

"Ormack doesn't belong in a Marine outfit," Wohl said. McLanahan wasn't coming after him again, but he was ready for a fight—his fists were raised at his sides, and he had dropped back into a wide, defensive stance. Wohl always figured there was a cauldron of emotion built up inside the powerful-looking man, but he never figured he'd actually let it out. "He failed the last obstacle. He's out."

"Like *hell . . . !*"

"As you were!" a voice shouted behind them.

The four men snapped to attention as Brigadier General Jeffrey Lydecker, the commanding general of the Combat Development Center, and Lieutenant General Bradley Elliott approached the group. Elliott returned their salutes, then stayed a few paces behind Lydecker.

"What happened here?" Lydecker asked. "We heard an explosion."

"Training, sir," Wohl replied immediately.

"Did you get permission to bring pyrotechnics out onto the course, Gunny?"

"Yes, sir," Wohl replied. He produced a sheet of paper. Lydecker examined it, then gave it to Elliott. Elliott shook his head and looked at McLanahan—this wasn't going to go down well for him at all. McLanahan would be lucky to hold on to his commission now. "Very well," Lydecker said. He paused, looked at McLanahan, then looked at the left side of Wohl's jaw. "What happened to your face, Gunny?"

"Slipped on one of the obstacles, sir."

"Bullshit, Gunny," Elliott interjected. "Tell us the—"

"Excuse me, sir, but I'll handle this," Lydecker interrupted. Elliott fell silent, scowling at McLanahan. "Tell us the truth, Marine. What happened to your face?"

"I slipped on one of the obstacles, sir," Wohl repeated. "I think it was on The Tough One."

"We *saw* the whole—" Elliott began.

"If one of my Marines says he slipped, sir, then he *slipped,"* Lydecker said. "Report on the results of the final obstacle course, Gunny."

"I'm sorry to say, General Ormack failed the final test," Wohl said. "He slipped off the rope when I applied the pyrotechnics on the final obstacle. Colonel McLanahan and Captain Briggs performed to minimum standards. I respectfully recommend that General Ormack be excluded from all further activities with any Marine Recon units."

Lydecker fell silent for a moment. Then he straightened his shoulders, looked at Elliott, then to Wohl. "Unfortunately, the timetable of the operation has been moved up. We have been directed to get these three officers ready to deploy with the 26th MEU immediately. There won't be any more training."

Wohl looked panic-stricken. "Excuse me, sir, but you *can't* send General Ormack . . . you can't send any of these men in the field with a Recon unit as they are *now*. They're a danger to themselves and anyone around them. Your mission won't have a chance."

"That will be all, Gunny. Have them report to my office ASAP. Send someone to pack their gear."

"Who's going to complete their training program? The Recon unit won't have time to—" Wohl stammered.

"You are going to complete their training, Gunny," General Lydecker replied. "We're sending you TDY with the 26th MEU. While en route, you will conduct training classes on unit tactics and mission essentials. Your orders are with my clerk. You'll depart in four hours. General Elliott will interface with you and the MEU operations staff. Close up shop and move out."

Wohl looked stunned, but recovered quickly enough to reply with a loud "Aye, aye, sir." Lydecker shook hands with General Elliott and departed, leaving an utterly speechless gunnery sergeant with the smiling three-star Air Force general.

"Well, let's get started, Gunnery Sergeant," Elliott said.

"Excuse me, sir, but I am going to make this appeal to you one last time," Wohl said. "I mean no disrespect—in fact, I have to give your men a lot of credit. They are raw, completely untrained in small-unit tactics, and very much out of shape, but they made it through by helping one another.

"I don't know what's going on, but I've gathered enough over the past few days to understand that you've got another officer trapped somewhere, and these men will accompany a Marine Force Recon team to go get him."

"You'll know when it's appropriate, Gunny."

"I expect I will, sir," Wohl replied, "now that you got the big man to make me nursemaid here. My point is, you could end up with the entire unit, myself, and all four of your officers dead if you allow these men to go on this mission—and I for one don't like it when *outsiders* tell me to stick my head in a bear trap without a fighting chance. Captain Briggs has the best chance of surviving—he can probably keep up with a Recon unit, although he knows nothing about their tactics. McLanahan is strong and he's driven to succeed, but it'll take more than just desire to complete a mission. General Ormack has no chance. None. And small units are only as effective as the least-capable member. If you have to extract an injured or immobilized person, it'll slow you down even more. I cannot in good conscience commit highly trained Marines to a dangerous mission deep within hostile territory, and then saddle them with three untrained, out-of-shape flyboys."

"You have no choice in the matter, Gunnery Sergeant."

"Sir," Wohl continued, ignoring Elliott's interjection, "if you're going someplace hot enough to send a Marine Recon unit, your boys will not keep up. They'll be left behind and probably die." Wohl saw Elliott's eyes flare at that remark, and he quickly lowered his voice. "I'm not trying to be a doomsayer or give you any interservice-superiority bullshit, sir; I'm giving you my professional opinion. Your mission is doomed to failure if these men are allowed to go."

Elliott let his words sink in for a moment. Then he said, "All right, Gunny, I've heard you out. Now you listen to me. I'll tell you what the objective is—since I've had you assigned to lead this operation, you might as well know."

Elliott told him about Luger and the Soviet stealth bomber, the main objectives of the mission. When he was finished he said, "Now, if you knew anything about experimental aircraft, Gunny, maybe I'd consider letting you and your men go in alone. But you don't. I'm told you're the best aggressive personnel-extraction man in the country, so you got the job. Maybe what I heard is wrong. Say the word and you're out."

Wohl looked at Elliott, then stepped closer to him, just close enough to Elliott's face to intimidate without threatening or assaulting him. He was half a head shorter than Elliott, but in his hard, chiseled face Elliott saw nothing but pure, white-hot fury simmering just beneath the surface.

"You can't bully me, sir," Wohl said in a low, growling voice. "You can try, but you will fail. Here at SOTG, my word is law. Wonder why Lydecker departed so fast, sir? If the General saw you talking to me like this, you'd be out of here faster than your two skinny legs could take you."

Wohl felt a surprisingly strong hand wrap around his left wrist. Before he could pull away or resist, Elliott had clamped hold of Wohl's wrist and had pulled his hand right onto Elliott's right thigh. A shiver ran unbidden down Wohl's spine as he heard the faint *clunk* and felt the rubbery coating over a piece of cold metal where Elliott's right leg should have been. Wohl snapped Elliott's grip away easily, but the message was received loud and clear: the three-star Air Force officer had an artificial leg. Wohl had seen the man wandering around the training facility now for two days, but he had never noticed it before.

"I got that fighting a war you'll never hear or read about, Sergeant," Elliott said. "Not Vietnam, not Grenada, not Libya, not DESERT STORM. Ormack and McLanahan were with me. They saved my life, but Luger saved all of our lives. I was one of the lucky ones: I only sacrificed a leg. Luger didn't just save me or the other members of my team—he saved all of us from a nuclear war. And I'll tell you right now, Marine: we're going to go in and bring him home with or without you.

"Now load up your gear, assemble your men, and be out on the flight line in four hours, or step aside and let someone else fly with us. Either way, we've got a job to do."

"Yes, *sir,*" Wohl said. "But I've got a reminder for you, sir: once your men are out in the field, they belong to me and the task force commander. What *we* say goes. I noticed that your name is not in the chain of command in this operation, not even as an observer, technical consultant, or as an interservice adviser—you will have no authority over me, just as their rank will mean nothing to the task force members. If you want any hope of bringing your men back alive, I would advise you not to interfere with Marine Corps professionals involved in a Marine Corps operation, *sir.*" Wohl saluted, spun on a heel, and jogged quickly away.

Elliott was contemplating chewing on Wohl a bit more, especially after that last tirade, but there wasn't time—and he knew Wohl was right. Elliott had arrived at Camp Lejeune completely unannounced, only to check up on his three officers. Lydecker had patiently extended the utmost courtesy and attention, just as he might any three-star visitor, but in the end Elliott's presence was just slowing down the works. The President's National Security Advisor, George Russell, said it best: "You're not in charge here and your services are not required."

I may be just in the way here at Camp Lejeune, Elliott reminded himself, *but at the HAWC,* my *word is law.* It was time he returned to Nevada and saw to his own plans for locating and rescuing David Luger.

OUTSIDE THE FISIKOUS INSTITUTE
5 APRIL, 1330 VILNIUS (0730 ET)

"Vakar Ignalina! . . ."
  "Rytoj Denerokin! . . ."
  "Vakar Ignalina! . . ."
  "Rytoj Denerokin! . . ."

The cry of "Yesterday Ignalina! Today Denerokin!" from a thousand throats echoed across the low hills and lush forests of southeastern Lithuania. The rallying cry—a reference to Ignalina, Lithuania's Soviet-built, Chernobyl-like nuclear power plant closed the previous year by popular referendum because of its repeated leaks and safety hazards—was not one of anger or frenzied retribution, but of controlled, sincere emotion. The people of Vilnius did not want to storm Denerokin, they wanted the powers-that-be to hear their concerns. That distinction was coming through loud and clear.

An hour into the demonstration and General Dominikas Palcikas was pleased with how things were working out. He had a line of spit-and-shine soldiers of the Iron Wolf Brigade, standing proudly at parade rest, arranged a dozen meters away from the massive concrete-and-steel fence of the Denerokin Nuclear Research Facility. The flag of the Lithuanian Republic fluttering in the breeze was positioned to the right of the entrance gate to the facility. To the left was the Iron Wolf Brigade's adopted standard, the Vytis—a knight mounted on a rearing charger, carrying an upraised sword and a shield with a double-barred cross on it.

Just as he had promised Anna, there was no overt show of force displayed by his men. Batons were under the soldiers' coats, dogs were in the buses—nearby, but out of sight—and baseball caps with ear protectors were worn instead of riot helmets. No tear gas, no guns.

Anna, who was standing with General Palcikas, was clearly impressed, and had told him so several times.

And Palcikas was becoming increasingly impressed with Anna. Ever since the day he'd met her on her father's farm, he had taken a liking to her. True, they saw so many things differently, but his respect, even admiration, for her was growing. As was his fondness toward her.

A huge crowd of about three thousand protesters moved in waves and surged across the street from the Denerokin gate. Near the gate, a small handful of them, no more than a hundred, were standing a few meters in front of Palcikas' soldiers on the other side of a small barrier of yellow-and-red sawhorses. The protesters were loudly singing the hymn *"Nebeuztvenski upes begimo"* (Rebirth of a Nation), a song which was becoming the Lithuanian's version of "We Shall Overcome."

Occasionally a woman or child would come forward and present a bunch of flowers to one of the soldiers, who gracefully accepted it, went to the steel fence, and laid the flowers at the foot of one of the massive concrete buttresses supporting it. A moment ago a woman had given a soldier some flowers . . . and a kiss. "You said nothing about that little display, Miss Kulikauskas," Palcikas said, trying not to smile.

"Purely spontaneous, I assure you, General," she replied. "It wasn't planned."

"We don't need spontaneity this afternoon. We need control," Palcikas said.

"It was harmless, General."

"First flowers, then a kiss; now some in the crowd want the woman to bring that poster to lay in front of the fence," Palcikas retorted. "What will it be next? A bucket of sewage? A barrel of burning oil?"

"You don't need to exaggerate, General," Kulikauskas interrupted. She raised a walkie-talkie to her lips. "Algimantas? Anna here. Tell Liana not to bring anything else to the police line. Pass the word to all section leaders—no one else approaches the police line." She paused, glanced at Palcikas resignedly, then added, "This is from me, not the General."

"Thank you," Palcikas said. "The fewer surprises for my men, the better."

"I agree," said Anna. "But everyone needs a kiss now and then."

Palcikas acknowledged her with a smile, and she returned his with a dazzling one of her own and a twinkle in her eye.

They were on a reviewing stand about two hundred meters from the outer gate of Denerokin, in the parking lot belonging to the rail terminal across the street from the Fisikous facility, accompanied by about two dozen individuals including the Vice President of the Lithuanian Republic, Vladas Daumantas; the chairman of Sajudis, the chief political party in Lithuania; and several local officials. Also on the podium were a few Polish and English Secret Service agents, ready to take their position when their respective dignitaries arrived. The guest of honor was an American senator, Charles Vertunin, from the state of Illinois, a first-generation American from a Lithuanian immigrant family and a strong supporter of increased trade and relations with all the Baltic states. Surrounding the podium was a throng of several thousand, all waiting to hear the distinguished guests speak.

Palcikas turned to Kulikauskas. "So. I understand you are going to get yourself arrested this morning. Do you think it's wise, Anna, for the event organizer to get arrested? Doesn't that send the wrong message to your members?"

"This time it's more of a protocol arrangement," Anna said, "because Senator Charles Vertunin, the senator from America, is going to get arrested too."

"What?" Palcikas gasped, whirling to face her. "The American is getting arrested as well? I wasn't told this."

"It was his idea," Kulikauskas said. "Don't worry—it's been cleared through the State Department and the Senator's office. You don't have to do anything special for him."

"Miss Kulikauskas, this is not a joke," Palcikas said, pulling Anna away from the others a bit. "We all know this is just a protest for the TV cameras. It was your idea to stage the arrests, and I agreed because what I want more than anything right now is *no surprises*. I get control, and you get your publicity. Now you tell me an American senator is going to be arrested? Were you trying to see how embarrassed I could get?"

"General, you can do to him whatever you were going to do to us . . . or me," Kulikauskas said.

Palcikas had left the platform to alert his squad leaders and was walking just behind the row of soldiers, heading toward the front gate, when Major Kolginov ran up to him. "Alexei, we have a small change to the program," Palcikas said.

"I'll say we do, Dominikas," Kolginov said. "I just got a report from the border patrol post at Salunianiai." Salunianiai was the largest border-patrol post in Lithuania, situated on the border between Lithuania and Byelorussia. "Four attack helicopters were seen heading west."

"What?" Palcikas exploded.

"Not only that," Kolginov continued, "the helicopters have made contact with MSB security forces inside Fisikous. The attack choppers were on a routine training mission over Byelorussian airspace when someone from inside Fisikous reported that armed intruders were storming the facility. The helicopters copied a distress message and are responding."

"Who made the distress call from Fisikous?"

"The report I got said it was Colonel Kortyshkov," Kolginov replied. "He said that Gabovich was hurt in the exchange."

"Kortyshkov must be insane!" Palcikas thundered. "He'll start a riot out here—and we've got an American politician that wants to get arrested."

"You're kidding."

"No, I'm not. Alert the squad leaders. Tell them quickly but carefully, and I mean *carefully,* move the crowd out *away* from the fence. Across the road at least, and preferably into the railyard parking lot. I'll get back to Kulikauskas and tell her about this. She has a pretty good radio net set up with her organizers."

The crowds had gotten thicker and more restless as Palcikas made his way back to the platform, but by that time the speeches were over and the foreign dignitaries had made their way from the podium and down onto the road leading to Denerokin's front gate.

Anna Kulikauskas, accompanying the American senator, noticed Palcikas scuffle with the Secret Service agents, excused herself from Vertunin, and trotted over to Palcikas. "What are you doing, General? We agreed that you were not to be here when the arrests are made."

"I came to warn you," Palcikas said.

"What about?"

"Someone from inside Fisikous made a distress call," Palcikas explained.

The ambassadors and the American senator continued to greet well-wishers, walking briskly toward the Denerokin gate, waving at the OMON security guards inside the facility. They did not notice that the guards had unslung their weapons and were now holding them.

"Anna, someone inside said armed intruders were storming the facility, which is ludicrous. But four attack helicopters are on their way."

"Attack helicopters? From Lithuania?"

"No! I don't know who they're from—the Commonwealth, or from Byelorussia. Either way, we've got to clear this crowd away from the gate before—"

But it was too late.

Anna turned and looked out over the crowd as a deep, rhythmic *whapwhapwhapwhapwhap* of rotor blades could be heard.

Palcikas did not have to look to tell what it was: a formation of four Mil-24P attack helicopters. Each aircraft looked like a huge, deadly bird of prey. Each had two fixed wings on the sides just aft of the engine pods, where rocket pods and fuel tanks were mounted. There were two 30-millimeter cannons on the starboard side of the nose. They were among the deadliest ground-attack helicopters in the inventory—and they wore Byelorussian flags on their fuselages.

Anna turned back toward Palcikas, horror slowly giving way to fury. "What in hell are those things doing here, Palcikas?" she cried over the growing noise of both the choppers and the crowd. "We agreed no show of force, no guns, no intimidation. Those things . . . my God, they're carrying *bombs!*"

"I was trying to warn you," Palcikas shouted over the din. "I knew nothing about those choppers! I only heard about it—"

"Order them out! This is a peaceful demonstration."

"I have no control over them!" Palcikas shouted. "General Voshchanka and Colonel Kortyshkov of OMON control those helicopters."

"I don't care *who* controls them. I want you to order those helicopters to leave this area!" Kulikauskas shouted. "This is outrageous! If a riot breaks out, with all these dignitaries here, it will be *your fault!*" Kulikauskas made a hurried apology to Senator Vertunin, then keyed her microphone and asked all the protesters to move away from the fence and sit down.

As the thunder of the choppers intensified, Palcikas began to hear another strange sound—singing! The protesters had sat down and were beginning to sing "Rebirth of a Nation." A few in the crowd actually began waving to the pilots and gunners who could be seen peering out the Plexiglas canopies and standing at the open doors of their attack helicopters.

"General . . . look!"

Palcikas followed Kolginov's warning shout and his heart skipped a beat. Senator Charles Vertunin and a group of about fifty protesters and security agents were continuing up the road toward the Denerokin gate.

At the same time, Palcikas could see OMON troops rushing toward the gate on the other side, weapons at the ready.

"Move out! Move out!" the loudspeaker blared.

Heavily armed troops were rushing out of the security headquarters building, rifles and tear-gas launchers at the ready. They carried steel batons, and the dogs on their leashes were in full view and ready to attack.

Colonel Nikita Ivanovich Kortyshkov of the MSB was at the microphone, shouting orders to his forces from atop the glass-walled security control tower that rose above the main gate area. To the young officer who had never commanded a combat unit and had been in Lithuania only a few months, the sight of hundreds of people outside his gates had thrown him into a state of sheer panic. Their Lithuanian chanting sounded like angry, threatening cries of death. Every time a citizen approached Palcikas' line of soldiers, he expected the rest of the crowd to follow and storm the fence. That would be disastrous. Not that Fisikous was in any danger of being overrun, but losing control of the situation would not help Kortyshkov's career one bit.

General Gabovich wanted Kortyshkov to be firm, to take charge, and that's exactly what he was going to do. Making a full sweep of the perimeter and checking to see that the helicopters were moving into position, Kortyshkov got back on the radio and ordered, "I want that crowd moved away from the open area. Signal the helicopters to dust them. Out."

It was exhilarating to watch. The huge Mil-24 attack helicopters swooped down, hovering less than ten meters above the crowd sitting in front of the main gate. The dust and gravel in the perimeter open area flew first, the tiny stones becoming shotgun-like projectiles battering the protesters. Next went their banners and posters—Kortyshkov saw a few cardboard-and-wood signs whipping around the heads of the screaming protesters, flying through the air like magical axes before being tossed against the gate itself. The impact of those posters and signs against the gate set off the intrusion alarms, and Kortyshkov ordered the horn cut off in the security control tower.

Next to go flying were the people themselves. The blast first knocked them backwards and on top of each other; then, as they tried to rise, the rotor wash threw them off their feet and sent them hurtling into the air like scarecrows caught in a tornado. A few tried to crawl away, but as more helicopters joined in the fray, even those who tried to crawl away close to the ground were sucked into the air and sent tumbling across the gravel. Kortyshkov especially delighted in seeing Palcikas' men being tossed around as they, too, were caught in the rotor wash—that will teach them, Kortyshkov thought, to not wear their protective riot gear. Without face guards, they were as blind and as helpless as the protesters.

Kortyshkov then reached for a walkie-talkie clipped onto his belt and spoke just one word: "Engage." He then put the transceiver back on his belt and watched.

Somewhere in the crowd, several Byelorussian soldiers, disguised as Lithuanian Self-Defense Force soldiers or Lithuanian policemen, withdrew American-made M-79 grenade launchers from hiding places, raised the guns toward the Denerokin security gate, and fired. One grenade was deliberately aimed at one of the hovering attack helicopters so that it would hit the rotor disk. The ten grenades launched at the MSB troops guarding Denerokin were American-made Mk-23 gas grenades, dispersing a mild blister agent. The prevailing winds and the rotors of the attack helicopters would spread the gas away from the MSB troops inside Denerokin and out over the crowd. The guards inside Denerokin put on gas masks as soon as they saw the white propellant arcs heading inbound, and all the Black Beret troops inside the compound were protected when the gas grenades hit.

"Gas!" someone cried out.

Kortyshkov picked up the command-wide radio microphone. "All units, all units, full-assault response, full-assault response. Open fire."

Confusion and shock grabbed the crowd as shots rang out. The one gas grenade that hit the Mil-24's rotor disk made a big, spectacular white cloud over the crowd, and blister-agent droplets rained down on the helpless crowd. Although the gas was not debilitating and dispersed rapidly, its effect was worse than tear gas as the agent was inhaled and caused instant blistering of the trachea and bronchia. The four Mil-24s climbed to a safe altitude, joined, then started an attack run on the crowd.

Palcikas had rejoined Kolginov at the security communications truck near the front gate when he heard the horrifying sound of an AK-74 assault rifle on full automatic.

Just fifty meters away, a line of dust geysers sprouted out of the asphalt and grit around the compound perimeter, finally intersecting paths with the line of distinguished visitors and protesters in front of the main gate. Their bodies exploded in chunks of bloody gore as high-velocity 7.62-millimeter shells found their targets.

"Cease fire!" Palcikas shouted, ducking for cover behind the truck, issuing orders even before realizing that it could not be his own men doing the shooting. He peered around the truck's bumper and, to his horror, saw more and more troops inside the Fisikous compound shooting into the crowd. "Cease fire, *damn you!"* Palcikas shouted above the gunfire. "Those civilians are unarmed!"

A few soldiers paused, looking at Palcikas and considering whether or not to obey his orders—after all, he *was* a general—but they quickly remembered who their real superior officer was, and continued firing through the fence into the screaming crowd outside. Palcikas had to duck back down behind his communications truck as an errant bullet whizzed by his head.

Then Palcikas realized that his own troops were taking hits—from Kortyshkov's troops inside the compound! Stationed between the shooters and the crowd and barely visible in the confusion and swirling dust, the OMON troopers were shooting Lithuanian troops in order to clear a fire lane for themselves. Palcikas saw one OMON trooper with his AK-74 on full automatic, sweeping his muzzle in a short arc near four Lithuanian soldiers who were lying flat on their stomachs.

Palcikas had no choice: he pulled his 9-millimeter Makarov automatic pistol from his holster and fired, aiming at a spot well above the man's head but close enough for him to feel the rounds whizzing near him and duck for cover. The bastard dropped to the ground, tried to reload, fumbled the magazine, and chose to simply lie down on the ground and cover his ears with his hands.

The noise swirling around him finally began to subside, and Palcikas took advantage of the relief to clear his head—before realizing that the reason the noise had subsided was that the Mil-24s had moved out of position. All four of them had suddenly wheeled away and flown to the south. Against the bright April sun, it was hard to see what the big choppers were doing.

But Palcikas soon found out.

The choppers had turned, formed up in a V-attack formation, and were coming in fast over the crowd. From about five hundred meters away they suddenly let loose with a volley of 30-millimeter cannon fire from underwing gun pods and nose cannons. The attack pass chopped a one-hundred-meter-wide bloody trail of destruction and death across the mass of protesters. The lead helicopter fired several rounds from the UV-32-57 rocket pod, barely missing the distinguished-visitors' platform, but the platform was set instantly ablaze, and VIPs and security agents were being tossed around like dolls from the force of the explosions. The chopper's target was the crowd nearest the fence, not the platform, and the huge 30-millimeter cannons were the preferred weapons. The big shells, huge steel sausage-sized bullets weighing as much as a can of soup, killed with utter devastation.

Kortyshkov watched with fascination as the Mil-24s turned away into the sun, then wheeled and dove out of the sun on their deadly run. The devastation was incredible—from relatively long range, protesters were being hit with uncanny accuracy, being lifted off their feet by the force of the heavy 30-millimeter shells' impact before being tossed, quite dead and most completely dismembered, onto the ground. It was the most exhilarating sight he had ever seen in his life.

But then Kortyshkov saw the Lithuanian peasant Palcikas, firing a pistol *toward* the compound! Unbelievable! He raced over to another window and saw one of his OMON troopers drop to the ground. There was no doubt in his mind that he had been Palcikas' target. Palcikas was shooting at the OMON soldiers!

Sporadic gunfire still erupted from somewhere inside the compound, and the sound of the helicopters' rotors was so loud as they passed overhead that Palcikas wasn't sure if the pilots had heard his orders—but a few seconds later the helicopters wheeled to the west, took spacing, and set up a protective formation among themselves as one by one they lined up for landing inside the Denerokin compound. The attack had lasted less than thirty seconds, but Palcikas could see dozens of men, women, and children lying dead on the ground outside the compound.

No, not just dead—obliterated.

Palcikas and Kolginov were numb. Both had had experience in Afghanistan, fighting guerrilla attacks across the border during the conflict, and both had seen the aftermath of a Mil-24 attack. But to have it happen right in front of your eyes—bodies shredded into hamburger not fifty meters away—it was too horrible for words.

Palcikas grabbed the radio microphone, keyed in the Commonwealth's aviation-command channel, and screamed in Russian: "All aviation units near Fisikous, this is General Palcikas. Disengage immediately! No hostile forces outside the security compound! Unarmed civilians only! *Disengage!*"

Kortyshkov couldn't believe the balls Palcikas had as he heard Palcikas on the aviation-command radio net, ordering the helicopters to break off the attack. After identifying himself as a general, and after receiving no threatening return fire, the pilots had no choice but to comply. "You bastard!" Kortyshkov cursed. "You cowardly bastard." Pushing past a sentry, Kortyshkov picked up his AK-74 from its rack near the door and stepped out onto the catwalk surrounding the outside of the security control tower.

Palcikas had returned to cover behind his communications truck outside the front gate, so Kortyshkov didn't have a clear shot. Leaning over the catwalk railing, he shouted to his troopers, "Sergeant! Take two squads, arrest the protest leaders and General Palcikas! On the double!" Thirty Black Berets quickly converged on the OMON master sergeant, received their orders, and moved toward the front gate in two single files.

The devastation was horrifying, and Palcikas and Kolginov could do nothing else but stand in sheer disbelief at the piles of corpses all around them—women, children, old people, and their own Lithuanian Self-Defense Force troops, cut down like wheat under a combine. Every groan, every scream of pain, every spasm from that horrible mess tore at Palcikas' heart like a razor—and it opened something within him.

No Russians died here, Palcikas realized.

Only Lithuanians.

As it had been throughout Lithuania's one-thousand-year history, the people were worth nothing. Despite all of Palcikas' power and influence, he could do nothing to save them.

"Call Trakai," he murmured to Kolginov, forcing himself to take command. "Get ambulances, buses, trucks—anything that will hold litters. Alert the hospitals . . . Jesus . . ."

Through the screams and cries of the dying he heard a woman's voice cry out to him. He saw Anna Kulikauskas, her dress, hair, face, and hands covered with moist blood, half-walking, half-stumbling over to him. She was carrying the body of a child, a girl no more than twelve years old. The child's neck, face, and chest were horribly swollen and purple—the child had literally drowned in her own bodily fluids as she inhaled the deadly gas. Alexei Kolginov ran over and took the limp, bloody body out of her arms—Kulikauskas didn't have the strength to resist. "Palcikas . . . Palcikas, you bastard!" she cried out. "What did you do? What in God's name did you do . . . ?"

"Anna! Are you hurt?"

"No . . . I don't think so . . . Jesus, Palcikas, they're all dead! All of them—"

His eyes widened. "Not—"

"Yes, yes . . . the ambassadors, the American senator . . . they ran toward the front gate. The Black Beret soldiers were shooting at them. Then the helicopters . . . cut them down one by one . . ."

"Stay here, Anna. You'll be safe."

"What did you do?" she repeated, almost hysterical. "Why did you order those troops to open fire? Why did you order those helicopters to attack . . . ?"

"I didn't issue those orders! Those troops belong to OMON, not to Lithuania!"

"I saw the grenades when they were fired—they came from *your* soldiers!" Kulikauskas stumbled over to him, grabbing his coat with trembling fingers. "You're a murderer, General. You've killed dozens of innocent people here today."

Kolginov had just set the child down and had motioned for a medic to help him when he glanced up at the security control tower over the front gate to the Denerokin compound. To his horror he saw Colonel Kortyshkov himself, aiming an AK-74 at Palcikas. "General! *Cover . . . !"*

Palcikas looked at Kolginov, then followed his gaze up to the security control tower and saw the AK-74 aimed at him. He grabbed Anna, tossing her behind the communications truck, just as he heard the automatic gunfire. He fell heavily against the truck and turned in time to see a spray of bullets pepper Kolginov from stomach to head. Holes as big as a man's fist were ripping open over Kolginov's body, and one round to the head sprayed the entire contents of Kolginov's skull all over.

"Kortyshkov, *you bastard!*" Palcikas screamed. He tried to rise, drawing his Makarov sidearm at the same time, but at that moment a dozen rifles surrounded him and his arms were pinned to the ground from behind.

"Lie, still, General," the squad leader ordered. "You are under arrest. Struggle and my men will kill you."

"You can't arrest me, you ass! I'm a Lithuanian Army officer! This is *my* country."

"You will do as you are ordered, General."

"No!"

It took most of them to subdue the big Lithuanian, but finally the Makarov automatic was pried from his fingers. A man knelt on Palcikas' neck, pressing his head into the asphalt, so the only thing Palcikas could see as his hands were secured behind his back was Kolginov's bloody, headless body lying a few meters away. He let out a loud, animal-like cry of fury and frustration. One of the Black Beret troopers plunged the butt end of his AK-74 against the back of Palcikas' head, throwing him into tortured darkness.

SMORGON ARMY AIR BASE
NORTHERN BYELORUSSIAN REPUBLIC (BELARUS)
7 APRIL, 1840 MINSK (1140 ET)

They looked very, very unimpressive, General Lieutenant Voshchanka thought. Perhaps he expected to see them glowing blue, like he saw in foreign science-fiction movies; at the very least he expected them to look like artillery shells or rocket warheads, with pointed noses, fuze-setting rings, fins, thrusters, and all that. Instead, the three objects displayed before him looked like car transmission units, with funnel-shaped fittings attached to cylindrical units with tubes and knobs attached. He wondered half-seriously if he should take them home and bolt them up under his car rather than to five-million-ruble missiles. "Those are the oddest-looking missile warheads I have ever seen," he told General Viktor Gabovich skeptically. "They don't look very lethal."

"Lethal?" Gabovich looked at the old Byelorussian general with complete surprise. Could the old fart really be this naive? "General, these are not only lethal, they're devastating. The Fisikous KR-11 warhead is the state of the art in battlefield thermonuclear warheads. It's a totally self-contained warhead, guidance unit, and fuzing mechanism in an ultracompact package. You do not need a separate guidance and fuzing system on your missiles, only a proper interface between the warhead and flight controls."

Like a butcher trying to sell a strange cut of meat, or a man trying to sell a Romanian car, Gabovich stepped over to one of the warheads, patted it, and explained, "The guidance unit is in the back end, which would be near the center of gravity of the missile. It is a ring-laser gyro, capable of almost instantaneous leveling and coarse true-north alignment—you can race the transporter-erector-launcher over hundreds of miles, bang it around for hours, and park the vehicle with the motor running on uneven ground, and the gyro will still align itself to true north within sixty seconds. It can withstand forty Gs and very austere conditions, and it's powered by chemical batteries that need no service or replacement. The inertial-measurement unit needs only two minutes of no motion for full fine alignment before launch."

He could tell Voshchanka was still unconvinced. *The old fool.* So he continued, "The warhead itself is in the center section. It is a ten-kiloton FFF, or fission-fusion-fission device, one of the smallest and most efficient of its kind, with a plutonium-239 implosion device surrounding a deuterium fuel cell core, all surrounded by a uranium-235 shell. The initial implosion of the plutonium creates a fission reaction which burns the deuterium fuel, creating a large fusion reaction which burns the uranium casing to produce a sustaining fission reaction to fuel the—"

Voshchanka waved a hand dismissively in front of Gabovich's face. "I don't understand half of what you're saying, Gabovich," he said irritably. "Can you put all that into terms an old tread-and-boot soldier can understand?"

"Of course, General," Gabovich said a tad condescendingly. Voshchanka was as stupid as some of those idiotic Lithuanians Voshchanka had gunned down at Fisikous the other day. "The result is an explosion nearly as large as the ones that destroyed Hiroshima and Nagasaki, in a package that you can practically pick up and carry with you. If you program a ground burst—the detonation on impact—the fireball would be approximately two kilometers in diameter, with absolute vaporization for all but deep, extremely hard targets. With a five-thousand-meter-altitude airburst, there would be absolute destruction of all aboveground things for a diameter of five kilometers."

"Then what about fallout?" Voshchanka grumbled.

"Fallout is not as great a problem as you might expect," Gabovich replied matter-of-factly. "The yield of these weapons is relatively low—these are not 'ground-digging' weapons—so the fallout is minimal for high airburst attacks. In a ground burst, the fallout of these weapons would spread for approximately twenty to thirty kilometers, depending on winds and weather."

"Thirty kilometers! Lithuania is only three hundred kilometers wide!"

"Well, of course any use of nuclear weapons must be judicious and carefully planned," Gabovich said easily. "In any case the radioactivity decays ninety-nine percent after only two days, making it safe to move about with protective clothing and respirators." He motioned to a truck parked nearby and added, "In that truck I've provided you with five hundred sets of full nuclear/chemical/biological protective suits and masks, all manufactured at Fisikous with raw materials from Lithuania. More is on the way, plus I'm sure you have stockpiles of older Soviet equipment. After two weeks, unprotected soldiers can move about for a limited time."

Voshchanka still looked skeptical. With a wry smile, Gabovich said, "General, for purely practical and political reasons, the facts about nuclear war have been one of the best-kept secrets of our time simply because if more generals knew the truth, more generals would use nuclear weapons. In fact, the proper application of low-yield nuclear devices can actually *spare* lives.

"Everyone believed that a nuclear detonation would create untold havoc all over the globe: melt the ice caps, encircle the globe with radioactive death, create a new Ice Age, and render the earth uninhabitable for thousands of years. That may have been true for a large-scale intercontinental exchange of thousands of the original atomic and hydrogen weapons that had yields of one, ten, or even one hundred megatons. Weapon development has moved from the realm of bigger bang for the buck to smaller, cleaner, more precise weapons. Why blow up the whole battlefield when you just want to take out a few tank companies?"

Voshchanka rubbed his chin, thinking . . .

"Look, with proper planning, modern weapons like the KR-11 can end a large-scale conflict long before it starts. And in today's world, governed by bleeding-heart liberals and environmentalists, nuclear retaliation following a limited nuclear release is practically unthinkable. You'll be able to effectively hold the entire world hostage with a small amount of weapons. You know why? Because you'll convince them that you have *more* weapons and that you will not hesitate to use them. Do that and no one will dare challenge you."

"You make it all sound so easy," Voshchanka said. "It is not easy. It is an awesome challenge." He reached out to touch one of the warheads, but could not make himself touch the shiny metal casing, as if tiny rads of radiation might be leaking from the casing.

Gabovich suppressed an amused smile. The old war-horse looked like some Neanderthal who was watching a light bulb for the first time. *How in hell does this man command soldiers on the modern-day battlefield if he's afraid to touch an inanimate object like that?* Gabovich finally motioned to the technicians that the warhead shrouds be replaced and the SCA-RAB missiles be reassembled for transport.

"You don't have to use them, you know," Gabovich finally said. "But having them around does make a difference—it's an important factor in your campaign planning." Gabovich paused, smiled mischievously, and added, "And for the man who instrumented that armed response at Denerokin the other day, I would dare say that the employment of small-yield nuclear weapons is a decision you can make. I must say, even I did not anticipate that you would use *four* Mil-24 attack helicopters on that crowd. It was a stroke of genius. You will be feared throughout Europe, I can guarantee you." Gabovich handed Voshchanka a large briefcase, moved in a bit closer so no one could overhear, and said, "You have greatly impressed my principals at Fisikous. They are prepared to back you all the way. As we agreed: one million kroner."

Voshchanka accepted the briefcase with a satisfied smile on his face. He had done it! he said to himself. He had not only convinced those Fisikous scientists to give him nuclear weapons and hard cash, but at the same time he had effectively silenced the Commonwealth of Independent States' Council of Ministers, engineered a series of sweeping military maneuvers throughout Belarus, Kalinin oblast, and Lithuania, and convinced his own government to back him. In just a few days he had moved from being a disgraced, unemployed general officer to military leader of one of the greatest military takeovers in modern time.

Now he had the power to hold off any large-scale response until he consolidated his gains and improved his strategic position. "Yes," Voshchanka nodded, clearly pleased with himself, "if we were to make others believe that Lithuanian and foreign terrorists were running rampant in Lithuania, my response had to be quick and massive. I would have sent an entire aviation company if I had had it available."

"Your response was perfect, General," Gabovich enthused, reminding himself not to lay the compliments on too thick or Voshchanka might think he was not being sincere. "Too little force would not have called attention to the incident; too much force would have directed attention to your real motivations. I congratulate you. You are well on your way to total victory. But let us return to these little marvels of technology, shall we?

"You must keep these missiles under tight control, guarded closely night and day, and you guard your command and control center even tighter. You will control them from your headquarters in Minsk, I assume."

"I have an alternate command center here in Smorgon that I shall use for this campaign," Voshchanka said, "and Smorgon is defended much better than the bases in Minsk. We shall install the command-and-control system for the missiles here."

"There should be a remote-command center," Gabovich suggested, "so that if your headquarters is attacked, you will not completely lose control of the weapons."

"There is no time to set up an alternate," Voshchanka said. "My operation to take Lithuania and Kalinin oblast starts immediately. Once Minsk is secure and the Commonwealth forces removed from there, I will set up an alternate command center."

"Very well, then. Security is paramount," Gabovich said. "There are a lot of missiles, a lot of warheads, but only one commander. You are now it." He withdrew a thick silver chain with two large flat rectangular keys on it. "The usual procedure is to use two-man control, and that is how I propose to install the command and control system in your headquarters. Your president has one key, you have the other, and both must—"

"No one will have the other key," Voshchanka said firmly. "I alone will control those weapons."

Gabovich's eyes were riveted on Voshchanka. "But . . . General, if you are captured or betrayed, you lose all control of the weapons."

"I will not be betrayed," Voshchanka said confidently, "and if I am captured or killed, then I don't care what happens to the weapons, do I?" He reached for the chain but Gabovich pulled the keys away from his grasp.

"One last thing before I give you the keys to the gates of hell, General," Gabovich said with an amused smile. "We have an agreement, a bargain. You will crush the Lithuanian and Byelorussian opposition and expel all Commonwealth forces from Lithuania and Kalinin oblast, but you will keep Fisikous, myself, and the persons I have designated free and undisturbed. And you agree to provide full security for Fisikous and its workers and guarantee access to food, creature comforts, services, and raw materials to us throughout your occupation. These three missile warheads and nine more within the next thirty days, along with technical assistance on the operation of the fifty Soviet missiles you have in hiding, are our payment for this protection. All other weapons we provide are to be purchased from us on a cash basis. Agreed?"

"I already said I would agree."

"Swear it," Gabovich said. "You believe in God and Jesus Christ and the saints and in heaven—swear to God and Jesus Christ that you will abide by our agreement."

It was Voshchanka's turn to smile. "You sound as if you don't trust me, General Gabovich."

"I do not."

"That is wise," Voshchanka said smugly. "I do not trust you either. I will test the systems you are installing in my headquarters, and after we learn how all this equipment operates, we will change its location and operation so that you cannot alter them."

"And we will devise safeguards to be sure that it will never happen," Gabovich said. "You will have control of the weapons to use against your enemies, but we will have control to be sure that they are not used against *us*. And the first Byelorussian soldier that enters Fisikous without permission will end our agreement, in which case my associates and I will turn all our attention and efforts, not to mention our weapons, against *you.*"

"Other men may swear to God and the saints, General, but I swear by something I *truly* believe in . . . this!" Voshchanka laughed aloud, then placed his right hand over his crotch. It was the ages-old symbol of *testificari,* in which a man seals his promise by nothing less than his manhood. "We will all need a great big handful of these to make it through this war, will we not?" He laughed again and slapped the former KGB officer on the back when he saw Gabovich's shocked expression— Gabovich wasn't about to shake Voshchanka's hand after *that.* "I swear to abide by our agreement, General Gabovich. Perhaps I cannot trust you, but as long as I understand that you are not to be trusted, I can deal with you. Our glorious offensive to reunite the empire of Belarus begins immediately."

THREE

The President of the United States squinted.

The glare of the television-camera lights beating down on him made the large-print cards lying on the podium in front of him hard to read. No TelePrompTers here, this was an "informal" press conference in the East Room of the White House. Usually these gatherings were held in the press room, but shortly after taking office the President privately told his aides that he found that room too hot, too claustrophobic. So they switched him to the much larger, gold-gilded East Room, where Ronald Reagan and Richard Nixon had held so many of their televised conferences. It was a beautifully appointed, elegant room that gave the new president, his staff felt, a more commanding presence.

And he certainly needed that presence today, facing his first major international conflict since taking office in January.

"The events last week in Vilnius, Lithuania, underscore this administration's great concern over the future of the Lithuanian Republic and all of the free Baltic states." Unlike his predecessor, who was an expert on international relations and policy, this studious-looking chief executive's expertise was in domestic affairs and the economy, which was why he got elected. Even after the previous administration had presided over the collapse of world Communism, the country's glaring domestic problems had created an upset in the elections.

But today he was going to have to give foreign affairs his best shot. He even wore a black ribbon pinned to the lapel closest to his heart in memory of Senator Charles Vertunin.

"The loss we have all suffered with the death of Senator Vertunin has shown once again that, even in this era of peace and sweeping embrace of democracy, we must be on guard to combat treachery and oppression.

"At this time, the Joint Military Command of the Commonwealth of

186

Independent States has imposed a temporary flight restriction for all flights, military or civil, through the Baltic states—Latvia, Lithuania, and Estonia—without prior permission," the President went on. Also, the Commonwealth Army appears to be active, especially in Lithuania, with thousands of troops moving across the countryside.

"So far, we see no reason for this obvious aggression in an independent republic, and it is a clear violation of the treaty between the Commonwealth and Lithuania. The reasons for these actions are ones we can only guess at, but they are horribly reminiscent of the actions by Saddam Hussein and the Iraqi Army in the weeks preceding the invasion of Kuwait. The Lithuanians and Estonians are free, law-abiding, peaceful citizens who embrace many of the same ideals as America.

"We want to make clear to all that the United States is prepared to act, with diplomatic means at first, with economic sanctions, and with force if necessary.

"In keeping with our policies in this region, I have ordered Secretary of State Danahall to draft and introduce a resolution in the United Nations Security Council today, calling for the immediate, full and unconditional withdrawal, under United Nations supervision, of all foreign military and paramilitary forces from the Baltic states. I understand the tenuous nature of the situation in the Baltic states in terms of the orderly transition of Commonwealth of Independent States–flag troops out of formerly occupied Lithuania, but this transition must be accomplished by peaceful, non-military means. The United States is ready to assist. We believe this can be handled peaceably."

Questions flew at the President from the press corps. Since he and his advisers had yet to put together a firm plan of action beyond what he'd just described, he really didn't want to take questions. But he knew they wouldn't let him walk out of the East Room without some answers. It was times like this when he wished the podium came equipped with an air bag, anything to survive a head-on with the press. More often than not, the press seemed like characters out of a Clint Eastwood movie—good, bad, and ugly. He winked at his press secretary. A silent signal to cut this off after five minutes.

"Mr. President," a reporter from CNN asked, "you say this can be handled peacefully, but Belarus is claiming the United States is planning a military operation in Lithuania in retaliation for the attack in Vilnius. Is that true?"

"Ah . . . I'm calling on the government of Belarus to conduct a full investigation into the attack at the Denerokin nuclear power plant," the President said, "and an investigation to find those responsible for the death of Senator Vertunin. So far all I've heard from Belarus is a lot of posturing and a lot of threats of retaliation. We have no plans to retaliate.

But we may be forced to act if the Commonwealth of Independent States does not cooperate with the investigation and insists on sealing off Lithuanian airspace to commercial carriers."

"Mr. President," an NBC reporter asked, "you appear to be comparing President Svetlov of Belarus to Saddam Hussein. Do you see Svetlov and Belarus as threats to peace in Europe? If so, what do you expect Svetlov to do and are you prepared to go to war to stop him?"

"Your question has a lot of 'what-ifs.' It's just too speculative," the President declared. "I repeat—this government and this nation reject any attempt by any foreign power to exert its influence over peace-loving, democratic people. I don't want to intervene, but no one is being given any other alternatives here."

"So you *do* plan on going to war with Belarus or the Commonwealth?" someone from ABC pressed.

The President was beginning to get a little perspiration on his forehead and upper lip, which he quickly dabbed with a handkerchief. *Jesus, this room is almost as hot as the press room.* He made a mental note to tell his press secretary to keep the goddamned air conditioning way up during these events.

Smiles spread across some of the older reporters' faces, ones who'd covered a lot of administrations. The East Room setting and the sweating President offered a curious déjà vu very much like the old Nixon days. Some things, a few of them mused, never change.

"I don't want war. No one does," the President finally said. "Uh, naturally we'll be sure to examine all the relevant options. War is certainly far, *far* down the list."

More questions flew at him from all directions. The President quickly scanned the faces and raised hands and pointed to a *Washington Post* reporter.

"Mr. President," the *Post* reporter asked, "what about President Svetlov's reported threat to use nuclear weapons to defend Belarus? Does Belarus have nuclear weapons, and if so, do you believe he'd launch an attack against American forces or against Lithuania?"

The President cleared his throat. "We received assurances in early 1992 that all nuclear weapons belonging to the former Soviet Union were being destroyed or returned to Russia. Now, if Belarus is saying they have nuclear weapons, then they've either obtained them from Russia or never returned the ones they originally had. In either case it's a clear violation of international agreements. I only hope that a threat to use these weapons is nothing more than rhetoric."

The President's press secretary stepped forward and put an end to the press conference, claiming an earlier commitment. The President fielded some questions as he backed out of the East Room, made carefully worded replies shaded to avoid details, and left a moment later.

He went directly to the Cabinet Room next door to the Oval Office, where his Cabinet officers from Defense and State, the Chairman of the Joint Chiefs, the National Security Advisor, the Director of Central Intelligence, the Vice President, and their aides had gathered. He motioned everyone to their seats after he took his.

"Excellent press conference, Mr. President," Secretary of State Dennis Danahall said loud enough to be heard by all in the rather small room. "Quick, to the point, clear and succinct."

"Thank you," the President replied, not believing a word of it. Danahall *would* kiss a little ass after his own had just been put on the griddle before millions of American viewers. To his Chief of Staff he said, "I'll need details on Vertunin's memorial service—Arlington, if I'm not mistaken. And he'll lie in state under the Rotunda, of course."

"Yes, Mr. President."

"Good." Coffee was served in silence. After the stewards left the room and the Secret Service men secured the doors, the President said, "All right, let's discuss the military option. I'll tell you right now I'm opposed to it. I still think force won't work in this situation, at least not as it stands now. But I want to find out about the Americans in Lithuania, what these Byelorussian forces are like, and exactly what military units we have in the area. You first, Ken. What have we got?"

Kenneth Mitchell, the Director of Central Intelligence, or DCI, looked at some notes in front of him. "Mr. President, we've got an estimated three hundred and twelve Americans known to be in Lithuania, plus an embassy staff of fifty. The diplomatic corps is at the embassy in Vilnius. All U.S. government employees are accounted for.

"We are trying to gather all the civilians together in the embassy grounds in Vilnius," Secretary of State Danahall added, "just to facilitate communications and make an extraction easier if it came down to it. But the Commonwealth's military commander, a Byelorussian general named Voshchanka, has warned all foreigners to stay in their registered homes or places of lodging—for their 'safety,' he says—and that's what we're recommending to them for now. It's disconcerting, but at least they're safe."

"Some of those Americans trapped in Vilnius are the cream of the American business crop," Vice President Kevin Martindale whispered to the President. "As in rich, as in political contributors and company presidents with lots of voters working for them."

The President nodded that he understood. Martindale was a young man in his early forties with very high, strong political ambitions himself, but wisely content to work for the real power-brokers until his own political net worth had grown. He was well familiar with the concept of policy influenced by politics, and so far it was working well. Martindale had become a bulldog in the White House and on the Hill, more than willing to engage in the back-room and cloakroom trench warfare to get the President's proposals heard—and put through—by Congress.

As if confirming the Vice President's comment, Mitchell continued: "There are a few Americans scattered throughout the country, but all just as influential. The CEO of Navistar International is in Kaunas, where he was about to cut the ribbon on a new joint-venture farm-machinery plant; half the legal staff of Pepsico is in Vilnius negotiating a bottling plant; Kellogg's is building a cereal plant north of Vilnius . . . the entire list is in the folder before you."

The President flipped through the blue-covered folder with the CIA shield on it, then he asked, "The Commonwealth government tells State that they're not in any danger as long as they don't travel? What's your assessment? Are they in any danger?"

"Not yet," Mitchell replied. "They're all in hotels or private residences, and so far all are in direct contact with the embassy. They haven't been approached or restricted in any way. Satellite imagery confirms that small numbers of Commonwealth troops have been on the move in Lithuania, but so far there's no indication that they're moving to reinforce or occupy the city."

"So are they in any danger from any sides?"

Mitchell shrugged, noncommittal. "There's no way to know, Mr. President. I think things may calm down after a short period."

"The Pentagon disagrees," Chairman of the Joint Chiefs Wilbur Curtis chimed in. "The presence of the Byelorussian attack helicopters over Lithuanian airspace, and the movements of Byelorussian troops—operating under the Commonwealth flag, but composed almost entirely of Byelorussian troops—is very worrisome. They're not large troop movements, at least not right now, but—"

Secretary of State Danahall shook his head. "General, there is a treaty in effect between the Commonwealth and Lithuania that allows the presence of Commonwealth-flag troops in Lithuania."

"I *know* that, Dennis," Curtis said. "But there have been repeated violations of the treaty, documented by reports from the Lithuanian Self-Defense Force to the United Nations, and the pattern is disturbing."

"What are you getting at, Wilbur?" asked the President.

General Curtis spread his hands and said, "I think there's a good possibility that Byelorussia, or secretly the Commonwealth, might try to make a grab for Lithuania."

"Shit," the President muttered. "Are you sure?"

"No, I'm not, sir," Curtis admitted. "But some observations Ken Mitchell briefed us on have me real worried."

The President turned to Director of Central Intelligence Mitchell, who nodded, saying, "General Curtis's theory has been borne out by a contact we have in Moscow, someone outside the Commonwealth but with strong connections. The contact is a former KGB bureau chief, a man named Boris Dvornikov. He is as wired as anyone from the old KGB can be. The possibility of a land grab *was* broached . . ."

"Why Byelorussia? I don't get it," the President said.

"There doesn't necessarily have to be a connection, sir," observed Curtis.

"But there is a very strong one," Mitchell said. "Historically, Byelorussia—what they call Belarus, which is closer to its historical name—was once united with Lithuania. Belarus was even the official language of the court of Lithuania for centuries. Together, Lithuania and Belarus were at one time one of the most powerful nations in Europe.

"You see, Belarus is landlocked and dependent on other countries—Russia, Lithuania, Latvia, Poland—for imports and exports. Belarus has always been dominated by Russia, and now they're dominated by a Commonwealth that caters more to Russia and the Ukraine, even though Minsk is the capital of the new Commonwealth. Plus, they have a *huge* military machine sitting around doing nothing—except whatever the Commonwealth orders them to do."

The President anxiously drummed his fingers on the table. "So this attack by Byelorussian attack helicopters was the prelude to a full-scale invasion?"

"I don't know, sir," Mitchell replied. "The Commonwealth is investigating the incident—they haven't said whether those chopper pilots were acting on orders of the Commonwealth or of Byelorussia. The problem is, they're the same—Voshchanka. He is the military commander of all Commonwealth forces in the area, and he is also commander of the Home Corps of the Byelorussian Army, based at Smorgon Army Air Base northwest of Minsk. Initial indications I've received from our bureau in Minsk say that Voshchanka is to be relieved of duty, so we should know more very soon."

"What about Voshchanka?" the President asked irritably. "Every time there's a problem in the region, he's at the heart of it. Is he another Saddam Hussein in the making?"

"Good analogy, Mr. President," Curtis said. "He's probably the most powerful man in the country next to President Svetlov. He's been responsible for the rapid buildup of the Byelorussian military since independence—and that makes him very popular in his country. He commands a total of about one hundred and fifty thousand troops and might hold the key to Byelorussia's nuclear arsenal as well."

"*Nuclear* arsenal?" The President sighed. "I thought that reporter was just baiting me. He really *does* have nuclear weapons? Those reports are true? Didn't they withdraw *them?*"

"We don't think so, sir," CIA chief Mitchell said. "The intercontinental birds, the SS-25 road-mobile and SS-24 rail-mobile missiles that were garrisoned at Brest were removed—that was verified—but no one could account for the nearly three hundred SS-21 Scarab missiles scattered throughout the Red Army units in Byelorussia. They were supposed to be removed as well, but we believe there are some units still in place."

"How do you know? Can you see them with satellites?" the President asked, waving his hand as if satellites were in the room.

"Sometimes . . . especially when the Byelorussians forget to check our overflight schedule. More often, they move the missiles when one of our satellites goes overhead," Mitchell said. "The SS-21 is a little smaller than the SS-1 SCUD missile, which it replaced in the Soviet Union, and it's road-mobile. Very easy to conceal. Fortunately they have to move them a lot for training and to align them on pre-surveyed launch points, so as long as we keep the launch points under watch we can spot 'em. Voshchanka probably has about forty or fifty at Smorgon, of which perhaps half are serviceable."

The President was thunderstruck. "I can't believe it," he said. "We've known about this and we haven't *done* anything to take those fucking weapons away from them? What are we doing, just sitting around all the time with our thumbs up our asses?"

"The SS-21 is not a threat to anyone except other Commonwealth countries or the Byelorussians themselves, sir," Mitchell said patiently. "And I'm sure the Commonwealth knows of the missiles' existence in Byelorussia. They simply choose not to acknowledge it."

"Well, they're a threat to *us* now, aren't they?" the President grumbled. "If the Byelorussians decide that our forces in Lithuania are a threat, they can lob a few into Vilnius pretty easily, couldn't they?"

Mitchell looked surprised at that question. "I think that's pretty unlikely, sir," he said. "It would not be a factor in a large-scale war."

"But in a small conflict, especially what this is shaping up to be," the President said, "it could be devastating. I need a plan of action on how we'll deal with those things. If Byelorussia shows any signs of trying to move against Lithuania, I want to be assured that those things will be neutralized. Is that *clear?*"

"I'll have a plan drawn up for presentation by tomorrow morning, sir," Curtis said, relieved that the President moved a lot faster than his wishy-washy predecessor.

"Good. Let's get back to the problem at hand—the Americans in Lithuania," the President said. "We've determined they're not in any immediate danger, and they're not being held against their will, at least not right this minute. Am I right?" A nod from Mitchell, Curtis, Russell, and the others. "All right. If they're not released or escorted safely to a neutral border, what do we do? Wilbur?"

"An airlift is still the best way," General Curtis replied. "If we can get permission to land a few airliners at Vilnius International, and if we can get assurances the planes can land safely, we can get everybody out in one day. If no commercial carrier wants to do it because of liability problems, we can contract with one of the air carriers under the Civil Reserve Air Fleet. The government would then assume the liability.

"Next choice is a military airlift," Curtis continued. "General Lockhart of our European Command has already briefed me on his proposal. Air Mobility Command can give him six C-130 transports from Rhein-Main Air Base near Frankfurt immediately. What he needs, though, are C-17 Jupiter transports—they don't require as much ground support and have better passenger and cargo capacity than the C-130. They also don't require the long runways and special handling of the C-141 Starlifters or C-5 Galaxys. With three C-17s and two crews per plane, Lockhart says he can pull all the Americans out of Lithuania in one day. I'd prefer the commercial carriers because the Commonwealth soldiers probably won't get as spooked by the sight of a civil jetliner flying overhead. But we can get him the C-17s from McGuire Air Force Base in New Jersey within twenty-four hours."

The short, squat, wide-bodied C-17 Jupiter transport plane, a smaller version of the C-5 Galaxy transport, was some of the best money the American taxpayers ever spent, and one of the best airplanes American industry ever developed. The Jupiter had so much power and was so well constructed that, literally, anything that fit inside it could be taken, and it could take off or land on any surface—sand, snow, dirt, broken pavement, unimproved runways—that could support its nearly half-a-million-pound gross weight. Every theater commander wanted to use them because they gave the commanders almost unheard-of speed and mobility. Theater commanders called the aircraft "Mighty Mouse" because the deceptively small-looking plane could transport an entire two-hundred-person flying squadron, with all its equipment and personnel, anywhere around the world in a matter of hours—even to places that didn't have runways or airports. It made the commanders look very good whenever they were tasked with a difficult assignment.

"Can you cut the C-17s loose from whatever they're scheduled to do to have them available for an evacuation?" the President asked.

"Yes, sir."

"Then do it. Get six of them so we have spares handy, and make sure double crews are available. When we get the word to go, I want the Americans pulled out in *less* than one day."

"You got it, sir," Curtis said, wishing he could light up a cigar, but knowing the President hated smoking.

"And what if they close down the airport?" pressed the President.

"In essence, the airport is already closed down—by orders of General

Voshchanka," Curtis said. "If negotiations fail to reopen it so we can evacuate our people, we look at forcible entry into the country to get them out."

The President shook his head, wishing he could escape all this. Instead, he listened to Curtis go on.

"We have four military operations to examine sir: an embassy reinforcement operation, an NEO, or non-combatant-evacuation operation, a security operation to open the airport for our aircraft, and possibly an emergency foreign intervention and defense operation.

"But there is one other event driving our recommendations for military action—the REDTAIL HAWK extraction mission."

"Oh, Christ. I forgot all about that, dammit," the President muttered. He remembered now that his National Security Advisor, George Russell, and General Curtis had briefed him on it shortly after Russell had approved the mission. He believed in giving people latitude, especially people like Russell, but now he wondered if this thing wasn't going to come back to haunt them. "When do they go in?" He looked at his watch, made a mental calculation. *Tomorrow* night, right?"

"Yes, sir," Curtis replied. "Conditions are very good for the extraction despite the increased alert status in the country. A pretty good spring storm that's brewing should ground all Soviet aircraft and reduce radar scanning range to minimum—the Special Forces teams on the ground will take out the transmission towers and transformers to the Soviet air-defense bases. Won't shut 'em down completely, but they'll disrupt things enough to let our troops slip in. We've got the Delta Force Silver team moving toward the research center, ready to do the same thing at the facility. The Special Forces units will be right behind them, softening up the area defenses for the assault team. The SEAL teams are taking out the radar sites along the coast."

The President's skepticism was growing. "I really think this one should be canceled, Wilbur, given the—"

"On the contrary, sir, not only should REDTAIL HAWK proceed, but it should be expanded to include the embassy-reinforcement mission," Curtis said.

"What are you driving at?" the President asked. "You want to use this terrible incident at Denerokin to help a covert spy mission? So we have *two* operations going at *once?* Jesus, the region's already explosive enough. You'd better rethink this one, Wilbur."

"The main objective is to move in swiftly and reinforce and secure the embassy," Curtis continued. "We have an advantage right now because we are in contact with the embassy and they know the whereabouts of ninety percent of the Americans in Lithuania. It's important to maintain that advantage."

"And at the same time, the plan to rescue Lieutenant Luger from the Fisikous Institute continues—except under the guise of the embassy reinforcement," National Security Advisor Russell said. "Sir, your main problem with REDTAIL HAWK from the beginning was the use of American troops in a non-hostile environment. Well, things have changed. Now we can cover our use of special-operations troops under the embassy-reinforcement operation."

The President was silent, feeling increasingly as if things were going to spin out of control. "Let's keep with the problem at hand, gentlemen, which is the Americans in Lithuania. Wilbur, continue with your briefing. Who do we have in place to spearhead this thing . . . ?" He paused, glancing at his Secretary of State, then added diplomatically, ". . . *if* we decide to go in."

"The main spearhead force involved is still the 26th Marine Expeditionary Unit, and they've been given the warning order to stand by—they only need the execution message, sent when you sign the executive order, to go into action," Curtis said. "That's about sixteen hundred Marines, four hundred Navy personnel, and six ships, including the Marines' newest amphibious-assault carrier, the *Wasp.* Two more MEUs, the 20th and 16th, would deploy from the U.S. East Coast upon receipt of a warning order. The recommendation from General Kundert of the Marine Corps is the same as before: we should issue the warning order for the entire Second Marine Expeditionary Brigade and put them on standby alert for deployment to their staging bases in Germany and Norway. This is because this Byelorussian general, Voshchanka, is warning us not to land U.S. military forces in the area."

"And no one should tell us what to do when the safety of our citizens abroad is concerned," Secretary of Defense Thomas Preston said. "This is not an internal affair or a civil war, Mr. President. This is an act of aggression against a neighboring country. This is Afghanistan all over again. This is another Kuwait."

Danahall looked at the National Security Advisor, George Russell. "The situation is close to defusing itself, George, and you know it," Danahall said. "If you send in troops, we destabilize the entire scenario. Now, we agreed it was best to announce only the U.N. draft resolution."

"And I agreed," Russell said. "And you agreed that we go ahead with alerting the 26th MEU. But we can't move nearly two thousand men and six warships without it going public. We need to start getting the American people behind us."

"The President hasn't made a commitment to starting a shooting war in Lithuania," Danahall said. "We shouldn't—"

Curtis interrupted, "And remember, there's REDTAIL HAWK."

The President turned to Curtis and Russell. "This may affect the status of your REDTAIL HAWK out there, gentlemen. I may have no choice but to cancel the mission."

"Lieutenant Luger is in danger, Mr. President," Curtis said firmly. "That much we know from the CIA and ISA contacts that have reported back to us. We have a team moving in, ready to snatch him. The mission has been executed—"

"You can cancel it at any time, General," Danahall said. "Don't try to make it seem as if the execution order is irreversible at this stage."

"That was not my intention, Dennis," Curtis said. "But timing is critical, and Lieutenant Luger is undoubtedly running out of time. We have to move."

"The Commonwealth, Byelorussian, and Black Beret armies are obviously alerted," Danahall said. "The extraction team won't risk going in now."

"On the contrary, Dennis, they've got the latest information on the attack and the latest info on the Byelorussian troops moving within Lithuania, and they're ready to go," Curtis said. "They've got the best intelligence data we've got, and they say it's a go."

"They'll get mowed down for sure."

"I and General Kundert disagree," Curtis said confidently. "The Marine Corps classifies the REDTAIL HAWK rescue mission as a high-risk but high-percentage operation. Until the Byelorussian forces move into Lithuania in greater numbers, their assessment still stands." He turned to the President, deciding to plead his case directly to the man once again. "Mr. President, you can't mean to abandon Lieutenant Luger, risk losing that brave airman, simply on the hope that if we do nothing then everything will be all right . . . ?"

"I think we should give the REDTAIL HAWK mission a try, Mr. President," Russell interjected. "Our boys won't get a better opportunity. They can complete their mission to retrieve Luger and then land in the embassy compound in Vilnius to make it look like they're reinforcing the Marines in the embassy—which they will do, of course."

"That won't stand up to scrutiny," Danahall insisted. "It takes time to move a Marine special-operations force into position to run an operation like this. Certainly the Russians can figure out our timetable. They'll know we didn't go in to support the embassy."

"It doesn't matter," Russell decided. "Lithuania is a sovereign country, and relations with us are good. We can go in anytime."

"This situation is special," Danahall said. "Lithuania may be an independent, but they're still under Commonwealth influence. Any action we take could be perceived by the Commonwealth as an act of aggression."

"Enough, enough," the President said. He fell silent for a moment, then said, "Look, I want the embassy protected—that's job number one.

But use that mission as a jumping-off point to continue REDTAIL HAWK. Get your man Luger out if you can, but the embassy reinforcement comes first. If your special ops guys get caught in the Fisikous Research Center, understand that I'll call it an unfortunate error on their part—they got lost, confused, made a mistake, got themselves killed. I'll take the heat, but I'm going to dump it right back on your Marines and your special ops troops."

"Yes, sir," Curtis acknowledged, silently breathing a sigh of relief.

The President continued. "Along with the near-term military response is what we should be thinking about in the longer term, especially in light of the Byelorussians' buildup and this nuclear arsenal. General Curtis has suggested the possibility of a land grab, and CIA concurs. What do we lose if this comes to pass? Why should we be worried about this? Dennis, what's your thoughts on this?"

"Lithuania is one of those countries that, because of its strategic position, its climate, its arable soil, and its cultural mixture, will always be subject to whichever neighbor is most powerful," Secretary of State Danahall replied. "It has seaports that do not freeze over, lots of fertile farmland, lots of potential wealth, a rich history, and strong, well-educated citizens. They also have a very strong national identity and a real desire to become independent, free, capitalistic, and democratic.

"The bottom line: we have an opportunity to help Lithuania grow. I'm not advocating that we occupy the country, but I think it would be in our best interests to help Lithuania resist occupation from outside forces counter to our own. Lithuania is democratic, they have a lot to offer us and the rest of Europe, and we can help them do it.

"There are other motivations for us as well: with the emergence of the European Community and the loss of American markets in unified Europe, Lithuania may become the first real trade toehold we can develop in Europe. The same holds true for the other former Soviet republics."

"This sounds like stuff we need to discuss later on," the President said. "But I gather you're going to tie this in to the present-day situation. What is it?"

Curtis said, "You're right, sir, this does tie in. We've received full overflight permission from President Kapocius of Lithuania, and his government seems pretty amenable to our military operations over there. They're being threatened by Byelorussia, and the Commonwealth seems to be dragging its collective feet on withdrawing troops. This might be the time to suggest full military assistance to Lithuania. We should request permission from Kapocius to send transports, fighters, attack helicopters, and antiaircraft-missile batteries to Vilnius, Kaunas, and Liepaja, the three main cities."

"Kapocius has already said he doesn't want foreign military aircraft near his civilian airfields except in an emergency," Secretary of State Danahall said. "We've got to respect that or we won't get any more cooperation from him."

But the President was intrigued. "What is it you're after, Wilbur?" the President asked.

"A trip wire, Mr. President," Curtis replied. "A way for the United States to get immediately involved in protecting Lithuania and the other Baltic states, and ensuring that our own interests are protected in the region in case the CIS or Byelorussia tries a quick strike into Lithuania.

"We'd set up a staged approach to sending military assistance and sweeten the pot with economic assistance," Curtis continued. "My staff's plan was to form first an evacuation center for Americans, then a relief center for Lithuanians, a civil-and-industrial-assistance center, and finally a military-training and cooperative-defense base, all at Vilnius International Airport. We'd use the Army's Third Brigade from Germany—their troops, armor, aircraft, and air-defense systems—along with transports from 21st Air Force. The presence of several thousand American troops will certainly deter anyone from further aggression in Lithuania, and of course the hard-currency investment in Lithuania won't hurt Kapocius or his government."

"This sounds bad, General," National Security Advisor Russell interjected. "It sounds like another Beirut 'peace-keeping' mission. These trip wire tactics never work—if a conflict breaks out, or if one side resorts to terrorism or fanaticism, our people get clobbered, and public opinion usually forces the Administration to pull forces *out,* not put more forces *in.* Soldiers die for no reason. I recommend against such a plan."

The President considered the suggestion momentarily; then, after no other comments were put forth, said, "Let's put that one on the back burner for now, Wilbur. It's a good idea, but I'm concerned about Kapocius. The man's really under the gun—he lost his vice president, several foreign diplomats are killed in his capital city, he's got foreign troops all over his country, he's got inflation, he's got shortages—and the last thing he'll want to hear is our plan for an occupation force. For the near-term, though, what else are we going to need?"

"Right now I think all we need is more reconnaissance assets up," Secretary of Defense Preston said. "General Curtis and I have discussed putting Special Forces troops on the ground trying to find those nuclear-capable Scarab missiles and destroy them if necessary—I think we should talk about moving that plan forward. We also talked about more recon planes over Lithuania—with overflight privileges granted, we can keep a pretty good eye on the Russians and the Byelorussians."

"What kind of recon planes?"

"Sir, we've got pretty good satellite imagery of Lithuania," Curtis said, "and we've got pictures of bases and large concentrations of troops, but not enough electronic-monitoring-and-analysis information and not enough near-real-time targeting-quality imagery, the kind of stuff we'll need to give to air crews and fire-control computers if we ever have to go out and blow them up. A constellation of small radar satellites, like the NIRTSat system, would be perfect. Also photo-and-electronic-reconnaissance aircraft like an RC-135 RIVET JOINT, TR-1, or TR-2 stealth recon plane. We have a briefing prepared for you whenever you'd like."

These days the President almost never haggled about sending out reconnaissance forces anywhere in the world. He had seen the value of constant, real-time intelligence during the Gulf War, and he had become a firm supporter of new state-of-the-art technologies in the field of intelligence-gathering. This was no exception: "Pencil in a briefing time on my calendar with Case, but consider your plan approved. Any other trouble so far?"

"Small problem with one of our Intelligence Support Agency units, sir," Russell interjected. "They're the ones that we sometimes call on to insert agents into a country when the normal military or CIA channels are being watched. One of the members of that unit, called MADCAP MAGICIAN, might have compromised himself. DoD is conducting an investigation."

"Then bust him hard," the Vice President chimed in emphatically. "Keep him incommunicado until this is over with. We don't need anyone scuttling these operations before they get started. Lives are at stake."

"The breach occurred at General Elliott's unit at Dreamland," Curtis said quickly. "So General Elliott is handling the investigation. If you want the doer scrambled, Mr. Vice President, Brad Elliott's your man."

The Vice President nodded in agreement. He and most of the Cabinet members present knew Elliott was one tough son of a bitch with security violators.

"I can brief you on the other Special Forces teams' progress and the support units at any time," added Curtis.

"Speaking of Elliott," the President said, "he's been very quiet lately. Has he been briefed on the progress of his people and the status of REDTAIL HAWK?"

"He's not on the list for update briefings, sir," Curtis said. He glanced at George Russell when he said that—it was Russell who decided that Elliott should be cut out of the information loop. "Do you want that directive modified?"

"Elliott can get the information on his own," Russell said irritably. "I'll bet you Elliott's just as informed as we are—isn't that right, General Curtis?"

Curtis did a slow burn. "His group designed the aircraft that'll fly the

Special Forces troops into Lithuania," Curtis said. "He also designed the satellite-reconnaissance and mission-analysis system sitting down in the Situation Room. He's got four of his top officers, including two men that saved his life, involved in a mission eight thousand miles from home. Now, apart from the fact that he and his unit could be of enormous assistance to us in case this situation blows up in our faces, Mr. Russell, I think the man deserves to be kept apprised of the status of this mission."

"Okay, okay," Russell said with resignation. "I didn't know you two were once joined at the hip. Put him on the damn Priority Two notification list."

"Let's get at it, then," the President said, thankful this meeting was over. "I can see already that this is going to be one hell of a night."

TRAKAI CASTLE CHAPEL, NEAR VILNIUS, LITHUANIA
12 APRIL, 1213 HOURS (0613 ET)

It was the first funeral of a Knight of the Iron Wolf in over two hundred years—and today, twenty-three Lithuania knights were being buried. In the center of the chapel in the main residence section of Trakai Castle, the coffins of the dead were draped with the red Grand Duke's battle flags, the Vytis, and surrounded by tall candles on gleaming gold antique candleholders. As senior officer, Major Kolginov's casket was at the head of the group, and it was his flag-draped coffin on which the Lithuanian Sword of State had been placed. Four fully armored knights stood guard, each with a long-handled ax in his hands. Slung over their shoulders and hidden, but within easy reach, they also carried AK-47 assault rifles. Tradition and ceremony were still observed in mourning the dead, but the army of Lithuania was on a war footing, even the honor guards.

Mass for the rest of the dead soldiers from the Denerokin massacre had been held earlier in the day, and the final Mass for the knights was scheduled for that evening, at midnight, as were all other rituals of knighthood. It was at the chapel, after the service for the other slain soldiers and citizens, that Anna Kulikauskas found General Dominikas Palcikas, kneeling in the first row of pews in the chapel. She genuflected when she reached the row, then stood silently and waited for Palcikas to look up at her. He was dressed not in his red cassock but in full black "midnight" battle-dress uniform, with a Makarov sidearm and full combat harness. He looked as though he were one minute from going into battle. An American-style helmet, a walkie-talkie, and a loaded AK-47 were lying on the pew beside him.

"Your guards let me in," she said. "They recognized me from the other night." No response. "I am very sorry for your loss, General."

"So why are you here? You dislike our 'perverse' rituals so much—well, this is just another one of them. Or have you come to prefer charges against me for causing the deaths of these men?"

"Please don't hate me, Dominikas," Anna said. "I was in shock out there. I was terrified. You had represented all that was bad, all that was distrustful, in Lithuania. My God, I saw that dead child lying on the ground like a sack of wet garbage . . . please forgive me, Dominikas. I forgot that I had learned to trust the military . . . to trust you."

He nodded, then turned to her and said, "I suspect you had something to do with the testimony before the Commonwealth Council of Ministers regarding the incident. I have you to thank for gathering those witnesses and testifying on my behalf."

"I tried to identify the soldiers that launched those grenades—I was sure they were Lithuanians," Anna said. "But after talking with other witnesses and examining photographs of all your men, we realized they were not. I was afraid of what they had done to you. I couldn't believe they were actually clubbing you and dragging you away—you, a Lithuanian citizen and our highest military officer, being dragged away by foreign troops like a road kill! I had to do something. We took our information to the Commonwealth Council of Ministers and demanded your release."

The Council of Ministers and the Inter-Republican Council for Security immediately sent representatives to Vilnius to investigate the incident. The Lithuanian government, led by Anna Kulikauskas, argued for Palcikas' release; their pleas were punctuated by the people of Vilnius themselves, backed up by Self-Defense Force troops, who were ready to take to the streets if Palcikas was not let go. He was released shortly after midnight the following day. "Were you badly treated?"

"I think I would be dead right now if you had delayed any longer—or if you had continued to insist that I had something to do with the attack," Palcikas said. Anna finally realized that if she had insisted that Palcikas was responsible for the attack, as she first surmised, the Byelorussians or the OMON Black Berets inside Fisikous would have killed Palcikas to "placate" the citizens of Lithuania. She had come very close to assassinating Palcikas herself without ever pulling a trigger.

"I was taken inside Fisikous by the Byelorussian and MSB soldiers. There was no interrogation, only complete isolation. They were looking for the right opportunity to do away with me. If you hadn't alerted the rest of the Self-Defense Force and the Parliament after my arrest, I might not have made it out of the stockade at Fisikous."

"Those bastards! I'm so sorry about what I said, what I thought. I'm so fearful of all the bad things a strong military can do in a country that I forget about the good you can do as well. I know I can trust you now.

I'm so sorry about Major Kolginov . . . my God, I don't think I'll ever forget that moment." She paused, unable to continue as the memory of watching Kolginov die before her eyes returned.

"Thank you," Palcikas said quietly. "Alexei was a good soldier and a good friend—he will not be forgotten." He touched her hand, and that simple gesture made her smile. The bond between them had finally returned, even amidst the confusion and danger that surrounded them. "We will need your trust, and the trust of all the people and the government, to carry us through the next few days. We need to prepare to defend the country if the Byelorussians continue to insist that this riot was the prelude to full-scale terrorism against the Commonwealth. What have you heard lately, Anna?"

"The Byelorussian Army was conducting a search of the city," Anna said. "An investigation for the Commonwealth, they called it."

"It was a good opportunity for them to search for weapons that we might use against *them,* should they mount a full-scale invasion," Palcikas said. "Unfortunately, my men have no evidence to link the weapons or the grenades to anyone. The MSB said they found several homes in Vilnius with stockpiles of blister-agent grenades."

"Obviously planted by the Byelorussians or the MSB."

"It is only circumstantial evidence, but it points to your organization as the cause of the riot," Palcikas said. "The end result is that everyone is confused, which will mean the investigation will stall. Nothing will be done to avenge our dead. Meanwhile there are Byelorussian troops all over the countryside, gearing up for war. The time has come to act."

Anna looked at Palcikas in surprise, her eyes wide and fearful. "What do you mean?"

Families of the dead had begun to file in, so Palcikas crossed himself, stood, and retrieved his helmet, radio, and rifle. "Come with me, Anna," he said, then left the pew. He stopped to say some comforting words to the families, then departed the chapel and headed to his office.

Anna followed quickly behind.

Palcikas' office had made a dramatic conversion since Anna had seen them last. Banks of telephones, radios, and computers were set up in the outer office. A large emergency-power generator was standing by in a corner of the outer office—Anna had seen several since coming to the castle—and stacks of small explosive charges could be seen piled everywhere so the staff could easily destroy all the computers and any secret documents if the castle was attacked. Charts of Lithuania, Latvia, eastern Poland, Kalinin, the Baltic Sea region, and northern Byelorussia were everywhere.

Several desks had been set up in Palcikas' office along with a dozen large charts. Several clerks, all dressed in combat fatigues and wearing telephone headsets, were busy collecting information and entering it into the computers for processing by the General's staff. An officer that Anna did not recognize threw a black cloth cover over one chart when he saw her enter the office. "Anna Kulikauskas, my new deputy commander, Colonel Vitalis Zukauskas. Colonel, Miss Anna Kulikauskas." Zukauskas gave the woman a tentative nod, which she returned. "Anything come in, Vitalis?"

"Several items, sir," Zukauskas replied, handling Palcikas a small handful of notes. He looked at Anna again and said, "I think we'd better ask Miss Kulikauskas to wait outside."

"No. I brought her here to hear our plans."

"Do you think that's wise, sir?" Zukauskas asked, wide-eyed. "If I may speak candidly, Miss Kulikauskas' antimilitary reputation is very well known."

"All the more reason for her to hear our plans," Palcikas said. "We need her support. If we can't get it, we may have to rethink our plans. Anna, please sit right there. Colonel, if you don't mind, give us an update on Operation Stronghold."

Zukauskas still looked skeptical, but he stepped over to the large briefing board beside Palcikas' desk and removed the black cloth cover. It revealed a chart of Lithuania. Slowly, carefully, he began to explain what Operation Stronghold was all about. . . .

Five minutes later, when the briefing was finished, Anna sat in shock. "Do you have the authority for an operation like this?" she asked.

"I think I do," Palcikas said. "I was commissioned to protect this country and that's precisely what I'm trying to do."

"What if Parliament decides not to endorse your operation or the foreign assistance your colonel just said you'll need?"

"If we don't get foreign aid, we continue the operation anyway," Palcikas said. "But if we don't get unanimous approval from Parliament, we will withdraw. I'm not trying to stage a military coup or act without the sanction of the people or the government. If they tell me to stop, I will stop."

"What kind of assurances do we have that you *will* stop?" Anna asked.

Palcikas raised his eyebrows over that remark. "Learning to trust me must be so very difficult for you, Anna," Palcikas said. "What has the military done to you to make you hate us?"

"It's a legitimate question, General," Anna said, "and if you take it personally, that's your problem. But I'm sure the President and the Prime Minister will want an answer. What is it?"

Palcikas paused for a long moment. It *was* a legitimate question. The military sometimes could not be trusted. Entire nations have been brought down by corrupt military officers, and the Lithuanian Republic was never so vulnerable as it was right now. "Wait here," he said, then exited the office at a fast trot.

A few minutes later he returned with an armed soldier at his side. Staring at Anna, he said, "Corporal Manatis, give it to Miss Kulikauskas."

The young soldier stepped forward. In his hands, partially covered by a red battle flag of the Grand Dukes of Lithuania, was the Lithuanian Sword of State.

Colonel Zukauskas was stunned. "General, what in hell are you doing . . . ?"

"This is my promise, as keeper of the regalia and as a knight and champion of Lithuania," Palcikas said. "Anna, I give you the Sword of State of Lithuania, and the Vytis from Major Alexei Kolginov's coffin." He reached into a pocket of his blouse and withdrew a dark metal bracelet. "This is Alexei's military I.D. bracelet. I took it from his body just now." The pale face of the young corporal beside Palcikas told Anna that he was telling the truth. Palcikas snapped the bracelet onto the hilt of the Sword of State so it would not slip off.

"You now have everything in this world I hold dear, Anna—the Sword of State, symbol of the nation that I cherish; the Vytis, the symbol of the heritage and traditions that I follow; and a possession from the body of my closest and dearest friend. There are only two ways you would have gotten these things—if I had given them to you or if you had pried them from my dead fingers. Corporal Manatis has been permanently assigned to look after you and guard these items with his life as long as they are in your possession. I have known Georgi and his family since he was a child, and I trust him with my life—as I now trust you to take care of these things, Anna.

"You will take these things to the President as proof of my pledge to him and to the country that Operation Stronghold is in the best interests of Lithuania and that if I do not receive overwhelming support from the people's elected representatives in Vilnius, I will terminate the operation, withdraw my forces, and obey whatever legal commands are given me— including an order to resign my commission and be relieved of command if that is their wish. If operational demands allow it, I will repeat my pledge to Parliament, but I anticipate that I will be very busy once Operation Stronghold begins."

Palcikas covered the sword with the flag, and Manatis wrapped the package in a waterproof canvas duffel bag to protect it. He then stepped closer to Anna, away from the others, and said, "I would give anything to earn your trust . . . but I've given away everything I own of real value. Tell me what I have to do."

Anna Kulikauskas was close to tears. For the first time in these past few days she felt she finally understood him. He was a rough-cut soldier who seemed out of place in time, but what he really was was a man who truly loved his country and was willing to sacrifice his career, his life, even his soul, to protect it.

"General—I mean, Dominikas—no one . . . no one has ever trusted me with so much." She looked at the duffel bag holding the sword, now slung securely over Corporal Georgi Manatis' shoulder, then looked up into Palcikas' steel-blue eyes and said, "I do trust you, Dominikas."

"Then I've got all the weapons I'll need to fight this battle, Anna," he said, a smile growing on his chiseled face.

HIGH TECHNOLOGY AEROSPACE WEAPONS CENTER, NEVADA
12 APRIL, 0800 PT (1700 VILNIUS)

"I still don't believe it, General," Colonel Paul White said as General Brad Elliott entered the office in which White had been working for the past several days. The office walls were lined with all kinds of charts and satellite photographs of different projections and scales, with prominent landmarks highlighted. "You've got a satellite that you can launch within a few hours, and these satellites can locate an object the size of a truck from four hundred miles in space and then transmit that information directly to a B-52, which can hit it with a bomb a few minutes later?"

"Yup," Elliott replied. White noticed a message form in Elliott's hand but did not mention it—Elliott would get to it in good time, White surmised. "We've been playing around with it in a series of classified situations and it's worked beautifully. The satellite booster is carried on a modified DC-10 airliner, then dropped and fired off into space. We call 'em NIRTSats, for Need-It-Right-This-Second Satellites. They're made by a company called Sky Masters."

"Well, then, what do you need MADCAP MAGICIAN for?"

"Because the system only works when the area that the satellite is flying over has only bad guys in it," Elliott explained. "The system has trouble differentiating between a Soviet and an American truck. We need someone on the ground to say, 'Those are the bad guys there, but stay away from the good guys here.' Given a clear-fire area, of course, we can easily strike all targets within that area, but there aren't a lot of battlefields so cleanly delineated that you can just pick any target area and say they're all bad guys."

"Gotcha," White said. "So then these satellites upload the information to your war machines out there, and the crew computes an initial point and target area for the missiles?"

"The bombing computers pick the IP for the crew," Elliott explained.

"The MARS missiles can update their target data base with targeting information from the NIRTSats. We can update that data base right up until seconds before launch, and the missile will take into account the travel time and adjust the target coordinates."

"Well, what happens if the missile adjusts the target coordinates right on top of a column of good guys?"

"We need to plan this thing so there won't be any conflict," Elliott said. "No good guys within ten miles of the 'basket,' or the missile might— check that, it *will*—go after them."

"That doesn't leave us too much room," White said. "Lithuania's only one hundred and eighty miles wide. With a couple dozen missiles in the air, we might put good guys at risk no matter what we do."

"Then we decrease the number of missiles," Elliott said. "But I think we can create a lot of havoc with a small number of MARS missiles overhead, even if we won't destroy every bad guy. Remember, we also need to deconflict the area with friendly aircraft, since these missiles will be loitering in the area at different altitudes and changeable ground tracks. No fixed- or rotary-wing aircraft in the target basket when MARS missiles are flying."

"Makes you want to put the 'man-in-the-loop' back in again, doesn't it?"

"The objective is to interdict armor columns at long range, far enough away so the missiles won't threaten friendly forces or the launch aircraft," Elliott said. "Remember, MARS was developed for use during the air-campaign portion of DESERT STORM, to face off against four thousand Iraqi armored vehicles with no Coalition ground forces committed yet. Once friendly forces got into the mix, MARS would have been targeted farther north."

"What a nightmare for our ground forces," White exclaimed. "Deconflicting air traffic means that troops near a target—the guys that'd be marking targets for the satellites—will lose their air support for several minutes after the MARS missiles are on the way. If the time between target marking and missile-away is too short, they'll be stuck until the missile clears out. And there'll be a shitload of MARS missiles in the air—God, there could be dozens of them. We'll have to restrict all of Lithuania."

"It shouldn't be too difficult. Since MARS flies faster than a tilt-rotor aircraft, they can head in toward the target area at the same time if they start from the same IP," Elliott said. "By the time the missile finishes its attack and re-attack, it'll be down and the tilt-rotor can extract the ground forces. If we're careful planning, we can plot a safe ingress route for the tilt-rotors so they can avoid all the target baskets—as soon as one missile goes down, the tilt-rotor moves into that sector. By the time the aircraft makes the pickup and transitions to the next sector, the missile in that adjacent area should be down."

"I'm really glad you got all these computers doing the planning for us," White said. "I never thought a lot about deconfliction before—I always thought the sky was big enough to hold everybody."

"Not when everybody wants the same piece of sky," Elliott said. He stepped over to White and handed him the message form. "And it looks like the sky's going to get a bit more crowded. We just intercepted that from MILSTAR. It looks like the 26th MEU has been activated."

MILSTAR was the newly established worldwide satellite military-communications network.

White studied the message for a moment. "I think you're right. We can't know for sure, General—they change their code words all the time—but it looks like they've been activated."

"But the team that is supposed to rescue Dave was already activated—they got the message while I was at Camp Lejeune," Elliott said. "This looks like another warning order. It's got to be for the rest of the MEU, not just the task force going after Dave."

"It could have something to do with the riot at Denerokin," White said. "Maybe the White House authorized another operation out there . . . a show of force or an embassy reinforcement. The Byelorussians and the Commonwealth really cracked down on foreigners in Lithuania, closing the airport and all that—maybe the President wants to show his displeasure. The MEU is the best unit to send in for something like that."

"They want to send in an entire MEU while Dave is being held at Fisikous?" Elliott asked incredulously. "They can't do that! They're sacrificing Luger's life. If the Soviets in Fisikous see a thousand Marines coming ashore in Lithuania, they'll dispose of Luger for sure." He motioned to the message and asked White, "Any idea from that message when they go in?"

"Impossible to say, General. It depends on what the deployment order said. You can pretty much bet it'll be at night, but which night is anybody's guess. If this is a warning order, it takes place no less than six hours prior to H-hour, but it could be as much as seven days ahead of time. The mission might not start for weeks."

Elliott looked depressed. "Christ, I've never felt so damned helpless before. Three of my men going in to rescue another one of my men and I'm thousands of miles away and unable to help."

"I think what we've been doing here during this time constitutes help, General," White said. "I've worked with Marines for a couple years now. Don't you believe any of the 'dumb lug' and 'jarhead' jokes about these guys—they're as smart as they are tough. They'll protect your officers and get Dave, don't worry."

"I know they're good," Elliott said, remembering Gunny Wohl, "but I'm usually in charge of these kinds of missions. Sitting on the sidelines isn't my idea of fun." He thought for a moment, then said, "Hell, I'm not going to guess about when the rescue mission starts. We've got enough information ready, the crews are ready, we've got landing rights and hangars for my planes."

"Yeah. And I'll bet they're thrilled to be deploying to Thule Air Base in Greenland. Didn't you say it was only a thousand miles from the North Pole?"

"Nine hundred miles to be exact," Elliott said with a smile. "The base has actually expanded operations in the past few years with the return of Strategic Defense Initiative research, and although there haven't been any B-52s based there in over twenty years, the facilities are still there and have been taken care of by the U.S. and Danish governments. My organization has authority to use that base, so we'll stage out of there. The Sky Masters' NIRTSats network can be launched with only six hours' warning, and we'll have around-the-clock access to the satellites within twelve hours. I'm recommending we execute *our* project."

"I'm ready, General," White said enthusiastically. "My boys've been ready ever since you came up with the project. They can have the *Valley Mistress* fueled and stocked by the time I get out there. All we need is clearance from Washington to proceed—" But White stopped when he saw the look on Elliott's face—it was that sort of dreamy, faraway look visionaries often have. Paul White shook his head, then smiled. "Uh, Brad, you *are* planning on getting permission from Washington to do this, aren't you?"

"Paul, you've got a hundred highly trained Marines on board that ship of yours," Elliott said. "You know the Security Facility, part of the Fisikous Institute, as well as the 26th MEU does. Our own intelligence sources say that the Commonwealth troops are on the move—they could be massing for an invasion of their own."

"You don't have to convince *me,* Brad," White said. "Hell, I came to you with this nutty idea. I was ready to go last week and so were my troops. But I wasn't flying B-52s and carrying all these smart cruise missiles. I had a good chance of sneaking in and sneaking out again. But this . . . well, you're a three-star, Brad, so I shouldn't tell you your business, but I think we need permission to take this show on the road."

"Let's look at it this way, Paul," Elliott began. "First, the MEU will go in at night—only at night. Right?"

"No question. Everyone fights at night."

"So the thing kicks off either tonight or tomorrow night."

"It could be next *week,* Brad."

"If that's true, then we definitely go ASAP," Elliott said. "In all probability Dave hasn't got that long to live. The informants in Fisikous report that Ozerov is being sequestered—he's alive but his whereabouts are unknown. I think our contact in there has been blown."

"I agree."

"Okay. So we're agreed that we need to make our move if we want any chance of rescuing David," Elliott said. White nodded. "Then we launch and execute our mission tomorrow night. If the MEU goes tonight, we'll find out about it and turn around. If the MEU goes tomorrow night, we'll be in a position to assist or we can abort and recover."

"We go nose-to-nose with our own forces?" White asked incredulously. "I don't like that idea. If the amphibious-assault ship *Wasp* sees us coming, they'll send a Harrier jump-jet after us and shoot us down. Hell, we could end up shooting at each other if MADCAP MAGICIAN and the 26th MEU end up in Fisikous at the same time."

"We can decide to contact the MEU or Joint Task Force and tell them we've arrived," Elliott suggested. "They'll tell us to get the hell out of the way or they'll give us an order. But either way, we should—"

The yellow light on the telephone in Elliott's private conference room illuminated. Elliott knew that only the most important phone calls would be allowed to go through during their meeting, so he didn't hesitate to pick it up. "Elliott here."

"Brad, how the hell are you?" boomed Wilbur Curtis.

White saw Elliott's face brighten with surprise, and he looked at White with a smile. "Why, General Curtis, we were just talking about you." Now it was White's turn to be surprised—just as they were thinking about breaking the law and taking a strike force overseas without permission, the Chairman of the Joint Chiefs of Staff himself was on the phone.

"I'll bet you were—my ears were burning." Curtis laughed. "How are you?"

"Couldn't be better, sir."

"Can the sir stuff, Brad. It's me. Or are you calling me sir to butter me up for something?"

"My, but you're very suspicious today, Wilbur."

"Comes from dealing with you all these years."

"Do you have news about the MEU mission?"

"First briefing on it will be at H minus twelve hours—that's about an hour from now," Curtis said. "You're back on the list. Priority Two."

Elliott's heart leaped when he heard that he was being included on the briefing list, but he quickly recovered when he learned it was Priority Two—classified top secret but usually delivered by the Pentagon press secretary (the Chairman of the Joint Chiefs of Staff if he was available) after the National Command Authority and National Security Council. He had about the same status as a senior Congressional committee chairman—high, but not anywhere near the decision-making loop. "What's the word from the team?"

"Preparations are under way, everyone's doing fine, everyone's in place," Curtis said. "So far, so good. What have you been up to? You've been awfully quiet these days. That tends to make, uh, people at 1600 Pennsylvania a little nervous."

Elliott looked at White with a smile and replied, "Does it now? Well, I'm not up to anything special, Wilbur. Same old stuff."

"Same old stuff, huh? How's the investigation going on Colonel White and his group?"

"I was speaking with White when you called. He's right here."

"He's still in Nevada? That's interesting."

"Why?"

"Because my sources say that his ship has left port and is heading east through the Baltic Sea," Curtis replied.

"Part of the investigation, sir."

"Oh good, we're back to sir again. That's probably best," Curtis noted. "Not only has the *Valley Mistress* left port, but it has a full contingent of Marines and two, count 'em, *two* CV-22 PAVE HAMMER aircraft safely stowed on board. Now would you mind explaining why?"

This was a good time, Elliott decided, to cut the innocent routine. "You know as well as I do what's going on, sir," he said. "I wasn't convinced that the White House was actually going to go through with the mission. If they ran into any trouble, which appears to be the case, I wasn't convinced they'd follow through. I didn't know what you had moving in that direction and I wasn't going to wait until it was too late to find out . . . Sir."

"So you set up your own rescue operation, using MADCAP MAGI-CIAN as your assault team," Curtis said. "When the White House finds out, they'll skin you alive, *then* court-martial you." There was an exasperated sigh over the secure telephone line; then: "So you cut White loose?"

"Well, White was never really under investigation," Elliott said. "He brought the news about Dave Luger to me because no one had done anything about Dave for several months. It was White's contacts in the embassy in Moscow that got things moving. Not Russell. Not the Defense Department. If he hadn't done anything, Luger might be dead now."

"So instead of bringing him up on charges of revealing classified information, you decided to work together to rescue Luger? Dammit, I should have known you were going to do this." There was a pause; then: "You haven't sent any Megafortresses or Black Knight bombers over there, have you?"

"We were just about to start engines."

"General, I hope you're kidding," Curtis said in a low, serious tone, then: ". . . but I know you're not. What have you got? What's your plan?"

"Six EB-52 Megafortresses—four primaries, two spares," Elliott said. "Air support against the CIS radar sites, antiair units, and base defenses in Fisikous. Two CV-22 PAVE HAMMER aircraft, with fifty Marines."

"Just amazing. I should have *known* you weren't going to sit still and sweat it out with the rest of us. And when were you going to tell me about all this?"

"I wasn't," Elliott said. "I was going to go when my team was ready. If the MEU was inbound, I'd turn around or stand by in case they needed my help. If they weren't going in, I'd continue my mission."

"With B-52 bombers flying over Lithuania? How did you ever expect to get away with *that* . . . ?"

"The odds were that my Megafortresses would never be detected," Elliott explained. "I had enough standoff weapons to grease every long-range surveillance radar and fighter-intercept radar in the region, and my planes have the power to jam all the others. Fighters were not a big concern—at night, with no GCI, and as long as I was no threat to Kaliningrad or Minsk, no enemy fighter jock was going to mess with me at low level. SAM sites, optically guided antiaircraft artillery, and the odd missile-equipped attack helicopter were the big concerns, but we felt confident enough that we could take enough of them out and avoid the rest. Using the EB-52 for the heavy threats and the guns and rockets on the CV-22s, we'd drop White's Sparrowhawk team in and take that security building."

"That's some pretty big ifs there, Brad," Curtis grumbled. "But if anyone could pull it off, it's you. Then MADCAP MAGICIAN was going to pull Luger out?"

"Exactly. We'd take him to the embassy if necessary, but our destination was Norway or Belgium or Germany—any friendly territory we could set down. If the tilt-rotors and the EB-52s got out okay, the entire incident could be deniable by the White House—"

"And if one or more of them got shot down, you and White would take the heat yourselves," Curtis interjected. "But you'd totally embarrass the government and shoot our credibility as a nation to hell for at least ten years!"

"I believed that the White House would just as soon let Dave Luger rot than risk embarrassment," Elliott said resolutely.

Curtis had to admit that Elliott's observation was correct—the White House was just looking for an excuse to cancel the REDTAIL HAWK extraction.

"I'm expendable—throughout my entire career I've always been expendable," Elliott said.

"Don't give me that martyrdom crap, Brad. The White House doesn't trust you because you pull shit like *this*. Now just keep your mouth shut and I'll tell you what you will do next:

"I'm ordering you to contact the *Valley Mistress* and tell her to return to port immediately," Curtis said. "I will contact General Kundert and advise him that two CV-22 PAVE HAMMER aircraft and the Marines on board that cargo ship are available for duty with the 26th MEU if necessary. Your Megafortresses will stand down immediately. All training flights are suspended—if I hear of *one* EB-52 launch from Dreamland, I'm going to place you under arrest. Is all that clear, Brad?"

"Yes, sir."

"It better be. You and Colonel White sit tight in Dreamland and don't do a thing. I'll be in touch when the briefing starts. Listen, but don't say anything, or I may be forced to tell the White House about your plan. Is that clear?"

"Yes, sir."

Elliott's responses immediately told Curtis that Elliott hadn't heard one word he was saying. "I'm serious about this, Brad. Don't launch those bombers or you'll be raking stones at Fort Leavenworth by week's end. I've never threatened to arrest you before, but this time the threat is *real*. Sit tight and be good."

"Yes, sir."

Orders and threats meant nothing to Brad Elliott, Curtis decided—he was going to do exactly what he wanted anyway. Shit. Well, it was his neck he'd be stretching. Curtis terminated the call.

"You're smiling, Brad," Paul White said as Elliott hung up. "What did General Curtis have to say?"

"He said stand down. He ordered us to return the *Valley Mistress* to port."

"Oh, terrific. That was our last shot." White picked up the phone. "Get me a satellite channel to MADCAP MAGICIAN," he said to the operator. To Elliott, he asked, "How did Curtis find out? Did he discover the *Mistress* in the Baltic?"

"He didn't say." Elliott was staring straight ahead, elbows on the table, fingers massaging his chin. White saw that expression on his face. "Uh, oh . . . umm . . . what do you have in mind?"

"Order the *Mistress* to turn around," Elliott said, "but send it someplace for repairs or refueling—someplace very close. Stockholm, perhaps, or Visby."

"Both places are too obvious *and* too far away," White said. "My favorite place is Ronne, on Bornholm Island. It's Danish, not Swedish, so we shouldn't have any difficulties bringing armed aircraft into port. Best of all, it's only sixty nautical miles from the original staging area."

"Do it, then," Elliott said. "I've got no choice but to stand down the

Megafortresses, but we'll keep the *Valley Mistress* on station as long as we can. Dave Luger's not out of Lithuania yet, and I'm going to keep this force in operation until he's back. Fuck 'em."

LISTA NAVAL AIR BASE, VESTBYGDA, NORWAY
13 APRIL, 2300 NORWAY (1700 ET)

"Jammed weapon . . . go."

Patrick McLanahan lowered his M-16 rifle. Bracing the rifle against his right thigh, he used his right hand and slapped upward on the magazine, then pulled the charging handle on the back of the rifle all the way back and inspected the chamber. Finding it clear, he released the charging handle with a loud *snap,* shoved forward on the bolt-closure assist lever, and raised it once again to firing position.

"No, sir, that's wrong," Gunnery Sergeant Chris Wohl interjected, but not to McLanahan. Wohl was sitting beside John Ormack, carefully watching his actions. Out of a corner of his eye he saw Hal Briggs execute the SPORTS actions for clearing a misfired M-16 in two seconds, which was Marine Corps standards. McLanahan was a bit more deliberate, but his actions were correct. But Ormack still didn't have it down. "Don't ease the charging handle back into place, sir. Let it snap back," Wohl told him. "You can jam another round in the chamber if you don't let the handle pump that next round in."

Ormack nodded, but his frustration level was obviously high.

"Try it again, General. Ready? Jammed weapon . . . go."

Ormack lowered his weapon, pulled back on the charging lever, checked the chamber, hit the bolt-clearing lever, and raised his rifle.

"Wrong again, sir," Wohl said. "Slap the bottom of that magazine first before pulling the charging handle. If the magazine's not in properly, you'll reseat it—pulling the charging handle will do no good if you've got a round jammed in the magazine or a bad magazine. Let's try again . . ."

"I'm beat, Gunny. Let's bag it for tonight."

Ormack was definitely tired, McLanahan thought—the long plane rides from North Carolina to this isolated Norwegian naval base at the very southern tip of Norway; the jet lag; the endless training and conditioning sessions; and a feeling of utter helplessness had taken their toll. As hard as Ormack tried, he just wasn't picking up on the routine stuff. "Give me a stick and throttle and I'll be okay. One lousy rifle and I turn into a blithering idiot."

"Few more minutes, sir," Wohl said. "This stuff is important. You'll jam a weapon about once per fifty rounds, which is almost once every magazine. If you practice this enough, you won't panic when you pull the trigger and nothing happens. I understand they can make a monkey fly a plane, sir, but no monkey I know of can fire an M-16. Try it again." His attempt at humor was completely lost on the Air Force one-star general. To McLanahan, Wohl said, "You just fell into a river, sir. Your weapon was submerged. When you reach the shore, you get ambushed. You return fire—"

"Not before clearing the rifle," McLanahan replied, anticipating Wohl's characteristic real-life, rapid-fire quiz. "Firing a bullet now can cause the thing to blow up in my face."

"Very good, sir. Show me the procedures for clearing your weapon."

Patrick lowered the muzzle of his M-16 and recited, "Point the muzzle down to drain water. Pull charging handle rearward two to three inches. Allow water to drain. Release charging handle and push bolt-assist lever to seat round and lock the bolt. Then clear drainhole in butt and drain water."

"Why do you pull back on the charging handle?" quizzed Wohl.

"Because a round fully seated in the chamber will prevent all of the water from running out the barrel, like a straw that stays full of water when you put your finger over the top end. Pulling the charging handle will partially unseat the round and allow water to run out."

"Very good. I'll make a Marine out of you yet—if you can ever learn to shoot." To Ormack he said, "Keep practicing, sir. Major Briggs, watch him. Both you guys, listen up while you practice. Colonel, draw your knife."

They were all wearing a nylon web LC-2 harness secured on their torsos, covering thick black cotton-and-nylon coveralls—with no military uniforms or insignia. The harness had what seemed to be an endless array of things attached to it—ammo pouches, first-aid kits, canteens, flashlights, a compass, a length of rope, a radio, and a holster for a sidearm. On the right-side suspender hung a fifteen-inch Bowie-style knife with a parachute-cord-wrapped handle, a serrated and straight-edge spine, and a thick steel hammerhead pommel. McLanahan flicked off Velcro straps and the knife dropped into his right hand. As he did so, he crouched low and moved his left foot back into a defensive knife-fighter's stance.

"Good. Keep your left hand farther back so your opponent can't slash it," Wohl said. "Now, we didn't go into knife fighting that much. You've got a sidearm and a rifle, so use them. Never discard your weapons. Fill your ammo pouches every chance you get." Unsaid was the thought, *with your dead buddy's ammo if necessary.* "But don't carry more than normal.

"But if you run out of ammo or lose your weapons, and you're confronted by an attacker who hasn't shot you dead yet, draw your knife, attack to kill, and then get the hell away." Wohl's knife suddenly appeared in his hands, as quickly and as naturally as he extended a finger. The knife flashed out at McLanahan as he spoke: "Strike at the face, the eyes, the hands, the neck. Every cut weakens him. If your opponent goes down, cut his neck or eyes deep. Don't try to stab him in the heart or guts. He's probably wearing a flak vest or layers of clothing that'll protect him, and even if it penetrates it probably won't kill him unless you're lucky and pierce the heart. Even a tiny button can deflect a knife point. Slash his neck or his eyes deep, then get away from the area. You're not Rambo— you can't take on an army with just a knife. Use it to escape.

"If you're confronted by a guy with a knife, my advice is to get the hell away from him. Several reasons why: one, if he's not within arm's reach of you, he can't hurt you; two, he doesn't have a gun, so he's just as disadvantaged as you are; and three, if *he* stays, he's probably a skilled knife-fighter and will skin you alive if you stay. All three are good reasons not to hang around and fight it out with knives.

"But if you have no choice but to fight, remember three things. One: never fight on equal terms. Use rocks, stones, dirt, sand, water, rope, or noise to distract him and make him lose concentration. Spit, scream, yell, curse, act crazy. Two: commit yourself to kill. Three: attack, then depart. If he comes after you, start the whole process over again. If he doesn't pursue, you've won. Knife fighting is survival, not tactics or strategy or position."

Wohl paused and looked at his three charges. McLanahan was attentive, but Wohl could tell by reading the young officer's eyes that he wasn't thinking about survival or fighting—he was thinking about getting his buddy. Briggs, he knew, understood what he was saying—he had been trained to the point where he could let the mechanics and techniques of martial arts happen naturally. Ormack, although very intelligent and dedicated, was simply not cut out for this line of work. He could probably explain the physics and pneumatics of how an M-16 worked, but the thought of killing someone with it was patently abhorrent to him. Ormack would have to be protected and led—something that a Marine Force Recon unit was not accustomed to doing. But it would have to be done nonetheless.

A few moments later one of Wohl's NCOs came into the room with a message on a strip of computer paper. He read it, breathed deeply, and handed the message form to Ormack.

"We've been executed," Ormack said simply. His throat seemed to go instantly dry, his voice tight and raspy. "Mission begins tomorrow tonight."

"What that means, gentlemen, is that the National Command Authority has given its permission for us to proceed," Wohl said immediately. "It is not, I repeat *not*, an authorization to do something we're not prepared to do. I've trained you all I can in the time I was given. You've spent long hours studying, training, rehearsing—but *you* have the final say on whether you go or not."

"We go, then," McLanahan said, sheathing his knife resolutely.

Ormack was on his feet, looking at the message form as if it had eyes and was looking back at him. He did not reply—he was looking at the paper, but Wohl knew that Ormack was really looking inward, at himself. He was faced with the question he didn't want to answer. When he looked up at the rest of them, he nodded assent, but it was clear that he felt he wasn't ready—and, Wohl thought, he was right.

Briggs was watching Wohl, who looked with great concern at Ormack. "Do you think we're ready?" Briggs asked the Marine.

"Do I think you three are ready to participate in an extraction mission with a Marine Force Recon team? No way. It takes months of training and years of practice to do that. Do I think you can keep up with my team on an extraction mission? No. You're not in shape and you don't have the skills.

"But do I think my team can lead you into a hostile area? Yes. Do I think that, once we have neutralized opposing forces, you can operate in that hostile area and accomplish your mission? Yes. Do I think my brother Marines can lead you out of the hostile area after you have accomplished your mission? Yes." He paused, then added, "I suppose it's all how you look at it. You three showed me a lot in the past few days. But I'm not prepared to risk my life and the lives of my men to save you, just so you can be heroes and get your buddy out of hock. So let *me* tell *you* how we are going to do things from now on.

"I will be in command of this mission. Rank disappears as of right now. My word is law, punishable by death." No one there even raised an eyebrow at that last statement, because they all knew it to be true. "You do as I say, when I say it. When I say 'stay,' you stay and keep as quiet as if you were dead and buried. When I say 'run,' you run until you drop. When I say 'no,' it means *no*. You touch nothing unless I say to—that goes for your crew member in hostile territory. What I say and do goes. Do you understand?"

All three Air Force officers nodded.

"All right. You've come this far—and the boss says you'll go—so you're going. Now go get some sleep."

Ormack handed the message form to McLanahan and hefted his rifle. "I think I'll practice my procedures with the M-16, Sergeant."

"I just told you what to do, Ormack," Wohl snapped. "You will report to your barracks and lights-out. And I am still 'Gunny' to you, although you are no longer 'General' to me.

"You listen to me good, all of you. The two skills I think you three have learned in this short time with me is how to listen and how to obey orders to the letter. I guarantee that no matter how much high-ranking horsepower you three have, if I go back to my CO and inform him that you cannot take an order from me, this mission will be terminated immediately. Few organizations in the world risk dozens of good men in peacetime to rescue one; my unit is not one of them.

"That is the last time I will repeat an order—next time you're out on your ear. Ormack, if you don't know your shit by now, you never will. I'm betting that all these lessons and all the work we've done will surface when the shit hits the fan, but if it doesn't, you and probably a few of us will be dead. Hopefully, some brass somewhere will remember I told 'em so—I hope one of my brother Marines will carve it on my headstone. But that's none of your concern—or mine.

"Safe and stow your weapons, then hit the rack. I'll come get you in the morning and we'll do a final inspection and dry run before the mass briefing. I know sleeping will be difficult, but try it anyway. And *that's* an order, too."

FISIKOUS RESEARCH INSTITUTE SECURITY CENTER
VILNIUS, LITHUANIA 12 APRIL, 1400 VILNIUS (0800 ET)

During the past couple of weeks, especially since the encounter with the orderly in the dining hall, Luger was able to run a few extra dekameters every day; today, he had run a full extra kilometer more than he had just four weeks earlier. His strength was better, and his alertness and attention spans were better. He looked thinner, but his muscles were wiry and tough, like a marathon runner's. But he was not quite getting along with the rest of the staff, and he was growing irritable and quiet.

It was during Luger's exercise treadmill one day that Viktor Gabovich's attention was attracted, and he made the decision to confront Luger.

The reason for the change was eventually found during a routine urine specimen test—Luger had been given a drug antidote that reacted with an entire spectrum of psychoactive drugs and induced vomiting. It must have been secretly administered by the Lithuanian agent, Gabovich guessed. The antidote had worn off within a week, but by then Luger had developed a severe case of bulimia—alternating food binges with vomiting—and now he was lapsing into anorexia, refusing to eat altogether. Obviously now he distrusted all food, so he was refusing to eat anything that he even thought was tainted. He had lost so much weight from refusing to eat that he was in danger of hospitalizing himself.

Gabovich entered the small one-room gymnasium where Luger trained, just as Luger was finishing his treadmill run. Teresov was behind him and stayed near the door, carefully watching Luger. "I see you are feeling better, Doctor Ozerov," he said to Luger. No response. "Is something wrong?"

"No," Luger replied in Russian. "Nothing."

"You must be more forthright with me, Doctor," Gabovich said, carefully adding a bit more authority to his voice. "You were virtually no assistance to the security units on finding this orderly, who was obviously an intruder. Your safety, as well as the success of your projects, rely on accurate and timely informa—"

"I told you I don't know anything," Luger suddenly blurted out in English. He stared at Gabovich for a few moments as if thinking about continuing his tirade, then turned away and toweled off his face. "I'm going to take a shower."

"What did this man say to you, Doctor?"

"Nothing."

"You are lying."

Luger suddenly turned and threw the towel in Gabovich's direction, but not directly at him. Teresov drew a sidearm from a shoulder rig. That action, Gabovich knew, would bring the security guards running as soon as they saw it on their closed-circuit monitors. No matter. This game was finally at an end.

"You lie to me all the fucking time!" Luger shouted. "You tell me I'm a Russian citizen, that I was born in Russia, but I stay here all the time. I can't control anything around here! I haven't seen the damned sun for weeks! I want—"

Three security guards burst into the room, sidearms holstered but batons at the ready. One rushed Luger while the other two stood squarely in front of Gabovich, shielding him. Gabovich pushed them aside slightly so he could watch the other guard restrain Luger.

"I knew this place was bugged," Luger said, a satisfied sneer on his face—until the guard pinned his arms behind his back, causing a very painful grimace. "I thought I'd give it a try."

"An interesting notion," Gabovich said. "Fortunately, you will not have to worry about it any longer. This is the last you'll see of this room."

"You think I give a shit?" Luger said. "You think I care about what you do to me? I'm a traitor ten times over. I deserve to die."

"You will get your wish, then," Gabovich said with a smile, "but not until we explore the value the United States has placed on your head. Obviously if they expended the time and took the risk of planting an agent inside this facility, they hold you in some regard. They may pay handsomely for you. If not, you will simply answer as many questions as you can about the High Technology Aerospace Weapons Center and the Single Integrated Operations Plan."

"I'm not going to tell you a damned thing," Luger said. "You've already bled me dry. There's nothing you can do to me that will make me talk to you. Period."

A smile crept across Gabovich's face. "Oh, really? Why, I forgot, Lieutenant. You have no recollection of our unique little apparatus for making you talk, do you? You were in a coma when we dragged your battered body out of Siberia, and you are usually sedated before you are placed in the isolation system.

"Well, we have a real treat in store for you today. You will see first-hand the apparatus—designed by myself, I must tell you—before we hook you up in it. And since we no longer need the services of the esteemed Doctor Ozerov, we can leave you connected to the device for an extended period of time. We will have the opportunity to extract every little erg of knowledge from your brain; we will expand our knowledge of sensory deprivation by seeing how long a human being can tolerate a state of complete and total mental isolation; and he will undoubtedly discover what happens to him when he snaps. It will prove very interesting. Take him away."

THE WHITE HOUSE, WASHINGTON, D.C.
12 APRIL, 1312 ET (1912 VILNIUS)

General Wilbur Curtis and his Pentagon staff were briefing the President and his Cabinet on the embassy-reinforcement operation and on RED-TAIL HAWK.

The briefings were essential because it was important that every government member understand exactly what forces were in place and the reason for their presence. Because military forces usually travel quickly and react to situations autonomously, these briefings had to be frequent and comprehensive—tough to do when the President wanted to maintain a business-as-usual façade while military intrigue was going on in the background.

Before any American military member can cross a foreign border, for whatever reason, he or she must have permission from the National Command Authority—the President and the Secretary of Defense, the civilian overseers of the American military machine. In the case of the Baltic states, the original order to send troops into Lithuania came months earlier, in the form of an Executive Order authorizing increased surveillance of the Baltic states during the transitional period while Commonwealth forces and foreign nationals were withdrawing from the former Soviet republics. These forces had originally been CIA agents and informants, the same HUMINT (human intelligence) sources used for eons.

The President had authorized the upgrading of HUMINT resources to direct military surveillance several weeks before the Denerokin riot, when it was obvious that something was going on inside Lithuania between the Commonwealth and Byelorussian military forces. This upgrade consisted of increased satellite and aircraft surveillance of the Baltic states and expanding to the nearby republics, with special emphasis on military forces and extra-special emphasis on the location and disposition of nuclear-capable forces.

When the REDTAIL HAWK mission was authorized, the President signed another Executive Order authorizing direct military action within Lithuania, Russia, and Byelorussia, but concentrating on small covert-action groups that would collect information by direct observations. The HUMINT resources took the form of Army Special Forces groups hiding in several locations within Lithuania, operating in concert with the U.S. European Command, the Marines, and U.S. Special Operations Command to provide intelligence information and other forms of support; and by U.S. Navy SEAL teams that would deploy from ships in the Baltic Sea and attack targets near the Lithuanian, Latvian, and Kalinin coast.

Code-named AMOS, these teams had been in place for several days, getting into position to best observe the embassy-reinforcement operation and the rescue mission and to help any way they could.

It was the status of the AMOS teams that Curtis was talking about that afternoon: "We have a total of twenty-four AMOS teams in position, and all are ready to go," Curtis concluded, an unwrapped and unlit cigar in his right hand. "Most start their actions about six hours before the embassy operation commences.

"Six SEAL teams will take out Soviet radar and surface-to-air missile sites in Latvia, Lithuania, and the Russian city of Kaliningrad. Simultaneously, ten Army Special Forces teams will destroy or disable several key Commonwealth military installations within Lithuania, with special emphasis on air bases and army-aviation bases. There are two Marine Corps and Ranger AMOS teams outside Vilnius who will prepare a marshaling and refueling area for the Marine Corps helicopters coming out of the embassy. Finally, there are six Special Forces teams within the city of Vilnius itself—two stationed in the city in case our forces need help, two keeping watch on the U.S. Embassy, and two keeping an eye on the Fisikous Institute. All teams are in contact with the embassy—it's not constant contact, considering the situation some of these team members are in, but they can all react fairly quickly if the need arises."

"What sort of situation do you mean, General?" the President asked.

"Some of the AMOS teams are in hiding near their assigned targets, sir," Curtis replied. "Two guys have been holed up in the roof of a warehouse. Two teams have been hiding in a cellar. We were lucky enough to have a few go in as tourists—they were in fact real tourists that were given an unexpected mission while on vacation. They are staying in youth hostels and hotels. Others are not so lucky. Some of the talented Army troops are hiding in camouflaged holes in the ground—they call them spider-holes. Very appropriate name—two guys living in an eight-foot-diameter hole. They sometimes dig several such hiding places to avoid detection."

"Incredible," the President said. "I'd like to meet these gentlemen after this is all over with. What a sacrifice they're making."

"But as you pointed out, General, special operations are important these days," Vice President Kevin Martindale reiterated. "The victory in the Gulf War would have been impossible without the covert-action groups that were sent into Iraq and Kuwait long before the air war began."

"Exactly, sir," Curtis agreed, noting the concurring nod of agreement by the President. Unknown to the President, the Vice President's remark had been well rehearsed by him and Curtis—they were in collusion on a new development that they both wanted to see put into motion. It was important that the President agree with the Vice President because they were going to have to convince him of something they were sure he wasn't going to like.

"All of the units are safe and in good shape," Curtis concluded. "They are standing by for their execution order. When they receive it, they'll begin moving toward their objectives. The SEAL teams need their order first. They deploy from the amphibious-assault ship *Wasp* by helicopter until they're just outside radar range of shore, then they'll come ashore in rubber boats. They travel less than thirty miles, but it'll take them nearly four hours to reach their target."

"But it's one of the most important targets," the Vice President said. "Those coastal radar sites can detect incoming aircraft nearly a hundred miles away."

"I still don't like the idea of blowing up actual radar sites and missiles," the President said uneasily. "The radar is used for air-traffic control, I understand, and the missiles are for use against high-speed, high-altitude aircraft at long range. They're defensive weapons. Why worry about them?"

"They can blow this entire operation, Mr. President," Martindale explained. "Those radars can practically see our helicopters lifting off the deck of the *Wasp* and track them all the way to Vilnius. And those missiles are an obscenity. They're not Lithuanian missiles, and they're not manned by Lithuanian crews. It would be as if the Russians had a missile base in Norfolk, Virginia. It should have been dismantled—we're just helping them along."

The President chuckled, a short, rather nervous laugh, and nodded again. He was convinced, and the Vice President had convinced him, Curtis noted.

Perfect . . .

The President opened the red-covered folder containing the prepared executive order. The paper document was a formality, a holdover from Revolutionary and Wild West times when orders from the President of the United States really did emanate from the Oval Office and were transmitted via paper documents carried by couriers to soldiers in the field. The actual mission descriptions and orders were contained in several documents, pre-planned mission packages and regulations throughout the U.S. military. The President signed the document, had it witnessed by the White House counsel and by Secretary of Defense Tom Preston, whom he gave it to. "Get the ball rolling, and let's hope we can defuse this damn thing before everyone gets too nervous or excited. Anything else?"

"There is one other point I'm concerned about, General Curtis," the Vice President said pointedly. "What if we run into severe opposition from the Commonwealth or from these Byelorussian troops? What other forces do we have in the region? I think we need something to prove to those warlords out there that we mean business."

Curtis looked taken aback and a little apologetic, which immediately caught the President's attention. Curtis fiddled with his cigar. The President narrowed his eyes with concern. "Wilbur? What about that?"

"Well, sir, our forces in the area are pretty sparse right at the moment," Curtis replied. "The 26th MEU in the Baltic Sea is the closest combat unit—"

"That's it?" the President asked, alarmed. "A thousand Marines and a few Harrier jump-jets?"

"Of course, aircraft and troops from Germany can respond . . . given time," mumbled Curtis.

"How much time?" the Vice President pressed, staying with the pre-agreed script.

Curtis shrugged his shoulders, which only made the President that much more concerned and aggravated. "Probably forty-eight hours for an initial response," said Curtis.

"Forty-eight hours! *Two days?* That's unacceptable!" the Vice President retorted. "If they wanted, the Russians could overwhelm the entire city of Vilnius in six hours, including the American Embassy! We'd have another hostage crisis on our hands!"

"We're trying to keep this crisis as low-key as possible," said Curtis.

"And meanwhile we lose another embassy, this time to renegade military forces," the Vice President said. "That is completely unacceptable." To the President, he said, "Mr. President, I think we need some more firepower in the region—small, unobtrusive, easily recallable, nothing extravagant—but we need them there *now*. We're betting a lot on the actions of a handful of Marines against the full might of the Red Army. They need some backstops."

"But we don't have *time,*" the President said irritably. "You heard the General—two days. We're out of position . . ."

Now for the telling blow . . .

After a short period of silence, when the Vice President was looking angry and frustrated and the President was looking worried, Curtis said, "Well . . . there is one possibility, Mr. President. Some Air Battle Force aircraft from Nevada and South Dakota were scheduled for a deployment to Thule, Greenland, as part of a Rapid Deployment Force contingency exercise. The exercise has been scheduled for months in advance, so it can't be considered an escalation of forces, and the exercise involves only six strike aircraft plus support aircraft—tankers, radar planes, a transport, that sort of thing. We can divert that group and send them into international airspace over the Baltic Sea, close enough to help out but far enough out so it won't seem like we've got a guillotine blade hanging over the Russians' heads."

"What sort of strike aircraft, Wilbur?" asked the President, wishing like hell he were on the tennis courts instead of in this damned briefing.

"They're B-52s, sir," Curtis replied. "Modified B-52s, carrying defensive weaponry and antiarmor cruise missiles."

Modified?

He just bet they were.

It was then that the President figured out that he'd been had—this was General Brad Elliott's unit. Elliott could have been involved in the real Air Battle Force, the rapid-response composite air-combat group stationed at Ellsworth Air Force Base near Rapid City, South Dakota—but this operation smelled just like Brad Elliott. The President didn't change his expression, but he nodded thoughtfully and said, "Okay, I'll think about it."

The Cabinet meeting was adjourned, but the President asked that Curtis, Preston, National Security Advisor Russell, and the Vice President stay.

"All right, what the hell kind of game are we playing here—pull the wool over the old man's eyes? Pretty good acting job, Kevin, until Wilbur mentioned the modified B-52s. You're talking about Brad Elliott's hybrid Death Star whatchamacallits, right?" He turned to Secretary of Defense Preston. "Tom, did you approve of this operation?"

"I did not," Preston replied. "The General and I discussed it. I refused to endorse the idea—I didn't think we needed the Air Battle Force or Elliott's group. Elliott's planes should still be in Nevada."

"They are," Curtis interjected. "But they are formed up and ready to go."

"Ready to do *what?* Go *where?*" the President thundered.

"Sir, I felt it important to formulate a contingency plan in case things began to get out of hand, as the intelligence summary indicates," Curtis replied. "We don't have any heavy striking units closer than two days from Lithuania. If the embassy-reinforcement and REDTAIL HAWK operations proceed, and the Russians or Byelorussians escalate this into a full-scale conflict, they can operate anywhere in Europe completely unopposed. We have drawn down our forces to the point where response times are very, very slow. There is a real danger that nations with democratically elected governments friendly to the United States can be overrun by renegade or adventuristic powers. Brad Elliott's unit may be able to stop them."

The President looked at Curtis and the ambitious Vice President with a warning eye. With irritation dripping in his voice, he said, "I don't like being manipulated by my own fucking advisers. You got something to say to me, say it. But I won't tolerate any ploys or gimmicks, and I *will not* tolerate any secret agendas. I run this show. If you don't like it, run for President and collect fifty percent of the popular vote. See how easy it is."

The President paused, letting his words sink in a bit, then added: "It so happens that I agree with what Wilbur just said. I do think the Byelorussians are up to something; I think the Commonwealth of Independent States may support it, or at least not oppose it; and I think we have an obligation to not only save our interests in the Baltic states but to assist. And I may not like Brad Elliott personally, but the man does seem to position himself and his forces in just the right place at just the right time, God help us.

"So sit down, all four of you, and let's walk through this little operation Brad Elliott has concocted. And let's pray that when the rescue operation starts, we don't have to use Elliott's cockamamie mutant warplanes."

PALANGA BREAKWATER, LITHUANIAN REPUBLIC
13 APRIL, 0309 VILNIUS (12 APRIL, 2109 ET)

Some of the most beautiful beaches in northern Europe are located in Lithuania near the resort city of Palanga, on the Baltic coast nine miles south of the Latvian border. In summer, tourists from all over the Baltics, the Commonwealth states, and southern Scandinavia flock to a seven-mile strip of white sandy beaches north of the city. An extensive network of sea walls, vacuums, and tidal booms, along with hundreds of workers, were pressed into service to filter the polluted water of the Baltic Sea and to keep as much waste and debris off the beaches as possible, and to restore the former port city to a semblance of its pre–World War II grandeur. As a result, the Palanga Breakwater beaches were some of the purest in the industrialized world. A summer-long circus, an amusement park, folk art and crafts shops, and a glass-blowing factory that produces fine crystal and stained-glass windows enhance the attraction and charm of the small Lithuanian seafront community. It was often called the Riviera of the Baltics, although while under Soviet domination the name hardly seemed appropriate.

But the area was home to still another presence—the Commonwealth military. Drawn by the beaches and attractions as well as the tactical placement, the Soviet Troops of Air Defense built an airstrip, a long-range radar site, and an advanced SA-10 surface-to-air missile site just north of the beaches, on a section of oceanfront land almost as nice as the famous Palanga beaches. Not coincidentally, they also built a lavish resort base for their senior officers. The small base's manning swelled from just a few dozen in winter to several hundred in the summer as general officers brought their wives and families to "inspect" the air-defense facility. Of course, when the facility reverted to Commonwealth control, it was not shut down or deactivated.

Until late spring, the Palanga Breakwater is deserted, and except for a skeleton caretaker crew, the same holds true for the air-defense site. The pristine white beaches that are choked with people in the summer are raw, cold, sometimes snow-covered, and very empty this time of year. At night, when the bitterly cold winds blow down from Siberia and out across the Baltic, it can feel like the loneliest, most isolated spot on earth . . .

. . . Perfect for Petty Officer Brian Delbert and his SEAL demolition team.

The howling wind, which created wind-chill factors well below zero, would also mask the sound of their outboard engine as they approached the shore. A Boston Whaler insertion craft, armed with an M-60 heavy machine gun mounted on a steel frame just forward of the helmsman, carried twelve SEALs and over a thousand pounds of equipment. The team was dropped by a Marine Corps CH-46 Sea Knight helicopter twenty miles offshore to the southwest, just out of range of Palanga's big radar net. The Boston Whaler had a heavily muffled forty-horsepower outboard motor that propelled the craft at over twenty miles an hour, but the run to shore took almost two hours because they would stop the motor anytime they were near fishing boats or military vessels. There were plenty of patrols, but apparently none that used night-vision devices while on lookout.

Delbert, nicknamed "Command," was the commander of the raiding team that would go ashore to the objective. The entire group was commanded by a Marine lieutenant, nicknamed Wheel, who would stay with the Boston Whaler and wait for the team to return after dropping them off on the beach.

Every piece of skin on their bodies was covered. All but two SEALs wore thick Mustang suits, with cold-weather fatigues and long underwear underneath, a black insulated balaclava with eye holes big enough for the PVN-5 night-vision goggles they all wore, thick wool gloves with leather shells, and insulated waterproof boots. Two SEALs, in the "swimmer scout" positions, wore black Neoprene wet suits, gloves, and boots under their swimming fins. The SEALs carried their standard assault weapons—Heckler & Koch MP5KA4 9-millimeter submachine guns with thirty-two-round magazines and suppressors; Heckler & Koch P9S 9-millimeter automatic pistols; and a variety of flash-bang, smoke, gas, and incendiary grenades. The swimmer scouts, who would move to the objective on the point position, carried M-37 Ithaca 12-gauge shotguns in waterproof bags. The SEALs also carried six square canvas haversacks resembling Boy Scout camping packs. Each pack was an Mk133 demolition-charge assembly containing eight blocks of M5A1 composition C-4 high-explosive.

Brian Delbert was the oldest and shortest man on the entire team. He was quite different from most of the men who were accepted as Navy SEALs—he was not tall or muscular; he did not look like a triathlete or linebacker. He won his place as SEAL team leader not by physical strength—although he was as powerful as a man fifty pounds heavier—but by brains and resourcefulness. Besides his nickname, he was also known as Weasel, and he preferred that name to any other name or title. Despite his experience—six years as a Navy commando—this was his first team command overseas.

"H-hour is in about two hours," the Lieutenant announced. Delbert, steering the Boston Whaler, nodded that he understood. The timing was close, but they would be able to make it if their intelligence information was at least close: no opposition, no beach patrols, no perimeter patrols, and only a cursory maintenance patrol around the SA-10 missiles and the radar. Dogs were a possibility—satellite phots of the installation clearly showed kennels, and a short inner fence had been set up to keep the dogs away from the taller, motion-sensitive outer fence—but even dogs disliked cold, wet weather. Only U.S. Navy SEALs liked nasty weather.

When within two hundred yards of shore, just outside the surf line,

Delbert killed the outboard motor and dispatched the swimmer scouts to check out the beach. The swimmer scouts were the key to the entire operation. They were often the strongest and smartest men on the team as well as being the best swimmers. While the rest of the team used their paddles to maintain position, they waited for the scouts to check the landing area.

The entire assault team used small wireless FM transceivers called "whispermikes" to talk with each other. Whispermikes operated at very low power and at very short ranges, and were taped to the head and ears. The first message came through a few minutes later: "Command, scouts, all clear," came the report from the scouts. Using flashlights with special lenses that made the light visible only to those wearing night-vision goggles, the scouts directed Delbert onto the beach. Delbert saw that they had picked a pretty good landing zone, or "strongpoint"—between two clusters of rocks, in a narrow sandy inlet that afforded good cover from all sides. Delbert recommended that the scouts' choice of strongpoint be adopted, and "Wheel" agreed. Word went around to memorize the location of the strongpoint.

As soon as they were in knee-deep water, Delbert and five SEALs jumped out of the small black rubber raft and sprinted for shore, being careful to step in each other's tracks to try to disguise their number. Establishing the BDP, or Beach Defense Perimeter, was the most critical step in any amphibious landing in enemy territory—the mission could be ruined in seconds if the team was discovered, especially so close to a military installation. Two SEALs joined the two swimmer scouts and acted as flanking guards, two on each side, scanning down the beach for any sign of discovery. Delbert established the center defense position. Three other SEALs, called the "powder train," carried the Mk133 assemblies onto the beach and took cover behind Delbert. Their weapons were slung on their shoulder straps—their job was not to carry a rifle, but to carry and protect the explosives.

Delbert raised the microphone of his tiny transceiver to his lips. "Beach team, report."

"Right flank secure."

"Left flank secure."

The two flanking guards had dashed out about seventy-five yards from the strongpoint, then separated from each other by about twenty-five yards and set up for overlapping fields of fire on either side. Delbert had to concentrate to find the well-concealed SEALs.

"Copy flanks. Center is secure." He turned and received hand signals from the three men in the powder train. "Train's ready. Scouts, move out. Flanks cover."

The eight-man assault team headed inland, following the dim outlines of the scouts as they checked their maps and compasses and moved toward the air-defense base. Meanwhile, the Lieutenant took the helm of the Boston Whaler, and the last SEAL, called the "cover," used a rake and a small canvas water bag to erase the footprints on the beach. When that was done, they pushed the Boston Whaler into the surf and motored out away from shore, monitoring the progress of the team and watching for any signs of discovery.

Once they were a few hundred yards outside the base, in a well-concealed position, Delbert gathered the team together and gave them another short briefing. Then one scout, one powder carrier, and one flanker split off from the group. They were the backup team, ready to create diversions, mount a flanking assault on a security team, or if necessary attempt to carry out the mission if the main group was trapped or captured. Delbert and his four-man team continued on to their penetration point on the extreme easternmost side of the base, while the second team moved northward to the more populated part of the base, where the headquarters and security buildings were located.

Security at the small base was mostly concerned with tourists wandering into the place during the summer months, so the SEALs found nothing too difficult to defeat. Getting into the base itself was absurdly easy—they could hop the two-meter-tall chain-link fence with ease, hiding between conveniently located scrub oak and cypress trees. It was a quarter-mile fast jog between darkened, deserted buildings to the small airfield, where the team split into two again. One two-man team would jog around the runway to set charges at the radar facility, while the last three-man team, led by Delbert, would set charges on the nearby SA-10 surface-to-air missile's radar and command-control-communications equipment.

The SA-10 "Grumble" surface-to-air missile was the most advanced air-defense missile now deployed outside the Commonwealth. The big missile, resembling an enlarged version of the U.S. Patriot, was stored in a four-round, side-by-side box-launch magazine which was mounted on a trailerable platform. It was capable of destroying both high- and low-altitude aircraft, and its advanced pulse-Doppler tracking system and autonomous radar seeker head made it difficult to jam and almost impossible to evade. Two four-round launchers were set up inside a fenced compound, ringed with sodium-vapor floodlights. Because the missile launchers could be depressed to very shallow angles for use against sea-skimming targets, the compound was clear of any obstructions all the way to the fence. But their objective was not the missiles themselves—it was the plain gray concrete building just outside the fence. Disrupt the equipment inside that building, and the eight SA-10 missiles would be blind.

Weasel and his men waited in the shadows of a radio air-navigation facility to rest and wait for the rest of the team to get into position. The sounds of the Baltic Sea crashing on shore and the sharp ocean breeze made them feel almost relaxed. . . . Almost. The sharp, insectlike *chirp chirp* of Delbert's miniature tactical transceiver cut that image off right away.

"Team Two's in position," he announced. Team Two had run all the way around the base, entering from the north side, and had moved up to within striking distance of the base headquarters building, which conveniently housed the base security office and command post. If they had time and the opportunity, they would set some explosives on vehicles, near doorways, or on communications aerials, trying to disrupt a security response as much as possible. Their objective was not to kill as many soldiers as possible, but to reduce their response effectiveness should the demolition team be discovered before they could set the timed charges.

A few minutes later, a triple *chirp* was heard, and Delbert reported that Team Three was in position around the radar site. The site had three large white radomes—one held the long-range Echo-band search radar, one a Lima-band missile-guidance radar for the SA-10 missiles, and the last a backup Hotel-band radar for both long-range surveillance and missile guidance. The sites were fully automated, lightly patrolled, and minimally manned. Setting explosives to eliminate them would be easy.

He waited a few more minutes, allowing each team a few precious minutes to recheck their weapons and catch their breath, then swung his microphone to his lips to issue the command to attack . . .

He was interrupted by a *chirp chirp . . . chirp chirp,* the *chirp chirp chirp chirp* on the whispermike.

All of Delbert's SEALs froze.

Team Two had issued a warning message and now wanted to talk via voice—only the most serious development could prompt Team Two to break radio silence.

Delbert raised the radio to his lips: "Go."

"Five trucks, thirty armed soldiers, heavy weapons, headquarters building. Mikey's on the roof."

Delbert felt a prickle of sweat start to itch under his collar.

Mike Fontaine, one of the four SEALs in Team Two, had made his way up to the roof of the headquarters building—probably to set time-delay charges on the antennae up there—when a large convoy of trucks had unexpectedly pulled up to the building. Now he was surrounded by troops. Their satellite and HUMINT intelligence had said to expect only minimal activity around the headquarters building all night—no more than a few night-duty officers ever went near the place after hours.

Who the hell were these guys?

"Any sign we've been discovered?"

"Negative." There was a pause, then: "Look like six, maybe eight soldiers staying outside, acting as guards. The rest entering the building."

Twenty soldiers going into the headquarters building? If they were a response team to the SEALs' infiltration, they weren't acting too excited. Maybe they're all getting coffee before hunting down—

"Shots fired—inside the headquarters building!" the Team Two leader suddenly radioed. "I can hear grenades going off . . . shit, a grenade . . . two grenades went off *inside!*"

"Mikey okay?"

"Not directed at Mikey . . . no one's going near the roof . . . hold on . . . Weasel, we gotta get Mikey off the roof. Something serious is going down."

"Time?"

"A minute. No more."

"Hold your position," Delbert said. "In sixty seconds, create a mess and scatter. Copy?"

"Copy."

To his team, he said, "We got thirty seconds to get inside the missile-control center." He outlined exactly how he wanted to do it, a slight variation of the plan devised a week ago from satellite photos and diagrams provided by agents and defectors. He took twenty seconds to explain his ideas, then drew his H & K P95, fitted its suppressor in place, and growled, "Let's go!"

The three-man team split up. One man circled around the perimeter of the control building, out of the glare of floodlights, while Delbert and his partner sprinted for the fence.

The missile-control center was surrounded by a three-meter-high chain-link fence, topped with razor wire and illuminated by floodlights, and there was a thirty-meter clear-fire area from the tall grass and weeds of the runway perimeter to the fence. Delbert took five shots to blow out three nearby floodlights, throwing his section of fence into complete darkness; a few seconds later four more lights soundlessly winked out on the other side of the building. There was no reaction from the building's occupants as they raced across the clear-fire area. Five seconds had elapsed.

Delbert reached the fence and withdrew a small, battery-powered metal saw from his knapsack. The saw was about the size of a Thermos, with a powerful three-inch circular blade. One swipe against the fence, with his partner providing cover, and he had cut a gap in the fence big enough to crawl through. Ten seconds total had elapsed, and still no reaction from the building.

They raced across the clear-fire area.

There were several thin gunports around the building, but all were covered with metal grates—odd. No guards, no patrols, no dogs. Delbert carefully went around to the front of the building. There was a large bulletproof glass window in the front, with a large gunport beside it so the guards could pass identification papers in and out, and beside it was the steel-sheathed front door with a thin, heavily scratched Plexiglas booth around it to keep the chill winter air from rushing in when the door was open. Delbert rolled under the window and carefully checked around the side to be sure the third man was in position. He was already at the side door to the control building, crouched down below another closed gunport.

Delbert gave the signal and the riggers opened the Mk133 packs and broke out the L-shaped hunks of plastic explosive. Each bar weighed forty ounces, and its puttylike consistency made it easy to stuff into the doorframe. Every SEAL qualified in demolitions knew the formulas for determining how much explosives to use—the basic breaching formula ($P = R^3KC$), the conversion factors for a steel door, and the tamping factors for charge placement. A priming adaptor threaded into a hole in each end of the bar, an electric blasting cap pushed into the priming adaptor, and the leg wires from each blasting cap were connected with "Western Union" splices and connected to a standard "hell box" blasting machine with sixty feet of firing wire. The wires from the explosives set on the side door were then led to the rigger and connected to the same hell box. The rigger made a quick continuity check of all wires with a tiny galvanometer circuit-tester and gave Delbert a thumbs-up. Twenty seconds total had elapsed.

When he was ready, Delbert signaled his teammates, and the rigger flipped the safety switch off and threw the "hell handle." The explosives ripped the thick steel doors out of their frames and threw them inside. Even with earplugs, the sound was jarring—but it was far worse for the building's occupants. Delbert threw his body onto one remnant of a door hinge that hadn't completely sheared off its frame. It broke free, and Delbert was flat on his stomach, lying atop the shattered door. But he knew what was going to happen next, so he stayed down and covered his eyes and ears with his arms.

Delbert's partner was right behind him. He tossed in a flash-bang grenade, waited for the nova-bright burst of light and the lung-popping *booom!,* then hopped over Delbert and swept the front room with his submachine gun, looking for targets.

The flying front door had caught one soldier from behind, and he was unconscious in the front area. The security guard just inside the door was a shattered mess. There was a narrow hallway past the security area, two doors on the right, one door on the left, and the main control room straight ahead. Delbert's teammates had entered the control room directly when they blew their door, so Delbert and his partner checked the three other rooms in front before entering it. By the time he finished and joined his teammates in the control room, forty seconds had elapsed—he was ten seconds behind schedule, but they were in without casualties.

Delbert's teammates had scored big in a very short period of time. Two soldiers were lying unconscious on the floor in the control room, one was attending to his minor wounds from another flying door, while three others were already lining up facing a wall with their hands on their heads, coughing from the smoke that partially filled the room. Delbert's rigger was pat-searching the men along the wall, shouting, *"Meznah! Meznah obay ya kochutnya viznuh!"* which was Russian for freeze or he would kill them. The SEAL from the second team was looking around the control room in puzzlement, and Delbert's flanker began doing the same. "Let's go, you guys. Set the charges and let's split."

"Check this out, Weasel," the rigger said. He was pointing at one control console. The radarscopes were smashed in and several removable components in the console were lying in twisted, broken heaps on the floor. A sledgehammer was lying nearby—obviously it had been recently used. "These guys looked like they were busting up the place already."

It was hard to believe, but he was right—the control room looked like it had already been effectively destroyed. The place looked like a country-western saloon after a big fistfight. "Set the charges and let's go," Delbert repeated. The rigger did as he was ordered. "Johnny, guard the front. I'll take the side."

A few minutes later Delbert heard over his whispermike, "I heard an explosion on the other side of the runway. Team Two . . . ?"

"We're out of time," Delbert said. "Set the last charges and let's move out." The process was slow because, for safety's sake, one man only set charges and rigged the leg wires.

One of the captives turned his head and said in rather good English, "Who are you? Are you Americans . . . ?"

"Shut him up, Doug . . ."

"Weasel, look," the SEAL named Doug said. Delbert went over to the men being frisked. "These aren't Commonwealth or MSB uniforms—"

And then Delbert saw it—the gold, blue, and red flag on the man's upper-left jacket sleeve. They all had one. Other patches had been ripped away, and these little cloth flags sewn on in their place. "Lithuanian flags? They're wearing Lithuanian flags . . . ?"

"We are *Lietuvos,*" the soldier said in broken English. "Soldiers from *Lietuva.* You are Americans . . . ?"

"I don't care if he's the king of Sweden," Delbert said angrily. "Team Two has started breaking out of the headquarters area, and the assault team flies within radar range in less than twenty minutes. Cuff these guys, set the charges, and get them out of here. We're behind schedule as it is. Move out."

The initial shock of seeing what appeared to be local militia commandos in a Soviet defense site wore off quickly, and the SEAL team set to work.

In two minutes the rigger had set and programmed over one hundred pounds' worth of composition C-4 high-explosives in the consoles, electrical-junction boxes, data-transmission cable boxes, and every piece of communications gear they could find, and had wired the whole thing to an electronically controlled hell-box firing trigger. They used the Lithuanian commandos' own green and black "tiger stripe" combat jackets to secure their arms, and phone cords to gag the prisoners, then led them outside, through the cuts in the fence, and out across the end of the nearby runway and back across the base perimeter.

Ten minutes of hard running later, they were back outside the small base and hiding in a small supply shed in a stand of trees about five hundred meters from the beach. Delbert ordered a rest stop and an equipment check, and got on the whispermike. "Team Two, report."

"We're clear of the base," Team Two's leader replied. "Moving to the strongpoint."

"We heard your explosions. Did Mike make it out?" asked Delbert.

"Negative," the leader reported. Delbert could hear the team leader's labored breathing as he continued his run to safety, but he could also hear the tension, the frustration in his voice. "That wasn't us. The guys that stormed the building blew it up. Mike was just making his move when the whole building went up."

Ah, shit, Delbert thought grimly. *You always expect to lose a couple of guys on a mission like this, but when things go smoothly you start believing that everything's going to be okay. Just when you start thinking that, the shit hits you in the face.*

"Copy," Delbert said. He took a breath, then continued: "We got a bunch of those guys with us. Looks like they're Lithuanian commandos."

No reply, just a double *chirp* on the radios. He obviously had no more stomach for talk.

Delbert checked in Team Three and coordinated an ETA for the rendezvous and pickup with "Wheel."

"What are we going to do with these guys?" one of the SEALs asked.

"Leave 'em here," Delbert said. "We're not going to risk discovery by letting them go." He sat close to the one who appeared the oldest and asked him, "What unit are you from?"

"We are the Grand Duke's First Dragoons," the man replied in pretty good English.

Delbert felt a flush of anger heat up his face, but he held it in check. Something was going on here, and beating this guy around wasn't going to help. "What is that? Is that Troops of the Interior? Border guards? Internal Security . . . ?"

"We are *not* Soviet," the man spat. "Not Commonwealth. We are Lithuanians. We are now the Grand Duke's First Dragoon Guard of the Lithuanian Republic. We are the Iron Wolf Brigade."

"You mean you're in the Lithuanian Army?" one of the other SEALs asked.

"Lithuania doesn't have a fucking army," Delbert hissed.

The captive smiled, then puffed out his chest with obvious pride. "We do *now,* my friend," he said. "We are the first army of the Lithuanian Republic since the glory days of the Grand Dukes. The Iron Wolf Brigade was the finest army in all of Europe. We will repel all invaders and make our republic a proud nation once again."

The other SEALs were shaking their heads—some in amazement, others in amusement. Delbert was worried about the upcoming mission. "How many men do you have in this First Dragoon Guard?"

It was obvious that the man was hesitant about revealing any more information about his unit. Instead, he tried to put on a jovial tone and said, "You Americans? You can join us. America, land of freedom. You help us drive out Soviets—"

"I asked you—how many men do you have?"

Delbert's tone of voice was definitely threatening, and the Lithuanians, happy enough to have completed their mission and not to be dead or captured by the Soviets, were in no mood to resist. "Eight thousand, maybe ten thousand men," the Lithuanian replied. "A few would not join. Russian traitor dogs. But most all do join. We find more in the cities and villages. Find more from the other Commonwealth units. Men all over are proud to join."

"Who is your commanding officer?"

Another hesitation—but it was obvious again that the pride this man had in his unit and his commander outweighed all other concerns. "Our commander, General Dominikas Palcikas, may God preserve him."

Delbert did not recognize the name.

"We are fighting men from Lithuania. We follow General Palcikas. We carry the Grand Duke's war banner and stand for freedom."

The English language was getting tiresome for this guy, and Delbert thought he was starting to rant. It was almost time to go. Just a few more questions: "Are you a guerrilla army? Guerrilla army?" That term was difficult for the man. "Hide, then strike? Do you have a headquarters? Where is your headquarters?"

The Lithuanian man smiled broadly, then said, "Fisikous."

Delbert almost dropped over backwards from surprise. "Did you say *Fisikous?* The Fisikous Institute near Vilnius?"

The man clasped his hands and nodded enthusiastically. "Site of the last slaughter of our people by the Byelorussians will become birthplace of rightful Lithuanian Republic and headquarters for the Grand Duke's First Dragoon Guard," the man said proudly. "Even now we are capturing that place and claiming it as our own. We are also destroying other defensive-weapon sites, communications centers, command posts, airfields, supply depots, and barracks. With God's help we will succeed in freeing our country."

Delbert shook his head in surprise, then silently ordered his SEALs to pack up and head on out to retrieve the raft—the charges back on the base were set to explode in ten minutes, and they needed to be off the beach and headed out to sea before they blew. "You just might get your wish, my friend," he said as he stood to depart. "A little help from God—and a lot of help from the United States Marine Corps."

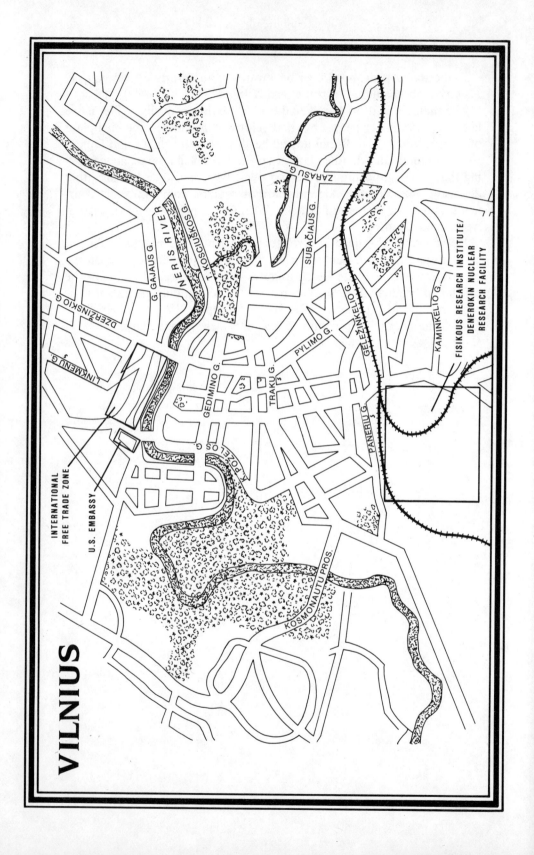

FOUR

Vadim Teresov had only one goal in life—make a man powerful. Be a kingmaker. He had no desire to be the King, but he wanted to make himself indispensable to the King, to be the one who saw to it that the King stayed in power. The perquisites were there, with none of the responsibility.

In Lithuania, and soon in Moscow, the King of the MSB, the Commonwealth's Inter-Republican Council for Security, was Viktor Gabovich. Gabovich was an obsessive micromanager, a stickler for details. Everything had to run just right. The fewer surprises Teresov could lay at Gabovich's feet, the better he liked it.

Gabovich was to arrive at the Fisikous Research Center at six A.M. to interview the chief designers of the Fisikous-170 stealth bomber. The Fi-170 was only a few weeks away from its maiden flight, and Gabovich wanted everything to be perfect—and he wanted to brief them on the deal he had struck with General Voshchanka of the Byelorussian Army. In exchange for supplying weapons, the researchers at Fisikous were going to be allowed to continue working, at full salary and benefits, for as long as they desired.

Teresov had called a meeting at five A.M. to conduct a pre-interview of the entire design team. Any problems would be aired then, the serious problems worked out, the not-so-serious ones discarded, and everyone carefully rehearsed in what they were going to say. No surprises. And for a five A.M. meeting to take place, Teresov had to be in his office at four and on the phone at four-thirty, reminding all of the usually scatter-brained scientists to be on time. He had plenty of leverage with them all—as the man who controlled what Gabovich saw and heard. Many of these scientists realized early on that it was in their own best interests to make Teresov happy.

237

Teresov was about five miles from the Denerokin gate to the facility when he came upon a long line of military vehicles with MSB marking on them. Most of the vehicles were light- or medium-duty trucks, perhaps carrying troops or supplies, but the tail-end vehicles carried old, nearly obsolescent T-62 main battle tanks and combat-engineering vehicles—big vehicles that looked like tanks but carried short-range demolition cannons, dozer blades, and cranes. The convoy was moving at a very rapid clip, nearly fifty kilometers per hour. Although Teresov was the aide for the commander of all MSB units in Lithuania, he did not recognize any of the vehicles in this column.

Security patrolmen on motorbikes—a few with sidecars with PKM machine guns mounted on them—zipped in and out of the convoy, examining side roads and stopping traffic. Several times a security policeman would drive beside Teresov's car, and the soldier in the sidecar would shine a flashlight inside. Teresov would flash his MSB identification card and the soldier would salute and speed off. A security policeman would then return to escort Teresov's car around trucks when it was safe to pass.

By the time Teresov passed through the middle of the convoy, his eyes grew wide in surprise: he saw his first ZSU-23-4 mobile antiaircraft-artillery vehicle.

The squat, beetlelike vehicle looked like a small tank, but instead of one big howitzer cannon the ZSU-23-4 carried four small antiaircraft artillery guns in a quad mount on the forward part of the long, flat turret. On the back of the turret was a radar disk that looked like a large inverted saucepan. Even rolling down the highway, the thing looked lethal. But seeing such an awesome weapon so close to Fisikous made Teresov think back, and to his recollection he had not been briefed on any scheduled troop movements. Were all these vehicles headed for Fisikous? Unlikely—he had heard nothing about reinforcing the one-thousand-man Black Beret garrison there. The Commonwealth Army base at Darguziai was thirty kilometers south of Vilnius, and this road would take them there in about an hour. Was it their destination . . . ?

Better to find out than to sit idly trying to guess the answer. He picked up his UHF radio microphone: "Control, this is Unit Four-One-One, priority three call. Over."

There was a slight delay, then: "This is control. Stand by, Four-One-One."

Teresov waited.

The convoy passed the last major turnoff for Highway 11 to Darguziai—they were headed for the Fisikous Institute, no doubt about it.

Something was definitely wrong here, and the size of this convoy made it imperative that Teresov find out what was going on. Gabovich would certainly want to know. "Control, Four-One-One, priority two." Using priority two was permitted for him, but only for extremely urgent requests. The chance had to be taken . . .

"Go ahead with your priority-two call, Four-One-One."

"Requesting security-clearance records on reinforced infantry unit, perhaps a battalion, traveling down the Sziechesi Highway toward the Fisikous Research Institute. Commanding officer's name, date of request, commander reporting to, and name of approving authority."

"Four-One-One, we cannot comply at this time," the radio-net controller responded. "All channels are tied up with military traffic. Expect a ten-to-twenty-minute delay."

"What's the reason for the delay?" Teresov demanded before stopping himself—he knew what the answer would be.

"That information cannot be released on an unsecured line, Four-One-One," the voice sneered. Whatever pull being Gabovich's assistant and using Gabovich's radio call sign had, went out the window when he made that technical blunder—he would be lucky to get the time of day from them now. "Make your request later or on a secure landline. Control clear."

Damn them, Teresov thought. First this huge convoy of MSB vehicles rolling down the highway, then suddenly all the radiotelephone lines are jammed by the military. What in the hell was going on? And why hadn't he been briefed?

The first opportunity he had, he raced around the last remaining vehicles and zoomed to the head of the convoy. He saw several MSB officers in a large camouflaged van in the front, and for an instant Teresov considered ordering the driver to stop and interrogate the commanding officer for his orders. Finally he saw a face he recognized—Colonel Igor Murzuriev, the chief of logistics for the Inter-Republican Council for Security, based in Kaliningrad. What in hell was *that* paper-pusher out here for? Murzuriev was famous for nothing but his aversion to any sort of hard work. He still considered stopping the van and asking Murzuriev what he was doing—if for no other reason than to find out who or what could have prompted this lardass to get out of bed at this hour and drive all the way across Lithuania to lead this column of equipment.

But he needed to get to the Institute, and being reproached by the radiotelephone operator on a security question that he should know like his own name had taken the fight out of him.

Teresov roared on ahead of the column.

The answers would come soon enough.

OVER THE BALTIC SEA, NEAR THE COAST OF LITHUANIA
13 APRIL, 0309 VILNIUS (12 APRIL, 2109 ET)

The KC-10 Extender aerial-refueling tanker aircraft dropped off its four receivers sixty miles off the coast of Lithuania after giving the planes— two fixed-wing and two hybrid tilt-rotor—a final fill-up. The refuelings were all accomplished at low altitude—about one thousand feet above the Baltic—because they had to try to avoid the dozens of air-defense radars scanning the skies all around them, from long-range search radars to patrol boats with sea-scanning radars; and they had to fly well below any commercial and military aircraft approaching Riga, Klaipeda, or Kaliningrad.

The KC-10—a huge, modified DC-10 airliner carrying almost enough fuel to take the four aircraft all the way back to the United States—was uniquely suited for this mission, not only because of its massive fuel-transfer capability, but because it could service two different kinds of receiver aircraft on the same mission. The KC-10 had a boom-type refueling probe, a fast, high-volume system standard for larger Air Force aircraft, in which a nozzle at the end of a long boom is inserted into a receptacle in the receiver, and it also had a drogue-type refueling system, common on carrier-based aircraft and helicopters, where a nozzle on the receiver aircraft is inserted into a lighted, basketlike drogue on the end of a long, four-inch-diameter hose reeled out by the tanker.

The Extender accomplished a gentle turn to the north, headed toward Stockholm and away from its five charges, then began a steep climb. As the assault aircraft moved inland, an Air Force E-3C AWACS Airborne Warning and Control System radar plane that had been flying at thirty thousand feet over the Baltic moved along with them, scanning the skies for any sign of attackers or conflicting aircraft in the tanker's path and keeping the Marine assault package advised of any hostile aircraft nearby as it crossed the Lithuanian coastline. The long-range APY-2 radar on the AWACS plane could maintain radar contact with the Marine Corps aircraft throughout their mission inside Lithuania.

Patrick McLanahan, flying in one of the tilt-rotor assault aircraft, could see the tankers turn away from the formation out the starboard side windows. There was always this feeling of impending doom every time strike aircraft left their tanker, as if the tanker were the last thin string from order to chaos, from peace to war. When the aircraft you rode in did not turn with the tanker, as it sometimes did during training missions, you knew you were heading off into battle. . . .

Before this mission, that usually just meant flying toward a simulated target, wrapped in a fast-moving jet aircraft with stealth hardware and electronic jammers and other crew dogs with their eyes and ears open, scanning for the enemy. It usually meant that McLanahan had his hands on the controls—if not on the flying controls, at least on the controls to a whole planeload of sophisticated attack avionics. Right now all he had his sweaty, clammy hands on was his lap, trying as best he could not to show the others that they were trembling.

Of course, McLanahan had been in combat before. That was how they lost Dave Luger. But putting your life on the line in a high-tech B-52 bomber, skimming the earth at eight miles per minute, was a lot different from going face-to-face with a guy with a rifle. In air combat, nerve was something you needed just to get into the aircraft, or to keep your aircraft flying and fighting when your equipment was going to hell on you. Nerve was something a fighter pilot needed for a split second to try that one last maneuver or one last jink—if it didn't work, he bugged out and the fight was over.

Nerve was what had earned McLanahan his reputation as the best bombardier in the United States, a fact demonstrated time and time again by long lines of trophies he'd received in navigational and bombing exercises as a B-52 crew member. Pretty good for a guy who wasn't an Air Force Academy grad, or an engineer, or a test pilot. Unlike most of the pilots at HAWC, who were usually flashy, cocky, and swaggering, McLanahan was quiet, efficient, and totally professional. But a hell of a crew dog. His prowess with the B-52, lovingly called the BUFF (for Big Ugly Fat Fucker) was what had originally brought him to the attention of HAWC's commander, Brad Elliott, who was developing the Megafortress.

But out here, exposed and vulnerable, McLanahan was finally beginning to realize that nerve was something the infantryman needed every second. It sustained you, protected you, gave you the energy and conviction to go forward. There was no fibersteel skin, no speed, no electronics to protect you out here. Once you were on the ground, you were alone.

But McLanahan wasn't going in alone—the United States Marines never did anything alone. This assault package contained some of the world's most sophisticated war machines, all preparing to converge on the capital city of Lithuania.

The lead aircraft in the assault package was an Air Force MC-130H COMBAT TALON II. It was on the books as a cargo aircraft, a typical "trash hauler," but it was anything but typical. It was fitted with the world's most sophisticated airborne navigation, terrain, and weather-avoidance systems, along with special target sensors, worldwide communications capability, electronic-warfare jammers and decoys, and special support equipment that allowed it to fly into very heavily defended areas and deliver supplies or insert (or retrieve) personnel. It carried twenty thousand pounds of supplies, mostly for the special-operations troops on this mission, but some were destined for the American Embassy personnel in Vilnius.

The number-two aircraft in the formation was an AC-130U Spectre gunship. The Spectre carried three big guns—one 25-millimeter high first-rate cannon for ground troops and light vehicles, a 40-millimeter cannon for use against light armored vehicles, and a huge 105-millimeter bunker-buster howitzer for buildings and heavy armor, all firing out the left side. The guns were remotely aimed by sensor operators using heat-seeking sensors, telescopic low-light television cameras, and all-weather high-resolution radars. Orbiting over a target area, the Spectre could rain death and destruction on hostile forces with great precision, in any weather. It also carried twelve Hellfire laser-guided rockets, six on each wing on pylons near the wingtips, that could destroy tanks and other targets at much longer range than the cannons.

The last two aircraft, call signs Hammer Three and Four, were not technically part of the assault team, and would not show up on the roster of "Congo" aircraft or crews involved in the mission. Spread out on the right trailing position of the assault formation were two Marine Corps MV-22A SEA HAMMER tilt-rotor aircraft. The MV-22 was the Marine Corps version of the Air Force CV-22 PAVE HAMMER, and the replacement for the venerable CH-46 Sea Knight troop-transport helicopter, which was slated for retirement. Based at Cherry Point Naval Air Station and used extensively on Marine Corps amphibious-assault carriers like the USS *Wasp,* the MV-22 could take off and land vertically like a helicopter but had the speed, range, and cargo-carrying capability of a turboprop fixed-wing airplane. These two aircraft were modified for low-altitude, terrain-following navigation, precision airdrops, electronic warfare, and fire suppression.

Unlike their Air Force brothers, these SEA HAMMER aircraft had far more weapons aboard, to provide more close air support for the Marines they carried along. Along with the 20-millimeter Hughes Chain Gun cannon pod on the portside sponson and one twelve-round Stinger heat-seeking missile pod on the starboard-side sponson, which were targeted by a PNVS/NTAS (Pilot's Night Vision System/Navigation Targeting Attack System) imaging infrared sensor aimed by a head-pointing fire-control system, the MV-22 also had one 7.62-millimeter Minigun in the starboard-side entry door and one Minigun centered in the rear cargo ramp, all to support the Marines.

The first SEA HAMMER carried eighteen Marines, part of the 26th Marine Expeditionary Unit (Special Operations Capable), members of the Marines' elite Assault and Building Clearing Units; the "Hammer" assault team leader, Marine Corps Captain Brian Snyder, his radioman, and his executive officer were riding in the first MV-22. They would command the overall strike on the Fisikous Research Center from the SEA HAMMER aircraft. These Marines were specially trained to enter and search a building. Back at Camp Lejeune, they had trained for over a week on a building similar to the target building in the Fisikous compound. Instead of standard combat BDUs and Corcoran jump boots, they wore black flashsuits with Kevlar body-armor vests and lightweight HiTech sneakers. They wore the new INVADER helmet, nicknamed "Darth Vader" or simply "Vader," a helmet resembling a bug-eyed pilot's helmet and oxygen mask. The Vader helmet combined a set of removable night-vision goggles, a gas mask, and a tiny VHF whispermike communications set in a single bug-eyed bulletproof Kevlar helmet.

Their standard weapons were MP5SD 9-millimeter assault submachine guns with infrared flashlights and sound suppressors, and .45-caliber Colt Government Model 1911A1 automatic pistols—Special Operations Capable forces were the only Marines that carried the old "slabsides" .45 automatic. Four Marines carried Hydra automatic grenade launchers, a weapon with a large twenty-round rotary drum that contained high-explosive and fragmentation grenades—the desired-type grenade could be selected and launched with a simple flick of a switch. All of the Marines carried "flash-bang" stun grenades, fragmentation grenades, and CS tear-gas canisters.

Riding in the number-two MV-22 aircraft were another eighteen Marines who composed the landing-zone security team for the Fisikous operation. It was their job to set up a secure landing pad for the two MV-22s. The individual weapons were heavier, designed for better, more sustained hitting power—M-16A2 rifles, 9-millimeter M9 Beretta automatic pistols, 5.56-millimeter M249 FN Minimi Squad Automatic Weapon (SAW) machine guns, LAW antitank rockets, shoulder-fired Stinger antiaircraft missiles, and M79 and M203 40-millimeter grenade launchers.

Under the direct supervision of Marine Gunnery Sergeant Wohl, Patrick McLanahan, John Ormack, and Hal Briggs were assigned to this platoon. It would be their job to identify Dave Luger when the assault team brought him out, and then once the building was cleaned out they would go back in to get any files they could find on the Fi-170 Soviet stealth bomber until things got too hot for the small team. The three officers were also assigned to carry extra grenades and cans of extra ammunition for the SAW machine-gun teams.

As part of the landing-zone security team, the three Air Force officers were armed like any other Marine on their team. They all carried 9-millimeter automatics as sidearms, and Briggs and McLanahan carried M-16 rifles. But because Ormack could never work out the intricacies of the standard infantry rifle, he was given an MP5 9-millimeter submachine gun with thirty-two-round magazines instead—the German-made weapon was virtually soldierproof, very jam-resistant, and easy to operate.

Each officer also had a standard Kevlar infantry helmet, painted black, with infrared I.D. tape on the back, strapped down tightly on his head. An NVG-9 night-vision goggle assembly was attached to the helmet on a swivel mount, with the battery cable leading around the helmet and down the back of the neck to the battery pack on the back of the ALICE harness. Their ALICE harness contained first-aid kids, a KaBar knife, water canteens, extra ammunition, infrared chemical light sticks and tape, and minimal survival gear. Standard-issue Marine Corps fatigues, boots, and gloves—along with carefully applied camouflage makeup—completed their outfit. Like the Building Clearing Team troops, the three Air Force officers wore full Kevlar body armor, front and back. The SAW Security Team Marines wore only lightweight flak vests for protection against flying debris or shrapnel.

Briggs couldn't wait to get into the action, and he looked it—he seemed to wear the gear comfortably, almost casually. But McLanahan and Ormack were unaccustomed to going into a fight with so much shit strapped to their bodies, and they had trouble making even simple movements like climbing an aircraft boarding ladder or adjusting a lap belt.

Gunnery Sergeant Wohl noticed all this, and the more he noticed the more worried he became.

The infantry company commander in charge of the Fisikous security team, an impossibly young-looking Marine first lieutenant, was on board as well. Wohl and the company commander had been speaking for quite some time when Wohl finally squeezed between the Marines jammed in the cabin and sat down next to the three Air Force officers.

"I thought about this for a long time, sirs," Wohl said to Ormack and the others after refueling was completed. "I finally spoke with the platoon sergeant and the one-LT."

Patrick glanced over at the commander of Alpha Company, 2-5 Marines, First Lieutenant William Marx. The guy looked like he was about sixteen years old, with a Kevlar helmet that appeared three sizes too big for him and wearing a .45-caliber Colt automatic on his hip that looked too heavy for him to heft. But he commanded one of only three infantry companies in the 26th Marine Expeditionary Unit that had qualified as special operations capable, which was one of the greatest achievements a young commander could aspire to in the Corps. If Wohl, a fifteen-year veteran of the Marine Corps, showed obvious respect for the man,

McLanahan had to be impressed. The platoon sergeant, a huge, somber, mean-looking black gunnery sergeant by the name of Trimble, hadn't spoken two words to the three Air Force officers the entire time they were together.

"The one-LT agreed with my decision," Wohl continued. "I hate to do this to you, but you two"—he pointed at Ormack and McLanahan—"are not carrying a rifle."

McLanahan couldn't believe what he'd just heard. It was as if Wohl had just insulted him. And worse, McLanahan had just started getting used to the thing, although he was far from a master or even qualifying with it. Not being allowed to carry it hurt. But there was no argument— everyone had learned well not to argue with Wohl.

Ormack picked up his MP5, removed the magazine, opened the breech so Wohl could double-check that no round was in the chamber, and handed it over.

McLanahan did the same with his M-16.

Wohl gave the weapons to an Air Force crew chief, who stowed them in a rack within easy reach of the MV-22's door gunner. "You've got your sidearm, and you tested pretty good with it. Captain Briggs will help you guys out."

McLanahan had the feeling that Wohl was silently saying, *And I pray you losers will never have to draw it.*

"I didn't want to carry the damn thing anyway," Ormack said as he began to unclip the ammo pouches from his ALICE harness and handed the stuff over to Wohl to redistribute through the platoon. "Never got used to it." His voice seemed distant and hollow.

Hearing Ormack scared McLanahan a bit. Would his own voice sound that way if he spoke right now? He didn't want to find out, but he *had* to talk about it. McLanahan nodded toward the other camouflage-suited Marines around them and said to Ormack, "Let those guys handle the shooting. We'll keep our heads down and get Dave."

Ormack seemed to like the logic in that, although his averted eyes and hesitant nod showed how many doubts the man really was carrying around inside of him.

The MV-22 made a steep turn and seemed to settle even closer to the ground. Patrick, who was accustomed to flying big aircraft at very low altitudes, didn't think they could get any closer to the ground, but they did. The winds were gusting and the ride was bumpy, and for the first time in his career he felt the odd queasiness of airsickness.

Hal Briggs seemed to notice it right away, even in the dim red light of the crew cabin. "You're lookin' a little green, Muck," the Air Force security officer said. "Think of eating a lemon—that always helps me."

"I'm used to flying low, at night, and in shitty weather," McLanahan said, "but I'm usually at the controls, or at least I can see outside. Being chauffeured like this isn't fun. I need a window."

"I can tell you barf stories that would curl your hair," Briggs said with a smile, "but that won't help your stomach. Think of Dave. We'll see him soon."

That was their small group's battle cry over these past few weeks. Whenever they felt like quitting, or were getting frustrated from lack of knowledge, or couldn't perform some task or feat, to themselves or to one of the others they would say: Think of Dave.

Sometimes, McLanahan thought, life takes truly strange courses. Three weeks ago he was working on modifications to the B-2 stealth bomber they had received in Dreamland. Two weeks ago he had learned that Dave Luger was alive, and hours later he was shooting an M-16 rifle for the first time—the *very* first time. One week ago he was up to his knees in mud being screamed at by some deranged Marine gunnery sergeant. Now he was sitting in a web seat on a special operations aircraft, wearing a knife and camouflage paint on his face and a big 9-millimeter automatic pistol at his side, flying into Lithuania.

A strange course of events, indeed.

And now he didn't have the damned rifle anymore. Whether that was an improvement or not, he wasn't sure.

A few moments later Lieutenant Marx got to his feet and faced the rear of the SEA HAMMER. Holding on to handrails on the cabin ceiling against the constant sway and chopping motion of the plane, he shouted, "Third platoon!"

The Marines responded with an animal-like growl—even the three Air Force officers could not help but let out a yell. After being with the Marines for two weeks, everything about this elite group of warriors rubbed off on them.

"We're about ten minutes out. Gunny Wohl will go over last-minute instructions. Our mission is simple: go in, locate and secure the zoomie, and control the situation while these three Air Force officers rifle some desks. Fifteen minutes on the ground and then we'll be off and outta here."

McLanahan's ears burned when he heard Marx refer to Dave as the zoomie, but other Marines made it very clear that Luger was little more than a target, a guy to be located and "secured." But their first priority was to look out for themselves and their buddies. A Marine would risk his life to accomplish the mission, but he would not sacrifice it.

"The Soviets in this research facility hold an American Air Force officer, and they have imprisoned and tortured this officer for many years. The Soviets have denied the existence of this man, but we know he is there. We have been ordered to locate him and retrieve him. Once inside the facility, your actions will be swift, decisive, powerful, and deadly. We will enter their facility, destroy all opposition, take what is ours, and leave. Above all, use your heads. Think. Stay aware of the situation around you. Communicate. Act. Is that *clear?"*

There was another loud animal-like growl from the squads.

"What are your questions?"

There were none.

"Gunny Trimble, continue the briefing and prepare your men to attack."

The four-aircraft assault formation was not the only mission going on that night—in fact, it was not even the largest or the primary one. The reinforcement and resupply of the U.S. Embassy in Vilnius was the primary mission, and that had been under way long before the two Marine Corps and two Air Force fast-movers crossed into Lithuanian airspace. The attack on Vilnius had actually started hours before the four aircraft finished their refuelings.

Launching off the Marine amphibious-assault ship *Wasp,* on station in the Baltic Sea and guarded by six Navy escorts, was the main body of the assault package: eight Marine Corps helicopters. The two Air Force and one Marine Corps fixed-wing aircraft would sweep in over the Lithuanian capital several minutes ahead of the helicopters, making a vital airdrop of supplies into the embassy grounds and countering any ground defenses. Then, when the Marines in the embassy compound were resupplied and ready, the eight-helicopter Marine embassy-reinforcement task force would make their assault.

The armed-escort duties of the Marine-helicopter assault package were handled by four Bell Helicopter-Textron AH-1W Sea Cobra helicopters. The AH-1W was the standard Marine Corps tactical assault-escort helicopter, armed with a steerable 20-millimeter gun in a nose turret, four laser-guided Hellfire air-to-ground missiles for use against heavily armored vehicles, and two AIM-9L Sidewinder heat-seeking air-to-air missiles. These Sea Cobras, call sign Rattler, were also equipped with two external fuel tanks to help extend their range for the long flight through Lithuania.

The primary troop carriers for the assault package were four Marine Corps CH-53E Super Stallion helicopters, call sign Manta. Two of the four huge forty-thousand-pound machines, nicknamed Echoes, carried fifty Marines—two reinforced fire-team companies—and a crew of six, including two pilots, a flight engineer, and three door gunners armed with 7.62-millimeter Miniguns for ground-fire suppression. Instead of troops the third Echo carried thirty thousand pounds of supplies, all for the Marines who would be reinforcing the embassy, plus logistical equipment; and the fourth Super Stallion carried three large, round, rollable fuel bladders, each containing sixteen hundred gallons of jet fuel. Each Super Stallion could be refueled inflight, even at very low altitude or while under attack, by Marine Corps KC-130 tanker aircraft launched out of Germany.

The commander of the entire operation, Marine Corps Major Richard "Boxer" Jurgensen, and three members of his senior staff, rode in the number-one Super Stallion. After years of leading amphibious assault teams, Jurgensen, a tall, lanky, fifteen-year Marine Corps veteran, was leading his first heliborne assault. He was not a tremendous advocate of the Marine special operations concept, and his only concern was that the secret operation over Fisikous not interfere with what he perceived as his number-one priority—the embassy-reinforcement operation.

The five fast-moving aircraft arrived over the city about ten minutes before the helicopters. The AC-130 Spectre gunship arrived over the embassy grounds first and set up an immediate attack orbit five miles in diameter, centered on the embassy, which was in the northwest corner of the city. Bounded by Vytauto Avenue, Tarybu Avenue, Ziugzdos Avenue, and the Neris River, the embassy grounds were easy to spot on radar—especially since the Marines already in the compound put large radar reflectors and infrared beacons on the embassy rooftops to direct the assault formation. The sensor operators on the AC-130 began tracking all known Commonwealth and Byelorussian troop concentrations, storing each discovered weapon and vehicle location into the fire-control computer. With a huge data base of targets already pre-stored in the computer, gathered from satellite surveillance of the area, the weapons operator could begin his attack by hitting a single button.

Force timing was perfect—as soon as the two armed aircraft set up their defensive orbits, the MC-130 COMBAT TALON was ready to begin its run. It came in from the northwest, turned, and headed east after crossing Paribio Avenue and the complex of thirty 20-story apartment buildings that overlooked the city and continued east away from the embassy. This was an attempt to fool any pursuers that their target was not the embassy. But there was no pursuit. The COMBAT TALON aircraft headed out another seven miles, paralleling the Neris River, which ran through the northern part of the city, until they passed the Sports Palace and were abeam Gediminas Tower—the medieval castle built by the Grand Duke—before making a sharp 180-degree left turn and heading for the embassy. Intelligence photos taken by KH-12 satellites showed that Commonwealth troops had lined Dzerzinsky Avenue, the main north-south street in and out of the city, so the COMBAT TALON crews hoped that flying over those troops' positions from two different directions would confuse them.

Careening in from the northeast now, the MC-130 swept in over the City of Progress free-trade zone and headed toward the embassy. The embassy was located just outside the southwest corner of the City of Progress, on the banks of the Neris. As it came over Lvovo Avenue, the street that defined the northern boundary of the free-trade zone, the MC-130 opened its cargo doors. At Ukmerges Avenue, the MC-130's crew began ejecting large, parachute-equipped fiberglass cases of food, supplies, water, and weapons into the embassy. Several cases went into the trees, and a few landed on rooftops, but most of the supplies hit their marks perfectly, impacting in the open park/clear fire zone around the ambassador's residence. The cases were retrieved and dragged inside immediately.

The Marines and embassy personnel already in the compound went to work next. While the Marines set up an aircraft-defense perimeter around the landing zone, the embassy personnel laid out two sixty-foot landing zones, using infrared chemical illumination sticks staked to the ground. One eight-inch-long chemical light stick, visible only by those wearing night-vision goggles, was enough to illuminate the landing zone. As the other Super Stallions orbited nearby, the first helicopter, carrying fifty Marines, Major Jurgensen, and his command staff, landed on the embassy grounds. Racing off the chopper, he trotted over to the set of stairs leading up from the park toward the ambassador's residence, where a small crowd of people was waiting. Manta Three landed a few moments later.

"Where's the ambassador?" Jurgensen shouted over the roar of the helicopter.

"Here!" a voice replied. Ambassador Lewis K. Reynolds, a short, mustachioed black man with short salt-and-pepper hair, and glasses, went over to the Marine. "Glad to have you here. You are Major Jurgensen . . . ?"

"Yes, sir, I am. Is everything set up as I requested?"

"Main communications center has been moved to the roof, as you asked," Reynolds replied. "The Marines set up another desk with radios downstairs, right inside that door." He pointed toward his residence. "They will act as your flow control for the evacuation."

Just then, Major Jurgensen's executive officer came up to him and said, "Sir, Manta Three is down." Manta Three was the CH-53E that carried the fuel bladders. "Hydraulic leak."

Jurgensen cursed softly. They always planned on losing a certain number of aircraft in every operation, usually every one in four, but when it actually happens it gets frustrating and it always feels as if it's totally unexpected. "They got an ETIC for me?"

"Two hours' minimum."

"Crap." Jurgensen glanced at the stricken helicopter, then at Reynolds. "Is everyone ready to go?"

"Yes, Major. The embassy lieutenant has the list of people going, and here's the list of people staying. It's been approved by the State Department."

"How many to go altogether?"

"Two hundred and three."

Jurgensen frowned. "That's about sixty more than they told me about, Ambassador."

"More civilians showed up than we were told at first," Reynolds replied. "All women and children. No men."

Jurgensen paused for a moment, then said, "Well, we just lost one of our evacuation helicopters, so it's going to be a very tight fit, but we can take them. No one brings any luggage. No carry-ons at all, just themselves."

"I told them that already," Reynolds said. "I was in the Marine Corps, back in Vietnam. I know the cargo capacity of the Sea Stallion."

"Very well. We'll take sixty-eight per Echo. As soon as we off-load our gear, we'll start loading up the helicopters." To his executive officer, he said, "Fold the rotors on Manta Three and get it off the landing pad so we can get the other choppers on the ground. Move."

Using Jeeps and trucks from the embassy parking lot, the stricken Super Stallion chopper was unceremoniously dragged off between a few trees to make room for other helicopters, its refueling equipment hastily unloaded. The second Super Stallion was refueled, and it lifted off to make room for another bird. Soon the third Super Stallion was on the ground off-loading Marines, and the fourth chopper landed on the second pad and immediately began unloading equipment and supplies. The second helicopter made random orbits over the area, searching for any sign of hostile action. So far, nothing.

When refueling was completed, they began loading civilians onto the helicopters. People had to double up on seat belts and hold on to children, and Marines unceremoniously grabbed large bags and briefcases from staffers ignoring the ambassador's instructions not to take carry-on luggage, and tossed them onto the embassy grounds. A few staffers and civilians refused to go on the crowded helicopter, and they were removed and a man put in their place. The last helicopter swooped in after the first two lifted off, refueled, another sixty-eight Americans were loaded aboard one of them, and the three helicopters with civilians on board lifted off and headed southwest, being careful to stay away from the Fisikous Institute and the airport on the south side of the city.

"Super Stallions are at the rendezvous point," Jurgensen's executive officer reported.

"Good. Bring 'em in," Jurgensen ordered.

The three Super Stallions would wait in a large clearing far northwest of the city, a spot already selected by satellite reconnaissance and patrolled by Army Special Forces troops on the ground. The AC-130 gunship would set up a protective orbit over this spot, destroying any ground vehicles that looked as if they might be a threat. Once the Sea Cobras were refueled, the rotary-wing aircraft would all form a massive air convoy and head for the Polish border, where the unarmed aircraft had already received permission from the Polish government to land. Because the Polish government would not allow any foreign armed aircraft to cross into its airspace, the Sea Cobras and Spectre gunship would continue out to the Baltic Sea, and the AT-1Ws would land on the USS *Wasp.* The AC-130 gunship would return to the embassy to search for any hostile forces moving toward the embassy, then continue on to Rhein-Main, Germany, for recovery. One by one the fuel-starved Sea Cobra attack helicopters came in for refueling.

Jurgensen asked, "What's the status of the Hammer assault team?"

"Still a go," the executive officer replied. "All birds in the green."

"Then be sure to leave enough fuel for them, at least three thousand pounds per," Jurgensen said. "Reduce the number of Sea Cobra escorts if you have to. Washington wants those Marines and their stuff out of the country."

The Marines had enough fuel left over to completely top off only two Cobras, so the other two helicopters took reduced fuel loads only. Those two Cobras that were fully fueled would launch and escort the Super Stallions back to friendly airspace. The others were made ready to launch from the embassy grounds, awaiting orders from the White House for any other missions they might be given.

The evacuation had attracted the attention of a large crowd of Lithuanians outside the gates of the embassy, who watched with fascination as the women and children were flown out. They waved gaily at the Sea Cobras flitting overhead, and they cheered as the last Super Stallion lifted off. A few Lithuanian Self-Defense Force soldiers had appeared, but they cheered just as loudly as the rest, looking on with admiration and envy at the well-disciplined Marines at work.

Within forty minutes after the first chopper hit the ground, and without firing a shot, over two hundred American civilians—all of the embassy personnel dependents and a few civilians and staffers—were being flown to freedom. Escorted by the MC-130 COMBAT TALON aircraft and two AH-1W Sea Cobra attack helicopters, the three Super Stallions immediately headed southwest to the Polish border city of Suwalki, only ninety miles away.

* * *

When the embassy assault package turned north to begin its south-westerly run on the embassy grounds, two aircraft—the two Marine Corps MV-22 SEA HAMMER tilt-rotors—peeled off to the south and headed through the center of the city itself. With Gediminas Castle and the wispy, delicate-looking spires of St. Anne's Church on the right and the hulking twin towers of the Church of Saints Peter and Paul to the left, the two aircraft sped just thirty feet above the apartment buildings, churches, and office buildings of downtown Vilnius. Past Iron Wolf Hill, the birthplace of the capital city of Lithuania, the SEA HAMMER aircraft sped above the Lithuanian Art Museum and the State Youth Theater of Lithuania building, two prominent land-marks, before picking up the railroad tracks in the southern part of the city.

A few minutes later the pilots could see the three huge buildings and hourglass-shaped cooling towers that made up the Denerokin Nuclear Research Facility. "Two minutes to first drop," they reported.

The announcement surprised McLanahan—in the darkened cargo hold of the SEA HAMMER aircraft, being tossed, turned, and tilted so often, he completely lost all sense of time. He checked that his shoulder harness and lap belts were tight—no need to check his rifle on SAFE anymore, since he wasn't carrying one—and he gave his Kevlar helmet strap another tug.

Less than sixty seconds to go . . .

He was really doing it.

They were going to invade . . .

A few seconds later the rear cargo ramp began to motor down, and McLanahan got his first glimpse of Lithuania—and his first realization of exactly how damned *low* they were! Their forward velocity had slowed a bit, but that only served to increase their vertical velocity as the pilots dodged power lines, buildings, and floodlight towers. The noise was incredible. His memory flashed back to a visit of Niagara Falls as a kid, and the sound from the SEA HAMMER's twin turbo-props was very similar to the roar of the falls. A railroad-yard light tower flashed by not twenty feet away, and in the glare of the sudden illumination he could see John Ormack staring straight ahead, his eyes glassy, his left index finger twitching on his lap. McLanahan looked at Briggs, and even without the light he could see a shit-eating grin across his face. Hal Briggs was enjoying the hell out of this. Hal Briggs was *made* for this kind of action.

Hal gave McLanahan a thumbs-up and another grin. Patrick noticed that Hal's right index finger was already exposed through the tiny shooter's slit in the glove's finger—they hadn't even hit the ground yet and he was ready to pull the trigger.

FISIKOUS RESEARCH INSTITUTE
13 APRIL, 0315 VILNIUS (12 APRIL, 2115 ET)

Teresov stood before the incredible monstrosity and shook his head with an absolute feeling of awe. *Yes,* he thought, *I can see why some men would kill another human being to see this thing fly.*

He was standing before the Fisikous-170 *Tuman* stealth bomber. *"Tuman"* means "fog," and the name was appropriate—it looked like a huge gray fog bank. The bottom of the fuselage was well over five meters above ground, and the huge, gracefully curving body stood on tall, thick, landing gears. It was almost sixty-one meters wide, far larger than the American B-52 Stratofortress or B-2 Black Knight stealth bomber, and it had 50 percent more weapons payload capability than the B-2. The manta ray–like body looked thick and not very aerodynamic, but on closer inspection one could see that the fuselage, except along the center, was very thin. The wingtips curled down in a sexy arc, making it appear that the manta ray was flapping its undulating wings.

Teresov smiled, thinking that what was even more surprising than the machine itself was the fact that for the past ten years it was constructed in total secrecy. There had not been, he thought smugly, one word about it in the Western press or in the reports that were sometimes intercepted from Western intelligence agencies on new Soviet equipment. There had been lots of speculation about what was going on inside the three Fisikous hangars, naturally, but nothing else. Even during the political upheavals in Lithuania, the lid had always stayed screwed down tight on Fisikous. It was a testimonial, he thought, to the extraordinary security measures instituted by Viktor Gabovich. Gabovich had his fingers in every government organization in the ex-Soviet Union—anything that had to do with Fisikous, from any branch of the government, went across his desk for review and approval.

Of course, the minute they rolled out the monster from its lair, the secrecy would be over. But with the American B-2 stealth bomber project stalled at only fifteen planes—one squadron, a laughable amount for so advanced a warplane—and numerous other aircraft and weapons programs canceled, the Fi-170 would be a tremendous shock to the world. When they realized that it was truly as effective as it looked, it would throw the Soviet Union—or the Commonwealth of Independent States, or the Belarus Republic, whomever Gabovich and the scientists at Fisikous decided to support—right back into the forefront of modern military-technical leadership.

Teresov sensed the approach of the security force commander, Colonel Nikita Kortyshkov. "What did you find out, Colonel?" Teresov asked without taking his eyes off the magnificent machine before him.

"The radios are jammed with traffic," Kortyshkov replied. "Some breakdown in communications between several outlying bases. Partisan guerrillas may be involved."

That was a better explanation than others he'd heard—solar flares, a Baltic Sea Fleet exercise, a few others. The people of Lithuania were getting restless. They needed to be taken down another peg, starting with their hometown hero, Dominikas Palcikas. General Voshchanka had to make an example of Palcikas. "I'm interested in that convoy, Kortyshkov, not in the radios."

"I could not find any specific details on the convoy you saw, sir," Kortyshkov said. "But there is a general Commonwealth mobilization under way in the northwest parts of the country, so they may have been deployed very recently."

"Why has a Commonwealth mobilization been called?" Teresov asked. He still did not know the identity of the MSB troops heading toward Fisikous, but they must be part of whatever was happening tonight. "I was not informed."

"As I said, sir, the radios are messed up. Several bases are not reporting, and the command network has been disrupted. There's quite a bit of confusion out there. I think the central telecommunications facility in Kaunas has probably had an overload—"

"I'm not interested in your speculation," Teresov said impatiently. "I need concrete data. You can get it for *me* or you can stand before General Gabovich and try to give him lame excuses and useless speculation. Now about that convoy: did you at least discover if it is destined for Fisikous?"

"Yes, sir. They are approaching the Denerokin gate right now."

Teresov was already running late—Gabovich would be arriving in a little more than an hour and he hadn't met with the chief engineers yet. Well, the deployment of MSB troops wasn't Teresov's concern right now. No one would get inside Fisikous without proper orders. Teresov would see to it that Gabovich was not delayed when he arrived.

"I want you to personally see to it that whoever commands that convoy has proper orders before he brings one truck inside the gate," Teresov said. "I will accept nothing less than General Gabovich's signature on the orders. In the meantime make sure that the road is clear for General Gabovich's arrival. And double the guards around the *Tuman* until the situation with the radios has been resolved."

DENEROKIN SECURITY GATE, FISIKOUS RESEARCH INSTITUTE
13 APRIL, 0320 VILNIUS (12 APRIL, 2120 ET)

The Commonwealth security radio command net was buzzing with orders, queries, and general confusion. "What in hell is going on?" one MSB corporal asked his supervisor.

"They keep on saying there are helicopters over the city, but they're not sure where or how many," the sergeant in charge of the security detail, Sergeant Vladimir Mikheyev, replied. "First they say over the Sports Palace, then over the parliament building, then over the City of Progress—wait a minute . . . now they're saying four helicopters over the City of Progress and a big fixed-wing over the parliament building. Hell, who knows?"

"Should we ask for confirmation?"

"We already did that and they told us to stay off the air," the sergeant replied. "No aircraft have been reported south of Traky Avenue, so we don't go into stage-two alert."

"Is it the Commonwealth Army? Is it the Byelorussians? What are they doing over the city . . . ?" asked the corporal.

"They never tell us anything anyway—why should they tell us now?" He was interrupted by a telephone call from the outer security gate near the highway. "Sergeant Mikheyev . . . what? Reinforcements? Yes, that peacock—Major Teresov did mention the convoy. How many trucks . . . ? What do you mean, you don't know? At least thirty . . . with a tank and antiaircraft artillery? Led by a colonel? Colonel who? Logistics commander . . . Murzuriev? Yes, Teresov authorized it, if he's got orders from Gabovich. Yes, send him on in. Does he want to bring every truck in? Yes? Why doesn't he bring them in through the south gate . . . ? Don't be a smartass, Simikov . . . no, I don't need to talk to him. I'll check his orders here. Just remind him we'll have to check each vehicle individually and it may take a while . . . yes, *you* tell him. Out."

Mikheyev replaced the handset. "Well, something's going on. Headquarters is sending in a reinforcement company and a colonel, Murzuriev, to deploy around Denerokin. Get me Murzuriev's access badge."

The corporal turned to a cabinet with row after row of plastic-laminated restricted-entry badges with small black-and-white photos on them. Anyone wishing entry to the Denerokin facility would have to produce a matching I.D. card and exchange it for the badge. The guards inside the security compound would examine the badges to be sure they matched, then compare the photo to the bearer. The corporal pulled Murzuriev's photo badge. "I've never met Murzuriev before. Wonder what he's like."

"He's a staff weenie that was probably the only one sober enough to do this job when they called," Mikheyev said. "Just alert the rest of the compound that we've got a headquarters colonel coming in. Then call Teresov and tell him the convoy has arrived. We'll have to secure an area for them to bring their stuff in until the entire crew is checked out."

Used only by engineers and technicians assigned to the nuclear power plant itself, the northeast Denerokin gate was nonetheless the most heavily guarded entrance to the entire facility. Once past the outer guard post, vehicles entering the plant were stopped inside a large entrapment area, where the occupants were removed and the vehicle searched from top to bottom. The entrapment area ensured that at least one heavy gate was closed at all times on both personnel and vehicles.

A few minutes later the lead truck stopped outside the outer entrapment area gate. An officer dressed in standard green fatigues, wearing a large infantry helmet with MSB insignia, walked to the smaller personnel entry gate. Because he wore the stars of a colonel, he and four other officers—five was the most persons allowed in the badge-check area at one time—were admitted immediately to the entrapment area, but the outer gate remained closed.

The sergeant inside the security bunker saw that the officer wore a thick gray scarf around his neck, partially covering his chin, and the helmet was pulled down low over his eyes, so he couldn't readily recognize the man—he had the same general height and build of Colonel Murzuriev, and he had Murzuriev's thin little mustache, but it was still hard to be sure. The Colonel stepped up to the large thick bulletproof glass wall in front of the security bunker and said, "Sergeant, Colonel Murzuriev with the reinforcement company from headquarters. Start admitting my trucks immediately."

"Yes, sir." The sergeant opened a small "ticket-door" opening in the glass. "Your badge, please."

"We're in a hurry, Sergeant," Murzuriev said. He had removed his black leather gloves, placed them on the sill in front of the window, and was fishing around in his fatigue jacket pockets for his I.D. card. "You should have been notified of our arrival by headquarters ten minutes ago."

"The radio net is jammed with traffic, sir," Mikheyev said. "We were ordered to stay off the net. If a message came in, we did not hear it. It will take some time to admit all your vehicles." Just then Mikheyev noticed that all four of Murzuriev's officers accompanying him were crowding around the bulletproof window, watching what was going on. "Sir, please remind your staff to stand behind the yellow line. One person at a time near the window."

Murzuriev motioned for his men to step back. He seemed to be surprised at the news Teresov told him. "What radio traffic? What's going on?"

"Seems to be helicopters over the city, sir," Mikheyev replied. "We can't get any details."

Murzuriev's eyes were narrowed in confusion, but he quickly shook it off when he noticed Teresov staring at him. He slipped his photo I.D. card into the ticket-window slot. "I'm not sure what's happening, either," he said, "but it probably has to do with why we've been called out here. Hurry it up, Sergeant."

"Yes, sir." *Great,* Mikheyev thought. *Even a headquarters commander hasn't a clue as to what's going on.* Mikheyev examined the I.D. card and Murzuriev—they matched. He then put the I.D. card and the restricted-area entry badge together to compare the photos.

They did not match.

The photo I.D. and the restricted-area entry badge had been made at the same time, with copies of the same photo to ensure security. Something was wrong here. Not only did the photos not match, they weren't even relatively close to being similar. Mikheyev couldn't see the man's eye color, but the shape of the face was wrong, and the Murzuriev in the restricted-area badge was chubby and soft. This man was big-boned, square, and hard as a rock, although the mustache was similar.

Don't panic, Mikheyev, the security sergeant told himself. *It's probably a screw-up, or it could be a security test. Headquarters pulls this stuff all the time.* Mikheyev could see the man's sidearm, a Makarov pistol, plus an AK-47 slung over his shoulder—unusual for a battalion commander to be carrying a rifle, Mikheyev thought—but if the stranger was afraid of being discovered, he was making no move for either weapon. They were older weapons, not currently issued or made, but they all looked serviceable.

Mikheyev reached for the alarm button under the table, felt for it, and flipped off its safety cover, but did not press it. If this was a true screw-up, blowing the facility-wide alert horn would be the kiss of death for his career. Better try one more tack to fix this problem—call for a supervisor. "Sir, there seems to be something wrong here," Mikheyev said, trying to get his young corporal's attention—it wouldn't look good for the corporal's back to be turned if this was a test. "Did you have your I.D. card changed recently?" It looked fairly new, and Murzuriev hardly ever came to Denerokin.

"Yes, I have, Sergeant." If this was an intruder, Mikheyev thought, he was as cool as an icicle. Not one twitch, not one nervous swallow, not one millimeter's move toward a weapon. Murzuriev continued. "Everyone has his badge changed every year—you know that. Now let's get going. I have to report in to headquarters in three minutes."

"Your restricted-area entry badge was not replaced when your photo I.D. card was changed, sir," Mikheyev said. "I'll have to call my shift supervisor. Please stand by."

"This is ridiculous, Sergeant." Murzuriev motioned to the line of trucks outside the entrapment area. "I've got an entire *battalion* waiting."

"This will only take a minute, sir. I only need approval from my superior—there will be no delay." The four officers accompanying Murzuriev had stepped back away from the window, back almost to the outer gate, ten meters away. Why had they done that? Mikheyev wondered. Then he looked outside the tall fence and saw over a hundred soldiers from four of the trucks outside the entrapment area quickly jumping out of their trucks, rifles in hand. They tried to hide behind the trucks, out of view of the security cameras, but not all of them succeeded.

A surge of panic seized Mikheyev. Momentarily forgetting about the alarm button, he looked at Murzuriev inquisitively. "Excuse me, sir, but what are your men—"

"Is there something wrong, Sergeant?" the Colonel asked.

"No, sir. Please stand by." The phone was a few meters away from the desk. Hit the alarm button or call the duty officer? Mikheyev opted for the latter. But when he tried to close the "ticket" window, he found that Murzuriev had placed the fingers of his black leather gloves in the slot, preventing the metal door from completely closing. "Sir, please remove your gloves from the slot . . ."

Instead, Murzuriev stuck a large knife in the slot, jamming it completely open. Before Mikheyev could pull his sidearm or hit the alarm button, Murzuriev had rolled a tear-gas canister inside the slot. The gas instantly filled the security bunker with a blinding yellow fog. He then withdrew his knife to prevent any of the gas from escaping. In fifteen seconds, unable to see or breathe, the two OMON guards had no choice but to open the door—but not before sounding the alarm.

Dominikas Palcikas, who had disguised himself as Murzuriev, turned to the four officers behind him and said in Lithuanian, *"Now."*

Simultaneously, snipers arranged along the outer fence shot out security cameras inside the fence that scanned the entrapment area. At the same instant, explosives were stuck onto the remote-controlled locks on the gates, and seconds later the entrapment area was wide open. Trucks began rolling into the compound immediately.

Palcikas cut open the locking mechanism to the steel turnstilelike gate to the inner driveway beside the security bunker, then used a small amount of composition C4 explosive and blew the lock on the door to the security bunker. He rushed inside just as the direct phone to the security headquarters building near the aircraft-design area rang. With his scarf over his nose to block the gas, he picked it up and said, "East gate. Sergeant Mikheyev."

"Mikheyev?" The person on the other end immediately questioned the voice he heard, but he was obviously too excited to pursue his doubts. "We lost contact with five of your forward surveillance cameras, and the status indications on your gates all show red. What's going on?"

"All under control here. Inadvertent alarm. I've got video on my monitors, and all my lights are green. I've got all gates closed and one truck in the entrapment area. Must be a circuit problem at your end. Should I hold Colonel Murzuriev's detail outside until you get it checked?"

"Of course. That is the proper procedure. Stand by for authentication."

"East gate standing by." Palcikas knew that each guard detail had a code that was changed every shift, and it was simple enough to be memorized. Mikheyev wouldn't have written it down—he was too experienced for that. The young corporal might have written it down, but there was no time to search for it. Palcikas dashed out of the bunker just as the last truck was rumbling inside. He withdrew a radio from a coat pocket: "Battalion two, report."

"Main gate secure," came the reply. "Minimal resistance."

"Battalion three, report."

"Southwest gate secure. No resistance. Rail yard secure."

"Battalion four, report."

"West gate secure. Still moving in." Battalion four's target was the Fisikous aircraft-design facility; because this was guarded even more heavily than Denerokin, Battalion four had an extra five hundred men along, which slowed them up considerably. But they were armed more heavily than any other strike unit and outnumbered the Black Beret troops stationed there at least three to one.

"BTR incoming!" someone screamed. Palcikas whirled around. The breach in the entrapment-area gate brought an immediate response—a BTR-60PB armored personnel carrier careened down the main road from its position watching the gate and opened fire on the trucks rushing through the gate.

The first truck, carrying sixty Lithuanian soldiers, was raked with 12.7-millimeter cannon fire.

Palcikas' security teams opened fire with their heaviest antitank weapon, an antitank grenade propelled from an AK-47 by firing a bullet which ignited the grenade's rocket motor, but the projectiles all missed or the gunners were cut down by machine-gun fire before they could get into position.

"Move the T-62 up here. Now!" Palcikas ordered. "Take it through the fence!"

Palcikas' troops had already unloaded the T-62 tank from its flatbed trailer. It was an older, less capable version of the Soviet Union's main battle tank, and in a pitched battle with other tanks it would come out the loser; but in urban warfare, with room to maneuver, it was a devastating weapon. The T-62 rumbled off its flatbed, wheeled left, and plunged through the twelve-foot-high chain-link fence as if it were made of pine pickets. The main cannon of the BTR-60 swung around and began peppering the T-62 with shells, which allowed the Lithuanian gunners to surround the BTR, refine their aim, and make a few direct hits on it. The armored personnel carrier unloaded ten Black Beret soldiers just as the T-62 opened fire with a single high-explosive round, which blew the BTR-60 over in a spectacular backwards cartwheel.

Bent on revenge, Palcikas' men made short work of the Black Beret soldiers who tried to find cover.

Palcikas tried not to look, but his eyes were drawn to the truck that had been hit by gunfire from the BTR. He saw at least ten dead and all the rest wounded, some horribly so. So far the task he had set out for himself and his men had seemed relatively easy. They had captured dozens of communications centers, armories, air bases, supply depots, and garrisons that night, with only minor casualties—but now the full force of what he was doing began to hit home. Lithuanians, mostly seasoned troops but some just wide-eyed boys, were dying and being maimed in large numbers that night. And for what? For his own revenge? For some unattainable dream? What right did he have to do this . . . ?

But his men answered that question for him. Despite their first horrible taste of battle, despite their sudden, shocking losses, the men began to cheer as the Vytis, the war banner of the Grand Duke of Lithuania, was hoisted above the security bunker. This was what they were fighting for, Palcikas reminded himself. Lithuania would never be free until the people threw off the tyrants that invaded their homeland, until they developed the strength to fight off their enemies. That was what he was doing. He was driven by revenge, by the urge to punish the Soviets for holding his people hostage and murdering them indiscriminately. But he was doing this for Lithuania's future. Nothing more.

"All right," Palcikas shouted to his officers, "they're going to sound the alarm any second. Battalion four is not in position yet, but we can't wait for them. Take your positions and get ready to repel enemy forces. I want—"

Just then, Palcikas' radioman reported, "Helicopters approaching, sir. No I.D. made yet, but definitely heading toward Fisikous. Not scouts—full-sized choppers. Five minutes out, no more."

"All right. Alpha Company continues to the security headquarters building at top speed," Palcikas ordered. "Bravo Company splits up into platoons and surrounds the power plant on the north, east, and west sides. Charlie Company sets up right here, right now. Air-defense batteries first, then antiarmor stuff. Let's move it—time is running out."

* * *

Just outside the northeast gate of the Fisikous complex, atop the low railroad-yard warehouses on Dariaus Avenue, two figures dressed in ordinary worker's blue coveralls lay in a tiny crawlspace in the attic of one of the older, abandoned warehouses.

But they were not workers.

"Shit the bed, looks like half a battalion going in the Denerokin gate," Sergeant Charles Beaker said. He was peering through a large StarLight night-vision telescope at the scene at the northeast gate, furiously writing down everything he saw on a thick pad of paper.

"I need numbers and I.D., Beak, not your damned commentary," Sergeant First Class Ed Gladden said. He and his partner were members of a Special Forces "A-Team," part of a U.S. Army Special Forces Group scattered throughout Lithuania, Latvia, Russia, and Byelorussia and assigned to various places to conduct surveillance on key parts of the city and the surrounding area. They and almost one hundred other Special Forces members had been camped out in various hellholes like that warehouse crawlspace, reporting everything they saw to U.S. Special Operations Command headquarters in Germany via satellite uplink.

In preparation for the assault on the Fisikous facility and the embassy reinforcement, several Special Forces A-Teams—fluent in Russian and Lithuanian and specially trained in intelligence, engineering, and covert reconnaissance—had been sent into Vilnius to prep the area for the American troops' arrival by reporting on Soviet troop movements and positioning. Gladden was preparing another report on the appearance of troop-carrying trucks at the Denerokin security gate. "Whatcha got?"

"Thirty-four vehicles, Sarge," Beaker replied. "One Jeep with the commander, one two-ton van that looks like a radio or command post van, three tracked vehicles that look like . . . Jesus, they look like Zeus-23s."

"Get off it, Beaker."

"That's what they look like to me, Sarge. Like a ZSU-23-4 gun. There's a ten-ton truck following behind that looks like it could be the ammo truck."

Gladden was beginning to get very, very nervous. Beaker was excitable, but he was trained and disciplined to be accurate as well. The ZSU-23-4, nicknamed Zeus, was a Soviet tank that had four 23-millimeter cannons mounted on its turret. Guided by radar or heat-seeking sensors, it could fire a lethal cloud of bullets out to two miles and was a threat to any aircraft flying below twelve thousand feet. Zeus was standard armament for a Commonwealth Army infantry battalion. Why would the MSB— the interior security forces, consisting mostly of ex-KGB and Soviet Troops of the Interior soldiers—have such a weapon?

Beaker continued. "Four ten-tonners that could be power generators or ammo trucks, nineteen five-ton troop carriers, a couple water trucks, a fuel truck, a flatbed with a bulldozer, and a flatbed with a T-62 tank. They all got MSB markings on them."

Gladden was encoding the data as quickly as he could—Beaker could help, but he had to keep on watching the gate. The MSB, the newly formed Inter-Republican Council of Security, was the Commonwealth organization that had replaced the Soviet Troops of the Interior, the KGB, and GRU, or military intelligence. Their responsibility was mostly internal and institutional security. But because of their violent, repressive heritage, the MSB's activities in the Commonwealth had been severely curtailed, and in independent Lithuania they had been all but outlawed. Now this MSB unit had heavy infantry weapons. How? Why . . . ? "A tank, troops out the wazoo, and air-defense guns? Sounds like an invasion force," grumbled Gladden.

"No, *we're* the invasion force," Beaker said. "Looks like the Commonwealth found out about us. This is the stuff I'd send to fight off a Marine Expeditionary Unit invasion."

Beaker was right on, but something still nagged at Gladden's mind. "But the other squads tracked this convoy coming out of the south barracks and out of the Nemencine reserve barracks to the northeast, not the central barracks," Gladden mused, remembering the coded messages received earlier from the other Special Forces units. "If there was an alert, why wouldn't we have heard from our unit covering the central Vilnius barracks before now?"

"You got me," Beaker said. "Maybe they're saving the central corps for something else."

"There is nothing else more important than Fisikous and Denerokin," Gladden said. "The Commonwealth would order the MSB to protect Fisikous at all costs. What gives?"

"A little disorganized, that's all," Beaker offered. "They're still responding, with really heavy shit, and responding pretty damned fast. This is going to be . . . *holy shit!*"

"What?"

"Riflemen coming out of the trucks . . . trying to get a count . . . ten, maybe a dozen . . . but they're aiming *into* the security compound!"

Gladden resisted the urge to tell Beaker to move aside so he could look through the StarLight telescope—Beaker was trained at observation and grabbing the 'scope would waste time. "Are the Marines over the compound yet?"

"No, no sign of them," Beaker replied. "They . . . damn, they're shooting! *They're shooting out the security cameras!*"

Gladden immediately wrote a PAUSE, then a STBY ACTION message in code and sent what he had already coded. The U.S. Embassy would receive the transmission, and their computers would automatically relay it to other units and to U.S. European Command headquarters in Germany. The STBY ACTION phrase would let them know that something else was happening and that important details would follow. "What do you got, Beak?"

"Something's happening at the guard bunker . . . I can barely see it, but . . . I see flashes of light near the gate. There might be a firefight going down, or small explosives . . . gate's opening . . . outer gate is open . . . inside gate is open too. Trucks are rolling inside."

"That's a major breach of security," Gladden said. "We've never seen both gates open at once like that."

"Guys are just running in and heading off towards the power plant," Beaker said. "Trucks are rolling in fast. No I.D. checks, no badge swaps—they're just barreling in as fast as they can move. They . . . holy shit, the newcomers are getting hosed by an armored personnel carrier! A BTR from inside the compound is shooting at the newcomers! What in hell is going on?"

"What else is going—"

"Oh, man, the T-62 engaged . . ." Gladden heard a tremendous *boom!* followed by a crash of steel on steel and a thundering explosion. "Christ, the T-62 just blew the BTR away. Man, that was awesome . . . the newcomers are mopping up the crew from the BTR. Who *are* those guys?"

Gladden was considering breaking cover and trying to get closer to the gate—a foolish idea, but under the circumstances it might be necessary—when the PRC-118 command radio crackled to life. It was the first time either of them had heard uncoded voice messages on that radio: "All units, this is Yellow, I've got at least a battalion entering the west gate near the hangars. Two T-62s, several combat tractors, and what appears to be antiaircraft-artillery vehicles. Firefights inside the facility. The newcomers have raised some kind of Lithuanian flag and are attacking the guard posts and MSB positions."

No one ever wanted to be the first to break radio silence, but once it was broken, it was best to get your info out as fast and as orderly as possible, then strive to regain radio silence. Gladden found the microphone and began: "All units, this is Blue. I've got at least a half battalion entering Denerokin gate. Thirty-four vehicles, estimated one thousand troops. Heavy fighting between defense forces and unidentified newcomers. I've also got a T-62 and four ZSU-23-4 antiaircraft-artillery batteries moving into the compound. I say again, antiaircraft-artillery batteries inside the compound . . ."

"Hey, he's right—they raised a flag," Beaker called out excitedly. "It's not a Lithuanian flag, but it's that other one—what do they call it?—the red one with the knight on a charging horse?"

"A Vytis," Gladden told Beaker. "Shit, this looks like a civil war busting out." He keyed his microphone: "I concur with observations—these newcomers appear to be Lithuanian partisans engaging MSB troops. God help us."

**INSIDE THE FISIKOUS DESIGN-BUREAU SECURITY FORCE HEADQUARTERS
SECOND SUBFLOOR "ZULU" AREA
13 APRIL, 0320 VILNIUS (12 APRIL, 2120 ET)**

The lights flickered momentarily, then brightened, then dimmed, then went out for several seconds. Emergency battery-powered lights snapped on. Over the buildingwide public address system came the announcement: "All personnel, report to briefing room. All personnel, report to briefing room immediately."

The lone guard outside Luger's cell leaped to his feet at the announcement. What in hell was going on? PA announcements were never heard in the Zulu area—this must be a real emergency. He picked up his AK-74 rifle, then went over to the locked cell where the prisoner was being held and opened up the eye-level shutter to check on him. What the guard saw in that miserable little cell made him sick despite himself.

It was not really a cell, only a ten-by-ten windowless room hastily built with concrete blocks along one wall of the lowest subfloor of the building's basement. It had no heat, no lights, no water, nothing—four smooth walls, a low smooth ceiling, and a steel door that swung outward. The prisoner—the guard did not know who he was, but heard that he was one of the scientists assigned to Fisikous—was lying on a waterbed, with only thin Velcro restraints across his chest and arms. His eyes and nostrils were taped closed, a pair of headphones were taped to his ear, and a large plastic tube was taped into his wide-open mouth. A strange electronic contraption intravenously pumped liquids from plastic bags into his body—amphetamines or some other psychoactive drugs, the guard surmised, because he thought the prisoner was never allowed to sleep. The electronic device also controlled the cassette tape recorder, and the guard guessed that the device had been pre-programmed to administer drugs, noise, and propaganda to the prisoner. Occasionally the guard could hear faint sounds from the headphones, a cacophony of loud music, voices, sounds of violence and death, and then nothing.

Whatever the drugs and the music were, it was making the prisoner's body twist in sheer agony, but he had no strength to break free of his bonds. His head would thrash about from the pain, and sometimes the convulsions that racked his body were severe enough to double him up, but he never rolled off the bed. The prisoner was rail-thin, gaunt, with horribly sunken eyes, a thin neck, and crusted and swollen lips. He shivered constantly. The prisoner was never given any solid food, so the guard never recalled seeing the KGB medics cleaning up after him.

"Attention, all duty personnel, report to the first-level ready room immediately!" the announcement repeated. "All special-duty personnel, report to the third-floor director's office." The guard was sure there was trouble now—he had to report to Gabovich's office. He shook his head and snapped the inspection shutter closed, silently praying that he would never do anything so dumb or screw up so badly that General Gabovich would ever subject him to torture like *that*.

What the guard failed to notice, however, was that when the lights went out briefly in the subfloor of the Fisikous Design Center Security Building, the computerized monitoring device turned itself off, and it failed to automatically come back on when the power came back.

For the first time in many days, the barrage of electronically delivered noise in David Luger's head stopped.

David Luger was awake—in fact, he had not been allowed to sleep since he was brought down to that chamber of horrors. When the noise would stop and he would drift off into sleep, the voices would speak to him, softly and slowly at first and then louder and faster, until he would be awakened, screaming, to unrecognizable sounds of chaos. The pattern would repeat itself over and over. His mouth was dry from breathing through the tube. He could feel restraints on his chest and wrists, but they felt incredibly heavy, like huge steel manacles.

But now, there was an unearthly silence, and he was awake. Luger consciously forced himself to breathe easier and try to relax. After several long minutes—even noticing the passage of time was an incredible relief—he was able to poll his own body and take stock of himself. His muscles trembled as if he were on a severe caffeine buzz, but his fingers and toes seemed to respond. He was not blind—his eyes were covered, as were his ears. He strained against one of the restraints on his wrists and heard the familiar rip of Velcro. In seconds, with happiness and a surge of power flooding through his head, he ripped his restraints free, and moments later Luger was free. He ripped the headphones and eye coverings loose, then carefully withdrew the intravenous needle from his right arm.

He had never heard a public-address loudspeaker announcement down here in his cell. Except for the Russian language—now as understandable to him as English after all these years—it sounded . . .

. . . *Exactly like the announcements he used to hear at the B-52 alert facility back at Ford Air Force Base in Sacramento.*

God, he thought, that seemed like another lifetime ago. What was that announcement about? It must be serious, because Luger had never heard any others until now.

Luger allowed himself the luxury of a little hope. Was it a rescue attempt? Would they find him down here? He had no way of signaling anyone, no tools or devices to make noise against the eight-inch-thick concrete. It was hopeless. There had to be hundreds of troops in this building. It would take a full-scale infantry assault to breach the security here, and the United States would never attempt such a thing to rescue one long-lost man whom they probably suspected of being a traitor, or worse, had simply forgotten all about.

Luger shook his head, trying to remain positive. Stuck in isolation, in the dark, in these conditions, it was easy to let supposition and negative thoughts overwhelm you, but he was determined that it wouldn't happen to him. He remembered his POW training, and held fast to the tenets of survival that he'd learned then. He'd been down for so long now, the only way to go emotionally was up. After the Lithuanian agent had made contact with him—God, how many weeks ago was *that?*—Luger had stopped eating the tainted food Gabovich had put in his diet and the drugs had finally washed themselves out of his body. They had obviously been drugging him again—he could feel the amphetamines coursing through his body, making his eyelids and fingers twitch—but physically he felt all right. It was important to guard his mental health now. Whatever was happening now, whatever was in store for him later, Luger knew he had an opportunity—now was the time to take it.

The primary thing he had been telling himself was not to let his own fears condemn him. Survival was primary. Survival was everything. He had to concentrate on preparing himself for rescue. When the rescue attempt came—and he had a feeling it would be soon—he had to make sure he would not burden his rescuers. If they had to carry him out, it could mean death for all of them.

Luger struggled out of the waterbed and stumbled to his feet. His legs felt rubbery and weak, but he was standing upright and he could feel that shakiness slowly leaving his tortured body. He even attempted a few simple stretching exercises, and found his back and his arms wobbly but strong. But the most important exercise was the one going on inside him, the one that said over and over: *Don't Give Up. Don't Give Up. Don't Give Up.*

The number-one MV-22 SEA HAMMER aircraft, carrying the Marine First and Second platoons, raced across the railroad yards northeast of the Fisikous compound, across the northeast gate, just north of the Denerokin nuclear research facility, and arced south toward the three large buildings on the west side—the two aircraft hangars and the engineering center that made up the Fisikous Aircraft-Design Bureau. Just to the northeast side of the fenced-in compound was the security force headquarters, including the Fisikous security detail's arsenal, communications center, and detainment facility. This was the assault team's target.

"Hammer flight, Congo Two," the AC-130 Spectre gunship radioed to the second MV-22. "I'm showing several columns of vehicles surrounding your target area. Be advised, I think your PZ may be hot. Repeat, your PZ may be hot . . ."

"Message from Congo Two, sir," the radioman passed along to Lieutenant William Marx, the commander of Alpha Company in Hammer Four. "Clear-text messages from field units. He's tracking several columns of vehicles surrounding the Fisikous target area. He thinks the pickup zone may be hot. Vehicles include a ZSU-23-4 air-defense artillery."

Patrick McLanahan's ears pricked up when he heard *that*—every flyer in the world knew about the ZSU-23-4's murderous reputation.

First Lieutenant Marx shook his head in disbelief. "Where the hell did all these extra vehicles come from?" he murmured.

It was the most agitated McLanahan had ever seen the young officer. Special operations with small, lightly armed forces relied solely on two things to ensure success: scrupulous intelligence and precise knowledge of the objective, and speed. Having a large, as yet unidentified force suddenly show up right under your nose, especially with such a devastating weapon as the ZSU-23-4, which was usually not deployed inside the Fisikous compound, is a special ops commander's worst nightmare. "Satellite photos don't show a thing except for the regular Commonwealth garrisons in the city. He got a count yet?"

"Just coming in. He's saying one, perhaps two battalions, sir. Over a hundred vehicles on all sides. Some already in the facility."

"Two battalions? That's impossible. The Commonwealth had only two battalions in the entire *country* twelve hours ago! I can't believe it, but it looks like the Soviets might have moved the Byelorussian Army in on us. That's the only army that could have mobilized and moved into the area so fast."

"But how?" Gunnery Sergeant Wohl asked. "It takes time to move that many troops from the frontiers into the city. The embassy would have reported something, and sure as hell our satellite imagery would have spotted them."

"Well, they didn't," Marx said irritably. "The old heads keep on telling me not to trust the 'birds' for Intel, and I'm starting to believe them." He thought for a moment, then turned to Trimble and Wohl and asked, "Well, Snyder's going to call any second. What do you want to do?"

"We got no choice," Trimble said, his voice ringing with authority even over the noise in the SEA HAMMER's cabin. "The gig is blown. Let's land in the embassy, get reports from the Special Forces guy in the city, and replan."

"But Luger dies in the meantime," Patrick McLanahan interjected.

Marx riveted McLanahan with an exasperated glance and said, "This doesn't concern you, McLanahan."

"Like hell, *Lieutenant,*" McLanahan said. He was unaccustomed to pulling rank on anybody, but Patrick thought this was a good time to try it even though he had felt vastly inferior to everyone he had encountered in the past three weeks. "Your mission is to get David Luger out of that prison."

"The Lieutenant said *button* it," Trimble growled.

"Your rank means nothing here, McLanahan," Marx said, cutting off his platoon sergeant, "as does your opinion. We'll decide—"

"An American military officer that has been tortured for years in that place will be executed if we don't go in there, Lieutenant," McLanahan shouted over the roar of the wind whistling in the cargo section. "We've come too far to turn back. Luger will die."

"He's dead already, McLanahan," Trimble said. "If the Byelorussian Army was ordered into Fisikous, the first thing they'd do is execute all foreign prisoners."

"You don't know that," John Ormack interjected.

"That's standard operating procedure for them," Trimble said.

"We've got to go in anyway," McLanahan insisted. "We can't leave him, not when we're so close."

"It doesn't work that way around here, McLanahan," Marx said. McLanahan could tell that he hit a nerve with Marx by continually referring to Luger by his human name instead of the "target" and the "objective." Trimble was completely unaffected. "If there's any hope for success, it has to be planned to the smallest detail. Men will die if we don't take everything into account."

"A man will die if you *don't* finish the mission," McLanahan said angrily. "Send in the AC-130 to suppress fire around the security building—the embassy evacuation and reinforcement should be over by now. Call in your air cover. The AV-8s can be over the city in fifteen minutes!"

"We're not authorized to use the fighters," Marx explained. The AV-8B Harrier II "jump jets" were deployed on the USS *Wasp* amphibious-assault carrier stationed in the Baltic. The upgraded Harrier attack jets could attack heavily defended targets with pinpoint precision at night or in bad weather, they could take off and land like helicopters, and they could put a lot of bombs and rockets on target with pinpoint precision—they were designed from the start to support Marines during an invasion. "The Harriers are on standby to support the embassy reinforcement only. This is a non-mission, McLanahan, and we can't just start sending in planes."

"Then we'll forget about stealing stuff on the Fi-170 stealth bomber. The building clearing and I.D. is supposed to take seven minutes. Seven minutes to save an American's life. We can get Dave Luger out and be off before they know what hit them."

"Shut your mouth, McLanahan," Trimble ordered. "You don't know shit about this operation!"

"Let the Colonel talk, Trimble," Hal Briggs said, rising to his feet and staring down Trimble. Hal did not need to hold on to a handrail or the bulkhead to steady himself—it was as if all turbulence and noise had vanished when he stood.

The challenge was unspoken but obvious. Briggs was as tall but not as big as Trimble, but apparently Briggs's reputation preceded him—or else it was the surprise of seeing the Air Force officer challenging him. In either case, Trimble hesitated, his eyes briefly wide with surprise, before saying, "You wanna fuck with me, Briggs? Go ahead. Take your best shot."

It seemed like a ridiculous scene—they were speeding over a foreign and hostile country, enemy soldiers below them, aerial death on the way, noise and vibration so great that it was hard to think straight, mere feet away from hitting a tree or crashing into a five-hundred-year-old castle, and Trimble was trying to goad Briggs into taking a swing at him. But life and death was a serious affair for these Marines, and they didn't want hassles from three outsiders. Briggs had little chance against a trained killing machine like Trimble, but Trimble's slight hesitation in front of Briggs spoke more than any threat or action.

Marx defused it: "Shut the fuck up, all of you, right now." Just then, the radioman handed Marx the radio handset, and Marx took it as Trimble and Briggs glared at each other, practically nose-to-nose in the cramped, soldier-filled compartment. "Hammer Four, go."

"I'm recommending we abort," Marx heard Captain Snyder say. Marx looked at McLanahan, then at Trimble, thought for a moment. "Hammer Four, you there?" asked Snyder.

"Affirmative . . . I recommend we proceed. Our pax want to proceed as well. Suggest we bring in Congo Two over the target for fire support."

"We're showing a battalion of hostiles rushing into the facility, Hammer Four. We've lost touch with the situation."

Marx could tell that Snyder wanted to continue as well—the Captain was never this indecisive unless logic and the book were conflicting with his gut feeling. If he really wanted to abort, he would have just ordered Hammer Three to turn around—Hammer Four would have followed, and the mission would be over. Marx said, "Our timeline is still intact as long as the newcomers don't storm the target building. With Congo Two we can keep the bad guys away until we get the target. I recommend we proceed."

The pause was only momentary this time: "Stand by." There was dead air for about fifteen seconds; then: "Hammer Four, we'll take one extra turn around the city to let Congo Two in. I'll be on the horn with home base. Stand by."

The five-hundred-man Black Beret security force on duty at the headquarters was prepared for all sorts of emergencies, especially after the riot at the Denerokin facility. They had contingency plans for saboteurs, terrorists, accidents, natural disasters, civil disturbance, even a hostile occupation by well-armed left-wing radicals—everything but a full-scale military invasion force. Fisikous was supposed to be impenetrable. Who would dare try to take the base? Even without the pledge of support from the Byelorussian Army—which was supposed to begin an invasion of Lithuania—the security forces under General Gabovich and Colonel Kortyshkov were ready for any eventuality . . .

. . . But they weren't ready for an invasion by the Lithuanian Self-Defense Force under its charismatic Soviet-trained leader, General Dominikas Palcikas.

Palcikas didn't want a bloodbath in Fisikous, but with unknown and potentially hostile aircraft on the way, he wasn't going to play games with the garrison at the Denerokin facility. Third Battalion had joined up with Fourth Battalion, and they were going up against the Black Berets' heavy armor protecting the Institute. Second Battalion joined up with Palcikas' First Battalion, and Palcikas quickly surrounded the garrison building. The faster he could capture the Black Berets' security-force headquarters, the faster the remaining forces would surrender.

Palcikas pulled one of his T-62 main battle tanks up in front of the commander's front window, lowered the four-and-a-half-inch muzzle, and blew out the entire office and part of the front of the building with a single sabot round. The Soviet security-force commander immediately ordered his men in the garrison to surrender. Good thing they did, because except for a few white phosphorous rounds, the T-62 had no more ammunition.

The siege had lasted only a few short minutes. Palcikas' men, forgetting caution and procedures in their happy rush toward their objective, rushed the garrison en masse with guns blazing. The sloppy but direct approach worked. A few Lithuanians were wounded, but it was obvious the troops inside were not aching for a fight after being rattled by a T-62 wakeup call, and the OMON Black Beret troops surrendered.

Palcikas soon faced the OMON deputy commander, Lieutenant Colonel Ivan Ivanovich Stepanov, who had been dragged out of a basement backup communications facility. "Greetings, Colonel Stepanov," Palcikas said when the Black Beret commander was dragged before him. "You and your men will surrender to me immediately."

Stepanov was so shocked and disoriented that for several moments he could do nothing but gape at Palcikas. After a few moments of stuttering he cried out, "Palcikas, what in hell do you think you are doing?"

"I am in command of this facility now, Colonel," Palcikas said. "I order you to—"

"You . . . pompous . . . strutting . . . Lithuanian bastard!" Stepanov shouted. The guards tightened their hold on Stepanov's arms, but he continued. "You will release me and my men and lay down your weapons *immediately!*"

"No, Colonel. The Black Berets no longer control Fisikous or any of the Soviet defense posts in Lithuania. My men control them."

Stepanov looked skeptical at first, but seeing the sheer number of men Palcikas had and how well they were armed seemed to slowly convince him.

To Colonel Zukauskas, his second-in-command, Palcikas said, "See to it that all prisoners are strip-searched for weapons and all are handcuffed. Secure the officers in a separate room and post guards inside and out. Colonel Stepanov will be secured by himself in a separate room." To Stepanov, Palcikas said, "You will be allowed to speak with your men before being separated from them, Colonel. I advise you to tell them not to resist. I will give my men specific instructions to shoot any man, officer or enlisted, who fails to follow orders. If you do not resist, I promise that you will not be harmed, you will be treated fairly, you will be given rations and personal items equal to my own men, you will not be used as hostages or human shields, and at the first opportunity those who wish to leave Lithuania will be safely escorted to the Russian border. If you resist, you will be treated like barnyard animals and caged up. Is that clear?"

"You will be executed by firing squad for this, Palcikas!" Stepanov cried as his hands were secured behind his back by plastic handcuffs. "You will be executed for this!"

"This is not treason—this is a revolution, Colonel," Palcikas said simply. "We will show you the difference. Now, where is Colonel Kortyshkov? I wish to pay my respects to him as well."

"Go to *hell,* Palcikas!"

"No doubt I will see you all there," Palcikas said. "Where is Kortyshkov?"

"We will not cooperate with you, Palcikas! You've never dealt with OMON before. We don't crack like you Lithuanian tit-suckers." A deranged smile ran across his face; then: "We don't bleed like you Lithuanian faggots do, either—"

A lifetime's worth of rage finally burst from Palcikas' heart, and before anyone could stop him he had grabbed Stepanov away from his guards, lifted him in his left fist, and had flattened him with a single punch from his right. His nose shattered, dazed and bleeding, Stepanov collapsed onto the floor in a heap.

"Secure him in his own stockade," Palcikas ordered. "Find who is second in rank and bring him to me." Stepanov and his officers were led away.

"The arsenal was stocked for World War Three," one of Palcikas' officers reported a few minutes later. "We'll be able to keep the battalion armed for at least three days. We even have a few more rounds for the tank."

"Have the armorers and ordnance disposal teams check it out before distributing it," Palcikas warned. "Every captured weapon and round has to be checked—they could have sabotaged it while we were surrounding the place. Get on that right away."

Zukauskas relayed the orders to the unit NCO, then added, "We also have almost a hundred MSB and OMON soldiers that say they want to defect, including two officers. How do you want to handle these men?"

"The same as the others. They can join us if they meet my conditions," Palcikas replied. "We'll accept only men with Lithuanian names and who kept their Lithuanian citizenship. If they swear loyalty to me in front of the other captives, we'll separate them from the others and give them preferential treatment. But we can't afford to give them a rifle in here— too many chances for cold feet and second thoughts. First chance we get, we'll bus them out to Trakai and screen them, but in here they'll have to be locked up."

"Yes, sir," Zukauskas said. He relayed that order as well, then commented happily, "It's even more promising than I imagined, Colonel. Ten, twenty, even thirty percent of every unit we've encountered want to join us. I could only pray that we'd ever find this kind of support. There are many that I'd trust with my life right now, men that I know."

"I know, Vitalis," Palcikas said. "I recognize many as well—some of the officers captured here are from my hometown, and some had relatives that died during the Denerokin riot. But we can't be too careful. There will be time to recruit soldiers from the prisoner ranks, but for now we secure our objective and prepare for the Soviet counterattack. Third and Fourth battalions still are engaged with Black Beret forces."

A few moments later another soldier ran up to Palcikas, saluted, and said, "Sir, Charlie Company guards report a single fixed-wing and two heavy rotary-wing aircraft inbound. Negative identification. Alpha and Bravo companies report engaging security patrols but expect to be set up for antiair operations soon. Charlie Company reports ready for antiair and antiarmor action. Our company stationed near the parliament building is reporting considerable air activity near the City of Progress. They are investigating, but they believe it is the Byelorussian Army aviation units, possibly the heavy attack squadrons from Smorgon."

"Make sure the antiaircraft artillery is deployed as planned as soon as possible," Palcikas said, remembering the power of the attack helicopters that had slaughtered so many civilians just last week. "I need the report from Third and Fourth battalions as soon as possible. They are the key to this entire operation. If the Soviet helicopters attack before they get into position, we'll lose our left flank. There won't be anything to stop the Commonwealth from overrunning our position then."

Dominikas Palcikas paused, scanning the faces of those around him. They showed shock, apprehension, and fear when they heard "Byelorussian Army." The horrors of the Denerokin massacre were still too fresh on their minds as well.

"You men listen to me, and listen well," Palcikas said. "You have done the impossible tonight, but the job isn't done yet. You have marched a considerable distance through occupied Lithuania; successfully mounted attacks on dozens of Soviet military and Commonwealth bases; and occupied the strongest and most important Commonwealth facility in all of the Baltic besides the Baltic Sea Fleet headquarters itself. Our exploits tonight will go down in history as the most sweeping and successful raid by a Lithuanian army since the siege of Minsk by the Grand Duke Vytautas himself. What the Commonwealth used as a base of operations to slaughter our innocent, peace-loving people, we now control.

"We are not some rabble protest group throwing stones at soldiers and dodging rubber bullets. We are not revolutionary hotheads who want nothing but to see everything burn just for our amusement. We are liberators. We are protectors. We are the right arm of the free Lithuanian people, holding the sword of liberty in defense of our country for the first time in centuries. We are the Grand Duke's Iron Wolf Brigade, and we have been blessed by God and christened in the fire and blood of the ones that died at Denerokin to carry the sword.

"We anticipated the arrival of the Commonwealth Army. We prepared for it. We occupy or destroyed all the Soviet aviation and infantry-support infrastructure in Lithuania, so when their counterattack comes it will be blunt and cannot be sustained. We knew the aviation units would begin the counterattack; in the same way, we know where the infantry and armor units will begin their counterattack, and we have aligned the Second Regiment against them."

He paused, staring each one of his officers and senior NCOs in the eye, and concluded, "I don't want you looking defeated. Look at what we've accomplished. You all know our operations plan for this evening; you computed the expected losses, recommended where the units be deployed, suggested what equipment to bring. Your estimates were perfect. Our goals for this one evening are being met and exceeded. So it will be with the rest of our plan. Get your heads up, get your men together, and execute the plan that we have prepared. If you truly believe that what you are doing is right, for yourself and for your country, then you will prevail."

THE NATIONAL MILITARY COMMAND CENTER
THE PENTAGON, WASHINGTON, D.C.
12 APRIL, 2120 ET (13 APRIL, 0320 VILNIUS)

Via MILSTAR, the satellite military communications network, Chairman of the Joint Chiefs of Staff Wilbur Curtis, National Security Advisor George Russell, CIA Director Kenneth Mitchell, and Secretary of Defense Thomas Preston heard the report from Hammer Three at the same time Colonel Albert Kline, commander of the Amphibious Task Force of the 26th Marine Expeditionary Unit aboard USS *Wasp,* got the message.

"Jesus, what a mess," Russell said. Despite his outburst, he found himself undecided about what to do. "Tom, what are you going to recommend?"

Preston, the grizzled old veteran of the White House Cabinet, rested his chin on his fist, considered the words, then said, "My impulse is to yank them out of there back to the embassy and see how this thing rinses out. But I hate to leave my boys out there with their dorks hanging out. Wilbur?"

"I agree with you, sir," Curtis replied instantly. He had a phone to Camp Lejeune cocked in one ear, waiting for General Kundert to get on the line. "I've got a call in to Vance to get his opinion, but my impression is to finish the raid on the research institute."

"I agree," Mitchell replied, "but I'm sure not for the same reason."

Curtis turned an angry stare at Mitchell. "I get it," he said. "You want to be sure Luger's dead, don't you? Only the Marines can tell you that. You probably instructed them to bring back evidence—what? His tongue? His vocal cords? His fucking *head?*"

"Don't get dramatic, General," Mitchell said, rolling his eyes. "Business is business."

"We're trying to rescue the man, not recover his body," Curtis said irritably. He knew Mitchell was locked into a different version of this Lithuanian mission, one in which Luger was a heavy liability and worth far more dead than alive. "The forces are in place, Tom," Curtis said to the Secretary of Defense. "The aircraft are over the target. At least let them give it a try. The on-scene commanders can call the abort if they feel it's hopeless. The AC-130 gunship has completed its sweep of the Super Stallion loading zone—let's divert him over Fisikous to help the Marines."

"I'll need the President's okay on that."

"The tilt-rotors will bingo if they have to stay in the air to wait for word from the President," Curtis said. "Let's get them moving toward the objective. Let the on-scene commander call the shots."

Tom Preston thought for a moment; then: "All right. Let them proceed." He picked up the direct line to the White House at the same time Curtis gave the orders.

FISIKOUS AIRCRAFT-DESIGN BUREAU SECURITY FACILITY
FISIKOUS RESEARCH INSTITUTE
13 APRIL, 0330 VILNIUS (12 APRIL, 2130 ET)

"Move it! Move it!" Colonel Nikita Kortyshkov screamed. The commander of OMON security forces at the Fisikous Aircraft-Design Bureau, brandishing an AK-74, shoved passing soldiers in the back to move faster. Even with five hundred heavily armed soldiers on duty, they were practically defenseless unless they could get into proper position in time.

Kortyshkov had screwed up badly, but he told himself it wasn't his fault. He had heard the first radio reports of a large number of intruders in the base and passed that off as an exercise. The Design-Bureau security force was never involved in any large-scale exercises, but Denerokin and the rest of the base performed security evaluations and realistic invasion exercises all the time. It was never announced as an exercise, but Kortyshkov assumed it was anyway because they were saying that upwards of three battalions were storming the base.

That was ridiculous, or so he thought.

Minutes later, a loud cannon shot rumbled throughout the base. A few frantic radio reports said that a huge enemy force had entered the base, that the base headquarters had been destroyed, that half the security force had been killed, and that soldiers were ready to attack the design bureau. How much was fact and how much was fiction, Kortyshkov couldn't tell. But at this late stage of the game, he had better assume the worst.

"I want a platoon up on the roof," he said to his NCO in charge of the security detail, "along with four machine guns. Break out the night-vision equipment in case the lights are taken out. Have communications been restored with the headquarters building or with Stepanov? Why are all these men running around like this . . . ?"

Just then Kortyshkov recognized Vadim Teresov, the assistant to the senior KGB officer on the base. Teresov's office and that of his superior officer, Gabovich, were on the top floor of the security building, and Teresov was often here many hours before Gabovich arrived at six A.M. Kortyshkov tried to ignore the man, tossing orders left and right, but it was obvious Teresov was looking for him and would not be deterred.

The KGB officer walked over to Kortyshkov and said in a low voice, "I will speak to you, Colonel, right now."

"Not now, Comrade . . ."

"*Right* now, Colonel." Teresov pulled the OMON officer aside into a doorway. "Have you carried out the Zulu directive?"

The Zulu directive stated simply that all prisoners kept in the lowest level of cells in the security facility, called the "Zulu level," will be executed in case of an attack, riot, or disturbance. The directive was initiated after the Denerokin riot, when it was obvious that had the Black Berets not cracked down on the rioters, the base could have very well been overrun and the politically sensitive prisoners released. The prisoner was to be removed from his cell, killed by a gunshot to the head, and thrown into the incinerator on the same level, two floors down below street level.

Currently, there was only one prisoner in the Zulu level: Dr. Ivan Sergeiovich Ozerov.

Kortyshkov searched his fading memory; then the realization of what Teresov was talking about hit hard. "The prisoners . . . !"

"Quiet, you fool," Teresov said as soldiers rushed past within listening range. "Yes, the damned prisoners. Now carry out the directive immediately."

"I don't have time to butcher the pris—to supervise the directive," Kortyshkov stammered. It was immediately obvious to Teresov that Kortyshkov was completely unprepared for the assault currently under way, and he was virtually frozen with fear. He looked as if he was about to shoot himself in the face with his AK-47 any second. "I have lost contact with Colonel Stepanov, and my Thirty-second Armored Company is getting ready to engage enemy forces west of the runway."

"You asinine fool, your first responsibility is to the KGB and to General Gabovich!"

Kortyshkov's eyes widened when Teresov said "KGB"—but of course everyone knew that the "old" KGB had never gone away. The new MSB, of which Kortyshkov was a part, was nothing more than a leaner, meaner *Komitet Gosudarstvennoy Bezopasnosti.* This only served to confirm that suspicion. "My first responsibility is to stop those invaders," Kortyshkov snapped. "Now get out of my way."

"You idiot! You will be executed for your insubordination if you do not—"

Then Teresov stopped. Kortyshkov had a strange, detached expression on his face. The beleaguered OMON officer was beginning to tune out all voices, all sounds. Some voice in his head was overriding all else, and right now that voice was telling him to remove all blabbering sources of distraction. Kortyshkov actually swung the muzzle of the AK-47 slowly in Teresov's direction, and Teresov knew that at the slightest provocation—a word, a sudden noise, even a glance—he was going to pull the trigger. Kortyshkov would die for killing a senior KGB official, but that was little comfort because Teresov would be just as dead. The KGB officer stepped back a pace and moved his hands away from the holster under his jacket that he saw Kortyshkov glancing at.

"Leave me alone," Kortyshkov said in a low, trembling voice. "Leave me alone. I *must* supervise the base defense. Carry out your directive yourself if you have to, but leave me *alone.*" Kortyshkov turned and rejoined his executive officer, throwing commands at everyone.

Teresov was left alone in the doorway of a darkened room. *Damn him,* Teresov cursed silently, thinking about the hell Gabovich would make Kortyshkov pay for his insubordination.

But Teresov's first responsibility was to his superior officer. Gabovich had to be found and escorted to safety. Holding a KGB general would be an immense victory for whoever was staging this invasion, and Teresov had pledged to lay down his life for his superior officer.

His second responsibility was to see that all of Gabovich's plans and programs were secure and uncompromised during this emergency, and Gabovich's most important covert operation was the American, Luger, being held prisoner in the basement. It was obviously too late to get Luger out of the facility and into hiding or across the border to Byelorussia.

The only option was to execute him.

Teresov had developed a comprehensive procedure to be followed for disposing of Luger's body—burn it in the incinerator on Subfloor 2, the same floor as Luger's cell. But he never intended on doing the thing himself. Murdering a helpless prisoner was a job for brainless louts, not for officers. More importantly, it was vital that all possible traces of Luger's presence and death could never be traced back to Viktor Gabovich.

Better get started locating Gabovich, Teresov thought, and hope to hell that the incompetent fool Kortyshkov could hold off whoever it was out there until all traces of First Lieutenant David Luger's presence here in Fisikous could be properly and efficiently destroyed.

CONGO ZERO-TWO, USAF AC-130U SPECTRE GUNSHIP
OVER VILNIUS, LITHUANIA
13 APRIL, 0340 VILNIUS (12 APRIL, 2140 ET)

"I say again, your primary target is map coordinate zulu-victor-five-one-four-three, clear an area for one hundred meters around the building," the AC-130U Spectre gunship's electronic-warfare officer read, after decoding the updated targeting instructions received from the Marines. "Second target follows. Clear a one-hundred-meter area around grid coordinates bravo-lima-three-seven-seven-zero for pickup zone. Establish security perimeter of two thousand meters around coordinates of primary target. Over."

In the cockpit, sitting behind the copilot, the AC-130U's navigator quickly plotted the grid coordinates on his chart, then punched the PRESENT POSITION button on the Global Positioning System satellite navigation computer, plotted the aircraft's present position, and computed a heading to the target coordinates. "Pilot, give me a heading of one-niner-five, targets at your twelve o'clock, eight miles."

The navigator immediately transposed the target coordinates onto a detailed map of the Fisikous Research Institute, derived from satellite photography, showing the layout of every building and every landmark in the complex, and passed it to the fire-control officer (FICO) beside him. It was the FICO's job to locate and identify the target building himself. He had control of the Spectre's AN/APG-80 high-resolution radar, and he could call up the scene from either the low-light TV or forward-looking infrared scanner. He also controlled the twelve laser-guided Hellfire missiles, and could direct a laser designator beam on any target he saw in his screens.

The Spectre crew had been briefed on the Fisikous Research Institute as a possible target, and the navigator, FICO, and the two sensor operators had spent long hours going over the layout of the complex and the possible targets to hit. "Our objective is the design-center security building," the FICO announced. "Keep all vehicles away, clear personnel off the roof, and clear an LZ for the Marines." That was all he needed to brief—the sensor operators would do the rest.

"Sensors copy." Once they were briefed on the area they needed to secure, and which targets needed to be hit and which did not, the sensor operators went to work locating targets. At six miles' distance, the forward-looking infrared (FLIR) scanner could pick out individual heat-generating targets, and the fight was on.

It was, as they say, a target-rich environment. The FLIR operator selected several hot targets. "FLIR's got a column of light armored stuff and maybe tanks," he reported.

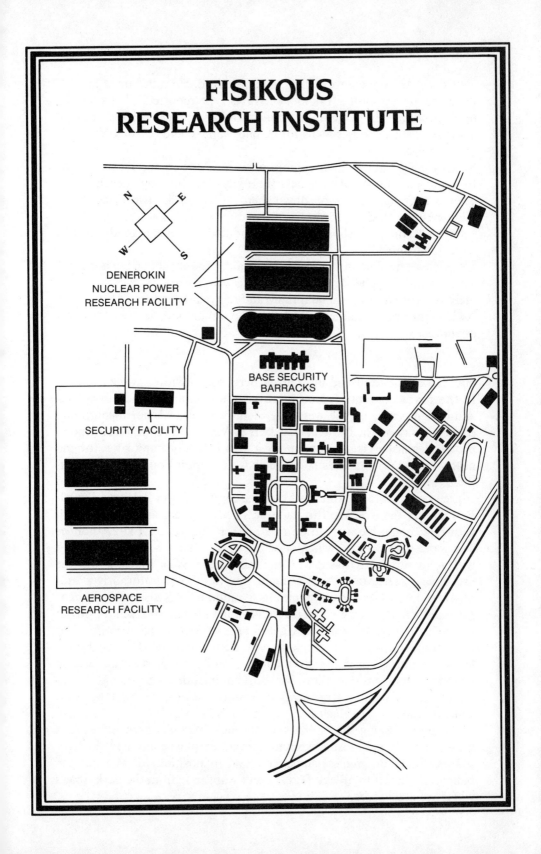

FISIKOUS
RESEARCH INSTITUTE

N E

W S

DENEROKIN
NUCLEAR POWER
RESEARCH FACILITY

BASE SECURITY
BARRACKS

SECURITY FACILITY

AEROSPACE
RESEARCH FACILITY

"Copy," the fire-control officer acknowledged. He called up the FLIR image on his monitor. "Looks like BTRs," he reported. "Let's lock it up." He locked the target in the fire-control computer, which automatically provided steering signals to the pilot so he could set up a left orbit over the area.

"Hey, STV's got another column of armor," the second sensor operator reported. "Looks like . . . hey, these guys are shooting at each other! There's a firefight going on down there. It looks like two mechanized infantry units slugging it out."

"What?" the pilot shouted on interphone. "You mean good guys?"

"I don't know."

"Well, we need to find out," the pilot said. "E-dub, get on the horn and get the word from headquarters." The electronic-warfare officer immediately switched to his command radio and relayed the request. "FICO, get back on the primary target and let's clean it out until we decide who's who down there."

Half of the one-thousand-man Black Beret security force at the Fisikous Institute was concentrated on the two-hundred-and-fifty-acre research-and-design center on the west side of the complex. A north-south-oriented runway on the far west side, part of Vilnius International Airport, provided a wide clear-fire area, so it was virtually impossible for the nearly two thousand soldiers of Palcikas' Battalion Four to sneak in on the base unobserved.

Lieutenant Colonel Antanas Maziulis, commander of Palcikas' Fourth Battalion of the Iron Wolf Brigade, scanned the area east of the runway with binoculars. He was sitting in an old, Polish-style AFD-23 mobile-command-post vehicle, which was little more than an old rickety Jeep with a tin box in the back with the radio gear. With Maziulis was his executive officer, Major Aras Drunga, plus a radio operator, driver, and observer/gunner/co-driver manning a mounted AKSU machine gun. Maziulis, a father of eight and an old veteran of twenty years in the Soviet Army, including four years in Afghanistan, was one of the first officers to retire from the Soviet Army and join the Lithuanian Self-Defense Force. He was rewarded by being given command of the largest strike force in this very important operation. Maziulis commanded a battalion of over a thousand men and a large array of armored vehicles, a few T-62s, and combat-engineering vehicles.

"They're keeping the ballpark lights on," Maziulis observed. "That must mean no night-vision equipment. Call Dapkiene and have him get sharpshooters or grenade-launcher crews in position to take out the ballpark lights. If the Black Berets don't want to fight in the dark, that's where we *want* to be."

"Echo Company reports one of their BTRs has a broken axle," Major Aras Drunga, Maziulis's executive officer and deputy, reported. "Echo Company platoon ten unloading, proceeding on foot."

Maziulis swung his binoculars northward to the very edge of light on the ramp. Sure enough, the Black Berets had spotted the breakdown as well, and were moving a BMP-90 armored combat vehicle opposite the Lithuanian foot soldiers. "Tell Captain Haviastir to get an RPG up front. He's got company. Get me a report from Third Battalion and find out where the hell they are."

A few moments later the response came: "Third Battalion is moving into position. Ready in two minutes."

"Shit. What's taking them so long? They had a highway to drive on—we made better time and we went cross-country." Two minutes was far, far too long. The command net had First Battalion streaming in through the northeast gate, and Second Battalion was moving toward the security headquarters. He couldn't wait any longer. "Radio Third Battalion and tell them to stick it in high gear. We're attacking. Signal to all units, stand by. Signal to Alpha and Bravo companies, attack."

"Aircraft inbound!" the radioman reported.

"Aras, get that report," Maziulis said. He wasn't going to take his eyes off his spearhead. "C'mon, boys, pop those mortars loose or you'll get hosed. Radio Bravo Company to get his mortarmen working. Where are my snipers?"

"First Battalion observers say a large fixed-wing aircraft will be over the base in thirty seconds," Drunga reported. "Identification unknown. Suspected cargo aircraft, possibly carrying paratroopers."

"Drop paratroopers right in the middle of a battle zone? Let 'em. We'll finish them off too. Tell Alpha Company to watch out for those BMPs to the south, they've got 73-millimeter guns. Mortars and speed, in that order. That's what I need."

Suddenly Maziulis heard the first *pwoof!* bursts of mortar fire. At the same time, two lines of Lithuanian armored vehicles, led by a line of six T-62 main battle tanks, rushed onto the clear area just to the west of the runway and headed across. "Too early. Mortars haven't hit yet . . ."

When the mortar rounds hit, Maziulis nearly leaped out of the truck in shock. Every round landed short, some by dozens of meters. A few landed so short that they came closer to the Lithuanian tanks rumbling across the runway than they did to the Black Beret infantrymen. Maziulis shouldn't have been too surprised—the men manning some of the heavier infantry-support pieces were young soldiers who'd never fired those kinds of weapons except on the training range. He should have had them pop a few smoke rounds to get their distance, then lob in a few HE rounds. Well, too late now . . .

"Tell those mortarmen to adjust their aim!" Maziulis screamed.

"Charlie and Echo companies! *Move! Move! Move!* Alpha and Bravo need cover fire! Tell Third Battalion to move at best speed or we'll lose the west flank!"

ABOARD THE AC-130U SPECTRE GUNSHIP

"Units on the ground reported Lithuanian partisans trying to attack the Commonwealth troops on the base," the electronic-warfare officer on board said. "The ground units said that partisans surrounded the base and appear to be converging on the security headquarters building. They are heavily armed, including tanks and Zeus-23s."

"That doesn't help us much," the pilot grumbled. "Who are we supposed to blow away? And—"

"Triple-A search radar, ten o'clock!" the electronic-warfare officer reported. "Another triple-A up . . . looks like a Zeus-23-4." The electronic-warfare officer on the Spectre centered a circle cursor on the two "A" antiaircraft-artillery symbols on his radar threat-scope. That action fed position information to the Spectre's targeting computer and instantly computed the position of the ZSU-23-4 mobile gun. "Target feed on the triple-A coming in."

"I got it," the FLIR sensor operator said. The targeting computer slaved both the low-light TV and infrared scanner to the new threat, and the FLIR operator saw the distinctive outline of the quadruple guns on the armored vehicle. "New primary target, FICO."

"I got it," the fire-control officer reported. "Laser firing. Range, three miles . . ."

"Ground forces said the Zeus belongs to the partisans," the electronic-warfare officer said.

"I don't care if they belong to the goddamned Pope," the pilot said. "If they try to lock me up on radar, they die. FICO, clear to launch."

"Missile away," the fire-control officer reported. At that, he unlocked a red-guarded switch on his control panel and pressed a trigger. One Hellfire missile, this one from the right wingtip, leaped from its rail and streaked earthward. Following the guidance signals from the laser beam, the missile hit dead-on. The crew was rewarded with a spectacular sight in their TV monitors of a deadly antiaircraft-artillery vehicle disappearing in a cloud of fire.

"Sweet kill," the FICO confirmed. They could hear cheers from the four gunners and the loadmaster/spotter in the back of the aircraft. The fire-control officer hit a button, and all the sensors returned to the target-building area to search for more targets.

"Looks like a column of troops moving in on the security building from the east, another group trying to approach from the west, and a group of defenders on the east side of the runway trying to hold 'em off," the STV sensor operator summarized. "Call it, someone."

"Our target is the security building," the fire-control officer reiterated. "The troops defending it must be the bad guys, and the ones attacking it must be the good guys. I say we target the defenders."

"Agreed," the navigator said.

"I'll buy it," the pilot said. "As long as they all stay away from the security building. Anyone who comes near it, unless they're U.S. Marines, we hose. Coming left."

The pilot began a slow, 20-degree bank turn to the left over the security building, then transitioned from his forward HSI to the low-light TV monitor-and-attack-coordinator mounted on the left window. By following the steering cues, the pilot set up an orbit precisely eight thousand feet above ground level.

From this point on, the sensor operators, the navigator, and the fire-control officer picked and attacked targets, with occasional warning messages from the electronic-warfare officer. The two sensor operators had almost complete control of the 25-millimeter cannon, letting loose with one- to two-second bursts at any group of soldiers that might be a field commander or communications crew, heavy-machine-gun nest, mortar crew, or rocket-propelled grenade-launcher crew. The FICO picked targets for the 40-millimeter cannon, alternating control with the sensor operators as they located suitable targets.

The pilot adjusted his orbit over targets designated for the 105-millimeter cannon, attacking tanks and destroying buildings close to the security building that might screen oncoming enemy troops from the Marines. The pilot felt a rush of adrenaline as he watched the incredible sight through his TV monitor. The power unleashed by that simple action of his left thumb was truly amazing. One squeeze of a trigger, and huge armored vehicles thousands of feet below him simply mushroomed into twisted hunks of burning metal. "Target destroyed," he announced calmly, choking back the urge to cry out an excited "Yes!!!" Instead: "Safeties on. Gun secured, clear for safety check. Gimme the next target."

"Clear."

"I got another Zeus-23!" the electronic-warfare officer shouted.

The crew's attention was diverted instantly—the ZSU-23-4 could easily bring down a Spectre, and the standing order was to destroy or avoid them at all costs. The fire-control officer immediately slaved the sensors to the threat-warning receiver, and four sets of eyes searched for the tiny white dot that might be the deadly tracked weapon. "I can't see it, dammit, I don't see it . . ."

Suddenly, a fast *deedledeedledeedledeedledeedle!* erupted on the intercom, and a flashing AAA LOCK light appeared on every instrument panel in the plane.

The ZSU-23-4 was just off to the right and close—too close.

"Triple-A lock!" the electronic-warfare officer shouted. "Break left!"

The pilot threw the AC-130 gunship in a tight left turn—with the big cannons hanging out the left side of the aircraft, left turns in a Spectre gunship are always tighter than right turns—and the EWO ejected radar-decoying chaff from the right-side ejectors.

"I see it! Continue left turn . . . roll out!" the copilot cried out as hundreds of winks of light and beads of death curled up from below, heading right for the aircraft. The beads swept across the right wingtip, and the entire aircraft shook as if a giant hand had kicked the plane like a child's toy. "We took a hit on the Hellfire pylon!" the copilot cried out. Flames and bright bursts of light enveloped the right wingtip. "Jettison right weapon pylon!"

The fire-control officer immediately opened a clear cover over an illuminated button that read RT WPN PYLON FIRE, reached in, and pressed the button. The right Hellfire-missile pylon popped off its hardpoint seconds before one of the missiles cooked off and exploded.

"I can't roll out," the pilot said on interphone. "I've got a jammed aileron . . . copilot, get on the controls. Help me straighten out . . ."

Immediately they heard, "Rattler Three cleared in hot, continue your left turn to clear." One of the four Marine Corps AH-1 Sea Cobras that had stayed behind in the embassy compound had launched from the embassy, rendezvoused with the AC-130, and now dove in on the second ZSU-23-4 mobile gun. With the antiaircraft gunner's full attention on the bigger target, it was too easy for the Sea Cobra's weapons officer to find the target from the flash of its four guns, lock on to the target with its laser designator, and fire a single Hellfire, destroying the target instantly. "Target down," the Cobra pilot reported. "I've got a visual on you, Congo Two. I see large sparks on your right wingtip."

Even a one-second burst from a ZSU-23-4 was menacing—that meant two hundred radar-guided shells as big as a hot dog peppering your aircraft. The murderous fire from the second ZSU-23-4 created a massive fuel leak from the right wing. "Congo Two is hit," the pilot radioed on the command channel. "No engine fire, but we're leaking fuel."

Everyone on the two Hammer aircraft knew what that meant—the Spectre was going home. An AC-130 gunship was too valuable and too high-profile an aircraft to lose over Lithuania.

LITHUANIAN SELF-DEFENSE FORCE BATTALION FOUR
13 APRIL, 0340 VILNIUS (12 APRIL, 2140 ET)

"Aircraft opening fire on First Battalion artillery units," Drunga reported. "Heavy cannon fire. One antiaircraft artillery unit destroyed. Rotary-wing aircraft inbound."

Maziulis felt a flush of fear run through him, but he pushed it away. It was sooner than expected, but they did expect a counterattack. "Where's Third Battalion . . . ?"

Suddenly the night sky illuminated from the bursts of several large-caliber cannons firing at once, and a few seconds later the ear-shattering reports roiled across the runway. Several T-62 tanks and Lithuanian armored vehicles exploded. The drivers were temporarily blinded and confused as they crossed the path of their own mortars, and the smoke from the mortars screened their gunners from taking aim on the line of Black Beret armored combat vehicles. But as soon as they emerged from the smoke, the Commonwealth gunners had them cold and opened fire.

Many Lithuanian units were killed before they could get a shot off.

Maziulis grabbed the command-net microphone and yelled, "Echo and Foxtrot companies! Fake north, wheel east, and engage! Delta Company, release from the line, stunt circle north, and flank those BMDs!"

He scanned his line with the binoculars. Echo and Foxtrot companies, far to the south, were moving, but Delta Company, located just a few hundred meters away, hadn't moved backwards yet. Maziulis turned to Drunga and yelled, "Aras, run over to the Rover and have him go over to Delta Company lead and tell him to stunt north and cover Alpha and Bravo. Find out what's wrong with his radio."

Drunga threw off his headset, grabbed an AK-47, and jumped off the radio truck and sprinted over to a small four-wheeled vehicle, flagging it down.

He had taken perhaps eight steps away from the radio truck when a scream of compressed air and a terrific explosion threw him off his feet. He flew for perhaps five meters into the air, then was thrown across the ground amidst shards of red-hot metal and waves of superheated air. When he looked back at the radio truck, nothing was there except a blackened metal skeleton with the broken and mutilated bodies of Maziulis and the others scattered around the area like dolls tossed by the wind.

* * *

"Congo Two, can you give us some fire support on the Hammer target area against the heavy stuff before you split?" Captain Snyder asked from Hammer Three.

"Can do easy," the AC-130's pilot reported. "Our tanker is heading back to join with us, and our fuel loss is minimal right now. There's no sign of engine fire. We've got about five minutes more on station before we bingo."

"Copy. Hit the heavy armor first, then soften up the area around the two target areas. After that, give us a sparkler and you're cleared to depart. Open her up, Congo Two."

"Copy all, Hammer leader. Watch the sky."

The OMON Black Berets had its front-line men and equipment protecting the research center, including six BTR-60PB armored personnel carriers, each fitted with two heavy-caliber machine guns and able to transport fourteen soldiers at speeds up to sixty miles per hour; three BMD tracked combat vehicles, fitted with a 73-millimeter cannon and wire-guided AT-3 antitank missiles; and infantry units armed with grenade launchers and RPK and PKM heavy machine guns. This formidable line of vehicles, arrayed against the advancing Lithuanian forces to the west, became easy targets for the Spectre gunship.

No Spectre crew liked to bring back unspent ammo from a live fire mission. This crew was determined not to bring back one round. Using the two rapid-fire cannons, the Spectre began chewing into the Black Beret troop positions. The 25-millimeter cannonfire ripped apart smaller armored personnel carriers and Jeeps, while the 40-millimeter cannon destroyed or disabled the larger armored combat vehicles. They were careful to keep the gunfire away from the security building, where Luger was being held, as well as the hangars where the Soviet stealth bomber was supposedly kept. The sensor operators and fire-control officer also tried to stay away from the troops he felt were the "partisans."

There were enough good targets everywhere below, especially the heavy vehicles and armor. A few times the pilot opened up with the 105-millimeter howitzer, creating large antivehicle pits around the planned pickup zone while being careful to keep fences intact. The crew liberally sprayed the MV-22 landing site with 25-millimeter and 40-millimeter cannonfire in case any troops tried to hunker down in those areas. The Spectre then made another circle over the city, selecting targets for the twelve remaining Hellfire missiles on the left wingtip, destroying any heavy armored vehicles identified by the Marines in the embassy compound as threats.

Once again, they headed for the area near the Fisikous Institute to deliver their *coup de grâce.* . . .

LITHUANIAN FOURTH BATTALION

More cannon fire erupted—the shock waves and ear-splitting noise all around Major Aras Drunga was like an iron-gloved fist, driving him to the ground. Drunga crawled to his hands and knees, trying to move closer to the bodies, to see if any needed help. Then he saw the rows of Black Beret armored combat vehicles begin to move across the aircraft parking ramp toward him. They were less than three hundred meters away, and they were hammering the Lithuanians with volley after volley of cannon fire. The charge was a failure. General Palcikas' west flank was going to disintegrate.

Suddenly, it looked as if one of the BMD armored combat vehicles simply lifted straight up in the air, like a frog jumping off a rock. When it fell to earth again, flames and burning fuel were spilling out a gaping hole in its turret. A few seconds later, another vehicle, a BTR-60 armored personnel carrier, seemed to split apart like a ripe melon, spilling pieces of Black Beret soldiers who'd been chopped up by artillery fire. The young officer didn't know what was happening, but whatever it was, it was accurately and effectively wiping out the best of the Black Berets' offensive punch.

Every Spectre mission-planning session includes a "sparkler," a target that is so large and filled with so much explosive or flammable material that it provides maximum shock value and disorientation, allowing aircraft to escape, friendly troops to move in, or helps to demoralize the enemy. Even though a sparkler may not be a high-value target or related to the sortie's main objective, it is kept in the commander's "hip pocket"—in this case programmed into the targeting computers—and made ready for use at any time.

Now was the time . . .

The Spectre swung out of its orbit around the Fisikous Institute compound, headed south, and made a left bank around its final target. The sortie's sparkler was a fuel-storage area a few miles south of the facility near the railroad yard.

The 105-millimeter howitzer found its mark, and as a final parting shot created a spectacular fireball and a terrific rumbling explosion by sending a dozen high-explosive shells into that fuel-tank farm.

The concussion knocked over tank cars and engines on their tracks and shattered windows ten miles away. Then, with two Sea Cobra helicopters acting as escorts, the huge attack plane climbed into the night sky and was clear of the city a few minutes later.

* * *

The AC-130 gunship orbiting over Major Aras Drunga destroyed half of the Black Berets' armor in the few short minutes it orbited over the Fisikous compound. With the former KGB and Soviet Troops of the Interior forces being decimated by the gunship, the surviving elements of the Lithuanians' Fourth Battalion were able to sweep across the runway and rout the Black Beret security force. The control tower and radar facilities were captured intact, as were the underground fuel-storage tanks and aircraft-refueling facilities.

Dominikas Palcikas led one company each from First and Second battalions in a flanking maneuver to try to disrupt the Black Berets' resupply routes to the east, but it proved to be unnecessary. Palcikas' forces had surrounded the design center and security facility before he realized how far and how fast he had moved across the base. He met up with the remnants of the Fourth Battalion streaming in from the northwest. Third Battalion was mopping up the survivors of the gunship attack. "Third Battalion reports several vehicles escaping out the south gate," the radioman reported. "Lieutenant Colonel Manomaitis is pursuing."

"Tell him to let all but the heavier vehicles go," Palcikas said. "Setting up the perimeter defense is more critical than chasing down a few platoons. Tell him to set up his security teams along the south highway and seal it up tight. We'll get Second Battalion to join up with him to the southeast as soon as possible, but he's responsible for warning us of an immediate Soviet counterattack from the Darguziai Army Barracks."

A few moments later a driver brought Major Drunga, the deputy commander of Fourth Battalion, up to Palcikas in a Commonwealth Jeep flying a red Vytis. "Good job, Major. Where's Colonel Maziulis? We need to set up his security team for that runway." Then Palcikas realized why the deputy was reporting to him: "What happened, Aras?"

The young officer, barely thirty years old, was covered with blood. His jacket was missing, his hands were trembling uncontrollably, and he was bleeding heavily from a cut on his left temple. "Medic!" Palcikas shouted as he took off his jacket and threw it around Drunga. "Talk to me, Aras." No reply—only a stunned, vacant expression. Palcikas raised his voice and shouted, "Major Drunga! *Report!*"

That shook Drunga out of his catatonia. He straightened his back by force of habit and even tried to salute, but Palcikas held his hand down as a corpsman began treating his head wound. "We were hit by a round from one of the BTRs, sir," Drunga said. "The shell sliced the whole top off the Colonel's armored car. The Colonel . . . he lost . . . the shell took off . . . my God, the Colonel's blood was *everywhere!*"

"What's the status of Fourth Battalion, Aras? Give me a report."

"Fourth Battalion . . . the battalion is heavily decimated but currently on station, sir," Drunga said shakily. "Alpha Company . . . Alpha Company was nearly wiped out in the initial assault. Colonel Maziulis ordered Bravo to sweep north to flank the MSB armored line and break it, and they were nearly cut down as well before the aircraft came in. That aircraft saved us, sir. It saved us."

"Yes, it did, Major," Palcikas agreed. "Major Knasaite . . . ?"

"Dead, sir. Everyone in Alpha Company . . . almost everyone . . . dead."

"Major Balzaraite?"

"Dead, sir. Captain Meilus commands Bravo Company, but he's hurt, too . . . God, he lost his left hand . . ."

Drunga finally realized that Palcikas was gently coaxing a full report out of him, that he was in effect commander of Fourth Battalion, so he straightened his shoulders a bit as he continued. "Bravo Company is about thirty-five percent manned, sir; they are regrouping to surround the design center and security facility as ordered. Major Astriene of Charlie Company is leading the security team to seal off the south gate. I recommend . . . I'm sorry, sir, but I recommend that he be placed in charge of Fourth Battalion."

"Only until you are better, Major Drunga. Only until you are better." The medic was easing Drunga down and wrapping blankets around him to ward off shock. "Take care of him, and find Captain Meilus and tell him to report to the aid station. Find Lieutenant Dapkiene or Lieutenant Degutis and put them in charge of Bravo Company." Palcikas rubbed his eyes wearily and turned to Zukauskas. "My God, I'm having to put my lieutenants in charge of entire infantry companies. Three weeks ago their biggest concern was filing a report in the right folder—now they command hundreds of men."

He paused, willing the numbness and exhaustion away. The officers of Iron Wolf Brigade were the only family he had had in many years, and to see them decimated like this was difficult. He called them by their rank and surname when speaking with his subordinates, but he knew them as Anatoly, or Danas, or Vytautas, or Karoly. He knew their individual quirks, their leadership style, their strengths and weaknesses. Maziulis had eight children back at his home in Siauliai. Drunga was Mister Spit and Polish. Meilus was the ladies' man, the peacock strutting around the bars and cafés of Kaunas showing off his awards and medals to all the young ladies . . .

They were all dead now, dead or horribly maimed or shocked into virtual catatonia by a civil war that he, Palcikas, had started. He could do nothing else but replace them with an even younger, probably more scared officer, and when he died he would have to be replaced by someone younger and even less experienced. When the officers died out, then he would have to promote noncommissioned officers to company grade rank, and the cycle would start again . . .

"Sir . . . General Palcikas, Fourth Battalion is awaiting orders. Shall we proceed to the security building in the aircraft-design area?"

"Hold off on the assault on the security building until we get the command straightened out," Palcikas said. "The building is surrounded—they are not going anywhere."

"Sir, what was that aircraft? Why did it first attack us, then attack the Black Beret armor?"

"Either it was a Commonwealth Air Force strike aircraft that made a horrible mistake," Palcikas speculated, "or some other power has gotten itself involved in our battle. I think it detected the ZSU-23-4 because it detected its tracking radar and judged it to be a threat, but then it judged the armored units defending the aircraft-design compound to be a threat as well—it left our armor alone. It doesn't matter, though. It saved our lives tonight, and we don't want to anger the powers that control it.

"Now," Palcikas continued, "I need a report on our antiair-artillery units, and I want a report on the position of that gunship and any other aircraft in the vicinity. But we've got to consolidate and reinforce our hold on the complex before the Commonwealth counterattack begins. I want the commanders of—"

"Helicopters inbound!" someone cried out. "From the north!"

Heads swung in that direction, but the night sky revealed nothing. Through the occasional bursts of cannon or gunfire on the base, they could hear the beat of fast helicopter rotors coming closer. "Slow rotors . . . heavy helicopter—attack, or troop carriers," Lieutenant Colonel Simas Zobarskas, commander of First Battalion, said. "One, perhaps two. Flying over the aircraft-design compound. Whoever it is, they're not attacking, at least not yet."

"All these overflights seem to be concentrating on the aircraft-design center," Palcikas said, his curiosity up. He pointed toward the huge howitzer craters surrounding the four-meter-high security fence around the design-center compound. "Look at those craters—they are aligned precisely around the fence, but they did not destroy it. They look like tank traps . . ."

"Tank traps?" Zobarskas asked incredulously. "Against our forces . . . ?"

"I don't know," Palcikas said, mulling it over. "But if they wanted to stop us or our armor from coming any closer to the compound, they could have done it more efficiently—"

"Namely, by hitting *us* with those bombs," Colonel Zukauskas exclaimed.

"It was not done with bombs, Vitalis," Palcikas said. "I distinctively heard cannon fire during that gunship attack. The same gunship that was firing antitank machine guns at the MSB was shooting a large-caliber cannon—it probably was responsible for the explosions in the fuel depot as well. I know of only one aircraft in the world that has that capability—"

"Company Alpha-Charlie reports heavy rotors inbound, fifteen seconds behind the light helicopter," a radioman reported. "They are requesting permission to engage."

"Stand by," Palcikas said.

Up until now, the means to secure the objective were plain—all military units and equipment not belonging to the First Iron Wolf Brigade were considered hostile. But that was no longer true anymore—or was it? The unidentified fixed-wing gunship attacked only the Commonwealth armor units and the ZSU-23-4 guns that were engaging it—other than the anti-aircraft-artillery units, it stayed away from Lithuanian units and concentrated its deadly accurate fire on the Black Berets.

Now more unidentified aircraft were coming.

Could the newcomers be friendlies? If they were unidentified friendlies, Palcikas could be hurting his own cause by attacking them. Would a Commonwealth Air Force gunship have behaved as the unidentified gunship had? Probably not—the Commonwealth armor units were definitely defending the Soviet installation, and the Lithuanians were definitely attacking. There could be no mistake about it—the gunship saw the defenders as the enemy and the Lithuanians as friendlies.

If he was wrong, he could be letting the Byelorussians or Russians reinforce the Soviet defenders here in Fisikous. Even two or three companies inside that design-center compound could wreak havoc on Palcikas' soldiers. But Palcikas knew something else was going on. The security building was a target for something, or someone, else entirely . . .

"No," Palcikas finally answered. "No one will engage without my specific orders. Pass to all units: do not engage any aircraft over the complex without my specific orders. I want a positive identification of the inbound aircraft immediately."

ABOARD HAMMER FOUR

The only eyes they had on the assault zone now, the two AH-1W Sea Cobra helicopters that had been escorting the Spectre gunship, were departing after only one pass over the aircraft-design research compound. It did not belong with the Hammer aircraft, because on this particular mission the Hammer aircraft did not exist.

The MV-22s had to finish the assault alone.

"Hammer, Rattler, I see ground forces, perhaps two to three hundred, dispersed to the east and south of your LZ," the gunner on one of the AH-1 Sea Cobras reported on the command network. "Additional forces, perhaps another battalion, converging in light vehicles and trucks from the south. The battalion that was hit by the base defenders is regrouping and is setting up a perimeter defense to the west. I see one Zeus unit on the move, but its guns are raised, repeat, raised, in service position. Over."

"Well, what the hell does *that* mean?" Lieutenant Marx asked.

"It means they're servicing their guns," Gunnery Sergeant Trimble said impatiently. He was still angry at being taken down by his commanding officer in front of the three outsiders. "A Zeus 23-millimeter cannon has a very short barrel life, perhaps three thousand rounds, which is just a few engagements. The barrels have to be changed frequently. That thing is still alive."

"We're not reporting any triple-A signals," McLanahan said. "The radar is down."

"That don't mean shit, either, McLanahan," Trimble said. "If I was servicing my own rig, I wouldn't have my radar on either—they know we can home in on their radars by now."

McLanahan lowered his eyes and did not reply—he knew that what the big Marine said was true. Getting Luger was blinding him to the dangers they faced. He had to face reality: Luger was probably dead.

Trimble turned to Marx. "Sir, the LZ is *hot.* This is a special ops mission, not a MAGTF mission. This team only has thirty-three members, and there's at least a battalion down there. We got no choice but to recommend an abort. You can't risk an entire company for this zoomie—"

McLanahan's nostrils flared, and Briggs was ready to get in Trimble's face again, but this time Lieutenant Marx held up a hand quickly and said, "You're right, Gunny, you're right." He turned to McLanahan and Ormack and, feeling guilty enough to offer an explanation, said, "If the Spectre took out more of the triple-A batteries, we could proceed, but there's still live Zeus-23s down there. The SEA HAMMERs wouldn't stand a chance over the security building with that thing nearby." Marx reached for the command net microphone and depressed the mike button: "Hammer Lead, this is Four. Over. . . ."

"Hammer units, monitor UHF GUARD channel and stand by," came Snyder's call a few seconds later. Up in the cockpit of the second MV-22 SEA HAMMER, the copilot switched the radios so the Marines in the cargo section could hear the universal emergency channel:

"Attention inbound helicopters, attention inbound helicopters, this is General Dominikas Palcikas," a message came over a few moments later in heavily accented English. "I am the commander of the Grand Duke's First Iron Wolf Brigade of the Lithuanian Republic. My forces now occupy the Fisikous Research Institute in Vilnius and other defense installations throughout the republic, in the name of the people of Lithuania. The Black Beret troops defending this installation have been removed. I seek only to return the Lithuanian Republic to the people of Lithuania.

"I order you to identify yourself immediately or you will be fired upon without further warning. If you are friendly, and if you will comply immediately, you will *not* be fired upon. I will repeat this message in Russian. This will be my final warning. Identify yourself immediately." The message paused, then repeated in the Russian language.

The shock of that short message had quieted everyone in the cargo section of the MV-22. Finally Trimble retorted, "What is this shit? There's no such thing as the Grand Duke's Iron Wolf Brigade in Lithuania."

"Palcikas . . . Palcikas . . ." Marx muttered; then, recalling his background intelligence briefings, announced, "Palcikas! Dominikas Palcikas, the commander of the Lithuanian Self-Defense Force!"

"He's staged a coup," Wohl said with admiration. "A damned Lithuanian Army general has staged a coup."

"Not a coup. A military takeover," Marx said. "If what he says is true, he's commanding those troops down there."

"That means we can proceed," McLanahan said. "We're Americans. We're not trying to take over Fisikous." He hesitated; then, with a shocked expression, he realized what this *really* meant to their mission. "Jesus . . . Luger . . ."

"Looks like Palcikas may have caused the death of the zoomie after all," Trimble said. "If they had orders to kill their prisoners in case of a rescue attempt, he's dead."

"Shut up!" McLanahan shouted, ready to take a swing at Trimble.

"We can't go down there now," Trimble said, ignoring McLanahan. "We've been blown for sure. This is supposed to be a covert mission. We can't have a fucking audience watching us touch down on that rooftop."

"We can't leave until we get Luger," Ormack said. "Dead or alive, we've got to get him."

"Like *hell.*"

"Palcikas is giving us clearance to overfly the compound," McLanahan insisted. "If we show we're not hostile to his forces, we can keep going."

"And what if it's *not* this Palcikas character?" Trimble retorted. "What if it's just the Black Berets trying to lure us down there? Those Zeus-23s will hose us if we get too close. I recommend we abort, Lieutenant. Follow the proper procedures, sir. Let's get the hell out of here—now!"

FISIKOUS DESIGN-BUREAU SECURITY CENTER

"That's right . . . you heard what I said!" MSB Major Teresov screamed
into the radio microphone. "Fisikous has been surrounded by armed
Lithuanian peasants, and some unidentified aircraft has just bombed the
base . . . no, you asshole, this is *not* an exercise! I don't care if this is an
unsecure channel! I want a fucking helicopter-gunship squadron with
antiair support deployed to Fisikous immediately, and I want a full
Commonwealth battalion with assault gear and armor sent as well! Alert
the Commonwealth Army corps commander in Riga that Fisikous is
under attack. Request infantry and security support . . . yes, Corps
headquarters directly, under General Gabovich's authority." He knew he
was stretching the limits of his authority once again, but this was getting
very serious . . .

"What do you think you're doing, Teresov?" Colonel Kortyshkov
interrupted. A junior NCO had led the design bureau's security forces
commander to where Teresov was talking on the portable UHF transceiver—Teresov made a mental note to have that soldier carry Kortyshkov's cold-weather gear to Siberia when this was over. "You are not
authorized to order air cover or anything from Corps headquarters, and
I gave orders that no communications are allowed out of this building
without my specific approval."

"Your approval is the least of my concerns," Teresov said dismissively.
"The defense of this base and the safety of the projects here are my only
concern." He finished his conversation with the radiotelephone operator
he had managed to reach, then faced Kortyshkov with a stern glare and
asked, "Has General Gabovich been located yet?"

"I am not yet in contact with the south gate or with Colonel Stepanov—"

"Then you have failed again," Teresov said. "It is imperative that
General Gabovich be found and warned to stay away from the base."

"Then I suggest you run out and find him, Comrade," Kortyshkov
said. "Or are you still debating whether or not to carry out your Zulu
directive? Let me help you with both missions." At that, Kortyshkov
reached into his NCO's holster, withdrew a Makarov PM 9-millimeter
automatic pistol, and slapped it into Teresov's hand. Pointing toward the
barricaded front door and then toward the stairwell that led to the two
subfloors, Kortyshkov said, "Your general is that way, your helpless
victim is that way. Let's see how well you carry out either mission."

"I order you to carry out the Zulu directive, Colonel."

"And I refuse," Kortyshkov replied. "My men tell me that the man
down there is an American military officer. He's not a traitorous Soviet

scientist, but an American! An *officer!* I have seen filthy pigs kept in better condition! You—" And then Kortyshkov stopped, his eyes wide with fear and realization: "Oh God, those are the Americans outside! They're probably here to retrieve their officer!"

"Don't be an idiot! Have you lost all of your senses?" Teresov demanded. He couldn't wait until Gabovich sent this insubordinating moron to Anadyr or some other hellhole base.

"You think I'm being a fool, Major? *Think* about it."

And it was then that Teresov realized, with a growing sense of dread and horror, that Kortyshkov was right. It was the only possible explanation for this cockeyed series of events. The fucking Americans were raiding the Institute! And at the same time they were probably aiding and abetting that Boy Scout army, the Iron Wolf Brigade, to liberate Fisikous. Teresov cursed the heavens, wishing this day had never dawned.

"If you want to kill a defenseless military officer, damn your eyes, then do it yourself! Thanks to your treachery, Major Teresov, I have to defend this installation against an American invasion force!" Kortyshkov then turned and departed, leaving Teresov angry enough to shoot the pompous, weak-livered officer in the back and end his useless existence. But the mission had first priority.

By then, Kortyshkov's soldiers had closed and locked the ground-floor doors and had placed tables against the windows and in the hallways to provide cover. Teresov realized he was not going to get out of the building. Gabovich had to help himself now—there was nothing more that Teresov could do for him until these Lithuanian rebels were squashed.

That left only Luger to contend with.

Grimly, Teresov tightened his grip on the Makarov and headed for the stairs that led to the subfloor detention center. The first thing Gabovich would want to ensure was that Luger was disposed of—and that was what Teresov had to do right now.

FIVE

General Wilbur Curtis's custom Lincoln Continental staff car—nicknamed the "JokerMobile" because of its gaudy purple leather interior, inch of bulletproof Kevlar plating, and sophisticated communications equipment—skidded to a halt at the entrance of the White House East Wing. The Chairman of the Joint Chiefs of Staff and his aide, Air Force Colonel Andrew Wyatt, were stepping out of the big car before the wheels had even stopped rolling. Through the double doors, past the security station, left down the Lady Bird Hallway, left and up the Grant Staircase, the General and his aide hurried to the "ground floor" of the White House, in the Oval Office anteroom.

Tonight was a "constituents' evening" photo opportunity, when carefully selected senators were "rewarded" by the President for supporting certain legislation or siding with the President's party, by bringing constituents in for a brief reception in the White House and pictures with the President in the Oval Office. The Oval Office anteroom was filled with people, all dressed in their Sunday best, looking nervous and excited.

On strict orders of the President's chief of staff, and to maintain all outward appearances of business as usual, Curtis had to stop and greet the senators and their guests, which he did as politely but as quickly as he could possibly manage. As soon as he could, he broke away from the crowd, hurried past the Cabinet Room, and waved at the Secret Service agents who admitted him immediately into the Oval Office. Wyatt plugged his portable Pentagon command-post transceiver into a wall outlet in a nearby office and waited.

The President was sipping coffee at his desk. His jacket was off and his light-blue silk shirt underneath was wrinkled and tired-looking, but his tie was still straight, his hair was neatly in place, and he looked as perky and energetic as ever. He glanced at his watch when Curtis entered. He and Secretary of Defense Preston, along with National Security Advisor Rus-

296

sell, had been briefing the President every thirty minutes on the progress of the Marines' mission in Lithuania, and Curtis hadn't been due for another update for a long time—getting an early one could only mean trouble. The President waved at the Oval Office photographers to leave by the door to the Cabinet Room, then asked, "What have you got, Wilbur?"

"Good news and not-so-good news, sir," Curtis replied. "The embassy staff who evacuated tonight from Vilnius are safely in Polish airspace and have rendezvoused with an Air Force KC-10 tanker for refueling. No sign of pursuit. They have received clearance across Poland for a landing in Warsaw. The embassy staff in Poland is standing by. Bad news, though— one embassy staffer's wife had a heart attack and died on board one of the choppers. Robert Massey's wife, Rebecca."

"Oh, Lord, Rebecca Massey. Jesus . . . couldn't anybody do anything? No doctors or medics on board?"

"It was sudden and quick," Curtis said. "They were jammed into this helicopter like sardines—one Super Stallion broke down, as we told you earlier, so they had to double up. By the time the Marine corpsman reached her, she was gone. Nothing could be done."

The President nodded, obviously not happy, but realizing there was nothing he could do about it now.

Curtis continued. "A few minor injuries, getting on the helicopters and such, none serious. Otherwise everyone else is fine. I think I'll have the Marines create a training course for all embassy staffers on helicopter operations during evacuation procedures. A few ladies refused to get on, and others simply had no clue."

"Evacuation procedures, helicopter operations . . . sign of the times, eh, Wilbur?"

"Sign of the times, Mr. President."

The President felt bad about Rebecca Massey—he had known the tempestuous Washington insider for years—but he was also relieved that she was the only casualty. Something had told the President that he might expect dozens of Americans to die in Lithuania tonight. "What news from the embassy? What are the Soviets doing?"

"So far no sign of excitement," Curtis replied. "I expect you'll be getting a call from President Kapocius of Lithuania. The wire services are reporting that he will make an announcement about the raid in about an hour. Nothing from the Commonwealth at all. The Marines in the embassy are hunkering down and waiting for trouble."

"I will call President Kapocius," the President said. "He should be briefed on the progress of the mission. He took a big chance authorizing our aircraft to fly over Lithuania. I could give President Miriclaw of Poland a hug for all he's done."

"I'd wait until you hear what he'd like in return before you hug him,"

Curtis said wryly. "Poland has been clamoring for additional farm and industrial credits, including rebuilding that nuclear power plant in Gdynia, which we've opposed in the past. Payback may be a bitch on this one."

"Right now he deserves it," the President said. "Stepping on the Commonwealth's toes like this isn't going to be popular in his country or his government. We'll have to make it up to him." The President paused, looking at Russell with a wary eye. "Okay, what's the not-so-good news?" Before Curtis could speak, he said, "The rescue mission to Fisikous? Something went wrong . . . ?"

"We're not sure yet," Curtis replied uneasily. "It appears that the Lithuanian Self-Defense Force, of all things, has staged a series of military raids on Byelorussian and Commonwealth military bases in Lithuania. The self-defense force is led by General Dominikas Palcikas. The main thrust of his attack was on the Fisikous Institute of Technology itself—"

"You're saying that a Lithuanian military unit stormed Fisikous?" he asked in alarm. "Don't tell me they went in at the *same time* as the Marines . . . ?"

"That appears to be the case, sir."

"What? They decided to finally toss out the Byelorussian and CIS troops the same night we go in? Jesus," the President muttered. "Boy, I'll never play cards again—the long odds are really going against me." He was silent for a moment, then said, "Well, if the wire services got the news, I'd better drop the all's-quiet routine." He buzzed the outer office. "Nancy, cancel all other appointments tonight with my sincere apologies."

A few moments later the chief of staff, Robert "Case" Timmons, hearing the President's instructions on the intercom, knocked and entered the Oval Office.

"Case, get the NSC and the White House staff over here, and put a call in to the leadership. Tell them I'll have news for them in a couple of hours."

His longtime aide and protégé hurried off to his office to make the calls, leaving the Chairman of the Joint Chiefs of Staff alone with the President.

The President poured himself another cup of coffee, then motioned Curtis to a chair. "Might as well be comfortable, Wilbur. This is shaping up to be a very long evening. Details, please, from the beginning."

"The Special Forces assaults inside Lithuania all went off without a hitch, with the exception of one Navy SEAL," Curtis said quietly. "He was killed while attempting to cut down some communications antennae on a headquarters building. The building was blown up under him—blown up, it turns out, by the Lithuanian Army. We got one report from a Special Forces team about a strange incident at one air base, but then we lost contact—the Army guys were heading for cover. Then we received the first indications of something happening from the Navy SEAL Gold team, the same one that lost one of its members, when they demolished a radar site and found a small Lithuanian commando unit already trashing the place. Other Special Forces and SEAL units have been encountering what we thought were small Commonwealth patrol units all over the country. But each of these small units was carrying an ancient Lithuanian war flag, which this General Palcikas has adopted as his banner of liberation."

"What about this Palcikas? What's the word on him?" the President asked, sipping his coffee.

"Director Mitchell will be giving you a complete briefing on him, sir," Curtis said. "But in my estimation he's one of the good guys. He's Lithuanian-born but educated and trained by the Soviets. Veteran of Afghanistan. He's powerful, well liked in Lithuania, and he's enamored of Lithuanian history. He has called his unit the Iron Wolf Brigade, after one of Lithuania's medieval rulers."

"He doesn't think *he's* a Lithuanian king, does he?" the President worried.

"I don't know, sir," Curtis said. "I think he's got more on the ball than that. More likely he invokes images of the Grand Duke as a clever marketing ploy to rally popular support to his side."

"If President Kapocius tells him to disband, do you think he'll do it?"

"I don't know, sir. Ken Mitchell and his staff will be prepared to answer that question. A better question for us to consider is what this government should do about Palcikas, and how it affects both the U.S. Embassy reinforcement and the Fisikous extraction."

"Nothing will affect the embassy reinforcement," the President said firmly. "Those Marines will stay until all dependents and non-embassy personnel are out of Lithuania and the situation has stabilized. I will not stand for another embassy-siege drama played out on television. We have the right to use military force to protect our embassies, and by God we're going to use them. There will be no doubt about *that.*" He paused, and Curtis could see the first hints of hesitation on the President's face. "We'll wait and see what President Kapocius does about Palcikas. If he embraces him, we'll support Kapocius. If he doesn't, we'll stay out of it. Now, what's going on with the REDTAIL HAWK rescue mission? Have the Marines aborted the mission?"

"No, sir," Curtis replied. "They are continuing to orbit the city, and they requested instructions."

"You're sure they're Lithuanian soldiers involved in those firefights in Fisikous?"

"There's no way to be positive, sir, without face-to-face contact. They're heavily armed, much more so than what we thought the Lithuanian Self-Defense Force had, but they have not fired on our aircraft. Radio contact has been made between the Marines and a man claiming to be General Palcikas himself. His forces did battle with the Black Berets in Fisikous. All evidence points to those troops being Lithuanians."

"What about the Black Berets? How strong are they in Fisikous?"

"Perhaps a few hundred, most concentrated in one section of the base," Curtis replied. "The Spectre gunship shot them up pretty well. The only ones left are in the design-bureau security facility—"

"The same place as Lieutenant Luger." The President nodded. "What are the chances Luger is alive?"

The question was obviously painful for Curtis. "Hard to say, sir . . ."

"Don't crap out on me now, Wilbur," the President said. "I trust your judgment—don't let it be clouded by what you feel for Luger. Do you think he's still alive?"

Curtis sighed. "I feel it's a sixty-forty chance he's still alive, sir. If what our informants and agents said is true, then Luger—who they call Ozerov—was one of the Soviets' most important engineers. He advanced the Soviet state-of-the-art several years. His value is incalculable. They might try to save him, smuggle him out, something. If not—if the Soviets find out that we're specifically going after Luger—then they may use him as a bargaining chip to effect their own escape."

"I disagree, Wilbur," the President said. "I think the chances are very good that they'd dispose of Luger to hide the fact that he was ever there. If it ever came out that the Russians inside Fisikous were hiding an American flyer for all these years, our invasion would be instantly justified and they'd be finished, shut down. If Luger is not found, we've committed an act of war by invading a Commonwealth research facility."

"I understand that, sir," Curtis said, "and I must agree with you. But there is one more thing to consider: We owe David Luger this effort. We *must* try to rescue him. World opinion be damned for once—we know what we're doing is *right.*"

The hesitation was longer this time, Curtis observed.

"This parallel operation at Fisikous *is* different," the President finally said. "What the Soviets have done to this Air Force flyer is terrible . . . monstrous . . . but"—he paused, weighing his words—"I won't go to war with the Commonwealth to get one man out of there, Wilbur. The Commonwealth is on the verge of cracking apart, and the flying pieces can cripple the entire world. I'm not going to push them to the brink of all-out war, even over your Lieutenant Luger."

He went on: "I understand that Secretary Preston authorized the use of the Spectre gunship to support the rescue operation. That's fine. But the Marines get one shot at it. If they can't get Luger on the first try, Wilbur, I don't want heroics."

"Mr. President, you know my view on David Luger." Curtis sighed. "I think the opinions that the NSC staff presented are a bunch of bull. Luger is an American hero. The previous president gave Patrick McLanahan—the man who destroyed the Kavaznya laser site and brought the bomber home safely—the Air Force Cross for what he did on the Old Dog mission. He probably deserved the Medal of Honor. Now it's time we—uh, you, sir—do something for the man that saved Patrick McLanahan."

"I understand what you're saying, and I do sympathize," the President said. "But Lieutenant Luger is already a dead man—he's been dead for years. I'm not going to pull punches or spare your feelings here, Wilbur. *Luger is already dead.* If the Soviets do him in for real, nothing will change. The problem for this administration is not preventing his death, but justifying his existence. Have you thought about what you'll do if Luger *is* rescued?"

"Of course, sir . . ." Curtis replied, somewhat hesitantly, darting his eyes away for a moment.

The President nodded knowingly. "I thought so. You just can't bring him back, can you? He's got a grave, a headstone, the works, right? The other crew members of the Old Dog were explainable, accountable—but not Luger. Everyone thought he was dead, so you made up a cause of death—in a plane crash in Alaska—and doctored hundreds of documents, records, and pages of testimony to make it real, all in the attempt to keep the Old Dog mission secret. How do we explain his reappearance? Resurrection? Cloning?"

"We can sequester him until the incident is unclassified," Curtis said. "The first automatic declassification review of the records is in only six years."

"I know you can work the problem out, Wilbur," the President said, "and I'm not saying that I'd prefer the man were dead. What I am saying is this—Luger's life is not worth the lives of dozens of Marines. I would give a lot to get Luger or any American serviceman who was captured by the enemy in the course of his duty—trade, prisoner swap, make a deal, even pay a ransom—but I won't risk young lives for a man we gave up for dead years ago. I *can't.* I'd see the faces of those dead Marines in my sleep. And when their wives and mothers ask me why I had to order their husbands and sons to die, what do I tell them?"

"Dave Luger's life is worth something too, sir," Curtis replied quietly.

"Yes, it is," the President agreed, his patience beginning to wear thin, but knowing he was going to have to toss Curtis a bone after the successful embassy evacuation. "Okay, it's worth a shot—*one* shot. The Marines get one try at getting Luger. If they withdraw without making contact, they will withdraw to the embassy and stay there. Period."

Curtis merely nodded his head, signaling that he understood.

OUTSIDE THE FISIKOUS DESIGN-CENTER COMPOUND
VILNIUS, LITHUANIA
13 APRIL, 0347 VILNIUS (12 APRIL, 2147 ET)

"Here they come!" General Palcikas' radio operator shouted as the message was relayed to him by the Iron Wolf Brigade's outer security units surrounding the periphery of the Fisikous compound. "Enemy aircraft inbound! All air-defense units, stand by to engage enemy aircraft!"

Four hundred rifles raised toward the bright morning "star," the planet Venus, which could barely be seen though fast-moving clouds to the east. The sound of an approaching heavy helicopter grew louder and louder. Dominikas Palcikas plugged his left ear with his left index finger and squeezed the radio handset closer to his right ear. He could feel his breathing quicken in anticipation of what was about to appear . . .

When the sound grew almost intolerable, he ordered into the radio: "Stop your position! Rotate left ninety degrees, decrease altitude to twenty meters, turn on all exterior lights, and translate right until I order you to stop."

Dust and debris curled up from the ground, and Palcikas could feel the power of the machines approaching him. They were *big* helicopters, gunships in every sense of the word. They had to be . . .

"Look! There they are!" Palcikas saw them then as the two war machines slid right toward the spot where he was hiding. The first thing he noticed was the size of the rotors—they were huge, at least eleven or twelve meters in diameter, slow-moving but so broad of chord that they stirred up a tornado of dirt despite their relatively slow speed.

"Hold position!" Palcikas ordered into the radio. The machines stopped and hovered just out of ground effect firmly, without wobbling or swaying, as steady as if set on an invisible shelf. They were like nothing any of them had ever seen. They looked like small cargo planes, like a cantilevered twin-tail Lockheed Hercules, Aeritalia G222, or Soviet Antonov-12 transports, but then there were those two big rotors mounted on the plane's wingtips, swiveled upwards to act like a helicopter's rotor. Palcikas saw the weapon pods on the wheel wells on each side, and the sensor dome under the nose with its mechanical eye staring right back at them. "All right, Major Dukitas, what the hell is it?"

"It's a V-22 Osprey," Dukitas, Palcikas' intelligence officer, replied, wearing a broad smile as he watched the extraordinary spectacle of these two machines, as foreign as alien spacecraft, obeying Palcikas' every word. "Tilt-rotor design. Those engine nacelles can swivel downwards, turning those rotors into propellers."

"An American aircraft?"

"Yes, sir. Used primarily by the American Marine Corps and Air Force as a covert-operations troop carrier. Twice as fast as a conventional helicopter, large payload, long range, but with vertical takeoff and land capability. Judging by its paint scheme, I would say those are American Marines."

"Well, this is a strange and pleasant surprise," Palcikas said. "The Americans appear to want Fisikous as much as we do."

"What are we going to do, sir?" Zukauskas, Palcikas' executive officer, asked. "Are they after us or the Soviets? Will they attack . . . ?"

"We will find out right now," Palcikas said. "Radio to all units: stay clear of the two aircraft over the security building. Continue to your assigned positions and await further orders. All other unidentified aircraft are to be considered hostile except for the two subject aircraft over the design center. They are to be monitored but not interfered with." On the portable radio, Palcikas said simply: "Proceed as desired, gentlemen. Welcome to Lithuania."

At that, the two tilt-rotor aircraft wheeled to the right in unison and lifted into the night sky. The first aircraft disappeared from sight while the second accomplished a tight turn around the security building inside the design-center compound.

"Should we monitor the first aircraft's position, sir?"

"I think both aircraft will stay very close," Palcikas said. "I want all units to monitor for signs of Soviet counterattack. It will do neither us nor the Americans any good to be caught unaware now. And the Soviets *are* coming. I can feel it."

ABOARD HAMMER FOUR

"I don't fucking believe what we just did," Gunny Trimble muttered— loud enough to be heard by everyone, but addressing no one except the shades of lucky Marines all throughout the Corps' history.

McLanahan didn't dare open his mouth, but inwardly he was beaming. Captain Snyder, the task-force commander aboard Hammer Three, had done what no one expected he would ever do: he had intentionally exposed both MV-22 aircraft to unknown, possibly hostile, forces. He had allowed the voice on the radio who claimed to be a Lithuanian Self-Defense Force general to see both secret special-operations aircraft, and even to position them the way he wanted. Snyder had ordered both SEA HAMMER aircraft to hover right in front of Palcikas and his men, in plain sight, with lights flashing, completely vulnerable to even light ground fire.

And it had worked. When that voice on the radio said, "Proceed as desired, gentlemen. Welcome to Lithuania," the thrill of anticipation McLanahan felt was unbearable.

Lieutenant Marx was on the command radio talking to Snyder. He lowered the phone, stood, and balanced himself in the aisle so he could speak with everyone in the cargo section. "Listen up. Slight change of plans. The Captain doesn't want any Hammer aircraft on the ground—too risky with all those troops hanging around. Also, the security building is still heavily occupied with Black Beret troops. The LZ security team will set up on the roof. Gunny Wohl, get your officers ready to fastrope. They're going on the rooftop."

"Hoo*rah*," Wohl yelled, pleased that he was going to see a bit more direct action instead of sitting with the security team near the MV-22. Wohl got to his feet and stood in front of McLanahan, Ormack, and Briggs, and withdrew a large canvas bag from an underseat compartment. "All right, sirs, the one-LT says we're going on the roof. I showed you how we fastrope, and you've all tried it during training.

"Remember the briefing on this rooftop: it's got only a two-foot rim," Wohl continued. "Perfect for falling off. Just follow me. You'll all have night-vision goggles, and the place will be illuminated by infrared lights. Don't walk under the engine nacelles. If you get confused or disoriented, just drop to one knee and look for me. I'll be looking for you." From the canvas bag, Wohl withdrew several sets of thick leather-and-cloth "reactor" gloves, specially made for fastroping.

"Remember, you do everything the jumpmaster tells you—no more, no less," Wohl said as he watched McLanahan and Ormack suit up. "There will be a Marine jumper on the rope across from you, so just watch him and descend with him. When he slows down, you slow down. If you freeze up, listen for me on the ground for distance calls, but continue your descent or you'll be hanging from the rope when the aircraft climbs away. Got it?"

"Got it, Gunny," Briggs replied, all fired up.

"I'm ready. Let's do it." McLanahan gave Wohl a thumbs-up, looking Wohl right in the eyes.

Wohl liked that. If there was any fear, Wohl could not see it.

Ormack too made eye contact with the Marine instructor, but he muttered his "Okay."

"General, you up for this?"

Another slight reply and a nod.

"You better speak up, General, or you'll be riding instead of jumping."

Ormack raised his head. His eyes were round with fear, and his expression appeared pained, almost nauseated. But he answered, "Yes, I'm ready."

Wohl nodded. He knew he should abort Ormack. He *knew* it. But there was going to be only one jump, and they had come too far for a little anxiety to jeopardize this mission. Wohl said, "Very good, sir. Remember your procedures, take a deep breath. You'll do fine."

As Hammer Four departed on a seven-minute orbit around the rural area south of Vilnius, Hammer Three swept around the security building from the east, the side of the building where intelligence reports and photoreconnaissance had shown there were more blocked windows and fewer offices.

For maneuvering and landing, the SEA HAMMER pilots and crew chiefs/door gunners wore a set of improved NVS-13 night-vision goggles, which gave them better depth perception for tricky landings and hard maneuvering. The copilot had control of the PNVS/NTAS system, which projected digital imagery taken from both the FLIR sensor and the attack radar onto his goggles; the copilot could aim the FLIR and both the Chain Gun pod and Stinger rocket pod by simply moving his head.

"I've got two machine-gun nests on the rooftop!" the copilot shouted. He quickly slaved the steerable M242 Hughes Chain Gun pod to the FLIR sensor with the press of a button. "Target!"

The pilot quickly searched the area on either side of the building. No other forces in sight. It would not be wise to have friendly troops nearby when the Chain Gun opened fire. "Jumpers clear the doors. Clear on the sides?"

"Clear left," the left door gunner replied.

"Clear right."

"Clear to shoot," the pilot said. The copilot squeezed the trigger, and a stream of 25-millimeter bullets raked the rooftops, peppering the OMON machine-gun emplacements with pinpoint accuracy. Not expecting an attack from the air, the soldiers manning the nest could not raise their heavy machine guns fast enough to take aim at an aircraft, and they were forced to leap away from the hailstorm of hotdog-sized bullets showering down on them. The gunners on the second nest got off a few shots at the MV-22 with rifle fire, but the SEA HAMMER's copilot quickly centered the gun on the second machine-gun nest, and it was destroyed seconds later.

"Enemy troops on the rooftop!" one of the door gunners shouted on the interphone as he watched the OMON troops alternately scurrying for cover and taking potshots at the SEA HAMMER in the darkness. "Taking ground fire. Target!"

"Clear to shoot," the pilot repeated. The Marine door gunners sprayed rounds on the survivors from their door-mounted M134 Miniguns. A single two-second burst from the Minigun sprayed a cloud of one hundred 7.62-millimeter shells on the retreating troops.

The MASTER CAUTION light, a large yellow push-to-reset light in the top center of the instrument panel, snapped on. The big light commanded instant attention. The pilot reset it, then both pilots quickly scanned the instrument panel, looking for the malfunction. Another yellow caution light was illuminated on the center console: it read RT OIL PRESS. The copilot punched buttons on one of his multifunction displays and scanned the graphic engine instrument readouts. "Got it. Oil-pressure drop on the starboard engine," the copilot announced. "Still in the green band, but two . . . now five PSI lower than the port engine."

Another MFD automatically displayed the proper malfunction procedures checklist. The copilot accomplished the first four items—checking other engine indications, turning on auxiliary pumps, and inspecting the engine visually for signs of fire—then got to step number five: "Next item is ENGINE SHUTDOWN INFLIGHT checklist, Ken."

"Flag it," the pilot replied. "We've still got a few minutes before it seizes up. We'll finish the infiltration, then head for the embassy. Give Jurgensen a holler and tell him to make a ready deck." On interphone, he said, "Jumpmaster, get your boys on the roof. We've got maybe two minutes before we have to bug out."

Once over the building, the first MV-22 hovered just twenty feet above the rooftop. Four thick ropes were tossed out—two from the cargo ramp between the door gunner just inside the cargo door and one from each port and starboard entry door—and within ten seconds all eighteen Marines had fastroped down to the rooftop. Rappelling was usually too slow for this kind of work—fastroping used no carabiners or lowering devices. It was more akin to sliding down a fire pole; the descent was controlled by hands and feet only, usually resulting in faster descents.

It was soon obvious that the OMON defenders had no night-vision equipment—the troops on the roof were stumbling around blindly, searching for the aircraft overhead, and the Marines now on the roof were able to literally walk right up to the OMON troops. The Marine Building Clearing Team's MP5 submachine guns made quick work of any surviving OMON soldiers on the rooftop, but not before one Marine was hit in the leg as he slid down his rope.

The MV-22 pilot was about to peel away from the roof and head for the U.S. Embassy when he heard on the assault channel: "Marine down! Marine down! Stand by to medevac!"

But the pilot had his own problems. The oil pressure on the right engine was definitely dropping, and now a fuel-pressure problem was developing on the same engine. "Christ, I knew it!" the pilot cursed. "He might be safer on the roof than with us." But he clicked on the interphone and yelled, "Guide me down, door gunners, and let's make it snappy. I didn't bring my American Express card."

With the Marine door gunners acting as spotters, the MV-22 settled down to within two feet of the roof, and the wounded Marine was helped up onto the cargo ramp and pulled inside. Thirty seconds after that radio call, the wounded man was being treated by a medical-trained door gunner. The pilot immediately climbed to five thousand feet, as far from any threat of ground fire as he could. By then the oil pressure had dropped to the red line. "Okay, Jim, give me the shutdown checklist," the pilot said. Following the checklist, the pilot put the MV-22 in full helicopter mode and manually crossed over power from the portside engine to both rotors, allowing the SEA HAMMER to fly on only one engine. Once they were sure that both rotors were under control, they shut down the starboard engine seconds before all oil bled out.

Back on the roof of the Fisikous security building, four Marines set up machine-gun nests and scanned for any sign of counterattack, and Captain Snyder and his executive officer set up a communications link with the Embassy and the other MV-22 orbiting safely over the city. The other eleven Marines disabled the elevator from the roof, then blew the door to the stairwell open and rushed inside.

Floor by floor, the Marine Assault and Building Clearing Team members swept down the stairwell. Stealth and speed were important, so no heavy explosives were used. At each floor, a subsonic round from their suppressed MP5 submachine gun took out the stairwell lights and any guards in the stairwell. In sixty seconds the stairwell on the four aboveground floors was controlled by Marines. With three Marines acting as guards on the stairwell, four two-member Marine clearing teams were poised at each aboveground-floor doorway ready to enter each floor.

With five radio beeps over the whispermikes, the teams on each floor simultaneously began their attack.

The doors on each floor leading from the stairwell were all steel-sheathed fire doors, locked on the inside, so the Marines went in the easy way—two rapid-fire rounds from the Hydra rotary-drum grenade launcher punched man-sized holes in the doors and walls, shorting out most of the lights and creating enough smoke, noise, and debris on each floor to make the OMON soldiers and KGB officers inside bolt in confusion. Several carefully placed shots destroyed the battery-powered emergency lights, and using their night-vision goggles the Marines operated in total darkness.

The target floor was the fourth floor, the floor which had been con-verted into some sort of bizarre facsimile of an apartment complex. A reception area with couches and solid wood desks was in front, with two pine-paneled hallways left and right. Upon inspection, only one room had actually been converted into an apartment—the rest of the rooms had monitoring equipment, a medical facility, an interrogation center, and a control room. Whoever came up the elevator would see only this reception area and would never know that he was in a military detention facility—it appeared just like a standard Soviet apartment building, right down to the little "floor mother" room down the hall. The prisoner could be kept in this same floor for years and be made to think that he was transported to many different places.

The apartment had a small kitchenette, a small living room, and an even smaller bedroom with a lavatory. It very closely resembled a stan-dard government-built apartment—small, sparsely furnished, cramped but comfortable.

The apartment was empty. It had obviously been empty for some time.

The assault-team leader clicked open the radio channel in his VADER helmet: "Hammer Three, this is Assault. Target area empty. Continuing search." The target was not where intelligence said he would be. Al-though that was normal—it was too much to expect everything to be where you expected—it only meant more danger for the assault team because now the entire building, including the two below-ground floors, had to be searched.

The third floor, the one below the "apartment-complex" floor, was an office area for the KGB contingent that controlled security at the design center, with only a graveyard shift of workers and perhaps a small Black Beret guard unit expected there. The entire floor had to be sealed as quickly as possible to allow the Marines free access to and from the roof. With one security-team member guarding the stairway door, one assault member would blow a wall or door apart with a grenade round, and the other used his suppressed MP5 submachine gun to neutralize anyone left standing in the room. Using an infrared flashlight, the third team member quickly searched each room, tossed a sleeping-gas canister inside to dis-able anyone hiding inside, closed and jammed the door shut with a jamming spike, marked it with infrared tape—visible only with night-vision goggles—and the team would move on to the next office. Each room would take about five seconds to search and clear. When an assault-team member would encounter someone in the room or hallways, he would study his face for about two seconds in the light of their infrared flashlights before shooting. Anyone that looked even remotely like Luger was searched more carefully—after he was down.

The OMON security force's arsenal was on the second floor, which was arranged differently than the other floors. The offices of the officer in charge of the arsenal, his NCOIC, and his clerks flanked the hallway as they entered, but the rest of the floor was divided by a long steel counter-top, with sand-filled weapon-clearing barrels, cleaning-solvent tanks, and gun-cleaning benches along the windows. Beyond the countertop was a brick wall with a single vaultlike door, and beyond that was the arsenal. After leaving two Marines to guard the stairwell in case any enemy soldiers straggled out, seven Marines congregated on the securely locked door to the arsenal and began their assault on this important floor.

This was where the first serious firefight between the Marines and the Black Berets broke out.

Several OMON soldiers had grabbed machine guns, automatic rifles, and shotguns and were hiding behind the counter, ready to take on the invaders. They began firing as soon as the Marines' grenades punched holes in the door and walls. One Marine was hit in the stomach by heavy AKMS rifle fire as soon as he jumped through the hole they blasted in the wall, the high-velocity round easily piercing his Kevlar vest, and he was dragged back into the stairwell by another Marine while the others provided covering fire.

The Marines could not afford to waste time in a prolonged gun battle with these soldiers. Speed and shock were their only allies, and if they lost those two important elements the entire battle was lost. With these heavily armed soldiers on this level and over fifty more soldiers on the ground floor, the greatly outnumbered Marines could lose the entire building very quickly if they allowed the situation to get out of hand. The two Marines on the ground floor had already begun their assault, but there was return fire already. The Marines had to wrap up this assault quickly.

The decision on how to handle the arsenal floor was made several days earlier. If Luger was being held on this floor, he was going to die. There was nothing the Marines could do about it, because the arsenal and everyone inside had to be neutralized, swiftly and completely, at all costs.

The Marines first shot several CN tear-gas grenades into the room, followed by a volley of six fragmentation grenades, and then two Marines entered the room. A few shots rang out, but none were aimed at them—they heard nothing but coughing and screams of pain from the wounded. The three front offices were searched and sealed, and slowly the Marines approached the counter behind a cloud of slowly dissipating tear gas . . .

Suddenly an OMON soldier popped up from behind the counter.

It was obvious he'd been close to one of the exploding grenades, because he was covered with blood, and the right side of his face and neck looked like the remnants of a fresh road kill. The Soviet soldier screamed and opened fire, spraying the entire room with full-automatic fire. With his unprotected eyes closed and burning from the gas, he still did not miss. Two Marines were riddled before the others finally silenced the last survivor.

The rest of the bodies behind the counter were searched and then the vault door to the arsenal was checked. It was thankfully unlocked—they were not carrying enough explosives to blow a thick steel door and destroy the arsenal. Two Marines quickly checked for booby traps, then cleared the rest to proceed.

"Command, Assault. Great arsenal they got here, sir," one of the Marines radioed to his commander on the roof. At the same time two Marines carried the bodies of their dead comrades upstairs to the rooftop.

"Follow the plan, Murphy," Snyder, the overall task-force commander, radioed back. "Set the charges, block the doors, bring your casualties up, and do the rest of the building. We'll blow the arsenal if things get hairy."

"Roger. Three casualties coming your way. Target not yet found. Proceeding to ground floor and subfloors. Out." After the explosives were set, the remaining eleven Marines rushed downstairs to continue their assault.

The stiffest resistance for the Marines was on the ground floor, but by that time—only four minutes since they first blew the stairwell-roof door off—the lights were out all over the building and the explosions in the upper floors had created a panic. Half of the men on the ground floor were trying to get a clean shot off at their attackers in the darkness, and the other half were trying to surrender. Most of the Black Beret soldiers were armed with rifles or handguns and taking cover in the doorways of offices along the long central hallway on the ground floor.

The Marines first shot in tear-gas canisters to make the soldiers pull back out of the hallway, then used their rifles to shoot out the emergency lights that illuminated the hallway. But it was still too dangerous to go into the hallway to start clearing out the offices, so the Marines did the next-best thing—they re-entered the stairwell, used their grenade launchers to blow holes in the walls, then rushed into the adjacent offices. One by one they cleared a room and then, instead of going down the hallway and through the office's front door, simply blew holes through the connecting walls into the next office.

Watching a man through night-vision goggles as he tried to do something in total darkness was a painful, horrifying experience—it was akin to watching a young blind child in an unfamiliar room and not lifting a hand to help. Every sound was an enemy to him, and many of them took shots at every creak and groan in the place, often hitting one of their comrades, and the screams of those accidentally shot only served to increase the fear and confusion. Once-familiar surroundings were unseen enemies, ready to trip you up. One Black Beret stuck his hand in a flower pot, turned, and fired four shots from a pistol into his own hand—his screams of terror and pain continued until a Marine was close enough to the man to finish him off. The Marines could see the whites of the men's eyes, see the terror in their faces, watch their hands trembling, their eyes darting frantically back and forth at every sound, or watch them weep or urinate uncontrollably. When a Marine raised his weapon and fired, he was often just a few inches away from his victim, and the enemy had no sense of his killer's nearness when he died. The expression of sheer surprise the Marines saw through those night-vision goggles when the Black Beret felt the bullet hit was something none of them would ever forget.

The resistance got stiffer the farther down the hallway they went, but the darkness and the tear gas took their toll quickly on the confused OMON soldiers. In two minutes the three Marines had swept through the entire floor, killing or incapacitating the entire Black Beret contingent.

Snyder and his executive officer were busy dressing one of the Marines' wounds—the other two were dead when they were brought up to the roof—when the NCO in charge of the Building Clearing Team radioed up to Snyder: "Command, this is BCT. Upper floors secure and charges set."

"Copy, BCT," Snyder replied. He switched channels on his tactical radio, then keyed the mike. "Security, this is Command," Snyder radioed to the other MV-22. "Upper floors secure. Move in."

ABOARD THE MV-22 HAMMER FOUR

On the rear cargo deck, on either side of the MV-22 SEA HAMMER crew chief manning the Minigun, were Hal Briggs and Gunnery Sergeant Wohl. They were holding tight onto one-inch-thick "Marine green" ropes, ready to fastrope to the roof once the MV-22 tilt-rotor aircraft was in position. Two more Marines, one on each door on the port and starboard sides, were ready to go as well. Right behind Briggs was McLanahan, with another Marine corporal ready to fastrope behind Wohl, and right behind McLanahan was Ormack. Lieutenant Marx was standing beside the jumpmaster, ready to fastrope down with Ormack. The jumpmaster would lower Marx's radio to the roof after everyone else had departed.

Through his night-vision goggles, McLanahan could see other Marines already on the roof of the design center, using axes and wire cutters to chop down radio antennae that might be tall enough to hit the tilt-rotor aircraft. Three-man SAW security teams manning heavy M249 machine guns and M203 grenade launchers were on each corner of the roof. Most of the Security Team members from Hammer Four had already fastroped to the roof, jumping down as soon as word was received from the Building Clearing Team that it was safe to occupy the upper floors.

When McLanahan flipped his NVG out of his eyes, everything disappeared in the blackness. He could see nothing outside—no roof, no men, no machine-gun nests. The feeling of vertigo was very real and gut-wrenching, so he put the NVGs back in position real fast. For safety and security reasons, the MV-22 had changed positions on the roof after unloading the first twelve Marines on board, because an enemy could have easily drawn a bead on the hovering aircraft. Now Hammer Four was maneuvering back into position to off-load the three Air Force officers and the rest of the Marines in the security-team platoon.

"We're going to approach the roof tail-in," Wohl said to his three Air Force officers, "so remember, when you get off the rope, turn immediately towards the center of the roof. It's real easy to get confused when you leave the chopper, so if you get disoriented, just step clear of the rope and drop to one knee. I will grab you and tell you where to go. Don't get confused and run off the edge of the roof. Remember to step clear of the rope because the next Marine will be coming down right on top of you. Look before you move."

The MV-22 stopped its forward motion, swung left so the nose was facing out away from the building, and translated backwards until the cargo ramp, and then the crew doors, were over the edge of the roof. Spotter/gunners in each door guided the pilot to the proper position.

When the MV-22 was positioned properly and stabilized in a hover, the jumpmaster yelled, "Jumpers, go!"

Wohl and Briggs pulled themselves onto their ropes. Like the hot dog he was, Briggs held on to the rope with one hand and gave McLanahan a thumbs-up and a big smile, then disappeared below the edge of the cargo ramp.

The jumpmaster yelled, "Jumpers, ready on the rope!"

McLanahan shuffled forward onto the cargo ramp, careful not to cross his feet in case the motion of the MV-22 caused him to trip. He reached out and grabbed the thick, soft nylon rope. Someone down below was holding the bottom, and the tension against him made McLanahan feel as if he were going to be pulled off the cargo ramp, so his grip involuntarily tightened. This was it. The noise was almost unbearable. McLanahan was afraid he wouldn't hear the commands because of the rotor noise and the roar of the blood pounding in his ears, but three seconds later, the jumpmaster yelled, "Jumpers, g—"

The SEA HAMMER tilt-rotor suddenly heeled upwards so hard that McLanahan's knees buckled. The aircraft then swung hard left, lifting up some more, swung hard right, and then the 25-millimeter Hughes Chain Gun pod on the left-side sponson opened fire. McLanahan's feet left the deck, and he found himself hanging for dear life on to the rope, dangling away from the cargo ramp, being swung so violently that he could not reach the ramp.

The MV-22 flew away from the rooftop, picking up speed and altitude fast to fight off a sudden attack.

"Patrick!" General Ormack yelled. He was on his hands and knees on the cargo deck, being pulled back against the web troop seats by a Marine. The Marine on the other fastrope on the cargo ramp was nowhere to be seen—McLanahan realized with a thrill of terror that he probably fell off the rope when the SEA HAMMER made that violent swerve. That tightened his grip on the rope even more.

The jumpmaster, who was secured by a safety line, edged his way to the back of the cargo deck. He motioned with his hands to his ankles. McLanahan immediately understood. Holding on tightly with his hands, he wrapped his left leg around the thick rope, letting it twist around his leg and rest against the inside of his left sole, then pressed down on it with all his might with his right foot. The rope and his left foot formed a firm step that McLanahan could use to relax his hands and take some of the press . . .

A streak of yellow fire suddenly arced away from the aircraft hangars to the right. The MV-22 made a sharp left turn, but the streak of fire was too fast and hit the right engine nacelle. The nacelle exploded in a ball of fire, showering McLanahan with flying pieces of metal and white-hot flame. A shoulder-fired surface-to-air missile, probably a Soviet-made SA-7 or SA-11, had hit the right engine.

They were going down.

The MV-22 swiveled to the left. Still dangling on the rope, McLanahan had no sense of up or down anymore. His knuckles and cheeks were flushed with pain from the burning right engine. He hit the side of the cargo door as the SEA HAMMER nosed up. When the nose suddenly came back down, the whipcrack was too much.

McLanahan was thrown off the rope like a pellet from a slingshot.

INSIDE THE FISIKOUS DESIGN-BUREAU SECURITY FACILITY

The explosion from the Marines' three simultaneous attacks from the stairwell nearly threw Vadim Teresov, who was rushing down that same stairwell to the second subfloor, off his feet. *Damn them!* he cursed. *That was close!* Bits of concrete and insulation dust dropped from somewhere above him, and the lights flickered, then went out completely.

Teresov found himself leaning in a corner of the stairwell against a wall, shaking his head to clear the ringing. The emergency light over the last door below him snapped on. He took a few moments to let his head clear, then gripped the Makarov tightly and headed toward the light. At first he swung the pistol overhead, aiming it at the stairs, deciding that he was going to shoot anyone who appeared—if they were attackers they were his enemies, and if they were Soviets they were cowards, and both had to die. But when he reached the door to the second subfloor, he found all his concentration swinging toward the grim task at hand, and he forgot about all else.

Teresov looked through the wire-reinforced window in the door. The guard's desk near the door was unmanned, the door locked. He quickly unlocked the thick gray-steel fire door with his pass key, closed it behind him with a dull echo, and locked it again. The basement of the security building was a maze of heating ducts, machinery, leaking pipes, and sounds of all kinds. Only a few emergency lights were on down here, so Teresov unclipped the light from its bracket over the doorway and used it as a flashlight to find Luger's cell.

The Marine Corps pilot of the stricken MV-22 SEA HAMMER tilt-rotor aircraft had by force of habit lifted the nose to gain altitude when the missile hit the starboard engine. That was a mistake that he almost did not live to regret: when you suddenly have no flying speed left, you don't raise the nose, which bleeds off more airspeed—you *dump* the nose to try to regain airspeed. Realizing his error, he immediately dumped the nose and stomped on the right yaw-control pedal to counteract the spin to the left. Without forward airspeed of 60 knots or more, the SEA HAMMER wasn't going to autorotate no matter how perfect his procedures were, but with a few extra knots of airspeed in the fall, he might have enough speed to keep the aircraft upright in the crash landing. A V-22 must crash-land upright and level—anything else would mean serious fuselage stress, rupture, and fire.

The V-22 has a system that can apply power from one engine to both rotors at the same time, and in most conditions the aircraft can stay controllable; the crossover was supposed to happen automatically, but the third item in the bold print (must-be-committed-to-memory) checklist for engine failure inflight, after POWER-MAX and AIRSPEED-60 KIAS, is EMERGENCY CROSSOVER—CHECK XOVER.

"Check emergency crossover!" the pilot shouted to the copilot.

The copilot had immediately run the same checklist in his head, so he was on the same step as the pilot, looking at the illuminated status light. "Linkage shows crossover!" the copilot yelled back. That interchange took one-half second. They had another five seconds before they'd hit the ground.

The explosion had momentarily cut off all power to the instruments, so the pilot couldn't see his airspeed gauge, but he knew he didn't have flying speed. Time for a new bold-print emergency checklist—crash landing: "Fire T-handles, pull!" he shouted. There was no time to complete the rest of the bold-print items because the MV-22 hit the ground at that instant.

But the pilot did just as he had hoped. When the MV-22 hit the ground just a few seconds later, he had enough airspeed built up to lift the nose and prevent his aircraft from burrowing the nose, or "augering in." The MV-22 hit the ground at nearly 40 miles an hour, in a nearly level pancake crash. The extra weight on the left wing threatened to flip the aircraft upside down, but luckily it stayed upright.

On the end of the thirty-foot-long rope, Patrick McLanahan was flung through the sky for several seconds like a leaf fluttering in the wind, until that final snap when the MV-22's nose came down and he could no longer hold on. But the aircraft was only a few feet above ground, so his ballistic trip through the air was short but spectacular. McLanahan landed several dozen feet away from the MV-22's impact area, hitting on his left side and cartwheeling along the ground several more yards.

Dazed and confused, McLanahan picked himself up off the ground and checked himself over. His night-vision goggles were history, twisted pieces of the instrument hanging off his helmet, so he unstrapped the helmet and tossed it aside. His left shoulder felt wrenched where he had landed on it, but it did not appear broken or separated. His feet and ankles were working.

The only light nearby was from the slowly burning wreckage of the MV-22's right wing. McLanahan ran over to check on the crew. He could feel something snapping along the ground near him, digging up patches of asphalt and grass—was it his Marines shooting at him or was it the enemy? He had no way to find out. But he made it safely to the rear cargo hatch of the stricken MV-22 and yelled, "Hey! Marines! Anybody in here . . . ?"

"Patrick!" It was John Ormack. He was bending over another Marine—the jumpmaster, Patrick realized—checking his wounds. "My God, I don't believe it! I never thought I'd ever see you alive again! Are you all right? Where's your helmet?"

It's funny what an excited man will say sometimes, McLanahan thought—John Ormack saw McLanahan flung off into space from the back of an aircraft, and he wanted to know about his *helmet!* "I trashed it. Are you all right?"

"I'm not sure," Ormack said. "Hey, nice fastrope job. You made it down safe and sound."

"Gunny Wohl will be pissed. My one real try at fastroping and I screw it up."

Ormack laughed, then pulled up in pain. "Dammit, Patrick, don't make me laugh. I think I cracked a rib." He motioned toward the front of the aircraft. "The jumpmaster is hurt real bad. He pushed me onto the web seats, then got flipped around the cargo hold. Lieutenant Marx." He pointed to the soldier lying in the web troop seats along the fuselage, the one that was supposed to jump with Ormack. "Goes in and out—he might have a concussion. I'll drag these guys out. Check the cockpit!"

The MV-22 had landed slightly nose-low, crumpling the left-front portion of the nose. In the glow of cabin emergency lights, it appeared that the copilot's harness had failed or he had taken it off to activate a switch, because the copilot was dead, his body smashed against the left forward windscreen.

He had seen to the dead—now to see to the living. His first concern was the stricken V-22. Fortunately, McLanahan had a lot of experience with V-22-series aircraft at the High Technology Aerospace Weapons Center, developing the weapons suite for Air Force and Border Security Force versions, so working in the dark cockpit was easy for him. McLanahan averted his eyes from the corpse, reached over, and made sure that both fire T-handles on the top of the instrument panel had been pulled. He found the battery switches on the overhead console and shut those off as well, then retarded the power control to IDLE, released the idle latch, and moved the power control to CUTOFF. It was easy to retrieve the semiconscious pilot from the right side of the cockpit and drag him out, just as it was awful to drag the dead copilot out.

"The copilot didn't make it," McLanahan told Ormack when he reached the cargo hold.

"Dammit," Ormack muttered. "Let's get the others out of here." Ormack tried to drag the jumpmaster out while helping Lieutenant Marx to his feet, but his ribs creaked and he moaned in pain.

"You help Marx to the security building," McLanahan told him. "I'll get the jumpmaster and the pilots."

As Ormack assisted the semi-lucid Marine out, McLanahan grabbed the two unconscious Marines by the backs of their jackets and unceremoniously dragged them across the pavement and bits of frozen lawn to the side of the design-center security building. Ormack had found a side door and had placed Marx beside it.

"Try the door," McLanahan said.

Ormack did—it was locked.

"I'll get the copilot. Shoot the lock off if you have to." McLanahan ran off to the stricken MV-22, which had crashed about fifty meters away from the building, between it and the aircraft hangars.

McLanahan was breathing heavily and had slowed down to a trot when he felt, rather than heard, gunshots hitting the ground near his feet. He didn't know if it was friendly fire, or the Lithuanians, or the Black

Berets, but whoever it was definitely was getting a bead on him. With a surge of adrenaline, he sprinted for the MV-22, dodging every time he heard the *pop!* of gunfire.

Back in the cargo section, McLanahan was about to grab the dead copilot by the jacket and drag the body to the security building, but the shooting outside gave him a better idea. He went to the forward part of the cargo bay and grabbed two MP5s and two web belts full of ammunition from the crew chief's gun rack. He clipped one ammo pack to his own ALICE harness. Instinctively McLanahan immediately opened the bolt of one of the rifles, checked it in the dim glare of an emergency light, pulled out a magazine, tapped it, inserted it into the breech, slapped the bottom to seat it properly, then flipped the bolt closed. The actions seemed so natural, so fluid, that McLanahan surprised even himself. McLanahan put the weapon on three-shot semiautomatic and, with the gun in his right hand and dragging the dead copilot with his left, began his dangerous trek back to the security building.

This time he could tell that the shots aimed at him were coming from the aircraft hangars. McLanahan moved as fast as he could, not daring to take a rest, and firing at every muzzle flash he saw. Halfway along he had to stop to reload and rest his left arm. This time the enemy fire seemed closer, and he thought he saw movement near the burning MV-22. No clear targets presented themselves, so he grabbed the dead copilot and began dragging him . . .

. . . when suddenly two soldiers appeared around the back of the MV-22's rear cargo door, aiming what looked like AK-47s with long, banana-shaped magazines at him. Their outlines were clearly seen in the glow of the burning left engine, and Patrick realized that he must be easy to see as well. Shots rang out, and McLanahan instinctively dropped to the ground, using the corpse as a shield in front of him. But the enemy soldiers were only a few dozen yards away—they couldn't miss.

Teresov had to walk across half the length of the building to reach the 3-by-3–meter concrete-block cells that had been constructed by the KGB many years ago. The guard post here was deserted as well—Luger could have been alone down here ever since the alarm was sounded. No matter. He would—

Another explosion, this one dozens of times more powerful than the first three combined, made Teresov drop the flashlight in terror. Was that the arsenal? Three hundred weapons and thousands of rounds of ammunition were undoubtedly gone in that one. Two major explosions in just the time it took Teresov to walk from the door to Luger's cell. Whoever it was, Marines or devils, they were moving fast.

Thankfully, the emergency flashlight hadn't broken when he dropped it, and there were other emergency lights on nearby, so the entire subfloor itself wasn't completely dark. He made his way to the proper cell door, opened the shutter, and, holding the emergency light up to the opening, peered inside.

The cell was empty. The shadows were thick because the light was too weak to illuminate the entire cell, but Luger could not be seen. The bed was empty, the computerized vital-signs monitor and environmental regulator were off. Luger was free but nowhere to be found.

Teresov felt a chill of panic. What condition would Luger be in—was he deranged or dead? Teresov needed help. He tried the phones on the guard desk in front of the cells—all dead. No walkie-talkie. He was alone. No lights except for the one he held in his hand and another farther down in the subfloor. Searching the desk, he found no tear gas, stun guns, or anything else he could use to subdue the prisoner singlehandedly. Well, he decided, a lie was as good as anything else.

Teresov returned to the cell and, hefting the big Makarov PM pistol, said in English, "Lieutenant Luger, this is Major Vadim Teresov, General Gabovich's aide. I have been directed to take you upstairs. Come out so I can see you. Immediately."

No response.

From somewhere overhead, a series of loud *booms* reverberated throughout the building—two, four, maybe ten of them, all in a loud, terrifying string, like massive firecrackers going off. Teresov felt moisture on his palms, and he dried his hand on his pants before tightly gripping the pistol again. "Do you hear that, Lieutenant? We have been ordered by an American Marine Corps rescue detail to destroy our weapons and bring you to the ground floor for a prisoner exchange. If you do not comply with my request, the Marines will assume you are dead and destroy this building. You and everyone inside will die. So close to rescue, do you want to risk dying? But I do not want to risk dying either. Come out where I can see you and I will escort you upstairs."

Still no response.

Luger flattened himself against the door to the cell, staying as far out of sight as possible. *No more passive, drugged-out, mind-fucked prisoner,* Luger told himself. *Teresov is here to kill you. Fight with everything you have left, Dave, because there won't be a second chance.*

Luger knew there was one dead-bolt lock and two sliding cylinder bolts on the door. The door would withstand an impact with two of the three bolts in place, but with only one he might be able to break it. He started to summon all his power, all his courage, all his being into concentrating on what Teresov was doing out there. He would have only one chance.

* * *

Shots rang out and McLanahan's body jumped at each burst—but they were not from in front, they were from *behind!* John Ormack, still wearing his helmet and night-vision goggles, had run up beside McLanahan, firing away with his 9-millimeter automatic.

"Those sons of bitches," huffed Ormack. Patrick heard the loud, dull *click!* as the slide locked open—Ormack had run out of ammo.

As Ormack hurriedly reloaded he shouted, "Patrick! *Run!"*

The two enemy soldiers had ducked behind the fuselage of the MV-22, so McLanahan took the opportunity, scrambled to his feet, and dragged the corpse back to the building. McLanahan heard Ormack eject a spent magazine, snap a new one in place, and begin firing again.

Ormack used several shots from his Beretta to break open the lock on the door, and then closed it behind them. The hallway was completely dark. McLanahan used the grisly, broken body of the Marine copilot to barricade the door. "Jesus, John, you came along just in time," McLanahan said, breathing heavily. "I owe you one."

"Forget it," Ormack said. He examined the copilot through his night-vision equipment. "Yeah, he's dead, poor bastard." He lowered him gently to the floor in front of the steel door, then withdrew his FM radio from his ALICE harness. Ormack tried several times to raise someone, with no luck. "Try your radio, Patrick." But it was obvious the instant he withdrew it from his harness that the radio was shattered.

"What do you see around here?" McLanahan asked. "Where are we?"

Ormack withdrew an infrared chemical light stick from a pouch, bent it until a vial inside the soft plastic tube cracked, and shook it. McLanahan could see nothing at all, not even his hand in front of his face—to him, it was pitch black. But to Ormack, with his night-vision goggles, the hall and stairwell were brightly illuminated. "There's no other door here—this entrance only leads to the subfloors," Ormack said, peering around them with the goggles. "There's only a staircase that leads down."

"Well, we can't stay here. Those jokers outside may be coming after us," McLanahan said.

"Let's leave the copilot here—we've done all we can for him, and I'll need help with the injured," Ormack said grimly. "Let's head down with the others and find a place where we can cover the stairwell and lower floors at the same time until help arrives."

"Sounds like a plan to me," McLanahan said. "Lead on." McLanahan first withdrew a door-jamming spike from the semiconscious Marine's ALICE harness pack and hammered it into the doorframe with the shattered remains of his FM radio. Anyone trying to open the door would have to break it open, and they would hear it and be ready. He also applied a small strip of infrared tape with his element number and the date-time group on it to the doorframe, and rubbed it with his gloves to activate the tiny chemical beads in the tape to make it glow. Anyone with night-vision goggles—hopefully, the other Marines in the assault force and not the Black Berets—would see the otherwise invisible tape and know who had been there and when. McLanahan then hoisted the unconscious jumpmaster onto his shoulders, and with Ormack painfully helping the other semiconscious Marine, they made their way downstairs.

Damn you to hell, Luger! Teresov raged inside. But Teresov was really angry at himself. *Why didn't I think of bringing a soldier down here, or a grenade, or some tear gas?* Teresov opened the magazine on the Makarov and counted the rounds—seven, with one in the chamber. *I didn't even think to bring extra magazines.*

His anger boiling over, Teresov snapped the magazine back into the gun, stuck the muzzle into the shutter, and fired four rounds blindly into the tiny concrete cell. He was rewarded after the second shot with a blood-curdling scream, like a badger caught in a trap.

Well, well, Teresov thought with relief.

The screaming continued unabated—Luger barely had time to draw breath before another scream echoed throughout the subfloor. Teresov had heard men scream before—in pain, in fear, in sheer terror, when they know death is only a fraction of a second away—and Luger's scream was real. A ricocheting bullet must have hit him in a serious but obviously nonlethal place.

Teresov eased the bolts off the door, leaving one in place, then flashed the light inside the cell. He could see a foot at the very bottom of the shutter—Luger must have been hiding directly underneath the shutter. The foot was trembling uncontrollably, as if in death throes. Perfect. Teresov inserted the key into the lock. No hurry now. Let Luger become weak from loss of blood.

When he opened the door, Luger would fall right into his waiting arms.

The first subfloor door was locked. Their intelligence briefing said that this floor had some offices but was mostly file and furniture storage. They decided not to shoot it open, for fear of attracting the attention of any enemy soldiers that might be nearby, so McLanahan applied another jamming spike and infrared tape to the doorframe and they made their way downstairs to the last subfloor.

The door here was locked as well. There was no other way out—it was either through the door or back upstairs. Their intelligence briefing said that the second subfloor was heating and cooling equipment, incinerators, and water heaters. No reason to enter that floor either. "We'll hide back in the corner so we can cover the stairs and the door," McLanahan said, handing a submachine gun to Ormack. "I'll go upstairs and check to see if any Marines have—"

Suddenly they heard four shots, followed by the most bone-chilling scream either of them had ever heard. The screaming continued, increasing in pitch and intensity. It was coming from inside the door to the last subfloor.

"Christ, what was that?" Ormack whispered.

McLanahan's mouth dropped open in surprise. "It's Dave," he said. "That was Dave!"

"What? Are you sure?"

"I've heard him scream like that before—when we got hit by the missile, on the Old Dog," McLanahan said. "It nearly blew his right leg off. He screamed just like that. It's *him!* He's in there!" He raised his MP5, set it to single-shot semiautomatic, and aimed it at the door handle . . .

"Wait, Patrick. What are you going to do?"

"Get Dave, that's what. Step back."

"But you don't—"

"I said step back, John, goddammit!"

Ormack dragged the two Marines away from the door just as McLanahan fired several shots at the handle. After several seconds of frantically pulling at the hot metal, the door wrenched free. McLanahan snapped a fresh magazine into the submachine gun and made ready to go through the door.

"Wait, I'm going with you," Ormack said.

McLanahan was about to argue, but he changed his mind—he knew he needed the backup.

"Here." Ormack removed his helmet with the NVG-9 night-vision goggles and gave it to McLanahan, who strapped it tightly on his head. "You're better at this infantry shit than me." But when Ormack handed him the infrared light stick, McLanahan refused it.

"If his guard's got night-vision equipment, I'll be a good target for him," said. "There's supposed to be boilers and incinerators down there—I should have enough light. Leave it here but bring a few more new ones."

Ormack picked up the second MP5 submachine gun, checked the magazine, set it to single-shot semiautomatic as well, and nodded to McLanahan.

With Ormack behind him, McLanahan crouched down and slowly pulled the steel-sheathed door open. No sign of response. He slowly moved it all the way open and applied the doorstop to keep it open. There was a small ledge just inside the door, a small staircase leading down, and a dark maze of pipes, conduits, and huge pieces of equipment inside. The screaming had subsided somewhat. Judging by the sounds, the person was not too far away. McLanahan crouched, partially shielded by the steel railing surrounding the ledge, and carefully scanned the entire subfloor, watching for any movement that might reveal Luger's captors. Nothing. There was a small light far off in the distance, toward the source of the screams, and McLanahan thought he saw the light move.

McLanahan figured that David Luger's captor obviously knew they were there, so all chances of surprise were gone. McLanahan filled his lungs with air, then yelled, "United States Marines! You are surrounded! Surrender!" Then, switching to Russian—hastily taught by Wohl and the other Marines back at Camp Lejeune—he yelled, *"Stoy!* United States Marines! *Pahsloshightye myenyah! Bistrah!"*

The screaming stopped abruptly. McLanahan's heart was in his throat—he thought Luger's captors had killed him. McLanahan gripped the gun, ready to rush toward the light—

—but a distinct voice cried out, "PATRICK! I'M DOWN HERE! HELP ME!"

Damn, damn, damn it! Teresov swore.

American Marines *were* invading Fisikous—and they were *here!* Worse, Luger—that shit—was still alive! He had to finish him off before they arrived. He would put a bullet in Luger's head, then wound himself, get rid of the gun, and pretend that he was a prisoner along with Luger. Perhaps the Marines wouldn't kill him right away if they saw he was wounded. Hefting the gun, Teresov snapped open the last bolt on the door and—

—the door suddenly burst open, and David Luger came flying out and landed on top of him.

The presence of the Marines, along with seeing Luger's foot flopping around and hearing him scream like a wounded cat, made Teresov sloppy, made him think only of himself and not of his captive.

Luger was not injured, and now he was fighting for his life.

The emergency flashlight went flying under the desk. Luger had hit Teresov low, right around the knees. Teresov crashed back against the guard's desk but stayed upright. Luger was a wild man, his bony fingers digging into Teresov's flesh, screaming like an animal, writhing and snarling. He had grabbed on to Teresov's right wrist and was squeezing like a man possessed. A hand raked across Teresov's eyes, into his nostrils, pulling at his ears. First a fist, then an elbow, then another fist hammered his face.

But none of his blows caused any pain—Luger was simply too weak, too emaciated, to hurt anyone. Teresov's right arm broke free of Luger's grasp, the Makarov in Teresov's right hand came down hard on Luger's skull, and the American officer crumpled. Teresov swung with his left arm, and the skinny, half-naked body flew across the basement, hitting hard against the open cell door.

Luger dropped to one knee, dazed, but he raised his head—and Teresov freaked. Even in the dim glow of the emergency light he had never seen such wild, murderous eyes before in his life. They were wide open, spinning, gleaming and terrible. Luger's lips were pulled back in an animal-like snarl, his brown teeth bared. Blood flowed from a head wound, covering Luger's hideous death-mask of a face with rivulets of bright-red blood. Teresov knew what it was like to have just cornered an injured wild animal. There was nothing human about that skinny, disheveled figure before him.

That made it that much easier for him. Teresov raised the Makarov, aimed, and—

"NOOOO!" someone screamed behind him.

Teresov jerked his head around, saw a dark figure running out of the shadows, carrying a submachine gun. Teresov squeezed off two shots at Luger without aiming—at this distance, he could not miss—and turned to face his new assailant.

Three shots rang out from an automatic weapon. Teresov could feel the slugs whiz by him, walking up from about waist level to well over his head, could feel the shock and heat of the muzzle blast, but he was unhurt. A clean miss, at very close range—sloppy work for one of the legendary U.S. Marines. He whipped around toward the gunblast and fired the last round from his Makarov. A figure leaped out of the darkness, tackling Teresov and shoving him hard down the hallway in front of the other concrete-block cells. Teresov let his body go limp, cushioning his head with his left arm as he hit the concrete floor.

To his surprise, however, the figure was off him immediately. Teresov could see a solidly built man in dark-green baggy fatigues, wearing a bulky "Third Reich"–style Kevlar helmet with boxy fittings attached to it—night-vision equipment, Teresov guessed—crawling over to where Luger had collapsed. He seemed to have forgotten all about him. Scrambling to his feet, Teresov wheeled around and kicked as hard as he could into the newcomer's midsection.

The soldier grunted, the air popping out of his lungs in one great *whoosh,* but he crawled to his hands and knees and got to his feet . . .

. . . just as Teresov kicked again, using a snapping karate side kick.

Teresov saw that the Marine was festooned with weapons and hardware—a big sidearm, a thick flak vest, a knife in a shoulder harness, pouches and utility bags filled and attached all over his body, and an MP5 submachine gun carelessly tossed aside—but he seemed to have forgotten about all of them. Who was this guy? The Americans actually sent an untrained, unskilled boob to rescue Luger! Teresov's kick landed squarely on the Marine's head, bowling the guy over and dropping him. But the big guy was up again, struggling to his feet, almost as wild and possessed as Luger. The Marine's helmet was nearly turned sideways on his head from the force of the kick, and he pulled it off, revealing a mop of short blond hair and a round, almost boyish face. Teresov guessed his age at forty-something, well-exercised and big-shouldered but not hard and lean. A pretty soft-looking Marine.

Teresov danced easily around the lumbering Marine. "They should have sent a better-skilled soldier to do the job, pretty boy," he said gaily in English. He made another whirling roundhouse kick to the right side of the Marine's head, and the guy slumped to his knees. This was fun!

Seeing his opportunity, Teresov stepped forward, reached into the Marine's holster, and pulled out his sidearm. He recognized it instantly—a 9-millimeter Beretta automatic, standard issue from the U.S. Marine Corps. He cocked it, held the Marine's head steadily with his left hand, and pointed the big pistol at the helpless Marine. *"Doh svedanya, Master Marine . . ."*

A shot rang out, a booming, heavy explosion, very close. Teresov jumped, dropped to one knee, taking cover behind McLanahan, and pointed the pistol toward its source. He should have guessed there might be another Marine down here, but if he was as incompetent as the first he should have no trouble dispatching him.

The first shot, and now a second shot, both missed, flying well overhead. Teresov looked up and saw the second Marine, a short, goofy-looking man with no helmet, short brown hair, aiming a pistol unsteadily at him. He simply emerged from the shadows, now about forty feet away, not bothering to take cover. The second Marine took a third shot, and that one missed as well.

This is ridiculous! Teresov aimed his captured weapon at the second Marine and fired, hitting him squarely in the chest and dropping him easily. Two down and one to go . . .

But he had ignored his other captive far too long.

McLanahan grasped Teresov's left hand with his own left hand, twisting him around so the Russian was facing the floor, then he reached up to his left shoulder with his right hand, withdrew his KaBar infantry knife, and plunged it into Teresov's belly, thrusting upwards with so much power that the point of the big knife protruded from the Russian's back.

Teresov stiffened, all feeling and breath draining from his entire body, and dropped the gun.

McLanahan tossed the dying man away from him and left him lying in a pool of his own dark, warm blood.

McLanahan crawled over to the inert form lying against the thick cell door. "Dave? Dave?"

It was him, all right.

He was thinner than he'd ever imagined, and his head and chest were covered with blood—but it was warm, red blood, not dried blood, which meant that Luger's heart was still beating. McLanahan felt around Luger's bloody chest, and finally found the wound, high on the left side. One shot had missed, and Luger's clavicle had deflected the other bullet up and away from his chest. A quarter of an inch lower and it would have deflected into his heart. While pressing his left hand hard into the finger-sized wound, McLanahan retrieved his first-aid kit from his ALICE harness and withdrew a thick combat dressing pad. When he pressed it into the wound, a low moan escaped from Dave Luger's crusty lips.

"Dave? It's me, man—Patrick. Wake up!"

Luger's eyes fluttered, strained to focus in the dim light. He blinked, eyes scanning the bloodied, exhausted face before him. *"Shto?"* Luger asked in Russian. *"Kto tam . . . ?"*

"Dave, it's me, *Patrick,*" McLanahan said. "You're okay. It's me. Your partner—Patrick."

Luger's eyes opened wider, and Patrick was surprised to feel a hand on his face, brushing away bloodstained hair. "Pa . . . Patrick? Is that *you?*"

"Yeah, Dave," McLanahan said, his heart so full of joy that he almost burst out crying. "Yeah, it's me . . ."

"How very touching," a weak voice said. Behind Patrick, Vadim Teresov had somehow gotten to his feet, the 9-millimeter automatic in his hand. The KaBar infantry knife was still sticking in his stomach, the blood-covered, parachute-cord-wrapped handle protruding from his belly like some sort of hideous organism. "So . . . you two are old friends, eh?" Teresov gasped in English. "Well, you can join me in hell." He raised the pistol in shaky hands and aimed it at the back of McLanahan's head. "Good-bye . . ."

"Good-bye to *you,* motherfucker," General John Ormack said. He leveled his MP5 at Teresov and pulled the trigger. Thirty-two rounds of 9-millimeter death on full automatic took about three seconds to empty into Teresov's body, and this time when he fell, he was dead. He did not have the luxury of a thick Kevlar flak vest to protect him, as Ormack had had when Teresov's earlier shot had hit him.

"And good riddance," Ormack said. "Who says I can't hit the broad side of a barn?" He dropped the spent weapon and knelt at Luger's side. "Luger, is that you? Are you all right, Lieutenant?"

The burst of automatic gunfire seemed to have fully revived Luger, because his eyes widened in shock and disbelief when he turned to face Ormack. "Colonel . . . Colonel Ormack, is that you? You're here too . . . ?" It was like a dream from long ago and far away.

"You bet I am," Ormack said proudly. "And you can call me General, son."

"Right," Luger said with a weak smile. "Right. General. I should have known that. Patrick?"

"Right here, Dave."

Ormack handed over his first-aid kit and Patrick applied it to the exit wound in Luger's back.

"Are we going home now?"

McLanahan didn't have a chance to answer. He heard a footstep in the shadows. Quickly he reached for the fallen automatic, turned, and aimed it into the shadows.

"Nice move, Colonel," Gunnery Sergeant Wohl said as he stepped into the light. Instantly, the area was filled with three other Marines. Wohl raised his night-vision goggles and said with a hint of a smile, "For a second there I thought these goggles were defective—you looked like a real Marine there for a second." He motioned to Luger and said, "Who is this? Is this REDTAIL HAWK?" He then saw Teresov's body, a mangled heap of tissue a few feet away, and shook his head. "I hope *that* wasn't him—"

"*Shot?*" Luger asked.

"Oh, great. You bagged a Russian . . ."

"No, this is him," McLanahan insisted. "Gunnery Sergeant Wohl, meet First Lieutenant David Luger, U.S. Air Force. Dave, Gunny Wohl. I need some help with this chest wound."

"Rourke, front and center," Wohl said, motioning to a Marine carrying a green canvas medical bag. Wohl stooped down and patted Luger on the leg, giving him a nod and a reassuring smile. "Nice to meet you, Lieutenant. I'm glad McLanahan and Ormack found you—and I'm glad we found all of you alive." Wohl then looked at Ormack, who was lying against the cell wall trying to massage away the pain of the bullet impact on his chest, and added, "Sheesh, General, Luger's even skinnier than you are! What is it with you Air Force pukes, anyway? You have an aversion to pumping some iron?"

Hal Briggs suddenly appeared beside Luger, and he shook Luger's shoulders and his hands until Luger rolled his eyes in pain. "Dave Luger! Goddamn it, Luger, you're alive . . . I mean, damn, man—it's good to see you!"

"Hal . . . *Hal Briggs?* God, I don't believe it. You're here, too?" He looked at McLanahan and said, "Can I see Wendy and Angelina now?"

"Not for a while, partner," McLanahan said, thinking Luger looked like a kid at Christmas. "We've got a long way to go yet."

"You got that right, Colonel," Wohl said.

Luger looked at McLanahan. "Colonel? You made *colonel?*"

"Quit gabbing and save your questions until later, Lieutenant," Wohl said. "We ain't out of this shithole yet."

Luger's face turned very tight and grim, and he leaned his head back as if resigned to die—as he always thought he would.

"Don't let him get to you, Dave," Briggs said with a smile. "He's a Marine. He has that effect on everyone."

"You can button it too, Briggs." Wohl watched as the corpsman finished his work, then asked, "Is he okay to move?" The corpsman nodded, then turned to examine Luger's head. "Then let's get the hell outta here, boys."

McLanahan and Ormack first led two Marines to where the injured jumpmaster and the last Marine security team member were, then made their way upstairs to the ground floor.

Gunnery Sergeant Trimble was with the radioman when he saw the group emerge from the subfloors. He stood as they approached him and said, "Report, Wohl."

"Second squad and I, along with Captain Briggs, made a search of the first subfloor, as you directed," Wohl replied. "During our search we found a door-jamming spike and activated infrared tape with Colonel McLanahan's ID number on it. We tracked McLanahan down to the second subfloor and found McLanahan and General Ormack with this individual, whom they've identified as REDTAIL HAWK."

"Well, no shit," the big Marine exclaimed. Trimble stepped over to where Luger was lying on the floor beside the other injured Marines. "Your name?" he asked.

"Myeenya zahvoot Ivan Sergeiovich . . . I mean, my name is Luger, David," Luger replied. He turned, smiled still in disbelief at Patrick McLanahan, then added, "United States Air Force."

"Why is this man speaking Russian? Are you sure you got the right man, McLanahan?" snapped Trimble.

"He's the right one," McLanahan said. "He's been brainwashed into thinking he's some Russian scientist."

Trimble looked completely unconvinced. "Right. We'll interrogate him later. Search him for weapons or transmitters."

"Search him?" McLanahan asked. "He's not wearing anything but a pair of torn-up trousers, Trimble."

"I don't care if he's buck naked. He's a foreign unidentified individual until an intelligence team tells me otherwise. Search him, handcuff him, and post a guard. And that's the last outburst I'll tolerate from you." Trimble turned away from McLanahan and checked Lieutenant Marx. "What's the one-L-T's condition?"

"Looks like a severe head injury, Gunny," the corpsman replied. "He needs to be medevaced immediately. Sergeant McCall will be okay.

Major Cook has a broken left leg and head injuries also." He motioned to the copilot, whose face was being covered by someone's fatigue jacket. "Captain Brandt was KIA."

McLanahan looked down the corridor and saw another four covered faces and three more wounded. Out of a total of forty-eight Marines on this mission, including the air-crew members, eight were dead and eight were injured badly enough to place them out of commission. He could see several others, perhaps a dozen, with bandages wrapping head, hand, leg, and shoulder wounds.

"We sure took a beating just for one Russian-speaking flyboy," Trimble said, shaking his head angrily. He glanced at McLanahan and Ormack and added, "At least you went back and got the injured." That was all the thank you they were likely to get. "All right, children, we've got thirty-two Marines to hold this building until our pickup arrives. I've got four SAW squads and a Stinger squad on the roof. I want two in the stairwell. I want the subfloor door sealed and booby-trapped. I'll set up a four-man patrol to check floor to floor. The rest will be on station on the ground floor. We'll set up SAW squads on each side of the hallway and in front of the main entrance.

"You three," he said to Briggs, Ormack, and McLanahan, "will go through each and every desk and each and every file cabinet in this building, upper floors only. You will have one B-4 bag each, and you will report to me when your bag is full. That bag becomes your responsibility, and it adopts a higher priority than yourselves—if there's no room on the chopper, you stay and the bag comes with us. If we have to sacrifice Marines to get you in there, dammit, you're going to make it worth our while."

Briggs was ready to chew on Trimble for those remarks—speaking like that to an officer, even a noncombatant, was far, far out of line—but he held his anger in check. Trying hard to keep his temper, Ormack asked, "How long do we have until the Sea Hammer comes back?"

"Hammer Two landed in the embassy grounds for fuel and some repairs," Trimble said. "They are scheduled to be back over the roof in fifteen minutes. Since we've lost one SEA HAMMER, he'll need to make two trips—the first will be for the wounded and dead and for the BCT, and the second for the security team. You should have about thirty minutes altogether."

"Thirty minutes!"

"What the hell did you think, sir?" Trimble retorted. "Did you think the MSB and the Commonwealth were going to give us a week or two to go through their shit? We'll be lucky if you *get* ten minutes. My Marines aren't accustomed to sticking around when a job is done, especially when the bad guys know we're here—we kick ass, then split. But not tonight.

Now we have to wait on you three. Now get moving, sir. You will collect important data on this Soviet stealth bomber until I order you to cease activities and report back to the roof for evacuation. Is that clear, sir?"

"When do we go to the aircraft hangars?" McLanahan asked. "The bomber itself is supposed to be—"

"If you want to go there right now, sir, be my guest," Trimble interrupted, maintaining his version of military decorum by remembering to append "sir" to most of his sentences. "You may get your ass blown off, but you'd have your adventure. This complex has not been secured."

"But the aircraft itself is the real target," Ormack said. "If we get pictures of the Soviet stealth bomber, it'll be the biggest intelligence coup—"

"Besides, this is just the security facility," McLanahan interjected. "They may have some documents in storage here, but they're bound to be outdated or useless to us. The stuff we need to see is in the offices in the hangars. We need to—"

"Dammit, sir, I'm not interested in your coups or what you think is the real target," Trimble growled. "Your opinions don't mean shit to me—can't you officers get that into your thick skulls? My orders were to rescue REDTAIL HAWK and allow you time to search for records pertaining to this experimental aircraft. No one said a word to me about taking pictures or seeing a stealth bomber, and they did not specify how long I had to stay to allow you to rifle through desks. They left that decision to Captain Snyder and me. Now *move.* When I call you upstairs to get on the chopper, your bags should be as full as Santa Claus leaving the North Pole."

CONFEDERATION JOINT ARMED FORCES (WEST) HEADQUARTERS
KALININGRAD, RUSSIA
13 APRIL, 0450 KALININGRAD (**12 APRIL, 2150** ET)

General Anton Osipovich Voshchanka hung on to a leather strap bolted on to the interior of his Zil staff car as the driver negotiated a tight turn in the streets of Kaliningrad. It was about four-thirty in the morning, and already the streets seemed more crowded than usual. People that were out stopped and pointed at the large, dark-blue sedan, as if they could see its occupant. *Do the citizens know?* Voshchanka thought to himself. News, especially bad news, usually travels very fast. The big military car, sealed and armored on all sides and weighing several hundred kilos more than a regular automobile, fishtailed a bit on the icy streets. Voshchanka tightened his safety belt and tried to pay attention to his executive officer briefing him:

". . . No more than a series of hit-and-run strikes," his exec was saying, "but the Lithuanians knew where to strike. They went after power transformers, radars, communications facilities—not just the easy stuff like the antennas or transmission lines, but the relays and control centers. They also blew up several key rail and highway bridges. Very little loss of life, but damage was extensive and complete. Entire bases are still out of direct radio or telephone contact, and it's been over an hour since the first attacks."

"Has a general alert been broadcast?" Voshchanka grumbled.

"Yes, sir, but we've received acknowledgment from only thirty of the largest bases and installations," the executive officer replied. "Small installations and outposts have not reported in. Of the ones that did acknowledge the alert, all but three say they were under attack or had already suffered some damage."

"Palcikas is going to pay for this," Voshchanka said under his breath. "God, I am going to make him pay! Who does he think he's playing with? I want his location, and I want him placed under arrest—"

"General Palcikas is believed to be in the Fisikous Research Institute."

Voshchanka's mouth dropped open in surprise: *"Fisikous* was attacked?"

"Not just attacked, sir," the exec replied. "It has been taken. It is the only installation where Lithuanian troops have invaded and then occupied. They have an estimated four to five thousand troops inside the facility itself and on the airport, plus another one to two thousand patrolling the capital."

"You said that American Marines were over the city and in Fisikous," Voshchanka said. "So the Marines are working with the Lithuanians to attack our bases and facilities?"

"It is not known yet what the link is between the Lithuanians and the Americans," the executive officer replied. "But it is too much of an extraordinary coincidence. They've got to be working together."

"Any word from the Americans? Anything on television or from Minsk?"

"Nothing, sir."

"Incredible," Voshchanka mused. "America attacks Commonwealth and Byelorussian bases and facilities without a declaration of war—and does it hiding behind little Lithuania's skirts!" Despite his bravado, Voshchanka was worried—if the Americans were involved, he stood a very good chance of losing his command, not to mention his life. He'd almost lost his command a few weeks ago after Palcikas had complained to the Lithuanian President. But he'd convinced the Commonwealth Council of Ministers to keep him on—and after the riot at Denerokin they were glad they had. They would never know of his involvement in *promoting* the massacre. The Americans were proven to be tenacious, punishing fighters. "Are they still using the embassy as a base of operations?"

"Yes, sir. There are at least two small attack helicopters, identified as Marine Corps AH-1 Sea Cobras, both fully armed, and one supply helicopter, a Super Stallion, that appears to be damaged or under repair. A contingent of at least one hundred Marines landed in the embassy, which would bring the total contingent to about one hundred and fifty. Three Super Stallion helicopters airlifted civilians out of the embassy grounds."

A security officer in the front seat, acting as radio operator as well, handed the executive officer a message.

"Another aircraft sighted in the embassy, sir, identified as a Marine Corps MV-22 tilt-rotor aircraft, nicknamed the Sea Hammer. It too appears damaged. Four casualties were observed being taken off the aircraft."

"Did it come from Fisikous?" asked Voshchanka.

"Yes, sir. This would seem to confirm the identification of the aircraft that was shot down inside the Fisikous Institute as a V-22 tilt-rotor. A modern Marine Corps composite helicopter squadron usually has six to eight such aircraft, along with the Sea Cobra and Super Stallion helicopters."

"Any firm estimate on how many Marines are in Fisikous?"

"None, sir. The Commonwealth's MSB had some forces still inside the facility with a radio, giving some intelligence information on the forces inside, but they were routed out by the Lithuanians. But each MV-22 aircraft holds up to twenty combat troops plus a crew of six."

"So we may assume that there are at least thirty-six Marines still inside," Voshchanka said. "A pitifully small force."

"There has been no word from the MSB forces inside Fisikous," the executive officer reminded his superior, "and there were several hundred troops there. That may mean that those forty Marines defeated ten times their number when they took Fisikous."

"With help from the Lithuanians," Voshchanka said, shaking his head. "What a debacle! This must be the worst defeat Soviet troops have suffered since Afghanistan."

The executive officer had taken another message from the radioman in the front seat, and he interrupted Voshchanka with it: "Sir, General Gabovich of the MSB is on line one."

"Gabovich? How did he get this number?" But there was no use asking that—he was KGB, after all. He probably had the President of the United States' bedroom phone number in his coat pocket. Voshchanka hit the line button and picked up the phone: "General Voshchanka here."

"What in blazes are you doing, Voshchanka?" Gabovich asked in Russian. "What in hell is going on? Are you on duty or aren't you?"

"What are you talking about, Gabovich?"

"General Palcikas and his street-gang members have raided the Fisikous Institute," Gabovich raged. "There are helicopters all over the city. I have lost contact with my aide and my military commanders in Fisikous—I think they've all been slaughtered by Palcikas."

"They've been attacked by American Marines," Voshchanka said.

"What? *Marines?* In Lithuania . . . ?" On the other end, Gabovich wondered if Voshchanka had been drinking.

Quickly, and without too much detail, Voshchanka told Gabovich about the series of raids all throughout Lithuania, and some details about the embassy reinforcement and the raid on Fisikous. Why he did this, he himself wondered. "So," Voshchanka said, after finishing his short briefing, "this seems to destroy your little plan for dealing with the Lithuanians, doesn't it?"

There was silence.

Voshchanka was considering hanging up on the pretentious Russian.

Gabovich finally said, "No, General, this is *the* perfect opportunity. You must launch your attacks now. Move your forces from Kalinin and Byelorussia *now*. There will be no better time."

"Now see here, Gabovich—" But Voshchanka froze, realizing Gabovich was right. With all the confusion over the raids, Voshchanka, as commander of all Commonwealth forces in Lithuania, could—no, was *expected*—to respond in order to safeguard lives and property. These were obviously terrorists operating in Lithuania. The word was that they were Lithuanian soldiers, but there was no word from the Lithuanian government about the threat of such attacks. Perhaps they were not under government control—Palcikas could have gone insane or was operating independently. Maybe *he* was trying to stage a coup or take over the high-tech weapons in Fisikous for his own use! Yes, perhaps that was it. Or at least what he would tell the Council of Ministers if he had to.

In any case this was the perfect time to move. With the communications infrastructure in Lithuania disrupted, news of his troop movements would be delayed, perhaps by hours, even in daylight. In that time his troops could take over the entire country. He felt his face flush with anticipation.

But was he ready to do it? Where was Gabovich and the MSB going to be when the shooting started? He wondered . . . maybe it would be best to wait. "What if the Americans are assisting the Lithuanians?" Voshchanka asked. "The Americans could retaliate with force. I need time to mobilize my troops."

"Your troops should have been ready to move, General," Gabovich hissed. "I'm willing to bet they're ready—it's *you* who are hesitating. I've seen your forces maneuver for best position over the past few days, barely within the constraints of the treaty. Your aviation units must have updated their data base of landmarks, assault locations, rally points, and landing spots—I have seen their activity across the border more and more.

"The time is now, General Voshchanka. You *know* it is. Quit vacillating. This opportunity may not come along again in years." There was a pause, Voshchanka still having second thoughts, when Gabovich added, "You must also attack the American aircraft on the embassy grounds."

"Attack the American Embassy?" gasped Voshchanka.

"Well, you say there are three, perhaps more, attack helicopters on the embassy grounds. They must be destroyed, General, before our troop movements are detected. You must also demonstrate to the Americans that we will deal harshly with *any* military force that tries to interfere with our plans."

Voshchanka should have known that Gabovich was manipulating him, saying "our" and "we" when it would clearly be only Voshchanka's troops on the firing line—but in his excitement, Voshchanka ignored the real impact of Gabovich's words. It *was* a delicious opportunity. Far better than even he had expected. If it worked, it would ensure Voshchanka of the chance to create a new, stronger empire. One in which he would have to answer to no man or council . . . and he would rule with an iron fist. Without another word, he handed the receiver back to his radioman. He thought for a long moment, then turned to his aide. "Get me Colonel Tsvirko at the Fifty-first Air Army. I want to speak with him immediately. Have the Order of Battle for the Fifth and Seventh armies ready for me when I arrive at the office. And use the siren to clear that traffic out there, driver, or I will pull out a rifle and start clearing them away myself."

FISIKOUS DESIGN-CENTER SECURITY FACILITY
13 APRIL, 0408 VILNIUS **(12 APRIL, 2208** ET**)**

"Here it is," Ormack shouted. "I got something!" He was poring over a file-cabinet safe full of materials that Briggs and one of the Marines had broken into with a small piece of C4 explosive. McLanahan and Briggs ran over to him. "Look—it looks like a briefing package, as if the scientists were going to brief government officials on the project. I got slides, videotapes, handouts, cost projections, the works."

"I got something, too," Briggs said. "Looks like a security—inventory logbook, with lists of publications and documents and which drawers they're in. I'll get Sergeant Haskell to translate it for us." The Marine

Special Purpose Force such as the one that invaded the Fisikous Research Institute usually carried at least one man who was very familiar with the local language. The assault team's man was Andrew Haskell, one of the Marines patrolling the stairwell.

As McLanahan and Ormack piled files and videotapes into their green canvas bag, McLanahan said, "Christ, John, can you believe we're doing this? In a top-secret Soviet research lab, trashing the place? And we found Dave. I just can't believe it."

"Me either," Ormack huffed. "I just wish we'd get out of here. If we can't get into the aircraft hangars, what's the use? We got Dave and he's okay. Let's get the hell out."

"Yeah—but wouldn't you love to get a look at that bomber?"

"Look at this," Ormack said, ignoring the question. "This is a briefing slide on . . . man, this is a slide on a test flight for the bomber! It even has a date on it . . . hey! That's only a week and a half from today! That thing must be ready to fly!"

"Let's ask Captain Snyder for permission to go over there," McLanahan insisted. "I hate going over Trimble's head, but his head has been up and locked this entire night. These Marines are tough sons of bitches, John, but if it's not in the game plan, they won't allow it."

"Look, I'm not gonna argue with their game plan, Patrick, because they got us in here alive," Ormack said. McLanahan nodded his assent. "But I don't have any trouble going to Snyder. We've got a job to do, and Snyder runs this show, not Trimble."

They packed all the documents they had collected into one B-4 bag, then went out to the main stairwell where the guards got clearance for them to head upstairs to the roof. A cold drizzle had started to fall in the pre-dawn hours, which only served to heighten the feeling of nervousness and dread.

Ormack dropped the stuffed green canvas bag near the elevator-shaft door under an overhang, which would provide a bit of protection from the rain.

Captain Edward "Breaker" Snyder was huddled under a low poncho tent, sitting beside a suitcase-sized portable radio, a headset in one ear. His executive officer was flipping through a small notebook, reading. Occasionally Snyder would raise a pair of night-vision binoculars and scan the nearby buildings and the aircraft hangars. He lowered the binoculars when Ormack and McLanahan approached.

"You gentlemen done already?" Snyder asked. In the pre-dawn light, Ormack could see the exhaustion and worry on Snyder's face. Ormack didn't know if this was Snyder's first actual assault, or if he had done dozens of them in the past, but from his stooped shoulders and sagging mouth, the pressure was definitely affecting him.

"There was nothing on any floor except for the third floor," Ormack replied. "We've gone through the file cabinets and safes, and we got everything there is."

"Then go through the desks and the lockers on the first floor," Snyder said. "You have some time."

"What we'd like to do is go over to the aircraft hangars," Ormack said.

Snyder took a deep, exasperated breath. Before he could speak, Ormack interjected, "Captain, the plane is over there. The tech orders are over there. We need to—"

"Captain, vehicles approaching from the south!" the executive officer shouted. Snyder jumped at the announcement, whipped off the headset, then crawled over to the south edge of the roof and peered over. The two Air Force officers did the same.

An armored troop carrier was slowly rumbling down the ramp area in front of the aircraft hangars, heading toward the security building. Atop the APC was a large red flag, the Vytis, fluttering on a radio mast. There was also a white flag tied to the muzzle end of an AK-47, being held aloft by a soldier in the cupola of the vehicle.

"Radio message coming in from that vehicle, sir," the executive officer said. "On the emergency channel. Unsecure." Snyder crawled back to the radio tent and held the headset up to his ear:

"Attention please, American Marines. Attention please," came the heavily accented voice. "I speak on behalf of General Dominikas Palcikas, commander in chief of Lithuanian Self-Defense Forces. The General sends you greeting and would like to inform you that all Soviet security forces have been removed from Fisikous. I repeat, all Soviet OMON troops have been captured or killed inside Fisikous. My commander requests to speak with the commander of your forces, please."

The APC was still moving forward toward the security building. Snyder clicked on the radio: "Armored vehicle with the Lithuanian flag, hold your position." He lowered the handset. "Range from the APC to the building?"

"Fifty meters," one of the SAW squad members shouted back. "Vehicle has stopped."

"Weapons visible?"

"Only the rifle," the squad member shouted back. "Four . . . five . . . six gun ports closed . . . machine-gun mount empty."

Snyder picked up another handset. "Trimble, I want a SAW squad on that APC. If it moves any closer to the building, blow it away. You got that?"

"Trimble copies," came the reply.

Snyder and his executive officer dragged the radio over toward the edge of the roof so he could watch and talk at the same time. A tall, beefy soldier had emerged from the rear of the APC, accompanied by a younger man with a portable radio slung over his shoulder. After the two dismounted, the vehicle backed up about twenty meters. The soldiers were alone, with only sidearms visible. The big soldier boldly stepped right up to the front door of the security building; the radioman was a bit less determined, but he kept up with the big strides of his partner. Ignoring the guns, barricades, and determined Marines challenging him, he walked right up to the shattered front door of the facility, a cocky smile on his face.

"That's far enough," Trimble challenged them. "Step aside so I can see your APC." The radioman translated for the other man, and with an amused smile on his face, the two soldiers complied.

"My name General Dominikas Palcikas, commander of military forces of *Lietuvos,*" the big man said in halting English. "I wish speak with your commander, please." He apparently recognized that Trimble was not the leader of this unit.

"Captain, the guy says he's General Palcikas," Trimble radioed up to Snyder. "Wants to talk with you."

"He wants to talk?" Snyder repeated incredulously. Ormack and McLanahan could see the crushing strain on Snyder's face—the guy looked like he was having a heart attack. "Take them into custody. If they resist, kill them. If that APC moves, blow it away. I'll be down there in a minute."

"You're going to arrest the commander of the Lithuanian military?" McLanahan asked. "Why?"

"How do I know he's really Palcikas? How do I know he's with the Lithuanian Army? Lithuania isn't supposed to *have* an army—only a militia, a bunch of rough, ill-equipped volunteers. This group has got tanks and antiaircraft weapons." Snyder took a drink from his canteen, water spilling out the side of his mouth. He turned to Ormack and continued: "I don't give a shit about arresting anybody. But I'm going to follow procedures. Lots of spies have just walked into a camp waving a white flag. I'm going to secure him, isolate the two individuals, and interrogate them, just like Trimble and Haskell did with Luger.

"But what I really care about, sir, is getting *off* this fucking roof. The Soviets are going to dump on us any minute, and we're standing around with our thumbs up our asses, about to have a tea party with the locals." He dropped the FM radio handset and picked up the UHF command radio. "Dockside, Dockside, this is Hammer. Status of our transport. Over."

"Hammer, this is Dockside, estimate ten mike for your ride. Over."

"Copy ten mike," Snyder acknowledged, swearing to himself again. He glanced at his watch. In their coded phraseology, "ten mike," or ten minutes, needed to be multiplied by whatever number the minute hand was pointing on at the time of the transmission. In this case, he needed to multiply by two—they were estimating twenty minutes before the MV-22 would be back to pick them up. He put the handset back in the radio. "We're going to lose daylight at this rate—the chopper won't be back for at least twenty minutes."

"I know you got a lot on your mind, Captain," Ormack said, "but this is a great opportunity for us. The Lithuanians down there seem to have control of the entire facility, and the SEA HAMMER's been delayed. We don't need any other Marines to help us."

"Oh, is that so?" Snyder asked derisively. "So now you guys are experts in securing buildings, huh?"

"I'm not trying to tell you your business, Captain," Ormack insisted. "I'm trying to say we're willing to take the risk. You've got the important data from this building in a bag right there, and you've got REDTAIL HAWK downstairs in custody."

"So you think you can go trotting off anywhere you please, and I'm not responsible for you and I shouldn't care what happens to you, right?" Snyder asked, clearly distraught. For the first time, the two Air Force officers saw real concern in the Marine captain's eyes. He really felt exposed, unprotected, completely alone out here, his thirty-some Marines against the full might of the Commonwealth Army that might be bearing down on him at any moment. "Well, I *am* responsible for you, dammit. I'm responsible for all the men here. It's my ass if I get anybody killed on this mission."

He removed his helmet, scratched his head irritably, sprinkled a bit of water on his head, and strapped the helmet back in place. Taking a deep breath, he gave Ormack and McLanahan an icy stare; then: "Look, just finish up your search of this building—collect any data you can. Hopefully by the time you finish, the SEA HAMMER will be back and we can get the hell out of here. With the Lithuanians in charge, maybe you'll get invited back to get the rest of the data. But I'm more concerned about this assault team. With only twenty-eight combat-ready troops here, we're sitting ducks for any sort of counterattack. Hell, one bomb can take us all out." He turned over control of the radios to his executive officer and headed downstairs.

Ormack and McLanahan followed.

The two Lithuanians were seated on small wooden chairs in the main ground-floor hallway. Their wrists and ankles were bound by plastic handcuffs. They wore no hoods, blindfolds, or gags, but they were seated facing a blank wall, separated from each other by a few feet. One Marine was examining the radio, copying down all the frequencies and channel numbers imprinted on it. Sergeant Haskell was standing by, ready to help translate; he also carried a black-and-green leather pouch that contained the unit's intelligence records—the photos and briefing notes used by the unit for reference during the mission. Gunnery Sergeant Trimble was examining the two soldiers' identification papers; he handed them over to Snyder as the three officers approached. "Haskell?"

"We don't have a photo of Palcikas, sir," Haskell said. "I'd like to request the embassy fax us a copy from their files."

Snyder picked up his portable radio: "Bob, get on the horn to the embassy and tell them to fax us a picture of General Dominikas Palcikas of the Lithuanian Self-Defense Force. Out." The PRC-118ED UHF radio had a built-in fax modem on which documents could be printed out and transmitted from across town or, via satellite, around the world. "You got anything on him?" Snyder asked Haskell.

"Nothing on Palcikas himself except for his name, rank, and age. I got his unit's approximate troop strength, headquarters, staff . . . not much more than that," Haskell replied. "General word is that Lithuania's not supposed to have an army. Total strength of about two thousand, small arms, some APCs. No aircraft, heavy armor, artillery, or air-defense weapons. Border guards, ceremonial, government security only."

Snyder nodded to Trimble, and a guard swiveled Palcikas' chair around so he faced into the hallway. He wore a slight smile on his dirty, tired-looking face. "Do you understand English, sir?"

"Yes. Little," Palcikas replied. He noticed the dark-blue bars on Snyder's collar, looked at Snyder's face, and his smile broadened a bit. "You are commander here?"

Snyder ignored the question. "Sir, how many troops do you have here in the Fisikous Institute?" he asked.

"You say 'sir' with very little respect in your voice, young captain," Palcikas said. "You must be American Marines." Palcikas had trouble with his English, but the other Lithuanian, still facing the wall, translated the question into Lithuanian and helped his superior with his translation: "I had four battalions here, about three thousand five hundred men. Two battalions, no more. Organized three battalions, each eight hundred men."

"Jesus," Snyder said. He had lost a third of his forces, as had Snyder, but this man had lost a hundred times more souls. "And I thought *I* lost a few men."

Palcikas looked at Snyder and nodded, as if he could see the fear and pain that the young Marine captain was trying to hide. "War is a difficult thing, is it not, Captain?" Snyder made no reply. "You are very young to command American Marines, are you not? But then, some of my officers are very young as well."

"What is your objective here?"

"Fisikous will be headquarters for my troops during attacks," Palcikas explained with help from his radioman. "My headquarters in Trakai not good against air attacks. Fisikous very good, very strong."

"But what is your objective? Why are you doing this? Why are you attacking Fisikous?"

"To drive foreign troops out of my country," the man replied. "I destroy communications centers, missile bases, power plants, and airfields—now I take my stronghold and plan my next offensive. Fisikous now belongs to Lithuania." He paused, scanning Snyder carefully, then asked, "And what is *your* objective here, Captain?"

"That's classified, sir." Haskell handed Snyder a printout. It was the fax from the Embassy with a recent photo of Palcikas. It matched. Snyder showed Trimble the printout, then showed it to Palcikas. "Release him—but don't give him back his weapons until they're ready to leave."

Palcikas smiled at that extra bit of caution. He had a chance to look around after he was cut free and his equipment, minus his weapons, were returned to him: "Ah. Secret invasion. Small force, limited objective, few casualties. Hostage rescue? You steal secret formulas, like in James Bond movies?" He looked at the other men around him, his eyes falling on Ormack, McLanahan, and Briggs. "These men not Marines. CIA? You spies?" He shook his head, deciding they were not. Then he stared at Ormack and nodded his head. "No, not spies. But you are main man. You are commander here? You look like commander."

Snyder gave Ormack a warning glance—no names, we're not even supposed to *be* here—and Ormack nodded that he understood. "Perhaps someday we can be formally introduced," Ormack said, extending a hand. Palcikas grasped it in his huge hand. "But it's a pleasure to meet you, and I've admired you ever since you left the Red Army and returned to Lithuania. You are an inspiration for a lot of people in America."

"You smart guy!" Palcikas said with a laugh, a broad grin on his face. "I first think you general like me, but you too smart for general—maybe gunnery sergeant, no?" The Americans around him laughed aloud—Palcikas' charisma was infectious. "No names, classified mission, and you know of me—maybe you all spies." He shrugged nonchalantly, then added, "No matter. You shoot the right soldiers—you shoot OMON Black Berets here in Fisikous. I thank you for assisting me. What are your intentions?"

"Right now, my intention is to get *out* of here," Snyder said.

"Easy," Palcikas said, clapping Snyder and Ormack on the shoulder. "You go. We take you. You go to embassy? City of Progress? Yes, we take you to embassy. Heavy guard, hide in trucks, you stay secret. Okay?"

Snyder was about to say, "No, we're waiting for our people to come get us," but he paused and thought about the officer. A SEA HAMMER or Super Stallion would have to make at least two trips to retrieve all the Marines trapped inside Fisikous, in broad daylight; each trip would be a hundred times more perilous than the previous one. Plus they would ruin any chance they had of keeping this mission into Fisikous a secret. He turned to Trimble and together they stepped away. "What do you think, Gunny? I hate putting our lives in the hands of people we don't know, but they *are* locals. Enlisting the assistance of locals is part of the SOP. And if the Echos or the Hammers come get us, they'll be under the gun the whole way."

"I think any way we look at it, sir," Trimble said, "the faster we can get out of Fisikous, the better. We've accomplished our mission—we got the zoomie and we got the classified stuff. Let's split."

"I'm all for that," Snyder said. He turned to Palcikas and said, "We accept your offer, General. We'd like a few conditions: I want to know the route of travel we'll take, no one is blindfolded or restrained, we have full access to our weapons, and we have an equal number of Americans and Lithuanians in each vehicle."

The radioman translated Snyder's words, and Palcikas nodded. "Very cautious of you, Captain, but I approve of your caution. Your conditions we will meet."

"Good. Perhaps you can use some of the weapons on the second floor of this building—they have enough ammunition and weapons for a battalion."

"We can always use more bullets, young captain," Palcikas said with a smile. "If you will allow it, I will bring troops to carry it out."

"When we depart, you can have all of it," Snyder said. "Not until."

"You very cautious man. I like. Very well. You don't blow up. I take when you leave. Good." He issued orders to his radioman, then turned to Ormack and the other Air Force officers. "And what of you three unnamed spies? Will you go with Marines to the embassy or do you wish to see the rest of the facility? I have not been there yet, but I am told a fantastic and beautiful bird lives in the east hangar out there. I make a guess and say that was your objective, no?"

Ormack couldn't hide his excitement from Palcikas, but Snyder, who was already on his walkie-talkie to his executive officer on the roof, said, "No, General, they *will* be accompanying us," with emphasis, for Ormack's benefit, on "will."

Palcikas nodded and issued orders to his radioman, then said to Ormack, "Do not worry, General—and I know you are a general, despite taking orders from young captain—I will take good care of the bird, and my staff will take nice pictures. Perhaps you will see the pictures in *Aviation Week and Space Technology* next week, no?"

THE WHITE HOUSE OVAL OFFICE, WASHINGTON, D.C.
12 APRIL 2157 ET (13 APRIL, 0357 VILNIUS)

When a call from overseas comes into the White House Communications Center and is accepted by the President of the United States, he is not the only one who picks up the phone and says "Hello." An incoming call is usually delayed a few minutes, no more than three or four, while an entire army of people gets on the line.

On this call from the Byelorussian capital of Minsk, two interpreters were quickly put on undetectable "dead extensions"—a Russian interpreter and, in this case, a Byelorussian interpreter. The Russian interpreter, a naval officer assigned to the White House, was on permanent assignment to the President's National Security Advisor and ordered to stand by when the embassy reinforcement commenced; the Byelorussian interpreter, a civilian State Department employee born in the former Soviet republic, had been summoned shortly before the operation began, when it was obvious who might be calling.

Along with the interpreters, there were engineers who would use sophisticated computers to analyze the line and would determine the origin of the call and how many ears might be listening on the *other* end; there were psychologists who would analyze the stress in the voice of the caller and determine if he was being truthful, or sincere, or desperate, or ready to concede, or to identify any attempts by the caller to use tricks like hypnosis or autosuggestion; there were intelligence officers and engineers who would identify the caller by his voice and also try to identify any other voices or sounds in the background that might give a clue as to the caller's real intent; and of course there were the President's advisers, in this case several members of the National Security Council, listening in on "dead extensions" so as to not be heard or detected themselves.

When his staff indicated that everyone was ready, the President punched the line button and introduced himself . . .

. . . and no sooner had he done so than the president of Byelorussia, Pavel Borisovich Svetlov, shouted in the telephone in his native tongue. The volume was electronically toned down a bit, and the female voice of the interpreter said almost simultaneously, "Mr. President, why are you aiding these Lithuanian terrorists? Why do you have American Marines in Vilnius?"

On the left side of a computer screen on the President's desk was the near-real-time translation and transcription of the conversation, with the staff's comments on the other side. "He's going to play the terrorist gambit," one of the psychologists typed on a computer screen in front of the President. Another wrote, "Might be slightly intoxicated." A CIA staffer wrote, "He was briefed to say 'terrorist.' Briefed by whom?"

"If you are referring to the action over the American Embassy, President Svetlov," the President of the United States said, "we received permission from President Kapocius to fly our aircraft over his country several days ago. The Council of Ministers of the Commonwealth of Independent States was notified by telegram of our overflight request." That was a slight stretch of the truth—in fact, the telegram had been sent only a few minutes before the phone conversation, along with copies to most other countries in Europe. "I am not aware of any terrorist actions in Lithuania."

"Several Commonwealth bases were attacked last night, resulting in the deaths of several hundred soldiers, most of whom were from my country," Svetlov thundered.

A staffer immediately wrote, "Clear casualty inflation." The interpreter went on: "We have information that bands of Lithuanian terrorist guerrillas perpetrated these raids. Is the United States a party to these terrorist activities?"

The President released the "dead man" button on the phone, which cut off the mouthpiece so he could confer in private: "Has President Kapocius made his statement on the attacks yet?"

Someone replied, "Yes."

"When?"

"About ten minutes ago."

"He says Lithuanian troops are involved?"

"Yes."

"And General Palcikas? Did he mention Palcikas?"

"Yes, sir. The General received a full endorsement."

"Good." The President pushed the dead man button: "President Svetlov, President Kapocius of Lithuania announced just ten minutes ago that he ordered Lithuanian Self-Defense Force troops to strike those bases. General Palcikas is taking his orders from President Kapocius. That is not an act of terrorism."

It was hard enough to talk on the phone with the typical two-second delay in the overseas phone line, but when one party decides to interrupt, it makes it even worse—before the President could finish, Svetlov was talking, and the interpreter was saying, "I have been charged by the Council of Ministers of the Commonwealth of Independent States to maintain law and order in the Baltic states during the transition period specified in the Treaty of Cooperation. Your interference and your support of this terrorist insurrection threatens the peace and security of not only Lithuania, but of the Commonwealth of Independent States and of Belarus."

Immediately, comments like "Sounds very serious" and "Prelude to something????" appeared on the screen.

"Stick with your policy, Mr. President," George Russell, the National Security Advisor, said aloud. "We're evacuating Americans and reinforcing the embassy against civil unrest. Everything else can be handled by the U.N."

"Don't put up with his shit, either, Mr. President," Vice President Martindale inelegantly added.

The President nodded his assent to both those suggestions. "Mr. President, I will not sit here and listen to threats," the President of the United States said to Svetlov. "You will allow our embassy-reinforcement operation and noncombatant operation to continue unimpeded. As far as the attacks on Commonwealth bases, that is best handled in the United Nations. All sides in this matter have suffered legitimate wrongs. The United States will not use military force to harm Commonwealth noncombatant forces unless our forces are fired upon first. I urge you not to respond with military force within Lithuania."

"I will not stand by while the United States and Lithuania destroy my volunteer army and the peace that we have tried to achieve," Svetlov huffed. "Belarus is dependent on the peace and security of the Commonwealth of Independent States for trade and necessary goods. We have an important interest in the affairs of Lithuania, and its terrorist guerrilla army—"

One CIA analyst typed, "Key phrases! Dependent on Lithuania . . . important interest in Lithuania . . . prelude to war!?"

Svetlov continued. "—and I tell you, Mr. President, my government is prepared to act if these attacks do not stop. Peace must be restored." His voice was more agitated, his tone rising in anger. "We will use all resources to establish peace in the Baltic region. *All resources.* Leave Lithuania and do not interfere or your people will suffer the consequences."

At that, the line was disconnected.

The computer immediately displayed a word-count and call-duration, followed by a stream of analysis from all those technicians listening in.

Without even reviewing the CIA and psychologists' evaluations, Secretary of Defense Thomas Preston said, "I think he means business. I think he's going to move against Lithuania."

"It's got all the elements, Mr. President," National Security Advisor George Russell added. "He's painted a no-way-out picture—terrorist guerrillas, peace is threatened, his country is dependent on Lithuania, his country has special interests in Lithuania—it's all there. He can take the transcript of this conversation and go on television to explain his actions."

"But his only authority for his military presence in Lithuania is from the Commonwealth," the President said. "What will the Commonwealth say? What will *they* do . . . ?"

"I don't think it matters anymore, sir," Chairman of the Joint Chiefs of Staff General Wilbur Curtis said, chomping on his cigar. "He mentioned the Commonwealth once, but after that it was all Belarus. I think he's prepared to act without the Commonwealth's sanction."

Heads nodded at that—everyone seemed to agree.

The President felt a deepening knot growing in the pit of his stomach. He could feel events beginning to spin out of his control—there was nothing he could do to stop Svetlov from moving against Lithuania if that's what he was going to do. "All right," he said, collecting his thoughts. "What will he do? Where will he move first?"

In a flash Curtis had a notebook open to his staff's research notes. "Our analysis reveals three likely striking points, based on the deployment of his forces at the present time:

"The primary thrust will come from Smorgon Army Air Base in northwestern Byelorussia, with one armor brigade of fifteen thousand troops and two hundred tanks, one air brigade with about sixty attack aircraft, and one infantry brigade, with about fifteen thousand troops. They are all within two hours' travel time of Vilnius, with the exception of the attack helicopters, which can be over the capital in less than thirty minutes and a few fixed-wing attack aircraft that can strike within ten minutes.

"The secondary strike will be within Lithuania itself. Byelorussia has approximately ten thousand troops stationed throughout Lithuania. Depending on the extent of the disruption of communications caused by our raids and the Lithuanian raids, they can be mobilized in as little as one hour.

"The third strike will come from the territory of Kalinin, the little slice of Russia southwest of Lithuania," Curtis continued. "Most troops there are Byelorussian, under direct Russian supervision. The Byelorussians have been reinforcing their base at Chernyakhovsk, in the center of Kalinin—they now have at least a full air brigade stationed there, with at least a hundred fixed- and rotary-wing aircraft, and they've been swapping out their usual light transports with attack and troop assault helicopters. They can strike the city of Kaunas and the port city of Klaipeda in about thirty minutes. This unit has a very small infantry group with it, but they can do considerable damage from air strikes and then reconfigure for parachute drops and troop transport."

"So in less than an hour," the Vice President calculated, "the Byelorussian troops can be on the move all throughout Lithuania, and in just a couple of hours they can be attacking them in force?"

"I'm afraid so, Mr. President."

There was silence in the Oval Office.

The very event that all of them had feared from the beginning was happening—Lithuania was under attack.

"Case, get President Kapocius on the phone for me right away," the President ordered.

"We're trying," Timmons, the chief of staff, reported. "Lines have been disrupted. We're patching through the U.S. Embassy, but things are pretty scrambled there, too."

"He may have evacuated the capital as well," Secretary of State Danahall offered.

"I want to talk to Kapocius," the President repeated. "I need his direction. Jesus, I can't make this decision for him . . ."

"You have to respond, Mr. President," the Vice President said. "Gintarus Kapocius authorized American military aircraft to overfly his country. He was counting on us not only to rescue our own people, but to protect his country. We have the authority."

"I want to hear it from *him*," the President snapped. "I'm not going to start a war on his soil without full and unequivocal permission. Especially with the threat of a damned nuclear release! Christ, what a fucking mess."

"Sir, we've got a contingency plan for this," Curtis interjected. "General Lockhart of U.S. European Command would gain the Twenty-sixth Marines, the Seventh Fleet detachment in the Baltic Sea, the Third Army, and Seventeenth and Third Air Force—we can put all those units on full alert immediately, along with the Air Battle Force in South Dakota. That's twenty thousand troops, two thousand Marines, four fighter wings, six light and medium bomber wings, electronic-warfare support, communications, transportation—"

"For God's sakes, General, hold on a minute," the President ordered. "I know you have a contingency plan. I need to *think*." Everyone fell silent. The President rose from his chair, paced the Oval Office for a few minutes, and stopped at the doors leading to the Rose Garden. He stared at his own reflection in one of the bullet-resistant polycarbonate windows and then returned to his desk but did not sit. "With our forces in Germany, how long would a mobilization take?" the President asked.

"We can begin limited air operations—reconnaissance and limited air strikes—over Lithuania in about ten to twelve hours," Curtis replied. "However, realistically we'd have to wait until tomorrow night, since we couldn't have anything put together tonight and we'd have a much tougher time in daytime operations. In three days we can begin full air operations.

"Ground operations are tougher unless we get permission to cross the Polish border into Lithuania, and that's very unlikely. It'll take the Marines' Second Marine Expeditionary Force, about forty thousand Marines, at least a week to set up for an amphibious assault."

"So at least ten hours for any combat air operations, and possibly not for another twenty-four to seventy-two hours," the President summarized. "And the Byelorussians, if they decided to invade now, would use all tomorrow to drive across Lithuania. They could take the capital before we'd get one plane off the ground."

"We could run air operations in the daytime, sir," Curtis said. "I don't have a current weather report, but if the weather is poor we'd stand a better chance. But casualties will increase in daylight operations until we take control of the skies. Without forward bases or overflight privileges over countries like Poland or Latvia, neither of which I think we could get, our aircraft and helicopters would have to fly hundreds of miles overwater from Denmark, Norway, or Germany."

"And that's if *those* countries will allow us to stage combat forces from their territories," Danahall interjected. "They very well may wait several days, or wait for a United Nations Security Council resolution, before allowing us to launch strike aircraft from bases in their countries."

The President looked at Curtis, and for the first time Curtis saw the strain of the situation in the President's eyes. "You mean we could very well watch the Byelorussians or the Commonwealth of Independent States overrun Lithuania—and there's nothing we could do about it?"

"I don't think that's realistic, Mr. President," Secretary of Defense Preston said. "I think all those countries would support us if we decided to go ahead—England and Germany, certainly, considering what the Soviets and Byelorussians did to the ambassador from Iceland and the Vice President of Lithuania—not to mention one of our own senators—during that so-called riot at Denerokin."

"The distances may be too great for helicopters right away," Curtis added, extinguishing his cigar, "but F-111 bombers from England, A-10 and F-16s configured with Maverick antitank missiles from Germany and Denmark have plenty of striking power and range to do the job. It'd take several days to deploy F-117 stealth bombers and F-15E bombers from the mainland. The Air Battle Force can be tasked to launch within a day, but we'd need forward basing for them to make them effective."

This was the telling moment when he had to decide whether to send young men off to fight, perhaps to die, in a foreign country, the President realized. Before, it was just a handful of Marines to reinforce the American Embassy in Vilnius and a few more to find an American. Sneak in, sneak out. Both noble goals, both low numbers of men, both in darkness, both low-risk operations. This new scenario was shaping up differently—now he had to send more men, more equipment, and all in daylight, with the enemy troops fully alerted.

"I need better options, General," the President decided. "I need better direction from all the parties involved. I need to know what President Svetlov has in mind. I need to know what President Kapocius wants. I need to know exactly what we're facing. Otherwise I'd be throwing away American lives in a conflict, and that I will *not* do."

Curtis remained silent for a moment, running through his own list of options—and, every time, he came up with the very same answer:

"Sir, even if you decide to begin air operations over Lithuania immediately, it'll take time for our European units to organize effectively for a heavy enough strike," he said.

The President looked at him with wary, accusing eyes. The President knew what he was going to suggest.

The Chairman of the Joint Chiefs thought, *Well, might as well get it out. . . .* "As I said, the Air Battle Force from Ellsworth will need at least twenty-four hours to deploy, and then would require substantial forward basing, in Norway or England for example. But, as it happens, we have one unit ready to deploy immediately and that has a plan of action developed for precisely this contingency—"

"Elliott," National Security Advisor Russell said in disgust. Obviously, everyone had been dreading—or hoping?—the same thing. "Brad Elliott's unit, right?"

"I spoke with General Elliott shortly before the reinforcement operation began," Curtis explained, "after he was granted priority-B notification status. He was, you'll recall, being unusually quiet for a man who had four of his top officers involved in this mission. Upon further inquiry, General Elliott briefed me on an operation he had devised as a backup to the REDTAIL HAWK mission. Should that one fail or get canceled, General Elliott's group, along with an Intelligence Support Agency operations unit called MADCAP MAGICIAN, was going to go and attempt a rescue."

"On *whose* authority?" the President thundered.

When Curtis did not answer promptly, the President's eyes widened in understanding and aggravation. "I see. *No one's authority.* Elliott was going to launch this mission by himself, right . . . ?"

"I ordered him, upon penalty of immediate imprisonment, to stand down his operation and return his forces to base," Curtis said. The President's question was answered without explanation, which only made him angrier. Curtis continued. "His units have complied—"

Russell was shaking his head. "Is he crazy? Has he gone off the deep end? Who in the hell does Elliott think he is? He shouldn't be imprisoned—he should be taken out and *shot* . . . !"

"Perhaps." Curtis nodded. "Except for one thing, George—he's the best we've got right now. What he's done is assemble an incredible air, sea, and ground assault force that is completely covert, deniable, stealthy, and powerful. He's got a hundred Marines, two tilt-rotor assault aircraft, and six modified B-52 bombers that don't exist on the books. He's briefed me on a plan to destroy half of Byelorussia's invasion force *in one night* and to yank the remaining Marines out of Fisikous and into the embassy or out of Lithuania. My staff has studied his operation, and we've concluded that with a little luck and some help by the Lithuanian militia he can do it. Not only that, he can do it in about fourteen hours."

"Fourteen hours!" the President said in disbelief. "But I thought you said it would take a minimum of twenty-four to seventy-two hours to get a full air operation into motion."

"Sir, General Elliott has already mobilized *his* forces," Curtis explained. "Within HAWC, he commands a group of highly skilled flyers, engineers, and scientists, along with an arsenal of high-tech experimental aircraft and weapons. Elliott has run that place for years—he's the heart and soul of the people who work there. The Old Dog mission was their greatest triumph. When he told his people he wanted to save the hero of that mission from imprisonment in Lithuania, his people responded. On a wartime footing, his research center becomes just as powerful, perhaps even more so, than any other combat unit in the United States.

"By early tomorrow evening Lithuania time—by three P.M. tomorrow afternoon, Washington time—we can have a heavy strike force over Lithuania," Curtis concluded. "I'd like to brief you and the staff on his proposed operation, and I recommend that we authorize his aircraft to launch from Nevada and deploy to its staging point over the Baltic Sea. If the situation improves, we can recall his unit or deploy them to a forward base—England, or his planned deployment base at Thule, Greenland."

Curtis paused and assessed the mood of the President and the rest of his advisers. The President appeared dubious, angry, and ready to chew on steel and spit nails—but he was quiet, not railing against Elliott as Curtis expected. Everyone else had been quiet, waiting for a decision from the President on how to proceed—now, faced with this very real, very tangible option, they were both conflicted and hopeful, but still afraid to side with such a bold but potentially dangerous crackpot like Bradley James Elliott.

"Dammit, General," the President cursed, shaking his head in total exasperation, "how does Elliott get away with this shit? And please don't tell me we *need* guys like Elliott—he does nothing but give me nightmares."

Curtis didn't dare answer that one.

The President ran a hand across his face, trying to wipe away the tension he felt in his eyes and neck, then said with a sigh, "Get Elliott in here ASAP. And this better be good."

THE UNITED STATES EMBASSY
CITY OF PROGRESS, VILNIUS, LITHUANIA
13 APRIL, **0502** VILNIUS (**12** APRIL, **2302** ET)

Major Jurgensen looked at the MV-22 SEA HAMMER and shook his head in disgust. The starboard engine nacelle looked like a dead flower—its rotors folded, the nacelle turned horizontally, and access covers pulled off the nacelle, the doors hanging like bark stripped from a tree by a beaver. The once immaculately groomed lawn outside the embassy was stained and mushy from hydraulic fluid, oil, and boot prints. "All that damage from small-arms fire, Sergeant?"

The Marine plane captain in charge of the damaged aircraft cursed silently and said, "The golden BB theory is still running true to form, sir. It's not the massive assault that'll get you—it's the one lucky shot. He couldn't have placed that round any better if he tried. It's as if he knew exactly which line would be the hardest to replace in the field, and hit it deliberately."

"Did you try swapping parts with the Echo?" Jurgensen asked, nodding toward the damaged CH-53E Super Stallion. Its crew had abandoned it several minutes ago, watching with dismay as parts were pulled off to go into the MV-22. Jurgensen had made the decision to cannibalize the Super Stallion to fix the SEA HAMMER because it would be better suited for evacuating the recovered Air Force officer and the classified materials all the way out of Lithuania—the tilt-rotor aircraft could go farther than the Super Stallion with the small amount of fuel they had left in the embassy.

"We did that," the plane captain replied. "There's not many parts in common between the two, but fortunately hoses are pretty common. The Hammer will be as good as new when it's finished, sir—this is no temporary fix." The captain frowned at the engine, then added, "You know, sir, we should submit a suggestion to Patuxent River to consider putting some Kevlar on these engine shrouds near critical points."

"Later, Sergeant. I want to know how long before we can pick up the assault team."

"It should only be a few more minutes, sir, and we'll start buttoning it up and doing a ground check. After that we need to reinstall the weapons—that should only take a few minutes. Say another ten to fifteen minutes."

Jurgensen had already figured out that a more reasonable number might be twenty to thirty minutes, especially after seeing the numbers of panels and cowlings open on that engine nacelle. "Advise me when you're ready to crank," Jurgensen said. "We'll forgo the weapons pods and launch the Sea Cobras for air support. Do it." Jurgensen was then summoned back to the scrambled UHF radio station set up just inside the back entrance to the embassy. "What have you got?"

"Encoded message from the BCT, sir," the radioman replied, handing Jurgensen the decoded message form.

Jurgensen's eyes lit up when he read the message. "Outstanding, Breaker," Jurgensen exclaimed aloud, as if the Building Clearing Team leader could hear him. To the radioman, he ordered: "Reply to the BCT in code: 'Your idea approved, send transfer plan and route soonest, revised ETIC to Hammer launch twenty mike. End.' " He turned and saw Ambassador Reynolds. "Excuse me, Mr. Ambassador. My assault team over at Fisikous has made contact with General Palcikas of the Lithuanian Self-Defense Force. Palcikas has apparently offered to escort the Marines secretly to the embassy. They may be ready to move within fifteen minutes. Do you see any problems?"

The ambassador thought for a moment, then shook his head. "No, Major, I don't. Your men must wear their uniforms at all times, and they must avoid offensive actions. That is *very* important. If we want to be able to prove to the world that we are not an invasion force, your men must keep their fingers off the triggers. We have to do everything we can to prove this is a defensive mission. Having Palcikas' cooperation is excellent, but if he's in charge, let *his* men do the fighting. Of course your men can defend themselves."

"I understand," Jurgensen said. "I'll need a detailed map of the city, or a large-scale photograph if you have—"

"Choppers!" someone screamed. "Heavy choppers inbound from the east!"

Jurgensen dashed outside and picked up a pair of binoculars, scanning the horizon, checking around the area of the rising sun first. Sure enough, there they were—four Mil-24 helicopter gunships, NATO nickname Hind, coming in out of the sun. They were distinctive with their stub weapon pylons, resembling short slanted wings, carrying what could easily be seen as an enormous amount of weaponry, and of course by their incredible low rhythmic beat, like a thousand African war drums bearing down on you, loud enough now that the sound seemed to interfere with the beating of your heart.

Jurgensen was on his walkie-talkie in a flash. "All crews, all crews, air-raid procedures, air-raid procedures. All noncombatants, get into the basement shelters. Scan for flankers—I don't want everybody fixating on the Hinds and letting a smaller gunship sneak in from behind. Rattlers, prepare for takeoff! Stinger crews, sing out when you acquire—"

"Major, you can't attack those helicopters!" Ambassador Reynolds said, placing a hand on Jurgensen's shoulder.

"Say again?"

"You can*not* fire on those helicopters from this embassy."

The roar of engines firing up on the AH-1W Sea Cobra gunships echoed in Jurgensen's ears, making him shake his head as if he had not heard Reynolds' incredible statement. "You have *got* to be joking, Mr. Ambassador."

"I am deadly serious, Major," Reynolds said earnestly. "Don't you understand? We enjoy diplomatic protection here in this compound only because we maintain a purely defensive posture and we protect the lives of our own citizens here. Furthermore, we have not received permission from Washington or from the President of Lithuania to conduct any offensive acts."

"Those helicopters *are* a threat to my troops."

"Helicopters in flight are not legally a threat to anyone until they attack, Major," Reynolds said. "You have no choice—you cannot fire unless we are fired upon first. An attack on the embassy is considered a declaration of war, according to executive order, but an attack staged from an embassy in peacetime is a serious violation of international law."

"So what do you expect me to do? Just stand here and watch them attack . . . ?"

"You have no choice," Reynolds said. "You can only prepare to defend the embassy and pray they aren't foolish enough to attack."

"I am *not* going to sit around and wait for an attack!"

"I don't know if I have any more influence over you, Major, but as U.S. ambassador to Lithuania and senior government officer in charge of this facility, I order you *not* to fire on those helicopters unless we come under attack ourselves."

Jurgensen was shocked speechless. The Hinds were getting closer— Jurgensen could now see that they were older Hind-D gunships, with a 12.7-millimeter Gatling-style gun in a steerable nose turret, two 32-round 57-millimeter rocket pods, and at least four antitank or antiaircraft missiles. The Hinds had moved into staggered trail position, one behind the other, with the first and third helicopters a bit higher than the others—it was a classic head-on attack formation, in which the first and third helicopters act as spotters and the second and fourth act as shooters, presenting the smallest possible profile to guard against missile attack.

"It's a rocket-and-strafing-attack formation, Ambassador," Jurgensen said. "We've got to do something!"

"You cannot attack, Major," Reynolds said, almost pleading. "I understand what you're feeling—I'm a lawyer and an ambassador now, but I *was* a Marine. If those helicopters goad you into attacking first, they can slaughter everyone inside this compound and reduce this embassy to rubble—and they would be entirely within their rights to do so, acting in self-defense. Legally, you cannot even raise those Stinger missiles at them—that can be construed as an act of war in itself! If they photographed you doing that and published the photos, we would all be out of a job."

"Fuck, fuck, fuck!" The Marine major had never felt so hamstrung in his entire life. "I am not taking my Stinger crews off watch—I don't care what happens to me, but those Stingers are our only hope against helicopter gunships."

The Hinds were in optimal Stinger-missile range—it was now or never.

Jurgensen got on the radio. "All units, now set condition green. Do *not* attack. No one opens fire unless I give the order. Repeat, no one opens fire unless I give the order." To Reynolds, he said, "There's nothing that says I can't launch my Sea Cobras, is there?"

"We have permission to overfly Lithuania, Major," Reynolds said. "You can do whatever you want with the Cobras. But the same rules apply—no one can fire unless fired upon. I would, uh, recommend that you follow international aviation rules as well." Reynolds couched that last warning in less definite tones, because those Soviet-made helicopters were getting real close real fast, and Reynolds didn't want to risk talking Jurgensen out of *not* launching the Sea Cobra gunships.

No danger of that right now. "I'm sick of following rules right now, Ambassador," Jurgensen said. On the radio, he ordered: *"Rattlers only,* repeat, *Rattlers only,* now set condition yellow and launch. I want you to tail those Hinds. Do not attack unless fired upon first. Repeat, *do not open fire unless fired on first."* Jurgensen studied the inbound attack helicopters with his binoculars, then handed the binoculars to Reynolds. "Sir, tell me if you can make out that flag on the second helicopter. It looks like a tricolor, but I can't make it out."

Reynolds took the binoculars and peered intently at the gunships. "I can't see the colors yet. All of the republics' flags except Moldova and Georgia have horizontal bars, but I can't tell if this is from Russia or—"

"Please keep looking. We have to identify them." Reynolds was more than happy to be asked to participate—it was just like the old days in Vietnam.

The Sea Cobras, which had just completed engine start, were beginning to spin their rotors up to lift-off speed when someone shouted, "Missiles in the air! Missiles in the air!"

Jurgensen's worst fears had come true.

The number-two Hind-D gunship had fired two fast-moving missiles toward the embassy—not the laser-guided AT-6 "Spiral" or radio-controlled AT-3 "Sagger" antitank missiles that he was expecting, but smaller, faster SA-7 "Grail" heat-seeking missiles. One Sea Cobra helicopter lifted off and skidded right, and a missile missed it by several yards, but the second Sea Cobra was still on the ground, not yet up to lift-off speed, when the SA-7 missile slammed into the rotor and exploded. The helicopter ripped apart like a burst balloon, the blast and fireball so intense that Jurgensen and Reynolds, both at least four hundred feet away, could feel the heat.

"All units, *open fire!* Now set condition *red* and *open fire!*" Jurgensen screamed into his radio as he and the ambassador dove for cover behind a thick concrete planter box. "All units, *open fire!*"

The first salvo of Stinger missiles launched by the embassy Marines took several seconds to react, but at about a half-mile range, two missiles screamed into the sky.

Seconds after they were launched, the Hind helicopters let loose a salvo of 57-millimeter rocket fire on those same positions, uprooting trees and blasting the embassy wall apart.

One Stinger missile hit, blowing out an engine in the number-two Hind-D, and the huge machine wobbled, spun nearly in a complete circle, and descended rapidly, but managed to keep on flying until it landed with an incredible crash and a cartwheel onto the embassy grounds, finally coming to rest in a fiery ball near the broken Super Stallion helicopter. The fire from the Hind immediately threatened to set the CH-53E on fire, but all Jurgensen's Marines were occupied with the air raid and could not put it out.

The second Stinger launched did not hit, but was decoyed away by bright magnesium flares dropped from the Soviet-made helicopters.

The number-four Hind-D gunship had one target only—the Super Stallion and SEA HAMMER aircraft. With rockets and cannon fire, both aircraft disappeared in blinding bursts of fire. The gunners did not waste one rocket or one shell—every round hit home with pinpoint accuracy.

The number-one and number-three Hind-D helicopters immediately peeled left and pursued the AH-1 Sea Cobra. Although the Sea Cobra was faster and more maneuverable, it could not get into proper attack position before one of the eight SA-7 missiles launched from the two Hind-Ds hit. Jurgensen did not see the hit—he saw the Hinds move away, saw the missiles fly, and lost contact with Rattler Four. After that all he saw was a column of black smoke several miles away.

The attack was over almost as soon as it began. The other two Stinger missile crews never got clean shots off at the attackers before they disappeared, so they saved their weapons for the next attack. The first two Soviet attackers were obviously under strict orders not to attack the embassy structure itself, because except for the rocket attack against the two Stinger positions and the attacks against the helicopters on the ground, nothing else was struck.

In the space of thirty seconds, four aircraft had been destroyed, with a loss to the Soviets of only one helicopter.

Jurgensen and Reynolds both looked at the devastation around them with stunned expressions. Where once they were surrounded by well-groomed, shady trees, and green grass, it was all obscured by clouds of thick, oily smoke and debris. The cries of "Help! Over here!" and "Medic! Corpsman!" shook Jurgensen out of his stupor. On his walkie-talkie, he ordered, "Radio, send a priority-one message to the Twenty-sixth and advise them that the embassy came under attack by four Hind-D helicopter gunships. Casualties unknown but light. Moderate damage to embassy. Four Marine helicopters destroyed. One Soviet helicopter down—"

"Make that a Byelorussian helicopter," Ambassador Reynolds interjected.

"Stand by, Radio," Jurgensen said. To Reynolds, he asked, "Are you sure, Mr. Ambassador?"

"I got a good look at the two that chased the Cobra," Reynolds said. "I'm positive—the bastards that did this were from Byelorussia. The Byelorussian flag is the only one that has a vertical bar on the staff side as well as horizontal bars."

"How can you tell if they were Byelorussian or representing the Commonwealth?"

"Commonwealth aircraft from the various republics, except for Russia, have a large white diamond painted around their national flags or insignia," Reynolds said. "That allows easy identification from the air and ground, and allows aircraft to freely fly over foreign airspace. There wasn't a white diamond around those flags. They could be Russian, but the glimpses of the colors in the insignia said they weren't. They were Byelorussian. I'm positive."

"Radio, append to message: identification of helicopter gunships verified by Ambassador Reynolds to be from Byelorussia, repeat, *Byelorussia*. One gunship crashed in the embassy compound; we will examine the wreckage to verify country of origin. Send it."

Jurgensen was on his way down to direct his Marines to extinguish the fire around the downed Hind when his walkie-talkie buzzed again. "Sir, message in the clear from Amos One-Zero." Amos was the call sign of the Army Special Forces troops scattered throughout Lithuania in support of this embassy-evacuation-and-reinforcement operation. "They report troops on the move, at least a brigade, traveling west at high speed from the Byelorussian military base at Smorgon." Smorgon, an Army Aviation base in northwestern Byelorussia, was only thirty nautical miles from the Lithuanian border and only fifty-five miles from Vilnius. "Transmission ended during report of precise troop strength. Amos Ten reported fourteen rotary-wing aircraft inbound before transmission terminated."

"Copy all," Jurgensen replied. *Jesus fucking Christ—the Byelorussians are going to do it—they are going to invade Lithuania. All the troop movements, the reinforcements, the maneuvering we've seen and had been reported was all a prelude to this. Of all the fucking days, they had to choose this day to roll their armies across Lithuania.*

"Clear a direct scrambled priority channel to the Twenty-sixth MEU, urgent, and radio a warning message to the Assault team over at Fisikous. Looks like their ride's been canceled. Advise them of the air activity inbound. Tell them to hotfoot it over to the embassy as fast as they can, by whatever means possible. Send it."

NATIONAL MILITARY COMMAND CENTER, THE PENTAGON
12 APRIL, 2202 ET (13 APRIL, 0402 VILNIUS)

General Wilbur Curtis was surprised to see Brad Elliott dressed in a flight suit when he walked into the Pentagon's National Military Command Center. "We going flying, Brad?" Curtis asked slyly.

Elliott respectfully stood when Curtis entered the room, but did not reply. His features were taut, his jaw and lips firm. Curtis thought Elliott was in pain but knew better—he was angry. Really angry.

Curtis found the three-star chief of HAWC in the Support Section of the Command Center, the large, auditorium-like conference room where the Joint Chiefs of Staff and their staffs managed combat operations around the world. The Support Section was a soundproof, glass-enclosed balcony overlooking the main Command Section, used by observers and secondary staff members as necessary; it could be isolated from the main floor by closing the remote-controlled shutters. Right now the Support Section's window shutters were open, so Elliott could see the Big Board, the Command Display System, a set of eight huge digital-computer screens on which the whole spectrum of information, from real-time satellite imagery to checklists to television to digitized charts, could be displayed. The board was displaying a few charts of the Baltic Sea region, Lithuania, the capital city of Vilnius, and some weather depictions.

Curtis waved Elliott back to his seat and dismissed the one command-center staff officer assigned to escort Elliott. "How you doing, Brad?" he asked.

"I've done better," Elliott admitted tightly.

"You didn't check in for the last few situation updates. I guess I know why now. You should tell me when you're on your way to Washington."

"We need to cut the small talk here, sir."

"Don't call me 'sir,' Brad," Curtis said, still trying to inject a little humor into the situation. "You know better." Elliott only scowled at his superior officer. This was the showdown that he had been dreading, Curtis thought. *Might as well get it over with . . .* "What do you do, Brad, when a man you thought you knew for years isn't the same guy anymore? I've seen men change—war, promotion, demotion, disillusionment, anger, joy—but some guys you think are old enough or experienced enough to never change."

"I'm not sure if I know *you* at all, *sir,"* Elliott said bitterly. "Suddenly it seems as if the whole military establishment is just shuffling its feet."

"Not really, Brad . . ." offered Curtis.

"What is it, General Curtis? Is it the end of the Cold War? The peace dividend? Has the military's will been cut along with its budget? No one seems to have any sense of what's right or what's wrong. I get the feeling you're just letting my people hang in the wind out there in Lithuania. No support. No backup. No options. I trusted Lockhart and Kundert—I trusted *you*—to protect them."

"They're being protected, Brad," Curtis said patiently. "The Twenty-sixth MEU is the best special-operations-capable unit in the Marine Corps. Your officers will be just fine."

"While Lithuania burns down around them," Elliott said. "I get MIL-STAR data just like the other units in the field do, Wilbur. The team's in trouble. They lost one SEA HAMMER and the other one's damaged. I saw something else about President Svetlov on the board, so I assume he knows about the operation and very well might be responding."

"Good observations," Curtis said, "and all true."

"Then what in hell are you doing about it?" Elliott exploded. "I haven't seen any other mobilizations since this operation began. Have you sent in the rest of the Twenty-sixth MEU? I've heard nothing from the First Marine Expeditionary Force, nothing from Third Army, nothing from the Air Battle Force. What will the President do if something blows up in Lithuania, Wilbur? If something happens, it'll take hours until a sizable force can react. You guys are just sitting on your hands."

"In fact, something has happened," Curtis said. "We've detected the Byelorussians moving on Vilnius. At least a brigade from the east and perhaps two or three battalions from the south."

"Shit. I knew it," Elliott cursed. He waved at the National Command Center down below—except for a few staffers and some maintenance personnel, the place was empty. "You haven't called in the battle staff? Who's running this show—announcers in the booth at RFK Stadium?" He paused, then narrowed his eyes at Curtis. "From the east? Smorgon? The Byelorussian Home Brigade has activated?"

"You know about the Home Brigade?"

"Dammit, Wilbur, of course I know!" Elliott said angrily. "It was one of *our* major targets. MADCAP MAGICIAN was going to send two platoons to take out the headquarters building and the command-and-control facility. My Megafortresses were going to make the building secondary targets. They have to be taken out if there's any threat of the Byelorussians getting involved, Wilbur—the rumor is that they've got nuclear-tipped Scarab missiles at Smorgon. I didn't want to go over the border, but if there's any possibility that they'd use those missiles, they have to be neutralized. Two SLAM cruise missiles against the power facility near the town, two more against the buildings themselves—"

"Christ, Brad." Curtis shook his head at Elliott's words. "You were going to have yourself a big day, weren't you? Billions of dollars' worth of destruction, all on *your* say-so."

"The employment of air power is an essential part of our national security," Elliott argued, "and it's part of my job as director of HAWC to plan, organize, and execute highly dangerous missions in order to safeguard—"

"Get off it, Brad. You've never used jingoistic prattle to justify yourself before, so don't start now," Curtis said. The Chairman of the Joint Chiefs shook his head and said, "Jesus, Brad, I never thought even *you* would have the audacity to invade another country without even notifying or clearing your operation with me or the White House."

"Hey, I briefed you on my plan, and I canceled it when you said no-go," Elliott said. "My hesitation will probably get Luger killed. You've left it wide open for the Byelorussians to attack Lithuania, but I'm doing as you ordered."

"In case you forgot, Brad, that's the way it's *supposed* to work," Curtis said. *"We're* supposed to give *you* orders, and *you* carry them out. Having military officers plan and execute military missions without government approval is what they do in military dictatorships and *coups d'état,* not in constitutional democracies."

"And our military leaders in Washington are not supposed to abandon American servicemen being tortured and imprisoned in foreign countries while in the service of their country," Elliott retorted, "unless the military leaders in charge have turned into political ass-kissers!"

"You can call me names all you want, you old fart," Curtis said. "You know I won't fire you—I'll leave that to the President, who's ready to do it at any moment now. But you can't just go off and build a brand-new Old Dog mission whenever you feel like it."

"Don't bring up that mission, Wilbur," Elliott said angrily. "You know the reason I did the Old Dog mission, along with the fact that I had the greatest crew a pilot could want, is that I thought we had seen the beginning of a new era. The new military. We were finally going to shoulder the responsibility that God gave us—protectors of freedom and democracy in the world. Libya, Grenada, the Middle East, the Philippines—things were changing. We were finally snapping out of our Vietnam funk. But then *you* abandon Dave Luger. You send a handful of troops into hostile territory to rescue him. Now you're abandoning Lithuania, and possibly the rest of the Baltic states."

"Everyone wishes they could simply launch a bunch of high-tech B-52s and bomb the bad guys," Curtis said. "Unfortunately, it's not that easy. The civilian leadership in this country has more to account for than one man's guilt and ego."

"Guilt? Ego? What are you talking about?"

"I'm talking about you, Brad," Curtis said. "You wear the Old Dog mission on your chest like a medal. It's a chip on your shoulder that you dare everyone to knock off. Your artificial leg is some kind of monument to a mission *that you screwed up.*"

"I didn't screw up a thing, Curtis! We accomplished the mission! We got Kavaznya!"

"You bombed the target because you had professionals like McLanahan and Luger and Tork and Pereira and Ormack on board," Curtis said. "You were out of it: in pain and shock for most of the mission, half-unconscious during the bomb run, and completely unconscious after you left Anadyr. You weren't even at the controls after the refueling at Anadyr—McLanahan, an untrained radar navigator, brought that bomber home! You didn't contribute to the mission—in fact you nearly killed everyone on that mission and started World War Three *yourself!*"

"You don't know what you're talking about!" Elliott said, so angry, so flustered, that he could barely respond. "You weren't there . . ."

"I reread the Defense Intelligence Agency's analysis of the mission, Brad," Curtis went on. "I reread the testimony from the other crew members. Everyone on that crew, *everyone,* thought the mission should have been aborted because of the damage to the aircraft and because of your worsening condition. You had no charts, no helmets, no classified documents, no safety equipment. The mission should have been aborted. But you said 'go' . . ."

"We made that decision together, as a crew."

"What did you expect your crew to say, Brad? Did you really expect them to quit? McLanahan, the best bombardier in the whole damned world? Luger, probably the best navigator in the world? Ormack, a deskbound frustrated war hero? No way, Brad. None of them would quit.

"It was up to you to abort the mission. As aircraft commander and mission commander, it was *your* responsibility. But there's no glory in quitting, is there? You don't get any respect by turning back."

"You're dreaming, Curtis. That's not how it was."

"What would you get if you turned back? Nothing. Dreamland was blown wide open after the terrorist attack. They would have closed it forever. You'd be out of a job and probably forced to retire. If you went ahead and got killed during the mission, you'd be a hero—a dead hero, but still a hero. But if you succeeded, you'd be set for life. You'd be the one who fought off the Soviets and won. Beginning of the end of the Cold War. Champion of democracy over communism. Defender of the faith. Unfortunately you didn't think about your crew. What if they got killed? You didn't care what happened to them—you only thought about *your-self."*

"Bullshit . . ." Elliott said in almost a whisper. His eyes no longer bored into Curtis's, but were vacant, far away . . .

"You killed Dave Luger, Brad," Curtis said. "You put the crew into a situation where one man had to sacrifice his life to save yours. Your fault. No one else's. Did you ever wonder why you never got a decoration after the Old Dog mission, why McLanahan, an O-3 senior navigator, got the Air Force Cross, while you, an O-9 command pilot, got a Distinguished Service Medal?" The sudden pain in Elliott's face told Curtis that he had just hit a very big, very painful nerve with him. Good . . . "It's because your role as commander of the Old Dog mission didn't stand up to scrutiny. There were too many questions about your judgment, your leadership.

"And look at what you're doing now. Six EB-52s ready to launch. MADCAP MAGICIAN, which I ordered you to stand down, is missing somewhere in the Baltic Sea. You're in your flight suit, trying to prove to me and to the White House that you mean business. You're not medically cleared for aviation duties, so there's no reason for you to be *in* a flight suit. Furthermore, you know as well as I that utility uniforms are not allowed to be worn in the Pentagon. But here you are, *wearing a flight suit.* It's nothing but a clown's costume you're wearing, Brad. It's pitiful. It's the mark of a tired old man afraid to die alone and unrecognized.

"You don't care about the consequences—war in Europe, a nuclear exchange between us, Byelorussia, and the Commonwealth. You don't care whose lives you waste as long as you get your chance to save the man that saved your ass. You probably have Wendy Tork and Angelina Pereira in one of those EB-52s, don't you?"

"I . . . they said they wanted to serve, wanted to go . . ."

"You sonofabitch," Curtis exploded. "How dare you risk their lives again like that? What would you do if they died on this mission? Or didn't that matter to you? As long as you got Dave, as long as you *tried* to get Dave, your conscience would be clear. You'd go to the funerals, say a few words, toss in the first handfuls of dirt into the grave, then congratulate yourself on staying alive."

"Is that what you think I do?" Elliott retorted, his eyes suddenly shiny in the light of the Support Section. "Do you think I lie awake all these years since that mission, congratulating myself because I made it out alive? Those faces haunt me, Wilbur."

"So you think taking your flight suit and your crews and your Mega-fortresses and going off to war, with or without permission from the government, is going to help you sleep at night, Brad? Think about it, dammit. Think about what's gnawing at you. Success or failure isn't the issue. You have always been a success. But you've always been alone, also. You're a loner afraid of being alone. You're a warrior afraid of dying.

"Look at what's happening here, Brad. General Voshchanka of the Byelorussian Army Home Brigade is ready to occupy Lithuania, on his own authority. No permission from his government—he just fucking decided he was going to do it. Svetlov had no choice but to agree to the operation. Svetlov now has to be spoon-fed by Voshchanka on what to say and how to act, or Voshchanka has, I'm sure, threatened to take over the capital.

"Now, just about the same time we decry that action and think about countering Voshchanka's aggression, here we've got *you* doing the very same damned thing," Curtis went on. "What's the President supposed to do? How's he supposed to react? When I tell the President that I have control and you will calm down and do as you're ordered, what sort of guarantees does he have that you'll behave? None, that's what!"

"My job is not to *behave,* General," Elliott said. "My job is to plan, prepare, and execute—"

"Your job is to follow orders and obey the law!"

"All right, Wilbur, all right. If you think it's necessary, I'll admit that I assembled an assault team without consulting the Pentagon and I was going to execute a military operation without permission. Let the legal weasels decide if it was legal or not. But let's not waste time arguing that. Let's do something to get Ormack, Briggs, McLanahan, Luger, and those Marines out of Lithuania—right *now.*"

"What you *will* do, General Elliott," Curtis said angrily, "is tell me the precise location of each and every element of your assault team—especially MADCAP MAGICIAN. Since I gave you an order to recover that vessel to port, it hasn't been seen or heard from."

"I ordered that ship to withdraw, and it did."

"You stretched the meaning of my orders to you," Curtis said, "and I'll bet you told Colonel White to lay low someplace in the Baltic, within striking range of Vilnius. Just another example of your blatant disregard for my orders.

"You will sit down on the MILSTAR channel with representatives of European Command in Germany and with the Twenty-sixth MEU aboard the USS *Wasp* and describe your mission, reveal where the SS

Valley Mistress is located, and explain in detail exactly what you intended to do with MADCAP MAGICIAN. And you'd better be truthful and up front with me and with everyone in my chain of command. I think it's about time you stopped playing lone wolf and started acting like a true United States military officer, General, or by God I'll put you in hack myself."

"Don't Dave Luger and the others mean anything to you, Wilbur?" Elliott asked. His eyes were softer, his voice pleading. "I have the ability to help. I have the capability to hold off a Byelorussian invasion. I have a deniable, powerful, stealthy assault team ready to roll, and I have my neck on the chopping block stretched to the maximum. Doesn't any of that matter to you?"

"Yes, it does." Curtis sighed. "You have a lot to contribute. Everyone recognizes your potential, even the President. But no one likes a loose cannon. Your plan is to be implemented immediately, and your aircraft will be directed to launch and execute their assigned mission. But I'll be the one giving the orders, with the full sanction of the National Command Authority."

"My plan—what?"

"It's what I've been trying to tell you ever since I pinned on your third star, Brad," Curtis said. "You can be a real asset to this government and to the country, but you've got serious internal conflicts that need to be resolved. I used to think it was just a huge chip on your shoulder, but now I think it's more . . . you really walk on the edge.

"Now you've got the only small, heavy attack group that's mobilized and ready to act. You're out of the picture, but your team's been activated. The Megafortresses launch immediately. They've got full MIL-STAR and NIRTSat access, and MADCAP MAGICIAN is cleared in-country. You and I will watch from the Command Center here and pray we're not too late."

Elliott couldn't believe it. After this major ass-chewing, the National Command Authority—the President—was actually sanctioning his mission!

FISIKOUS RESEARCH CENTER, VILNIUS, LITHUANIA
13 APRIL, 0407 VILNIUS (12 APRIL, 2207 ET)

"Choppers inbound!" the radioman shouted. "Take cover!"

A small convoy of trucks and armored vehicles were at the Denerokin gate to the Fisikous compound, heading out to evacuate the Marines to the embassy across town when someone in the truck's cab shouted the warning. Hal Briggs and John Ormack, flanking Dave Luger in the back of a Yugoslavian-made truck, were nearly knocked to the ground when the alarm was sounded and Marines started jumping off the truck and scattering—they didn't even wait for the trucks to come to a stop. The Air Force officers followed. With Luger between them, Ormack and Briggs dashed a few hundred yards clear of the twenty-vehicle convoy, toward the relative safety of a line of low wood-and-brick storage sheds. McLanahan and Gunnery Sergeant Wohl were right behind them, carrying four heavy canvas sacks filled with classified manuals and other documents taken from the design-center security building.

"For a minute I actually thought we were going to make it," Luger said, sounding defeated. But at least he was looking better the closer they got to the gate and freedom. His left shoulder was heavily bandaged, his skin devoid of any healthy color, and his arms and legs shook from pain and weariness, but otherwise he was acting stronger and moving with very little help.

"We *will* make it, bro," Briggs said. "You just hang in there." Briggs was carrying an M-16, and he had it raised to the gradually dawning sky along with the other Marines surrounding them—as with the others, he assumed any aerial assault would come at them from the east, with the sun at the backs of the attacking pilots. McLanahan and Ormack carried only sidearms and knives—they were still not allowed to carry any weapons that might harm a nearby Marine if used improperly.

They saw the Marines' response before they saw the threat—a flash of light and a streak of smoke arced toward the horizon as a Marine, one of six still on the roof of the design-center security facility building, fired a man-portable Stinger at the incoming enemy helicopters. Their eyes followed the missile's smoke trail, and they saw three huge Soviet-made helicopters, now in steep bank turns, ejecting missile-decoying flares.

"Shit," Wohl cursed, "who told that guy to launch a missile? Snyder must be getting antsy. Now those things will be after us like stink on shit."

"They look like Mil-24 Hind-Ds," McLanahan said. "Rocket pods and antitank or heat-seeking missiles."

"Just keep your heads down and don't fire that rifle," Gunnery Sergeant Wohl said. "If they see the muzzle flash, we're all dead meat."

"What do we do? Run?"

"We make like we're not here," Wohl said. "If they don't find any more resistance, they'll go after the trucks and hopefully leave after reconnoitering the area. If they try to land or unload paratroopers or infantry, we'll go after them then—those things are very vulnerable on the ground. Otherwise we're no match for attack helicopters." Wohl was already thinking attack even as the big assault helicopters moved closer, their array of weapons hanging from the winglike weapons pylons now clearly visible.

Sure enough, all three Hind-Ds managed to evade the Stinger fired at them and continued their run toward the Institute. They opened fire at about five hundred yards' range with rockets and machine-gun fire, one after another, slicing the truck convoy apart with ease.

"They didn't go after the Marines on the roof," Briggs observed.

"They must have orders not to shoot the place up, to pick their targets carefully," Wohl said. *"Now* I hope Snyder attacks—"

Sure enough, a few seconds later the Marines launched a second Stinger at the trailing helicopter, and this time the tiny missile flew straight into an engine exhaust baffle and exploded. The helicopter's huge rotor simply stopped turning when the missile hit, engulfing the entire fuselage with fire, and the machine dropped out of the air like a poorly punted football wobbling through the air. It crashed just a few hundred yards outside the Denerokin security gate, near the railroad yards.

"Got one!" Briggs shouted.

"That was our last Stinger," Wohl said. "Those flyboys will be pissed now. Get ready to run if they come after us. Try to find a cellar or an open door. Stay out of the open."

The first two helicopters swooped in over the base, and the destruction really started.

Despite their enormous size, the Soviet-made helicopters wheeled and moved with incredible speed and agility. These older-model helicopters had a Gatling-style gun in a chin turret, and the gun seemed to move in every direction at once. Every time a man moved, the turret turned in his direction and let loose with a one- or two-second burst. The flimsy wood-and-brick buildings they were hiding behind were barely enough to protect them.

The Byelorussian crews saved their 57-millimeter rockets for the armored vehicles and heavy trucks, and they rarely missed—every long, low *whoosh!* was followed a split second later by a powerful explosion and the crunch of steel. Trying to return fire with rifles was as fruitless as it was dangerous—the big helicopters moved like prizefighters, darting up and down, wheeling and spinning and darting back and forth, exposing first a door gunner, then the chin turret, then a rocket pod, then another door gunner to threats.

The crews aboard those enemy choppers were good—very good.

The Lithuanian soldiers kept the situation from turning into a bloodbath. Just one of their ZSU-23-4 antiaircraft-artillery units was operational, and it had only a small amount of ammunition remaining, but a single two-second burst of fire from the deadly weapon was enough. The burst from the Lithuanians' ZSU-23-4 hit the hub of the lead Mil-24's tail rotor, causing smoke to stream from the tail. It had obviously hit something vital, because the Hind-D did not try to attack the ZSU-23-4—it wheeled away and climbed, escaping while it could still fly.

A Lithuanian soldier was sprinting across the road near where Wohl, Briggs, McLanahan, Ormack, and Luger were hiding. McLanahan stepped forward away from the building they were hiding behind and yelled, "Hey! Over here!"

Gunnery Sergeant Wohl grabbed McLanahan by the jacket and dragged him back to cover. "Get back here, McLanahan!"

But Wohl's warning was too late. The second Hind-D spotted the soldier, and the Gatling gun chattered. The soldier's entire torso exploded like a rotting pumpkin hit by a baseball bat.

The helicopter wheeled to the left and took aim at the maintenance building. Like kicking down a sand castle a bit at a time, the maintenance shed the five men were hiding behind began to disintegrate around them under a sudden barrage of gunfire.

Wohl grabbed the three officers and yelled at them over the roar of the helicopter's rotors, "Run!"

McLanahan, by force of habit, automatically picked up the two canvas bags full of documents, but Wohl knocked them out of his hands and with surprising strength, fueled by fear, pushed McLanahan away from the building and yelled, "Leave the damn bags and *run!*"

Their brief but intense Marine Corps training paid off, because none of those three healthy Air Force officers could remember running faster in their lives, even carrying Luger between them.

The maintenance shed disappeared in a blinding cloud of smoke and flying wood seconds after they darted away. The rotor wash of the second chopper started to tug at their clothing—it was as if the big attack helicopter were hovering right over them, sucking them into cannon range, ready to pluck them off their feet. Bullets flew past their heads, snapped at their feet, churned up dirt directly in front of them as they zigzagged away, not knowing or caring where they were running. It was as if the gunners were toying with them, playing a deadly cat-and-mouse game. When they tired of the game, they would simply pick a weapon and do away with them.

Their headlong run to find shelter was short because they ran right into a deep, wide concrete ditch that surrounded the base just inside the tall perimeter fence. Half-tripping, half-tumbling, they threw themselves down into the ditch, their fall cushioned only by a few inches of mud and water. On the other side of the twenty-foot-wide ditch was the twelve-foot-high concrete-reinforced perimeter fence: trapped.

The big Hind-D headed right for them, no more than twenty or thirty feet high, and at a relatively slow speed.

The door gunners could not miss . . .

"No!" Briggs shouted. As the Hind cruised overhead, he raised his rifle, squinted against the rotor wash and flying debris, and fired. The star-

board-side door gunner clutched his chest, flew backwards into the helicopter, and then lurched forward again, hanging dead from his safety
harness in the slipstream.

The helicopter careened overhead, the sound so deafening and so tremendous that it seemed to suck the air right out of their lungs.

Briggs kept on firing, trying to hit the tail rotor, the engines, something
vital.

The helicopter banked left, rolled out, and banked again as if it were
unsure about what to do; then it banked slightly right and headed east-
ward. The other stricken helicopter followed a few moments later, and
together they retreated off toward the gradually brightening dawn.

The group spent a few minutes just catching their breath and waiting
for their pounding hearts to calm down before attempting to move.
Finally they began to show signs of life. "Jesus . . . Oh, Jesus," Briggs
gasped. "Man, that was close."

"Good shooting, Briggs," Wohl said. "That took guts. You can fire
when you feel it's necessary from now on, okay?"

Briggs was shaking too badly from their close call to respond.

"Everybody else okay?" asked Wohl. No one had suffered anything
more than a twisted ankle or banged elbow, and they were on their feet
and moving. "All right. Let's get back to the security building as fast as
we can and—"

"*Stoy!*" a voice behind them shouted in Russian. "*Nyee dveghightyes!
Nyee dveghightyes!*"

Dave Luger froze immediately and placed his hands on top of his head.

"What did he say?" Ormack asked. "Who is it?"

"He said 'stop' and 'don't move,' " Wohl said. "Briggs, drop the rifle.
Raise your hands."

"All right—who the hell are you guys?" The voice had changed from
a gruff, deep-throated warning tone with a Russian accent into a relaxed,
old-fashioned Brooklyn accent. The five men turned around to find a
single man, dressed in dark-blue coveralls, carrying a short automatic
pistol that resembled an Uzi with a long, thick suppressor attached.

"Wohl, Chris R."

"Marines?"

Wohl nodded and the man lowered the gun. "Gladden, Edward G.,
U.S. Army. Welcome to Lithuania. Having fun yet?"

Luger found himself giggling so hard from the stress that he could not
stop until Briggs patted him on the back. "Has the Army invaded Lithuania?" Ormack asked.

"I'm part of one of the A-Teams, stationed here to observe and assist,"
Gladden replied. "We were moving towards your convoy to see if we
could hitch a ride out of here when the helicopters attacked. That fucking

Hind almost crashed on top of my hiding place in the railyard. I figured with a downed chopper nearby that there were going to be too many soldiers snooping around, so I thought it was a good time to join the real world and maybe hitch a ride home. My partner is watching the airport side." He motioned toward the Air Force officers. "Who are *you* guys? You don't look like Marines."

"That's classified," Wohl said immediately. "They belong to me. How many more Special Forces guys out there?"

"Maybe a company altogether, scattered between Kaunas and the Byelorussian border," Gladden replied, pulling a cigarette from a pocket and lighting it. McLanahan could practically taste the acid in the smoke of the Russian cigarette from ten feet away. "Let's go talk to your CO about getting out of here."

"You have a plan?"

"We always got a plan," Gladden said proudly. "Lead on." As they headed back toward the security building, Luger asked Gladden a question in Russian. Gladden smiled, nodded, and responded in easy, fluent Russian.

"Button it," Wohl warned Luger. To Gladden, he asked, "What was that all about?"

"Your friend said that my parents must've had a real sense of humor to give their son initials like 'E.G.G.'" Gladden said. "I agreed. They teach you Marines pretty good Russian."

"He's not a Marine," Wohl said, "and I'd appreciate your not talking to them."

"Are they your prisoners?"

"They're pains in the ass, is what they are." But Wohl's smile made the Army Special Forces soldier even more confused.

"Through the sewers?" Snyder asked incredulously. "That's your big plan? You want us to get out through the *sewers?*"

Gladden was stuffing his face with Lithuanian black bread and brown honey, given to him by some of Palcikas' men, as if it were the first real food he had eaten in days—which it was. "Yes, sir, that's right," he mumbled between bites. "We discovered the link a few days ago, in preparation for your mission; we reported it to U.S. European Command, but I guess the word never got to you Marines. There's almost a direct line that runs under the city from Fisikous, downhill all the way, and comes out on the south side of the Neris River, right near the Vilniaus Bridge. You sneak across the bridge on the service catwalk—it's not lighted and very lightly patrolled after two A.M. or so—and you're in the City of Progress. One mile west on Okmerges Avenue and you're at the embassy. Or just jump in the river and swim towards the other side—it's only a thousand meters wide. By the time you make it across, the current has taken you right to the embassy docks opposite Tartybu Street."

"Is it safe down in the sewers?" Trimble asked. "What about untreated waste or chemicals?" The thought of swimming in shit or nuclear waste made him wince.

"Bastards that run Fisikous have probably been dumping contaminated water down that line for years, but we tested it and there's no harmful radioactivity," Gladden continued. "Most of the really bad sewers are farther west—we just have to contend with shit from the railroad yard, but that dilutes out after a few blocks. It's slippery, it smells like shit, and sewage is ankle-deep in some places, but you have plenty of chances to get fresh air through storm drains, so it's not too bad. Best of all, it's safe and fast."

"Is it big enough for us to carry wounded down there?"

"It's a tight squeeze for about twenty blocks north of Fisikous until we get to Traky Avenue—a single sixty-inch main, hunchback city for about three miles—but north of there to the river it's at least an eighty-inch main, and under Gedimino Boulevard it's practically Grand Central Station. My partner and I ride bicycles down there to get around, and we've taken shopping carts and little wagons down there to move our gear—"

"Okay, okay, Sergeant," Snyder interrupted. *This guy's been down in the sewer too long,* Snyder thought. "We've got wounded and dead to evacuate. Still think it's practical?"

"It'll take you a long time, sir, maybe three or four hours, until you can carry your wounded upright," Gladden said. "It's clean with all the winter runoff, and it's not flooded, but if you can wrap your wounded in plastic and blankets or a body bag it'd be better. But, yes, sir, I'd say it's double."

"All right," Snyder said. He thought about it for a moment. He had a momentary fear when he thought about traveling across the city in a small, dark, confining tube several yards underground, but the thought of facing those attack helicopters wasn't very appealing either. "We'll take the sewers, but not everybody's going to go that way," Snyder said. "The enemy will be expecting us to make a break for the embassy, and if they don't see activity in the streets they'll start looking for us in other places. I don't want to get caught in a firefight in the damned sewers.

"We'll split up. The dead, the seriously wounded, and some of the team will go by truck. Some team members will go by separate vehicles by parallel routes to cover the trucks. We'll take the walking wounded and the rest through the sewers, including the zoomies and the documents."

He turned to General Palcikas, who had been receiving a report from his radioman—a new one, Snyder saw. The other man was nowhere to be seen. "Sir, where is your other radioman?"

"Dead," Palcikas replied. "He shielded me with his body during air raid."

"I'm very sorry, sir," Snyder said. It was hard for Snyder to express any real emotions right now—he had seen more death that day than he had ever thought he would in a lifetime. "We will try again to take a convoy out of the Fisikous compound, but this time I'd like three separate convoys, taking parallel routes to guard each other's flank."

"I agree," the Lithuanian general said. "We have been in contact with many people . . . citizens . . . who will help now."

"Excellent," Snyder said. "What are your intentions, sir?"

"We will stay," Palcikas replied. "We will begin taking the ammunition from the security building and taking it to our underground cells in the city. I am in contact with my units across the country now, so I can direct defense from here. I deploy one battalion to oppose Commonwealth infantry base at Darguziai to south—they threaten capital first. One, maybe two companies to protect parliament building and communications center in capital. Then we fight the Byelorussian helicopters and infantry from Smorgon. Big battle tomorrow morning."

"I wish you luck, sir," Snyder said. "I will relay any requests you have to the U.S. Embassy, along with my full report on how you helped my unit."

"Pas deschaz," Palcikas said, waving a hand. "You help, I help. You good soldier. Good luck to you too."

"Thank you, sir." He turned to Gunny Trimble and said, "Pull out the maps and—"

"Captain, we're not going with you," John Ormack said.

Snyder turned toward the Air Force officers and flashed Ormack an angry glare, but acted as if he didn't hear what Ormack had said. "You're going with me, Ormack."

"That's *General* Ormack, Captain," Ormack said. Several of the Marines had encircled the group, wanting to hear more, and even Palcikas focused his attention on Ormack, a slightly amused smile on his face. Snyder turned and looked at Ormack in surprise and disbelief. "And I told you, Captain, we're not going back to the embassy with you. Not *yet.*"

Now Snyder was really angry, and Trimble looked twice as angry as his superior. "You have no choice in the matter, *General.* You are assigned to my unit. You have no authority to make decisions."

"I'm taking the authority right now," Ormack said. "Your orders were to break inside Fisikous, find REDTAIL HAWK, and allow us to examine the classified material in this place. Well, REDTAIL HAWK's been located, but we haven't seen what we want to see yet. As long as General Palcikas stays here at Fisikous, we're staying. We want to examine *Tuman,* the Fisikous-170 stealth bomber."

"*You* are trying to tell *me* what *my* orders are?" Snyder asked incredulously. "No goddamned way, Ormack. *I* am in charge of this detail. I make the decisions. If I say you go, you will go. If I have to put you in handcuffs and hogtie you, I'll do it. You can squawk all you want to the brass after we get home, but if I accomplish my mission successfully, nobody will say boo to me. Now I want you to pick up your damned classified and get ready to move out."

"For the last time, Snyder—we're not leaving," Ormack said finally. He motioned to McLanahan, Briggs, and Luger, and they stepped away from the circle of troops and headed for the parking-ramp area and aircraft hangars. "We'll be in the third hangar examining the bomber—"

"Gunny Trimble, put those four men in irons," Snyder said. *"Drag* them to the sewer manhole if you have to." Trimble was moving before Snyder finished speaking. He was smart—he reached for Hal Briggs first. Hal was ready for him. With a twist and a swing of his right arm, Briggs threw off Trimble's grasp. With a low cry, Trimble leaped on Briggs, trying to drive him to the ground . . .

Suddenly a hand clutched his jacket, and Trimble found himself being lifted away from Briggs as if hooked on to a hydraulic crane . . .

It was General Dominikas Palcikas who had hold of Gunnery Sergeant Trimble. The big Lithuanian officer had no difficulty restraining Trimble. The other four or five Marines in the group were too stunned to move, hesitant to gang up on any officer, including a foreigner on his own soil.

"I think that is enough," Palcikas said. As if he were separating two squabbling children, he firmly but gently shoved Trimble away. "You may not do this."

"General Palcikas, what in hell are you doing?" Snyder said. One hand slipped down to his holster. Palcikas saw the move, but only smiled. Snyder changed his mind. "Gunny, carry out your order."

Trimble tried to push past Palcikas, but the Lithuanian general stepped in between him and the Air Force officers. It was obvious from Trimble's eyes that he was deciding the best way to take out Palcikas, but instead of reacting he shouted, "Out of my way, son of a bitch!"

"This general has given you your orders, Sergeant."

"I don't take orders from him!" Trimble shouted. At that moment Trimble reached into his holster to draw his .45 . . .

. . . And Palcikas' Makarov was in his face long before his fingers touched the leather, the muzzle barely three inches from his forehead. A few Marines surrounding the group began to unsling rifles from their shoulders or draw pistols, but the Lithuanian soldiers with them already had their AK-47s at the ready—they were not aiming them at the Marines, but held them at port arms, fingers on the trigger guards. The threat was clear.

"Enough," Palcikas said sternly. He raised the muzzle of his pistol and released the hammer. It had grown quiet enough around that spot that the *click* of the hammer being lowered was clearly audible. None of the other Lithuanians moved; neither did the Marines.

"General Palcikas, what do you think you're doing?" Snyder asked. "I gave an order. These men belong to me."

"My English poor," Palcikas said, "but this man"—he pointed to Ormack with his Makarov pistol before holstering it—"is general officer, no? He gives orders. You obey."

"Not in this operation," Snyder said. "In this operation, I'm in command."

"You in command of Marines. These men not Marines. You in command because he say you in command, because you *kvalifitsiravany rabochiv, spitsialistaf,* commando soldier. Now, he gives orders. He superior officer, *direktaram.* You obey."

"Listen, Snyder," Ormack said. "You're trying to get out because you're afraid of getting clobbered here. I understand that. You guys are special ops, and you got no odds in your favor so the best thing for you is to get the hell out. Well, we're not commandos like you. We're scientists and engineers and crew dogs. We've got to see that bomber."

"You're not safe here," Snyder insisted. "Can't you bastards see that? The Soviets can overrun this base in an instant."

"Yes, they can," McLanahan said, "but they haven't. They want this facility intact. General Palcikas said that ground units from Darguziai and Smorgon are on the way, and tonight or tomorrow the battle will be on. That means we have time to examine that stealth bomber."

"My orders are to take REDTAIL HAWK and the classified material."

"I know what your orders say, Captain," Ormack said, "but this is totally different. I'm amending your orders. I'm a general, and I say Briggs, McLanahan, Luger, and I stay and examine the bomber—"

"And I say you will follow my direction or—"

"I'm giving you a legal order, Captain," Ormack said sternly. "I'm a brigadier general of the United States Air Force. You're a captain in the United States Marine Corps. I'm giving you an order."

"You are not authorized to issue orders, Ormack," Snyder said. "And keep your voice down. You can't reveal any names here."

"You will not speak to me like that, Captain," Ormack said in a loud voice.

McLanahan looked on with complete surprise—they had never seen or even *imagined* John Ormack throwing his rank around like this!

"You will address me as 'sir' or 'general' from now on, and you will obey my orders or I'll prefer charges against you upon our return. You may think otherwise, but if you try to disobey my orders I'll see to it that you spend the next ten years in prison."

Snyder was too shocked to say anything for several seconds. He tried his best to think of something, *anything,* to retain his control of this operation, but nothing was happening. Ormack *was* a general, despite being nothing more than a passenger on this mission from day one. Snyder and his men could risk their lives getting them out, only to have their careers ruined in a court-martial. "What are you doing, General?" Snyder asked, hopelessly frustrated. "Why are you doing this . . . ?"

"The damned Marine Corps has done a good job making me feel like a second-class citizen in the past few weeks," Ormack went on angrily. "I know I can't run twenty miles, shoot an M-16, run obstacle courses, or kill someone with my bare hands like you guys can. In that time you made me feel inferior, even unworthy to wear a uniform. But all that doesn't mean that we suspend military discipline, the Constitution of the United States, and the Uniform Code of Military Justice. Your insubordination will end right here, right now."

"Insubordination!" gasped Snyder.

"Captain Snyder, *I order you* to take your men, your casualties, and those four bags of classified material and make your way via the fastest and the safest way you can devise back to the American Embassy," Ormack said, "where you will report to Ambassador Lewis Reynolds and give him a full report on your assigned mission and our activities here. Now, what's it going to be? Are you going to obey my orders or are you going to disobey them?"

"I can make a call to the embassy," Snyder said. "They can patch me in to General Kundert or General Lockhart."

"Then do it if you think you have the time," Ormack said. "In the meantime I've given you your orders. Carry them out."

Captain Edward Snyder, USMC, was practically dizzy from the confusion and surprise. Like a fistful of fine sand slipping through his fingers, it seemed as if his entire world was slipping out of his grasp. Gunnery Sergeant Trimble could not believe it when Snyder hesitated without saying a word. "Captain, you are in charge of this mission!" he said. "Tell these guys to get in line or I'll—"

"Oh, shut up, Gunny," Snyder said. He looked at Ormack with pure hatred in his eyes. "I've got my damned orders from the General here."

"I can call the embassy, sir. We'll get orders from headquarters—hell, we'll get the Commandant himself on the line."

"No, I said. We're going to follow orders. Mount up and let's get out of here."

"But, sir—"

"I said *mount up,* Gunny," Snyder snapped. He stepped toward Ormack, glared at Briggs and McLanahan, then stared Ormack directly in the face and said disgustedly, "I'm sick of you three. I'm tired of dragging you halfway around the world and risking my life so you three can play hero. I have just one request. A lot of good Marines risked their lives so you can come out here and play army. If you make it back alive, you will attend their funerals, kiss their widows and mothers, and pay your respects to them. No celebrating, no partying. All three of you. You say thank you to the Marines who got you here."

"We'll be there, Captain," Ormack said, staring dead-on at Snyder. "Now get out of here."

"Aye, aye, *sir,*" Snyder replied, his voice dripping with disgust. He saluted Ormack, his lips drawn into a tight grimace, his left fist balled at his side. Ormack did not return the salute. Snyder turned and walked away, his men falling in behind him.

The place felt very empty and quiet as the group of Marines headed off—until General Palcikas unexpectedly slapped Ormack on the shoulder and said with a broad smile, "Good job, General! I knew you be good leader! Generals must take command. Good job! We go look at strange Soviet bird now."

"We can do more than that," Luger said. "We can fly it out of here."

Heads turned toward Luger in surprise. McLanahan asked, "What? Is that true? Will it fly . . . ?"

"I've flown *Tuman* at least eight times . . . uh, that I can remember," Luger replied. "Sure, it'll fly." He looked at Snyder, then at Ormack, then at his friend and longtime partner, Patrick McLanahan, and grinned. "If they got any weapons still stashed here, we can even launch a few missiles and drop a few bombs."

"Then let's get over there," Ormack said, rubbing his hands together. "It's about time that we get out of these infantry duds and get our asses back into the air."

SIX

"First we're going to cut it off; then we're going to kill it."

—GENERAL COLIN POWELL, U.S. Army, on
the eve of Operation Desert Storm

OVER CENTRAL KALININ OBLAST, RUSSIAN REPUBLIC
13 APRIL, 0847 (1247 ET)

General Lieutenant Anton Voshchanka, flying in a Mil-8D assault/ transport helicopter configured as a flying command center and communications aircraft, saw plumes of smoke rising from Chernyakhovsk Air Base in central Kalinin. After ordering his pilot to descend and get closer for a better look—they were at four thousand meters altitude, near the maximum service ceiling of the heavily laden Mil-8 helicopter, to avoid sporadic ground fire from Russian infantry—he saw tanks on the airfield itself beginning to take up what appeared to be defensive positions around the air base's perimeter. There was no mistaking the identification of those tanks—old, slow T-60s of his Thirty-first Armored Brigade, punching through what was very determined resistance by front-line Russian T-72 and T-80 main battle tanks. "Status of the operation against Chernyakhovsk?" he asked his executive officer.

The executive officer relayed the question to the radio technicians. "Very good, sir," came the reply. "The Thirty-first reports that it holds the CIS command post, radar facility, and flight line. Several skirmishes still being reported, including the bomb-storage area and armory building. Several aircraft escaped, but our forces are in control of the airfield."

"Casualties?"

"Light to moderate was the last report from Colonel Shklovski," the exec replied. "He'll have a detailed report for you, but he reports his unit is fully combat-ready and taking up defensive positions."

"Very good," Voshchanka replied. Speed and shock were key elements in this operation; by the time the Russians had realized what was happening, his forces were on top of them. Since Voshchanka hadn't ordered a slaughter of Russian soldiers, resistance was useless. "I don't want a bloodbath, and I don't want to lose those munitions if possible. Tell Colonel Shklovski to isolate those areas and take a surrender. We'll need those weapons." The executive officer passed on the order. "Report on the status of Seventh Division in Kaliningrad?"

"Not yet contained, sir," the executive officer replied, referring to his notes transcribed from radio messages constantly being received. "General Gurvich and Twentieth Amphibious Brigade control the headquarters building of the Russian fleet and have surrounded the base, and Thirty-third Armored Brigade controls Proveren Naval Air Base. Our aircraft attacked and heavily damaged one warship trying to leave port. The others are staying at dockside, except three that were repositioned, per your orders, to block the deep-water canal across Kaliningrad Bay. Most vessels examined report only one-third to one-half manned. Most soldiers and sailors are reportedly staying in their barracks or off-base and trying to decide what to do. This allows our forces more freedom to get in position. We control one television station and four radio stations in Kaliningrad. The city appears to be taking a wait-and-see attitude."

Voshchanka nodded—that wait-and-see attitude had come about after a very stiff price was paid. The commanders of Kaliningrad Naval Base and Proveren Naval Air Base, the two main Russian military bases in Kalinin oblast, had each accepted bribes totaling almost a quarter of a million American dollars to stay out of the conflict. One reason why the air base at Chernyakhovsk was aflame was that there was no more bribe money to be paid to that base's commander, and he resisted.

But it was money well spent.

One of the keys to his successful occupation of Kalinin oblast and Lithuania was the reaction from the Baltic city of Kaliningrad itself, the largest and strategically most important city in the Kalinin oblast and certainly the most important in this entire operation. With a population of over four hundred thousand in the city itself and nearly seven hundred thousand in the western half of the territory, including a great number of wealthy businessmen and retired politicians and military members, it was necessary to not threaten the civilian population while "subduing" the many military bases and installations in the area. Fortunately, because of the Byelorussian military presence on behalf of the Commonwealth, there were almost as many loyal Byelorussian soldiers in Kaliningrad as there were Russian soldiers and sailors. Voshchanka's troops also found a good number of Commonwealth soldiers and officers from many other republics that agreed with the reasons for doing away with the Commonwealth's influence.

His military takeover was beginning to turn into something of a revolution.

The work he was doing here in Kalinin oblast was not designed as a sweeping military victory: Voshchanka, despite General Gabovich's assurances of cooperation and assistance, harbored no illusions about the power of the Russian Republic. They would not think fondly of having Kaliningrad invaded and occupied. But it was necessary to put the Russians in Kalinin in a "clinch," tie them up, and take strategic pieces of ground so he would have very strong foundations to stand on when negotiations began. Russia and the Commonwealth of Independent States had no money and no stomach for battle; Belarus had nothing to lose.

Voshchanka would win in Kalinin if he could take important strides without looking like a mad butcher.

But Lithuania was different.

It was necessary to occupy cities and towns, gobble up territory, and establish firm roots as fast as possible. The world would not stay stunned forever—eventually they would act, and they may vote to try to expel Byelorussian forces from Lithuania. Voshchanka had to move swiftly to consolidate his gains, and then prove that any attempt to try to kick him out of Lithuania would do more harm to Lithuania and to the surrounding republics than to Belarus . . .

. . . and part of that threat was his arsenal of SS-21 Scarab missiles now being dispersed throughout northern Belarus. Those small, road-mobile nuclear missiles were the keys to his success. The three nuclear-tipped missiles delivered to Voshchanka were deployed under heavy guard at a secret launch base in northern Belarus, and the others were being dispersed throughout the countryside. But while dispersing them to various launch sites was important, maintaining radio contact with each one of them was even more important.

"I need a report on the SS-21 deployment immediately," Voshchanka ordered. It was risky using the radios to contact his headquarters about such a secret topic, but the pace of his deployment and what he would eventually order the Byelorussian president, Pavel Svetlov, to tell the world, all hinged on the successful deployment of those weapons. "Use the scrambled data link when we are within range."

"That will not be for almost an hour, sir, until we are closer to Lida Naval Base," the executive officer said. "The data link is not secure this far out."

"Very well," Voshchanka said. "But have that report ready as soon as we arrive." The faster he got those Scarab missile launchers safely tucked away, he thought, the faster this invasion could be completed.

OVER NORTHWESTERN BYELORUSSIA, NEAR THE CITY OF LIDA
13 APRIL, 0935 (0235 ET)

"Lida Naval Approach, this is flight seven-one-one flight of two, forty kilometers southwest, one thousand meters, heading zero-niner-zero— correction, zero-niner-five. Over." The young Belarus pilot who made the position report brushed an irritating drop of sweat out from under the hard rubber of his oxygen mask. The day's security procedures dictated that all heading reports on initial call-up be given in odd numbers—he had almost forgotten that. There were about a dozen surface-to-air missile batteries along the Lithuanian-Belarus border that would let him know immediately if he made a mistake like that again.

"Flight seven-one-one, Lida Naval, fly heading zero-four-five for five seconds for identification, then resume own navigation. Acknowledge."

"Seven-one-one acknowledge." Flight Lieutenant Vladi Doleckis used two fingers of his right hand to gently bank his Mikoyan-Gurevich-27 fighter-bomber to the northeast, counted the required time silently to himself, then resumed his original course. His wingman, Flight Lieutenant Frantsisk Stebut, flying in close formation off his left wingtip in a "carp-mouth" Sukhoi-17 reconnaissance fighter, responded. Staying in pretty good fingertip formation, Frantsisk looked as if he were dangling on a string far below Doleckis, although he was only a few meters away.

Air-traffic control in the outlying parts of Belarus was poor these days—obviously Lida Naval Approach was not receiving his encoded beacon, but a primary radar blip only—and such small diversions were commonplace. The young, blond-haired, blue-eyed fighter-bomber pilot didn't mind. Flying was fun for him, no matter what the rules and restrictions were, and he wasn't going to let a little radar breakdown spoil his day.

"Seven-one-one, radar identified. Advise before changing altitudes. Flight east of meridian twenty-six *prohibited* until further notice. Lida Naval out."

"Seven-one-one. I understand. Out." That was fine with him—he didn't want to get involved in the little skirmish brewing up in Lithuania anyway. The "ground hounds" of the Home Brigade from Smorgon were on the move to squash some sort of rebellion or uprising in Lithuania, and although the Smorgon air units had been activated and the Lida and Ross air bases were put on alert—General Voshchanka was in overall charge of all the northern Belarus military forces and was without question the most powerful and influential man in the Belarus military— Doleckis's unit had not been tasked. Sending in high-performance bombers against the Lithuanians was like killing an ant with a wrecking ball—it was a real mess for so little work. He knew that they'd be called up eventually, either to deploy to occupied Lithuania or to drive off attacks from the Commonwealth, from Russia, or from the Western nations. As much as he enjoyed the thought of pitting his skills against other MiG-27 pilots or foreign defense systems, he wasn't looking forward to a war.

"Lida Naval," Doleckis's wingman grumbled on the interplane frequency. "What a joke. When are they going to change that name?"

"Whenever the bureaucrats and politicians finally decide to get off their lazy butts," Doleckis replied with a laugh. The name of that base was one of the many incongruities of life in Belarus these days, one of the bureaucratic quirks that would one day be corrected.

Lida Naval Air Base, about one hundred and twenty kilometers west of Minsk and about two hundred and forty kilometers east of the Baltic, was once a large Soviet naval air base, in support of the Baltic fleet. Lida once had a squadron of twenty Sukhoi-24 fighter-bombers and MiG-23 fighter escorts, designed for tactical and naval reconnaissance, close air support, naval bombardment, and antiship missions in the Baltic. Of course, now independent Belarus had no navy and no naval air force, but Lida still held its "naval" designation. Stupid. One of the useless remnants of a defunct Russian society.

Well, maybe not everything about the Russians was so bad: they built some great warplanes, like this MiG-27 fighter-bomber. It was incredibly sleek and slippery, with a top speed of almost twice the speed of sound at high altitude and over Mach-1 at low altitude. It could carry over four thousand kilograms of external stores and it had a range in excess of six hundred kilometers with external fuel tanks. This older D-model MiG-27 was fitted with some pretty fancy hardware as well: Doppler automatic-navigation units, an attack radar and laser rangefinder in the nose, a Sirena-3 radar warning system that could warn of nearby enemy radars, an infrared scanner for searching and attacking ground targets, and the upgraded ASP-5R solid-state fire-control system for the weapons and cannon. His D-model MiG-27 still had the titanium "bathtub" armor around the cockpit, which combined with the external bomb load took away his supersonic speed with weapons on board, but it was still a real hot rod. The thing was nearly as old as he was, but Doleckis loved flying it.

First Lieutenant Frantsisk Stebut's single-engine, swing-wing Sukhoi-17 was a C-model, older than Doleckis's MiG-27. It was configured for close air-support gunnery, with two 23-millimeter SPPU-22 gun pods on each wing, two 30-millimeter cannons in each wing root, and one large fuel tank on the centerline hardpoint; two of the SPPU-22 gun pods were configured to fire rearward, so ground targets could be attacked even after the SU-17 overflew its target.

One unfortunate characteristic of Belarus's Air Force was the strange amalgamation of aircraft in its inventory—they generally flew the castoffs of the old Soviet Air Force or the old Warsaw Pact nations, sparingly flying the aircraft that were serviceable and cannibalizing the others for spare parts.

Doleckis, one of the best bombardiers in the Belarus Air Force, with or without a laser rangefinder, had been scheduled for one of his four-a-month currency flights, but when he arrived at the base the squadron was on alert and his orders had been changed. His MiG-27 was armed to the teeth with a dazzling array of weapons: four cluster bombs on rear bomb racks, each with seventy little antipersonnel bomblets; two 57-millimeter rocket pods on air-intake hardpoints; one external fuel tank on a center-line hardpoint; and two AA-2 heat-seeking air-to-air missiles on the small outboard wing pylons. The big 30-millimeter ground-attack cannon in the belly held three hundred rounds of armor-piercing ammunition. It was the most armament he had flown with since graduating from fighter-bomber school in Tblisi . . .

. . . and, just like after flight school, the arming switches for all the weapons were covered and sealed with small steel wires and maintenance lead seals. He had been given strict orders not to activate any switch without specific permission—even breaking a safety wire without permission would lead to disciplinary action. No matter. The switches were out of the way, so accidental activation wasn't usually a problem—but God, did he want to arm up those weapons and let 'em fly! Here he was, by himself, loaded with several thousand kilograms' worth of fine weaponry, but he had been given no orders except to stand by and wait. He knew he was being kept on hand in case he was needed by General Voshchanka, and he liked the idea of getting a frantic call for assistance from the General himself, but he knew that it was unlikely. Stebut's camera pod had film in it, but neither of them had been briefed on exactly what to do, so they did nothing but fly. Stand by and wait. Bore some holes in the sky . . .

"Flight seven-one-one," came the radio message from the approach controller from Lida, "fly heading three-two-zero, descend and maintain seven hundred meters and contact Lida naval command post on local channel nine. Acknowledge."

"Flight seven-one-one, three-two-zero, seven hundred meters. Going channel nine. Good day." Finally, maybe some action! This new vector would take him closer to the Lithuanian border, and the altitude would put him only one hundred meters above the highest terrain in the sector. A call to the command post while only a hundred meters above the beautiful forests of the Demas River valley meant something was happening . . .

Lieutenant Doleckis excitedly switched his radio to the new frequency: "Lida naval control, flight seven-one-one on channel nine. Over."

"Seven-one-one, control, roger," the silky female voice of their command post radio-duty technician replied. She was a red-haired beauty from Russia—another good Russian import—that Doleckis had been wanting to get to know for weeks. He could listen to her luscious voice all day long. Breathily, she said, "Seven-one-one, establish tactical orbit at coordinates poppa-kilo, kilo-juliett, five-zero, three-zero, and stand by. Over."

"Seven-one-one copies all," Doleckis replied, reading back the coordinates and pulling out a cardboard chart from his flight suit left-leg pocket. He found the coordinates on the chart, just north of a small village ten kilometers from the border. A standard tactical orbit was figure-eight racetrack with twenty-kilometer legs, 10 degrees of bank, no more than five hundred meters above ground level or as directed by tactical considerations. It was a good pattern for visually searching an area—he was definitely looking for something. He was allowed to vary the centerpoint of the orbit to avoid any chance of attack by enemy ground forces, but here there was little chance of that.

Doleckis configured his MiG-27 for a ground-attack patrol. He brought the power back to 60 percent, manually extended his variable geometry wings to full extension, and lowered one notch of flaps to maintain stability in slow flight—losing control at this relatively low altitude could be disastrous.

"Seven-one-one flight, flaps fifteen, wing sweep sixteen," Doleckis warned his wingman. He waited a few seconds, then checked to make sure Stebut was configured properly—the standard wingman's job was to "make your plane look like mine at all times," but sometimes wingmen got complacent.

Stebut was on the job, settled in nicely with his own flaps and wings extended. The Sukhoi-17 was actually larger, faster, and could carry more weapons than the MiG-27, but the newer avionics and much greater accuracy of the MiG-27 made it the aircraft of choice for most ground-attack chores, especially in situations where low collateral damage or the presence of friendly troops in the area were concerns.

Doleckis had no useful landmarks to use except for the village—it was all thick forests below, the northern part of the world-famous Berezina Preserve—and if he had to find someone or something down there, it was going to be tough. He set the Doppler navigation set to the coordinates so he wouldn't stray across the Lithuanian border. "Seven-one-one established in orbit," Doleckis reported.

"Flight seven-one-one, roger," the controller replied. "Report fuel status."

He had been airborne for only twenty minutes when he got the call, and he had an external tank nearly full of fuel—at this low power setting, and so close to base to begin with, he could stay aloft forever. "Seven-one-one fuel status two hours." His endurance was actually a bit longer, but if he said three hours they were probably going to be *up* there for three hours.

"Control copies, two hours," the red-haired controller replied. "Stand by . . . Vladi."

Well, well, at least she knows my name, Doleckis thought, forgetting about the fact that he could very well be doomed to orbit that spot for the next two hours. He was going to have to look up that gorgeous redhead when he got back.

The clearing had to be no more than ninety feet wide at its widest point, because when Major Hank Fell, the pilot of the CV-22 tilt-rotor aircraft, nestled his beast into that clearing, there was virtually no room between the rotor tips and the thick, gnarly branches of the pine and spruce trees nearby—and the CV-22 had a clearance of about eighty-five-and-a-half feet. A sudden gust of wind, an errant whipping of a branch by his own rotor wash, and one of those branches could easily hit them.

The crew chief and door gunner on the CV-22 aircrew, Master Sergeant Mike Brown, was outside the aircraft, near the nose, wearing his helmet, with a long interphone cord attached and plugged into the jack near the entry hatch. He was scanning the skies with a pair of binoculars when the jet passed almost directly overhead. There was no chance the pilot would see them through the foliage unless they were very, very lucky, but Brown still crouched lower and half-expected a bomb or something to drop on top of them at any second.

"Got a *real* good look at them that time, sir," Brown reported, breathing fast and shallow in the microphone, almost hyperventilating. He cupped his gloved hands over his mouth, breathing in his own exhalations for a few seconds, and waited for his pounding heart to calm down before continuing: "A MiG-27 bomber and a Sukhoi-17 bomber. The leader's outfitted for long-range close air support, and he's got Atolls on the wings as well. I couldn't tell what his wingman's got, but they could be gun pods. I don't think they saw us." He started a timer on his wristwatch. "I'll time their patrol pattern to see how much time we have to lift off."

Hank Fell and Martin Watanabe, the CV-22's copilot, were scared and nervous as well, so they knew exactly what Brown was feeling—they could easily hear the roar of those jets flying overhead, even over their own engine noise. "Copy," Fell said. "He wasn't transmitting anything, so I think we're safe for now. Be sure to check the undercarriage."

Fell, who had been flying the CV-22 PAVE HAMMER aircraft at treetop level since ten minutes before exiting Polish airspace for Byelorussia, had managed to drop his CV-22 into the clearing when they saw the Soviet-made planes suddenly pop into view about fifteen miles away.

Fortunately the fighters were in a gentle turn, so he had a few more needed seconds to respond. He picked the clearing and dove for it. No sooner had his wheels hit the soft dirt than the fighters appeared. The eighteen Marines on board immediately exited the aircraft and took up defensive positions around the clearing. One squad had a Stinger missile, and was tracking the bombers every second.

"Undercarriage is underwater," Brown reported as he examined the underside of the CV-22. The clearing was partially flooded by the spring rains, the nose gear was completely submerged, and water covered the lower part of the forward radome and bottom of the FLIR sensor ball. "Shut down the radar and FLIR or you'll lose them."

"Done," Watanabe reported.

Luckily the rear of the aircraft was high and relatively dry, so the aircraft was not completely buried in mud. "It might take a high-power setting to free the nose," Brown surmised, "but your aft trucks are free. It'll be a hairy lift-off."

"Great," Fell said. "How far are we from the LZ?"

Watanabe punched up the computer flight plan on one of the big center multifunction displays. "A good seventy miles," he replied. "Twenty to thirty minutes' flight time."

Fell looked out at his two rotors, spinning at idle power. A V-22 tilt-rotor aircraft burned a lot of fuel turning those big rotors, even at idle power, and that was something they could not afford now. Since lifting off from the U.S.S. *Valley Mistress* a few hours ago, they had flown almost three hundred miles in a circuitous route, avoiding radar sites in Kalinin and the Byelorussian military bases along the borders. The CV-22, with eighteen Marines and all their gear on board, had a combat radius of only five hundred miles—they carried no extra fuel and did not get an aerial refueling—but they were still a long way from their objective. Every minute they spent idling on the ground sapped a lot of their range, and no one relished the thought of walking through these swamps, being chased by the Byelorussian Army.

"We can't afford to wait," Fell decided. "Mike, get everyone back on board. When the Sukhois fly overhead heading eastbound, we'll be right behind them. Hopefully when he makes his turn back to the west, he won't see us."

The Marines had just hustled back on board and were strapped in when Brown tapped on the pilot's right-side windscreen and pointed to the sky. "Here they come!" he shouted as he dashed for the entry door. Fell pushed the power controls forward—60-, 70-, 80-percent power. Nothing . . .

"Overhead, ready, ready . . . now."

Fell pushed the power to 90 percent. The tail and main landing gear lifted off, but the nose gear was still stuck fast. He pushed it to 95-percent power. The tail swerved to the right from the rotor wash, and the aircraft began to vibrate so hard that the nose gear seemed as if it would snap off. "Careful," Brown radioed on interphone. "Trees hitting the rudder."

Fell pulled back on the cyclic-control stick to settle the main landing gears back on the ground. As he did so, the nose gear suddenly popped out of the mud and the CV-22 skidded backwards directly into a stand of pines.

"Tailplane in the trees!" Brown shouted. Stabilize! *Stabilize!"*

Somehow Fell managed to keep the CV-22 from whipping out of control. With the aircraft no more than a few feet above the ground, he nudged the CV-22 forward until the horizontal stabilizer was free of the foliage.

"I see a few branches stuck in the tailplane," Brown said. "Want me to go out and get them off?"

Fell briefly switched the flight-control system to TEST, which would momentarily switch him out of helicopter to airplane mode so he could test the elevator. He felt no serious resistance. "No. Stay put," Fell said. "I don't think they'll be a factor."

The two pilots were never so relieved in their lives as they were when they cleared the treetops a few seconds later.

Fell retracted the landing gear and rotated the nacelles down to 45 percent, to the point when the CV-22's computerized flight-control system transitioned from helicopter to airplane mode, then turned slightly right to get behind the Sukhoi-17 that they could see a mile or two in the distance. They stayed right at treetop level, flying so close to the trees that they were skimming the bottom of the fuselage right at the tree's tips.

Well, maybe it wasn't such a good idea to ignore the branches stuck in the elevator, Fell thought a few moments later. As the CV-22 transformed itself into an airplane, the effect of the tailplane and the branches stuck in it became more and more pronounced. "Shit. I've got some binding in the stick," Fell said on interphone. It took a great deal of pulling on the control stick to move the elevator. "Christ, I hope those branches blow off or something. It'll be a bitch to—"

"They're turning right!" Watanabe shouted. Fell immediately turned left, trying to stay behind the Sukhoi-17s as much as possible. The Byelorussian pilots were turning tighter this time, and it was impossible to stay behind them. "Want to find another place to set down?"

The trees were heavier than ever in this area. There was only one choice—the river itself. "Crew, stand by for wet landing," Fell shouted, swiveling the engine nacelles to go from airplane back to helicopter mode again. "I'm going for the river."

* * *

There was definitely something out there, Doleckis thought. For the second time since starting his patrol orbit, he saw a shape, moving down low over the trees. But every time he focused on that spot, nothing was there. Strange . . .

"Flight, did you see some movement over there at five o'clock position?"

There was a momentary pause; then: "Negative, lead. I don't see anything."

Doleckis keyed his microphone switch: "Control, seven-one-one . . . ah, are there other aircraft participating in this patrol out here?"

"Seven-one-one, negative," the redhead replied.

"Are you showing anyone else on radar?"

There was a slight pause; then: "Seven-one-one, intermittent primary targets in your vicinity, slow-moving, altitude unknown. Possible bird activity in your area. Use caution."

Birds? Possible, but not likely. It was spring, but not quite bird-migration time in northern Europe. "Control, I haven't seen any birds out here. What exactly am I supposed to be looking for out here, Control?"

"Seven-one-one, would you like to speak with Alpha for a clarification?"

Talking with Alpha meant talking with the fighter wing commander, and that was never a really good thing to do unless you had an emergency. "Negative, Control. But I would like permission to alter my patrol orbit to look up and down the river. Over."

"Request to alter patrol orbit on request, seven-one-one, stand by."

Stand by . . . for what? He cursed silently. *Christmas?*

Doleckis strained to look in the area where he thought he last saw the . . . well, whatever it was there was nothing now. He considered just heading off over there to check it out, but if the wing commander was going to act on his request, the first thing he would do is check his radar track. If he already showed off course, it would look bad for him. The Demas River also curled northeastward very close to the Lithuanian border, and if the wing commander saw him flying toward the border he might really get upset. Better stick with the directed orbit until told otherwise . . .

But that was not his way of doing things.

Doleckis made a gentle bank turn to the right, carefully scanning to the east at the spot he had been seeing the motion.

There was *something* out there . . .

But his wingman had slipped out of position in the unexpected turn and had disappeared from sight behind him. "Lead, pull a little power for me," Stebut radioed. Doleckis reduced power and made a few wide skidding turns, and Stebut eventually slipped back into formation, a bit wider and looser this time.

"Seven-one-one, Control, are you experiencing difficulty?"

Well, they noticed that I cut my orbit short right away, Doleckis thought. *Too bad . . .* "Negative. Seven-one-one is investigating a possible contact, near the patrol orbit reference coordinates. Will advise. Over."

"Seven-one-one, roger . . ." The controller hesitated, obviously not prepared to issue a clearance for that action but hesitant to order him *not* to do it either. "Say your intentions, seven-one-one."

"I intend to advise you when I've made contact or when I return to the patrol orbit, Control," Doleckis said—then, to add a bit of sarcasm to the conversation, he added, "Stand by."

Fell had maneuvered the CV-22 PAVE HAMMER to the south side of the river, as close to the trees as he could safely take it. The rear cargo door was open, and several people could be seen standing in it. While two Marines acted as helpers and another scanned the skies with binoculars, Sergeant Brown was trying to lasso the tree branch stuck in the elevator hinge. The CV-22 was still flying along at nearly sixty miles per hour, with the engine nacelles at 45 percent, and it made their efforts very difficult.

Brown had just looped his rope over the branch and was trying to decide the best way to work it free when the spotter pointed toward the sky. Brown followed his outstretched arm and gasped in surprise. "The MiG and the Sukhoi are back," he reported on interphone. "Six o'clock, about seven miles. They're low and slow. I wanna pull this branch out. Guard the controls."

"Do it, Mike," Fell said, "then close that cargo door!"

Brown took a good pull on the rope, and most of the branch came free. "There's still some stuck in the hinge, but I don't think it'll flutter on you. Cargo door clear to close. Five seconds and you're clear to maneuver."

Watanabe hit the switch to close the cargo door, then turned to Fell. "What are we going to do?"

"No use trying to outrun or outgun them," Fell said. "We hide." Fell continued on for a few more seconds until he found a slight right-hand bend in the river, did a fast one-eighth turn until he was facing the oncoming Byelorussian planes, switched to full helicopter mode, then translated left until the tips of his portside rotor were whipping into the trees. He descended until the radar altimeter showed zero.

Brown was quickly switching from window to window, keeping an eye on the position of his aircraft. "Belly wet," he announced. "Don't move any farther left or we'll be in the trees." He moved over to the right side of the PAVE HAMMER aircraft. The rotors were churning up the narrow river into a white froth. "Whipping up lots of water on the right—he'll spot that from the air."

Maybe hiding wasn't such a hot idea after all—we might have to fight our way out of this.

"Let's have the Stinger and gun pods, Marty. I'll take control of the aircraft and the Stinger pod; you got the cannon. Check our ECM and jammers are active." Watanabe deployed the two weapons pods from the side sponsons, and Fell lowered the Target Acquisition and Designation System visor over his eyes. A yellow round aiming reticle called the "donut" was superimposed over his visor, indicating the field of view of the Stinger heat-seeking missiles. Meanwhile Watanabe activated the radar jammers and the ALQ-136 INEWS infrared jamming system, which set up invisible spikes of energy in all directions to decoy infrared-guided missiles like the Soviet Atoll.

The two Soviet-made fighters were now in full view, and Fell realized how vulnerable, how exposed, he was. Out the starboard window he could see the froth and the waves bubbling across the narrow Nemas River, and out the portside window he could see his rotors churning and dashing tree branches around. They were like giant neon signs pointing right at them. This entire daylight insertion mission was turning into a major nightmare. Fell's thoughts drifted momentarily to the other CV-22 crew that launched from the USS *Valley Mistress,* tasked to approach Smorgon through northern Lithuania and southwestern Russia, and he hoped they were having an easier time of it.

"Stand by, crew," Fell warned over interphone as the Byelorussian jets drew closer and closer. "This could get hairy."

SMORGON ARMY AIR BASE, BYELORUSSIAN REPUBLIC
13 APRIL, 0947 (0247 ET)

One of the busiest spots on Smorgon base that morning was the base fuel depot. Two lines of twelve tanker trucks were waiting at the fueling station—there were only two stations operating, out of the six normally available—and the wait was long. One line was for jet fuel, destined for the aircraft and helicopters on the fuel line that could not use the in-ground refueling equipment, and the other was for diesel to refuel the numerous trucks, utility vehicles, and power generators throughout the base and in the Lithuanian deployment. The Home Brigade of the Belarus Army was taking nearly a hundred fuel trucks with it during the invasion of Lithuania to keep the convoys moving.

The fuel depot normally had two platoons manning the facility, but one by one the men had been reassigned to the convoys, so only a handful of workers and guards remained—most truck drivers ended up pumping their own fuel. So it was a great relief to the NCO in charge of the facility when a truckful of soldiers showed up and reported to him, saying they were ready to work.

"Excellent," the NCOIC, Senior Sergeant Pashuto, said to the NCO in charge of the detail. "Your men can begin by getting the paperwork ready from all those drivers, so when they pull up to the pumps they are ready to go."

The young detail leader nodded that he understood, saluted, and departed.

He wasn't very talkative, Pashuto observed, but that was the first salute anyone had rendered him in quite some time, and he didn't need another blabbermouth here anyway.

The operation went very smoothly after the fifteen-man detail arrived, so much so that Pashuto was able to sneak away for a cup of coffee and a few slices of bread while the detail worked. When he returned, the detail leader was back with a stack of fuel-authorization forms. "Good work, Corporal," Pashuto praised the young detail leader as he signed off the fuel-requisition forms. "You have a real talent for this. Who is your commander? I'd like to speak with him."

"Menako, cela," the detail leader replied, thanking him in heavily accented, slow Byelorussian. The man's voice sounded syrupy, hesitant, as if he were a bit retarded, but that certainly didn't match his performance. "My commander's name is White."

"White? I'm not familiar with that name." It was hard to understand the man because of his slow speech. "Please repeat your commander's name again?"

"My commander is Colonel Paul White, United States Air Force," the detail leader said, this time in very understandable Byelorussian. He withdrew a small submachine gun with a silencer from a small "fanny pack" and aimed it at Pashuto. "Raise your hands and place them on your head or—"

Pashuto didn't wait for the rest—he immediately turned and sprinted for the rear exit, diving for the door and trying to swing it shut behind him before the bullets started flying. But as he reached the door, he ran headlong into two Home Brigade soldiers who were entering the building from the back. "Commandos!" Pashuto shouted, pointing at the man in front. "American commandos in front! Give me a gun!"

"Sorry, Comrade, can't help you," one of the Home Brigade soldiers said in English. Pashuto didn't understand the words, but he knew he wasn't going to get any help. The first soldier grabbed him and pinned his arms behind his back, and the other soldier placed a rag soaked with some sort of foul-smelling liquid over his nose and mouth. The world immediately turned dark and silent, and he was out of the conflict for a while.

"Trucks secure, Wilson?" Marine Corps Sergeant Thomas Seymour asked the man out front. Other Marines, members of Colonel Paul White's MADCAP MAGICIAN strike team, entered the office and began checking desks and file cabinets.

"Yes, sir," Corporal Ed Wilson replied. "Drivers were sedated, and our team members are on board ready to go. We've got three trucks destined for the flight line, one for the motor pool, and eight for convoys."

"We'll need two more for the flight line and two for the command center," Seymour said. "The convoys won't get any, I'm afraid." He turned to one of the other Marines rifling through the desks. "You find those change orders yet, DuPont?"

"Got 'em," the Marine replied. He sat down in front of an old typewriter and began to type in the new information, using a map of the base behind the desk as reference. When he was finished with the new orders, he spent a few moments practicing Pashuto's signature until he had it down, signed the forms, then scuffed them on the floor a bit to make them look properly worn. Seymour found line badges and gate passes in a locked file-cabinet drawer and gave them to Wilson for distribution. Seymour briefed the plan one more time, then sent the Marines off to their destinations in the fuel trucks.

"About time you got here, Private," the Byelorussian crew chief of the Mil-24 Hind-D assault helicopter grumbled as the fuel truck pulled up. As the private handed over his orders to be countersigned by the crew chief, he said, "Everyone was waiting on you fuel handlers. What's the holdup?"

"Sergeant Pashuto made someone go back for proper orders," the driver said. He placed the truck in neutral, engaged the parking brake, then jumped out and placed tire chocks under the wheels of his truck. After that, he went to the right side of the fuel truck, where assistant crew chiefs had already begun unreeling grounding wires from it.

The crew chief walked back to the private and stuck the signed orders back in his pocket. "These orders are freshly typed," he observed, staring the private right in the eyes. "It was you who had the screwed-up orders, wasn't it?"

The Marine Corps special operations commando had to struggle to remain calm. "It wasn't my fault," he replied in hesitant Byelorussian.

"Of course not," the crew chief sneered. He looked the private over carefully. "You're new here, aren't y—"

Suddenly there was a cry from somewhere across the aircraft parking ramp. The crew chief looked toward the voices, saw men pointing off in the distance, and looked in that direction. A plume of dark smoke was pouring up from a radar dome a few kilometers away, on the other side of the runway. "A fire? Fire in the approach-control facility!" Just then a tremendous explosion tore the radar dome apart like a bursting dandelion, throwing off debris and pieces of radar into the sky like seeds. They saw the explosion before they heard it, but when the sound finally traveled across the runway it was as if a huge thunderstorm had just erupted right in their faces. "My God . . . !"

"I'll call it in . . ." the private said, but as he turned to run back to the truck to get his radio, the crew chief grabbed him by his shoulder.

"Wait a minute, Private. I don't know you. What's your name?"

"Sir, let me call in the fire and I'll call my NCOIC—"

The crew chief's grip tightened, and now others nearby noticed the commotion. "I said, what's your name, soldier? I don't recognize you, and your accent sounds foreign." He turned to one of his assistant crew chiefs. "Misclav, help me over here!"

Just then another cry was heard. Across the parking ramp from where the crew chief was wrestling with the fuel-truck driver, a torrent of jet fuel was gushing out from underneath a three-thousand-dekaliter fuel truck. A flood of jet fuel spread quickly across the parking ramp. "What in hell is going on—?" Suddenly, a soft *bang!* could be heard, and it seemed as if the entire contents of the fuel truck that they were standing beside emptied out onto the tarmac.

"Run!" someone shouted. A few more *bangs!* were heard as three more fuel trucks suddenly disgorged hundreds of tons of raw fuel onto the ramp. Soon all the Hind-D attack helicopters parked in that area were threatened by the fuel, their wheels several centimeters deep in it.

"Sabotage!" the crew chief shouted. The young private tried to run, but the crew chief held him fast. "No you don't, you bastard! What's going on?"

Marine Corps Corporal Wilson was not accustomed to being manhandled by anyone, and especially not twice in a row. While maintenance men and aviators were scattering to get away from the growing lake of jet fuel that was spreading across the entire parking area, the young Marine suddenly grabbed the crew chief in an iron grasp and, grabbing him as if he were pulling him away from the truck, thrust his right knee deep into the man's groin. The crew chief let out a loud *whoof!* as loud as a dog and collapsed in Wilson's arms. Wilson waited a few precious seconds until everyone else had run by, then prepared himself to make the run to the blast fence just one hundred meters away, behind the helicopters and in the opposite direction that everyone else was running. The crew chief was unconscious, slumped in his arms.

But as hard as Wilson told himself to just get the hell out of there, he couldn't just let the guy go. The crew chief was just doing his job—he didn't deserve to die in a fireball set by a bunch of foreigners. Instead, Wilson dragged the unconscious man back behind the Mil-24 and toward the fence. He told himself that if any of the guards took a shot at him, he was going to drop the crew chief—but not before. The man didn't deserve to die. . . .

It takes a very hot spark to ignite jet fuel—a small half-pound piece of C4 explosive, along with a white phosphorous charge did the trick—but the timer was set for only thirty seconds. Corporal Wilson should have set it for sixty. It was his last thought before there was an intense burst of light, a loud roar in his ears, and then a searing wall of fire engulfed them both.

Wilson never had a chance.

One by one, the explosion and fire ripped into the eighteen attack helicopters parked on this section of ramp, detonating the fuel in their tanks and adding more fire and fury to the holocaust. The fire trucks arrived a few minutes later, diverted from the radar site back to the aircraft parking ramp, but by the time they returned to the parking area all eighteen aircraft were destroyed or badly damaged. A few seconds later, the fuel depot itself was also destroyed by charges set by the Intelligence Support Agency Marines of MADCAP MAGICIAN.

The Marines, minus Corporal Ed Wilson, escaped the base and executed their pre-assigned escape plan. The second CV-22 tilt-rotor aircraft would pick them up in a few hours, and they would move on to their next target as nightfall grew nearer.

OVER NORTH-CENTRAL BYELORUSSIA
13 APRIL, 0947 (0247 ET)

"I see them!" Flight Lieutenant Doleckis cried out on his interplane frequency.

What he saw was unclear—he could clearly see one turning rotor, and by the way the trees near the shore were shipping around, it appeared as if another set of rotors was very close beside the first. Two helicopters, practically side by side, hiding in the trees?

"Control, this is flight seven-one-one, I have two helicopters very close to the water on the south bank of the Nema. My position is . . ." He checked his navigation set. "About fifty-three kilometers west-northwest of Lida Naval Air Base." By the time he made that transmission, they had flown over the sighting. "I will attempt to get a visual I.D. on the target. Recommend deployment of helicopter and infantry patrols to this location. Over."

"Copy all, seven-one-one," the female command-post controller replied. "Be advised, no other authorized aircraft have checked in. We are checking with Smorgon for possible patrols from Home Brigade. Maintain visual contact on the target and stand by on this channel. Acknowledge."

"Seven-one-one, I'll try," Doleckis replied. "We're heavy gross weight and low. Get some slow-movers or fling-wings up here to relieve us. Over."

"Control understands. Stand by."

There was obviously no one in the command post yet, Doleckis thought—they had been assigned a patrol without any command support. Great. "Control, I need an answer, dammit," Doleckis said irritably. "They can be over the border in sixty seconds if they make a break for it."

There was nothing on the channel for nearly a minute, in which time the stall warning horn blared once and Doleckis's wingman complained several times about his airspeed and tight turn radius. Warning calls on all frequencies, including the international emergency channel GUARD, were useless. The contact stayed in the trees, stirring up branches and river water, obviously in a hover and holding his position. Finally: "Seven-one-one, Control, Alpha advises you to visually identify the aircraft, report, and close-pursue to keep the contact in sight. Authority to cross the Lithuanian border is granted. Stand by to engage if necessary. Acknowledge."

"Visual identification, report, close pursue, Lithuanian border overflight authorized for seven-one-one flight of two," Doleckis responded. "Seven-one-one flight, take a high orbit at one thousand AGL."

"Two," Stebut replied. The Sukhoi-17 fighter-bomber dropped behind the MiG-27, made a shallow climb so he could keep Doleckis in view, and took up an orbit position over Doleckis, varying his orbit pattern slightly so that he could see Doleckis and the contact at the same time.

"Ten minutes to bingo fuel, Hank," Watanabe said cross-cockpit. "We gotta get out of here or we can't complete the mission." They also knew that if the fighter pilots spotted them, more aircraft and ground forces were on the way.

"Then let's do it right now," Fell said. On the cabin loudspeaker, he said, "Attention crew. We're going to lift off and try some low-altitude maneuvering to get away from these two fighters on our tail. Secure all loose items and double-check your seat belts. Review your escape-and-evasion plans in case we go in. Remember to exit the aircraft straight back if you have to get out—the rotors and engines off to the sides will be hot, and the cannon and missile pods will be deployed. Hang tight."

*   *   *

Doleckis could not believe his eyes—it was not two helicopters down there, it was *one!* "Control, seven-one-one, I see the bogey. It's . . . it's a large, cargo-type rotorcraft, painted in camouflage, with engines mounted on long wingtips. It's heading—"

And suddenly the thing made a sharp turn, then accelerated faster than any rotorcraft he had ever seen. Frantically he searched the skies for the thing. No helicopter could move like that—it had taken off like a rocket. "Control, I've lost visual. It turned northbound and accelerated out of sight. Seven-one-one flight, get on an eastbound heading and search for this thing."

"Two," Stebut replied.

"Control, I'm switching to Lida Approach for radar advisories. Seven-one-one flight, go button ten."

"Two."

Doleckis switched radio frequencies, checked in his wingman, then said, "Lida Naval, flight seven-one-one of two with you tactical. Requesting vectors to unidentified aircraft last seen heading northbound, altitude approximately twenty to thirty meters."

"Flight seven-one-one flight of two, understand tactical," the approach controller replied. After the "tactical" call, the controller's responsibility now was to clear the airspace around the two fighters and work with them to find the unknown aircraft. "I have you radar-identified. Have your wingman squawk normal if you are no longer in formation." A second later the coded identification beacon for the Sukhoi-17 popped onto the screen, flying nearly parallel with the MiG-27, but three hundred meters higher. "Seven-one-one Bravo, you are radar-identified."

"Bravo," Stebut replied.

"Be advised, seven-one-one flight, I show no other aircraft in your vicinity. If your contact is at thirty meters I will be unable to advise you unless he gets within thirty kilometers of Lida. Over."

Damn! Doleckis swore. They were right on top of him, and they lost him! "Copy, Approach. If you have any intermittent contacts, advise us immediately—"

"Bravo has contact on the bogey!" Stebut interrupted. "He's heading zero-four-zero, a few klicks north of the river . . . he's banking right, heading for the river again. Shit, Vladi, it's a tilt-rotor aircraft. He's switched to airplane mode. An American tilt-rotor!"

Doleckis frantically searched the sky above him for the Sukhoi-17, finally spotting it. "I've got a visual on you, Frantsi. You've got the lead. Stay on this freq. I'm going back to button nine."

"Copy. Bravo has the lead."

Doleckis switched his radio to the command-post frequency. "Control, this is seven-one-one flight of two tactical. We have contact with the bogey. It is an American tilt-rotor aircraft. It is crossing back and forth over the border, heading east-northeast at high speed. Seven-one-one Bravo has the pursuit. We are standing by to engage. Request further orders. Over."

This time a very familiar male voice came on the line—the air wing commander. Finally a senior officer had taken charge of the chase. "Seven-one-one, I want both of you on this channel. Bring Bravo to this frequency immediately. Over."

"Seven-one-one copy. Control, off frequency, monitor GUARD, report back." Doleckis went back to the approach-control frequency, told Stebut to switch to the command-post freq, then switched back himself. "Control, seven-one-one flight of two tactical back on your frequency."

"Seven-one-one, your orders are to force that aircraft down," the wing commander said on the command-post frequency. "Smorgon is sending attack helicopters to assist, but their ETA to your position is unknown at this time. Bracket him on both sides, give him warning shots, and attempt to disable him with cannon fire if you think you can do it without causing a crash. I want the tilt-rotor and its crew intact. Do you understand?"

"I understand," Doleckis replied.

"Bravo understands," Stebut replied. "Bravo's in a descent. I'll take the left, Vladi, you take the right."

"I've got a good visual on you," Doleckis said, swinging over to the right as the big Sukhoi-17 began descending behind the tilt-rotor aircraft. "Clear to descend on the left." Doleckis never practiced intercept procedures—he was an air-to-mud fighter pilot, not air-to-air—but it was clear what the commander wanted—he wanted that aircraft to . . .

Suddenly the tilt-rotor aircraft heeled sharply on its right wing, decelerated rapidly, and disappeared from view. It had been traveling nearly four hundred kilometers an hour, and in the blink of an eye it had slowed to half that speed and turned with an impossible tight turning radius. "Seven-one-one lost contact! Turning right to reacquire."

"Bravo lost contact," Stebut added immediately. "I've got a visual on you, Alpha, you're in the lead."

"I've got the lead," Doleckis acknowledged. *This cat-and-mouse game could go on for a long time,* Doleckis thought as he banked hard right and strained out his canopy to spot the American aircraft. But he also knew that the longer they had this guy turning and stopping, the greater the chances that he wasn't going to accomplish his mission. He was a very long way from home; and at that altitude, switching from airplane to helicopter mode the way he was, he was sucking a lot of gas.

But when he completed his turn, the tilt-rotor aircraft was nowhere to be seen. "Seven-one-one Alpha has lost contact."

"Bravo has contact on the bogey, Vladi," Stebut cried out on the radio. "He's hovering right below you. He turned and then stopped . . . hey, it looks like he's flying *backwards*. Damn, I'm going to overshoot . . . Bravo has lost contact. I've got a visual on you, Vladi, you're cleared to maneuver."

"I'm maneuvering left and up, Frantsi," Doleckis said. "Give me a few hundred meters."

Doleckis increased his airspeed to his maximum flaps-down airspeed, banked left, and climbed. He gained three hundred meters, continuing his left turn until his airspeed had bled off nearly to approach speed, then pointed his nose down at the ground—at the end of his turn, he should be aimed back at the target.

"Control, I need instructions," Doleckis radioed. "Fixed-wings are not going to be able to bracket him. We can keep him in sight, but we are not going to be able to fly with him. Request permission to—"

Just then Doleckis regained visual contact with the tilt-rotor aircraft, and at the same time he saw the Sukhoi-17 fighter-bomber peel off to the right, then swing back to the left to keep him in sight. The tilt-rotor aircraft was indeed hovering in place—and now he was pivoting to the left, tracking the Sukhoi with the precision of a radar-guided gun. "Bravo, tighten your turn, then reverse. It looks like that tilt-rotor is tracking—"

And at that instant a plume of smoke and a streak of light erupted from the tilt-rotor aircraft. A line of bright white smoke extended quickly right at the Sukhoi.

"Break, Frantsi, *break! Flares!*" Doleckis shouted.

Stebut tightened his bank to 60 degrees, but the tiny missile hit before he had a chance to pump out any decoy flares.

At first nothing happened—only a flash of bright light right near Stebut's tailpipe, but soon black smoke began pouring out of the engine. Before Doleckis could say anything else, he saw the canopy fly off the Sukhoi-17, followed later by the ejection seat flying clear of the aircraft on a plume of yellow fire. It was the first time he had ever seen a stricken aircraft, the first time he had ever seen anyone eject from an aircraft except in the training films. It was horrifying, like watching someone getting hit by a car or getting gored by a raging bull. Stebut's parachute opened, but it had time to swing only once or twice before it plunged into the trees. It looked like Frantsi hit pretty hard. The parachute disappeared in the foliage as if sucked inside by the trees.

"Control, Bravo's down! Stebut's down!" Doleckis shouted on the command-post frequency. "Position, approximately forty-two kilometers northeast of Lida Naval, north of the Nemas, almost on the border. Bravo was hit by a missile fired from the American tilt-rotor." He paused, momentarily unsure what he should do next—but when he saw Stebut's

Sukhoi-17 disappear into the trees a second later and explode in an oily ball of smoke, he knew what he was going to do. "Seven-one-one is engaging." If his wing commander said something over the radio in reply, Doleckis did not hear it.

FISIKOUS AIRCRAFT-DESIGN BUREAU, VILNIUS, LITHUANIA
13 APRIL, 0847 (1247 ET)

"I can't believe it," General John Ormack said from the pilot's seat of the Fisikous-170 stealth bomber. "I think I can fly this thing with my eyes closed." Hal Briggs, Patrick McLanahan, and Dave Luger were with him in the cockpit of the massive, exotic aircraft, marveling over the controls and equipment. "It looks like an exact copy of the B-52's cockpit. Everything's in place—everything!"

He was right. The pilot's left-hand crew station was an exact duplicate of a B-52's pilot's station, with the addition of one more cathode ray tube in the center of the instrument panel. The control wheel, throttle quadrant, arrangement of instruments, and even the material and shape of the aluminum-and-vinyl glare shield were all precisely the same as the B-52's at the High Technology Aerospace Weapons Center that Ormack and McLanahan worked with every day. But the more Ormack talked, the quieter Luger had become.

Patrick, sitting in the copilot/bombardier's right-side seat, noticed Luger's slumped shoulders and detached expression. "Dave, what's wrong? This thing is incredible! It's still flyable, isn't it?"

Luger raised his eyes long enough to scan the instrument panel. "Hit the battery switch and main bus switches," he said to McLanahan. The switches were on the copilot's side instrument panel, exactly like on a Boeing B-52.

When McLanahan flipped the two switches, the cockpit lights and battery-powered gauges came alive.

Luger scanned the forward instrument panel. "It needs fuel . . . looks like no weapons aboard . . . might be a few access doors open in the back. Otherwise, yes, it's flyable." He sat back down in the seat and stared at a spot on the floor, remaining completely emotionless.

"Amazing." Ormack sighed. "My God, I feel like double-oh-seven. Imagine . . . sitting in a Soviet bomber in a Soviet research lab. Man, I think I know how successful spies feel when they go back and see what their mission accomplished."

Luger looked at Ormack as if the General had slapped him, then turned away before Ormack looked toward him.

When Ormack saw Luger's ashen face he realized what he had been saying. "Hey, Dave, I didn't mean—"

McLanahan finally realized what was eating his friend. "Dave, forget it, man. You were brainwashed. We saw what those bastards did to you, that chamber of horrors they hooked you up in. There was nothing you could have done—"

"I didn't resist hard enough," Luger said bitterly. "I could have tried harder. They got to me and I talked—almost from the first fucking day."

"That's bullshit and you know it," Briggs said. "You were alone, and injured, and confused. You were ripe for the pickin'. There was no way you could have resisted."

"Yes, there was," Luger insisted. "I caved in. I thought of nothing, nobody but myself. I betrayed everything I believe in, *everything.*"

"Dave, that's not true—" McLanahan said.

"Look at this thing! Luger snapped, sweeping a hand across the cockpit. "I re-created the pilot's and radar nav's crew station from memory, in precise detail. I was obsessed with it. This isn't the work of a tortured POW, Patrick, this is the work of a *traitor.* If I had tried harder to resist, if I had just let them kill me, I never would have done so much work for them."

"Dave, you know as well as I do that it's impossible to resist them for any period of time—especially the kind of torture they were using," Ormack said. "You can resist for a few days or even a few weeks, but if they control your environment and your movements, eventually they'll control your mind. You can't resist. Eventually everyone talks, or they go crazy, or they die. You're not a traitor—you're a hero. You saved our lives and quite possibly helped fend off World War Three. So you helped build this thing? Well, now you can help *us* take it away from them."

"And maybe even use it to fight off the Byelorussian invasion if we can get some weapons loaded on it," McLanahan said. He searched out the cockpit windows. "Where did our Lithuanian helpers go? They were supposed to be wheeling some of those cluster-bomb missiles over here."

"I'll go find out," Briggs said. "Sittin' in this thing is makin' me nervous anyway, especially when you start talkin' about bombin' stuff." Briggs climbed down the short entry ladder and disappeared out the front end of the hangar. He returned a few minutes later with General Palcikas and an interpreter following close behind. Briggs donned a pair of crew-chief headphones connected by an interphone cord to the cockpit: "Bad news, boys," Briggs said. "It looks like the Lithuanians are leavin'."

"What?"

"Several long convoys of vehicles are heading out. Here's the General."

Palcikas put on the headphones, shrugging off his interpreter, and the crew in the cockpit had to turn down the volume to guard against Palcikas' booming voice: "Hey, you spies, you look good in strange Soviet plane. Good you up there. We go now. Over."

"This is General Ormack. Where are you going, General?"

"We going to meet *General-Leytenant* Voshchanka and Home Brigade in Kobrin town—or in hell," Palcikas said. "He has crossed border with forty thousand troops and many tanks. He is moving very rapidly . . . may take Vilnius before my Iron Wolf get position. More may come from Kaliningrad and Chernyakhovsk. Not good stay in Fisikous. Over."

"Can you spare some English- and Russian-speaking men for us? We'd like to load the plane and—"

"No. Very sorry, General," Palcikas replied. "Not possible. We leave demolition team only to destroy Fisikous if Byelorussian troops advance. No soldiers stay. Maybe you go to embassy now. We go now. Over. Bye-bye." Palcikas handed the headset over to Briggs, saluted the stealth bomber's cockpit, and trotted off.

"Well, it looks like we load the plane ourselves," Ormack said with resignation. "Dave, I'd like you to translate the refueling manual for Patrick first. Once we start pumping gas, Hal and I will see about loading weapons. Let's go."

Dave Luger was expending all his energy just climbing in and out of the aircraft and hobbling across the polished concrete floor of the hangar, and he had to rest several times as he explained the refueling process to Patrick. Finally McLanahan was unreeling the refueling lines from the pump bay and was pulling the hose across the hangar floor.

"Reminds me of when you did that in Anadyr, Patrick," Dave said, sitting near the single-point refueling adapter on the left-front side of the Fi-170.

"I'm glad I don't have to climb on top of this thing, that's all—and the weather is downright balmy now compared to then."

"You've got that right," Luger said. He regarded McLanahan for a moment, then added, "I see you got a little plastic surgery for your frostbite."

McLanahan touched the pieces of stiff plastic that now made up the tips of his ears—he had suffered only a little frostbite during the Old Dog crew's entire ordeal. "Courtesy of the Air Force," he said. "One less thing they have to explain to someone."

"Unlike me," Luger said.

Patrick looked at his friend sympathetically and wanted to say something, but nothing came out.

"What do you think they're going to do with me, Patrick?" Dave asked.

McLanahan hooked the hose into the refueling adapter on the bomber, activated the pump, then returned to monitor the fuel flow and switch tanks at the proper time. He carried one of the MP5 submachine guns left behind by the Marines. "Debrief you, I guess," McLanahan said. "Get inside your head, find out what the fucking Soviets did to you."

"Do you think they'll kill me?"

McLanahan pretended he didn't hear the question, not wanting Luger to see his own fear. Through all these weeks after he'd learned Luger was in Fisikous, through the training, the planning, all of it, McLanahan had consciously blocked out considering the consequences of Luger's return. He had no idea what Washington had in mind, but knowing the inquiry the Defense Intelligence Agency had begun, Luger might have to go through really intense questioning about the Old Dog mission *after* he finished his debriefing. The shit Luger might have to endure once he was back in the States—*if* they even made it out of here—might be worse than anything the Soviets could have done. But the last thing he was going to do was let Luger know, or even suspect, those fears.

"Hey." McLanahan smiled easily. "Don't torture yourself, Dave. Don't do a number on yourself, man. We got a job to do here."

"Patrick, you gotta tell me what you know, what you *think,*" Luger insisted. "I'm scared. I feel like I'm totally alone."

"You're *not* alone, Dave," Patrick said. "You have some pretty powerful friends. Wilbur Curtis is still Chairman of the Joint Chiefs, Brad Elliott is still at HAWC and still a three-star, and Thomas Preston is Secretary of Defense. They all owe you big time." He patted the smooth skin of the Fisikous-170 and added, "And, of course, helping to bring back this trophy won't hurt."

Dave said nothing just then. The original idea of actually launching *Tuman* instead of just stealing tech orders and computer data was of course Dave's, and after they checked the weapons available—AA-8 air-to-air missiles and X27 runway-denial cruise missiles, a free-flying version of the British Hunting JP233 mine dispenser—it was his idea to try to use *Tuman* to hunt down and strike the Byelorussian invaders. General Ormack had approved the idea immediately. He was a pilot, not a ground-pounder—they all were. Making war from the skies was what they did best.

Launching the Fi-170 created the first real glimmer of energy Luger had shown since his rescue—but now the fire was fading. The closer they came to launching *Tuman,* the more guilt he was feeling for ever having created it. That crushing guilt was threatening to throw Dave right into a serious depression, and they needed him sharp to help fly the Soviet stealth bomber.

McLanahan was no psychologist, but he knew he had to talk Luger out of his funk or this flight was going nowhere. "C'mon—let's get Hal started on those missiles," he said. Then, pumping every bit of enthusiasm he could into his voice, added, "Man, you're going to make the brass pee in their pants when they see us land this thing on a NATO base."

"I get the feeling," Dave said, "that they might prefer I never made it back."

"You're wrong, Dave," Patrick said finally. He realized that he not only had to conceal from his friend what he thought, but *convince* him: "They wouldn't have brought us out here if they wanted you eliminated."

"Maybe they thought we'd *all* get eliminated."

McLanahan's heart skipped a beat. The idea had never occurred to him. It was a ridiculous idea—or was it? "Dave . . . you're getting paranoid, man. Just chill out."

Suddenly they saw a large truck roll across the compound outside the security fence that surrounded the aircraft hangars. McLanahan could see a large-caliber gun sticking out of the back of the truck, and his blood froze. It raced along at high speed right for the closed and locked gate to the parking ramp and crashed through it. Patrick clearly saw the red star on the side of the truck.

"Heads up!" McLanahan screamed. "Soviet truck in the compound!" He pulled Luger to his feet and half-carried him to cover on the side of the concrete aircraft hangar, then took aim on the truck with his MP5. The gun in the back of the truck swung in his direction. All he had was two extra magazines, about ninety rounds total, to fight off an entire truckful of Soviet commandos.

"Hold your fire, McLanahan!" someone shouted. The passenger-side door swung open and Marine Corps Gunnery Sergeant Chris Wohl hopped off the truck. "Damn, Colonel, maybe you *were* listening during all my drills. I hate to say it, but you're starting to impress me."

"Wohl! What in hell are you doing here? I thought you'd be in the embassy by now."

"We *were* in the embassy, McLanahan," Captain Edward Snyder said, hopping out of the truck along with Wohl and Gunnery Sergeant Trimble. John Ormack emerged from the Fisikous-170's cockpit a few moments later and both Trimble and Snyder rendered him a salute. Ormack accepted it with a hint of surprise. "We made it to the embassy and we dropped off the wounded and the dead . . . and then we came back."

"What? Why . . . ?"

"Don't fucking ask, sir," Snyder said. He shook his head as he looked at the Fisikous-170 stealth bomber before him. "Maybe we wanted to see what was getting you all fired up, sir. Now I see why you decided to stay. This thing is cosmic." He shrugged his shoulders, then added, "And we also saw the Lithuanians packing up and getting ready to meet the Byelorussian Home Brigade coming out of Smorgon, and we figured you guys would be all alone out here and required some adult supervision.

"We're here and under your command, General. We don't have enough guys or weapons to secure this base or even this part of the compound, but if you're going to launch this thing we figured you could use some muscle and someone who can read Russian. Tell us what to do to get you and this black beast under way."

There was nothing the eighteen Marines aboard the CV-22 could do except hold on and pray—pray that their PAVE HAMMER pilot's luck would hold out once more. A few of the COBRA VENOM commandos were stationed in the windows and wearing headsets, using the age-old "Mk 1" threat-detection system—the eyeball—to spot the enemy fighter bearing down on them. Even though they knew they could be dead by the time they ever saw the fighter, they felt that searching for the enemy and calling out his position was a more worthwhile activity than just sitting tight and hoping to escape.

"I'm staying north of the border until we get closer to the LZ," pilot Hank Fell said on interphone. "Where is that bastard?" Fell had the graphic engine readouts on his primary multifunction display—that way he could see any severe changes in the engine's performance right away. On his IHDS, or integrated helmet display system, which projected electronic images onto his helmet-mounted targeting goggles, he had the graphic readout of the CV-22 millimeter-wave radar, an ultra-high-frequency, short-range radar that easily detected very small metallic objects in the aircraft's flight path, especially the scourge of low-flying special operations crews all over the world—power lines. Fell was flying the CV-22 literally at treetop level, and many times far below that, hedgehopping from clearing to clearing and changing directions constantly every time the MiG-27 pursuing them popped up on the threat-warning receiver.

"No contact," Watanabe called out. "Last bearing was off our rear port quarter, heading east. He may be abeam us." He had the INEWS (Integrated Electronic Warfare System) threat-warning receiver on his primary multifunction display—which indicated all radars in the vicinity—show the location of missiles fired at them, and even pinpoint and jam a targeting laser illuminating the aircraft. INEWS would send a different tone for every kind of threat it detected—radar, infrared, or laser—through the interphone system, and Fell would change directions, however momentarily to turn his engine exhausts downward, and dive for trees when he heard the warning receiver bleep. Watanabe also had control of the Stinger missile system—it was he who downed the Sukhoi-17, so he and Fell each had one enemy kill since joining MADCAP MAGICIAN—and could take control of the Chain Gun pod for attacking ground threats that might appear.

"Heads up on the portside," Fell said on interphone. "Find that damn fighter. Jose!"

"Go," replied Marine Corps Gunnery Sergeant Jose Lobato, the COBRA VENOM team leader.

"You give any more thought to the idea of hotfooting it the rest of the way?" Fell asked.

"I told you, sir, we're staying," Lobato said. "Me and the boys don't like the idea of slogging through fifty miles of Indian country. We paid for the plane ticket and we're staying."

"It's your funeral." He started a hard left turn and said, "Clear my left turn and find a clearing. We've got to—"

"Contact!" one of the Marines shouted on interphone. "Portside, high, about eight o'clock position, range three miles!"

Watanabe, sitting on the left side of the cockpit, saw the MiG-27 immediately. "Contact on the bandit. Break left, Hank!"

As he gave that command, he saw a flash of light from the MiG's left wingtip, and the INEWS threat-warning receiver blared out a warning— it must have been blanked during the hard left turn and didn't spot the radar-silent MiG-27 as it slipped within infrared-detection range.

"Missile launch!" Watanabe shouted.

INEWS had automatically activated its infrared jamming system, which modulated the head energy of the CV-22's engine exhaust to cause the heat-seeking missile to break lock, and it ejected an electronic ARIES (Advanced Radar/Infrared Expendable System) decoy from a right-side ejector chute. The ARIES decoy was actually a small glider that transmitted RF energy throughout the entire electromagnetic spectrum, from infrared to ultraviolet, making it much more effective than standard flares or bundles of chaff—ARIES could jam an enemy fighter radar for several minutes, and it could even *attract* missiles from long distances or attract a missile that had missed its target and was turning to re-attack.

ARIES worked perfectly on the first missile. Flight Lieutenant Doleckis could only watch, first with astonishment and then in absolute helplessness, as his R-50 heat-seeking missile gracefully arced to the right into empty space and detonated nearly a full kilometer away from the American aircraft. Although he saw no bright flare, his missile was obviously chasing a decoy; the R-50 was an older model (the Byelorussian military rarely received top-of-the-line Commonwealth weapons—they were reserved for the Russians) and very susceptible to decoys. When he tried to turn left and lock his last R-50 on the CV-22, the missile's seeker refused to stay locked on, even though he was less than four kilometers away from the target and right behind him. His radar-warning receiver was beeping at him, which meant the CV-22 was transmitting tracking or jamming signals.

Doleckis tried one last shot at a lock-on. At minimum range of about three kilometers, the last R-50 reported locked-on, and he fired. He immediately activated his radar in air-to-air mode, reset his heads-up display for aerial gunnery, and switched to his 30-millimeter cannon. Although his cannon had three hundred rounds, it usually jammed after one or two hundred were fired—but at close range, just a few of the sausage-sized rounds were deadly. Anticipating the CV-22's next move, Doleckis used a bit of right rudder to point his nose slightly right to get a lead point on the target, placing his aiming reticle at the point he thought the aircraft would turn in just a few seconds.

The CV-22 banked sharply right, as Doleckis knew it would. The last R-50 wobbled a bit in flight, as if it were trying to go after another decoy launched to the left, but it stayed locked on. But apparently it momentarily locked on to the sun, a glint off the river below, or the *first* decoy launched by the CV-22, because the R-50 careened right over the CV-22, not attracted to its engines at all, and flew for several dozen meters before exploding.

The *fwooosh!* of the R-50 flying over the cockpit made Martin Watanabe duck and turn away instinctively, just as driving in a parking garage with really low ceilings made him hunch his shoulders, so he was protected from the brunt of the explosion as the missile screamed over the canopy. Hank Fell actually watched the thing pass by, so he was looking right at it when the missile exploded just a few yards away. The explosion shattered the right-side cockpit windows and right-front windscreen, showering the pilots with shards of Lexan. Fell felt the acrylic windscreen bite into his head, then felt the heat and pressure of the explosion slam into him—then he felt nothing as the concussion nearly blew him out of his seat.

Watanabe screamed and grabbed for the controls. The left engine had immediately gone to full power; when the explosion of the R-50's fourteen-pound warhead destroyed the right engine, the computerized flight-control system of the CV-22 automatically applied full power to the good engine. The crossover linkage tried to apply power from the left engine to the right rotor, and when that did not respond, it unfeathered the right rotor and immediately began switching the flight controls from airplane to helicopter mode for a landing.

Watanabe had his hands on the controls, but he was not fully in control. The blast that had killed Fell and torn most of his face away had badly hurt the CV-22's copilot. He had just enough time to consciously keep the wings level and the nose up when the CV-22 hit the trees. It flipped up onto its nose and threatened to cartwheel, but after hanging tail-up for several moments it settled back to earth right-side up. The right engine smoked and burst into flames, and one Stinger missile popped out of its launch canister and cooked off along the ground, but the automatic fire-extinguishing system kept the fire from spreading to the wing fuel tanks.

"Target down! Flight seven-one-one, target down!" Doleckis crowed victoriously on the command-post frequency. *Damn,* he *thought. My first kill!* He was breathing so hard that he felt he couldn't draw enough air through his oxygen mask, and he whipped it off. God, was this exciting! Doleckis used to hunt deer and pheasant with his father and uncles in the Ruzhany forests of western Belarus, and he remembered the nearly overwhelming rush of excitement when he got his first kill, but this was a million times more exciting. All that heavy iron going down, all those souls on board screaming their last breath. He felt no remorse for them at all, only sheer happiness and elation that they had died by his hand. His persistence and patience had defeated America's best technology.

Doleckis radioed his estimated position, trying to pick out some definite landmarks and finally requesting a DF (direction-finding) steer to his position. As he flew closer to the plane's impact point, he noticed the CV-22 seemed relatively intact—one small fire visible, but still generally in one piece. There was still dark fuel smoke rising, but already white smoke was replacing it—that meant automatic fire extinguishers had been activated. He needed to shoot it up some more in case there were survivors.

The young Byelorussian pilot immediately lined up his cannon gunsight pipper on the downed airplane and fired off a two-second burst from his cannon—but all rounds missed, ripping up trees far above the CV-22. He finally realized he still had the gunsight mil settings for air-to-air. It was too late to correct by the time he dialed in the proper air-to-ground settings, so he overflew the target, banked right to keep the CV-22 in sight, and set up for another gun pass. The rockets and mines he carried would do too much damage—he was sure his commander wanted this aircraft intact.

He was on the downwind leg of his re-attack orbit when a puff of smoke and a white shoestring suddenly leaped out of the forest near the impact site. Immediately, Doleckis threw his MiG-27 hard right and hit his chaff and flare buttons, ejecting bright magnesium flares from ejector racks under the tail.

The white streak spiraled right toward him . . .

It was going to hit . . .

The missile's arc gradually became larger and larger. It zeroed in right at the trail of flares left in his wake and missed him by no more than a few meters. There was no proximity explosion. The crew of that downed CV-22 had fired a Stinger at him! Not only were the Americans not helpless and out of the fight, but they had attacked! "Control, seven-one-one, crew of downed CV-22 launched a man-portable missile at me! Advise all aircraft to exercise extreme caution." The missile launch was actually a blessing in disguise, because by the time he had turned onto the base leg and was lining up for a gun pass, the smoke from the crash had subsided but the residual smoke from the Stinger-missile launch pointed right at the crash site.

Doleckis started his cannon run at one thousand meters, four hundred kilometers per hour airspeed, at a range of ten kilometers. At eight kilometers he lowered the nose, centered the CV-22 in the pipper, and watched the range counter click down. The range counter suddenly stopped, then counted down rapidly, then stopped again—the ranging radar was being jammed. No matter. He simply waited until he could clearly make out the outline of the CV-22 in the pipper and, at the proper moment, squeezed the trigger . . .

A sudden flash of motion caught his eye as he fired. He glanced to the left and saw what appeared to be a large insect, skimming just over the treetops—then there were two, then three, then three or four more on the right side. One by one the tiny insects jumped at him, with two bright winking eyes focused right on him. Doleckis turned his attention briefly to his ammunition counter—one hundred and fifty rounds gone. The impact marks were walking perfectly across the target—a perfect gun pass. All the rounds were hitting squarely on target. Little puffs of black were popping atop the CV-22, and the right wing sagged and dropped to the forest floor . . .

A terrific shudder tossed Doleckis against his shoulder straps—it felt like a giant wrecking ball had hit the side of his MiG-27. He pulled back on the stick and saw the insects flitting across his windscreen again— except this time he saw they were no insects. They were small two-man helicopters, with two machine guns mounted on the skids. They were all over him, surrounding him like bees around a hive . . . he would pass five or six of them in a second, only to be confronted by six more, each firing their machine guns at him. The small-caliber bullets peppered the armored sides of the MiG like rapid-fire sledgehammer blows. Doleckis knew they would not penetrate the fifteen-millimeter-thick steel-and-ceramic armor around the cockpit or penetrate the bullet-resistant canopy, but the rest of his jet was thin steel alloy.

Warning lights flashed inside the cockpit. The cannon gunsight went

blank, replaced by a crosshatched caution bar. The banging that reverberated through the aircraft was now a solid shuddering. It was impossible to move the control stick, and even if he could, he could not hope to
counteract the shaking in the flight controls. Doleckis activated the auxiliary hydraulic booster pumps and tested the rudder pedals—they were
functioning normally. Already a little control-stick authority was returning . . . good.

Maybe there was time for one more pass . . .

Doleckis was so intent on saving his aircraft and making one more
cannon or bomb pass that he never noticed the warning lights that told
him his engine had been destroyed, never noticed the rapid loss of airspeed or altitude. He flew the MiG-27 right into the ground in a nose-high
left bank, scissoring through the trees and exploding in a large mushroom
fireball.

"I never believed in fucking Tinker Bell—until now," Martin Watanabe
said. He was lying on the soft mossy ground, being treated by Lobato's
corpsman for severe chest and facial wounds, but he was fully conscious.
He watched as several small, buglike helicopters turned and flitted above
them. "Who are they?"

"I don't know," the corpsman asked. "Gunny's going to meet up with
them." Jose Lobato was going out to meet one of the helicopters that was
landing in a clearing nearby.

With four or five helicopters hovering nearby—Lobato saw they were
McDonnell-Douglas Model 500 Defenders, two-man, American-made
light patrol helicopters, with an infrared scanner and two 7.62-millimeter
machine guns mounted on the forward part of the landing skids—the
leader of COBRA VENOM took cover behind a tree as one of the
choppers touched down in a clearing. A soldier with a Soviet-made pistol
drawn stepped out of the helicopter and approached him. Lobato raised
his rifle and shouted, "Stop!" in English and Russian.

The soldier ordered the helicopter to cut its engine, and he stopped and
raised his pistol. In a loud voice over the winding-down engine, he
shouted, "You COBRA VENOM? American Marines? COBRA
VENOM?"

"Who the hell are you?"

"I am *Mayor* Balys Pakstas, First Brigade of the Iron Wolf, Third Air
Infantry, Lithuanian Self-Defense Force. Are you Gunnery Sergeant
Lobato, COBRA VENOM?"

Lobato couldn't believe this guy had been out here looking for him and
his team, but he still wasn't ready to divulge any classified information.
"What do you want, Major?"

"I was sent to escort you to your landing zone at Krovo," Pakstas said. Lobato couldn't believe his ears—this guy knew the exact location of their intended landing zone, a hamlet hidden near a forested butte near Smorgon Army Air Base. Could someone in the other assault team have been captured? "You will ride with us to your landing zone. We will assist in your mission."

"I don't know what you're talking about," Lobato shouted. "You had better clear out or I'll order my men to attack."

"Gunnery Sergeant Lobato, I know your objective is to mark the command-and-control center at Smorgon for a laser-guided weapon attack and locate and destroy the SS-21 Scarab missiles garrisoned there," Pakstas said. His English was very, very good, which only made Lobato that much more suspicious—to his knowledge, only well-trained intelligence agents had a command of the English language like that. "We have been briefed by your Colonel White on your mission and we are prepared to assist or take over if you are unable to continue. I need to transmit your team's status to General Palcikas and to the American Embassy."

"What crazy motherfucker told you all this?" Lobato shouted.

"The same one that will kick your ass all the way to Peabody's Tavern when you get back," Pakstas replied. He holstered his pistol and raised the middle finger of both hands at Lobato. The Lithuanian officer smiled and added, "Do you understand the meaning of this message, Gunnery Sergeant?"

Lobato had to subdue a laugh. "I sure do, Major," he replied. He could see and feel every team member relax when the Lithuanian officer said those words and made that obscene gesture. One of Paul White's quirks was the insistence on code words and phrases, backed up by a coded gesture. "Kick your ass all the way to Peabody's Tavern" was a reference to a popular bar in Plattsburgh, the city in upstate New York where Lobato went to college—it was a code phrase that only White would use and only team members that knew Lobato would remember; and, of course, only Paul White would punctuate the message with the finger: not one, but two.

Lobato shouldered his rifle, walked up to Pakstas, and shook his hand. "We can sure use your help, sir. We have two injured, one seriously, and one casualty, and we need to destroy our aircraft."

"Not necessary," Pakstas said. "Golf Company will be here in five to ten minutes to transport your casualties. They have been briefed by your embassy on which black boxes to take from your aircraft in the event it was rendered inoperable. We'll even try to transport your aircraft out of the area before the Byelorussians get it, but no guarantees on that. But we need to get moving—we have two fuel stops to make before sundown, and then we have to sneak into Byelorussian airspace after nightfall so you'll be in position. With all your gear, we can only take one Marine per helicopter, but more are on the way."

"Very well, sir. Thank you." Lobato issued orders to his men, and they formed up to get on board the tiny Defenders. As the COBRA VENOM members climbed on board their assigned helicopters, Lobato asked Pakstas, "Your English is very good, sir. If you don't mind me asking, where did you learn it so well?"

"No big deal. I was born in America," Pakstas replied. "Shaker Heights, Ohio—my folks still live there. They were Lithuanian refugees from Hitler and the Russians in the thirties, just before the war. I grew up in Ohio but came back to Lithuania in 1991 after independence. General Palcikas made me an officer in the Self-Defense Force when I became a dual national. I graduated from Allegheny College, Meadville, Pennsylvania, class of 1978. Psychology major. I think I've even been to Peabody's Tavern in Plattsburgh on a road trip to Lake Placid once— right down the street from Mother's Night Club, right?"

"You got it, sir."

"*Sauletumas vandenys,* as we say in Lithuania. Awesome party town. When this is over, I'll take you guys to some clubs in Klaipeda—you'll think you're right back in Plattsburgh. We've got the best Feast of St. Patrick's parties this side of Dublin—nothing like Boston or Plattsburgh, but pretty close. Meanwhile we've got a long way to go before nightfall. We'd better get moving."

NATIONAL MILITARY COMMAND CENTER, THE PENTAGON
13 APRIL, 1245 EASTERN TIME (1845 VILNIUS TIME)

"The situation is changing rapidly, sir," the Pentagon "War Room" briefer said. His audience was very small—only four persons in all, not including aides and staffers—but it was the top military leaders and Presidential advisers in the United States of America: Chairman of the Joint Chiefs of Staff, Air Force General Wilbur Curtis; the Secretary of Defense, Thomas Preston; and the Commandant of the Marine Corps, General Vance Kundert. They were seated in the front row of the large, amphitheater-like National Military Command Center, the main communications center of the Pentagon. From here the decision-makers in the Pentagon and the White House could speak with almost any unit commander, any aircraft, or any foreign government or embassy, and receive real-time data on the progress of a military operation.

Right now the status of the Byelorussian invasion of Lithuania and the U.S. response were the main topics of concern. "As expected, the

Byelorussian Army's advance into Lithuania has taken place on two main avenues—externally and internally," the briefer said. "Internally, the advances have been very slow and rather disorganized, mostly due to the guerrilla raids accomplished by the Lithuanian Self-Defense Force. The Byelorussians are occupying big chunks of land around their air base at Siauliai, but most other gains have been slowed by miscommunication and poor coordination. Guerrilla attacks by larger and better-equipped Lithuanian forces are continuing.

"The invasion of Lithuania from outside, however, is progressing very well. Unexpectedly, the Byelorussian Army has swept aside all challenges from the Russians in Kalinin oblast and in Kaliningrad itself, which has allowed the Byelorussian Army to advance towards Lithuania."

"The Russians offered no resistance at all?" Kundert asked, astonished. "What the hell is going on here? Why did that happen?"

"We assume it was a combination of factors, sir," the briefer replied. "The Byelorussians' strikes were swift and decisive, and resistance was probably useless. We are also not discounting the possibility of a deal struck between Voshchanka and the Russian generals in Kalinin. The territory has always been rather autonomous from Moscow and even more so from the Commonwealth—many local warlords have emerged in the confusion following the end of the USSR and the beginning of the Commonwealth—"

"I thought Kaliningrad was a Russian stronghold," Secretary of Defense Preston interjected. "What makes it so divisive now?"

"Kalinin oblast has always been a part of Russia," the briefer explained, "but it was historically part of the Polish-Lithuanian empire. It was taken from Poland during World War Two when the Soviets recaptured Poland from the Nazis. Kaliningrad is very much a Soviet/Russian city, but after the breakup of the USSR and the weakening of the Soviet military, the ethnic forces have taken precedence."

"Faced with annihilation or cooperation, the ex-Soviet warlords in Kalinin obviously chose cooperation," Curtis summarized.

"The Byelorussian forces are continuing along three main fronts outside Lithuania: along the coast, target the port city of Klaipeda; from Kalinin oblast, target the city of Kaunas; and from the east, target Vilnius," the briefer continued. "Advance forces have already penetrated the border itself and are joining with supply groups from within Lithuania itself."

"So we're too late, then," Secretary of Defense Preston said. "Whatever we do, it won't stop the Byelorussians, will it?"

A second briefer stepped up to a podium on the other side of the stage, and the first briefer deferred immediately to him: "I don't think so, Mr. Secretary," Air Force Lieutenant General Brad Elliott replied. "My—

our—Megafortress strike force can slow those three advancing armies down considerably."

Preston inwardly scowled at Elliott's remark. He knew that something dramatic had to be done to stop this war, but accepting Elliott's plan and sending in high-tech B-52s was not his ideal solution. He disliked having to accept a military plan that he didn't devise, and now he disliked having someone else—especially Elliott—supervising it. But the President and Wilbur Curtis had been won over, and it was their main defensive force right now. "I understand the objective of the EB-52 strikes, General Elliott," Preston said, "but if the Byelorussians have advanced into Lithuania, what good are they now?"

"Satellite imagery reveals that the advance forces are light armored scouts, light vehicles, and helicopter patrols only," Elliott explained. "The main tank battle forces are still some hours away. We can still strike some Byelorussian armor units before they cross into Lithuania."

"With just a few B-52s? It doesn't seem likely," Preston said skeptically.

"The EB-52 Megafortress battleships each has the offensive punch of an entire wing of A-10 or F-16 tactical bombers," Elliott said. "They may not be able to stop the entire force in one night, but if the first wave can be decimated it might help to call off the entire invasion."

Preston grudgingly agreed with Elliott's assessment—but he wasn't about to tell Elliott that. Instead he said, "*If* the bombers find their targets. What's their status?"

"We can expect the primary group of four bombers to go feet-dry in about forty-five minutes—"

"Feet-dry?"

"Cross the Baltic coast and heading inbound," Elliott explained. "One Megafortress will travel across northern Lithuania to strike at the armored units coming out of Smorgon from the east. Two bombers will start across the north, but then cut through central Lithuania to strike at the Byelorussian air base at Siauliai and continue south to counter the armor units coming in from Chernyakhovsk against Kaunas. The fourth bomber will go against the armored units along the coast that are threatening Klaipeda. The strikes will occur within ten minutes of each other, approximately two hours after crossing the coastline."

"What about the COBRA VENOM units that are already in Smorgon?" General Kundert asked. "I thought we were going to have air support for them as well."

"Yes, sir, we will," Elliott replied. "We have two Megafortresses in reserve. While the four primary birds are withdrawing, the two spares will proceed inbound. They are configured for air-to-air combat as well as ground attack. They will be able to help cover the primary group's withdrawal, and they will establish contact with the Marine Special Operations teams within Byelorussia. Together, their task is to locate and destroy Voshchanka's command-and-control system, including his nuclear-weapon-control network."

"That is absolutely essential, gentlemen," Preston emphasized. "We can knock back Voshchanka's tanks and infantry all we want, but if he follows through on his threats and pops off a few nuclear missiles, we've lost the battle."

"Sir, we need all the help we can get to locate those nuclear missiles," Curtis said to Preston. "Secretary of State Danahall indicated that some State Department or embassy staffers from Moscow are trying to help. Is there any indication on their progress?"

"Well, our embassy's political affairs officer, Sharon Greenfield, is probably the best Company operative we have. And she's got a strong line into Boris Dvornikov, the former Moscow bureau chief of the KGB, but I wouldn't count on any help from Moscow," Preston said. "The President is counting on your Special Operations Marines and General Elliott's bombers to knock out Voshchanka's headquarters. If we miss, we could be looking at a full-scale nuclear war in Europe within a couple of hours."

HOTEL LATVIA, RIGA, LATVIAN REPUBLIC
13 APRIL, 1921 HOURS (1321 ET)

"A messenger from Moscow, sir," the doorman said on the intercom. "It is marked urgent, eyes only."

General Viktor Gabovich hesitated. He had relocated to the twelfth floor of the Hotel Latvia in downtown Riga, once a run-of-the-mill Soviet-run Intourist hotel and a former KGB safe house, now converted into a rather lavish joint-venture Western-style hotel run by companies from Sweden and Germany as well as Latvia itself. Gabovich had left the confusion and danger of Lithuania and had escaped to Latvia to wait out the results of the Byelorussian invasion and to try to get a reading on Voshchanka's actions from the Commonwealth ministers. Absolutely no one should have known that he was there. But he did expect that former KGB officers from around the Commonwealth would try to contact him, to try to get in line for their piece of the new communist republic that Voshchanka was forming, so the message was not totally unexpected. Gabovich pressed the intercom button. "Bring the message up."

"The messenger insists that he deliver it to you personally, sir."

"Who is the messenger?"

"He has no name, sir, but his credentials are in order."

That was the typical response for a KGB officer: no name, no identity. A KGB officer appearing somewhere in person would not want to identify himself to anyone not known to him personally or to anyone of lower rank, especially a doorman or guard—Gabovich would have been suspicious if the stranger had given a name. He said, "Very well. Show him upstairs." Gabovich wished the hotel had a video security system, but Western-style hotels did not have such things, and Latvia and the rest of the Baltic states were becoming more and more Western every day.

Gabovich drew a Beretta automatic pistol from a shoulder holster when he heard the knock at the door—four knocks, then one lower on the door, a standard KGB entry code. Pistol at the ready, Gabovich opened the door.

"Greetings, General Gabovich," came the hearty greeting.

Gabovich did not know whom to expect, but one person he never would have guessed would appear was General Boris Georgivich Dvornikov, the former director of the Moscow Central office of the KGB and once the highest-ranking field officer in the entire service. Dvornikov was now a top-level official with the Moscow City Police, though Gabovich knew from his own sources that Dvornikov did more than just handle police affairs. Rumor had it that he kept his hands in many pies after the collapse of the USSR, and his contacts were considered to be far superior and more loyal than even Gabovich's own. It was also known that Dvornikov could be duplicitous at will and had on more than one occasion bent over backwards to help out the Americans. It was said he had a hard-on for the U.S. Embassy's political affairs officer in Moscow, Sharon Greenfield. Gabovich could only imagine what a sadist like Dvornikov wanted to do to Greenfield. . . .

"Well, Viktor Josefivich, aren't you going to invite me in, or will we talk out here in the hallway?"

Speechless with surprise, Gabovich motioned for Dvornikov to enter.

"It has been a long time since I've stayed at the Hotel Latvia," Dvornikov said casually as he removed his black leather gloves and glanced idly around the apartment. "Not anything like it was when Intourist ran the place, is it? The Ministry of the Interior and we in the KGB knew nothing of running hotels." He noticed Gabovich's hand in his right front pocket, smiled, and said, "Are you still carrying around those delightful little Italian automatics? You always did go for the best."

Gabovich withdrew the pistol from his pocket and placed it back in his holster, snapping the securing band tightly. "This . . . this is a surprise, Comrade General . . ."

"Please, no more rank, Viktor," Dvornikov said in mild protest. "At least not until the Union is restored—and then I will probably be inferior in rank to yourself. Only you have had the vision to actually do something positive to restore the Union to its former glorious position." He hesitated, watching Gabovich's eyes brighten with a smile. Yes, Gabovich was truly proud of his deeds these past few weeks. Never mind that he could be pushing the entire world to the brink of war—that wasn't his concern. Dvornikov added, "I assume that is what you are doing regarding this pact you have made with General Voshchanka and the other berserkers in Byelorussia, no?"

Gabovich was clearly relieved. His plan, and so far its successful progress, had been noticed by one of the highest-ranking, most powerful men in the former Soviet Union. Dvornikov was actually *deferring* to him! "Y–yes, that is precisely what my plan was, Comrade General," Gabovich said proudly. "I'm very glad you approve."

"I should like to hear more, Comrade," Dvornikov said. He motioned to a portable bar set up in the salon. "Perhaps we can toast your triumph." Gabovich motioned to a chair in the living room, and Dvornikov took a seat. Gabovich poured him a snifter of brandy, and before he could say anything else, Dvornikov raised it to him. "To you and your operation, much success."

"To the new Union of Soviet Socialist Republics," Gabovich said confidently. He drained his entire snifter, not noticing that Dvornikov barely wet his lips with his.

"Yes, it is quite a feat you have accomplished, Viktor Josefivich," Dvornikov smiled. "Getting that pig Voshchanka to mobilize his troops against both Lithuania and Russia in the Kalinin oblast was a stroke of genius. Frankly, I'm surprised the old goat understood what you were telling him."

"I think Voshchanka may have some dim inkling of the idea of a new communist state and the reunion of the fraternal Soviet republics under one government," Gabovich said, "but what I knew he believed in was power. He was obsessed with it. Nothing was going to stop him. All he needed was the right tool, the right spark—"

"And you provided that," Dvornikov said. "As director of security of Fisikous, you had much to tempt Voshchanka's appetite, didn't you? One prays for such an array of weapons to offer for sale or exchange—especially nuclear warheads. The KR-11 was a Fisikous product, if I'm not mistaken, along with the X-27 air-launched cruise missile. That is what you offered him, was it not?"

Gabovich was not surprised that Dvornikov had figured out or discovered his plan—he had a ten-year reputation of such unerring data collection. "Yes, it was," he replied. "Not only the weapons, Comrade Dvornikov, but the command-and-control systems as well. A simple system, really, highly automated and—"

"How many warheads did you transfer to him?"

"Three," Gabovich replied, "with technicians to modify his existing nuclear-tipped SS-21 missiles to interface with the command-and-control system. Voshchanka has an option for nine more, as well as—"

"How many SS-21 missiles with nuclear warheads does Voshchanka have in the field?" Dvornikov asked, idly running his finger around the lip of his brandy snifter.

The repeated questions, and especially the last one, irritated Gabovich—and Gabovich also noticed that Dvornikov had not touched his brandy. This, he thought, was starting to take on the form of an interrogation. "Is there some problem, Boris Georgivich? Everything is proceeding according to plan. In just a few days Lithuania will fall. The Commonwealth will have no choice but to negotiate a peaceful settlement with Voshchanka and Svetlov."

"What were you going to get out of all this, Viktor Josefivich?" Dvornikov asked. "Fisikous has fallen to U.S. Marines and to Dominikas Palcikas—surely you know that by now—and the scientists there have been arrested by the Lithuanians. You could not have possibly expected Fisikous to stay intact once the invasion was on, especially after the massacre Voshchanka's troops engineered there—Palcikas made Fisikous Lithuania's equivalent of the Alamo or the Bastille. What did you hope to accom—" And then he stopped, finally realizing what Gabovich wanted, and it had nothing at all to do with Fisikous.

"I think you have guessed what I want—and I think you agree with me, Boris Georgivich," Gabovich said. "This damned Commonwealth, the weak-kneed Russian bureaucrats in Moscow, the pathetic sheep in the Council of Ministers in Minsk—they all know what will happen, what *has* to happen. The Commonwealth cannot survive. It will eventually tear itself apart. Riots in the Nagorno-Karabakh, civil war in Georgia, the war between Armenia and Azerbaijan, the eventual incorporation of Armenia and Turkmenistan into Iran and the incorporation of Moldova into Romania, absolute poverty all over the countryside, even the breakup of the Russian Federation itself—how can the Commonwealth hope to survive . . . ?"

"I agree," Dvornikov said, nodding. "The Commonwealth must eventually fail. But giving a megalomaniac like Voshchanka nuclear warheads? You know he will do only one thing with them."

"Yes. Use them," Gabovich said simply. "Against the Commonwealth armies, against the Russians, against Minsk, against anyone who dares attack him. And when that first warhead explodes, chaos will break out in all of Europe. The Commonwealth will rip apart."

"And you are here in Riga because . . . you expect Voshchanka to target Minsk as well as the Russian and Commonwealth armies?"

"Of course he will," Gabovich said matter-of-factly. "He has no military apparatus in Minsk—everything has been moved to Smorgon, and will soon be moved to Kaunas."

"Because Vilnius . . ." Dvornikov prodded. "He intends on destroying Vilnius as well?"

"All remnants of Russian influence will be destroyed, including in his own country," Gabovich said. "But he will have most of his one-hundred-thousand-man army and air force with him, deployed safely to western Lithuania and Kaliningrad."

"The Russians will crush him."

"Do you think Voshchanka believes that? He does not. He thinks he is invincible. He thinks God will guide his sword, deliver him from evil, and all that mythological crap. It doesn't matter if it's logical or tactically wise, Comrade, he will do it. I wouldn't be surprised if he has rolled a few missiles into Russia and has targeted Moscow."

"What about Riga? Latvia is almost as Russian as St. Petersburg."

"I think he harbors some thoughts about taking Latvia and Estonia," Gabovich explained. "In any case I am monitoring his SS-21 unit's movements. So far none of those units are within range of Latvia, except perhaps Daugavpils."

"So you know where the nuclear-tipped missiles are?" Dvornikov asked. "You can pinpoint their location?"

"Of course," Gabovich said, pouring another snifter of brandy. "I was very concerned that the old war-horse would try to come after me. I think he believes I am in Minsk, which is why he has moved all three nuclear-capable missiles to the pre-surveyed launch point in Kurenets—that is, within optimal range for both Minsk and Vilnius for the SS-21."

"And so you think that by killing several million persons and destroying two European capitals, the Commonwealth will end and the Union will be restored?" asked Dvornikov.

"Of course it will be restored," Gabovich said testily. "Russia will certainly occupy Belarus after the attack. After that, Russia will have no choice but to subdue all the other republics that still have nuclear weapons—the Ukraine, Azerbaijan, Uzbekistan, and Kazakhstan. The Commonwealth will end, to be replaced by a strong, dominant Russia—as it should be."

Dvornikov studied the dark amber liquid in his glass for a moment; then: "And the deaths of millions of people, including your fellow Russians, don't concern you?"

"Concern me? Comrade, I am counting on it," Gabovich said. "What better way to begin a fresh start than with a nuclear release? What better way to purge the land of reformists, reactionaries, nationalists, imperialist, and capitalists? Just as there are no atheists in foxholes, there are no liberals after a nuclear explosion. Imagine the ramifications: higher prices for Russian oil; newer, stronger military to counter the West, which will certainly want to rearm against the 'new Soviet threat'—the list is endless. The people will realize that a divided union will only lead to more chaos. Everything will be as it once was, with Russia regaining the respect and power and authority it once had, with the foreign influences removed and with the central government firmly in command."

Dvornikov realized now he was sitting across from a very cool, very collected, but totally insane man. Gabovich's reputation as a tough, no-nonsense officer had preceded him for years, but there had been hints, strong hints, that he was more than just that. He was, in fact, probably many times more mad than Voshchanka. And yet . . . there was a spark of logic in what Gabovich was saying. Was it possible that Gabovich's twisted plan could actually *work?* He wondered . . .

"I see your plan now, Comrade," he said finally. "I was very concerned about you for a while: I believed you were actually selling out to Voshchanka, selling out the Union—"

"Never!" Gabovich retorted.

"I realize that," Dvornikov said. "But how can you be sure that Voshchanka will turn the keys? He may be committed to his plan, but we have seen that he is not the most intelligent commander that ever got off the shitter. To say he's primitive is being kind. Where is his command center at Smorgon? Can he communicate with his forces and send a launch message via radio or data link to his command center?"

"Of course," Gabovich said smugly. "The Fisikous command network is the world's most sophisticated system. But I don't think you need to worry about Voshchanka pulling the trigger—he will do it. We will get a report in just a few hours that a weapon has been launched."

"I wish I had your confidence that all will proceed normally, Viktor Josefivich. I like to be sure."

"I doubt that. You want to know where the command center is because you really want to stop him from launching those missiles," Gabovich surmised. "But why? Why do you want to stop him? Don't you care about the Union, Comrade? You were a powerful man in the old Soviet Union, Boris Georgivich—would you like to see it come back?"

"I would feel better if those weapons were in your hands rather than a nut case like Voshchanka's, that's all."

Gabovich regarded him warily. The flattery didn't suit Dvornikov. It had, in fact, blown him completely. "Don't try and placate me," Gabovich snarled. "You're lying. You no more want me to have charge of those weapons than Voshchanka. You think I'm crazy, don't you? Fool! You don't want them launched at all, do you? You care nothing about the future! The glorious future that will be ours—*mine!"*

Gabovich reached for the pistol in his holster, but he was far, far too late. From his greatcoat pocket Dvornikov withdrew a Walther P-4 automatic pistol fitted with a large cylindrical suppressor that was longer than the gun itself and fired twice into Gabovich's heart from close range. The heavily suppressed, small-caliber subsonic rounds made virtually no noise. Gabovich stumbled backwards, his eyes wide with surprise and insanity; he was dead before he hit the floor.

"You had the power of life and death in your hands, you stupid bastard," Dvornikov said to the corpse, "and you screwed it up. I only hope Voshchanka goes through with his plan now, or all this will turn into nothing but an incredible waste."

Dvornikov holstered his gun and began rifling through Gabovich's papers. The fool had an entire stack of information on the weapons, including their location, in his briefcase—*I could have had the floor mother steal this stuff, for God's sake!* He removed the files, ripped them into several pieces, tossed them into a metal garbage can, and dropped a match onto the papers. *Well,* he thought wryly, *Gabovich wasn't much of a spy anyway, but his plan was going to go forward despite his stupidity. He was going to be sure that—*

"Freeze, Boris. Raise your hands and get away from that desk."

Dvornikov stopped ripping papers, dropped them, and raised his hands. "Well, well, Sharon," he said. Despite her warning, he turned and faced CIA agent Sharon Greenfield with his usual disarming smile. "At last we are alone, and in more pleasant surroundings."

"Get away from that desk, I said." He stepped away a single step, moving toward her. "Left hand, fingers only, remove your gun from the holster and throw it over here."

"Really, Sharon . . ."

"Now!" she ordered.

He shrugged his shoulders, reached down with his left hand, withdrew the gun from his holster, and tossed it to her feet. She stooped down and stuck it in her coat pocket. Greenfield then motioned to the other side of the room with her gun. "Move over there." He circled away a few paces, but he was still the same distance to her. "You're getting lax, Boris," Sharon said, going over to the waste can, kicking it, and stomping on the burning papers. "Former KGB honcho like yourself, getting caught by a tail like me. You were much slicker, more careful in the old days, Boris. But thank God you've gotten lazier. Makes my job a lot easier."

Dvornikov ignored the jab. "Sharon, you're really making a mess of the new carpeting . . ."

"Shut up, Boris." She checked Gabovich. The two bullet holes in his chest were hardly bleeding—he was very dead. His gun was still in his holster; she left it there. "Why did you kill Gabovich, Boris? If what our reports say is true, he might have sold nuclear warheads to Voshchanka in exchange for clemency after the invasion of Lithuania was completed. He might have known where the warheads are . . ."

"He knew nothing. He was crazy. He reached for his gun, and I shot him."

"How can you be so sure? Did he say anything to you?"

"Nothing."

Greenfield frowned at Dvornikov, not sure whether to believe him or not, then motioned to the bullet holes in Gabovich's chest. "Pretty good group, Boris. Did you ever think about putting that group in his shoulder or leg so we could question him?"

"Is that what you will do to me, Sharon? Will you just wound me or will you shoot to kill?"

She bent down to examine the burnt papers. The top papers were charred, but the bottom ones were still mostly intact. "Neither, if you behave." Her Russian reading skills were poor, but she soon recognized what the papers said. "Boris, these papers . . . they show the location of Voshchanka's missiles. Why were you—"

Dvornikov moved with the speed of a cheetah.

He kicked Greenfield's gun hand, sending the gun flying. One more step, driving with his legs and hips, and he punched at her face with an expert karate blow. She cried out and went cartwheeling over. He was on top of her, pinning her arms to her sides with his legs. He slapped her across the face once, twice, and finally felt the fight go out of her body.

"You have no idea, bitch, how long I've waited to do this," Dvornikov gasped. There was no hint of the civil, refined, sophisticated man-about-town anymore—now he was a shaking, wild-eyed attacker.

It was a side of Dvornikov Sharon had always feared but never actually seen. The times they had met on business over the years in Moscow had always included heavy-handed sexual inferences from Dvornikov, inferences Sharon had just as heavy-handedly rejected. Knowing his sadistic reputation both in his professional and personal life, she had always worried that he would someday pounce . . .

He pulled her coat open, then ripped her blouse apart, revealing her breasts. "Oh, yes, lovely Sharon. I knew you'd be this beautiful . . ."

She tried hard to concentrate, to distract him, refocus him, all the while squirming beneath him, not giving in. She had kept tabs on him since Moscow, tailed him all the way to damned Latvia, and she was sure as hell not going to let him blow her mission for a quick and unwelcome fuck.

"Why were you helping Gabovich?"

"Because I realized he was right," Dvornikov said. He groaned in ecstasy, trying to undo his pants. "Voshchanka is going to destroy Vilnius and Minsk. When he launches those missiles, the world will change—again—back to the way it was before all this reform and glasnost and openness and capitalism that has been creating so much confusion and disorganization in my country all these years. Russia will retake the republics and reassert its dominance over Europe once again—and I intend to be part of it. All I have to do is make sure no one finds out about the missiles. When I return to Moscow, I'll be the chief of the KGB."

He fondled her left breast, twirling the nipple between his thumb and forefinger. His grasp suddenly tightened, and she caught her breath as his fingers tightened. Dvornikov's eyes narrowed, and his lips twisted into an evil leer. "You want a little pain, dear Sharon?"

There were three short, muted *puffs!* of sound, but the ex-KGB officer's body jerked as if it had been hit by three consecutive hammer blows. Dvornikov's right rib cage exploded in a cloud of gore and bright crimson, and his eyes grew wide in shock. He looked down at his side, saw bone and pieces of his right lung hanging out of his body, then turned to Greenfield. "Sharon, my love," he croaked, blood flowing from his dying lips, "what did you do?" His eyes rolled up in his head and he slumped over.

She stayed on her back for several long moments, the smoking gun in her right hand, listening to his heavy, gurgling breathing. She did not move until the gurgling stopped. Dvornikov had forgotten about the gun that she had put in her coat pocket—his gun.

The sadistic bastard was finally dead.

When she felt strong enough to move, she crawled back to the desk and the pile of half-burnt papers lying on the floor. From what she could tell, these were Gabovich's notes on the sale of three nuclear warheads to General Lieutenant Voshchanka of the Byelorussian Army and surveillance records on the location and technical-system setup for the SS-21s on which they were to be carried.

Sharon moved painfully to her feet, buttoned herself up, collected the papers, stuffed them in her coat pocket, and left the room. The Byelorussian Army's attack was under way and the counterattack would be beginning shortly after sunset. If Voshchanka was going to make good on his threat to launch those missiles, he would do it then. She didn't have much time, but there was still a chance. She had to get the papers to the U.S. Embassy there in Riga, have them decoded and translated, and hope they could lead the Marines to the location of the missiles.

ALONG THE LITHUANIAN-BYELORUSSIAN BORDER
THIRTY MILES EAST OF VILNIUS, LITHUANIA
13 APRIL, 2214 (1614 ET)

The *Osmanskaja Vozvysennost,* or Osmansky Highlands, which lay between Minsk and Vilnius, was called the "Highway to Heaven" by the
people of northern Byelorussia because the rugged, rolling glacial valleys,
hills, and buttes led from the marshy, dark wetlands of central Byelorussia to the fertile, well-drained valleys and farmlands of Lithuania and
the Baltic Sea region. But the Highlands were also rugged, rocky, wind-
swept hills, which made it very difficult to bring wagons or heavily laden
horses across it. As such, they were a favorite spot from which to stage
an ambush. Between the tenth and fourteenth centuries, several key battles between the Lithuanian-Byelorussian defenders and foreign invaders
were won because the defenders swept down from the Highlands to
overwhelm the invaders traveling on the marshy, unprotected valley
plains below.

Lithuania's Grand Duke Gediminas's main castle was built on a hill
that was part of the western terminus of the Osmansky Highlands. The
Iron Wolf Tower, the main guard tower of the castle, was perched atop
the hill and was itself ten stories tall, making the tower the highest
elevation in all of Lithuania, with enough visibility to see nearly fifty miles
into Byelorussia north and south of the Highlands.

General Dominikas Palcikas had taken advantage of this and had put
an old war-surplus Royal Navy Type 293 air-and-surface-search radar
atop the main tower to track helicopters and vehicles traveling along the
highways and lowlands. Because the radar was old and very unreliable,
however, Palcikas, just like his warrior brethren of ages past, had not
forgotten to keep human sentries up on the tower to keep watch and
report any activity they saw.

Palcikas, being a student of history, assumed that all professional,
Soviet-trained generals were the same. It was a surprise, then, for him to
find General Voshchanka's Home Brigade moving rapidly along the main
east-west highway north of the Osmansky Highlands. All armies that
have taken the "low road" through Byelorussia—the Teutonic knights,
the Mongols, the Crusaders, even the Russian conquerors—have gotten
nailed from defenders coming out of the Osmansky Highlands.

Of course this was now the age of helicopter and jet warfare, of tanks
that could climb mountains and guns that could dig out even the most
entrenched troops. So it was not going to be an easy fight.

"Radar contact, aircraft, numerous targets, bearing one-zero-three degrees, range twenty-eight nautical miles," the radar controller in a van

parked on the grounds of the Lower Castle reported via radio. "Heading westbound at eight knots. They'll be over Vilnius East in a few minutes."

Dominikas Palcikas, on board his Mil-8 assault/transport/command helicopter, nodded nervously when the report was relayed to him. The helicopter, along with twenty others belonging to his First Battalion, were parked atop Dokshitsy Butte, ten miles east of the Lithuanian border. The Mil-8 was a standard attack/assault craft, carrying ten security troops, a battle staff of four, and four 57-millimeter rocket pods, but Palcikas had it upgraded with extensive communications gear to serve as his forward command ship.

With his air-cavalry unit were about two thousand troops and a hundred vehicles, from tanks to armored personnel carriers to World War II–era Jeeps, armed and ready to charge. "Ninety knots airspeed—could be attack helicopters," Palcikas mused. "But if our patrols haven't spotted the initial spearhead of tanks yet, those helicopters are probably scouts."

"No reports of attack helicopters up anywhere," Colonel Zukauskas, Palcikas' deputy commander, added. "Perhaps the American Marines' raid on Smorgon was a success?"

"Perhaps," Palcikas said with a dim smile. There was actually a lot of evidence that suggested that the Marines were very active in Byelorussia—the command team that was picked up by one of Palcikas' helicopter cavalry companies, the unexplained return of the Marines to Fisikous, and the reports he heard about a large-scale explosion and fire at Smorgon Army Air Base itself.

But the Byelorussian Army that was advancing on Vilnius from Smorgon was still large and very powerful; they had as many scout helicopters as Lithuania had helicopters of *any* type, and they probably had as many mechanics and garbage collectors as Palcikas had trained soldiers. There was no way that Palcikas could hope to face Voshchanka's army head-to-head. Voshchanka could lay waste to the city with ease, using just his helicopters . . .

. . . so Palcikas wasn't going to face Voshchanka's troops head-to-head. He had learned from long years of experience as well as from the realities of life that he had faced since becoming commander of Lithuania's young army that he could not do anything he wanted. No amount of prayer, positive thinking, or planning was ever going to make the Byelorussian Army turn tail and run. Palcikas needed an alternate plan, and he was putting that plan into motion at that very moment.

Despite the speed advantages for Voshchanka's troops of traveling on the superhighway that ran from Minsk to Vilnius, the one disadvantage lay in maneuvering—it was easy and convenient to leave the highway only in certain places. Trying to maneuver laterally once the convoy got moving was nearly impossible. Palcikas had decided to borrow a page from Byelorussia's early history:

When the Mongol invaders swept across the territory toward the Baltic, the Rus inhabitants were able to cut off their supply lines as well as their rear and flanking guards by making lightning-fast hit-and-run attacks down from the Highlands, then escaping back into the rugged hills. Using his light tanks, armored personnel carriers, and assault/transport helicopters, that was precisely what Palcikas had planned—instead of trying to face the Byelorussian Army head-on at the border, he had moved his entire division from Vilnius, nearly six thousand troops, across the border into the Osmansky Highlands of Byelorussia and was now in position to attack the troop column's flanks and rear. Visibility was poor, but through the cold, driving rain Palcikas could see the columns of tanks and armored vehicles speeding across the Minsk-Vilnius Highway westward.

The poor weather had obviously hampered Voshchanka's scouting operations, because at least one patrol helicopter flew within two kilometers of First Brigade's hiding place and failed to spot them. Now most of the scouts had moved ahead, tightening their search patterns as they moved closer to Vilnius.

"Radar reports more helicopters inbound," Zukauskas said. "Multiple inbounds, faster than the first group. It's got to be the assault helicopters. Position is very close to Third Brigade's."

"Signal Third Battalion to stand by to attack when the helicopters pass by," Palcikas said. Messages were sent between Palcikas' units via old-style field telephones, since a radio broadcast originating so close to the Byelorussian troops would have been detected and pinpointed immediately. Palcikas walked, then crawled over to a small knot of soldiers lying on the very rim of the butte, studying the Byelorussian armored column through a large telescope. "You got us a target yet, Sergeant?"

Sergeant of Infantry Markuc Styra looked up, saw that it was General Palcikas himself lying in the mud next to him, and gulped. "No, sir. I see the vehicles all right, but I can't make out the missile vehicles or ZSU-23-4 units." His telescope was a large, bulky, Soviet-made CSR-3030 night scope, able to amplify tiny amounts of light to illuminate the entire scene and allow them to "see in the dark." Unfortunately, the older device needed a lot of light to be useful, such as moonlight, and with a full-blown spring thunderstorm on top of them, it was going to be all but useless.

"Hang tight, then. We'll have to get you some illumination." He crawled back out away from the crest of the butte, then said to his deputy, "Colonel, get the helicopters ready to attack."

* * *

It was not any of the troops in the armored column below, but the weapons officer aboard a Byelorussian Mil-24 assault helicopter flying south of the highway who first issued the warning: "Brigade, brigade, this is flight one-five-four. Enemy helicopters atop the butte to the south. I have them in sight—closing to attack." The gunner had locked his infrared scanner on the very hot profile of the helicopter below. "Target!" he cried out.

"Call out range," the pilot responded. "Rocket pods coming hot." In a Mil-24, the gunner usually controlled only the infrared TV sensor in the nose and whichever weapon the pilot would let him have. But since most pilots did not like to retake control of a weapon only to find no more ammunition in it, most retained full control over all weapons—relegating the gunner to the role of a high-tech observer.

The gunner used an optronic device in the infrared scanner to judge range: "Estimated three kilometers . . . two kilometers . . . left three degrees . . . coming up on one kilometer . . ."

But something was wrong. The object he thought was a helicopter was not looking anything like a flying machine now. "Stand by."

It wasn't a helicopter! As they got closer, the gunner saw it was a truck, apparently with a broken axle or two flat front tires, with some ammunition crates behind it to form the outline of a large helicopter and some sort of weathervane-type device mounted on the roof to make it look like a helicopter's rotor. A few strategically placed flares made it look like an idling helicopter through the infrared scanner. "It's not—"

But he wasn't adamant enough about making the withholding call. "Missile away," the pilot said, and let fly a salvo of ten 57-millimeter rockets. The explosion was spectacular—too spectacular. The thing must have been loaded with oil or gasoline, because the truck exploded with a great big orange fireball that lit up the night sky like a beacon—it was bright enough out there to see the armored column a good two or three kilometers away.

"Good hit, good secondaries," the pilot radioed.

"It wasn't a helicopter," the gunner reported. "It was a decoy! Let's climb out of here and—"

It was too late.

The Mil-24 was hit a few seconds later by a Soviet-made SA-7 missile fired by one of Palcikas' infantrymen as the attack helicopter flew overhead—at a range of less than a thousand meters, even the relatively unreliable SA-7 Strela missile could not miss. The infantryman even knew enough not to wait until the helicopter passed by, but to hit it as it was moving abeam his position since the Mil-24's engine exhaust is diverted sideways and downwards to deter heat-seeking missiles fired from astern.

The Mil-24 continued flying after its destroyed left engine was shut down, but it crashed several kilometers away moments later.

But the downing of the Mil-24, although a real bonus for the Lithuanians, was not the main objective—Palcikas' men needed a big distraction and a bright source of illumination while they searched for specific vehicles in the armored column, and they found it after the gasoline-laden decoy went up in flames. Layered within most Soviet-style armored columns were air-defense weapons, usually surrounded by other vehicles to disguise and protect them—but when the column reconfigured to deal with the "attack" from the Osmansky Highlands, the protection broke apart.

The spotters on the ridgeline above the column finally saw their objective: spaced every ten vehicles or so were four SA-8 road-mobile surface-to-air missile units, with four short-range antiaircraft missiles per unit; every fifteen vehicles was one SA-6 tracked surface-to-air missile unit carrying three medium-range missiles, along with its "Long Track" and "Straight Flush" surveillance and tracking radars and maintenance-support vehicle chugging alongside; and spread out laterally from the column every five vehicles were two ZSU-23-4 air-defense-artillery tracked units.

As well as learning lessons from historical battles, Palcikas had learned a lesson from the more recent Persian Gulf War—hit an objective with heavy, sustained firepower, then move. That is exactly what he did. As soon as the air-defense vehicles revealed themselves, Palcikas ordered his tanks and attack helicopters to attack. The Lithuanians streamed out of the Osmansky Highlands, opening fire on the air-defense vehicles before they had a chance to react.

The Lithuanians had nothing more powerful than mortars, bazookas, and rocket-propelled grenades, but their targets were not heavily armored main battle tanks but the fairly lightly armored air-defense vehicles. The truck and Jeep-mounted RPGs did the most damage, moving in to very close range before opening fire, then darting away.

The ZSU-23-4s were hit hard.

Palcikas' few tanks, all older-model T-55 and T-62 units, created enough distraction to allow the smaller vehicles to close in for the kill. Once the ZSU-23-4s were out of the fight, his helicopters hit next, blasting the SA-8 and SA-6 units with cannon fire and 40-millimeter grenades launched by the copilots. The Byelorussian SA-8 and SA-6 missiles could be disabled by heavy-caliber gunfire or even a grenade exploding too close, and the SA-6 was vulnerable to a hit on its companion radar vehicle, so they were easily put out of commission.

The Byelorussian trucks were having considerable difficulty deploying to defend their column by the time Palcikas' troops all along the Osmansky Highlands completed their fast attack. There was a deep, water-filled ditch on either side of the highway, and tall, strong fences beyond that kept stray cattle and blowing dirt, rocks, and debris off the highway. Even the heavy T-64 and T-72 tanks had trouble crossing the wide, deep ditch, and the lighter vehicles had no chance. Any vehicle hung up in the ditch or the fence for even a moment was easy prey for the Lithuanian cannons and RPGs.

"We've got them pinned down!" Colonel Zukauskas said to Palcikas, now airborne in the Mil-8 patrolling the highway in search of any unit that needed help. "Third Battalion reports several fuel and ammunition vehicles on fire, and it appears that several vehicles in the lead have stalled or broken down. We can target the heavier tanks and APCs now."

"No," Palcikas said. "Issue the retreat order. Tell all units to pull back to the Highlands and rally at point Victory for withdrawal instructions."

"But, sir, this can be a great victory for you," Zukauskas said. "We didn't anticipate the success our first thrust would be. Our casualties have been very light, only a handful of vehicles from the entire division—now is the time to press our advantage."

"Our casualties were light because we did not engage the heavy armor," Palcikas said. "That was the plan. We cannot afford heavier losses. The tide can turn quickly on us, and if we are trapped this far in Byelorussia we can lose our entire force. As long as this thunderstorm continues overhead, now is the time to withdraw, not attack. We've accomplished our mission."

"With all due respect, sir," Zukauskas pressed, "our mission is to protect Lithuania. If we stop this armored column now, Lithuania is saved. I recommend we proceed with the attack."

"Your objection is noted," Palcikas said. "Now issue the retreat order immediately."

Zukauskas nodded, although he looked as if he was ready to continue arguing. But seconds after he turned back to the radio net, Zukauskas turned to Palcikas once more: "Sir, Third Battalion reports that they have crossed north of the highway and are beginning a rear attack on the main battle tanks. Colonel Manomaitis reports six T-72s destroyed or disabled."

"Damn," Palcikas swore, loud enough for the pilots to hear him in the front of the noisy cabin. "If Manomaitis doesn't die from his stupidity, I'll wring his neck when we get back!"

"We can tell him to withdraw," Zukauskas said, "but then we've got to support his withdrawal with elements of Second Battalion or with the helicopters. But if we re-engaged with all forces we could—"

"You're getting too blood-hungry, sitting up here warm and dry in a helicopter, Colonel," Palcikas said angrily, "while sixteen-year-old volunteers running through knee-deep mud are getting shot at by

Byelorussian tanks. The helicopters are running low on fuel and will have to return to Lithuania, and we don't have many more Strela missiles left—did you think of that? I want First Battalion to withdraw to point Whirlwind and turn to cover the west flank. Third of the Second will also withdraw and provide covering fire. Get Alpha and Bravo companies of Second Battalion moving east to help cover First Battalion's withdrawal. Then I want—"

The Mil-8 swerved and dipped precipitously as the hull was pounded by heavy gunfire. The cabin began filling with oily, stinging smoke.

"We're going in, General!" one of the pilots called back as the lights flickered, then died in the cockpit. "Brace for impact."

Palcikas saw the rocket pods being jettisoned as the pilots fought to find a safe, soft landing spot, as far into the protection of the Highlands as possible but not so far up that they would land on rocks.

The big Mil-8 assault helicopter landed hot and heavy, but the fixed tricycle landing gear stayed intact and the big helicopter remained upright. No one was hurt in the impact. With the ten security troops deployed as a covering guard, Palcikas and his battle staff collected their classified charts and papers, retrieved their portable communications gear, and exited the helicopter.

"Up the hill," Palcikas called out to his troops. "Radio, see if you can contact Colonel Manomaitis. Tell him we're on the ground and order him to supervise an orderly withdrawal to rendezvous point Lightning or Overlord. Then contact Sparrow Ten and have him pick us up. Use light signals—stay off the transmitter as much as possible or the Byelorussians will home in on your—"

The unmistakable impact of heavy-caliber bullets against rocks and dirt nearby made them all leap for cover. The Byelorussian armored columns were starting to organize their counterattack. Several T-72 main battle tanks were rushing toward them from the west—it was hard to tell distance at night, but Palcikas thought they were now less than four kilometers away, well within main gun range—and First Battalion was fleeing from their heavy 125-millimeter guns. Already two Lithuanian tanks had been hit and were burning fiercely. "Get up into the hills!" Palcikas shouted. "Stay hidden, but don't get caught in a crevasse. Move!"

Palcikas paused to count heads as they ran up the hill toward the summit of the Osmansky Highlands, then grabbed the radio pack from one of the security men. He had to risk a radio transmission or else they'd be gunned down or overrun within minutes. "Second Battalion, this is Alpha, free up Seventh Armor and move west to counter four to six T-72s heading east. First Battalion is trying to withdraw. He needs—"

Palcikas heard a loud *ccrrackk!* and he felt as if his left leg had been shot off—there was no pain, only numbness and a warm, damp feeling that began to spread. He hit the ground hard, and the pain hit with the force of a blast furnace. His left hand felt for the wound, and it was a big one—blood was gushing out of a two-centimeter-wide hole like a ruptured high-pressure hose. Never in his life had he ever felt such excruciating pain. He rolled on the ground, vomiting and screaming and choking, hoping that a Byelorussian tank would just roll over his writhing body and end it for him.

"General Palcikas!" someone shouted. It was Colonel Zukauskas. He had run back to find his commanding officer. Palcikas felt hands grasping the epaulets on his field jacket, and he was being dragged across the rocks and dirt behind a clump of boulders.

"No . . . no, Vitalis," Palcikas screamed, "don't stay here. Run. Take command of the brigade." But Zukauskas' hands were still on his jacket. "That's an order, Vitalis. You can't help me. You have command of the brigade. Go!"

Palcikas reached up to try to pull Zukauskas' hands off his jacket. One released easily. "Now go, Vitalis. That's an order." One hand was still on Palcikas' jacket, and that one would not let go—and Palcikas soon found out why. Zukauskas' head and chest had been chewed apart by machine-gun fire and he had fallen behind Palcikas with his hands still clutching his commander's jacket. The corpse was hardly recognizable as a man, much less a Lithuanian officer.

Palcikas dragged himself behind the boulders and retrieved Zukauskas' AK-47 and an ammunition pouch, but even as he checked the magazine and chambered a round, he knew any attempts at fighting were useless. He checked his aviation survival vest for some field dressings, but they had all been lost. He tried stanching the blood with his left hand, but that was useless as well—he finally grabbed a handful of mud and gravel and slapped it in place. If the loss of blood didn't kill him now, he thought wryly, the infection from the dirt would.

As his blood-starved brain fought to maintain consciousness, the commander of the Lithuanian Self-Defense Force thought about this, his greatest battle—and his worst defeat. How quickly the tide of battle can change. It was a bold plan, rushing nearly one hundred kilometers in less than eighteen hours across hostile territory, right in the face of an oncoming army at least ten times bigger than his own, just to specifically target its air-defense weapons. They had actually struck a hard blow against the column of tanks and armored vehicles. Palcikas counted at least two dozen destroyed or damaged ZSU-23-4 antiaircraft-artillery vehicles and mobile surface-to-air missile units, plus another dozen tanks and other vehicles and two Mil-24 attack helicopters.

Pretty good for a tiny band of patriots . . .

The patter of rain on his flight helmet was being displaced by the roar of approaching tanks and the chatter of machine guns. Palcikas recognized the sounds: the T-72 main battle tank had that characteristic high-pitched squeal when the turret was traversed, no matter how well you tried to keep the bearings lubricated, and its V-12 diesel engine always sounded like the wheezing of an old man. Palcikas peeked over his cover of boulders. My God, he thought, there were at least four of them, all less than two hundred meters away—he was close enough to see the red-and-green Byelorussian flag flying on the leader. Some infantrymen were following along behind the tanks, shooting into the hills. The tanks had to stop in a few meters, Palcikas thought, so the infantry would be exposed soon. He could pin down the infantry with his AK-47 until his ammunition ran out or until the main gun of one of those tanks blasted him out of his rock hiding place—no way in hell was he going to be captured alive by the damned White Russians . . .

The main gun on one of the T-72s fired, the blast dislodging rocks and dirt around Palcikas and causing him to scream aloud in pain. The sheer thunder of that blast numbed his entire body. He barely heard the scream of compressed air as the shell flew through space, then a flash of light and a huge secondary explosion from somewhere above him—the gun had found a truck or had finally destroyed his disabled Mil-8 helicopter . . .

. . . But the scream of the artillery shell seemed to continue, except it was no longer flying over his head toward the Highlands, but from the east *toward* the column of Byelorussian tanks. Palcikas saw nothing, only heard the strange screaming noise—then suddenly two of the T-72s right in front of him exploded in huge balls of fire. The massive explosions threw the other two tanks over onto their turrets and they began rolling down the canyon toward the highway, finally coming to rest on their blackened sides.

It took several minutes for Palcikas' head to clear after the maelstrom of fire before he could pull himself back up onto the rocks protecting him and look out over the Minsk-Vilnius Highway below.

What he saw was incredible. It seemed as if every armored vehicle in the Byelorussian Army's column was on fire.

It was like some eerie holiday lantern chain, stretching for thousands of meters. He saw rivers of burning fuel spilling out onto the highway, roasting the bodies of thousands of soldiers that were strewn about the roadside like so many stones. Ammunition was cooking off everywhere, and he had to take cover behind his rocks again to protect himself.

He was sitting deep in the crevasse, listening to bullets pinging off the rocks around him, when he looked up into the gray night sky and saw an incredible sight—a massive aircraft with huge wings roared barely a hundred meters overhead—it seemed as if it was close enough to touch, so low that he thought it was going to land on the highway.

It was obviously an American B-52.

It had released some kind of anti-armor mines or bomblets that had decimated the Byelorussian armored column in one swift stroke.

It was not until then that General Palcikas understood the meaning of the message he had received from Lithuanian President Kapocius, just before he left Vilnius on his way east to ambush the Byelorussian Army— Kapocius had told him that he had received word from an unnamed foreign source that did not want to be identified. It said that if Palcikas could attack and destroy the air-defense units belonging to the invading Byelorussian Home Brigade forces, help would arrive. Palcikas thought it would be help from Poland, or even Russia or the rest of the Commonwealth—he never expected help to come from the United States of America.

The sounds of explosion and popping ammunition subsided, to be replaced a few minutes later by the sounds of boots on rocks.

"General Palcikas!" someone shouted. "General! Where are you?" There was a slight pause; then the voice shouted, "I wish the punishment, so that I may prove myself worthy!"

Palcikas smiled, filled his lungs with damp, cold air, and shouted, "To receive the power!" It was his officers' personal code-phrase, borrowed from their knighthood ceremony. Soon he was being helped out of the crevasse, and medics were tending to his wounded leg.

"How bad is it?" Palcikas asked.

Captain Degutis, Palcikas' headquarters intelligence staff officer recently promoted from lieutenant after the Fisikous raid, held a poncho over Palcikas' face to keep the rain out. "Your leg is in bad shape, sir, but I think you'll be—"

"Not my leg, damn you, Pauli. *The brigade.* Do you have a report?"

"Sorry, sir. The brigade has formed up at rendezvous point Whirlwind and is proceeding back to Vilnius at best speed. We lost approximately three hundred personnel in the battle, mostly from First Battalion when the Byelorussian tanks in the front of the column turned and attacked. Second and Third battalions came out very well—there was enough confusion in the rear to allow Third Battalion to escape. Your helicopter and one Defender were lost, along with four tanks and eleven APCs and trucks. Would you like an estimate on Byelorussian casualties and an estimate of the Home Brigade's offensive capability, sir?"

Palcikas felt a needle prick in his left gluteus, and he knew that the medics had drugged him so they could start removing pieces of bullets from his leg. "Only . . . if you can make it . . . quick, Captain," Palcikas gasped through the pain as he felt forceps dig deeply into his left thigh and blood spill down his leg.

"Yes, sir, it'll be quick," Degutis said with a smile. "Home Brigade losses: one hundred percent. Unit offensive capability: zero percent."

OVER SOUTHWESTERN LITHUANIA
14 APRIL, 0054 HOURS (13 APRIL, 1854 ET)

"I've got sensor contact on the return," Patrick McLanahan reported. The Fisikous-170 *Tuman* stealth bomber's telescopic forward-looking infrared scanner, slaved to the attack radar, had picked up a column of tanks moving northeastward near the small town of Kazly Ruda, just twenty nautical miles from Lithuania's second-largest city of Kaunas. McLanahan used a tracking handle, very similar to the old ASQ-38 radar tracking handle in the B-52G bomber, to center a set of crosshairs on the lead tank, then pressed a trigger. A white box centered itself around the tank. "Locked on, showing one-fifty to go." He turned to General Ormack in the pilot's seat. "Any luck over there, John?"

"No, damn this thing," Ormack cursed. He was struggling with the electric trim button on the bomber, which kept on driving itself first to the full nose-down, then suddenly to the full nose-up position. "Dave, dammit, are you sure I can't disconnect the flight-control system?"

"Not until after weapon release, sir," David Luger replied, sitting in the instructor pilot's seat between Ormack and McLanahan. "Flight-control system needs to be in ACTIVE if it's not faulted."

"Well, can't you pull a circuit breaker or something?"

"I tried that," Luger said. He was dressed in no less than two flight suits and a thick, winter-weight leather flying jacket to keep warm—his emaciated body simply could not generate enough heat. "Something's still energizing the trim drive system. Try the secondary hydraulic-system switch again."

Ormack took a firm grip on the control wheel with his right hand, reached down to the instrument panel near his left knee, and flipped a switch. A red light on the forward instrument panel marked GEAR UNSAFE—in English, McLanahan was surprised to see—had been on since takeoff. The red light went out and a loud rumbling in the forward part of the Fi-170 subsided—for about five seconds, when the red light popped back on and the rumbling returned. "Nose gear flopped back down," Ormack said. "We'll leave it where it is for now. Any restriction on releasing weapons with gear down?"

"Maintain zero sideslip and no turns or descents for ten seconds," Luger replied.

"Easy for you to say," Ormack said. "I'm fighting this trim wheel. It'll kill us for sure."

"Just don't let it descend after release—a slight climb is okay," Luger said. "Patrick, you'll have to open the doors manually to avoid putting the whole hydraulic system into standby. The switch is right below the window lever, to the right of the weapons-selector switch."

"Got it. One-twenty TG." McLanahan quickly inventoried their remaining weapons: two semiactive radar-homing AA-8 air-to-air missiles in the far outboard weapons bays and two cluster-bomb cruise missiles in the center bomb bay. At first they had no intention of attacking anything—they were going to fly *Tuman* out of Lithuania and into Sweden or Norway. The bomber had numerous malfunctions, and as in the Old Dog mission of years past, they had no flying safety equipment, no charts (except for the computerized navigation system), and no real plan of action except to survive.

But as soon as they were airborne they heard radio messages from Lithuanian Self-Defense Force units all over the country, pleading for assistance.

Towns and cities were under attack everywhere, mostly from Byelorussian troops that were already stationed in the country as part of the Commonwealth defense forces, but more and more from Byelorussian armored units from Kalinin oblast. They had enough fuel for several hours of flying, and verified targets were popping up on radar and on the infrared scanner, so they went to work.

In less than thirty minutes McLanahan and crew had attacked a column of tanks close to Vilnius with two cluster-bomb units, and they had hit a Mil-24 attack helicopter with an infrared-guided AA-7 missile shortly after takeoff. One more attack and their debt to the Lithuanians for securing Fisikous would be paid and they'd be flying for themselves and their own survival.

"One hundred TG," McLanahan announced. "Center the needle, ten right." He did some rough mental calculations—range to the target, altitude, and speed—then designated a second target about three thousand feet from the first. He planned on dropping the second cluster bomb right at the edge of the bomb's destructive radius in order to take out as many of the tanks as possible. "I've got the second target set," he said. "TG is counting down to second weapon release." The time-to-go indicator jumped to one hundred and twenty seconds. "I'll drop the first CBU manually at thirty TG, then switch to auto for the last release. Our escape turn will be a right turn at max bank, heading three-four-zero, and a descent to four hundred feet—er, I mean one hundred and twenty meters."

"Our emergency MEA is four hundred meters," Luger added. "That'll clear all terrain and towers all the way to the coast."

McLanahan pointed to the threat-warning receiver as a circle appeared on the screen. On an American threat-receiver, a warning tone would be heard on the interphone and the threat would be identified by its radar characteristics—antiaircraft artillery, surface-to-air missile, fighter, or search radar—but since this was a Soviet aircraft, there was no warning, so everyone was watching the scope carefully: only "enemy"—i.e., American or NATO—threats would be identified. "There's a radar in that armored column, probably a triple-A. If we overfly that column, we're dead. They don't seem to be locked on us right now."

"Remember, guys, when the bomb doors come open, our radar cross-section will jump," Luger said. "The bomb doors are composites, but the bomb racks and inner structure are steel—our RCS will go up by six hundred—"

Suddenly a second circle appeared on the threat scope, this time behind them. "Got a radar behind us," McLanahan said. "He's changing positions back there . . . looks like a fighter." He made sure that the four push-on light switches underneath the radar-warning receiver's display unit were on. "Jammers are active."

"Remember, we've got track breakers only," Luger reminded them. To avoid being detected by undue electronic emissions, the jammers on the stealth bomber were rather simple "track breakers," designed to momentarily disrupt only missile uplink signals, not search or tracking radars. "He can still track us and close to gun range."

"Sixty TG. Doors coming open at forty TG." The small circle on the radar-warning receiver disappeared. "He's gone into standby—he might have us visual or locked up on infrared. You got an infrared-warning mode on this thing, Dave?"

"Mode switch to KF—don't ask me what KF stands for—and press the quadrant button on the lower-left side three times. It's a full three-sixty scanner but it only looks in one direction at a time." The screen changed—now it showed a simple T in the center of the screen, with a single bright dot at the two o'clock position. "It's like the AAR-47 now," Luger added, "so imagine you're sitting facing backwards, so when the dot is on the right side of the scope the threat is on the *left* side of the—"

Suddenly two large red lights began blinking just above the threat scope. "Missile launch!" McLanahan cried out. "Where's the chaff and flares . . . ?"

"Don't break!" Luger said. "Stay on the bomb run. We don't use flares. Hit that button right there."

From a launcher in the tail, a small, slender rocket shot into space behind the bomber. Steered by a small pulse-Doppler radar in the tail, the rocket maneuvered until it was heading directly for the incoming enemy missile; then, when it was within a hundred meters or so from the missile, it exploded. The ten-kilo high-explosive warhead ignited a cloud of aluminum powder, blinding the missile's seeker head, and the warhead also sent a cloud of small pellets into the path of the missile.

The crew didn't see any of that, however—what they saw was the bright dot on the infrared warning receiver wildly turn away until it was off the scope. "Whatever you punched out, it worked," Ormack said. "I'm centered up. Bomb doors!"

"Doors coming open," McLanahan acknowledged. He hit the electrically operated door-unlatch switch, which allowed the selected bomb-bay doors to free-fall open. "Centerline doors open . . . five seconds . . . three, two, one, release." He hit the MANUAL RELEASE button, letting the first Fisikous X-27 cruise missile fly.

Unlike its smarter cousins from the United States, the X-27 could fly only straight ahead, and it had to be pre-programmed for its release points, but once deployed it was a devastating weapon. Like the JP-233 cluster-bomb unit from England, the X-27 sowed several different types of bomblets in its flight path: antitank and antipersonnel bomblets and delayed-action antivehicle mines.

The X-27 covered forty thousand square feet with explosive devastation, punching holes in main battle tanks and destroying light vehicles; the delayed-action mines, spread out several dozen meters away from the cruise missile's flight path, would ensure that the entire roadway was closed off by destroying any vehicles that tried to pass around the destroyed or damaged ones.

Thirty seconds after the first missile was released, and just a half-mile from the column, the second one was released. McLanahan motored the bomb doors closed, and Ormack turned the American-designed, Soviet-made bomber northwest toward the Baltic. With the flight-control system out of BOMB mode, the flight-control computers could be deactivated and Ormack could hand-fly the huge bomber without the spurious autopilot inputs.

A few moments later the radar-warning receiver bleeped again. "Bandit at six o'clock again," McLanahan called out. "I think that fighter's back. Why is he tracking us so well?"

"That nose gear stuck down wipes out our stealth characteristics," Luger said. "He can track us around all day just locked on to our nose gear."

"Let's launch another one of those rear-firing missiles at him," McLanahan suggested. "We can't let him hang on our butts too long or he'll eventually close the distance and gun us down. Chop the power, suck the guy in, then fire a missile at him."

"It's worth a shot," Ormack said. "Dave, get ready to give me a hand with the instruments if I get bollixed up."

"Gotcha," Luger said. He turned to McLanahan and smiled. "Hey, Patrick, just like Bomb Comp, huh?"

"Yeah," McLanahan agreed, "except we're playing for real marbles now."

Ormack tightened his shoulder harness, trying to get comfortable in the narrow, stiff ejection seat. "Ready, Patrick?"

McLanahan put a finger on the missile-launch switch. "Ready."

"Power coming back . . . now." Ormack pulled the throttles back to idle power and raised the nose slightly. The airspeed bled off rapidly. As he pushed the throttles back up, he shouted, *"Now!"*

McLanahan hit the LAUNCH button—and suddenly the bomber shuddered, the tail flipped up as if caught in a huge tidal wave, and lights in the cockpit flickered and died. "Jesus!" Ormack screamed. "Lights! Dave, check my airspeed!"

Luger punched a button in the overhead instrument panel, turning on a bright-red, battery-powered emergency light. "We lost the number three and four engines," he shouted. "One and two are good. The missile must've detonated when it left the launcher. Get your nose down! You're still flying, but you need airspeed. You've got a compressor stall on three and four—the decoy exploding right on the tail must have stalled the engines. Throttles three and four to CUTOFF."

Ormack yanked the two right throttles to IDLE, removed a safety bar, and moved the throttles to CUTOFF.

"Good. Patrick, watch the EGT gauges." He pointed out their position on the instrument panel. "Ten seconds, if the temp doesn't come down out of the yellow range, we'll have to pop the fire extinguishers. I'll dial in your elevon trim for you, General. Watch your airspeed. Shallower banks—remember, the wings are supercritical. She flies like a pig on two engines, but she flies. Be careful."

"Sage advice," said Ormack.

"That fighter's got himself a nice bright target now," McLanahan said. He looked at the EGT, or exhaust gas temperature, gauges once again. "No luck—temp's still up. We've got a fire back there. Fire extinguishers, three and four." Luger guarded the one- and two-engine fire handles so Ormack wouldn't accidentally activate them, and watched as McLanahan pulled the fire extinguisher handles. "Pulled." All of the instruments—navigation, threat warning, bombing, weapons control—were dark. "How do I get my stuff back? Where's the generator-reset switches?"

"On two engines you won't get them back," Luger said. "The generator will stay in TIE, and all available power will go to the flight controls, radios, emergency equipment, and stuff like that. We're out of the bomber business. Our MEA is four hundred meters, General—we'd better get up there."

"That fighter is probably moving back in," McLanahan said. "If we climb, we're sitting ducks."

"I can't see a thing out there, Patrick," Ormack said. They were out of the clouds, but the ground was dark, the horizon was obscured by fog and drizzle, and the rain was pelting the bomber's windscreen hard, completely blotting out the view outside. "I've got no choice—we'll smack into the ground if we don't climb." Ormack pulled back on the control column and climbed to four hundred meters, the lowest they could fly safely without seeing the ground.

Luger was busy tightening up the straps of his parachute. "Well, this is one thing I've never tried in this thing," he said. "Manual bailout from a stealth bomber. Reminds me of training in the simulator with Major White, doesn't it, Patrick?"

"Jesus, Dave, I'm sorry we got you into this," McLanahan said, worried about Luger's physical condition. "We should have let you go back with the Marines. You'd be safe by now."

"Vi nyee ahshiblyees—uh, sorry—don't be crazy, Patrick," Luger said. "I wanted to go. I *had* to go. This was my way of getting back at those fuckers Gabovich and Teresov and all the sons of bitches who kept me locked up in Fisikous all this time, building this piece of shit. Maybe if I had built a *better* bomber, we'd be safe by now."

"Can you bail out of the bomb bay in this thing?"

"No access to the bomb bay from the cockpit," Luger said. "I guess they didn't want . . . holy shit, *look!"*

They looked out the right-side windows.

A MiG-29 Fulcrum fighter was flying close formation just forward of the Fi-170's right wing. It had a fighter-intercept identification light on its left side, which shined a bright light into the cockpit. "Man, this is just great. It's like déjà vu all over again. Wasn't it a MiG-29 that was chasing us around after the bomb run on Kavaznya? The one that blew my leg to shit?"

"That's the one," McLanahan said. As they watched, the MiG-29 let out a burst of cannon fire from its portside 30-millimeter cannon. The identification light blinked—once, pause, twice, pause, once, pause, then five times. "One-two-one-five. He's telling us to go to VHF GUARD channel."

"Maybe we can talk our way out of this one," Ormack said. "I don't think we can fly out of it." He switched over to the international VHF emergency channel, 121.5, and keyed the mike: "Attention MiG-29 fighter aircraft, this is *Tuman.* We are an authorized flight over sovereign Lithuanian airspace. State your intentions. Over."

The voice that responded was in Russian, with no English attempted. "He is from Byelorussia," Luger translated. "He says he has authorization to shoot us down if we do not follow him. He is ordering us to fly a heading of one-five-zero at an altitude of three thousand meters and lower our landing gear. He will pursue. If we do not comply, he will shoot us down."

The MiG-29 wagged its wings once, then disappeared from sight.

"I guess we don't have any choice," Ormack said. "We can't see him, and we're barely flying already as it is. What do you guys think?"

"I think we should make a run for it," Luger said. "Try to descend and try to outlast him. If he fires on us, you guys eject. They don't get the bomber, and you at least make it out."

"But you won't make it," McLanahan said. "Forget it, Dave. Let's put it down on the ground and—"

Suddenly there was a terrific explosion and a blinding burst of light. McLanahan and Luger strained to look out the right-side cockpit windows and saw a blazing ball of fire careening through the sky. "It's the MiG!" Patrick shouted. "It blew up! What's going on?"

"I think I found out," Ormack said. "Look over here."

A few moments later a huge object appeared out the left-side window, overtaking the Fi-170 and flying a few hundred feet above it. It was a dark, massive shape, flying close enough and with enough power to vibrate the crippled Soviet bomber.

"My God . . . I don't believe it!" Luger shouted. It was an EB-52 Megafortress, flying in tight formation with the Fisikous-170. It had sneaked up on the unsuspecting MiG-29 and used one of its heat-seeking missiles to blow the MiG out of the sky from behind. A few moments later a second EB-52 appeared off the right wing, flying alongside. It was one of the most incredible sights any of them had ever seen—three massive, futuristic bombers, flying near one another less than two thousand feet above ground. "Two of them! You built more Old Dogs?"

"Damned right," Ormack said happily. "I just never thought I'd see one this side of hell."

Unseen by them, two more were far above the low-altitude planes, acting as high combat air patrol as they exited Lithuanian airspace. They stayed off the radios to avoid being detected by the enemy, containing their joy at the unexpected escort. Minutes later the group was safely over the Baltic, on their way to Norway and a safe recovery.

KURENETS AUXILIARY AIRFIELD, BELARUS REPUBLIC
14 APRIL, 0304 (13 APRIL, 2104 ET)

The Byelorussian sergeant ran up to his unit commander, Captain of Rocket Troops Edlin Kramko, saluted, and gave him a message. He read it silently, then reread it. His NCOIC swore that his commander's face went white, even under his camouflage makeup and helmet. "Sir . . . ?"

"We've received the alert order," Kramko said. "All missiles are to be ready to launch within ten minutes. And we've received retargeting orders as well."

Kramko handed the message over to his NCOIC. His eyes bulged in sheer horror when he read the new targets. "Sir, this must be a mistake. The first two targets are the original ones—Vilnius and Jonava, in Lithuania—but this last target has to be an error. Machulische? That is a Commonwealth air base in *Minsk!* We must—"

"I will call for confirmation," Kramko said. "But this fits with the radio messages we have received about air raids and commando raids inside Belarus itself. These bases may have been overrun by Russians or Commonwealth forces—we've heard rumors that even Ukrainian bombers have crossed the border and are invading. If this is true, we may be the last line of defense for the capital."

"But we are *firing on the capital!*"

"That's enough, Master Sergeant," Kramko interrupted. "I will get a confirmation if it's possible—the radios have been heavily jammed all night—but in the meantime set these new coordinates and alert the detail to prepare the missiles for launch."

The NCOIC saluted and trotted off to the control trailer.

Kramko's company commanded a total of twelve SS-21 Scarab missile units, three of which had nuclear warheads. For maximum reliability, all twelve units were interconnected with each other and with the command trailer by an armored telephone cable as well as by standard VHF radio. A microwave data-relay system allowed the command trailer to exchange position, targeting, and atmospheric information with the headquarters command center, and that was what Kramko wanted to check first before risking a radio transmission for confirmation of the retargeting orders. "Status of the relay channel?"

"Open and active, sir," the launch technician reported. Kramko checked the targeting data himself—it was verified. The retargeting information he had received by radio was the same as what was being fed into the missiles by the microwave link—two independent confirmations. "All units acknowledging the alert order."

"Very well. Notify me on the pager when the spin-up order is received. I am going to inspect the special units."

The spin-up order was really the launch order, but the SS-21 missile system required widely varying time periods to spin up their gyroscopes in preparation for the flight—as short as three minutes, but as long as five, depending on the age and serviceability of the units and environmental conditions. The nuclear-armed SS-21s had the most reliable gyros. Kramko had set up the nuclear-armed SS-21s within a few hundred meters of the command trailer, mostly for security reasons, and he was going out to give them a once-over.

There was nothing more for Kramko to do except wait—wait and wonder what in hell General Voshchanka was doing aiming a nuclear warhead at his own capital, Minsk.

SMORGON ARMY AIR BASE, BELARUS REPUBLIC
14 APRIL, 0305 (13 APRIL, 2105 ET)

In a scene reminiscent of old World War II movies, Voshchanka had set up a room-sized map of Belarus and the Baltic region on the front "stage" of his command post, in the battle-staff area. Radio operators on the floor moved tiny blocks of unit and national flags around the map with long croupier sticks. He and his battle staff, sitting in a glass-enclosed balcony overlooking the stage, could easily watch the progress of the battle, like gods watching the human tragedy from Mount Olympus. Behind and above the stage were four rear-projection screens on which overhead transparencies, films, photographs, maps, and checklists could be presented.

The mood in the command center at that moment was one of incredible shock and surprise. The single crimson block representing the forty-thousand-man Home Brigade deployed from Smorgon had first been divided into six battalion blocks when the report of the Lithuanian commando attack had come in, with one battalion block removed and an RC, or "reduced capability," flag placed on two other battalions.

After a short time more RC flags appeared.

Suddenly, inexplicably, all of the battalion blocks were removed, to be replaced by two company blocks with RC flags on them. The air-battalion block from Smorgon had an RC flag on it as well, although it had been removed from the board almost from the outset after the commando attack on the airfield and fuel depot. The same thing had happened south of Vilnius—three battalions sent to attack the capital city of Lithuania had been suddenly attacked by unidentified aircraft.

"One aircraft was identified by our fighter pilots as a Russian experimental-research aircraft," the Air Force commander had reported. "The aircraft attacked Thirty-third Battalion with cluster bombs. The pilots spoke English but identified themselves as Russians."

Russian aircraft involved in this war—that was unthinkable, completely unexpected at this early stage. Although Voshchanka and his staff had no positive identification of the aircraft that had attacked the Home Brigade or the other Byelorussian tank columns, they were assumed to be Russian or Commonwealth bombers as well—there had been no radar contacts from aircraft trying to penetrate Lithuanian airspace from the west. That meant they had to come from Russia or the Ukraine, the only two republics that flew heavy bombers.

"Has Kurenets acknowledged the retargeting order?" Voshchanka asked.

His commander of rocket troops looked at his colleagues on the battle staff. They remained silent—they were not going to back him up. He decided to forge ahead anyway. "Sir, they have acknowledged the retargeting order, and the command channel is open and active."

"Good. Then I want—"

"But I must re-emphasize my objection, sir. The missile targeted on Machulische is less than five kilometers from Minsk. A direct hit will cause much damage and destruction in the city, and claim perhaps thousands of lives. But if the missile misses, or falls short of its target—sir, the devastation would be tremendous!"

"General, that base is the main Commonwealth . . . no, the main *Russian* military base in Belarus," Voshchanka said. "It has twenty thousand troops, two dozen fighters, and a hundred attack helicopters based there."

"None of which have been used, sir. The forces there have not even been put on alert."

"That can change very quickly," Voshchanka argued. "Moscow refuses to confirm or deny the presence of heavy bombers over Belarus and Lithuania—they say they are investigating. That is unacceptable. Completely unacceptable!"

"I urge you to wait for confirmation before attacking a Commonwealth military installation, sir. If you wish to attack now, then use the conventionally armed missiles. The aircraft at Machulishche are still on the ground and are vulnerable—a single high-explosive warhead can do great damage."

"If its accuracy is perfect. We both know the SS-21 is not an accurate weapon, especially with a conventional payload."

The much-heavier high-explosive payload on the SS-21 reduced its maximum range by one-half, and also doubled its CEP, or circular error probability. In contrast, the lighter, more advanced guidance system on the Fisikous KR-11 thermonuclear warhead actually increased the normal range of the SS-21 by 20 percent, to almost two hundred kilometers, and decreased its CEP to less than two hundred meters.

"Then we will fire a salvo on the base," the Air Force commander argued. "A volley of twelve missiles from Baranovichi or Kurenets will destroy all the aircraft and most of the aircraft-support facilities. Or we can stage our own air assault from Lida. But a *nuclear weapon . . ."* He had to hesitate—the very thought of releasing a nuclear device was unthinkable for him. "Sir, you must reconsider—"

A loud, insistent beeping phone interrupted him. Voshchanka scowled at his air boss as he turned to his operations officer, who answered the phone.

"Air-raid warning, sir," the operations officer said. "Numerous aircraft at low altitude, about twenty kilometers away, identification unknown."

The Air Force commander picked up a telephone that connected directly to his air division commander, based there at Smorgon. After a few seconds he reported, "We've got a brief radar plot on the target—they're probably helicopters, hedgehopping across the border. I've got Number Nineteen squadron dispatched to intercept."

As he spoke, a red block shaped like a five-blade helicopter rotor moved out from Smorgon—a composite air squadron consisting of six Mil-24 helicopters that had survived the attack on the flight line at Smorgon, and MiG-27 fighter-bombers from other bases in northern Belarus.

Voshchanka's earlier anger and frustration subsided a bit. Yes, they were knocked back on their heels a bit; yes, they had lost a lot of tanks and vehicles in a very short period of time. But he now took a moment to look at exactly what he *did* have out there—and it was still impressive.

Although Kaunas and Vilnius, Lithuania's two main cities, were still unthreatened—except of course by his SS-21 missiles—the port city and third-largest city in Lithuania, Klaipeda, was under virtual occupation by his forces, and the fourth-largest city in Lithuania, Siauliai, with its huge air base and high-tech electronics businesses, firmly belonged to him. That was the plan: his forces in western Lithuania would remain safe and secure while the bulk of the Lithuanian resistance was destroyed in the east. Along with the fact that Kalinin oblast and the city of Kaliningrad were virtually his, the entire operation was still going as planned. The involvement of Russian and/or Ukrainian troops and air forces was unexpected, but he still had enough troops in reserve to handle that threat.

All in all, the operation was still proceeding nicely . . .

"Perhaps it is a bit premature to launch the SS-21s," Voshchanka said. He could see a genuine sigh of relief from each and every one of his battle staff officers. "I will keep the units on alert status, but I will withhold the final launch-commit order until I speak with the President and representatives from the Commonwealth. I will not tolerate interference from anyone—the Commonwealth, Russia, Poland, or the NATO countries. If I cannot receive assurances of their noninterference, I will commit the SS-21s immediately."

There were approving nods all around the battle-staff table, punctuated by the rocket troops commander: "Very wise decision, sir. The SS-21s are a much more effective weapon of intimidation than an actual destructive weapon."

"Sir, radar reports the inbound targets are fifteen kilometers out," the operations officer said. "Seventeen Squadron is still two minutes from intercept. I suggest we go down to the air-raid shelter."

"Very well," Voshchanka said. The staff officers hurried to their feet, impatiently waiting for Voshchanka to leave. He purposely slowed his pace, watching with amusement as they jostled each other in their anxiousness to depart.

A heavy steel door sealed off the battle-staff area itself. Voshchanka led them through the doors and into the command post itself, which contained the main communications system for the base as well as the microwave data-relay system for the nuclear weapons. Voshchanka glanced at the one silver key already in the command panel—he had inserted it an hour ago and turned it, which activated the command channel to the microwave-relay network to the missiles. The second key, the launch key, was in his pocket. He wished President Kapocius of Lithuania, President Bykov of the Commonwealth of Independent States, President Svetlov of Belarus, President Miriclaw of Poland, and even the President of the United States could see that key in its lock—it, and the other key so readily available, were proof of his determination to succeed in this endeavor.

A light-steel-sheathed wooden door with a bulletproof window was at the entrance to the communications center, followed by a long corridor entrapment/inspection area, then a heavy steel grate door at the opposite end so security guards in the command post could see anyone entering the building. Another heavy steel door protected the other side of the entrapment corridor, but so many people were moving in and out of the command post that the door was kept open and a guard posted. Normally only one person at a time was allowed in the entrapment corridor, but when the senior staff was present they were allowed to go in and out together. Beyond the door was a small security office with a simple glass office door, and beyond that was the front foyer to the headquarters building. Several soldiers, heavily armed and outfitted for combat, were stationed both inside and outside the front doors to the building. Voshchanka could see all the way to the circular driveway and ceremonial flagpoles outside. He noticed it was dark outside and realized he had been hard at it for well over twenty-four hours—maybe he would just stay in the bunker, three floors down in the basement, and take a nap.

Voshchanka had just entered the corridor, and the guard at the other end had just opened the grate door for him, when a tremendous explosion shook the walls as if they were made of tin. A series of explosions had ripped open the front doors of the headquarters building, right in front of Voshchanka. The blasts shattered the glass doors of the security office, but he was not hurt. Smoke and debris flew everywhere. Shots were fired, most from soldiers inside the headquarters but some from outside.

Soldiers flooded into the foyer, taking cover against the wall. Several soldiers, carrying bulletproof shields, ran into the security office and pushed Voshchanka back inside the communications center. "You'd be safer inside, sir," one soldier told him. The members of the battle staff had already run back inside, and Voshchanka wasn't going to argue either.

He met up with his officers back in the battle-staff room. The radio operators on the stage had disappeared. The staff officers were herded back into the battle-staff room and the door was locked behind them, with one soldier on guard inside with them. Voshchanka was on the phone immediately. *"What's going on out there?"*

"Unknown, sir," came the reply from the chief building-security officer. "We're investigating the area of the senior-staff parking lot—one of my men thought they saw a muzzle flash. There's no large force and no sign of any other activity."

"Like *hell* there's no other activity!" Voshchanka screamed. "I want a full armored detail dispatched to sweep this entire area! I want this area *secured!"*

At that instant two tremendous explosions ripped open the ceiling just above the stage, virtually in front of the battle-staff officers. The glass surrounding the battle-staff area exploded, the lights snapped out, and the entire area began to fill with acidic smoke that burned the eyes, throat, and all the way into the lungs. Emergency lights snapped on. Through the smoke, flying debris, tears, and confusion, Voshchanka saw men descending by ropes onto the map stage below. The stage was soon filled with at least twelve or fourteen soldiers dressed in black, with gas masks and large bulbous devices over their eyes. Voshchanka saw them rush the doorway leading off the map stage just before one of them shot out the emergency lights, plunging the entire area in darkness.

The lone Byelorussian soldier in the area went a little crazy, sweeping the stage with automatic gunfire, but he succeeded in doing nothing more than pinning down the officers beside him—a single shot, so far the only shot fired by the enemy, killed him instantly. Voshchanka crawled past him, opened the steel protective door, and crawled into the communications area.

Those bastards, Voshchanka cursed. *How dare they attack my headquarters!* He did not know who the attackers were, but it didn't matter—he would deal with them right now.

Voshchanka crawled over to the communications panel, over to the microwave network-relay system for the nuclear-armed SS-21. Shaking—more from anger and excitement than from fear—he removed the second silver key from his pocket, stuck it in the communications panel, and—

"Stoy!" a voice shouted behind him in Russian. A black-suited soldier, wearing a weird helmet with large, bug-eyed goggles and a breathing apparatus, pointed a small submachine gun at him. Then, in what Voshchanka recognized as Lithuanian, the soldier shouted, *"Uzeiga Lieutuvos! Lithuanian Army!"* Then, in Russian again, he said, *"Nyee dveghightyes. Don't move!"*

"You are too late, you Lithuanian bastard," Voshchanka said—and he turned the key.

The soldier immediately ran over to Voshchanka and pushed him to the floor. More soldiers, all dressed in the futuristic garb, rushed in behind him. The first soldier turned the key and removed it from the panel.

"That won't help, you idiot," Voshchanka said. "The missile launch is unstoppable now."

Another soldier placed a large, backpack-looking device underneath the communications console and pulled a lanyard.

Voshchanka was dragged to his feet and half-dragged, half-carried outside.

Small helicopters, ones Voshchanka recognized as Lithuanian Defender light attack helicopters, were flitting all over the sky, shooting at Byelorussian troops on the ground. The soldiers knelt down near the doorway, taking cover as two more Defenders swooped across the parking lot, blasting away at anything that moved. There seemed to be dozens of the little two-man helicopters buzzing around. Just then a bright flash of light and a loud, rolling *boom!* made them all jump and take cover.

Voshchanka recognized it instantly: it was one of his T-72 tanks responding. He could see it speeding across the outer parking lot, going toward the headquarters building. Its 12.7-millimeter antiaircraft gun was blazing away, keeping the Defenders away. The small-caliber guns on the little Defender helicopters weren't going to stop it, Voshchanka gleefully realized.

Suddenly the tank disappeared in a terrific explosion—the turret popped right off it as if it had been lifted off by a giant can opener.

Seconds later, as the Defenders swept across the parking lot searching for advancing infantry, a massive aircraft appeared overhead. It moved incredibly fast, then suddenly stopped in midair and fired two missiles into the darkness beyond the outer parking lot. More explosions followed—obviously two direct hits. The huge rotorcraft wheeled and made a sweep of the area around the headquarters building before settling down on the grassy quadrangle outside the building. Voshchanka realized what it was when it turned on landing lights just before touching down— it was a CV-22, an *American* CV-22 tilt-rotor aircraft!

Men began running toward the open rear cargo ramp of the CV-22. Voshchanka knew he was next. He considered breaking free from the soldiers guarding him and making a run for it—but to his surprise the soldiers released him. One of them even saluted him and said in Lithuanian, *"Aciu,* General Voshchanka, *uzteks. Viso gero.* Thank you, General, we're finished. Good-bye," before turning and dashing for the CV-22.

His first impulse was to run into the headquarters building, but that would have been foolish—those were obviously bombs they had planted in there. He could do nothing but stand and watch as the CV-22 lifted off and, escorted by waves of Defenders, sped off to the west. As soon as they were out of sight, he hurried away from the building. He made it across the senior-staff parking lot when a tremendous explosion, then two, three, four, five more explosions, rocked the headquarters building. Sheets of fire flew into the sky, and the roof and several walls collapsed seconds later. The rumbling he felt beneath his feet told him that they had even destroyed the underground weapons-storage facilities, power generators, and alternate-communications equipment. In less than ten minutes his entire central-command facility was gone.

But he had the last laugh.

The SS-21s were in launch commit—nothing was going to stop them now. Vilnius, Minsk, and Jonava—in five minutes, they would be no more.

He heard helicopters approach and quickly darted behind a tree as they came closer. But these were not Defenders or CV-22s—they were Mil-24s! He ran happily out to the parking lot and waved for them to land.

Finally his men were responding . . .

But as the helicopters settled in for a landing, he realized they were not Byelorussian—they had Russian and Ukrainian flags with white diamonds on their fuselages. Commonwealth troops, but obviously not under his command any longer. Soldiers leaped out of the three helicopters that had landed. Voshchanka turned and hustled for the headquarters building—maybe he could lose himself in the ruins before the soldiers—

"General Voshchanka!" a voice called out to him. "Stop! This is General Ivashova!"

The commander of the Commonwealth Defense Forces—*here?* With Mil-24 attack helicopters and dismounting troops, Voshchanka knew Ivashova wasn't here for a social call, so he ran harder.

"*Stoy!*" a new voice shouted. "Stop! *Stop or I'll shoot.*"

Panic made Voshchanka run even faster now. He heard a sharp *crraack!,* then a dull *thwap,* then a sharp pain in his back. He never felt the pavement hit him in the face because he was dead before he even hit the ground.

KURENETS AUXILIARY AIRFIELD, BELARUS REPUBLIC
14 APRIL, 0323 (13 APRIL, 2123 ET)

Captain Kramko was on his way to inspect the second of the three nuclear-armed SS-21s when his walkie-talkie beeped. "Alpha, this is Control, commit message received at Zero-three-two-one," his NCOIC reported.

Kramko acknowledged the report. *Dammit,* he thought. *They've really done it. They're going to launch the missiles.* Unbidden, his eyes filled with tears, and a lump of sorrow formed in his throat. A nuclear war—begun by Belarus. It was too much to believe.

The horror that he was about to unleash was—

Suddenly a flash of light popped off to his left, and a yellow flare arced skyward, disappearing in the cloudy sky, then descended to earth on a small white parachute. It was a perimeter-warning flare—there were intruders nearby! A shot rang out, then the sound of a rifle on full automatic. Kramko instinctively ducked as he felt the pressure of slugs whizzing near his head. He pulled out his walkie-talkie: "Security, this is Alpha. Report!"

"Intruders in the perimeter, unit one, north of my position at about three hundred meters."

Oh shit, Kramko thought. *What a damned nightmare!* He didn't want the missiles to launch at all, but now that there was someone out there trying to stop the launch, he wanted them to fire off immediately! "All security units, set condition red," he radioed. "Stand by to repel. Missile launch in approximately two minutes. Alpha clear." Kramko then bolted for the security trailer.

A guard was hiding in the shadows near a tree a few meters away from the trailer, scanning the buildings near the airfield itself. *The rest of the guards must have gone to their defensive positions,* Kramko thought. He rushed into the trailer. "Status of the launch, Sergeant—?"

Heads turned toward him—but they weren't Byelorussian soldiers. They were dressed in black and wore thick bulletproof vests and face masks. Three men were sitting at the launch-control console with their masks off, talking in English. Two soldiers grabbed Kramko and secured his hands behind him with plastic handcuffs. *"Kto tam?"* Kramko said in Russian. *"Myneyeh ehtah nyee nrahveetsah.* Who are you? Stop what you're doing!"

"The thing's locked, Gunny," one of the soldiers said. "Won't accept operator inputs. I tried resetting the system but it's not responding."

"Great," Marine Corps Gunnery Sergeant Lobato said. He turned to Kramko and said in Russian, "Captain, we are American Marines. Do you understand me?"

Kramko's eyes widened with surprise. "Americans? Here? How did you get here?"

"Captain, do these missiles have nuclear warheads?"

Kramko hesitated. One of the soldiers slapped him in the chest. Kramko replied, "I will not answer. I am a Byelorussian soldier. I will not—"

"These missiles are going to launch in about forty seconds, Gunny," one of the Marines said. "I can't stop the countdown."

"Captain, you understand that if these missiles launch your country will have started a nuclear war," Lobato said. "You must help us stop the launch."

"Gunny, I got the target file. It's locked and I can't change it, but here's the target coordinates . . . hey! One of the missiles is heading *south!* These bastards are launching a missile south . . . no, southeast of here. The only thing within range is—"

"Minsk," Lobato said to Kramko. "One of those missiles has been targeted for Minsk. Do you understand, sir? You're about to fire a missile off at your own people."

Kramko was confused, and now frightened. "I am Byelorussian soldier . . . my orders come from headquarters . . ."

"Call off your security troops," Lobato told him. "We can stop the missiles from launching."

"No one can stop them!"

"We can stop it!" Lobato said. "A bomber is on station—it is ready to attack. But we need to mark the target. Call off your security forces. Let us get close enough to mark the target!"

Kramko hesitated. These American Marines could have killed him, but they didn't. They seemed as if they truly wanted to help. Could this be the help he was looking for? Could this be the way he could stop this madness?

"I will do what you ask," Kramko finally said. He motioned at his hands, and the handcuffs were cut off and his walkie-talkie returned to him.

"All units, all units, this is Alpha," Kramko shouted into the radio. Then, twisting away from the Marines that held him, he shouted, "Repel! American Marines on the perimeter! *Repel!"* Lobato snatched the radio away, and his hands were bound behind his back once again.

"You stupid fuck," Lobato said. "You just condemned millions of innocent people to death." His breathing was labored, as if he had just run a marathon. He reached into his ALICE vest pocket and withdrew a tiny transmitter.

The members of COBRA VENOM standing with Lobato were helpless—all their training, all their experience, were useless if they couldn't get near enough to the missiles. "What do we do now, Gunny?" one of them asked.

"Tsehrkahf," Lobato said in Russian, glaring angrily at Kramko. He raised the transmitter to his lips. "Pray . . . that the Air Force can find those fucking missiles down here." On his walkie-talkie, he said, "All units. Blanket the area. Flares and HE. If you get a position on those missile units, mark it. You got about twenty seconds. *Do it!"*

ABOARD AN EB-52 MEGAFORTRESS
OVER NORTHWESTERN BYELORUSSIA
14 APRIL, 0325 (13 APRIL, 2125 ET)

"Coming up on launch point," navigator Captain Alicia Kellerman reported. "Thirty seconds. Ready with final release check."

The pilot, Major Kelvin Carter, the senior project officer of the EB-52 Megafortress program from the High Technology Aerospace Weapons Center, looked at his copilot and frowned in his oxygen mask. In his unmistakable Louisiana bayou accent, he asked, "We get a confirmation message from those jarheads yet?"

"Nothing," his copilot, Captain Nancy Cheshire, replied. General Brad Elliott's classified-research group at HAWC was not a real combat outfit, so that many of its crew members were women—but the four women on board the upgraded Old Dog strategic-escort "battleship" aircraft were prime examples of the success of women in combat; they were highly intelligent engineers and scientists as well as fully qualified aviators. "We punch these puppies out anyway."

"Checks," Carter said.

"Final release check," Kellerman announced.

Step by step, Kellerman and radar-navigator bombardier Captain Paul Scott ran down the eight-step checklist in preparation for launching the AGM-145 missile at the target. The AGM-145, also called MSOW (Modular Standoff Weapon), was a small, turbojet-powered missile with a five-hundred-pound warhead and an imaging infrared (IIR) seeker that transmitted pictures of the intended target back to its launching aircraft. Like its predecessor, the AGM-65 Maverick missile, MSOW was a "fire-and-forget" weapon that allowed the EB-52 to attack from long range with pinpoint accuracy; but unlike Maverick, MSOW could actually *hunt* for targets. Its infrared scanner, combined with a high-speed artificial-intelligence computer, compared pictures of targets it found with a catalog of desired targets, and it would identify each target it discovered and report its findings to crew members on board its own plane, on another aircraft, or even to troops on the ground. It could select its own target based on a target-priority list, or humans could override the selection and choose the proper target. The EB-52 could "ripple-fire" several MSOW missiles at a selected area, and each would find its own target and report to the carrier aircraft what target it found; then it would pick the highest-priority targets and attack.

MSOW was perfect for this mission because Kelvin Carter's crew was not given a specific target. As one of the "flying spares" on this mission, it and another modified B-52H were not sent into Lithuanian airspace until well after the four other EB-52s used on the late-night raids into Lithuania and Byelorussia were safely out. But since there were still American Marines involved, Carter and his crew were sent back into Lithuania and Byelorussia. After they were airborne, they were ordered to attack a small airfield between Minsk and Vilnius—not Smorgon, which had been their original target, but a smaller airfield suspected of being a short-range-missile launch site. The order had come not from Washington, but directly from a female CIA agent in Latvia.

The EB-52 carried eight MSOW missiles for the attack on a rotary launcher in the forward part of their sixty-foot-long bomb bay; it also carried eight AGM-88 HARMs (High Speed Anti-Radar Missiles) missiles in a rotary launcher in the aft part of the bomb bay. All but two of those missiles had already been launched when the EB-52 penetrated the radar-dense combat environment of occupied Lithuania, destroying surface-to-air missile-site-tracking and guidance radars.

The Megafortress had also carried eight radar-guided AIM-120 Scorpion AMRAAMs (Advanced Medium-Range Air-to-Air Missiles) and four AIM-9R Sidewinder heat-seeking missiles on wing pylons; two Sidewinders and four Scorpions had already been launched by the crew "gunner," Dr. Angelina Pereira, a veteran of the original Old Dog mission. Pereira designed the Megafortress's unique guided-missile tail defense system that replaced the B-52's tail guns with accurate, destructive guided flak rockets.

"Ready for launch," Scott reported. The MSOW missile's maximum range was about thirty nautical miles; at twenty-eight miles, he hit the LAUNCH button. The four missiles went into five-second countdown cycles as aircraft position and velocity data was transferred to them. The missiles' batteries were activated and their gyros spun up, and their stabilization system was aligned and leveled. Then the bomb doors were opened and the missiles were ejected from the rotary launcher. The launcher rotated until the next missile was in position and then it too was ejected. In twenty seconds all four missiles were on their way, and the fibersteel radar-transparent bomb doors were closed.

"Missiles away," Scott reported. "Good track on all missiles." His large, four-color attack display activated, showing images transmitted from all four missiles. He immediately passed control of two missiles to Alicia Kellerman—Scott had, as radar navigator and bombardier, the final say on which targets were struck, but Kellerman was equally qualified to employ the missiles. "I've got good data from one and two."

"Good data from three and four."

"Message on the tactical channel," Dr. Wendy Tork, the fourth woman on board the Megafortress and the crew electronic-warfare officer, suddenly interjected. Tork, an electronic-warfare-systems designer, was another veteran of the Old Dog mission. "Button three, Kel."

Carter activated the channel-selector switch on his interphone panel. He heard: "Tiger, Tiger, Tiger, flares away."

He keyed his microphone: "Tiger, say target. Over."

"Tiger, thank God . . . Tiger, your target is three mobile missile-launchers. SS-21 missile launchers. We cannot designate them. Repeat, we cannot designate them. Hostile enemy forces in the vicinity. We have fired flares in the vicinity but we cannot pinpoint the unit's location. Are your missiles in the air? Can you identify them? Over."

"Tiger, I understand, SS-21 missile launchers," Carter repeated. "Stand by." On interphone, Carter said, "We're looking for three SS-21 launchers, Paul. They're wheeled mobile missile units. No designation for us, but he says he's fired flares in the area."

"Still looking," radar-navigator bombardier Paul Scott replied. "Still fifteen seconds of missile flight time." The scene on his attack monitor showed nothing but trees, farmland, and the airfield itself, all very plain-looking. Nothing of target value showed at all.

"I got something—it's a vehicle—no, a trailer," Kellerman announced. When MSOW spotted the target, it immediately zoomed into it so it would get a close-up picture, then zoomed back out to continue searching. The close-up picture was stored as a still image in one corner of Kellerman's attack monitor; Scott could transfer the image to his monitor to study it as well. "Designating missile three on the trailer. Pilot, try to get a bearing from—"

"I see gunfire!" Scott shouted. Only ten seconds to impact, several targets were popping up on the screen now. Suddenly one flare was fired across a section of a runway, and MSOW zoomed in on an SS-21 launcher unit highlighted by the glare. "I got one! Designating it on missile one."

"I got one also!" Kellerman said. Scott immediately cross-checked the two targets to be sure they weren't the same ones, but the artificial-intelligence computers that controlled MSOW knew precisely what each missile was looking at and had immediately concluded that they were different targets. "Designating missile four."

Scott's last MSOW missile didn't lock on until seven seconds before impact. "Tiger, Tiger, we got three SS-21 launchers and a command trailer!" Carter radioed back. "Stand by and—"

Suddenly the third SS-21 missile disappeared from the attack monitor in a bright flash of yellow fire. "Shit!" Scott cried out. "The third SS-21 blew up before missile impact!"

"No!" Cheshire shouted. "It launched! There it is!"

Directly ahead, about nineteen miles away, a streak of light pulled away from the dark horizon. It appeared to be flying directly overhead, heading west.

"Impact on missile three and four," Kellerman reported.

"Impact on missile one," Scott reported. "Where's that other one?"

Cheshire tried to watch it, but the SS-21 accelerated rapidly and quickly disappeared into the clouds. "Looks like we're too late."

"Tiger, Tiger, you gotta stop that missile!" Lobato radioed on the tactical channel. "It has a nuclear warhead on it and it's heading for Vilnius. *You gotta stop that missile!"*

Carter reacted instantly. He pushed the electronically controlled throttles to full military power, waited a few seconds to build up airspeed, then threw the Megafortress into a hard climbing left turn. "Wendy! Angelica! Lock on to that thing and nail it!"

Pereira immediately activated the Megafortress's APG-165 attack radar. The APG-165 was a derivative of the Hughes APG-65 dual-purpose fire-control radar aboard the F/A-18 Hornet fighter-bomber that could provide information for both air-to-air and air-to-ground attacks, with the addition of terrain-following navigation, computer position updates, and automatic landing modes. It interfaced with the Megafortress's AIM-120 missiles to provide initial target position. It took Pereira just a few seconds to find the SS-21 and lock on to it.

"I got it!" she announced. "Range is twenty-eight miles—that's near the Scorpion's maximum range." She didn't hesitate to fire off two of their remaining AIM-120 missiles at the SS-21.

The worst-engagement profile for an air-to-air missile chasing a target is a tail chase—the advantage is with the hunted and not the hunter. Both missiles were accelerating as they climbed, but the SS-21's larger booster motor gave it an advantage even though the AIM-120's top speed of Mach-4, or four times the speed of sound, was much faster than the SS-21.

"First missile's off course," Pereira reported. Carter had leveled off the EB-52—they had climbed to nearly ten thousand feet in the twenty seconds it took to launch the missile—and was now in a shallow descent back to low altitude. "Lost track . . . second missile tracking . . . active radar engaged . . ."

Unlike most air-to-air missiles, the AIM-120 used its own on-board radar to guide it into its target, and it used a boost-sustain rocket motor that powered the missile throughout its entire flight. It needed every erg of energy to catch up with the SS-21 and hit, just a fraction of a second before the motor was exhausted.

Suddenly, in the wink of an eye, it became daytime.

It was as if the sun were suddenly overhead and the clouds were gone—the light was as bright as high noon on a perfectly clear day. It lasted only a fraction of a second, but it flash-blinded everyone on the EB-52's upper crew deck. "Jesus!" Carter cried out. "What in *hell* . . . I can't see! Nancy, I can't see!"

"Me either," Cheshire said. "I can see the panel, but I can't read the—"

Just then an incredible rumbling, like the sound of an approaching freight train, could be heard throughout the bomber and the EB-52 heeled sharply over to the right. It seemed to be skidding, its nose pointed one way but flying in a different direction. Carter had no choice—because he was blinded, he didn't dare touch the controls to compensate for fear of sending the bomber into a spiral. With no visual references, flying by feel was deadly. "Nancy!" he shouted. "Don't touch the controls!"

"I . . . won't . . ."

The turbulence continued for a few more seconds. It took all of Carter's and Cheshire's willpower to stay off the controls. They were all praying that the bomber's natural stability would keep it upright until the turbulence passed. When he felt it was safe enough to move around the crew compartment, Carter clicked on the interphone: it was dead. "Station check!" Carter shouted at the top of his lungs. "Is everyone on? Report!"

"Offense is okay," Scott shouted back.

"Defense checks," Tork shouted in reply.

"Paul! Alicia!" Carter shouted. "Get up here and help us!"

Scott and Kellerman went upstairs. "Everything is out downstairs, and I mean *out*—not faulted, but *dead*. We got some of that light down there, but we're okay." He saw Carter with his hand off the single sidestick controller—he was afraid to touch the controls while he was blind, for fear of putting the plane into a dive or spiral. Scott saw that they were still in the clouds—it was imperative to reactivate the flight instruments before they crashed. "We're in the soup, Kel. What do I do first?"

"Check the controls," Carter said. "I can't see a damned thing, and I think the flight-control system is out."

"Defense is flash-blinded too," Kellerman said after checking Tork and Pereira. "I don't think it's too bad."

Scott shined a penlight at the electronic flight-information-system screens and digital engine readouts. "Everything is dead," he said over the roar of the engines. "EFIS is completely out."

"It sounds like the engines are still running," Carter said. He tried moving the electronic throttles. "I don't seem to have control of them—they must be in analog override. Check the standby gauges."

Scott checked the standby instruments, a row of conventional mechanical engine- and flight-information gauges. "Okay, Kel, it looks like you got a compressor stall on number eight, but I'll leave it for now. All the other engines look normal. The standby artificial horizon is dead. The altimeter reads nine thousand feet, the vertical velocity indicator says you're in a three-hundred-foot-per-minute descent, and the turn indicator says you're in a very slight right turn into the dead engine."

"Not too bad—we have a few minutes to get everything running again," Carter said. "Alicia, open the emergency checklist."

With Kellerman reading the checklists and Scott monitoring the aircraft, Carter and Cheshire reactivated the engine-driven generators, reactivated the flight-control system and autopilot, and managed to get the standby flight instrument and backup mechanically actuated throttles to respond.

"What the hell happened to us?" Cheshire asked.

"The SS-21," Pereira replied. "When the Scorpion hit it, it must've cooked off at least part of the nuclear warhead. It obviously wasn't a full yield—I don't think we'd be flying now if it was—and it was far enough away that it didn't do any real harm."

"But the electromagnetic pulse killed all our electronics that had antennas exposed to the outside," Wendy Tork added. "None of our experimental avionics are hardened against EMP—the only stuff that's hardened is the older flight-control system. The analog devices and mechanical systems aren't affected by EMP."

"That must mean . . . shit, that must mean electronic stuff is out all over the entire *region,*" Kellerman said. "All those troops out there, their radios, the telephone system, thousands of things—it must be like the turn of the century down there."

"Well, I think it's going to be a real quiet flight out of here, then," Kelvin Carter said. "It's a pretty good way to stop a war, too—everything on the battlefield with the exception of a rifle uses electronics, and the EMP would have fried most of it. We'll have to navigate visually. The bases of the clouds were about four thousand feet, and if I'm not mistaken we can fly all the way to Norway at four thousand feet and not hit any terrain."

"And as soon as we're out of range of the EMP effect, we can use the survival radios to contact someone," Tork said. "I just tried one, and it looks like it survived the EMP effects. I should be able to hook it into an external antenna and talk to someone on the ground."

The rest of the three-hour-long flight was made in virtual silence. They knew what they had done, and the crew realized what might have happened. It was far too terrible for words.

Epilogue

"I never thought I'd be thankful for a nuclear detonation," General Dominikas Palcikas said with a wry smile, "but this is an exception."

He and his executive officer were sitting in the Minister of Defense's office in the Parliament Building. Normally the Minister of Defense's office was at the Breda Palace, which housed the residence of Lithuanian president Gintarus Kapocius and the offices of the executive branch of government. But in the current nationwide power emergency, necessary government functions had been consolidated into one building to save energy. Palcikas had to smile at the bank of no less than ten old-style field telephones piled up on the Minister of Defense's desk—because the effects of an electromagnetic pulse can last several days, they had been forced to use the crank-type telephone to communicate within the building. After three days, however, the effects of the low-yield nuclear blast over northern Byelorussia had subsided, and portable radios were being used until the main phone circuits could be rebuilt.

The Minister of Defense, Dr. Algimantas Virkutis, a sixty-nine-year-old full-time physician as well as civilian administrator of the Lithuanian Self-Defense Force, was doing a very unpolitical task—he was busily examining Palcikas' wounded leg. "I must agree with you, Dominikas," Virkutis said. "They used to say an army runs on its stomach—these days I believe an army runs on electronics and microchips. The blast over Byelorussia stopped everyone in their tracks very effectively. You tried walking on that leg yet?"

Palcikas nodded his head but wore a pained expression as he replied, "Yes, but it hurts like hell . . ."

"I told you *not* to walk on it, General," Virkutis admonished. He gave the leg a friendly little slap, which predictably caused Palcikas to grimace in pain. "Jesus, Dominikas, when are you ever going to listen? You'll extend your recuperation a week for every hour you put pressure on that leg. Follow me?"

451

"Yes, Minister."

"And I told you to call me Algy here in the office. You still don't listen." He stripped off a layer of dressings and examined the wound, causing another surge of pain.

Palcikas was ready to cold-cock the old fart.

"Holy Mother of God, but that must've been a real stinger when that baby went into your leg."

"Sort of like it feels right now, Algy," Palcikas said. "Do you mind . . . ?"

"Stop being such a crybaby, Dominikas." He examined the wound carefully, nodded his approval, and reapplied sterile dressings from a medical bag beside his desk. "Those field medics did a bang-up job debriding your leg—in the dark, in the rain, and considering you mucked it up pretty good slapping that mud into it, they did a fine job."

"It was either that or bleed to death."

"Next time don't lose your first-aid kit," Virkutis said.

He had an annoying habit, Palcikas thought, of making one feel tremendously guilty for even the slightest error. "I thought we had business to discuss, Algy," Palcikas said.

"Oh yeah, business," Virkutis said. "Good news: we think we've got a cease-fire agreement put together with Byelorussia."

"That's great," Palcikas said. "Under what terms?"

"The United States has agreed to head up a United Nations peacekeeping force in Byelorussia," Virkutis said. "All Byelorussian and Commonwealth troops out of Lithuania and Kalinin, and all Russian and Commonwealth troops out of Byelorussia; supervised destruction of all nuclear weapons and inspection of weapon-storage sites, military bases, and government facilities; and unlimited reconnaissance aircraft overflights of all Baltic and Commonwealth countries. We've also agreed to more-favorable terms for transporting goods across Lithuania to Byelorussia."

"What about the Byelorussian Army?" Palcikas asked. "They'll still have hundreds of thousands of troops and a sizable ground force—they can threaten us with retaliation at any time."

"I think, with reactionaries like Voshchanka gone, the threat will be greatly diminished," Virkutis said. "In any case, world attention has focused on the problems we face around these parts. I think people are starting to realize that just because the old Soviet Union is dead, aggression isn't." He slapped Palcikas' leg again, stood up, and returned to his desk. "Plus it means we're still in the prepare-for-war business, my friend. That is, if you still want to be."

"Of course!" Palcikas said. "This little scratch won't keep me from performing my duties."

"Well, you won't be rappelling out of any helicopters for a while." Virkutis clucked. "But no, I don't see any medical reasons to exclude you from active duty. But you've been battered around a bit, Dominikas—some might say a little *too* much."

"What does *that* mean?"

"It means that people—and I mean those in government, in business, and prominent citizens in this country—think you've done a terrific job as leader of the Self-Defense Force, but you've got a fire in your belly now that perhaps isn't appropriate for what we need to accomplish."

"Are you asking for my resignation, Minister?" Palcikas asked angrily. "Are you?"

"No, I'm not, Dominikas," Virkutis replied. "But I want you to think about it, is all. You've always been a forward-thinking man, Dominikas, but with all you've been through, perhaps your outlook may be a bit clouded."

"I don't believe this, Minister!" Palcikas said angrily. "My career, my whole life, is the defense of my home and my country—now you're telling me that I can't do that effectively and objectively?"

"I'm telling you to think it over, Dominikas," Virkutis said. "I know you aren't good at listening to me, you young buck, but listen to this: I'm telling you that you've built a strong, proud country here, and now it may be time to step out of the trenches and smell the flowers in the fields instead of rolling tanks or landing helicopters on them. You understand, Dominikas? And stop calling me Minister or I'll stop assigning pretty nurses to you and start assigning some big, hairy-armed medics to look after you."

Palcikas couldn't help but smile at Virkutis's words. He nodded. "All right, all right. Maybe in a year or two I'll think about retirement. But right now all I want is to get my headquarters organized again. If there's nothing else, I'll get back to Trakai."

"Yes, there is something else." Virkutis pushed Palcikas' aide aside and took the handles of his wheelchair. He pushed it out into the hallway, down the elevator, down the main hallway of the Parliament building, and took a right turn toward a set of ornately decorated double doors. Two armed soldiers opened them.

"What in hell is this, Algy?" Palcikas asked when he realized where they were going.

"Call me Minister, General," Virkutis said. "Christ, won't you ever listen?"

Over two hundred men and women, the members of the Lithuanian Parliament, rose to their feet when Palcikas and Virkutis entered the Parliament chambers. Ceremonial trumpets sounded, and the sergeant-at-arms announced in a loud voice, "Mr. President, members of Parliament, distinguished guests and fellow citizens: the Chief of Staff of the Self-Defense Force, General Dominikas Palcikas!"

Thunderous applause erupted in the Parliament chambers, hands slapped his shoulders, and photographers snapped away as Virkutis wheeled Palcikas to the podium. The Lord High Minister of the Parliament raised his pommel staff for silence, but it was ignored for several long minutes as the applause continued.

"The chair recognizes the President of the Republic, the honorable Gintarus Kapocius," the Lord High Minister announced. Kapocius himself moved down from his chair beside the Lord High Minister and stood beside Palcikas.

"Lord High Minister, members of Parliament, guests and fellow citizens. I know this is not yet a time for celebration. Enemy forces are still on Lithuanian soil. Our country is still suffering the effects of the nuclear explosion, and it will take many days to assess the damage to our population and our nation.

"But we are here today to honor the man who by his courage and his leadership helped to save our nation from certain disaster. In the face of vastly superior forces, he led a small force in ambush raids and carefully planned and perfectly executed guerrilla-style attacks on the invading Byelorussian forces. He is a genuine hero to us all, and an inspiration for Lithuanians and free people all over the world."

The applause again lasted for several minutes until Kapocius finally quieted them down. "There is one more act of recognition I am obliged to perform. As a sign of his fidelity to the government and to the people, General Palcikas surrendered two very valuable things to a member of this Parliament. It is my happy duty to return these things to him as a token of our respect and pride in him and what he has done for our country. Miss Kulikauskas?"

From a side chamber, Anna Kulikauskas and Corporal Georgi Manatis walked to the podium. With the corporal holding the item, Anna unwrapped the Lithuanian flag that covered the Lithuanian Sword of State, and carefully presented it to Dominikas Palcikas once again. To the deafening applause of the members of Parliament, Palcikas held the Sword of State aloft for all to see.

But amidst the applause and adulation, Palcikas could see only one person: Anna. Her eyes were locked with his, and he knew in that instant that the growing love between them was unbroken and getting stronger each day. Perhaps there *was* something more important than fighting for one's country, Palcikas thought: perhaps one did not fight for a flag or a sword, but for the people and the loved ones that were family, friends, and fellow countrymen. And when the fighting was done, perhaps it *was* time for the older, more battle-weary soldiers to step aside and let the younger lions take their place. How else were they to learn the value of defending their homes, their people, and their way of life?

Palcikas saw that Alexei Kolginov's identification bracelet was still firmly locked on to the cross-hilt of the Sword. He touched it, a silent remembrance of his friend, but left it there as a symbol of the old and the new. He turned to Manatis and gave him the Sword. "Take good care of this, George." The young corporal was stunned, but Palcikas only smiled and offered no other explanation or orders. He motioned for Anna to move closer, and as she did, he kissed her cheek.

"Come with me, Anna," he told her over the cheers and applause of the Parliament. "Be with me."

She nodded, tears welling in her eyes, then returned his kiss. Firmly but politely, she pushed the Minister of Defense away from the handlebars of the wheelchair and pushed Palcikas out of the Parliament chamber and into the warm Lithuanian spring sunshine.

"I think," Dr. Virkutis said to President Kapocius over the whistles and cheering of the members of Parliament, "that boy finally decided to listen to me."

HIGH TECHNOLOGY AEROSPACE WEAPONS CENTER, NEVADA
28 APRIL, 0545 HOURS (0845 ET)

"This really sucks," Hal Briggs said bitterly.

Briggs, along with Brad Elliott, John Ormack, Patrick McLanahan, Wendy Tork, Angelina Pereira, Paul White, Kelvin Carter, and other senior officers and engineers at the High Technology Aerospace Weapons Center research center and the Intelligence Support Agency group MADCAP MAGICIAN were standing outside of the small base-operations building on the flight line one cold, overcast morning—even Lieutenant Fryderyk Litwy, the young Lithuanian security officer MADCAP MAGICIAN had rescued months before, was there.

Parked in front of the building was a C-22B transport plane—a modified Boeing 727 commercial jetliner with all of its Air Force markings erased, it looked like any other commercial or corporate jet ready to depart.

Deputy Director John Markwright, chief investigations officer for the U.S. Defense Intelligence Agency, turned with an angry glance toward Briggs and said, "What was that, Captain Briggs?"

"I said, this *sucks,* man!"

"Listen, you—"

"That's enough, both of you," Elliott said. "Hal, keep it buttoned."

Briggs turned and walked a few paces away, muttering something under this breath.

"You know, part of the problem around here," Markwright said with aggravation, "is a noticeable lack of *discipline,* General. I'm a deputy director of the National Security Agency and a direct Presidential appointee, and ever since I've arrived I've been treated like shit by your snot-nosed officers."

"Maybe we don't like what you're doing," McLanahan said evenly. "Maybe what we think you're doing is *wrong.* "

"The President disagrees with you, Colonel," Markwright said dismissively. "I'm doing this under his authority."

"But as part of *your* recommendations," Ormack added. "I don't think you considered one goddamn proposal of ours or of the Pentagon for dealing with Dave Luger."

"My staff and I read and reviewed every recommendation on dealing with this situation, including your half-baked ideas about leaving him here," Markwright said. "The consensus was to get him out of the country and into isolative custody until the security review has been completed and the Old Dog mission has been fully declassified—and until *my* investigations have been concluded." He affixed every one of them with a cold stare. "And while I'm conducting my investigation, it would behoove all of you to cooperate instead of jerking me around with all your damned clearances and security checks. I'm sick of it. I've got clearance to see and ask *anything* around here, and the sooner you all realize that, the better it'll be for all of us." He lowered his voice slightly and said to Elliott, "And if I get full cooperation from you, General—*full* cooperation—it might make Lieutenant Luger's life a bit more bearable as well. Where he's going, he could be a bit uncomfortable."

"Get away from me, you arrogant son of a bitch," Elliott snapped. "And if I find out that you've mistreated *Major* Luger, after all this group has been through, I'll personally wring your scrawny little neck."

Markwright stepped away from Elliott as if the three-star general had kicked him in the groin; then a mischievous grin spread across his face. "Where he's going, General, you won't hear or find out diddly," Markwright said smugly. "Luger belongs to *me* now, got that? And if you think he had it tough at the Fisikous Institute, you haven't seen anything yet. Whatever we need to find out from Luger, we *will* find out."

Elliott shoved Markwright away from him, but Markwright only straightened his suit jacket, smiled, and walked briskly away from the group toward the C-22B.

"I don't understand, General," Wendy Tork told Elliott. "We're all here, and we've got full freedom to move around—why does Dave have to be taken into isolative custody?"

"I'm not sure, Wendy," Elliott replied. "He's under investigation, and I think they're afraid of the brainwashing he's undergone. There's a very real possibility that he's been turned into a double agent. The difference, of course, is that we pronounced him dead after the Old Dog mission was over. We can't explain his reappearance without revealing everything— the Old Dog mission, everything about what we do here at HAWC, and everything we did over in Lithuania."

"But we have the capability to keep him isolated and secure here at Dreamland," Angelina Pereira argued. "We've had Russian defectors and Chinese scientists here for years without anyone knowing about it. Why not the same for Dave?"

"Because Markwright can see a career-enhancing step in this investigation," Ormack said angrily. "That geek is going to push his way to NSA director on the back of Dave Luger."

At that moment an ambulance drove up to the base operations building. The rear doors opened up and two plainclothes security guards stepped outside and stationed themselves nearby. A physician from HAWC's medical staff remained in the back of the ambulance, sitting on a long, wide, enclosed cargo bench that doubled as storage space for rescue equipment. He looked restless and wary, as if unsure about some action that he'd been asked to perform. He visually sought out Brad Elliott, but he said nothing to the three-star general when they locked eyes.

Dave Luger, wearing a plain white shirt, blue jeans, and tennis shoes, stepped onto the back step of the ambulance. The group of well-wishers pushed forward. The security officers told everyone to step back away from the ambulance, but they realized the group's emotions at the moment were very intense, so they weren't too insistent. Finally they decided to wait in the front of the ambulance to at least let them say their good-byes in private.

"I guess this is it," Luger said. Angelina and Wendy were the first ones to embrace him. "I never thought I'd ever see you guys again," Luger said. "I'm glad I could."

"You'll be okay, Dave," Wendy reassured him. "They'll take good care of you—we'll see to that."

"We'll never forget you, Dave," Angelina said, tears welling up in her eyes. "We still owe you a party. When you come back, we'll throw you a real doozy."

"I can't wait," Luger smiled halfheartedly. "But seeing you two again is the best celebration I could have."

General Elliott was the next one in line. "Hey, thanks for the promotion, sir," Dave said.

"You deserved it, Major, and much more," Elliott replied. "God, I'm going to miss you. I'm glad you're all right."

"What are you going to do with the Fisikous-170?"

"Everyone's denying the thing ever existed," Elliott said. "The Russians don't want it, the Lithuanians don't want it, so I'll keep it. When you come back, you can have it."

"No way," Dave said. "I'm sorry I ever had anything to do with it. I'm just glad *we* were the ones to use it."

They shook hands, then embraced one last time. "I'll be seeing you, sir," Luger said.

"Soon. Very soon," Elliott said confidently. "The security review will be over before you know it. And I'll be looking out for you. Don't let Markwright give you any shit."

"I've taken shit from the best," Luger smiled. "He won't be a problem."

Paul White, Kelvin Carter, the Lithuanian officer Fryderyk Litwy, Gunny Lobato, and some of the other officers and engineers came forward to say their good-byes. The press of well-wishers was so great that the ambulance was nearly surrounded, and after a moment the guards finally warned the crowd to step back. They did so reluctantly. Ormack, Briggs, and McLanahan were the last ones to step forward. "I can never repay you guys for saving my life," Dave said. "It's still like a dream—an incredible dream."

"We'll push for an early release, and visitation rights, and correspondence rights," Ormack said. "We'll make those bastards in Washington believe you're a hero, don't worry."

"Even if it means going out there and standing on some desks," Briggs said. "I'm so pissed I could take on the Prez himself."

"With guys like you behind me"—Luger grinned—"I've got nothing to worry about."

Finally it was just Luger and McLanahan. The two looked at each other, then gave tight, strong hugs. "This is the worst thing that's ever happened," McLanahan said. "We lost you, then found you, and now we've lost you again . . . Shit."

"You haven't lost me," Luger said. He was determined not to get teary-eyed, so he smiled. "Remember when you suckered me into coming to this place, Patrick? You said this was an opportunity I'd never forget. Well, you were right."

"Jesus, I've gotten you into a lot of scrapes, haven't I?" McLanahan asked. "The Old Dog, then *Tuman* . . . boy, what's next?"

"Whatever it is, I'm looking forward to it," Luger said. He paused, then glanced at the guards, who were now back and ready to close the ambulance doors. "Whatever they've got in mind"—Luger sighed—"I know it'll be an adventure. Good-bye, Patrick. I'll see you . . . whenever." Luger stepped back into the ambulance.

Patrick tried to climb in with him, but the guards pushed him away. "Let me ride with him to the plane, at least!"

"No one goes with him except for the doc," one of the guards snapped.

"Oh, fuck you!" exploded McLanahan, as Luger lay down on a gurney and the HAWC physician began attending to him. McLanahan shoved the guard aside and tried to climb into the back of the ambulance.

The guard firmly pulled him back. "Stay back, Colonel, or we'll place you under arrest. And I'd hate to do that."

"I can't even *ride* with him to the plane? What kind of shit is this, you motherfucker?"

"Orders," said another guard, now holding McLanahan from the other side.

McLanahan glanced at Luger, who was shaking his head. "Don't, Patrick. We'll see each other again. It's not worth an arrest." Luger smiled and gave a gentle wave to the crowd gathered around the ambulance, then lay back on the gurney for the short ride.

The doors were shut and the ambulance finally roared off down the tarmac. The guards held McLanahan until the ambulance was at the C-22 and Luger was being carried into the plane through the rear boarding stairway. He noticed that a white sheet had been pulled over Luger's face, completely shielding him from view.

"I can't fucking believe this!" raged McLanahan.

"He'll be all right, Patrick," Elliott said. He motioned for the guards to release McLanahan; they did so after seeing that Luger was safely on board the plane and the aft airstair was retracted. The guards scanned the faces that were still assembled near the base operations building. A few people had departed, including the one young officer with the foreign uniform that they had noticed earlier.

But something did not quite feel right . . .

"Baker, this is Markwright," a message suddenly announced. One of the guards pulled a small transceiver from a coat pocket. "What's your status?"

"Baker here. Slight difficulty with one of the officers—guy named McLanahan."

"Everything under control?" Markwright asked from the plane.

The guard hesitated, still wondering about the faces he didn't see, but replied, "Yeah, everything secure."

"We're ready for departure. Close it up and let's move. Out."

"Baker roger." The two guards trotted toward the plane, glad to be away from that hostile group.

"We'll be monitoring him, Patrick," Elliott was saying. "Don't worry. He'll be taken care of, I promise."

"Do you know where he's going? Did you bug the plane?"

"We thought of that," Briggs admitted. "We tried NIRTSats to track the plane, we tried microtransmitters implanted in his intestines, we tried bribing someone at the NSA. Nothing. He's going to be clamped down on, hard, until the security review is completed."

"That'll take years—at least six years before the board can meet—and who knows how many years after that?"

"Well, you'll be the General by then," Elliott said, "and maybe you'll even be the Chairman of the Joint Chiefs or even the President. Then you can decide."

"Dave thought that someone might try to do away with him, do away with *us*," McLanahan said. "He was afraid that he knew too much, that he wouldn't be safe *anywhere*. Brad, we've got to do something—"

"There's nothing we can do, Patrick," Elliott said. "Just be patient."

They watched as the airstair was closed, the engines started, and the C-22 taxied and launched several minutes later. The group slowly departed as the C-22 was lost from view. Wendy Tork took Patrick's hand, and together they left the flight line and headed back to their cars.

Paul White, Gunnery Sergeant Lobato, and Brad Elliott were the last ones remaining on the tarmac. After a few long moments of silence, Elliott said, "Paul, Jose, I want to thank you for all you've done. I'll never forget your service to me and my unit."

"We were glad to help, General," Paul White said. He clasped Lobato on the shoulder and said with a smile, "It was one hell of a ride, wasn't it?"

"It certainly was, sir. It certainly was." Lobato walked to the car, leaving White with Elliott.

After a few moments, when everyone was out of earshot, Elliott asked White, "So. Do you know where they're heading yet?"

"Not yet," White said. "Give me ten minutes and I'll find out."

"Okay." Elliott paused a bit. They watched the HAWC ambulance slowly return to the base operations building: it eased up to them, then passed without stopping. The HAWC flight surgeon in the front passenger seat nodded to Elliott, who then remarked to Paul White, "That Lieutenant Litwy is a hell of a nice guy, isn't he?"

"He certainly is," White agreed. "He certainly is."

THE WHITE HOUSE OVAL OFFICE, WASHINGTON, D.C.
28 APRIL, 1744 HOURS (29 APRIL, 0844 HOURS, EASTERN AUSTRALIA)

It was the last staff meeting of the day before the President's evening meal, and as usual the topic of conversation, as it had been for the past several days, was the press's treatment of the events in Lithuania and Byelorussia.

"You can say 'don't worry' all you want, Case," the President said to his Chief of Staff, "but I get hounded everywhere I go. The press has locked on to the story that we launched bombers in support of the Lithuanian attacks in Byelorussia. What am I supposed to do? Just keep denying it? If they ever find out, I'll look like a total jackass."

"I'm telling you, sir, the report will fizzle away," Case Simmons said reassuringly. "The story appeared two days ago, and it hasn't been confirmed by anyone. We admitted we had Marines and Special Forces troops in Lithuania, but they'll never find out about the EB-52s. Some reports are saying they were Americans, others say they were Ukrainians, and others say it was a Russian stealth bomber . . . they don't know shit—sir. It'll blow over."

"I damned well hope so." The President groaned. "I'm sick of this. Jesus, I want to get on with relations in Europe, and I can't function with the press hounding me on the bomber attack." He smiled, then added, "Although I do have to hand it to Elliott—the old war horse came through. Again."

"That he did," agreed the Chief of Staff with a wry smile.

There was a knock on the Oval Office door, and National Security Advisor George Russell was admitted. He strode right over to the President's desk, looking almost apoplectic.

"George, what's the matter?" asked the President, concerned.

"That bastard Elliott!" exploded Russell. "He's done it again! He's . . . he's, oh, fuck it. I'm going to kill him!"

The President and his Chief of Staff were staring at Russell. "George," the President said, hoping he would calm down. "What exactly has Elliott done?"

Russell gritted his teeth. "That crazy sonofabitch swapped prisoners on us! Sometime when David Luger was being transported to his plane, Fryderyk Litwy, the Lithuanian defector we picked up last October, was switched in his place. That fucking doctor must have been in on it, too, goddamn it!"

"What doctor?"

Russell scowled. "Oh, one of Elliott's staff physicians. They must have snuck Litwy in the cargo bench storage area in the ambulance, then made the switch on the way to the plane. Dammit, when I get my hands on Brad Elliott . . . ! This time he's gone *too far*. He thinks he can do *anything* he wants and I've had it. Sir, I want him court-martialed. I want his head on a platter! I want—"

The President was now laughing so hard that Russell looked as if he were ready to pull his hair out in frustration.

"Sir, I fail to see the humor—"

The President was laughing even harder now, tears welling up in his eyes. "Never mind, George. Never mind. Just forget about it."

"What? But, sir, Elliott—"

"—will take good care of Luger, and he'll see that he stays out of the public eye until the security review is completed. He knows what's best for his people, George. He always did. He's a sonofabitch, all right . . . but at least he's *our* sonofabitch!"